JULY 18

Avi Burra

Casanostra Creations

For Luna, Silly, and Julie, my most loyal companions, who taught me the true meaning of unconditional love.

PART I. INFERNA

CHAPTER 1. January 3

Ante colorum extasis transcendentale, est primum renaisus vernatum, sed ante id, necessi il abyssum inferna demitter.

The meaning was a phantom limb of the mind. The sense of it lingered – a perfect, crystalline shape that had existed for a single, lucid second before shattering into the meaningless dust of its syllables. It was gibberish now, but it hadn't been. For a moment, it had been Truth.

Who had spoken? Was it a voice or a thought that wasn't his own? An intruder in the quiet corridors of his skull. The memory of the meaning was already gone, leaving behind only the cold, unnerving proof that some other consciousness had just passed through him.

Oliver Battolo opened his eyes to the familiar gray of his bedroom ceiling. The corrosive loop. It had been happening for a week, ever since the neat boundary of his twenty-fourth birthday, the same time his guide, the Noncemeister, had vanished for good. The old world had receded like a forgotten tide, leaving behind only this cold, new territory of the mind.

These weren't just dreams anymore; they were fractures. Fissures in the foundation of himself, through which these voiceless words now seeped. And below it all, the familiar ballast. Not just a feeling, but a physical weight in his soul, a cold anchor pulling him down into a private and suffocating dark.

769735 (December 31)

"Hey, babe, did you pick up the champagne for tonight?" Daniela asked as Oliver walked into the kitchen.

He managed a smile that felt thin and brittle. "Better. Four bottles of the 2003 Dom Pérignon. The David Lynch edition." It had been a small, defiant act of theater against the crushing reality of his situation, a way to feel the part of a man with a fortune, even if he couldn't touch a single dollar of it.

Daniela's eyes widened. "Four bottles of limited-edition Dom? Oliver, that must have cost a fortune."

"Five hundred a bottle," he said, his gaze dropping to the floor.

"Two thousand dollars? How are you going to pay for that?" Her voice was quiet, but firm. "You know you can't touch any of your dad's money. Any movement in that wallet and the feds will be on you in a second."

"I'll figure it out," he said, the words tasting like a lie. The whole idea felt more impossible each day – this vast, untouchable ocean of wealth he was supposedly captain of, while in reality he was just a man drowning in it.

"Okay," she sighed, letting it go for now. "Let's see them, then."

Oliver opened a cabinet.

"I only see three," Daniela said, her eyes narrowing. "Where's the fourth?"

He didn't meet her gaze. "Drank it last night. You were at rehearsal."

"A whole bottle by yourself? Oliver, you've been drinking every day for two weeks. Are you sure you're okay?"

"It's the holidays. I'll stop in the new year," he replied, his tone clipped. She was right, of course. The wine had become less a comfort and more a necessary anesthetic, a way to dull the sharp, jagged edges of a world that no longer made sense.

He needed to change the subject. "So, this party tonight. Who are these people again?"

"Steve and Reza? My professor from NYU? I've told you about them."

"Right," he mumbled. The prospect of making small talk felt exhausting. It was like being an alien, forced to discuss the weather with a species that had no concept of an atmosphere. How could he talk about their jobs or their holiday plans when his own reality had become a conspiracy thriller whispered in a dead man's code? A party at a gay theater couple's house on the Upper West Side – at least the wine should be good.

Daniela watched him, then shifted gears. "I was thinking about that message from your dad's address. The one that came with the twenty-four bitcoin transfer."

Oliver shrugged, though the words in the *OP_RETURN* were seared in his memory. "Obelisk, 18 July. It has happened."

"And the response my uncle Rafael told me to use," she continued, her eyes brightening with a hope that felt dangerous to him. "'Yes, let us meet there and then at 10 p.m.' I've been thinking, Oliver. There's an obelisk in Montevideo. What if your dad wants to meet you there?"

A flicker of interest – wild, seductive and terrifying – sparked in him before he ruthlessly crushed it. Hope was a luxury he couldn't afford, an ember he wouldn't let her fan into a forest fire. He had already spent months cauterizing that wound; he would not let her rip it open again with a ghost story. "Don't be silly, Daniela. My dad's dead."

"Is he?" Daniela pressed. "The DoJ is hunting Dev_akshar. We both know that was your dad. What if he found out they reopened the case and staged his death to escape?"

"Daniela, stop." A hot flush of irritation rose in him. It was the anger of a man trying to hold a door shut against a gale. "I spent months mourning him. One cryptic transaction doesn't change that."

"But it all adds up! He knew my uncle from that ashram in India. Why haven't I been able to reach my *Tío* Rafael? Maybe because he's busy hiding your dad!"

"That's insane."

"Is it? He could be there right now! Alive!"

"I said stop!" Oliver's voice was sharp, crackling with a rage that surprised them both. "He's dead. End of story. Someone else has his keys, and I have to figure out how to get the rest of the bitcoin before they do. Your uncle is probably on vacation."

Daniela flinched. She recovered quickly, her expression softening. "Okay. I'm sorry. I was just excited. We can drop it."

Oliver just nodded, sullen. The anger drained away, leaving only a familiar, sour exhaustion. The weight of the secret, of the money, of his father's ghost – it was all there, a dead thing in the center of the room. He needed a drink, not for the party, but for the long, empty hours between now and then. An escape hatch from himself. "I'm going for a walk."

769739 (December 31)

O'Connell's Irish Pub was empty when Oliver walked in, the quiet amplifying the scent of stale beer and polish. He was greeted with a warm smile from the otherwise stern-looking woman behind the bar. Her red hair was pulled back in a bun so tight it smoothed the newer wrinkles from her forehead.

"Joining us for the party tonight, Oliver?" the bartender asked, her sinewy arms flexing as she wiped a glass.

Oliver felt a pang of genuine warmth seeing Aisling. This place, this friendship, was one of the few real things he felt he had left. "I'm afraid not, Aisling," he replied. "Heading to the Upper West Side for a party with Daniela."

"A shame. We're having Irish line dancers just before midnight, then a proper champagne toast."

Oliver chuckled. "Line dancers might not be my mood, but proper champagne sounds nice."

"Well, it's not really *champagne*," she admitted. "Just sparkling wine. I can't afford the real stuff ... Anyway, what can I get you?"

Oliver scanned the top shelf, the part of the bar reserved for celebrations and bad decisions. He was in the mood for both. "The 18-year Auchentoshan, neat. Water on the side."

Aisling raised her eyebrows. "Well, look who's getting fancy. You haven't ordered your regular lager in weeks."

He was playing a part, trying on the costume of a man for whom money was no object. The performance felt both necessary and pathetic.

"Actually, can you make it a double?" Oliver asked. "Need to get in the mood for later."

She pursed her lips in mock surprise. "Fifty-seven dollars. Leave the tab open?"

Oliver nodded, the price a small, sharp reminder of the fraudulent role he was playing.

"So," Aisling persisted, "what's with the expensive taste? Celebrating?"

"Not celebrating," Oliver said with a wry smile. "Just ... stepping up my game."

His mind snagged on something she'd said earlier. "Is it really that big a deal for a pub to order a case of real champagne?"

Aisling's grin faded. "It shouldn't be. But money's tight. The lease is up for renewal, suppliers are charging more ... and to top it all off, our insurance claim for my grandad's painting was denied last week."

Oliver shifted on his stool, the casual warmth of the pub suddenly feeling like a courtroom. The painting she meant – *The Toddler* – was wrapped in a comforter under his bed. Every word she spoke was an indictment, another brick in the wall of his guilt.

"Why did they deny it?" he asked, his voice feeling strangely distant. He took a large sip of scotch.

"We were asking for seventy-five thousand ... the buyer, a guy named Bojan, disappeared the second he heard it was stolen. It's a mess. We could have really used that money."

Oliver's stomach churned. This was his work. Her struggle was a direct consequence of a crime he had committed right here, in this place of comfort and friendship. "Have the police made any progress?"

Aisling rolled her eyes. "The great NYPD? They've stopped calling. I'm just about ready to sell this place and move on, Oliver."

"Don't say that," he exclaimed, the shock of her words eclipsing his own selfish relief.

"And I have corroding water pipes, a kitchen that needs a new stove, tables that are falling apart. That's a hundred grand in repairs. Selling that painting would have helped."

Her words were a litany of his sins. The guilt was a suffocating, physical force, a hand squeezing his throat. The words erupted from him, not as a choice, but as a desperate, involuntary reflex to make it all stop. "What if I gave you two hundred thousand dollars for the renovations?"

Aisling stared, stunned. "What are you saying, Oliver?"

He was kicking himself, horrified by the impossible edifice of lies he was now forced to construct. "I, uh ... I've had some investments work out pretty well," his mouth stumbled on, his rational brain screaming in protest. "I'd be happy to help."

"Oliver, I ... I can't take that kind of money from you." As she spoke, her eyes welled up.

The sight of her tears was a checkmate. It sealed the promise, transforming his reckless words into an unbreakable contract. He saw with sickening clarity the trap he had just built for himself: a fraud, paying for his own crime with money he couldn't access, all to preserve the friendship he had already betrayed.

He took a deep breath. "Trust me, Aisling. It's not a lot for me, and I genuinely want to help."

"Oh, my goodness," she said between sobs, rounding the bar to pull him into a tight bear hug.

Oliver gently extricated himself, his mind racing. He had nearly half a billion dollars in theory, and not a single legitimate dollar in practice.

"Listen, I'm closing out the last of those investments. It might take a couple of weeks to settle. Can I get you the money around mid-January?"

"Of course," she said, her face alight with a hope that felt like another accusation. "Take all the time you need."

It wasn't a reprieve, he thought as he ordered another double. *It was a deadline.* The quiet, ticking clock of his own impossible promise had just started.

Stepping out into the chilly afternoon, Oliver felt the scotch waging a losing war against the cold knot of panic in his gut. The promise he'd just made was an act of insanity, a check written against a phantom bank account. It was terrifying. It was embarrassing. And yet, beneath it all, a sliver of something else stirred – a strange, manic excitement. He had just thrown a lit match into the placid listlessness of his life.

For a moment, the warmth of the whisky won out, creating a brief, fragile illusion of peace, a fleeting sense that he was a good man doing a good thing. A lie, he knew, but for now, it was a lie he desperately needed to believe.

769800 (December 31)

"This is it," Daniela said, pointing to the grand four-story townhouse at 45 West 84th Street.

"Which floor?" Oliver asked.

"They own the whole thing, silly," she laughed.

Oliver stared, a wave of alienation washing over him before he even stepped inside. A whole townhouse here, a stone's throw from Central Park, felt like a different category of existence, a level of wealth so profound it was practically a different nationality.

"Theater money," Daniela smiled. "They bought it in the 90s when the neighborhood was rough."

As they climbed the granite steps, Oliver heard a rustle. He turned and saw a construction awning across the street, where the shadow of a person shifted restlessly. A ghost at the feast. He shrugged it off, a minor note of dissonance in a symphony of it, and followed Daniela through the ornate door.

He stepped into a space so grand it felt less like a home and more like a statement. A thirty-foot ceiling, a massive chandelier, and a dozen impeccably dressed guests already performing the intricate ballet of a high-society party. A tuxedoed man played a pop tune on a grand piano, but the sound felt thin, swallowed by the sheer volume of the room. *It's not even 9 p.m.,* Oliver thought. *The anesthesia hasn't kicked in yet. Give them a few drinks and they'll be belting out the tunes, pretending to feel something.*

Suddenly, a booming voice: "My dear, dear Daniela! My most favorite student of all time!"

A flamboyantly dressed man emerged, a peacock in a purple blazer and sequined trousers. *This must be Steve*, Oliver thought, observing him with the detached curiosity of an anthropologist.

"So glad you could make it, darling!" Steve gushed, rattling off details about a celebrity chef – Jean-Pierre Papin – with a breathless excitement that felt utterly exhausting to Oliver. It was all performance, every word a polished stone in the edifice of the evening.

"That's incredible, Steve!" Daniela said. "I want you to meet my boyfriend, Oliver."

Steve turned, his smile contracting slightly. He pushed his glasses down his nose and looked Oliver up and down, a clinical inspection that took in the button-down shirt Oliver had worn under protest. It was a uniform for a world he didn't belong to, and Steve's cold, limp handshake was the official stamp on his passport to nowhere.

As Steve led them to the bar and vanished, Oliver felt a familiar, pressing need. He scanned the wine selection, and his gaze fell on a 2006 Château Margaux. He felt a flash of grim satisfaction. He might be an imposter here, but at least he could recognize their expensive props. He accepted a generous pour, but before he could turn to Daniela, she was gone, pulled away by the party's gravity toward a friend.

He was alone. He wandered through the room, the exquisite wine a temporary shield. He felt like a ghost, a spy from another reality, observing the natives in their natural habitat. He spotted another ghost, a gaunt man in casual clothes, his face a mask of profound boredom. A kindred spirit. Oliver nudged his way toward him.

"Hi there, I'm Oliver."

The man introduced himself as Reza and shook his hand with a weak smile. "I live here, or so I'm told."

"Thanks for having us," Oliver said.

"I'm not having anyone," Reza sneered. "I fucking hate all these people. Society parasites." The bluntness was a relief, a blast of cold, clean air in the suffocatingly polite room. "You seem fine, though," Reza added, a mischievous grin cutting through his gloom. "Of course, you'll probably prove me wrong any minute."

Oliver felt a strange, intuitive flash – a former idealist wrapped in a shell of cynicism. The insight came from nowhere, another one of those mental fractures he'd been experiencing lately. "Daniela told me you acted in the 90s," he said, deciding to follow the thread.

Reza's eyes brightened for a moment, a brief flicker of a past self. "Ah, yes, those were good times. I'd just arrived here as a student from Iran, and I got a lucky break being cast as Bloom in an alternative adaptation of *Ulysses*." He drifted off for a moment, the memory feeling more real and vital than anything else in this opulent house. "An off-off-off-off Broadway play," he laughed softly. "In an abandoned warehouse in Hell's Kitchen, back when you had to step over junkies on the way in. It became a cult hit, and my career took off ..." His voice trailed away, the light in his eyes going out as he returned to the present.

"And look at me now," he said, his voice flattening into a monotone of resignation. "Sucked into this pretentious high-society, full of vacuous people whose sole aim in life is to be photographed next to someone famous for Instagram likes."

The candor was flooring. Oliver quickly finished his wine and flagged a waiter for another. Reza raised his glass in solidarity. Their shared need for an anesthetic was the only real thing connecting them. After Reza delivered a bitter, final monologue on the vacuity of his life, the waiter returned.

"But that's enough about me," Reza said. "What do you do, Oliver?"

The question felt like an interrogation. Who was he? He was no longer the sales engineer from BlockWaves. He was the secret heir to a digital ghost, a man with a fortune he couldn't spend and a truth he couldn't speak. He tried a joke about being a professional wine drinker. Reza's pointed look told him it didn't land.

Oliver sighed. "I'm a freelance tech developer."

"What kind of tech?"

He hesitated, the word feeling dangerous, a piece of a forbidden language. "Bitcoin."

The conversation that followed was a familiar ritual, an attempt to explain the cathedral to a man who had only ever seen the marketplace. He explained the difference between the pristine, logical architecture of bitcoin and the grimy, chaotic bazaar of "crypto." He recounted the FTX fiasco, the words feeling rehearsed, a catechism he had recited many times before. He felt a familiar, hollow satisfaction as Reza listened, the feeling of a missionary successfully planting a seed in barren ground.

Just then, Daniela and Steve returned. After Reza made a dry joke and graciously accepted a glass of the Dom Pérignon, he announced his departure.

"I've had one unexpectedly good conversation tonight," he said, looking at Oliver. "And I don't want to risk ruining the rest of my evening."

After he left, Oliver remarked to Daniela how much Reza reminded him of his father. "The dark sense of humor ... Dad wasn't as jaded, though. He was more uplifting." The comparison felt true and sad, a recognition of two men who had become exiles in their own lives.

As the night wore on and the wine flowed, Oliver's sense of alienation curdled into a quiet, simmering rage. Reza was right. These people were NPCs, non-player characters in the grand, meaningless game of society. Their chatter about fashion, sports and pop culture was just background noise, the ambient hum of the matrix. The Château Margaux roared in his veins as fuel.

By his eighth glass, he was introduced to Arman, an investment banker whose fitted suit and smug certainty represented everything Oliver now despised.

"I'm a bitcoiner," Oliver said, the words a challenge.

Arman's face scrunched in disgust. "Isn't bitcoin dead? Headed to zero. It should, because it has no intrinsic value."

The condescension, the sheer, unadulterated ignorance of the man, was the final spark. The wine and the rage combined into a volatile, explosive mixture. Oliver's careful performance of civility shattered.

"You have no fucking idea what you're talking about," he exploded. The room seemed to fall silent around them. "There is no such thing as intrinsic value! All value is intersubjective. But why the fuck would you know that? You work at a bank, sitting right next to the money printer ... your entire fucking industry depends on people not understanding value!"

He took a staggering step forward, the entire weight of his secret knowledge, his frustration, his grief, pouring out of him in a torrent of furious, drunken truth. "Yeah, laugh now, but your precious fucking US dollar is being printed to zero! You're parasites! Bitcoin is the only thing that's worth anything. Absolute. Fucking. Scarcity. It's rules without rulers. It's individual liberty. It's demonetizing war! It's world peace, and you don't have a single fucking clue!"

Arman stared back, his smugness replaced by shock. "Dude," he finally said. "You're drunk as fuck. You should go home."

The arrival of the bouncer felt inevitable, a physical manifestation of his excommunication from this world. He felt Daniela's presence, her horror a cold wave washing over him. He let them lead him out, the fight gone, replaced by a vast, hollow emptiness.

The cold winter air on the street was a slap, a brutal return to a reality he had just spectacularly failed to navigate. He sat on the bottom step, defeated. From inside, he heard a muffled cheer. Midnight. *A new year*, he thought. *A new circle of hell.*

Then, the rustle from across the street. The silhouette stirred and walked into the dim streetlight. It was the ghost from the feast, a terribly unkempt man who looked like he was woven from the city's grime. He mumbled something.

Oliver stood and walked into the street, drawn by a force he didn't understand. The man mumbled. For a fraction of a second, the words made a strange, perfect sense, a key turning in a lock in his mind, and then the meaning vanished, leaving only the sound of gibberish.

"*Ploos cycla inferna. Ess temper, eh innit? N'as it, ser!*"

"What?" Oliver asked, the single word a small, useless net cast into an ocean of meaning he couldn't grasp.

The homeless man simply repeated himself, his voice a gravelly chant, adding a second, longer phrase. "*Ploos cycla inferna. Ess temper, eh innit? N'as it, ser! Et possti inferna, est renaisus vernatum. Ess temper, eh innit? N'as it, ser.*"

Oliver felt a profound sense of vertigo as the words washed over him, their phantom meanings flickering and dying at the edge of his consciousness. This was it, the language of the fractures, the whispers from the other side, now given a human face.

"Oliver! What are you doing?" Daniela's voice shattered the spell. She ran down the steps and grabbed his arm. "You're standing in the middle of the road!"

"I was just listening to this guy," he said, turning to point. But there was no one there. "He was right here."

"Oliver, you're drunk. Let's go home," she said, her voice tight with embarrassment. When she mentioned apologizing to Arman, the raw anger returned.

"No fucking way I'm apologizing to that fiat fuck," he spat. "He had it coming. This is why I hate these normie events. They're trapped in the fiat matrix, and their entire reality would crumble if they understood one percent of what I'm trying to tell them."

Daniela's face told him it was futile. She stormed to a cab. Sober enough to know better than to let her go alone, he followed. They rode in a silence as cold and vast as the new year stretching out before them.

769851 (January 1)

"Where are you?" Oliver yelled into the darkness, his voice swallowed by a vast, indifferent silence. "Please! I need to talk to you!"

But the Noncemeister's world, with its familiar purple chaos, was gone. For weeks, his pleas had been met with only this new, empty territory – a deep and tranquil blue, tinged with a scintilla of fear that was as omnipresent as it was imperceptible.

"Ego ex inferna natium. Ego viliye in claritate lumiere ..."

A voice drifted through the mist. It was a physical presence, a warmth that seemed to seep directly into his skin, bypassing his ears entirely. For the first time, he sensed a body attached to these strange words, a consciousness shaping them. It was a woman's voice, a soft, sensuous resonance that felt like honey and smoke.

It continued, its strange syntax a hypnotic cadence. "Oliver, I am here to talk to you, I am. Are you there to talk to me, you are?"

Finally, he thought, a wave of profound relief washing over him. *A language I can understand.* Every syllable was a warm caress, every word a promise. "Yes," he replied, his own voice sounding crude and clumsy in comparison. "Of course I want to talk to you. Who are you?"

"I am the one you can never have, but always want, you do. For if you have me, I dissolve, I do," the voice answered, a beautiful, maddening riddle.

"I'm not sure I understand," he said. "Where are you? I can't see you."

Out of the blue shadows, she emerged. The white of her robe wasn't a color but a tear in the fabric of the mist, a perfect void from which she stepped. Her hair was a cascade of liquid light that fell upon her shoulders. And her eyes ... her eyes were a pair of turquoise shores, promising a warm, clear, and bottomless sea. She was, Oliver thought with a sudden, painful clarity, the most beautiful thing he had ever seen.

"Wh ... who are you?" he stuttered, his breath catching, the sight of her a physical blow.

"Anariadne, I am."

"Ariadne?" he asked, grasping for a familiar shape in this new, overwhelming reality. "Like in the Greek myth?"

"Those names, I do not know. Anariadne, I am, not Ariadne. And I am here because certain, you are not. And help you, I can."

"How can you help?" he asked, his own problems feeling small and distant. "I was looking for the Noncemeister. He's gone."

"Of this person, I know not. I am my own, and I will guide you in my way, I will."

"How?"

"How did you wish this other person to guide you?"

"The Noncemeister?"

"Yes, him."

"Well, it's ... it's a long story. It's about my dad's bitcoin ..." Oliver stopped, the word 'bitcoin' feeling profane in her presence, a clunky, technical term from a gray and boring world. *What am I doing?* he thought. *She's a goddess, a dream, and I'm about to explain a distributed ledger to her?*

"Yes, carry on," Anariadne urged, her voice a gentle pull. "Tell me about your father."

"Do you ... know what bitcoin is?"

"Of that word, I do not know, I'm afraid."

"Just like the Noncemeister, then," Oliver mused, finding a strange comfort in the parallel. "He didn't know the word, but he knew the timechain. Wait ..." He looked around the blue void. "We're not in the timechain, are we?"

"I know not of this place you speak of. I am only here to lead you where you need to go."

"Okay, so not the timechain," Oliver clarified, the logic feeling flimsy against the reality of her. "Where do you think I need to go?"

"To that place you do not know," she said, a mysterious half-smile playing on her lips.

Oliver felt a laugh escape him. From the Noncemeister, the words would have been infuriating. From her, they were an invitation, a paradox so beautiful he wanted to lose himself in it. He could listen to her speak these perfect, meaningless sentences forever. "Are you saying I need to go to a destination I'm unaware of?"

"That is the truth," she said. "And I can lead you there. But you must want it. In you yet, that I do not see."

"I only found out about this place ten seconds ago," Oliver said, still smiling. "I'm still trying to understand what it means."

"Until then, I am gone," she whispered. Her form began to dissolve, the light of her hair and the turquoise of her eyes bleeding back into the mist. The withdrawal was a physical sensation, a warmth leaving his skin, leaving him suddenly, terribly cold.

"Wait, come back!" he yelled, the desperation raw in his voice. "I haven't decided yet! That doesn't mean I don't want to go! Anariadne!"

But she was gone, and he was left alone, staring into a darkness that felt colder and emptier than ever before.

769918 (January 1)

"Okay, Oliver, I'll be back in a couple of hours," Daniela called out.

Oliver looked up from his phone. "Where are you off to?"

"Just meeting a friend," she responded, her hand already on the doorknob.

He watched her go. The soft click of the lock was a trigger, unleashing a familiar, corrosive paranoia. *A friend.* On New Year's Day. The words echoed in the sudden silence of the apartment. Was it Maren? The cold whisper of the thought was immediate and invasive. Was Daniela, his partner, his accomplice, now feeding his secrets to the enemy? He tried to crush the suspicion. He trusted her. He had to. It was crazy talk.

His phone buzzed, a welcome anchor in the spiraling quiet. It was a text from Vince, his friend from upstate. A lifeline. The one person connected to this strange new world who still felt grounded and sane. Vince was in the city; he wanted to meet. *Perfect*, Oliver thought with a surge of relief. *The exact guy I need to talk to.* He replied instantly, suggesting O'Connell's.

A few hours later, Vince was already at a table. As Oliver sat, his chair groaned and nearly collapsed beneath him. He grabbed another, only marginally more stable. Aisling was right – the whole place, like himself, felt like it was quietly falling apart.

After catching up, Oliver cautiously navigated the conversation toward the precipice. Every word felt like a risk, an exposure.

"Say, Vince ... I've been trying to find some information about this topic but have drawn a blank so far. If someone had a bunch of bitcoin in a known address and they wanted to move it without leaving a trail, how would they go about it? I mean, this is a purely academic question, of course. I'm researching some of the privacy tools out there." The lie felt clumsy and transparent, the words of a terrible actor.

Vince stared at him skeptically, then broke into a smile. "So, where did you get your hands on this stash?"

"Oh no, no, no," Oliver said, the denial coming out too fast. "As you know, I'm relatively new to bitcoin, so how on Earth could I have got hold of a stash? I'm just curious how good the privacy tech is these days."

Vince didn't look entirely convinced but decided to indulge him. "Well, the best way is to use CoinJoin. It's when you send your bitcoin along with several other people in the same transaction to one address, and you get your amount back in another transaction. Simplistically, it's like if a bunch of people throw twenty-dollar bills into a box, then give the box a nice big shake, and then each person takes a twenty-dollar bill back out of the box. You still have the same amount of money at the end of it, but it's almost definitely a different bill with a different serial number than the one you put in. The more people involved, the better privacy you get. Think of it as getting lost in a crowd – the larger the crowd, the harder you are to find."

The irony was a bitter pill. Oliver was a student being taught the architecture of a prison his own father had designed. *Get lost in a crowd.* It was exactly what he needed to do – to take this enormous, glowing target of a legacy and dissolve it into an anonymous mist. He listened as Vince, the homesteader, explained the elegant, dangerous machine that Dev_akshar, the ghost, had built. A machine for anonymity that had become a cage for his partner, Christiaan van der Dussen, a man now rotting in a real prison for moving these ghosts of value.

Vince wasn't finished, though. "The bigger the CoinJoin round, meaning the more transactions yours gets mixed with, the lower the probability that one of the outputs can be traced back to the original inputs. If you want to play it really safe, take the bitcoin that you get back out of the CoinJoin round and put it through another two or three rounds. At that point, it's nearly impossible to trace it back to the original bitcoin. Think of playing the twenty-dollar-bill-in-a-box game over and over with a different group of people each time. The probability that you leave with a note that has the same serial number as the original one you had is basically zero."

"Wow, I hadn't thought about that," Oliver said, the words an honest admission of his own novice status in this dark new world.

A mischievous smile spread across Vince's face. "And if you want to well and truly shut the door on any possibility of traceability, do four rounds of CoinJoin, and then take the subsequent bitcoin and send it in and out of the Liquid network," he concluded emphatically, referring to a bitcoin-pegged network, or 'sidechain' called Liquid, that offered confidential transactions.

Oliver stared at him, wide-eyed. He replayed the steps in his mind – a complex, multi-layered spell for invisibility. It was a dark art. Each stage was a deliberate act of obfuscation, a ritual designed to sever the present from the past. He would have to move the coins like a ghost through the machine, burying his father's digital signature under so many layers of cryptographic noise that it would effectively cease to exist.

Yes, it was convoluted. It would cost him a fraction of the fortune in fees, a small tithe to the gods of anonymity. But it was absolutely foolproof. No surveillance technology on earth could follow that thread. He felt a surge of manic energy, the giddiness of a man who had just been handed a map of the abyss and been assured he could navigate it without being consumed. A major part of his problem was solved. But it was only the first part.

"That's incredible, Vince," Oliver said, the manic energy from a moment ago settling into a sharp, focused calm. "But what if this person wants to convert the resulting bitcoin into dollars? Cash. A regular exchange is a non-starter; the KYC process would tie their identity to the transaction."

"It shouldn't be an issue," Vince said. "The final exchange transaction can't be connected to the original bitcoin."

But it was an issue. The thought of creating an account, of handing over his driver's license and social security number, felt like deliberately walking back into the prison he was trying to escape. He didn't just want to hide the money's past; he wanted to sever his own connection to the legitimate, surveilled world. "But what if the person wanted to get dollars without leaving any paper trail? A truly peer-to-peer transaction, the way Satoshi intended," Oliver asked, the reference a flimsy cloak for the raw need in his voice.

"Depends where you are. Only a handful of countries have easy cash-for-bitcoin exchanges."

"Let's say ... New York City," Oliver persisted. "Hypothetically."

Vince's eyes narrowed, the friendly, academic mood of the conversation suddenly evaporating. He looked at Oliver not as a student, but as a man standing on a dangerous ledge. "Oliver, what have you gotten yourself into?"

"Nothing!" Oliver replied, the denial automatic, unconvincing. "It's not me, I'm just curious. I want to understand the options." A prickle of panic spread through his stomach. He was a terrible spy.

Thankfully, Vince seemed to be in an indulgent mood. He took a long sip of his drink. "Listen. If you're in trouble, I don't want to know. I'm going to assume this is a hypothetical conversation. Unregulated cash-for-bitcoin services are illegal, and doubly so in the nanny state of New York City. I would never advocate breaking the law, you understand?"

Oliver felt his pulse quicken. This was it. The final door. "Of course, Vince. Just an academic conversation between friends," he replied, his tone equally pointed.

Vince nodded slowly. "However ... I believe there is an active underground market in the city. Malcolm Shabazz Market in Harlem, to be precise."

The name landed in the quiet pub like a thunderclap. Oliver fought to keep his hands from trembling. It was no longer a hypothetical. It was a real, tangible location on a map. "If someone were to – in theory, of course – want to avail themselves of these services, how would they go about it?"

Vince sighed, the friendly pantomime now completely gone. "Listen, Oliver, I don't know what this is about, and I don't want you in jail. More importantly, I have a family I want to stay out of jail for."

"Vince, please," Oliver pleaded, the mask of academic curiosity falling away to reveal the raw desperation underneath. The hope of keeping his promise to Aisling, of solving this impossible problem, was a tangible thing he couldn't bear to see slip away.

Vince seemed to sense his desperation and relented. "Okay, look. You did not hear this from me. Understood?"

"Of course."

"Malcolm Shabazz Market. 116th and Malcolm X. Go in, ask for Saleem Bhai. Fifth stall on the left as you enter." Vince leaned forward, his voice dropping, his tone now deadly serious. "He's going to ask you who sent you. Oliver, listen to me. This is the most important part. Under no circumstances can you tell him my name. You cannot reveal your source. Ever. That whole world runs on an honor system, and the very first test is to see if you'll give up the person who opened the door for you. If you do, it's not just that the deal is off. It's that you'll be marked. It will not end well for you, and it will be a big problem for me. Do you understand?"

Sobered by the gravity in Vince's tone, Oliver nodded. "Yes, got it."

"Saleembai?" he asked, confirming the name.

"Saleem Bhai," Vince corrected him. "Saleem is his name; *Bhai* is a title, means 'brother,' I think."

"So, I find him, and we chat?"

"It's more involved. He'll vet you, ask questions before he even admits to knowing what bitcoin is. Once he decides you're legit, he'll ask for the address you're sending from. He'll check the history. The cleaner the coin, the better. He might even give you a discount."

"A discount?"

"It's not a free service. He takes a cut. Usually eight percent," Vince said, as if mentioning the weather. "So, if you give him one bitcoin – about seventeen grand right now – he'll give you ... a little over fifteen and a half."

Oliver whistled. He'd just escaped the world of institutional rent-seeking, only to find the fees were steeper in the shadows. He wasn't sure he had a choice.

"That's the range we're talking about, right?" Vince asked with a grin. "Around one bitcoin?"

Oliver smiled weakly, knowing he'd revealed far too much. He had dropped the third-person pretense entirely. He wasn't prepared to tell Vince the real amount – a sum that would cover Aisling's two hundred thousand and his own looming debts – but the secret was partially out. "Yeah," he said with a shrug. "In that ballpark."

"Maybe one day you can tell me what this is all about," Vince chuckled. "But for now, I'm happy to say that academic discussions about bitcoin privacy are my favorite kind." He raised his glass.

Oliver gladly obliged, his gratitude mixing with the giddy, terrifying thrill of his newfound knowledge. He now held a key to a door he knew he should never open, but one he now absolutely had to walk through.

770240 (January 3)

He found himself captivated, haunted by a phantom presence. In the days since she had vanished back into the blue mist, Anariadne was a constant hum beneath the noise of his day, an image burned onto the back of his eyelids. Brisk walks, cold showers, hastily downed glasses of wine – nothing worked. She was an inescapable ache, a constant, perplexing yearning.

This is nuts, he thought, the guilt a sharp counterpoint to the obsession. *She's not even real.* But if she wasn't real, why did the thought of her feel like a betrayal? The question led, as it always did, to Daniela. He hadn't told her. He couldn't. What would he say? "Hey babe, a goddess appeared in my head, and I think I'm in love with her. Just thought you'd like to know." No. The secret was his alone.

And in the space that secret created, paranoia began to bloom like a toxic mold. In the brief moments his mind wasn't filled with Anariadne, it turned on Daniela. Her recent absences, her vague talk of "meeting a friend" – his mind twisted these simple facts into a narrative of betrayal. It had to be Maren. Maren, pulling Daniela's strings, turning his ally into a spy. Was she ever loyal? Or was this the long game, a beautiful trap laid to extract his father's secrets? The thought was a venomous feedback loop: his guilt over Anariadne justified his suspicion of Daniela, and his suspicion of Daniela absolved the guilt.

He paced the room, the logic of his own paranoia making his gut churn. He downed the last of the Dom Pérignon. It didn't help.

Finally, he collapsed in his dad's armchair. Daniela was out. The fight was over. He succumbed, willingly this time, to the temptation. He closed his eyes, not hoping, but calling. He was ready to see Anariadne again.

From the blue mist, she emerged, and the sight of her was a physical impact, stealing the air from his lungs. She was more real, more painfully beautiful than he remembered.

"Wanted me, you did?"

Her voice. It was a texture, a silken touch against his mind. Her strange, broken grammar was a kind of music, a hypnotic rhythm that bypassed reason.

"Yes," he mumbled, the single word feeling hopelessly inadequate.

"But on your mind, something is. Is there?" she asked, a mischievous twinkle in her turquoise eyes.

"You are," he replied. "I couldn't stop thinking about you. I wanted to see you again."

"Ah, but have me, you never can. *Ego viliye in claritate lumiere.*"

"Wait," he said, the phantom meaning of her words flickering and dying like a spent match. "I almost understood that. Why does that happen?"

"A way of knowing many things, you have," she replied, her smile enigmatic. "A way of unknowing them, too. Sometimes, both happen at once."

"I don't follow," he said, flustered. "And what do you mean I can't 'have you'? I'm not a creep."

"Ah, Oliver, always you seek me. My lead, you follow. For I am here to lead you. And yet, have me, you cannot."

"Okay, look ... Ana." The nickname was an attempt to make her real, to bring her into his world, to shrink her down to a manageable size. "Anariadne is a bit of a mouthful," he added with a nervous laugh.

"No," she replied. The word was not sharp, not cold. It was spoken with the gentlest firmness he had ever heard, the quiet, absolute authority of a fundamental law of nature. It was the sound of a door being softly, but irrevocably, closed.

"Uh, okay. Anariadne, then," he continued, mildly embarrassed by the gentle but absolute correction. "I still don't get what you mean."

"Shush, my darling. So many questions." Her voice was a soft balm on his confusion. "Work to do, we have." She gestured for him to follow, and he did, a willing captive drawn deeper into the blue haze.

The mist grew brighter as they moved, the light seeming to emanate from her. She turned, her gaze impossibly perceptive. "But tell me, Oliver. On your mind, there is something else. I can see it."

"I told you, I wanted to see you again."

"Ah, but before that thought, another one there was," she insisted, her voice soft but firm. "What was it?"

He felt his defenses crumble under her gaze. The paranoia he'd been nursing felt suddenly exposed, a squalid secret brought into her pristine light. "Oh, right. That. Well, I'm not sure it makes sense to talk about it here."

"Oliver, you come to seek me, you do. And I am here to guide you, I will." She drifted closer until her face was less than a foot from his. She tilted her head, and he felt as though her turquoise eyes were not just looking at him, but *reading* him.

He couldn't resist. The confession spilled out of him. "It's my girlf ... my friend, Daniela. I've confided all my secrets in her, and I have this feeling she's betraying my trust."

Anariadne shook her head, a slow, sad gesture of disapproval. "Not good, that is. How can you be sure?"

"To be fair, I'm not," he admitted, the paranoia suddenly feeling childish and foolish when spoken aloud in her presence. "It's just a suspicion. Now that I've said it, I feel silly."

"My darling, certain you never can be," she whispered, and the words were not a comfort, but a poison. A seductive, logical poison that went straight to the heart of his anxiety. "But a way to get closer to the truth, you can find."

As she spoke, a single, shimmering thread emerged from her robe and began to unravel, leading away into the mist. She gestured for him to follow, her form dissolving, leaving only the thread. Panicked at the thought of losing her, he hurried after it, following her deeper into the labyrinth of his own doubt. He caught up to her inside a thick blue cloud.

"You must observe her mind, Oliver," she whispered urgently, her voice seeming to come from all around him. "Her memories. Certainty, that is how you find it."

"Observe Daniela's mind?" he asked, confused.

"You know how. The doorways to her mind are open to you."

The implication dawned on him, cold and horrifying. "No. You're asking me to project into her mind. To spy on her. I can't do that, Anariadne. I promised her I never would. That's a total breach of trust."

She moved even closer, and the cool, ethereal air around her was replaced by a sudden, intoxicating warmth as her body pressed gently against his. She raised a hand, her fingers tracing a slow, electric line along the side of his face. She moved her mouth next to his ear, and her whisper was no longer just a sound, but a warm breath that sent a shiver through his entire being. "Oliver, certain you want to be if *she* has breached *your* trust, you do. Why not find certainty, when you are able?"

He gulped, his principles dissolving in the heat of her presence. He was grappling with the thrill of her breath on his neck, her body an inviting warmth against his, and the cold, sick feeling of the promise he was about to break.

She took a small step back and slipped her hand into his, her touch both a comfort and a capture. She gestured with her other hand into the space before them. "You see? It is right there. All you must do is walk in."

Oliver looked where she had gestured. The blue haze parted, not like a curtain, but like a wound opening in reality. Through it, he saw Daniela walking down a sunlit street – a memory from New Year's Day, pristine and real. He stared at the shimmering portal, a doorway to a profane act. He was tempted, but the promise he'd made to her held him back, a final, fraying thread of his honor.

Anariadne leaned in again, her mouth once more a breath away from his ear. "Go on, Oliver," she whispered. "It's right there. You know you want to." She brushed her lips against his cheek, a touch as light as a butterfly's wing and as final as a brand. Then she stepped back, letting go of his hand.

He stood on the precipice. On one side was the gnawing uncertainty, the poison of doubt. On the other, the abyss of knowledge and betrayal. He closed his eyes, and a final, desperate rationalization bloomed in the darkness, a justification whispered by the most cowardly part of his soul: *She was right. Why was he so worried about breaching Daniela's trust when she had most likely breached his first?*

He walked into the scene.

It was Gramercy. The memory was mundane, almost boring. Daniela walked into a boutique thrift store, picked up a green leather wallet with a six-hundred-and-twenty-nine-dollar price tag, and bought it. She then crossed the street to a small café. A short while later, her friend Sarah arrived.

Oliver listened, a voyeur in his own life. They were discussing a script for a play: *The Minotaur's Revenge*. There was no mention of Maren. No conspiracy. Only the simple, innocent reality of a woman meeting a friend to talk about her work. The banality of the truth was a crushing weight. He felt a wave of shame so profound it was nauseating, and he walked out of the scene.

Anariadne was waiting, twirling a golden lock around her finger. "Certain, are you now?"

"Yes," he said, his voice choked with distress. "Anariadne, I've made a terrible mistake. She's just working on a play. It has nothing to do with Maren. Oh God, what have I done? I promised her ... I promised I would never do this."

She raised a finger and placed it gently on his lips, silencing him. "Shush, shush, beautiful man. The right thing, you did. You were uncertain. You sought the answer. And now you have it." Her logic was a cold, perfect blade, cutting away his guilt and reframing his violation as a noble quest for truth.

He relaxed slightly at her touch, but the transgression still felt like a stone in his gut. "At what cost? I have to tell her."

She pressed her body against his again, a soft, irresistible weight, and ran a hand down his neck and chest. "You cannot, Oliver. About me, she cannot know. If tell her, you do, then I leave ... and she leaves."

The threat was absolute, a double-edged sword. He shifted backward, resisting the overwhelming urge to wrap his arms around her. "What do you mean you leave? Or her, for that matter?"

"*Ego viliye in claritate lumiere*," she replied, the mystery a wall he couldn't penetrate.

"What?"

"It is the way it is, Oliver."

He didn't know what she meant, but he knew she was right about Daniela. This was a profanity she would never forgive. He would have to carry this transgression alone, to his grave.

Anariadne stared at him, then moved closer, her lips millimeters from his, her hand gently cupping the back of his neck. "You were good today, Oliver," she breathed, the words a warm, electric whisper that felt like praise for a mortal sin. "And I will lead you to where you want to go."

Before he could close the distance between their lips, her hand fell away. She took two steps back and vanished into the blue nothingness, leaving him alone, victorious, and utterly damned.

CHAPTER 2. January 10

A man in his early thirties glanced out of the window of the Acela compartment he was in. The train was about to pull into Union Station in Washington, D.C. He got up from his seat, reached upwards towards the overhead baggage shelf and pulled down a sleek, dark brown leather briefcase and a carefully folded wool overcoat that had been placed on top of it. He set the briefcase down on his now empty seat, unfolded the overcoat and gingerly put it on over his light gray suit, cautiously keeping his balance as the train shuddered in deceleration.

If a contemporary men's fashion critic had observed the young man, they would have said the gray suit, while made of expensive material – a finely woven wool with an acceptably high thread count – was very poorly fitted. The shoulders were drooping, and the top button was a little too far down the torso. The tie was a shade of red that didn't belong anywhere near the earth-tone gray of the fabric. All in all, he seemed like a man of means, as illustrated by the fine material of the suit, but not of taste. A man who, in all probability, was very new to wearing suits.

He stepped down onto the platform with the rest of the denizens of the early morning Acela corridor and strode purposefully towards the taxi stand, requesting an Uber on his phone as he walked. A few minutes later, he located his car, stuck in the roundabout. The man peered inside.

The driver looked back. "Nice?"

"Excuse me?" the man replied, mildly surprised at the odd question.

"Your name Nice, right?"

"It's Nick," he said curtly.

The driver turned to look at his phone, which was attached to the car's dashboard with a cheap suction holder. He saw the name on the app and turned back towards Nick with a toothy grin, "Oh yeah, yeah. I sorry man. Nick, that's right. English, not my main language, you know what I sayin'?"

Nick gave a tight nod and got into the back seat. The driver hit the *start ride* button on his app to reveal the destination address. "950 Pennsylvania Ave," he said, reading off the screen. "Oh, Department of Justice. You must be famous guy, right?" he said, turning around to look at Nick with the same toothy smile.

Nick offered a polite, noncommittal smile.

"Okay, some traffic today. Usually take five, ten minute to get there from here, but maybe today it take twenty minute, thirty minute. You got important meeting you need to be on time?" the driver asked, as he waited to maneuver the car out of the packed taxi stand.

Nick had no desire for a freewheeling conversation. "I'm fine," he said. "My meeting is at ten." He opened his briefcase and placed his laptop on his lap, a clear signal. The driver turned back to the road, his expression slightly disappointed.

The taxi arrived at its destination a little over twenty minutes later. "Thank you, Mr. Nick. If you like, you give me five star, okay? I give you five star also," the taxi driver said in a hopeful tone, as Nick got out of the car.

Nick nodded and turned toward the building. As he walked up the large stairs leading to the front door of the impressive building on Pennsylvania Avenue, he pulled out his phone, tapped the Uber app, and gave the driver a single star. He slipped the phone back into his pocket without breaking his stride, his gaze fixed on the entrance.

After clearing security, he approached the front desk.

"ID, please," the front desk clerk said, not making eye contact with Nick.

Nick handed her his driver's license.

"State your full name, who you are representing and the name of the person you are here to meet," she recited in a robotic monotone.

"Nicholas Hernandez, senior director of chain intelligence at Chain Intelligence. I'm here to meet Mr. Jeremiah Howard for a 10 a.m. meeting. I'm a few minutes early."

"State his designation please," the robotic voice continued.

"He's uh ..." Nick tried to remember Jeremiah Howard's title but couldn't.

"Just a sec," he said to the clerk as he fumbled through his pocket for his phone. He found it and opened up his email app to find the latest email from Jeremiah Howard and scrolled down to the signature block.

"Ah, found it. He's the head of the cryptocurrency crimes unit. His title is deputy principal deputy assistant attorney general. Yeah, that's right, there's two deputies in there. His boss is the principal deputy assistant attorney general, and he runs the full crimes unit. Mr. Howard runs the crypto part of that; that's why there's an extra deputy in his title," Nick chuckled nervously.

The clerk-robot seemed unamused. With her impossibly long, perfectly manicured red nail, she deftly manipulated the pinwheel on the mouse, scrolling down as her eyes remained fixed on the computer screen. "Room 407," she said blankly, "take the second set of elevators to your left to the fourth floor."

She pressed a button on her desk with the same nail, and the sensor light on the turnstile changed color from red to green. Nick thanked her and walked past it and towards the second elevator bank.

He got to the fourth floor and walked over to room 407. After checking in with an equally robotic receptionist there, he was led to a room with a glass door. He knocked on it gently, and it was opened a few moments later by a man a little older than Nick, in a decidedly less expensive and even worse fitted navy-blue suit than his.

"Jeremiah Howard," the man said sternly, extending a hand towards Nick.

"Nicholas Hernandez, from Chain Intelligence. Pleasure to meet you, Mr. Howard. You can call me Nick," he said, as he shook his hand.

Mr. Howard settled into a chair behind his desk, then gestured to the seat opposite him. "Please be seated, Mr. Hernandez," he said.

As Nick lowered himself into the chair, his eyes swept across the room. The space exuded a minimalist elegance, blending modern simplicity with classical touches. A desk of high-quality, polished wood commanded attention, its rich grain complemented by the equally impressive chairs upholstered in supple green leather.

Mr. Howard seemed to notice the expression on Nick's face, and his own stern demeanor appeared to soften briefly, "Like what you're seeing?"

"It's really nice. Looks like taxpayer money is being put to good use here," Nick responded, with a nervous chuckle, unsure if it was worth making that joke right after the words came out of his mouth.

It wasn't. The momentary softening in Mr. Howard's manner vanished. "So, Mr. Hernandez, I requested you to come here because I felt an in-person discussion of your findings would be more appropriate than an email exchange. You were suggesting the last time we spoke that you're making progress on Dev_akshar's on-chain activity, is that correct?"

"Yes, sir. We actually have some significant updates," Nick said importantly, happy that the topic had quickly diverted to work from the uncomfortable small talk. He pulled out his laptop from his briefcase and opened up a PDF document. He glanced at it before speaking again. "As you know, in February of 2022, we were able to flag one bitcoin address with twenty-four thousand bitcoin in it as likely being one of the MixMarket addresses, and furthermore, likely belonging to Dev_akshar."

"Can I stop you there?" Mr. Howard interrupted.

"Of course."

"*You* found that address, or we did?"

"Well, to be fair, sir, that was before my time at Chain Intelligence. But I do believe our company was able to discern that and provide the information to your predecessor at the DoJ," Nick replied.

Mr. Howard nodded. "Understood. Please proceed."

Nick cleared his throat, "The last recorded transaction from that address up until that point was from December 2013. Then, on December 15, 2022, meaning just about three weeks ago, there were another two transactions. The first ones in nine years. One was to move twenty-four bitcoin to another address, which is now being actively monitored, and the second was an

OP_RETURN that seems to contain some sort of coded message. We were able to track down the IP addresses for both transactions, and we believe that it was one individual using a VPN for both of those transactions."

"Why do you believe that?" Mr. Howard asked.

"The first transaction was from an IP in Slovenia. The second, four minutes later, was from Canada's northern territories. The probability of two separate actors hitting a nine-year-dormant address from such disparate locations within minutes is extremely low. It's more likely a single actor switching VPN servers. Both IPs also fall into blocks we associate with known VPN providers."

Howard chewed on the cap of his pen, staring into the distance. "Mr. Hernandez, these transactions happened three weeks ago. Why are we only discussing this now?"

Nick shifted uncomfortably. "Sir, our systems detected it immediately. We reached out to your office, but we were told it had closed for the holidays. January 4th was the first day we could connect with your team."

"Good point," Howard said dismissively. "What else have you got?"

"The next step, sir, would be for the DoJ to issue subpoenas to three or four of the top VPN providers to identify which one of them the IP addresses originated from. Once you identify the company, you ask them to hand over their list of customers and their corresponding session information. You can use that to triangulate the identity of the user who made those transactions, which we believe is Dev_akshar. Of course, there are VPN providers on the dark web which you wouldn't be able to issue a subpoena to because you wouldn't know who they are, and it's reasonably likely that a seasoned operator like Dev_akshar would have ..."

"Mr. Hernandez," Mr. Howard raised his hand and interrupted Nick. "It is not your place to tell the Department of Justice how to do its job. My question to you was, what else were you able to determine as it pertains strictly to chain analysis?"

Nick gulped. "Got it. I was just trying to lay out ..." he stopped again, sensing Mr. Howard was in no mood to hear his justification. "Anyway, from our perspective, we will continue monitoring all the current bitcoin addresses and any future ones that arise from this transaction. If we get further insights on the investigation from either your office or your partners at the FBI, it will allow us to make our model even more robust."

"Again, Mr. Hernandez," Mr. Howard said firmly, "the FBI's involvement in this investigation is not your concern. Your company's contract is with the Department of Justice." He leaned forward slightly, his gaze sharpening. "Am I correct in understanding that you have no further updates beyond the two transactions you've tracked?"

Nick bristled at Mr. Howard's tone. It appeared the man was deliberately downplaying his efforts. He weighed the urge to protest, but decided it was futile. "That is correct, sir. I will leave this paper copy of the report with you." He took a binder out of his briefcase, thumbed through a few stapled pages, pulled out the five-page report, and placed it on the desk. Mr. Howard promptly flicked it aside with two fingers.

"We also sent your office an electronic copy yesterday via secure email," Nick concluded.

The meeting ended, and as Nick exited the office, they exchanged a distant handshake. The tension from the meeting lingered, following Nick as he made his way through the building. As he put his overcoat on near the exit, he became acutely aware of the perspiration that had soaked through his shirt.

He stepped out onto the street and felt the cool winter air wash over him – a stark contrast to the stifling atmosphere he'd just left behind. Nick was deeply disappointed. He had anticipated a warmer reception from Mr. Howard, perhaps even some appreciation for the efforts of his team. Instead, he'd endured thirty minutes of relentless scrutiny, emerging without so much as a perfunctory show of gratitude.

He started walking towards D Street, looking for a place to eat before his train back to New York. A new resolve hardened within him. Next time, he vowed, Mr. Howard would be hanging on his every word.

770656 (January 6)

As the northbound taxi approached the roundabout at 110th Street and Central Park West, Oliver's gaze drifted out the window. The avenue's name abruptly changed to Frederick Douglass Boulevard after passing the roundabout.

Glancing at his phone, Oliver reviewed the bitcoin addresses he'd recorded for the impending cash exchange. After much consideration, he'd settled on 125 bitcoin. With the current exchange rate of a little over $17,000 per bitcoin, that would leave him with approximately $2 million after factoring in the eight percent transaction fee for Saleem Bhai.

Getting all that bitcoin through the four-stage CoinJoin and then the Liquid network had taken a lot longer than he had expected. He needed to split the amount into several smaller transactions because there was no CoinJoin round that could accept such a large amount. He chose not to consolidate all the bitcoin into one address at the end and instead left it in 11 irregularly sized amounts in separate addresses. The fact that he had all those addresses controlled on a wallet app on his phone was insane to him. He was walking around with 125 bitcoin in a hot wallet on his phone, a laughably insecure and incredibly dangerous practice. But he didn't have a choice, given the job at hand.

Two hundred thousand dollars for Aisling, another $200,000 to pay off his student loans and credit cards, and the rest would cover his expenses for the next couple of years at least. He realized the loan paydowns would take a while, as any cash deposit above $10,000 in his bank account would trigger red flags, so he would have to tackle those piecemeal.

He had waffled for a while between $1 million and $2 million. His back-of-the-envelope math had yielded a weight of 44 pounds for $2 million in one-hundred-dollar bills. At one gram per bill, $2 million would be 20,000 bills at 20 kilos or 44 pounds. One million would be half that weight, obviously. Willing to deal with lugging the extra weight around, he picked an extra sturdy hardback suitcase for the job.

What the hell am I doing? Oliver asked himself as the taxi turned onto 116th Street and approached Malcolm X Boulevard. *I'm going to walk into a specialty*

African market in Harlem with an empty suitcase, talk to a complete stranger about sending him an ungodly amount of bitcoin, and hope to walk out lugging a suitcase now containing almost fifty pounds worth of Benjamins. This is completely insane. Who on Earth is this guy, anyway? What if he just takes the bitcoin and kills me?

The butterflies in his stomach were flapping like vultures as the taxi pulled up in front of Malcolm Shabazz market.

He got out, retrieved the empty suitcase and took in the scene. Green minarets flanked an entrance topped by a red and yellow awning that stretched the length of the block, casting a warm glow on the bustle inside. It was a vibrant slice of West Africa on a New York City street.

He stepped through the ornate entrance and was immediately engulfed in a cacophony of voices and the smell of incense. He scanned the labyrinth of stalls as he ploughed forward, counting the ones on his left. Vince had told him Saleem Bhai's stall was the fifth one past the entrance.

The fifth stall was large. Brightly colored batik fabrics hung from the rafters, their intricate patterns appeared to be telling stories of distant lands. Hand-carved wooden figurines stood sentinel on makeshift shelves, their eyes seemingly following his every move. The glint of silver caught his attention – delicate filigree jewelry lay nestled in velvet-lined boxes, each piece a work of art.

The air around the stall was thick with the aroma of shea butter and exotic oils, their scents mingling with the leather of handcrafted bags and sandals. A collection of djembe drums stood silent in the corner, seemingly pleading for happy hands to bring them to life.

But of Saleem Bhai himself, there was no sign. Oliver's brow furrowed as he scanned the empty stall. He poked his head between the draped fabrics and spotted a middle-aged man sitting on a stool, engrossed in his phone. The man, wearing a colorful kufi cap, looked up, saw Oliver, and jumped to his feet, hurrying towards the front of the stall.

"Eh! Sorry, young man, I no see you," he said with a sheepish smile, his accent thick and melodious. "You come for something special, eh? I have many fine things!"

Oliver cleared his throat. "Actually, I'm looking for Saleem Bhai. Is he around?"

The man's eyes twinkled as he wagged his finger. "Ah, Saleem Bhai? Maybe he come, maybe he no come. But look-look, you see this fine jewelry?" He gestured to a display of intricate silver pieces. "Very special, very powerful!"

"Thanks, but I really need to speak with Saleem Bhai. It's important," Oliver pressed.

"*Aiiii*, important like hot pepper soup on cold day!" the vendor chuckled, slapping his thigh. But Saleem Bhai, he like people who appreciate the beauty. You buy small-small, it help you. You understand?"

Oliver shifted uncomfortably, realizing that finding Saleem Bhai might require navigating more than just the physical maze of the market. "I understand, but ..."

"No but-but, my friend!" the man interrupted, holding up a vibrant batik fabric. "You try this, eh? Make you look sharp-sharp like big man! Or maybe you want hear this drum?" He tapped a nearby djembe. "Sweet sound, sweet like palm wine. You play music?"

Oliver found himself caught between amusement and vexation, wondering how to proceed in this unexpected cultural dance. He decided to go the direct route. "I want to talk to him about bitcoin," he said firmly.

The shopkeeper fell silent. His gregarious entrepreneur manner stopped dead in its tracks, and he stared intently at Oliver for a few moments. "What you talk crazy stuff, man?" He said in a far more serious tone. "This is West African shop, you understand? You want buy something here, special stuff from Senegal, Mali, Nigeria, yeah. Maybe you want something extra, I find for you inside from Dubai and Saudi. We don't know no other stuff, eh?"

The change in the shopkeeper's demeanor at the very mention of bitcoin was proof enough for Oliver that he was on the right track. He remembered what Vince told him, that they would initially deny even knowing anything about bitcoin.

"Listen," Oliver lowered his voice unnecessarily. The din of the market would have drowned out anything spoken from more than three feet away. "I need to do an exchange. I have my bitcoin ready; I have the addresses and transaction history with me. Everything is clean. It's not a small number." He pointed to his suitcase. "Can I please talk to Saleem Bhai?"

The shopkeeper fell silent again and stared Oliver up and down. "Okay," he finally said, reluctantly. "You come inside, yeah? I call Saleem Bhai. You go there, back room," he pointed to a corner inside the stall. "Wait there, he come for you."

Oliver stepped around the table fronting the stall and ascended two rough-hewn stone steps, pulling the empty suitcase behind him. Following the shopkeeper's gesture, he ducked into a cramped, austere room. The floor beneath his feet was uneven, raw stone, and the walls were bare brick – not the trendy exposed kind found in upscale lofts, but the neglected, utilitarian variety that spoke of age and disrepair.

The space was spartan, devoid of any unnecessary furnishings, creating an atmosphere that was both claustrophobic and strangely expectant. As Oliver's eyes adjusted to the dimmer light, he couldn't shake the feeling that he had stepped not just into a room, but into a world far removed from the bustling market outside, the noise and hubbub barely perceptible through the walls.

There was a desk in one corner of the room with an old computer on it and a pile of dog-eared files next to it. A solitary metal folding chair stood across the room. Oliver sat down with the suitcase next to him and waited.

Fifteen minutes passed in the stone-floored purgatory. Oliver got up, the silence of the room a stark contrast to the frantic beating of his own heart. He peeked out into the stall; it was empty. He could hear the distant, joyous cacophony of the market, a world he no longer felt a part of. He retreated back to the metal chair, a man waiting for a verdict.

Ten minutes later, footsteps. An NYPD cop stepped into the room.

The sight was a physical blow. Oliver's heart plummeted. This was the system he was trying to escape, the world of consequences and laws, manifesting here in this lawless space. The badge on his uniform read 'Aguilar'.

"All right buddy, it's over," Officer Aguilar said, his voice a low growl. "I was told you're here for an illegal cash-for-bitcoin exchange. You're gonna tell me who sent you here, and maybe you'll get off easy. If not, things aren't looking too good for you."

Oliver's heart hammered in his temples. Vince's warning – *Under no circumstances* – was a frantic, screaming alarm in his head. "I don't ... I don't know what you're talking about," he stuttered.

"Drop the act, kid," Aguilar barked. "Abubakar told me exactly what you said. You have the bitcoin on you, you have all the addresses, and you're looking for cash. Do you deny you said that?"

"I don't know who Abubakar is," Oliver mumbled, realizing too late it must be the shopkeeper's name.

"Do I look dumb to you?" Aguilar towered over him. "How the hell did you get in here if you didn't talk to Abubakar?"

"Officer, I'm sorry. There's been a misunderstanding," Oliver said, his mind scrambling for a plausible story as a vision of a prison cell – gray, sterile, a lifetime of meaningless minutes – flashed in his mind. The panic was giving way to a cold, absolute terror. "I'm a bitcoin educator. I was trying to teach him about it. He must have misunderstood."

"What the fuck is this suitcase for then?"

"I was going to buy things ... I needed something to carry them. Please, I've done nothing wrong," he pleaded.

"That's it, I've had enough of this bullshit," Aguilar yelled, kicking the suitcase aside. He kicked the leg of Oliver's chair, and Oliver flailed to keep his balance. "Guess you want to do this the hard way." He grabbed Oliver by the collar, lifted him effortlessly, and slammed him against the rough brick wall, pinning him by the neck.

The impact knocked the wind out of him. The world compressed to the rough texture of brick against his back and the crushing pressure on his throat. "This ... is police brutality," he gasped, each word a painful, desperate bid for air.

"One last chance, kid. Who sent you here? Or you're walking out of here in handcuffs and a neck brace, straight to Rikers." Aguilar's face was inches from his, a mask of pure menace.

Oliver closed his eyes as the world began to gray out, the air completely cut off. His thoughts, starved of oxygen, began to unspool in a strange, slow-motion clarity, set against a gentle, neural hum. A procession of ghosts from his past appeared before him: Mrs. Cheadle, the history teacher whose disappointment felt like a punch in the gut; Ian Wright, his old boss, whose authority he had never dared to question; Maren, whose quiet manipulations he had only recognized too late. His entire life had been a series of submissions to power, a quiet, polite surrender. It wasn't until the Noncemeister taught him how to be a man that he'd ever stood his ground.

And now, here you are again, a voice in his head whispered. *Back to square one. A hand on your throat.*

Time seemed to stop. The thoughts tumbled, no longer frantic, but slow and crystalline. *The Noncemeister. What would he say? You are the mastermind of your own reality.* The memory was an echo from a lost world, a lifeline in the suffocating dark. *He's gone now. All that's left is me. Me and this hand on my throat. I'm observing it. I'm observing my feelings. What are they? Panic. Terror. Fear.* He saw the feelings not as a part of him, but as objects floating in his consciousness. *There they are. They are not me. I am not the terror. I am the one who witnesses the terror within me.*

It was not a peaceful realization. It was a violent, desperate act of psychological self-preservation. A psychic severing. He cut the cord connecting him to his own fear.

A deathly calm fell over him. The panic, terror, and fear didn't just evaporate; they were ejected, jettisoned from the core of his being. He opened his eyes and looked directly at Aguilar. "Okay," he managed to croak, his voice ragged but imbued with a new, cold stillness.

Surprised by the change, Aguilar released the pressure, taking a small step back. "Good. You're ready to talk now? Let's hear it."

"Nothing," Oliver said, rubbing the bruised flesh of his throat.

"What? What the fuck do you mean nothing?" Aguilar's face was a mask of confusion and disgust.

"I have nothing to say," Oliver continued calmly, his voice steady. "Nobody sent me here. I came here because I wanted to."

Aguilar stared at him, truly seeing him for the first time. He seemed to be looking for the fear that was no longer there. Finally, to Oliver's disbelief, he gave a curt nod, turned, and walked out. "He's good. He's clean," Oliver heard him say to someone outside. "Two percent for this one, don't forget." The footsteps faded away.

A bearded man entered the room, his arms clasped calmly behind his back. He wore a flowing kurta and an Islamic skullcap. Abubakar, the shopkeeper, followed close behind. The newcomer's gaze was keen, traveling over Oliver from head to toe in a silent, thorough appraisal before he offered a curt nod.

"So, you good guy, huh?" he said. *Scratch Middle Eastern*, Oliver thought, the accent unmistakably South Asian. *That's Saleem Bhai.*

Oliver stared, his mind still a frantic scramble of adrenaline and shock from the encounter with Aguilar. He felt a profound sense of whiplash, from the brink of violent death to this moment of calm, businesslike scrutiny. "Are you Saleem Bhai?" he finally asked.

"Ya. Abu say you want to do the exchange. What you got?"

The casualness of the question was staggering. "What on Earth was that just now?" Oliver demanded, his voice strained. "Who the hell was that cop? He almost killed me!"

Saleem Bhai made a dismissive clicking noise with his tongue, a sound of mild, parental annoyance. "Oh, don't worry about that guy. He one of my guy, but he new. Sometime new guy get too rough, you understand me?"

"Too rough?" Oliver exclaimed, incredulous. "A few seconds more and I would have been asphyxiated! Now you're telling me he's not even a real cop!"

"When I told he not real cop?" Saleem replied, his tone utterly unbothered. "I need real NYPD guys working for me. It's like insurance policy for my business, you know what I saying?"

Oliver stared, trying to process the inverted logic. A real cop, a paid asset, had just assaulted him as a customer service vetting procedure. The world he knew, with its clear (if corruptible) lines between law and crime, seemed to be dissolving around him. "So, you're telling me you have real cops on your payroll to vet potential customers?"

"You need many friend in this business," Saleem said, as if explaining a simple truth of commerce. "Government no like this, so we need to do ... how you say ... background check on customer."

"That's hardly a background check," Oliver winced, the bruised flesh of his neck a tender reminder of the 'procedure.'

"Okay guy. Sometime new guy can be rough. But now we know you good guy." Saleem's gaze sharpened. "Who send you here?"

Oliver felt the question not as a simple query, but as the final lock he had to pass through. The cold, detached calm he had found while being choked was still there, a shield against the room's strange currents. He knew this was the good-cop chaser to the bad-cop mauling he'd just endured. "No one," he said, his voice solemn and steady. "I came here on my own."

Saleem Bhai raised his eyebrows, then turned to Abubakar with a small, satisfied smile. "You see this, Abu? I think we got good guy."

Abubakar nodded.

"Okay mister, we can talk the money, yeah? What your name is?" Saleem turned back to him.

"Oliver."

"How much you want?"

Oliver's mind raced. He had 125 clean bitcoin. Giving it all up now felt like a total surrender. After the violation he'd just endured, he felt a desperate need to hold something back, to retain some sliver of control in a situation where he had none. It was a small, strategic act in a world he was only just beginning to understand. "I have 85 bitcoin to exchange. That works out to roughly one and a half million dollars."

Saleem Bhai's eyes widened, and he let out a low whistle. He turned to Abubakar again. "Look this, Abu. We got big man here. I thinking he got one, two bitcoins, and now he's telling 85. This our biggest one, yeah?"

Abubakar thought for a moment. "Maybe second, maybe third biggest one. For sure biggest in last three–four years."

"You got the address?" Saleem asked Oliver.

Oliver opened the notes app on his phone, hiding the last three of his eleven prepared addresses. He held the phone out.

"What I can do with this?" Saleem chortled. "You got the Signal app?"

Oliver nodded. Another step into their world, another piece of his old life left behind.

"Here my account," Saleem showed Oliver his username. "You set the disappearing message to five minute, yeah? Then you send me this one."

Oliver found the account on Signal and, with a final, silent acknowledgment of the threshold he was crossing, sent the eight addresses into the encrypted darkness.

Saleem Bhai strode to the computer and turned it on. Oliver watched as he performed a strange, low-tech data transfer, moving the Signal message from his phone to the aging desktop.

On the screen, Saleem pulled up a block explorer Oliver didn't recognize – a stripped-down, professional-looking tool. He began to click through the transaction history of each address Oliver had provided. It was a nerve-wracking audit. Oliver felt like an art student watching a master critic inspect his work, searching for the fatal flaw, the single brushstroke that would reveal him as a fraud. Abubakar hovered close to the monitor, the two men exchanging hushed whispers and meaningful glances that were impossible for Oliver to decipher.

After a few minutes that felt like hours, Saleem turned, pursing his lips. He gave a slow nod of what looked like genuine, mild admiration. "You right, Oliver. Very clean. I can't tell where this money come from. You got 87 bitcoins total in those addresses. Easier you do full amount, yeah, not 85."

A wave of relief washed over Oliver, so potent it was almost dizzying. He had passed. He nodded.

"Right now, price is 16,877 dollar, yeah? I give you discount 'cause it's clean. We do seven percent, okay? Usually we do eight percent, but you good guy. Clean guy," he chuckled, and Abubakar joined in.

Oliver nodded again, the absurdity of the moment hitting him. He had just been physically assaulted as an entrance exam, and now he was gratefully accepting a one percent discount for good behavior.

Saleem pulled out his phone and punched the numbers into a calculator, flipping the screen to show the result: 1,365,518. Oliver's own calculation matched.

"Ok, looks good to me. Do you have the cash?" Oliver asked.

"Two hour you come back, okay? Oh no, maybe three hour. I forgot, Abu and I go for the *namaaz* at twelve o'clock."

Oliver didn't understand. The casual mention of an unfamiliar word in the middle of a multi-million-dollar illicit transaction was another disorienting detail in a morning full of them. Saleem saw his confusion and clarified, "We go for our Friday afternoon prayer. You come back here maybe three o'clock, okay?"

"Ah, got it. Okay, I will," Oliver replied.

"Wait," Saleem raised his hand as Oliver turned to leave. "First you show where the bitcoins you have. You just show me the address, boss. Now I need to see you have this bitcoins."

"Oh, right," Oliver said sheepishly. The transaction history proved the coins were clean, but it didn't prove they were *his*.

He opened the bitcoin wallet app on his phone and showed the balance to Saleem Bhai, who promptly burst out laughing. He gestured to Abubakar, who peered over his shoulder and began laughing as well.

Oliver stood in the middle of the spartan room, a silent audience to the minute-long spectacle of the two men doubled over, laughing heartily at his expense.

Saleem finally wiped a tear from his eye. "Look this crazy guy, Abu ..." his voice trailed off into another cackle.

After an awkward eternity, a fragile, laughter-free quiet settled on the room. "You crazy guy, man," Saleem said, his voice still high with amusement. "I never see nothing like this. You got the 87 bitcoins on the phone. I thinking you got the Ledger, Trezor, some hardware wallet ... but no, you got it all on the phone." He looked at Abubakar, and they both started laughing again.

They're right, Oliver thought, a hot flush of shame creeping up his neck. The laughter was the genuine, disbelieving mirth of seasoned professionals looking at an amateur who had somehow survived making a rookie mistake of catastrophic proportions. No one in their right mind carries this much value in a hot wallet. It was like walking through a warzone with a bag of gold chained to your wrist. He had passed their violent physical test only to fail this simple, technical one in the most comical way imaginable.

After finally regaining his composure, Saleem Bhai spoke. "Okay guy, you come back three o'clock, yeah? First you send me ten bitcoins advance now, then you go. I saw the second address you gave me has ten in it."

A cold dread washed over Oliver, erasing the brief moment of relief. "Wait, what? Why don't we do the exchange after you show me the cash?"

"No, that's not how it work," Saleem responded, his tone shifting from jovial to a steely firmness. "Yeah you show the wallet now, but we need to verify you really control it. For that, you gotta send advance payment."

"But how can I know that you're not going to disappear with it?" Oliver protested, his voice rising slightly.

"Brother, I think so, you not understand the *hawala*," Saleem said, his voice calm, almost paternal. "This system is first you trust. You no verify."

The starkness of the irony felt like a slap in the face to Oliver. *Don't trust, verify.* It was the central commandment of the world he had chosen, the bedrock principle upon which the entire edifice of bitcoin was built. And here, at the final gate, he was being asked to commit the ultimate heresy: to close his eyes and trust a stranger with a fortune, based on nothing more than a violent handshake and a vibe.

"Okay," Oliver said, the word a quiet surrender. He had no choice. He'd come this far. He had passed a brutal physical test to prove his credentials. There was no going back. "Where do I send it?"

Saleem Bhai gestured to Abubakar, who returned a moment later with a small, calculator-like hardware wallet and handed it over. Saleem took it to the computer and, after a few clicks, a QR code glowed on the screen.

"Send to this one," he said.

Oliver looked at the string of characters, a digital abyss waiting for his offering. He opened the wallet app, his hand hesitant, and scanned the code. His finger hovered over the send button. *I can't believe I'm doing this*, he thought. *One hundred and seventy thousand dollars, cast into the void on a stranger's word. A reasonable chance I'm burning the soundest money in the world for nothing.* He sighed and pressed the button.

"Now we wait ten minute, yeah?" Saleem said, seeing the unconfirmed transaction appear on his screen. "You stay here. Abu come back and check, then you go." He unplugged the hardware wallet and walked out, leaving Oliver alone with Abubakar and the weight of his irreversible decision.

A short while later, Abubakar returned, glanced at the screen, and noted the two confirmations. "Okay, guy, you go and get something eat for lunch, maybe? Leave your suitcase here."

"Do you know any good place around here?" Oliver asked, the simple question feeling absurd after the morning's madness.

Abubakar's eyes brightened. "You want try special food from my country?"

"Sure, I'd love to."

"My cousin has best Senegalese restaurant in city. 117th St and St. Nicholas. Five minute to walk from here," he said enthusiastically. "Actually, he got guy in kitchen from Cote d'Ivoire, so it's all West African food. You like it, I think."

Oliver, needing to escape the claustrophobic back room and his own racing thoughts, thanked him and walked out into the market, then onto the street.

He squinted against the low winter sun as he approached the aptly named West Africa Restaurant. Inside, the modest room was a warm haven of vibrant tapestries and the rich aromas of a world away. He settled into a worn wooden chair, its slight wobble a comforting, physical reality after the abstract terror of the transaction.

He picked up a faded, laminated menu. *Mafé* – a rich goat stew in peanut sauce. He ordered it with *attiéké*, a cassava couscous, and a Solibra Chill shandy. The meal, when it came, was a revelation. The complex, savory flavors, the texture of the couscous, the crispness of the shandy – it was a profound, grounding experience. For a few minutes, he was just a man enjoying one of the best meals of his life. He had a second shandy, paid his bill, and stepped back out into the cold.

With two hours to kill before returning to the market, Oliver decided to walk. The crisp air and the brisk pace helped to ground him as he wandered through Harlem, a tourist in his own city. He meandered for an hour, letting the rhythm of the street pull him along, until he turned onto a quiet block and froze.

Sprawled on the sidewalk was a familiar figure, fiddling with colored chalk. It was the man from New Year's Eve, the ghost from the feast. It felt like an appointment he didn't know he'd made.

Oliver stopped, his heart beginning to pound a slow, heavy rhythm. The man looked up, his dazed, cross-eyed gaze landing somewhere in Oliver's vicinity. "*Hessele tu rabey,*" he muttered.

The sensation was immediate and unmistakable, the same maddening mental vertigo he felt with Anariadne: a fleeting, perfect moment of understanding, a flash of pure meaning that was instantly and totally forgotten.

"I'm sorry?" Oliver asked.

"*Ah, et possti inferna, est renaisus vernatum,*" the homeless man replied, staring past him. "*Ess temper, eh innit? N'as it, ser.*"

They were the same words from New Year's, a cryptic refrain in a song he couldn't grasp. "I'm not sure I follow," Oliver said.

"*Hessele tu rabey?*" the man repeated, the statement now a question, as if Oliver was the one who was failing a simple test.

Oliver could only grimace in response.

The man's eyes widened. He raised a single, grimy finger, a gesture demanding attention. He picked up a piece of red chalk and drew a crude spiral on the sidewalk. He took a yellow one and drew another beside it. He proceeded with the four remaining colors, arranging the six spirals in a circle, then connecting each one to a central point.

Oliver stared, transfixed. It was a glyph, a piece of impossible geometry drawn in chalk on a dirty city sidewalk. He'd seen Celtic art with three spirals – the name slipped his mind – but never six. The shape felt ancient, significant.

"*Hessele tu rabey!*" the man exclaimed, pointing animatedly at his creation.

"I'm sorry, I don't know what you're saying," Oliver replied, at a complete loss. He noticed the man wore only the same tattered t-shirt, a pathetic defense against the biting 30-degree air. "You must be freezing," he said, his concern a jarringly normal emotion in this surreal encounter. "Do you want to go to a shelter?"

"*Ess temper, eh innit? N'as it, ser!*" the man sputtered.

"Hang on, let me see if there's a cop who can help." Oliver walked to the corner and scanned the avenue. Seeing no one, he turned back.

The man was gone.

That's impossible, he thought, his mind rejecting the evidence of his own eyes. *I was turned away for 20 seconds.* He walked back to the spot. The spiral drawing was still there, a vibrant, silent testament on the concrete. But the artist had vanished. He was too frail to have run, too slow to have reached the end of the block. He had simply ceased to be there.

Still shaking his head in bewilderment, Oliver took a photo of the drawing, a desperate attempt to anchor the impossible event to the digital reality of his phone. He checked the time. It was almost three. Time to return to the other side of the looking glass, back to Saleem Bhai.

Back in the market, Oliver's mind was still reeling from the encounter on the street. The impossible disappearance of the man, the cryptic drawing left behind on the sidewalk – it felt like a message from a world bleeding into his own. He walked over to the fifth stall. Abubakar was at the front, trying to catch a customer's eye. He noticed Oliver and gestured with his head toward the back room.

Saleem Bhai was there, waiting. "Look your suitcase," he said, pointing to the hard-sided case on the floor.

Oliver's heart hammered. He walked over and unzipped it. Inside were stacks and stacks of hundred-dollar bills, arranged in perfect, dense rows. He took a sharp breath, the sheer physical reality of the cash hitting him like a wave. It wasn't an abstract number in a wallet anymore. It was paper, ink and the weight of a hundred dangerous decisions.

"Is 1,365,520 dollar, ya? Each pack is hundred notes," Saleem Bhai said. "I give you two dollar extra because you clean guy." He looked at Abubakar and guffawed.

"Ok, let me count to make sure," Oliver replied, the words sounding foolish even as he said them.

"You crazy guy or what?" Saleem scoffed. "You count the number of packs, okay? There are one hundred and thirty-six pack inside and one more small pack. You count one-by-one, it take all day, and we got no time."

"How did you count it then?"

"We got the machine in the office, brother. It count fast."

"Can I have the machine?" Oliver asked, feeling himself being maneuvered into a corner of absurd trust.

"No machine here. Other office," Saleem retorted nonchalantly.

"Can I do a few random samples, at least?" Oliver insisted, needing some semblance of verification in this world of smoke and mirrors.

"Okay," Saleem relented. "Twenty minute. First, you send me the remaining 77 bitcoins." He pointed to a new QR code on the screen.

Oliver sighed. There it was again. The price of admission was always another leap of faith. He scanned the code and sent the remainder of the funds into the ether. He then picked out ten random stacks and began the painstaking process of counting. The bills felt real, smelled real. Each stack held a hundred notes. He counted the total stacks: one hundred and thirty-six full ones, and a final, thinner one with fifty-six notes – fifty-five hundreds and a twenty. *This is as close to certainty as I'm going to get*, he thought. He nodded at Saleem as he zipped the heavy suitcase shut.

"What you gonna do with the cash, brother?" Saleem asked, satisfied after checking the confirmed transaction.

"Oh, I've got some expenses to take care of."

"Ya, but you need the agents, no?"

Oliver didn't understand. "I'm sorry?"

"Brother, in the bank, no one gonna allow you to deposit more than ten thousand dollar. They ask you where the money come from. Then you tell my name, and my business is finished."

"Oh, yeah, don't worry. I know that rule," Oliver chuckled.

"Then what you gonna do?" Saleem's tone was mocking. "Buy tomato in farmer market? How many you gonna buy?"

"I'm not sure I follow. I'll just ... cover my expenses."

Saleem clicked his tongue impatiently. "You not understand. I wanna help you. I got the agents. You need to buy apartment, I got guy who take cash. You want buy ticket to Cancun, Hawaii, Abu Dhabi, I got the travel agent. All cash. You want Maserati, I got the guy. They take small fee, but no problem for big guy like you."

It dawned on Oliver, a slow, sickening realization. The transaction hadn't ended – his entrapment had just begun. The cash was just a different kind of cage. He couldn't spend it in the real world without raising alarms. He was now a citizen of this parallel economy, a shadow world of agents and fees that would skim from him at every turn.

"I might need the travel agent," Oliver said, the words tasting of defeat.

Saleem pulled a business card from a drawer. "This my guy. Habib. Flower shop on 28th Street. Tell him Saleem Bhai send you. You tell my name, he give you discount, ya?"

Oliver took the card: *Habib Florist. 51 W 28th St.* "Thank you."

He shook hands with both men and left, the suitcase now a tangible, forty-four-pound burden.

"You can come back any time!" Saleem called out. "Next time, no interview with Aguilar!" He and Abubakar erupted in laughter.

Oliver gave them a wry smile and walked out.

In the taxi back home, he stared out the window, the city lights blurring into a meaningless smear. He began a grim accounting in his head. *Money laundering, check. Art heist, double check.* The words were an epitaph for the man he used to be. He was no longer a civilian dabbling in his father's secrets. He was an active participant, a criminal. *What next?* he thought, a profound weariness settling deep in his bones. *God, Dad. How could you do this to me? I appreciate this fortune, but at what cost? What have you made me become?*

770995 (January 8)

Oliver walked excitedly towards O'Connell's, eager to see the expression on Aisling's face. He'd spoken to her the night before, and she had insisted he come over on Sunday before the bar opened. He had neglected to mention he was bringing cash – a sticking point he hoped wouldn't dampen the mood.

He was carrying $250,000 in his backpack. It wasn't as heavy as he'd feared, just five or six pounds of paper and ink. He had decided to include an extra $50,000 as a final, expensive coat of paint over the rot of his guilt.

The front door was locked. He knocked, and a moment later, it was opened by a woman in her seventies.

"Shannon!" Oliver exclaimed, giving Aisling's mother a hug. Just then, Aisling emerged from the kitchen and ran up to hug him as well.

She locked the door behind him, beaming. "We're preparing a feast for you today, and I've got a special treat in store." She walked behind the bar and pulled out an ice bucket containing a magnum of Taittinger.

"Tada!" Aisling said with a flourish. "After our conversation last week about real champagne, I decided to get this for our celebration."

"Oh, Aisling, you shouldn't have," Oliver said, genuinely touched by the gesture, a warmth that felt dangerously close to the fraudulent performance he was about to give.

"Oh, don't be silly, Oliver," Shannon interjected. "I insisted. It's the very least we can do." She turned to Aisling. "Darling, did you put the sign up that the pub opens at 1 p.m. today?"

"I did, mum," Aisling replied, popping the cork and filling three foamy flutes.

The three of them cheered and sipped the Taittinger. The crisp, clean taste felt like a lie on his tongue. He was a fraud, being toasted as a savior in the very place he had victimized. He beamed at them both.

"I'm sure you're anxious to talk about the money," he began. "As I told you, I've been fortunate with some investments. I initially thought I would donate $200,000 ..." He paused to take a sip, and in the sudden silence, he saw their faces fall, their expressions assuming he was about to walk back his offer.

"But I have good news," he continued quickly. "I've decided to donate $250,000 instead."

Aisling and Shannon stared at him in stunned silence. He watched Aisling's mouth go agape, her lower lip trembling as she processed the number. He had bought this. This pure, beautiful moment of relief was a product of a violent, terrifying back room in Harlem. The dissonance was a physical weight, a knot in his chest that the champagne couldn't dissolve.

"Oliver, I don't know what to say," she finally managed. "I have no idea how I'm ever going to be able to thank you or repay this."

His mind flashed to the stolen paintings. "Trust me, Aisling. You've repaid me in ways you'll never know. Besides, this is a gift."

Aisling stood to give him another hug.

"So, here's the thing," Oliver said after she was seated again. "I have the money with me, but it's in cash. I hope that works."

Her eyes widened. "Cash? I thought you crypto guys did everything electronically."

Oliver forced a laugh, a touch too loud. "Oh, you thought this was from a crypto investment? No, this was something else. A cash deal."

Aisling glanced at her mother, but Shannon just waved a dismissive hand. "Of course, cash is good. The construction business loves cash."

Oliver handed Aisling his backpack, grateful for the easy out Shannon had provided, and hating himself for it. "It's all in there. Twenty-five stacks of ten thousand."

Aisling took the bag and disappeared behind the bar. Oliver heard the trap door open and her footsteps descending. She emerged a few minutes later and brought out the first course. Oliver dug into the hearty feast, the richness of the food a welcome distraction from the poverty of his own character.

Towards the end of the meal, Shannon seemed to remember something. "Oh, right, Oliver. You're a fan of my dad's paintings, aren't you?"

He grew nervous. "Uh, yeah. I think he's a great artist," he replied cagily.

"I had completely forgotten, but he went through a phase of illustrating comic books. My nephew, Mike, saw a set of them in a record shop somewhere in Brooklyn."

The new information was a lifeline, a clean, academic puzzle that had nothing to do with cash-filled backpacks or the cold terror of a crooked cop's grip. It was a blessed distraction. Oliver knew about the secret fourth and fifth paintings, but the comic books were a new thread entirely.

"Wow, that's very cool, Shannon. Do you know where the shop is?"

"It just struck me we could get the set for you as a gift," she replied. "I need to check with Mike on the location – he said it was in Bushwick. I'll ask him to look into it for you."

"That would be wonderful, thank you!"

Oliver stayed until the bar opened, then thanked them for the meal. He walked out the door a little unsteadily, drunk not just on the magnum of Taittinger, but on the exhausting, dizzying performance of being a good man.

771287 (January 10)

Nick got up from his chair and walked to the conference room door, staring out impatiently. Seeing no one, he sighed and paced back to his seat. It was

9:02 a.m. A couple of minutes later, a man and a woman filed in and took their seats.

One of them noticed Nick glaring, "Sorry, Nick. The subway was running late today."

Nick gave a dismissive nod. "Ok, what have you got, Chandra?"

The man addressed as Chandra connected his laptop to a cable on the conference table and projected his screen on to a large TV screen in the room. He minimized a few windows on his screen until he found the one he was looking for. "Before I begin, I should caution that these are new AI models we are using, so there might be some room for error in the results."

Nick pursed his lips in acknowledgement and turned his gaze intently towards the TV screen.

"Yan ran these last night," Chandra continued, pointing at the other person in the room, a shy-looking Asian woman. "There were sixteen transactions that came out of Dev_akshar's address on January 5th for a total of one hundred and twenty five bitcoin. All of them went to separate CoinJoins. What I'm showing you here is the first of those sixteen transactions. The models were able to de-mix that CoinJoin with eighty-seven percent probability. We believe the resulting transaction from the CoinJoin went to a second CoinJoin. We de-mixed that one as well, but this time our probability dropped to seventy percent. The resulting bitcoin went to an unknown address and stopped there. We ran the same model against the remaining fifteen transactions with similar results. All of them seem to have two CoinJoins, with the probability dropping to seventy percent or below after the second one. All of them ended in unknown addresses, except for one."

"Which one?" Nick asked, his eyes lighting up.

"The seventh. The output from the second CoinJoin ended up in a known address linked to an individual in Dubai. It was for 6.7 bitcoin."

"Do we have his name?" Nick asked.

"Yes. He's a British expat – Darren Gooch. No known criminal ties according to our database. He has a small-time import-export business."

"No known criminal ties until now," Nick exclaimed. "We're going to extradite that son-of-a-bitch's ass stateside!"

"Nick, I really do need to emphasize that these are brand new models. We're of course proud of all the work our engineering team does, but every new model needs a validation period before we can use it in the wild. When you asked us to run this model last week, I told you the condition was that it would be for testing purposes only," Chandra said earnestly.

Nick stared at him contemptuously. "Let me ask you something. What was the date of the first of these sixteen transactions that came out of Dev_akshar's address?"

"January 5th."

"And what's today's date?"

"January 10th."

"So, let me make sure I understand this," Nick said, his tone slow and deliberate, as Chandra squirmed. "As I was presenting to the DoJ in D.C. and getting humiliated by them in the process, Dev_akshar was merrily pulling out his coins. It then takes us five days to figure out what the hell is even going on with those coins. Fifteen out of sixteen of those transactions are dead ends, and the one of them that is a hot lead, you're telling me not to make a big deal out of?"

"Nick, you know fully well why it's taken so long," Chandra replied, his voice tight.

"Because your models weren't ready," Nick retorted.

"No, that's an unfair characterization. We told you as soon as the transactions were detected on January 5th that they all went to CoinJoins. You wanted to know immediately about the CoinJoins. I told you that we had just deprecated our older model because it was inaccurate and were in the process of refining our latest one. We still had over a week's worth of work left on it, but you insisted that we accelerate that and deploy earlier. So, we did it. The build and release schedule takes time, and there was a weekend in between. This is the earliest possible time we could have produced any results," Chandra said, not without a hint of bitterness in his tone.

Nick waved off the explanation. "Ok, that's all well and good. Let me explain something to you. This DoJ contract is by far our biggest one. We've got to deliver results, do you understand? Right now, they're treating us like a joke. So, here's what I'm going to do. I'm going to take these results, present it to them and let them know that we've got our guy."

"Nick, you can't do that!" Chandra said, shocked. "There's a reasonable chance we're wrong and you'd be setting up an innocent person."

"Oh, come on! These are state-of-the-art AI models, aren't they? Why the hell do we have such a big R&D budget if these models aren't worth anything? Look, it all adds up in my mind. Dev_akshar is a smart guy. Of course, he was going to CoinJoin when he pulled the coins out. In fact, he's so smart, he CoinJoined twice. But we were able to unravel that thread, and it's pointing to this Mooch guy in Abu Dhabi."

"Darren Gooch and it's Dubai, not Abu Dhabi," Chandra muttered under his breath.

Nick ignored him. "Whatever. He's got to be Dev_akshar's laundering agent. Import-export, my ass. It all makes sense. Dubai is the perfect place to launder money. Next best place after Switzerland. For all we know, Dev_akshar is on a flight there right now, with a nice little suitcase of cash waiting for him at the pickup terminal. All right, send me the files and I'll make a report. Let's see Jeremiah Howard's face when I show him this," Nick said gleefully as he walked out of the conference room, leaving Chandra shaking his head in disbelief.

CHAPTER 3. February 7

N ick straightened his tie for the third time, the knot feeling impossibly tight, a silken noose of his own making. He was alone in the 'Kilimanjaro' conference room at the Chain Intelligence headquarters in Midtown, a sterile glass box with a view of a thousand other sterile glass boxes. He felt a surge of adrenaline, a clean, powerful hum that drowned out the low-grade anxiety that had been his constant companion since the FTX collapse. This was it. This was the moment the comeback began.On the polished mahogany table in front of him lay the report, a 15-page document bound in the firm's official navy-blue cover. Its title, printed in a crisp, authoritative font, read: Project Dev_akshar: Probabilistic De-anonymization and Attribution Analysis. It felt heavy in his hands, dense with the weight of its own importance. Inside was the key, the slam dunk, the silver bullet that would not only vindicate – but catapult him into a new echelon. He could already feel the phantom warmth of Jeremiah Howard's handshake, hear the grudging respect in his voice.

He glanced at his watch. 9:58 a.m. Two minutes to go. He'd insisted on a video conference, but Howard's office had replied with a curt email providing only a generic D.C. conference bridge number. A minor irritation, Nick had thought. In a few minutes, it wouldn't matter.

He smoothed down the front of his gray suit jacket. He knew it didn't fit quite right, a relic from his pre-crypto days, but today, it felt like a suit of armor. He was no longer a disgraced "crypto bro" who'd been wiped out by scammers. He was now Senior Director Nicholas Hernandez, a man who got results for the United States Department of Justice.

At 10:00 a.m. on the dot, he picked up the sleek conference phone and dialed the number.

A tinny, synthesized voice answered: "Welcome to the Department of Justice automated conference system. Please enter your conference ID, followed by the pound key."

Nick punched in the nine-digit code from the email.

"Please state your name after the tone, and you will be placed into the conference."

He waited for the beep. "Nicholas Hernandez."

Brief dead air was followed by the worst hold music he had ever heard, a low-fidelity, instrumental version of "The Stars and Stripes Forever" that sounded like it was being played on a dying calliope. He grimaced, tapping his fingers on the table. Even the DoJ's on-hold patriotism was designed to be a form of soft torture.

After two full loops of the march, a click, and a new voice, bored and bureaucratic: "Department of Justice, Operator 47B. Who are you holding for?"

"I have a 10 o'clock call with Jeremiah Howard," Nick said, trying to inject a note of importance into his voice.

"Spell the last name."

"H-O-W-A-R-D. Jeremiah."

"One moment." The calliope music returned, this time for a mercifully shorter thirty seconds.

"Sir," the operator returned, her voice unchanged, "Mr. Howard's line is currently busy. Please hold."

Before Nick could protest, he was back in musical purgatory. He rolled his eyes. Of course, it is. This was how they kept you off balance, reminding you of your place in the pecking order. He was just a vendor, a supplicant waiting for an audience. He took a deep breath. It didn't matter. What he had in that report would change the pecking order for good.

Another click. The music died.

"This is Howard." The voice was exactly as Nick remembered it from his D.C. visit: clipped, precise and utterly devoid of warmth.

"Mr. Howard, good morning. It's Nick Hernandez from Chain Intelligence. I'm calling with a significant update on the primary Dev_akshar wallet, the one that's been dormant since 2013."

"I'm aware of the wallet, Mr. Hernandez," Howard said. Nick could hear the soft tapping of a keyboard. "I assume you're calling because your systems flagged the activity from January 5th."

So, he already knew. Of course, he did. The automated alert would have gone to the DoJ the moment the transaction was confirmed. This was about providing the meaning, not breaking the news.

"Yes, sir," Nick said, his confidence unshaken. "But the alert didn't contain our subsequent analysis. My team has spent the last week running the outputs through our new proprietary de-mixing models. Dev_akshar was sophisticated. The initial sixteen transactions all went to separate, high-volume CoinJoins."

"We anticipated as much," Howard said, his tone flat.

Nick pressed on, his confidence unwavering. "Yes, but what he likely didn't anticipate was the power of our new AI clustering heuristics. We focused on the seventh transaction from the initial batch. Our model was able to de-mix the first-layer CoinJoin with an 87% confidence probability. The output of that was then sent, as we suspected, to a second-layer CoinJoin."

"And your confidence level on the second de-mixing?" Howard's question was sharp, precise.

This was the part Chandra had been so nervous about. Nick felt a flash of contempt for his analyst's cowardice. "Seventy percent, sir. Still well above the threshold for actionable intelligence."

"Is that so?" Howard's voice was unreadable. "And where did this 'actionable intelligence' lead you?"

Nick paused for dramatic effect, letting the question hang in the air. "It led us to a known address, sir. A direct deposit into a wallet controlled by a British national residing in Dubai. An importer-exporter by the name of Darren Gooch."

He had expected a reaction, a surprised intake of breath, a moment of reflection, perhaps even a grudgingly impressed, "Well done, Hernandez."

Instead, all he heard was the faint, ambient hum of the phone line. For a full ten seconds, there was nothing. Nick's confidence began to waver for the first time. Was the line dead?

"Mr. Howard? Are you still there?"

"I'm here," Howard said finally. "Gooch. You're certain he's the recipient, not just a pass-through?"

"As certain as the data allows, sir. The address has been associated with Mr. Gooch's other known accounts. It's our assessment that he is acting as Dev_akshar's primary laundering agent."

"And the other fifteen transaction trails?"

"They've run cold for now, as expected," Nick admitted. "Dev_akshar likely created fifteen dead-end trails to obscure the one real one. It's classic misdirection. He just wasn't counting on our ability to unravel the thread."

Another pause, longer this time. Nick could hear the distant sound of a siren in the background of Howard's office. He imagined the man staring out his window at the grand sweep of Pennsylvania Avenue, pondering the global implications of what Nick had just handed him.

"This analytical model your team used," Howard said, his voice cutting back in. "Has it been peer-reviewed outside of your organization?"

"It's proprietary, sir, but it's built on industry-leading machine learning principles. My lead analyst, Dr. Chandra, is one of the top minds in the field. He stands by the results." Another lie, or at least a gross exaggeration. Chandra had been practically begging him to add more caveats to the report.

"I see," Howard said. The two words were impossibly heavy. They contained no praise, no validation, nothing Nick could cling to.

Nick felt a sudden need to fill the void, to reassert control. "Sir, with this information, we believe you have sufficient grounds to begin the process of ..."

"I'm aware of what the process is, Mr. Hernandez," Howard cut him off, his voice edged with what seemed, for the first time, like impatience. "Your job is to provide the data. My job is to decide what to do with it."

"Of course, sir. My apologies." Nick felt his cheeks flush, the heat of the rebuke traveling through the phone line.

The rustling of papers again. Then, Howard's tone shifted, becoming purely procedural.

"This is a significant lead. I want a full, formal report on my desk by end-of-day tomorrow. Everything: your full methodology, the model's parameters, the raw on-chain data, and Dr. Chandra's complete confidence analysis. I also want you and Dr. Chandra in my office in D.C. at ten hundred hours next Tuesday to present this in person to the full oversight committee."

Nick's heart leaped. The humiliation of the rebuke instantly forgotten, replaced by a wave of pure, unadulterated triumph. The full oversight committee. This was it. This was the call-up to the big leagues. Howard was being thorough, not cold. This was how professionals at the highest level operated.

"We'll be there, sir," Nick said, trying to keep the elation out of his voice. "We look forward to it."

"See that you do," Howard said. And then the line went dead.

Nick slowly placed the receiver back on its cradle. He leaned back in his chair, a wide, triumphant grin spreading across his face. He looked at the report on his laptop, no longer just a document, but a trophy. He had done it.

He stood up and walked to the floor-to-ceiling window of the conference room, looking down at the yellow cabs crawling along the avenue below. They were ants, scurrying about their small, insignificant lives. He was up here, in the rarefied air of real power, moving global chess pieces. He thought of his former colleague and friend Oliver, teaching kids in some rundown school, clinging to his purist, naive ideology. Bitcoin ... hah! A fat lot of good bitcoin did Dev_akshar. And a fat lot of good it would do Oliver. This was the real world. This was where the real work was done.

He pulled out his phone and sent a message to Chandra:

Howard loved it. Book two Acela tickets to DC for next Tuesday. You and me. Time to take our victory lap.

He didn't wait for a reply. He knew Chandra would be nervous, that he would want to hedge and qualify. But that was the difference between an analyst and a director. An analyst sees risk. A director sees opportunity. And Nicholas Hernandez saw the opportunity of a lifetime.

773001 (January 21)

Oliver reached into the compartment under his bed to pull out the suitcase with cash in it. He counted ten hundred-dollar bills and put them in his wallet. He then zipped up the suitcase and slid it back into the compartment. He felt his hand brush another soft object. It was one of the Bryce canvases wrapped in a comforter. He hadn't looked at the paintings in weeks, the unsolved mystery of their hidden seed phrase a problem for another day, another life.

He pulled out the painting and unwrapped it. *The Toddler*. He stood it against the bedframe and stared, a grim smile touching his lips. It was a masterpiece, a beautiful thing born of genius, and he had stolen it. The thought, once a source of sharp guilt, now felt like a distant, clinical fact.

He walked into the kitchen to refill his wine glass. As he turned to head back, he froze mid-step in the corridor.

From this exact vantage point, the late afternoon sun streamed through the window, striking the canvas at a peculiar, almost deliberate angle. And in that light, a ghost appeared. A faint geometry he'd never seen before was embossed in the very texture of the brushstrokes, a secret that had been waiting for this precise alignment of time, light and perspective.

Oliver took a slow step forward, and the shape vanished, swallowed back into the paint. He retraced his steps, his heart beginning to pound. It reappeared, an apparition of light trapped in oil and canvas. The faint pattern spanned the entire painting, a spectral layer superimposed over the image of *The Toddler*.

He couldn't believe his eyes. It was the same impossible shape the homeless man had drawn with chalk on the Harlem sidewalk: the six intertwining spirals.

He pulled out his phone, his fingers fumbling as he scrolled to the photo. He held it up. He was right. It was the same symbol. The surrealism of the street, the madness he had tried to dismiss, had just invaded the physical reality of his home. How was this possible?

He ran to the bed, pulled out the other painting, and placed it beside the first. He walked back to the exact spot in the corridor, a pilgrim returning to a holy site. And there it was. The same shape shimmered on the surface of *It Is Time*, another ghost in another machine.

Oliver stood for a long time, the wine glass forgotten in his hand, trying to digest a discovery that felt less like a clue and more like a cosmological revelation. He went to his computer, with a desperate need to anchor this impossible event in the mundane logic of a search engine. He typed: "six intertwined spiral shape."

The results were a useless collection of tattoo designs and corporate logos. He tried again, modifying the terms, until a word surfaced from his memory. *Triskelion.* That was it. The shape had three spirals, not six, but the ancient, esoteric feel was the same. The search results spoke of life, death and rebirth – of the Holy Trinity. Ancient symbols for ancient truths.

But this was six spirals. A double triskelion? What on Earth could it mean? The known world's lexicon had no entry for the thing he had seen with his own eyes. And how could the homeless man, a prophet of the gutter, know a secret Bryce had hidden so deep in his work it required a specific angle of winter light to be seen? Was it even Bryce? Or was it someone else, another phantom leaving their mark?

Either way, the logical part of his brain, the part that had once navigated Python code and client meetings, was screaming. It made no sense. He was interfacing with a system of knowledge that operated on a plane he didn't understand, a truth whispered by madmen and hidden in the texture of paint.

He pushed away from the desk and walked back to the precise spot in the corridor. The apartment was growing darker as the January sun dipped below the neighboring rooftops, but the angle was still just right. The six-spiraled shapes shimmered on the canvases, not like paint, but like wraiths of light trapped in the texture of the oil and canvas. They seemed to hum with a silent, otherworldly energy.

His mind raced, trying to connect this new, impossible piece to the others. The Noncemeister had given him riddles. Anariadne spoke in seductive, cryptic verse. And the homeless man ... he had simply drawn a silent map on a dirty sidewalk. A map to a secret that had been hiding in plain sight in this very room for months.

How? How could a man who looked like he'd been forgotten by time itself know a secret hidden within it? Was he a projection, another figment like the Noncemeister? But the chalk drawing had been real. It had been there. Gritty, tangible and now, terrifyingly prescient.

Oliver's head was spinning. He was being fed information through channels that defied logic – dreams, visions, a madman's chalk art. He felt he should be used to it by now, but he wasn't.

The initial thrill of discovery began to curdle into a profound sense of isolation. He was the sole keeper of an incredible, world-altering secret. He possessed two masterpieces of surrealist art, held the keys to a digital fortune that could reshape economies and had just uncovered a symbol that felt more ancient than the paintings themselves.

And yet, he had never felt more alone.

The Noncemeister was gone. Anariadne was a beautiful but ambiguous enigma. And Daniela ... could he even explain this to her without sounding like he was losing his mind?

He walked back into the kitchen, the paintings disappearing back into their mundane state as he moved out of the light. He picked up the bottle of Château Margaux from the counter, the one he'd been saving, and poured a generous amount.

He returned to the armchair and sank into it, the wine doing little to warm the cold knot of uncertainty in his stomach. He was surrounded by answers that only created deeper, more complex questions. The paintings stood silent in the other room, guarding their secrets. For the first time, Oliver felt a sliver of understanding for Jonathan Bryce. To be a conduit for this kind of knowledge was a magnificent burden. And tonight, it felt heavier than ever.

773397 (January 24)

The Uber's suspension groaned as it navigated a pothole on E Street, jostling Nick and Chandra in the back seat. Nick barely noticed. He was staring out the window at the grand, imposing architecture of the capital, a landscape of limestone and authority that no longer intimidated him. Today, he was a part of it. He was a man with answers, and these magnificent buildings were merely the stage for his triumph.

"I'm telling you, Nick, the confidence interval is a problem," Chandra whispered for what felt like the dozenth time, his voice tight with panic. He clutched his own briefcase on his lap like a life raft. "A 70% probability on a second-layer de-mixing ... it's a strong signal, I agree, but it's not a certainty. There are scenarios, tail risks, where the heuristics could misattribute based on decoy timings. We should be presenting this as a potential lead, not a definitive conclusion."

Nick turned from the window and gave his lead analyst a look of deep disappointment. He saw a brilliant but timid academic, a man constitutionally incapable of seeing the forest for the trees. Chandra's genius was in building the engine; his own was in knowing how to drive the car.

"Chandra, relax," he said, his voice a smooth balm of supercilious calm. "This isn't a university symposium. This is an intelligence briefing. They don't want your caveats and your error bars. They want a name. We have a name. We're giving them a win. You need to start thinking about the optics, not just the code."

"But the optics will be catastrophic if we're wrong," Chandra insisted, his face pale.

"We're not wrong," Nick said with a finality that shut down the conversation. He turned back to the window. In his mind, he was already in the conference room, walking Jeremiah Howard and his team through the brilliant, undeniable logic of the AI's findings. He saw the grudging nods, the dawning respect in their eyes. This was the meeting that would make his career, the one that would erase the stain of his crypto past and rebrand him as a serious player in the world of national security.

They arrived at the Department of Justice and went through the familiar, soulless ballet of security. Metal detectors, ID scans, the bored gaze of the guards. This time, however, it felt different. It felt like a rite of passage. He was now an asset.

A junior aide met them past the turnstiles and led them through a labyrinth of marble-floored corridors. He didn't speak, which only added to Nick's sense of importance. Finally, they stopped before a set of imposing double doors. The aide knocked once and opened the door.

"Mr. Hernandez and Dr. Chandra are here, sir."

The conference room was vast and cold, dominated by a dark, polished table that seemed to absorb all the light in the room. At the far end sat Jeremiah Howard, looking exactly as he had sounded on the phone last week: severe, impatient, and utterly unimpressed. Flanking him were three other figures, a tribunal assembled for his coronation.

"Gentlemen, thank you for coming," Howard said, his voice flat. He did not stand. He gestured to the two empty chairs across the table. "Please."

As they sat, Howard made the introductions with a clinical brevity. "This is Eleanor Vance, our senior counsel for emergent threat vector analysis. This is Marcus Thorne, acting undersecretary for digital asset forfeiture. And this is Robert Downs, chief of staff to the principal deputy assistant attorney general."

Each of them gave a nod so slight it was barely perceptible. Nick felt a flicker of unease. There were no smiles. No handshakes offered. The air was thick with a frosty, bureaucratic indifference. Chandra, beside him, seemed to shrink into his chair.

Nick cleared his throat and reached for his briefcase. "Thank you for having us, Mr. Howard, Ms. Vance. We've prepared a full presentation on the de-anonymization of the ..."

"That won't be necessary, Mr. Hernandez," Howard said, holding up a hand to stop him. He slid a thin folder across the table. "We've had a productive week since your call. We took the liberty of expediting the verification of your lead."

Nick's heart thumped. They'd already moved on it. This was even better than he'd hoped. They were taking him seriously. "And?" he asked, a triumphant grin beginning to form on his face.

Howard leaned back in his chair, a slow, deliberate movement. He steepled his fingers. "Your intelligence pointed us to a Mr. Darren Gooch, a British national and proprietor of a small import-export business in Dubai."

"That's correct, sir," Nick said, unable to keep the pride from his voice.

"A compelling theory," Howard continued, his voice still a monotone. "It had only one significant, and I must say, rather glaring flaw."

"Sir?"

"It was, to use the technical term, complete and utter nonsense," Howard said. The words landed with the soft, devastating impact of a sniper's bullet.

The grin on Nick's face froze, then melted away. "I ... I don't understand, sir. Our model ..."

"Your model," interrupted Eleanor Vance, the senior counsel, speaking for the first time. Her voice was like chipping ice. "Has a predictive accuracy problem, Mr. Hernandez. Specifically, it has difficulty distinguishing between a clandestine money launderer and a keynote speaker at an international trade conference."

"A keynote speaker?" Nick repeated, the words feeling foreign in his mouth.

"Indeed," said Marcus Thorne, the undersecretary. He slid a glossy photograph across the table. It was a picture of a beaming, red-faced man in his fifties, standing at a podium. Behind him, a large banner read: DUBAI INTERNATIONAL JUTE AND FIBER SYMPOSIUM 2023. A timestamp in the corner of the photo corresponded to the exact minute of the bitcoin transaction from Dev_akshar's wallet.

"Mr. Gooch, as it turns out, is one of the world's foremost experts on industrial-grade jute," Howard explained, his voice laced with a dry, almost imperceptible sarcasm. "At the precise moment your model identified him as receiving illicit funds, he was delivering a ninety-minute address titled 'The Future of Burlap: Innovations in Tensile Strength' to an audience of over four hundred delegates, including the Emirati Deputy Minister of Agriculture. The event was live-streamed."

A suffocating quiet filled the room. Nick stared at the photo of the beaming jute expert. He could feel Chandra's gaze burning into the side of his head, a silent, searing "I told you so."

Robert Downs, the chief of staff, who had remained silent until now, cleared his throat. "The resources expended to verify this ... erroneous lead have been noted," he said, his voice carrying the quiet threat of a man who managed budgets. "International inquiries, man-hours, a rather awkward call with the Emirati attaché ... it all adds up."

Nick's mind was racing, desperately trying to find an explanation, a rebuttal. "It could have been a pre-signed transaction," he blurted out, the words feeling clumsy but necessary. "He could have had an associate broadcast it while he was on stage to establish an alibi. Dev_akshar is a sophisticated actor!"

Howard let out a small, weary sigh, the sound of a patient teacher dealing with a particularly slow student. He glanced at Eleanor Vance, who adjusted her glasses with a look of profound boredom.

"A sophisticated actor, you say," Howard mused. He tapped a command into the keyboard in front of him, and an image appeared on the large screen at the end of the room. It was a credit card statement.

"This," Howard said, pointing to a highlighted line item, "is a charge from the hotel gift shop at the Dubai International Convention Centre. It was made by Mr. Gooch five minutes after the bitcoin transaction was confirmed on the blockchain. He purchased a plush camel and a novelty pen. We have the security footage."

Nick stared at the screen, momentarily confused. "I ... I don't see the relevance, sir."

Howard leaned forward slightly. "Let me be clear, Mr. Hernandez. Your theory is that a master cybercriminal, the elusive Dev_akshar, executes a flawless, multi-million-dollar transfer designed to create a perfect alibi ... and the recipient's first action, minutes after the funds are secured, is to go and buy a stuffed animal? It strains credulity, wouldn't you agree?"

Marcus Thorne, the undersecretary for digital asset forfeiture, chimed in, his voice a dry rustle. "Behavioral analysis is a component of our work, Mr. Hernandez. The behavior profile of 'international money launderer' does not typically overlap with 'purchaser of novelty plush toys.'"

The comment was a stiletto, slid neatly between his ribs. Nick felt a fresh wave of heat on his cheeks. They were mocking him.

"The purchase is irrelevant," Nick insisted, his voice a little too loud. "The timing doesn't matter if the address was provided in advance. Gooch could have given Dev_akshar the receiving address weeks, even months ago. The transfer could have been initiated at any time."

He thought it was a solid point, a way back into the game. But Howard simply nodded, as if he had been waiting for that exact rebuttal.

"Another plausible theory," Howard conceded, his tone dangerously calm. "It would be, except for yet another technical detail your model appears to have overlooked." He clicked another key, and a string of alphanumeric characters filled the screen, highlighted in yellow. It was the receiving address. "The address itself, Mr. Hernandez. It wasn't pre-existing. It was generated less than fifteen minutes before the transaction was broadcast. We were able to subpoena the recipient's payment processor's server logs. A fresh address, never before seen on the network. How could Mr. Gooch have provided it to Dev_akshar weeks in advance if it didn't exist?"

The air in the room grew thin. Nick's mind went blank. The logic was a steel trap closing around his leg. He looked at Chandra, whose eyes were fixed on the table, his face ashen. He had warned him about the tail risks, about the possibility of misattribution. This had to be it.

But Nick's pride wouldn't let him surrender. Not yet. There had to be an explanation.

"Then ... then Gooch generated it himself!" he said, grasping at the last possible straw. "Right before he went on stage! He created the address and communicated it to the associate. It's the only explanation!"

Howard actually allowed a small, almost imperceptible smile to cross his lips. It was the smile of a chess master who sees a checkmate twelve moves away. He leaned back again.

"We considered that possibility as well, Mr. Hernandez. So, we had our liaison from the State Department, in cooperation with the Dubai police, pay a visit to Mr. Gooch."

He paused.

"It was a very illuminating conversation. It turns out Mr. Gooch has a son-in-law who is, in his words, 'one of those crypto-nuts.' For his birthday last year, the son-in-law gave him a helpful little primer on 'the future of money.' Mr. Gooch admitted to us that he tried to read it but gave up after the first page because he thought bitcoin was, and I quote, 'a type of vape pen.'"

Howard let the image hang in the air before delivering the final, crushing blow.

"The problem, Mr. Hernandez, is not that Mr. Gooch is a sophisticated actor. The problem is that your AI model is not. The address your model flagged does, in fact, have a connection to Darren Gooch. What your model failed to discern is that the funds that landed in that address did not originate from your target."

Nick felt a cold dread creep up his spine. "What are you saying, sir?"

"I am saying," Howard continued, his voice now a clinical instrument of demolition, "that your model connected the wrong input to the wrong output within the CoinJoin. Our analysts, using more traditional and, I might add, more reliable methods, traced the actual source of the funds that went to the Gooch-affiliated address. They came from the public donation wallet of the 'Fiber for the Future Foundation,' the official charity of the Jute and Fiber Symposium. Mr. Gooch is a prominent donor and a board member; it was a routine consolidation of charitable funds. Your target's funds ... went somewhere else entirely within that same transaction. Your AI simply saw a boogeyman and a burlap salesman in the same cryptographic room and decided they must be partners."

Eleanor Vance, the senior counsel, leaned forward, adding a final, devastating footnote. "So, your model isn't just generating false positives, Mr. Hernandez. It's constructing elaborate, incorrect narratives from coincidental data. It's writing fiction. And the Department of Justice is not in the business of prosecuting fiction."

This was it. The incontrovertible evidence. The "oh crap" moment that felt like a physical fall. The world tilted on its axis. The entire theory, his slam dunk, his comeback, had been built on a technological mirage. He had gone all the way to Washington, D.C., walked into the Department of Justice, and confidently accused a man whose alibi was a plush camel, all because his vaunted AI couldn't tell the difference between two separate people throwing money into the same digital box. He hadn't been outsmarted by a genius; he had been made a fool of by his own flawed machine.

Nick felt a hot wave of shame wash over him, so intense it was dizzying. He risked a glance at Chandra, who was staring fixedly at the polished table, his face a mask of grim resignation.

"Mr. Hernandez," Howard said, his voice pulling Nick back into the room. "Your company was contracted to provide us with reliable, actionable intelligence. What you have provided is a waste of our time and the taxpayers' money. As of this moment, our contract with Chain Intelligence is under immediate and serious review. You can expect formal correspondence to that effect." He stood up, a clear signal that the meeting was over. "Thank you for your time."

The humiliation was absolute. There were no further questions. No debate. Just a cold, clean dismissal.

Nick and Chandra rose from their chairs like automatons. They packed their briefcases in the grip of a dead, oppressive hush, the four figures at the end of the table watching them without a word. The walk out of the conference room felt a mile long. Every footstep echoed in the marble hallway, a funereal drumbeat marking the death of his career.

They didn't speak in the elevator. They didn't speak as they cleared security. They didn't speak as they stepped out of the grand entrance and back onto Pennsylvania Avenue, the cool January air feeling like a slap on his burning cheeks.

They stood on the sidewalk for a long moment, the sounds of the city traffic a jarring intrusion into their shared bubble of failure. Nick couldn't bring himself to look at Chandra. He just stared ahead, at the monuments of a city and a world he had so confidently, so foolishly, believed he was ready to conquer. His comeback was over before it had even begun.

774096 (January 28)

The Tignanello was a mirage in the glass, its deep ruby hue absorbing the last of the Saturday afternoon light that filtered through the large Chelsea windows. Oliver swirled it absently, watching the legs cling to the crystal before slowly succumbing to gravity. A perfect metaphor, he thought with a grim satisfaction. He was clinging too, to the edge of a discovery that refused to yield.

He'd spent the week chasing apparitions. The six-spiraled shape, the one he had dubbed a "double triskelion," was a closed loop, a perfect and maddening cipher. He had stared at the photos on his phone, then at the paintings themselves, propped up against the far wall of the bedroom, waiting for the right time of day when the sunlight was at the perfect angle for the spiral to appear, until they did and then seemed to spin and bore into his vision. He'd scoured obscure forums on Celtic mythology, ancient geometry, even fringe physics, looking for a reference, a key, a Rosetta Stone for the glyph the homeless man had scrawled on the sidewalk. Nothing. The trail, which had been a torrent of revelation just weeks ago, had gone cold, leaving him in a silent, gnawing stasis.

He took a long sip of the wine. It was an expensive yet poor substitute. What he really wanted was the familiar comfort of a worn barstool and a crisp Zywiec pulled by Aisling's expert hand. But O'Connell's was dark, its windows papered over, a sign promising a "Grand Re-Opening This Spring" hanging like an epitaph on the door. He'd walked by yesterday, a Pavlovian impulse guiding his feet toward a bell he knew wouldn't ring. The silence from the building was more jarring than the usual din of a SoHo afternoon. He missed the smell of stale beer and polish, the sound of Aisling's sharp laugh, the simple, grounding normalcy of it all.

And the irony was crushing. He had paid for his own exile. His gift, a stack of hundred-dollar bills born from a dangerous and surreal transaction in Harlem, had shuttered his only sanctuary. It was the Midas touch in reverse; the fortune he couldn't spend had transformed his one reliable comfort into yet another inaccessible space.

He swirled the wine again. There was that other place, of course. Pubkey. He'd seen the articles a few months back – a bitcoin-themed bar that had opened in the West Village recently. A watering hole for the faithful, a place presumably, where you didn't have to explain the four-year bitcoin cycle or the difference between a private key and a public address. He'd meant to go, to see if this new world he was a part of had a physical outpost, a place to feel a sense of belonging. But he hadn't. Going there felt too much like a commitment, an admission that there was no road back to the simple life of a sales engineer who drank lager at an Irish pub.

He could hear the faint hiss of the shower from the master bathroom. A sound that should have been a comfort, a simple domestic rhythm, but had instead become the ticking of a clock he couldn't read.

Daniela.

A wave of guilt washed over him, sharp and immediate. He saw her face from last night, laughing at some stupid movie on the couch, her head resting on his shoulder. In those moments, the suspicion felt like a poison of his own making, a sickness in his soul. She had been his accomplice, his partner. She had descended into the rat-infested tunnels with him. How could he doubt her?

God, the promise he'd broken. The one thing he swore he would never do. To just ... walk into her head. A trespasser. A thief of a private moment.

And for what? To watch her talk to Sarah about some dumb play? Anariadne had promised him certainty, but all he'd gotten was this cheap, tinny feeling of his own shame. It hadn't left him since. A cold stone in his gut.

How could he even look at her, live with her, knowing he'd done that?

His mind recoiled from the thought, scrambling for an exit. His grip tightened on the wine glass, the crystal cool against his suddenly sweating palm. Unless ...

He heard the whisper of Anariadne's seductive logic, a memory of temptation from the blue mist that felt more real than the promise he'd broken. Maren was Daniela's mentor, her family, almost. A bond forged over years couldn't be undone in a matter of months. Yes, maybe the meeting with Sarah on New Year's Day was innocuous, but there were many others. What was being said in these "meetings with friends" she was having more and more often?

He hadn't told her about Saleem Bhai. He couldn't. How could he articulate the terror of that backroom interrogation, the surreal sight of a suitcase filled with over a million dollars in cash? The secret was a wall between them, and he was the one who had built it. The weight of it was immense, a tangible pressure in the quiet apartment.

He drained the last of the wine from his glass and stared into the empty living room. He was a king ruling over a kingdom of secrets, sitting on a throne of inherited lies. The paintings stood silent in the other room, guarding their mysterious geometry. The silence of the apartment was a presence, an entity fed by everything he couldn't say.

Silence. That meant the shower had stopped. He turned around. Daniela was standing right behind him in a bathrobe, a towel wrapped around her wet hair like a turban. Her gaze went from his face to the empty bottle of Tignanello on the desk beside him, and her eyes widened with a familiar mixture of surprise and concern.

"Oliver, it's barely six o'clock and you've gone through an entire bottle of wine!" she exclaimed. "What about our dinner plans for tonight?"

Oliver forced a casualness he didn't feel, gesturing vaguely with the empty glass. "Our reservation isn't until eight. I'm fine. Just ... thinking. It helps me think."

The excuse sounded flimsy even to his own ears. Thinking. He had been doing little else, and the wine hadn't clarified a single damn thing. It had only amplified the noise, turning his anxieties into a roaring chorus.

Daniela walked closer, her brow furrowed. She picked up the bottle, her fingers tracing the label. "This is the '18. It's a good one. An expensive one. You said we were saving it for a special occasion."

"It's Saturday," he said with a shrug, trying for a lightness that felt like a lead weight in his throat. "Isn't that special enough?"

She didn't smile. She placed the bottle back on the desk with a soft, deliberate click that seemed to ring through the quiet room. "Are you sure you're going to be up for dinner, babe? A whole bottle ... that's a lot before we even go out."

"I'm fine, Daniela. Seriously." His tone was sharper than he intended. He hated this feeling, the sense of being monitored, of his choices being weighed and judged. "I'll take a quick shower, and I'll be ready to go. It's not a big deal."

She held his gaze for a moment, her own unreadable. He could see the argument she was choosing not to have, the words she was swallowing. He wished she would just say them. The unspoken tension was worse than any fight. She finally sighed, a small breath of air that was equal parts resignation and worry.

"Okay," she said softly. "But Oliver, can we talk about this? The spending. It's ... it's getting to be a lot."

Here we go. He felt a familiar tightening in his chest. It wasn't about the wine. It was never just about the wine.

"What spending?" he asked, feigning ignorance. "I'm not spending that much."

"The Dom Pérignon for New Year's was $2,000, Oliver. This bottle of Tignanello is over 200. The wine you brought home yesterday was almost 300. I saw the credit card bill last week ... you're maxing everything out. You don't have a job. How are you paying for all this? We have maintenance fees on this place, your student loans ..."

Her voice was pleading, not accusatory, but it grated on him all the same. It was the voice of caution, of limits, of a reality that felt insulting to him now. He had over a million dollars in cash hidden under his bed, and she was lecturing him about a credit card bill. The absurdity of it, the secrecy of it, fueled his irritation.

"I'm handling it," he said, standing up from the armchair, needing to create some distance. He walked over to the window and stared down at the traffic on 10th Avenue. "You don't need to worry about it. I've got things under control."

"What things?" she persisted, her voice closer now as she followed him to the window. "Because all I see is you spiraling into debt. It adds up, Oliver. And it's not just the money, it's ... it's what you're doing. You're drinking too much; you're not sleeping. I'm worried about you."

He snapped. The pressure of the last few weeks – the dead-end search, the guilt, the constant, low-grade fear – it all erupted in a single, reckless volley.

"You're one to talk," he spat out, turning to face her. "Worrying about my credit card bill when you're dropping over $600 on a wallet at some thrift store."

The words hung in the air between them, toxic and radioactive. He saw the confusion on her face instantly, a flicker of incomprehension before the dawning of a terrible, impossible realization. He had just detonated the bomb.

"What ... what are you talking about?" she asked, her voice small. "What wallet?"

Panic, cold and absolute, seized him. His mind raced, a frantic search for a lie, an excuse, a rewind button that didn't exist. *Idiot. Idiot. Idiot.*

"Nothing," he said, the denial clumsy and transparent. "I just ... I must have seen it in your closet, that's all. It looked expensive."

Her face, which had been a mask of confusion, now hardened into something else. A quiet, chilling certainty. She shook her head slowly, her eyes never leaving his.

"No, you didn't," she said, her voice flat. "It's been in my purse since the day I bought it. And I never told you how much it cost. I never told you where I bought it."

She took a small step back, as if creating a physical space to accommodate the monstrous truth that was now filling the room.

"The thrift store in Gramercy," she whispered, the words barely audible. "The green leather one. With the $629 price tag. You saw me buy it."

It wasn't a question. It was an accusation, a verdict, and a sentence all at once. The game was up. The floor had fallen away, and he was in freefall. His first instinct was still to deny, but he could see in her eyes that it was useless.

And just like that, the panic curdled into something else. A hard, defiant rage. If he was going to fall, he wouldn't fall alone.

"Yeah, I saw it," he said, his voice hard. "I had to. I had to be sure."

"Sure of what?" she asked, her voice trembling now, the shock giving way to a deep, visceral hurt.

"Sure that you weren't lying to me! Sure that you weren't running off to Maren the second my back was turned, feeding her every secret I've ever told you!" There was a small voice at the back of his subconscious that was telling him he was gaslighting, that he was twisting his violation into a justifiable act of self-defense. The words felt ugly and false as they left his mouth, but he couldn't stop them.

"You promised me," she whispered, a single tear tracing a path down her cheek. "Oliver, you looked me in the eyes and you promised."

"And what was I supposed to do?" he shot back, his voice rising. "Just trust you? After everything? Maren is your mentor, your family friend! She's after the same thing we are, and you're the only link between us. I had to know whose side you were on!"

The accusation, so baseless and cruel, seemed to strike her like a thunderbolt. She flinched, and for a moment, the fight went out of her. Her face crumpled, the anger dissolving into pure, unadulterated heartbreak. The single tear became a silent stream.

"I was on your side," she sobbed, her voice thick with a pain that cut through his anger and pierced him to the core. "I have always been on your side. I went into those tunnels with you. I helped you steal the paintings. I moved into your dead father's apartment to be with you. How could you think ... how could you do this to me?"

Her tears broke him. The rage, the self-righteousness, it all shattered, leaving behind only the raw, sickening shame he'd been running from for weeks. He saw the depth of the wound he had inflicted, the sacred trust he had irrevocably broken.

"I'm sorry," he said, the words feeling small and inadequate. He stepped toward her, but she recoiled, holding up a hand to stop him.

"It wasn't me," he pleaded, the desperation raw in his voice. "Babe, you have to believe me. It was Anariadne."

Daniela stared at him through her tears, her expression shifting from hurt to utter confusion. "Who? Who is Anariadne?"

And so, it all came pouring out. He told her everything. About the blue mist that had replaced the Noncemeister's timechain. About the beautiful, seductive woman with the golden hair and the strange, hypnotic voice. He told her how Anariadne had appeared to him, promising certainty, whispering doubts about Daniela's loyalty, goading him, tempting him to just take a quick look, to just be sure. He explained how she had opened a window into Daniela's past and pushed him through it.

He expected his confession to bring some measure of understanding, perhaps even forgiveness. But as he spoke, he watched the last traces of warmth and empathy drain from Daniela's face. Her tears stopped. The hurt in her eyes was replaced by something else: a cold, clear disgust.

She stood there for a long time after he finished, the air thick with wordless tension. "So, you're telling me," she said, her words clipped and precise, "that you were tempted by a magical, beautiful woman in your dreams, a woman who told you to betray me, and you did it."

"It wasn't like that ..." he started, but she cut him off.

"That is exactly what it was like, Oliver. I don't care if she's real or a figment of your imagination. It doesn't matter. You made a choice. You chose to believe a phantom over me. You chose to violate my mind because you were weak and paranoid, and you couldn't handle your own guilt."

She shook her head, a look of profound and final disappointment on her face. "I thought you were on a journey of self-discovery. I thought you were becoming a man. But you're not. You're just a boy, lost in his own fantasies, being manipulated by his own demons."

She turned and walked towards the bedroom, her movements calm and deliberate.

"What are you doing?" he asked, his voice hollow.

"I'm getting dressed," she said, without looking back. "I can't be here anymore, Oliver. I can't be with someone I can't trust. I can't be with someone who is so lost that he can't even tell the difference between a guide and a monster."

He followed her to the bedroom door and watched as she put on her clothes with a mechanical efficiency. She didn't look at him. She didn't say another word. She picked up her purse from the dresser, walked past him without a glance, and went to the front door.

"I'll come back for the rest of my things tomorrow," she said, her hand on the doorknob. And then she was gone.

The click of the lock echoed in the apartment. Oliver stood alone, the empty wine bottle on the desk a monument to his undoing. He had found a semblance of the certainty Anariadne had promised. It was the certainty of absolute, crushing loss.

He stood frozen for a long time, listening to the ghostly hush of her departure. The wine's warmth had vanished, leaving only a sour, hollow feeling in his gut. It wasn't enough. The Tignanello was a gentle anesthetic for a wound that required a cauterizing fire.

A memory surfaced, unbidden, from the depths of another, earlier grief. The memory of a different bottle. His father's gift for his 21st birthday.

He moved mechanically, a man seemingly possessed by a spirit. He walked to the liquor cabinet by the dining table, his hands trembling slightly as he opened the ornate wooden doors. He pushed past the gin, the bourbon, the vodkas Daniela had bought for their parties. And there it was, tucked in the back corner like a forgotten relic. The dark bottle of Lagavulin 16.

He pulled it out. The label was just as he remembered, a familiar crest from an Islay he'd never seen. About a quarter of the bottle remained, a dark, peaty amber that held the memory of a different sorrow. The first time he'd opened this, he had been mourning a man he thought he'd lost. Now, he was mourning a man he was becoming.

He didn't bother with a glass. There was no need for the ritual of water or the pretense of savoring. This was an annihilation, not a tasting.

He worked the cork free and raised the bottle to his lips. The first gulp was a shock to the system. An explosion of smoke and iodine, a beautiful, violent assault on his senses. It burned a fiery path down his throat, a stark contrast to the elegant smoothness of the wine. He gasped, the peaty vapor filling his lungs. He took another long, punishing pull, and then another.

He didn't sit. He just stood there in the middle of the living room, methodically finishing his father's gift, chasing a numbness that remained stubbornly out of reach. With every swallow, the image of Daniela's face – her shock, her hurt, her final, cold disgust – flashed in his mind, refusing to be drowned. He was not drinking to forget; he was drinking to punish the man who remembered.

Finally, the bottle was empty. He lowered it slowly, his grip still tight around its neck, and sank back into his father's armchair. He didn't feel drunk. He didn't feel numb. He just felt ... erased. A blank slate of shame.

★★★★

A lone, empty bottle of sixteen-year-old Lagavulin rested in the hand of the young man slumped in the armchair. It remembered this boy, though he had been younger then, writhing on the floor in a cleansing fire of grief. That night, its spirit had offered catharsis. Tonight was different. There was no catharsis in this. This was not a fire to cleanse, but a thick, peaty smoke to obscure. It had seen men drink to remember and men drink to forget. This one was drinking to become a miasma. A fine purpose for a fine spirit, it supposed. And so it watched, its duty done, as the young man sought the bottom of the bottle, only to find the fathomless depths of himself.

774884 (February 3)

The summons came not as a thunderclap, but as a quiet, three-line email from an executive assistant, its subject line a masterpiece of corporate ambiguity: "Catch-up with Arthur Sterling." Nick had stared at it for a full minute, a cold, heavy feeling settling in his stomach. He knew what it was. And yet, a small, hopelessly irrational part of him clung to the possibility that it wasn't. Maybe it was a strategy session. A post-mortem. A 'how do we fix this and win back the DoJ's trust?' meeting.

He walked the long, carpeted hallway to the corner office, the emptiness of the 35th floor amplifying the frantic thumping of his own heart. The door to the CEO's office was a slab of dark, polished cherrywood that seemed to absorb sound. He knocked once.

"Come in," a calm, patrician voice called out.

Arthur Sterling, the CEO of Chain Intelligence, was a man who looked like he had been born in a bespoke suit. In his late fifties, with a mane of perfectly coiffed silver hair and the easy posture of a man who had never once in his life had to worry about a mortgage, he was the platonic ideal of the Wall Street executive turned political power player. He was standing by the floor-to-ceiling window, looking down at the panoramic view of Central

Park, a view that likely cost more than Nick's entire crypto portfolio even at its peak.

"Nick, my boy. Come in, come in. Have a seat," Arthur said, turning from the window. His smile was warm, but it didn't quite reach his eyes. He gestured to one of the plush leather armchairs facing his massive desk. "Can I get you anything? Water? Coffee? A stiff drink?" He chuckled, a dry, rustling sound, as he gestured toward a crystal tumbler on a tray next to him. Nick was sure the scotch in it was at least aged three decades.

"I'm fine, thank you, Mr. Sterling," Nick said, sinking into the chair. The leather sighed under his weight.

"Arthur, please," the CEO corrected him gently as he settled into his own chair. He picked up a heavy paperweight from his desk that looked like a tungsten cube and began to turn it over in his hands. "I spoke to Rob last night. At the club. He sends his best. Asked how his star son-in-law was settling in."

The mention of his father-in-law was a casual, almost friendly blow. It was a reminder of how he'd gotten here, and a prelude to how he was about to leave.

"He's ... he's well, I hope?" Nick managed.

"Oh, splendid. His golf swing is a thing of beauty. A real artist on the back nine," Arthur said, his gaze fixed on the paperweight. An awkward silence descended, thick and suffocating. Arthur seemed to be searching for the right words, a man unaccustomed to delivering bad news to the son-in-law of a friend from the club.

"Look, Nick," he began, finally setting the paperweight down with a soft thud. "There's no easy way to say this. We received formal correspondence from the Department of Justice yesterday afternoon. I think it's best if I just ... read it to you."

He picked up a single sheet of heavy, cream-colored paper from his desk. It was embossed with the official seal of the Department of Justice. Nick's blood ran cold.

Arthur cleared his throat and began to read in a dispassionate monotone, as if reciting a particularly boring weather report.

"To the Office of the Chief Executive Officer, Chain Intelligence, LLC. Re: Contract Number DOJ-CI-22-7B. Pursuant to the review initiated on January

24, 2023, following the briefing provided by your Senior Director, Mr. Nicholas Hernandez, this letter serves as formal notification. The Office of the Deputy Principal Deputy Assistant Attorney General, in conjunction with the Senior Counsel for Emergent Threat Vector Analysis and the Acting Undersecretary for Digital Asset Forfeiture, has concluded its assessment."

Arthur paused, looking up at Nick over the top of the letter. "They do love their titles down there, don't they? Sounds like a Gilbert and Sullivan opera." He offered another weak, humorless chuckle before continuing.

"The assessment has determined that the analytical product provided by Chain Intelligence regarding the subject 'Dev_akshar' failed to meet the standards of evidentiary rigor required for federal law enforcement operations. The intelligence was predicated on a proprietary analytical model whose methodology was found to be ..." Arthur squinted at the paper, *"'computationally unsound and prone to significant categorical misattribution.'"*

He looked up again, a flicker of something that might have been pity in his eyes. "That's a new one for me. 'Computationally unsound.' Sounds rather final, doesn't it?"

Nick didn't respond. He just stared at a point on the wall just past Arthur's silver hair, his mind a hollow, ringing void.

Arthur continued reading. *"The subsequent misidentification of a person of interest, Mr. Darren Gooch, resulted in a non-trivial expenditure of departmental and international liaison resources. The lead was found to be –* and I quote the addendum from Mr. Howard's office – *'predicated on a series of cascading logical fallacies culminating in a conclusion that was, from an operational standpoint, laughably incorrect.'"*

Laughably incorrect. The words reverberated in the silent, cavernous office. It wasn't just that he was wrong. He was a joke. A punchline in a report that would now be entered into the permanent record of the United States government.

"Therefore," Arthur read, his voice now softer, almost apologetic, *"as of the date of this letter, February 2, 2023, the Department of Justice hereby invokes Clause 14-C of our agreement and terminates Contract DOJ-CI-22-7B for cause, effective immediately. We wish your firm the best in its future endeavors."*

He placed the letter down on the desk, perfectly aligned with the edge. He said nothing for a few moments that felt like an eternity to Nick.

"Well," Arthur said finally, breaking the spell. "That's that, I suppose. A bit of a sticky wicket."

He stood up and walked back to the window, turning his back on Nick. It was a classic power move, but it felt more like an act of cowardice, a way to avoid looking at the mess he was about to make.

"Nick, you know how much I value my friendship with Rob," he began, his voice muffled by the thick glass. "He was so proud when you came on board. He saw this as a real … a real fresh start for you after that whole crypto unpleasantness."

He turned back around, his face a mask of practiced, patrician sympathy.

"Unfortunately, the termination of this contract puts the company in a difficult position. It was our flagship public sector engagement. The board is … displeased. We're going to have to restructure the entire Cyber and Crypto Crime unit. Realign resources. A lot of good people are going to be affected."

Nick knew what was coming. He just sat there, a passenger in the slow-motion car crash of his own life.

"My hands are tied, my boy," Arthur said, his voice laced with a feigned, almost theatrical regret. "Given that you were the lead on this engagement, and given the … the very specific and rather colorful language the Department used in their assessment, your position has become untenable. We're going to have to let you go."

The words, when they finally came, felt strangely distant, as if they were happening to someone else. He had been expecting them, but the finality of it was still a physical blow, a hollowing out of his chest.

"I've already spoken to HR," Arthur continued, now all business. "They'll walk you through the severance package. It's quite generous, all things considered. We'll have you sign the standard NDA, of course. And they'll need your badge and laptop. Someone will be by your desk in about fifteen minutes to help you … you know. Pack."

He walked back to his desk and extended a hand across the polished wood. "It's not personal, Nick. It's just business. I hope you understand. And I truly wish you the best. I'm sure you'll land on your feet."

Nick stood up on unsteady legs and took the offered hand. It was dry and firm. He shook it once, a single, lifeless pump. He couldn't find any words. There was nothing left to say.

He turned and walked out of the office, closing the heavy cherrywood door softly behind him. He didn't look back. He just walked down the long, silent hallway, the faint scent of Arthur's expensive cologne clinging to him like the stench of his own downfall.

775521 (February 7)

The second bottle of Château Haut-Brion was breathing its last. Oliver held the glass up to the lamplight, admiring the deep, garnet color, the way it seemed to hold a dark, liquid history within it. The wine tasted of scorched earth, old leather, and a faint, lingering sweetness that felt like a cruel joke. It was a magnificent, complex thing, and he was drinking it like cheap table wine, one deep, unthinking swallow after another. It was a desecration, he thought, and the idea pleased him immensely.

Ten days. Had it only been ten days since Daniela had walked out? It felt like a geological age. The silence in the apartment had become a permanent resident, a roommate that paid its rent in suffocating emptiness.

He closed his eyes, and the memory played back for the hundredth time, a pristine, high-definition loop of his own disgrace. He hadn't moved from this very armchair. He'd just sat there the next day, nursing a hangover that felt like a physical manifestation of his own shame, and waited.

She had arrived around noon, not alone, but with Sarah in tow, a silent, grim-faced accomplice. They didn't knock. Daniela used her key one last time, a final, quiet assertion of a right she was about to relinquish. They came in carrying two large, empty suitcases, their wheels clicking softly on the hardwood floor.

He had wanted to say something, anything. I'm sorry. It was a mistake. Don't go. But the words were stones in his throat. He just sat there, a spectator at the dismantling of his own life.

Daniela hadn't looked at him. Not once. Her movements were a study in cold, efficient erasure. She went from room to room, gathering her things – the clothes from the closet, the books from the nightstand, the toiletries from the bathroom – with a speed and precision that felt like a surgical procedure. There was no sentimentality, no lingering over shared objects. Each item was just another piece of evidence to be bagged and removed from the scene of the crime.

Sarah had been the worst part. She'd kept glancing at him, her face a mask of theatrical pity. It was the kind of look you give a wounded animal on the side of the road, a pathetic creature you feel a momentary pang of sympathy for before driving on. He had wanted to scream at her, to tell her to stop looking at him with those sad, patronizing eyes. But he had remained silent, a statue of shame in his father's armchair.

They had filled the two suitcases in under an hour. When they were done, they walked to the front door. He had thought, hoped, that Daniela would say something then. A final word. An accusation. A goodbye. But there was nothing. She paused with her hand on the doorknob, and for a fleeting, foolish moment, he thought she might turn around.

Instead, she reached into her coat pocket and pulled out her set of keys. He recognized the small, silver key to the apartment and the heavy brass one for the main building entrance. She held them in her open palm for a second before placing them deliberately on the small entryway table.

They didn't make a loud noise, just a soft, dull clatter of metal on wood, but the sound was deafening. It was the sound of access being revoked, of a shared life being rendered null and void. A key was a promise of return, and leaving it behind was a statement of absolute finality. It was a sound that said, I no longer belong here. This is no longer home. The quiet little plop of those keys on the table was more brutal than a slammed door.

Then she opened the door, and they left. The click of the lock was just an aftershock, a mechanical confirmation of the severing that had already taken place.

He had opened his eyes then, and the apartment was just as it was now. Empty.

He drained the last of the Haut-Brion from his glass and stared at the two empty bottles on the desk. A monument to a wasted week. He had spent every night since she left trying to find his way back to the blue mist. Back to her.

The irony was a blade twisting in his gut. When Daniela was here, he had been consumed by a guilty obsession with Anariadne, a chimera he couldn't have. Now that he was single, now that he was free to succumb to that temptation without the pretense of betrayal, she was gone.

He had tried everything. He'd sat in this chair for hours, meditating, focusing, calling out to her in the silent space behind his eyes. He'd tried drinking himself into a state of projection, hoping the wine would act as a key. He'd even tried lying on the cold floor, hoping a change in physical state would trigger a change in his mental one.

But there was nothing. No blue mist. No seductive, broken grammar. No golden hair or piercing turquoise eyes. The doorway that had opened so easily before was now sealed shut, and he was left pounding on a door that wasn't there.

He was ready now. He was ready to follow her thread, to go to that place she had spoken of, that destination he didn't know. He was ready to be led away from certainty, to dissolve in her light, whatever the cost. But the guide had vanished, leaving him alone in the labyrinth he had created for himself. He had chosen the apparent over the phenomenal, and in the end, he was left with neither.

The weight of that final thought was an anchor, pulling him down into the dark upholstery of the armchair. The empty bottles on the desk stood like twin tombstones marking the death of a day, a week, a life. The Château Haut-Brion, a wine meant for celebration, for savoring over hours, had been consumed like a fire extinguisher – blunt, desperate, useless. Two bottles. A new record.

He felt the effects now, not as a pleasant, warming buzz, but as a hostile takeover of his senses. The edges of the room began to soften and blur, the lamplight across the room smearing into a hazy, indistinct wash. He tried to focus on a single point, a corner of a bookshelf, but the room began to spin, a slow, nauseating carousel. He closed his eyes, but the motion only intensified behind his eyelids, a dizzying internal vortex.

For ten days, he had fought. He had tried to meditate, to focus, to will himself back into the blue mist. He had strived and struggled and strained. Now, there was no fight left. There was nothing left to do but let go. He surrendered to the spin, to the alcoholic tide pulling him under. He actively embraced the dissolution, a quiet, internal plea to whatever abyss was waiting for him. Take me.

And then, it happened.

It was not a gentle transition. It was a physical, gut-wrenching lurch. The feeling of the armchair beneath him vanished, and the solid floor of his father's apartment gave way. He was falling. Plummeting through a cold, silent, and infinite nothingness. There was no wind, no sound – just a terrifying, weightless descent. The dizzying spin of his drunken state resolved itself into this singular, terrifying vector. Down.

He was a stone dropped into a bottomless well. He didn't scream. The surrender was too absolute for that. This was it, then. The end of the fall. The bottom of himself.

Then, through the abyss, a sound. A single, perfect note that cut through the silence. It was a voice, and it was a caress.

"Ego ex inferna natium ..."

The blue mist began to coalesce around him, a soft, ethereal glow pushing back the absolute black. The terrifying sensation of falling slowed, then stopped. He was suspended now, floating in a sea of deep, tranquil blue.

"Ego mai plenei absentum ..."

She appeared before him, not all at once, but as if the mist itself was weaving her into existence. First, the golden hair, then the piercing turquoise eyes, then the flowing white robe. Anariadne. She was more beautiful, more real, more painfully perfect than he remembered.

A wave of sheer, unbridled ecstasy washed over him, so powerful he could almost feel it deep inside his bones. The shame, the guilt, the crushing weight of his loss ... it all evaporated, burned away by the sheer, radiant fact of her presence. He had found her.

"You're here," he breathed, the words clumsy with relief. "I've been trying … I've been looking for you everywhere."

She regarded him with a cool, placid expression. There was no warmth in her eyes, no welcoming smile. She seemed to be studying him, a beautiful, indifferent scientist observing a specimen.

"Wanted me, you did?" she said, her broken grammar the most beautiful music he had ever heard.

"Yes," he said, a desperate laugh bubbling up from his chest. He felt an overpowering urge to move toward her, to touch her, to confirm that she was real. He wanted to close the distance, to take her in his arms, to lose himself in her. "God, yes."

Anariadne took a single, graceful step back, maintaining the space between them. The gesture was small, but its meaning was vast.

"But something is on your mind, there is?" she asked, her gaze unwavering.

The question sobered him slightly, pulling him back from the edge of his elation. He thought of Daniela. The memory was a sharp, sudden pain, but it felt distant now, a tragedy from another lifetime.

"She's gone," he said, the words coming easily, a confession to a new and higher power. "Daniela. She left me. I'm free now."

He said it with a hint of pride, of offering. He was untethered. He was hers now, if she would have him.

"Good, that is," Anariadne replied, her tone as flat and cold as a winter stone. There was no sympathy, no validation. Just a clinical assessment of a new fact.

The coldness of her reply was a shock, but he pushed past it. It didn't matter. Nothing mattered but her. "So now … now I can follow you, right? I'm ready. I can go to that place you talked about. The one I don't know."

She glided closer, her turquoise eyes scanning his face, searching for something. "Ready, you think you are?" she whispered, the sound a soft caress against his raw nerves. "Almost, you are. But fully, you are not."

A spike of frustration pierced his euphoria. He had done what she wanted. He had pushed away the one person who anchored him to the phenomenal world. He had betrayed his own heart at her silent, seductive bidding. And it still wasn't enough.

"What else?" he pleaded, his voice cracking with a desperation he couldn't hide. "What more do I have to do? Tell me. I'll do anything."

Anariadne simply smiled, a slow, enigmatic curve of her lips that offered nothing. She raised a hand, not to touch him, but as if to signal an end.

"You have taken the first step, you have. The descent, it is almost complete. My purpose here, for today, it is done."

"No, wait!" he cried out as he saw the blue mist around her begin to glow brighter, the edges of her form starting to soften and dissolve. "Don't go! Tell me what to do next!"

She did not answer. Her form became translucent, the golden hair and turquoise eyes fading back into the blue nothingness from which they had been born. Her final whispered words lingered in the now-empty space.

"*Ego viliye in claritate lumiere ...*"

And then she was gone.

He was alone again, floating in the cold, silent, now dark abyss. The brief, ecstatic warmth of her presence had been ripped away, leaving behind a cold that was deeper and more profound than any he had ever known.

He replayed her words in the silent void. *Almost, you are. But fully, you are not.*

It wasn't a definitive rejection. It was something far crueler. It was a question mark, left hanging in the infinite abyss where an answer could not be found. What more was there to give? He had surrendered his will, his certainty, his last connection to the phenomenal world. What else was left to surrender? Was this another test? Or was the true test what he would do now, in the cold, after she had gone?

CHAPTER 4. MARCH 2

The smoke from Nick's cigar, a robusto he'd forgotten the name of, rose in a lazy, unhurried spiral toward the stained, pressed-tin ceiling of Casa Argento. It was a good smoke, he supposed. Full-bodied, notes of leather and something vaguely like burnt coffee, curdled into ash and chalk – like the taste of ground error bars. He'd paid $35 for it, a reflexive act of a man who was still used to having an expense account. The reality of his new financial situation hadn't quite caught up with the muscle memory of his former life.

He was the only person in the main lounge. It was about 6:30 p.m. on Saturday in Hell's Kitchen, and Casa Argento was an abandoned galleon adrift in a sea of raucous, brightly-lit bars. The place had the bones of old-world elegance – deep leather armchairs cracked and fissured like ancient riverbeds, dark wood paneling that had absorbed decades of secrets and smoke, a grand, unlit fireplace that stood like a cold altar. But the glory had faded. The air, circulated by a ventilation system that hummed with a hollow, bronchial rattle that coughed dust from the vents, was thick with the scent of stale tobacco and the faint, sweet perfume of disinfectant and decay. It was a place where ambition came to embalm itself. It was perfect.

Across the cavernous room, in a far corner, sat the lounge's only other patron. He was a man of indeterminate age, dressed in a full, shimmering silver tracksuit, complete with matching silver sneakers. His face seemed to have a strange blue tint to it. He wasn't smoking. He was just sitting there, perfectly still, nursing a single, untouched glass of what looked like milk, a beatific smile on his face as he stared intently at the dead, black screen of a wall-mounted television.

Nick took a long, slow draw from his cigar. The smoke filled his mouth, a warm, acrid comfort. He had been replaying the last two weeks in a continuous, agonizing loop, a mental film reel that he couldn't turn off.

Laughably incorrect.

The words were seared in his memory, as sharp and clear as the day Jeremiah Howard had uttered them. It wasn't the firing that haunted him. That had been a quiet, almost gentle affair, a corporate mercy killing administered by Arthur Sterling with a practiced, sanitized sorrow. No, it was the humiliation in D.C. that had branded him. The clinical, systematic dismantling of his work, his certainty, his very identity, in that cold, silent conference room.

He had walked in there a titan, the man who had cracked the uncrackable case. He had the data. He had the AI model. He had the name. Darren Gooch. The Jute King of Dubai. It had been so clean, so elegant. A perfect narrative.

And they had shredded it. Not with anger or passion, but with a bored, bureaucratic precision that was infinitely more cruel. They had countered his state-of-the-art AI with ... a credit card statement. A plush camel. A novelty pen. They had made his life's work, his comeback, the punchline to a joke about burlap.

A waitress, a young woman with tired eyes and a tattoo of a weeping cherub on her forearm, materialized beside his chair.

"Sparkling or still?" she asked, her voice a monotone of practiced indifference.

"Excuse me?" Nick asked, pulled from his reverie.

"For your water. Do you want sparkling or still?"

"Oh. Still is fine."

She placed a coaster and a glass of water on the small table beside him. Her wrist flexed as she set the glass down, revealing a crack in the weeping cherub. She then vanished as silently as she had appeared. Nick stared at the glass. The banality of the question in the face of his existential crisis was a special kind of insult. The world just kept on turning, kept on asking if you wanted bubbles in your water, even after your soul had been flayed.

He took another puff of the cigar. The initial shock had worn off in the days since his firing. The shame was still there, a low-grade fever that he couldn't shake. But something else was beginning to grow in its place. Something hot and clean and sharp.

Rage.

It was a quiet rage, a simmering, seething thing that was slowly burning away the fog of his humiliation. He was angry at Chandra, the timid academic who had built a weapon and then been too afraid to let him fire it. "The confidence interval is a problem, Nick." Yes, it was a problem. The problem was that Chandra lacked the spine to trust his own creation, to take the leap.

He was angry at Arthur Sterling, the silver-haired snake, with his talk of the club and his friend Rob. He had pretended to be a mentor, a paternal figure, but the moment the contract was threatened, he had cut Nick loose without a second thought. *"It's not personal, Nick. It's just business."* Everything was personal.

But most of all, he was angry at Jeremiah Howard. He saw his face, the cold, unimpressed eyes, the almost imperceptible smirk as he delivered the final blow. Howard had enjoyed his failure. He had relished the opportunity to put the cocky, private-sector crypto bro in his place. *Fucking DEI hire, most likely,* Nick thought to himself in disgust.

The waitress reappeared, this time with a brass receptacle and feather brush. She expertly flicked the accumulated cigar ash from his ashtray into the bowl, and without a word, disappeared again. The interruption was a pinprick, a momentary distraction from the storm brewing inside him.

They thought he was a joke. A fool who had been duped by his own flawed machine. They thought the case was closed, another failed attempt to pin down the elusive Dev_akshar.

They were wrong.

The rage was burning away the shame now, leaving behind something hard and clear. A purpose. The DoJ had given up. Chain Intelligence had given up. But he wouldn't. He had been publicly disgraced for being wrong, and the only way to erase that stain was to be right. Spectacularly, undeniably right.

He wouldn't just find Dev_akshar. He would dismantle him. He would trace every transaction, unravel every CoinJoin, expose every shell company. He would map the man's entire financial soul and deliver it to Jeremiah Howard, not as a vendor, but as an equal. He would walk back into that office, not with a report, but with a head on a platter. It would be a reckoning, not a presentation.

The thought was intoxicating. It was the first real, undiluted feeling of hope he'd had in weeks. This wasn't a job anymore. It was a crusade. A holy war for his own redemption.

He would have to go rogue. He had signed an NDA, of course, a document that forbade him from using any of Chain Intelligence's proprietary data or models. But they had fired him. The contract was broken. In his mind, that made the NDA null and void. He had managed to transfer the entire Dev_akshar case file and raw on-chain data onto a personal drive before he was escorted out of the building. And he still had his mind. He wouldn't use the flawed AI. He would do it himself. The hard way. The right way. Through proof of work.

He took a final, deep draw from the cigar, the cherry glowing a fierce, bright red. He had the skills. He had the data. And now, he had the motive. A cold-blooded, all-consuming thirst for revenge.

He looked across the room at the man in the silver tracksuit. The man had not moved an inch. He was still smiling at the blank television screen, a picture of serene, incomprehensible madness. For a moment, Nick felt a strange kinship with him. They were both men who had become untethered from the consensus reality, each pursuing his own private, obsessive vision.

Nick crushed the cigar butt in the ashtray. The smoke continued to rise, but the fire was out. He stood up, leaving a $20 bill on the table for the water he hadn't touched. He walked out of the faded elegance of Casa Argento and into the cold, sharp air of the city night. He was no longer Nicholas Hernandez, the disgraced senior director. He was a hunter. He didn't have a job anymore. He had prey.

776200 (February 12)

The Sunday morning light was a pale, watery gray, filtering through the windows of the Chelsea apartment with a distinct lack of enthusiasm. Oliver lay in bed, the sheets a tangled mess around him, and scrolled through his Nostr feed on his phone. It had become a ritual in the days since Daniela had left, a way to feel connected to a world, any world, that wasn't the suffocation of his own four walls. The global, asynchronous conversational firehose of bitcoiners was a strange and noisy comfort, a digital whisper of the community he still felt too alienated to seek out in person.

He scrolled past a technical debate on Lightning channel capacity, a thread of memes mocking central bankers, and a link to a podcast about Austrian economics. Then, a crudely drawn image caught his eye. It depicted a dejected-looking ape, recognizable from the popular ape NFTs he'd seen his former BlockWaves colleagues obsess over, trudging away from a burning Ethereum logo and toward a pristine, orange bitcoin citadel. The caption above it read:

Well, shitcoiners couldn't do monkey jpegs on their garbage chains, so they decided to bring them to bitcoin.

Oliver frowned. *Monkey jpegs on bitcoin?* The phrase made no sense. It was a contradiction in terms, a category error. He knew jpegs passed off as nonfungible tokens were the domain of bloated, centralized blockchains like Ethereum and Solana, protocols that had sacrificed decentralization for the cheap transaction space necessary for such frivolities. Bitcoin was different. Bitcoin was serious. It was a settlement network. It was pristine, it was money. It wasn't for ... pictures of cartoon monkeys. He dismissed the post as a joke, a bit of low-effort trolling, and kept scrolling.

But a few posts down, the topic reappeared. This time it was a long, angry screed from a well-known developer, filled with technical jargon Oliver only half-understood – *witness data, taproot script-path, envelope op-codes.* The emotional gist, however, was clear. The developer was incensed about what he called "an attack on fungibility" and "the most idiotic, profligate waste of block space imaginable."

He scrolled further. Now the feed was full of it. It was a schism, an ideological civil war erupting in real-time on his screen. Some were defending the new methodology, called Ordinals, as a radical innovation. Others were decrying it as a cancer, a parasite that had attached itself to the host. Then he saw a post that made him stop, its language a strange and compelling mix of militant fury and absurdist humor.

The only way to fight monke jpegs is with gorilla warfare. Plebs, this is a call to action. Let a million memes bloom!

Gorilla warfare. The pun, so stupid and yet so perfect, cut through his morning haze. This was now a culture war, not a technical debate. The phone was too small for this. He needed a proper terminal.

He walked to his desk, sat down in the chair, and turned on the computer. For the next hour, he fell down the rabbit hole. He read the documentation for the Ordinals and the accompanying "inscriptions," his initial confusion slowly morphing into a cold, intellectual horror.

They were actually doing it. They had found a way to exploit the witness data field from the SegWit upgrade and the scripting flexibility of Taproot to inscribe arbitrary data – text, images, even entire computer programs – directly onto bitcoin blocks.

He felt a wave of something that felt like violation. The timechain, the immutable, sacred ledger his father had helped build, the very thing the Noncemeister had described as the collective consciousness of the universe, was being used as a digital billboard for pixelated garbage. It was a desecration.

Every satoshi, the smallest unit of bitcoin, was supposed to be the same, a fungible unit of pure, unadorned value. That was the whole point. But Inscriptions attempted to attack that. They turned specific sats into unique, identifiable "collectibles," as tainted and nonfungible as a dollar bill with a celebrity's autograph scrawled on it. The shitcoin casino, with all its grifters and its get-rich-quick NFT schemes – the very world he had just escaped from at BlockWaves – had found a backdoor into his new home, bitcoin. It was an invasion.

His hands clenched into fists. He thought of his conversations with Vince, of the elegant philosophy of a sound money built for the long term, of a system designed to encourage low time preference and responsible stewardship. And now this. A system that encouraged the exact opposite: frivolous, short-term speculation on digital trinkets.

He was livid. The personal misery of the last two weeks, the loneliness, the guilt, it was all suddenly eclipsed by this new, righteous, and wonderfully clean anger. It was an anger that had a target. It was an anger that made sense.

The apartment began to feel like a cage, the walls closing in on him. He couldn't sit here. He couldn't stare at the paintings or the empty wine glasses or the imprint of Daniela's absence in every room. He needed to move. He needed to burn this feeling out of his muscles.

He strode to the bedroom, pulled open the drawer under the bed, and grabbed the first two hundred-dollar bills his fingers touched from one of the stacks in the suitcase. He shoved them into his wallet without a second thought, pulled on his jacket, and left, the click of the lock snapping behind him like a trigger pulled on his inertia.

He hit the street and turned north on 10th Avenue, walking at a furious, punishing pace. The cold February air was a clean blade against his heated skin, but it did little to cool the furnace roaring in his mind.

Monkey jpegs. The phrase was an insult, a childish taunt spray-painted across a masterpiece. For months, he had been on a sacred quest, unraveling a mystery that felt ancient and profound, a journey that had led him to the very nature of time and truth. He had found a sanctuary in the elegant, immutable logic of the timechain. And now, the barbarians were at the gates. Not just at the gates, but inside, scrawling their crude, stupid cartoons all over the pristine walls of the citadel.

He dodged a group of tourists ambling near Chelsea Market, his shoulder bumping one of them without apology. *Gorilla warfare.* It *was* a war. A war for the soul of bitcoin. And he was a soldier with no army, a king with no kingdom, raging silently on a city sidewalk.

The anger was so pure, so clean. It was a relief after the murky, self-loathing swamp he'd been wading through for the past two weeks. The guilt, the shame ... this new rage was a fire that burned it all away, leaving only a sharp, righteous certainty.

But then, as he crossed 34th Street, the towering glass structures of Hudson Yards looming to his left, the certainty began to fray. Who could he even share this righteous anger with? A few months ago, he would have called Nick, ready to laugh at the latest shitcoin absurdity. Now Nick was on the other side, a sniper in the employ of the very system they used to mock. He thought of Vince, but Vince's calm, philosophical detachment felt like a distant planet. *Bitcoin is for anyone.* Was it? Was it for *this*? He made a mental note to reach out to Vince to hear his perspective.

The image of Daniela's face flashed in his mind, her expression of cold, final disappointment. He pushed it away, but it returned, persistent and painful. He imagined trying to explain Ordinals to her. She would have listened, her head tilted with that look of intense, curious empathy. She would have understood his anger, even if she didn't understand the technicals. And then she would have put her hand on his and told him it would be okay.

The thought was a physical ache in his chest. He had pushed her away, and for what? For a whisper in a dream. He had traded the warm, breathing reality of her presence for a seductive question mark from the blue mist, and now both were gone.

He reached 59th Street, the frenzied swirl of traffic a perfect mirror for his own internal state. He didn't break his stride, crossing the threshold where 10th Avenue seamlessly, almost magically, became Amsterdam. The city shifted around him, the industrial chic of Hell's Kitchen giving way to the pre-war residential grandeur of the Upper West Side, but he barely registered it. He felt like a spectator to his own life, a man walking behind a pane of glass, watching the world go by in muffled inaction.

What was he even doing with his life? He was a man with a $4,000,000 secret he couldn't spend, and a mission he couldn't complete. The six-spiraled shape on the paintings was a constant, mocking presence in his mind. A bizarre geometry. A cosmic lock with no key. It was another dead end, another beautiful, unsolvable puzzle.

He was unmoored. An exile in his own city.

He finally slowed his pace, his lungs burning, his legs aching. He looked up, disoriented, realizing he had walked over 50 blocks without any conscious thought. He was on 71st and Amsterdam. Across the street was a pub, its name, McGinn's, written in a faded, Gaelic-style font above a dark green door.

It looked like a decent, unpretentious place. An O'Connell's for a different neighborhood.

And then he saw him.

Loitering on the corner by the pub, his movements aimless and jerky, was the homeless man. He wore the same filthy, tattered T-shirt, completely inadequate for the biting February wind. He was muttering to himself, his gaze fixed on something invisible on the sidewalk, his body a portrait of derelict madness in the heart of one of Manhattan's most affluent neighborhoods.

Oliver froze mid-stride, the city's raucous soundtrack fading to a dull hum in his ears. It wasn't just a random derelict. It was *him*. The man from New Year's Eve. The oracle of the sidewalk, the one who had drawn the six spirals in Harlem.

A jolt, electric and cold, shot through him. This felt like a summons. He remembered how the man had vanished before, a wisp of smoke dissolving into the winter air the moment he'd turned his back. Not this time. This time, he would get an answer.

He strode across Amsterdam Avenue, dodging a taxi that blared its horn at him. He didn't care. He walked right up to the man, who didn't seem to register his presence.

"The spirals," Oliver said, his voice low and urgent. "The drawing you made in Harlem. I saw them. They're on the paintings. What are they? What do they mean?"

The homeless man stopped muttering. He slowly, deliberately, lifted his head and looked at Oliver. His eyes were a pale, cloudy blue, and for a moment, they seemed to focus with an unnerving clarity. He offered a slow, toothless grin.

"*Hessele tu rabey?*" he rasped, a foul puff of air hitting Oliver's face.

"What? I don't understand," Oliver said, his impatience mounting. "I need you to tell me what the six spirals mean."

The man ignored him. His gaze drifted from Oliver's face down to the gutter. With a surprising quickness, he bent down and picked something up. It was a shard of a broken beer bottle, a jagged piece of dark green glass. He held it up, pinching it between a filthy thumb and forefinger, and angled it toward the pale afternoon sun.

A small, distorted shape of light appeared on the grimy brick wall of McGinn's. It was a haphazard smear of weak, wintry colors.

"*Tu rabey ess ... sol ...*" the man whispered, his voice a dry rustle. He twisted his wrist slightly, and the smear of light coalesced for a breathtaking, surreal second. It formed a shimmering, watery projection of six distinct points of light, spinning lazily around a central, invisible core. It was a beautiful, ethereal three-dimensional snowflake made of winter light.

Oliver stared, transfixed. It was a magic trick. A beautiful, logic-defying piece of street magic. "How ... how are you doing that?"

The man's grin widened. He continued his chant, a string of broken, incomprehensible words that Oliver's mind grasped at and failed to hold.

"*Decem et ashta ... in Iulius ...*"

"What are you saying?" Oliver pleaded, taking a step closer. The desperation in his voice was raw, pathetic. He knew it. He was begging a madman on a street corner for the secrets of the universe. This was his life now. "Please, just tell me what it means."

The man lowered the piece of glass. The magical shape on the wall vanished, leaving only brick and grime. He looked at the shard in his hand as if seeing it for the first time, then tossed it back into the gutter with a clink. He looked back at Oliver, his eyes cloudy and unfocused again, the brief moment of lucidity gone.

"*Ess temper, eh innit? N'as it, ser!*" he repeated, this time with a note of finality.

"Oliver? My goodness, is that you?"

A familiar voice, sharp and laced with a theatrical disbelief, cut through the cold air from behind him. Startled, pulled from the strange, hypnotic encounter, Oliver turned.

It took his brain a moment to process the figure standing on the top step of McGinn's, silhouetted against the warm light from the doorway. The gaunt frame, the long graying hair, the look of wry amusement – it was Reza.

"Reza," Oliver said, a surprised laugh escaping his lips. "What are you doing here?"

"I could ask you the same thing," Reza said, descending the steps. He looked past Oliver to the spot where the homeless man had been. "You seemed rather engrossed. Staring at a hole in the pub's brickwork. Contemplating its structural integrity?"

"I ... I was talking to someone," Oliver said, his cheeks flushing with embarrassment. He turned to gesture toward the now-empty spot on the corner. "There was a homeless man right there. He just ..." He trailed off, seeing nothing but a windswept patch of dirty sidewalk. He had vanished. Of course, he had.

"Was there now?" Reza said, his expression unreadable. He didn't mock, nor did he press the issue. He simply clapped a hand on Oliver's shoulder. "Well, whoever your mysterious friend was, he seems to have fled. You look half-frozen. I was just about to have lunch. I won't have you suffering out here while I'm enjoying a perfectly good pint of Guinness. Come on."

He didn't wait for an answer, simply steered Oliver by the shoulder up the steps and into the pub. The interior of McGinn's was a warm, dark cocoon of wood and worn brass. The air smelled of fried food, old beer and the faint, sweet scent of whisky. It was the comforting, unpretentious smell of a real neighborhood institution. They took a small booth by the window, the vinyl of the seat cool against Oliver's legs.

A waitress with a weary but kind face came over. "Guinness for me," Reza said without looking at the menu.

"I'll have the same," Oliver added.

As the waitress left, an uneasy quiet fell between them. Oliver felt the need to clear the air, to address the elephant that had been sitting in his mind since New Year's Eve.

"Reza, listen," he began. "About that night. At your party. I was ... I was completely out of line. The way I behaved, what I said to that guy Arman ... it was inexcusable. I'm really sorry."

Reza took a moment before responding, his gaze fixed on a framed, faded photograph of a Scottish highland cow on the opposite wall. "I heard there was a minor skirmish," he said. "Steve was beside himself, of course. Thinks a raised voice at a dinner party is a prelude to the apocalypse." He leaned forward, a conspiratorial glint in his eyes. "Between you and me, Oliver, that entire room had it coming. A collection of the most insufferable, vacuous parasites I have ever had the displeasure of hosting. If you hadn't yelled at that pompous little banker, I probably would have. You did me a favor."

Oliver let out a breath he didn't realize he'd been holding. "Still. I made a fool of myself. And of Daniela."

"Nonsense," Reza said with a dismissive wave of his hand. The waitress arrived with their pints, the dark stout settling into a creamy, white head. "You spoke with passion. A rare commodity in a world of curated opinions and lukewarm convictions. In fact ..." he paused, taking a long, slow sip of his Guinness. "That night ... after hearing about your little outburst ... it kindled something."

"Kindled something?" Oliver asked, intrigued.

"I've spent the better part of two decades cultivating a thick, protective shell of cynicism, Oliver. A necessary armor against the sheer, unrelenting stupidity of the world. I retired from the stage, retired from the city, retired from myself. I was perfectly content in my magnificent jadedness."

The waitress returned. "Ready to order?"

Reza scanned the menu with a strange, intense curiosity. "What's the most ... authentic thing you have on here?"

"The haggis, sir. We import it."

"Perfect," Reza said, closing the menu with a decisive snap. "I'll have that." Oliver, feeling a sudden hunger, ordered the fish and chips.

"But your conversation that night," Reza continued, as if there had been no interruption. "Your belief in this ... this bitcoin of yours. It was so absolute. So full of hope and righteous fury. It reminded me of someone I had long forgotten. It reminded me of me, when I first arrived in this city from Tehran, a boy full of poetry and fire, believing I could remake the world on a stage in some abandoned warehouse." He took another thoughtful sip of his Guinness. "It made me realize that my cynicism wasn't armor. It was a cage. A very comfortable, well-appointed cage, but a cage nonetheless."

Their food arrived. The waiter placed a golden-brown slab of fried fish in front of Oliver and the haggis in front of Reza. It was a rustic, unadorned mound of oats and offal, served with neeps and tatties. Reza picked up a small bowl from the condiment tray on the table.

He took a dollop of green pickle relish and placed it neatly on top of the haggis. He looked up at Oliver, his eyes bright with a strange, new light.

"I find myself lately," he said, his voice taking on a lyrical, almost performative quality, "eating with relish, the inner organs of beasts and fowls."

Oliver stared at him, unsure of how to respond to such a bizarre declaration. He watched as Reza took a bite of the haggis and relish, chewing with a deliberate, almost sacramental slowness.

"I've decided to reexplore this city that I came to as a young man," Reza said after swallowing. "To walk its streets not as a recluse, but as an observer. To see it with new eyes. To see if I can find the boy who got lost in all the noise and success."

Oliver watched him, a quiet sense of awe settling over him. This wasn't the same man he'd met at the New Year's Eve party. The deep, weary cynicism he had seen in Reza's eyes that night was gone, replaced by a flicker of the old fire, a hint of the passionate young artist who had first arrived in the city full of dreams. He was witnessing a quiet beginning, and it was a strange and beautiful thing to behold. They ate in a comfortable silence for a few minutes, the pub a low thrum of clinking glasses and quiet conversation around them.

"This city," Reza said finally, pushing his plate away, "is a labyrinth of secrets. It always has been. Especially for exiles. We learn to hide things in plain sight."

"What do you mean?" Oliver asked, leaning forward.

"Artists, thinkers, refugees ... people who live on the margins. They develop a different language. A language of symbols, of layers, of hidden meanings. I knew a whole school of them back in the nineties. Surrealists. Mostly Eastern European expats. Their leader was a mad Polish genius named Kaminsky. Believed art was a form of alchemy."

The name sent a jolt through Oliver, a sudden, electric connection. *Kaminsky.* The sound of it thrummed in his memory, pulling him back to a warm summer day last year, to a pop-up tent on a pier, to a conversation that had felt strange and significant at the time but was now exploding with newfound importance.

He wasn't in the pub anymore. He was back at the 2022 West Village Surrealist Art Fair. He could see Daniela's friend, Megan, the organizer, standing under a tree, smoking a Virginia Slim. He could hear her voice in his head, clear as day. *We're really fortunate to have an amazing surrealist who agreed to join the curation team this year ... Luis Velázquez.*

He remembered the name. Velázquez. The elusive artist who was too reclusive to show his own work but had curated the entire exhibition. And then came the crucial link, the breadcrumb he hadn't even realized he'd been given. *Luis belongs to a school of surrealism started by his mentor, Krzysztof Kaminsky ... Disepinephrenetic Psychosurrealism.*

The thought hit him with the force of a physical blow. *Kaminsky was the source. Velázquez was the disciple.*

Reza was still talking, but his voice had become a distant murmur. Oliver's mind was racing, a torrent of connections forming, an intuitive leap that defied logic but felt as solid and true as the table beneath his hands. The Bryce paintings, the six-spiraled shape, the surrealist school of hiding art *below*, the voices in Bryce's head ... it was all part of the same hidden tradition. A tradition that Kaminsky had championed, and that Velázquez was now the living heir to.

If anyone on Earth understood the hidden geometry on those canvases, if anyone could decipher the secrets of the surrealist crypto-artists who had come before, it would be him. It was a certainty that bloomed in his gut, a piece of knowledge that felt as if it had been downloaded directly into his soul. He had to find Luis Velázquez.

"I have to go," Oliver said abruptly, the need to act on this new information overwhelming him.

Reza looked surprised but nodded, a knowing smile playing on his lips. "Of course. The wanderer must wander. The flower, I daresay ... must bloom."

Oliver wasn't sure what Reza meant by that odd ending to his sentence but didn't dwell on it. He threw a hundred-dollar bill on the table. "For lunch," he said, standing up. "And for the revelation."

"Revelation?" Reza asked, raising an eyebrow.

"You have no idea," Oliver said, a real, genuine smile spreading across his face for the first time in weeks. He finally had it. A path forward. A tenuous, perhaps insane, but undeniable next step. The quest wasn't a delusion. It was real. And now, he knew where he had to go.

777707 (February 21)

Oliver stood in front of the hall mirror, shrugging on his winter jacket. The man staring back at him was a stranger, all sharp angles and hollowed-out eyes. The last nine days had been a blur, a frantic, obsessive manhunt conducted from the confines of his apartment. He had subsisted on coffee, whisky, and the electric hum of a single, galvanizing purpose: find Luis Velázquez.

The name Kaminsky, dropped so casually by Reza amidst the clatter of the Scottish pub, had been the key. It had unlocked a memory of a warm summer day, of a pop-up tent on a pier, and of Daniela's friend, Megan. Megan, the organizer of the surrealist art fair. She was the only link he had to Velázquez, the elusive curator who was himself a disciple of Kaminsky's strange school.

But finding Megan had been its own labyrinth. A nine-day descent into the digital catacombs of New York City.

His first, most obvious path was blocked. He couldn't ask Daniela. The thought of calling her, of the cold, polite dead air that would follow his request, was unthinkable. He was on his own.

The first three days were a demoralizing slog through the obvious. The "Fifth Annual West Village Surrealist Art Fair" had a defunct website and an abandoned Instagram page. He'd spent hours scrolling through years-old posts, his eyes burning from the screen's glare, searching the tagged photos for a face he barely remembered. He found her name in a press release: Megan Connolly, event co-organizer. A name so common it was practically an alias. The trail went cold almost immediately.

The next three days were a descent into a deeper, more methodical madness. He pivoted to the NYU connection, plunging into the university's public alumni networks, searching for every Megan Connolly who had graduated from the Tisch School of the Arts in the last decade. There were three. He created a spreadsheet, a sad, meticulous grid of potential lives. He cross-refer-enced their names with every social media platform he could think of, sending out cautious, carefully worded messages that were met with a wall of silence or the occasional confused, one-word reply. *"Sorry?"* He was a digital stalker, a man chasing a ghost through a forest of dead-end profiles.

By the eighth day, he was exhausted, bleary-eyed, and close to giving up. The initial spark of revelation had faded to a dull, disheartening ember. He was slumped in his father's armchair, staring at the wall, when a random, useless detail floated up from his memory. Megan, under a tree at the fair, smoking a Virginia Slim.

It was a laughably absurd detail, the kind of thing his brain stored instead of important passwords. On a whim born of pure desperation, he typed "Megan Connolly" and "Virginia Slims" into a search engine. And there it was, on the fourth page of results: a link to a blog post from a small, independent art zine, reviewing the very same art fair. The author mentioned interviewing the "chain-smoking and brilliantly insightful organizer, Megan Connolly." The post included a link to her professional portfolio website.

He had stared at the contact page for an hour yesterday before working up the nerve to call. She had answered on the third ring, her voice wary, surprised to hear from him. He had stumbled through a half-true explanation, something about being a collector interested in Velázquez's work, omitting any mention of Daniela. To his immense relief, Megan had been helpful.

The memory of their conversation was a fresh, clean line of certainty in the tumult of his mind. Velázquez was alive and well, but reclusive. He was based in Montevideo, she'd said, consumed by a new piece of work and seeing almost no one. He lived in a loft in the city center. She didn't have an address, but she knew the neighborhood. It was enough.

Oliver pulled on his boots, the familiar movements grounding him. He knew his next step. Tomorrow. Tomorrow, he would walk into Habib's flower shop on 28th Street, his backpack heavy with cash from the suitcase under his bed, and he would buy a one-way ticket to Uruguay. The thought was both terrifying and exhilarating.

But tonight was for something else. A brief return to a world he was still trying to understand. Vince's text had been insistent. *"Big event at Pubkey. Two of the sharpest minds I know are speaking. You need to be here. Stop hiding."*

He had to admit, a sliver of excitement cut through his fatigue. He was finally going to see it, the physical embassy of this new, digital nation he'd pledged allegiance to. After the isolation of the past few weeks, the thought of being in a room full of fellow travelers, of listening to a conversation that wasn't just the discordant hum in his own head, felt like a lifeline. He just hoped he was ready for what they had to say.

The 20-minute walk from the quiet austerity of his Chelsea street to the vibrant hubbub of Greenwich Village was a journey between worlds. The crisp February air did little to cool the nervous energy buzzing under his skin. It was one thing to read about bitcoin, to live inside its logic on a screen or in a projection; it was another thing entirely to walk into its physical embassy.

He found Pubkey on Washington Place, a discreet, below-street-level entrance that felt more like a secret society than a bar. A stoic, bearded bouncer who looked like he could be a node operator in another life glanced at his ID and nodded him down a short flight of stairs.

The moment he stepped inside, a wave of warm, convivial energy washed over him. The place was a perfect fusion of a classic New York tavern and a cypherpunk's library. The bar was dark, reclaimed wood, the air thick with the smell of good whisky and the low, happy thrum of dozens of conversations. But behind the bar, instead of mirror-backed shelves of liquor, was a floor-to-ceiling bookshelf packed with familiar titles: *The Bitcoin Standard*, *The Sovereign Individual*, *Mastering Bitcoin*. In a small, brightly-lit alcove to the side, almost like a religious shrine, was a framed, museum-quality print of the original whitepaper. Below it, a single, gleaming replica Casascius coin rested on a velvet cushion under a glass dome.

Above the bar, an electronic ticker, built with old-fashioned, chunky red LEDs like a relic from a 1980s stock exchange, displayed the price. It read: BTC/USD $24,576. A healthy recovery from the depths of late last year. A sign of resilience. Oliver felt a sense of belonging so sharp and unexpected it was almost painful.

"Glad you made it."

Oliver turned. Vince was standing beside him, his expression a mixture of a welcoming smile and gentle concern.

"Hey, I was sorry to hear about you and Daniela," Vince said, his voice low. "You doing okay?"

Oliver forced a nonchalant shrug, putting on a brave front he didn't feel. "Yeah, man. I'm good. It is what it is, you know? Just focusing on other things now."

Vince seemed to understand he wasn't to press the issue. He nodded and clapped Oliver on the shoulder. "Well, you came to the right place to focus on other things. The talks are in the back room. We'll be starting in about 15 minutes, but I wanted you to see this first. To feel it."

The bar was filling up quickly, a diverse crowd of what Oliver could only describe as bitcoiners. There were developers in hoodies, finance types in sharp blazers, artists, writers, a cross-section of the new counterculture.

"I'm glad you came," Vince continued, his voice shifting to an enthusiastic, host-like energy. "I've put together a bit of a dialectic for tonight. Two speakers, two very different visions of the same truth." He gestured toward the back room, where people were now beginning to filter in.

"First up is Gideon Reed. Remember him from the Occupy Wall Street days? He was one of the main organizers down at Zuccotti Park. He's gone full maxi since then. He's going to talk about the defensive imperative. Bitcoin as a shield against the Wall Street-D.C. revolving door, the endless bailouts, the financial panopticon. He's ... intense. He still sees the world as a battlefield, and bitcoin is the only viable weapon for the individual."

Oliver nodded, intrigued. That was the version of bitcoin that resonated with his own recent anger.

"And after him," Vince's expression softened, "is Mateo Kovač. He's an Australian filmmaker, Croatian background. Makes these beautiful, slow-burn documentaries about things that last – ancient winemaking traditions, generational stonemasons, that sort of thing. He's going to talk about the creative imperative. Bitcoin as a foundation for a more peaceful, more beautiful world. Low time preference, the flourishing of art, the demonetization of war. He sees bitcoin not as a weapon, but as a seed."

"The warrior and the philosopher," Oliver said.

Vince smiled knowingly.

Just then, two men in their late twenties approached them. They were dressed in loud, brightly colored hoodies, one emblazoned with the logo of a cartoon dog, the other with a pixelated penguin. The lingering scent of the shitcoin casino.

"Hey, excuse me," the one in the dog hoodie said to Vince. "Is the crypto event back there?"

Vince's smile remained serene and welcoming. "The bitcoin event is, yes. Please, go on in."

Oliver felt a hot spike of irritation. Vince's gentle correction didn't seem to register with the two. He couldn't help himself. "Bitcoin, not crypto," he said, his voice a little too sharp.

The two men looked at him, their expressions a mixture of confusion and mild annoyance, as if a piece of furniture had just spoken to them. They shrugged and turned to walk toward the back room. As they did, Oliver overheard the penguin hoodie mutter to his friend, his voice a theatrical, exasperated whine.

"Does anyone know a project that won't end in a rugpull? Please ..."

The question, so earnest and so ignorant, was a match to the gasoline of Oliver's frustration. He muttered back, just loud enough for them to hear, "Bitcoin, you dumbfuck."

The two men stopped, turned, and glared at him before deciding he wasn't worth the trouble and disappearing into the back room.

Vince let out a low chuckle, placing a calming hand on Oliver's shoulder. "Easy, tiger," he said, his eyes twinkling with amusement. "I know the feeling. But this is an embassy, remember? We offer asylum to the weary, even the deeply misguided. Save your fire for the real debate."

He steered Oliver toward the bar, which was now three-deep with patrons. "Let's get a drink before we head in."

Oliver nodded, but the brief, irritating encounter had stoked the embers of the rage he'd been nursing all week. "Speaking of those guys," he said, his voice a low, disgruntled grumble as they waited for the bartender's attention. "Have you seen what's happening with this Ordinals stuff? The fees are spiking because these clowns are inscribing their monkey jpegs onto the timechain. It's a fucking desecration, Vince."

Vince didn't seem surprised by the outburst. He just nodded slowly, a thoughtful expression on his face as he finally caught the bartender's eye and ordered two glasses of a Japanese whisky.

"I've seen it," he said, once the drinks were in their hands. He led Oliver to a small, standing-room-only spot near the bookshelf. "I understand why you're angry. It feels like a violation, an invasion from the very culture we're trying to build an alternative to."

"It *is* an invasion," Oliver insisted. "It's the shitcoin casino mindset, the get-rich-quick NFT nonsense, infecting the one pure thing we have left."

"This isn't the first time, you know," Vince said calmly, taking a small sip of his whisky. "And it won't be the last. People were trying to embed arbitrary data with Namecoin and colored coins a decade ago. The protocol is permissionless. That means it's for anyone, even for uses we find frivolous or distasteful. The network is an organism, Oliver. When it's stressed or attacked, it finds a way to get stronger. It's antifragile."

"But the fees, Vince. They're pricing out regular people who want to use it for actual transactions," Oliver countered.

"And the fees are the immune system at work," Vince replied, his voice still a placid sea of reason. "That's the beauty of it. If these spammers – and it doesn't matter if they're just speculators or even malicious state actors trying to clog the network – if they want to price out sound money with their jpegs, they have to pay for the privilege. For a while, maybe they can. Their pockets might be deep. A few months, maybe even a year. But eventually, the economic reality asserts itself. The cost of frivolous spam becomes unsustainable, while the value of a global, neutral settlement transaction only grows. The fee market is the ultimate arbiter."

He took another sip, letting the point settle.

"And if it doesn't ..." he said, looking Oliver directly in the eye. "If, in the long run, the world decides that immutable monkey pictures are a more valuable use of this technology than a global, censorship-resistant, sound monetary network ... then bitcoin was never going to be what we thought it was anyway. This is a test. One of many. And I have faith the network will pass it."

Oliver listened, the clean, cold logic of Vince's argument cutting through the heat of his own anger. He was right, of course. On an intellectual level, it all made perfect sense. Bitcoin's incentive structures were designed to withstand exactly this kind of attack. But his gut still churned with a feeling of righteous indignation. It felt like watching someone use a Stradivarius to paddle a canoe. It might be allowed, but it was still wrong.

He begrudgingly nodded, the anger receding into a low, simmering discontent. "I hear you. I just don't like it."

"You don't have to like it," Vince said with a smile, finishing his whisky. "You just have to trust the code." He put a hand on Oliver's back. "Come on. Let's go listen to Gideon. A little fire and brimstone might be exactly what you need right now."

He guided Oliver away from the bar and toward a doorway at the back of the pub, from which a low, expectant murmur was emanating. They stepped through and into a different world. The back room was small, cramped, and packed with people, a tight squeeze of 50 bodies generating a palpable heat. The ceiling was low, the lighting dim, creating an atmosphere that was less like a lecture hall and more like a secret meeting in a revolutionary's cellar. A small, makeshift stage stood at the front, barely a foot off the ground.

"There's a seat for you right there," Vince said, pointing to a single empty folding chair in the middle of a tightly packed row. "I've got to be up front. Enjoy the show." He gave Oliver a final pat on the back and skillfully navigated his way through the crowd toward the stage.

Oliver squeezed his way into the row, muttering apologies as he stepped over legs and backpacks. He settled into the chair, the proximity of the people around him – their warmth, the smell of their coats, their quiet, focused energy – creating a sense of intense, shared anticipation.

Vince took the stage, briefly welcomed the crowd, and announced the first speaker with a simple, powerful introduction: "For those who believe bitcoin is a tool of peaceful protest, a weapon against injustice, here is one of its finest warriors. Please welcome Gideon Reed."

A wave of respectful applause filled the room as a man in his mid-30s took the stage. He was wiry and intense, with a shaved head and eyes that seemed to burn with a restless fire. He wore a simple black t-shirt and dark jeans, the uniform of a man who had long since dispensed with pleasantries. He didn't smile. He just gripped the sides of the lectern and scanned the crowd, his gaze landing on each person for a fraction of a second, as if taking a silent inventory of his troops.

When he spoke, his voice was not loud, but it was resonant, a low, gravelly hum that commanded absolute attention.

"November 15th, 2011," he began, the date hanging in the silent room. "Some of you were there. Most of you were not. It was cold. That pre-dawn, New York-in-November cold that gets into your bones. We were in Zuccotti Park. Two months we'd been there, a messy, chaotic, beautiful city of ideals, built on the doorstep of the financial heart of the empire. We were a joke to them, an annoyance. A bunch of dirty hippies the media could laugh at."

He paused, letting the memory settle.

"And then, they stopped laughing. At 1 a.m., they came. Hundreds of them. Riot shields, batons, helmets. An army. They didn't come to talk. They didn't come to negotiate. They came to erase us. I was 21 years old, full of a naive, beautiful belief that if you just spoke the truth loudly enough, the system would have to listen. I stood my ground. And for my trouble, I was rewarded with a blast of pepper spray that felt like chemical fire setting my eyes and lungs ablaze."

His voice didn't rise. It grew colder, harder.

"I was on the ground, blind, choking, trying to breathe through a universe of pain. And that's when I felt the first baton strike across my back. Then another. And another. And as this ... this *agent of the peace* was beating the idealism out of me in real-time, I had an epiphany. A moment of terrible, perfect clarity. I finally understood. The state, in its purest form, is not a collection of laws or ideals or services. It is a monopoly on violence. And it does not tolerate competition. It does not tolerate the truly sovereign individual. It doesn't just disagree with you. It *hates* you. It hates you for daring to exist outside of its neat, controllable systems. The beating was a theological statement. It was the state reminding me of its godhood."

He took a step forward, his voice gaining a raw, serrated edge.

"That was physical violence. Crude. Obvious. They don't need the batons as much anymore, do they? The violence has become more elegant. It's become insidious. They realized it's inefficient to beat us in the streets when they can simply enslave us in our homes. The baton has been replaced by the algorithm. The riot shield has been replaced by the digital ID. The prison is now a network you are born into.

"They are building a panopticon, a digital Zuccotti Park for all of humanity. A world where every transaction is monitored, every conversation is logged, every preference is catalogued, and every deviation is flagged. They want to give you a Central Bank Digital Currency, not for your convenience, but for their control. They want to be able to shut you off, to de-person you with the click of a button if you say the wrong thing, support the wrong cause, have the wrong thought. That is the new violence. It is a quiet, bloodless and far more terrifying form of control.

"And we are their willing accomplices! We trade our privacy for convenience, our autonomy for entertainment. The attention economy is a weapon of mass distraction. It's a digital coliseum where they keep us fighting over political circuses and celebrity gossip while they quietly dismantle the foundations of our liberty. It is the continuation of the same violence, the same hatred of the individual, just in a more subtle, more insidious form."

Gideon's voice was rising now, a crescendo of practiced, righteous fury. He was an incredible orator. Oliver was captivated, his own anger from the Ordinals debate feeling validated and amplified by this man's words. He felt the heat of the room, the focused energy of the crowd, the power of Gideon's conviction. The words – *panopticon, sovereign, violence* – resonated deep in his bones, striking a chord that had been vibrating since the day he'd found his father's bitcoin treasure.

"They want to own your money, your data, your very thoughts," Gideon declared, his voice a roar. "They want to put a cage around your sovereign mind ..."

The phrase hit Oliver with an unexpected force. *Sovereign mind.* He felt a strange, dizzying sensation, as if the room had suddenly tilted on its axis. The low ceiling seemed to recede, and the edges of his vision began to soften and shimmer. The angry, gravelly sound of Gideon's voice became a distant, resonant buzz, the words losing their meaning.

A familiar, ethereal blue mist started to creep in from the periphery, cool and silent, and yet, a stultifying fog in the hot, cramped room. He wasn't in Pubkey anymore.

He was standing on cold, silent stone. The air was still and carried the faint, salty scent of a distant sea. He recognized it instantly. The high, vaulted ceiling, the unadorned walls, the rhythmic, eerie crash of waves thundering from some unseen shore. He was back in the *Camara del Tiempo*.

He stood in the center of the pitch dark, vast, empty chamber, a solitary figure in a place outside of time. And then, it appeared.

Floating in the dead center of the room, suspended in the silent air, was a weightless, intricate lattice of light. Six luminous arms spiraled out from a central point, weaving through each other in a pattern of breathtaking complexity. It was a celestial compass, a radiant, geometric blossom pulsing with a gentle, inner energy.

His mind raced, trying to anchor the vision to something real. *That shape ... on the wall at McGinn's last week. The homeless man with the broken glass.* It was the same fleeting construct, but here it was stable, persistent. He stared at its otherworldly geometry. Could it possibly be the double triskelion? It bore a vague, dematerialized resemblance. The shape felt less like a drawing and more like a law of physics, a fundamental truth he was only just beginning to comprehend.

He was so mesmerized by the form, he didn't notice it begin to fade. The six arms of light grew dimmer, their rotation slowing until they were just faint, hanging sparks. Then, they dissolved entirely, leaving a lingering afterimage burned into his vision.

From the space where the light had been, two new forms began to coalesce. They were indistinct, forged from the deep shadows of the chamber, their features obscured. They were just silhouettes, devoid of detail, yet they pulsed with a palpable sense of intent.

His rational mind saw only shadows. But another part of him, the part that was attuned to this place, received something else. An uneasy download. An intuition that bypassed his eyes entirely. He couldn't see their faces, but he could *feel* their identities.

One felt like a bitter, wounded ambition. A desperate energy, resentful of a world that had dealt it a bad hand. *Nick?* The feeling fit. This was the energy of a man who had lost everything and would do anything to get it back. Why on Earth would Nick be here?

The other was a woman's silhouette. It radiated a sharp, obsessive determination. A feeling he had felt before ... in the cold basement of O'Connell's. In that sterile storage unit in Queens. *Adele.* Christiaan van der Dussen's sister! The memory of her piercing gaze, her veiled threats, was unmistakable.

The two shadows stood side by side for a moment. Then, the figure he sensed was Nick turned its head slightly toward Adele's. Though he heard no words, Oliver perceived a silent exchange, an imperceptible nod of agreement. A partnership forged in the shadows.

No ... it couldn't be, he thought, a wave of cold dread washing over him. *Them? Together?* The idea was absurd, illogical. There was nothing that could possibly connect their paths. But in this place where the rules of reality were suspended, their union felt like a terrifying, undeniable truth. The vision offered no explanation, only the chilling certainty of a new and formidable alliance forming against him.

Just as the thought crystallized, the figures wavered, their forms dissolving back into the darkness. The stone walls of the chamber grew translucent, the sound of the distant waves replaced by a rushing, angry roar that grew louder and louder until it was the only thing in the universe.

" ... and that is why we build!" Gideon Reed's voice slammed back into Oliver's consciousness. "We do not ask for permission. We do not wait for an invitation. We build the parallel system, the life raft, the citadel, because the world they are building for us is a prison. We build because our freedom, our very sovereignty, depends on it. Thank you."

The small room erupted in a thunderous wave of applause and cheers. Oliver gasped, his lungs aching, his heart hammering against his ribs. He was back in his chair at Pubkey, the heat and noise of the room a physical assault on his senses after the cold silence of the chamber. He had been gone for an age, or maybe only a second. He looked around. No one seemed to have noticed a thing. They were all on their feet, clapping, their faces lit with the fire of Gideon's sermon. Oliver remained seated, the applause a distant, meaningless noise. He was no longer thinking about the state's panopticon. He was thinking about the two shadows he had just seen, and the new, far more personal war that was about to begin.

The applause, a rolling wave of sound in the small room, slowly subsided. Vince stepped back onto the stage, a broad, satisfied smile on his face.

"Let's hear it one more time for Gideon Reed," he said, leading another, shorter burst of clapping. "Alright, we're going to take a 10-minute break. Grab another drink, use the restroom, stretch your legs. We'll be back shortly with our next speaker, Mateo Kovač."

A collective sigh of relief seemed to pass through the crowd as people rose from their cramped folding chairs and began to file out into the main bar area. The sudden movement and renewed chatter pulled Oliver back into his body. He felt an uneasy chill, a lingering residue from the cold stone of the *Camara del Tiempo.*

As he stood up to let the people in his row pass, he noticed the two men in the crypto-branded hoodies from earlier. They were pushing their way toward the exit, their faces wearing an expression of disappointment and disgust.

"What a fucking waste of time," the one in the dog hoodie muttered to his friend, loud enough for Oliver to hear. "Not one mention of a 100x coin. Just a bunch of angry anarchist bullshit."

His friend shook his head. "I told you we should have gone to that NFT meetup in Brooklyn."

Oliver watched them go, a small, grim smile touching his lips. They had come seeking alpha and had been served a dose of philosophy instead. They were tourists, and they had just realized they were in the wrong country.

"So? Did that light a fire under you?" Vince appeared at his side, handing him a fresh glass of whisky.

"Vince, hey," Oliver said, taking the drink gratefully. The cold glass was a welcome anchor to reality.

"What did you think of Gideon?" Vince asked, his eyes searching Oliver's face. "Powerful stuff, isn't it?"

Oliver felt a pang of guilt. He had been a passenger on a journey to a different reality for most of the speech. He'd only caught the beginning and the very end. He had to lie.

"Yeah, man," he said, trying to sound genuinely impressed. He grasped for a detail he actually remembered. "That line about the state's monopoly on violence ... that was incredible. Really powerful."

Vince nodded, satisfied. "He has a way of cutting to the bone, doesn't he? He's lived it."

The ten minutes passed in a blur of small talk and the general bustle of the bar. Oliver mostly just nodded along to Vince's conversations with other attendees, his mind still replaying the vision of the two shadowy figures. *Nick and Adele. Together.* What could it possibly mean?

Adele had fallen off the map since their last unpleasant encounter in the storage unit in Queens, but she obviously had to be hatching a plan to get her brother's bitcoin back.

Nick ... he hadn't had a proper conversation with him for a few months. Not since he started working at the chain analysis place that was now working for the government to hunt down his dad.

I suppose they both did have aligned motives, now that he thought about it. Seriously, how on Earth could they have found each other? If it was indeed true, he was dealing with formidable foes.

"Alright everyone, let's head back in!" Vince called out over the din. "Mateo is ready to go."

The crowd began to flow back into the small, hot room. Oliver found his seat again, the chair still warm. He took a final sip of his whisky, the peaty smoke a familiar comfort. He didn't know what Mateo Kovač would talk about, but he had a sinking feeling that another journey was waiting for him in the darkness behind his eyes.

Vince returned to the stage as the last of the audience settled in. The room fell into a respectful hush.

"Gideon Reed showed us the fire," Vince began, his voice calm and centered. "He showed us the necessity of the shield, the wall, the fortress. He spoke of the world we must defend ourselves from. Now, I'd like to introduce a friend who will speak about the world we are trying to build. He is a master storyteller, an artist who has spent his life studying the things that last. From the vineyards of Croatia to the outback of his adopted Australia, he finds the signal in the noise. Please give a warm welcome to Mateo Kovač."

A man in his late fifties walked onto the stage to a warm, appreciative applause. He was the complete opposite of Gideon. Where Gideon was a coiled spring of wiry, intense energy, Mateo was a figure of gentle, grounded warmth. He wore a comfortable-looking linen shirt and had a kind, lived-in face, framed by a cascade of graying hair and a warm, grandfatherly beard. He rested his hands softly on the lectern, as if greeting an old friend. He smiled, a genuine, easy smile that seemed to instantly lower the temperature in the room.

"Thank you, Vince. Thank you all," he said, his voice a rich, pleasant baritone with a soft Australian accent. "My friend Gideon is a hard act to follow. He speaks with the fire of a man who has stared into the abyss. And he is right to do so. The world he described ... the world of control, of surveillance, of violence, both overt and insidious ... it is very real."

He paused, letting his eyes drift over the crowd.

"But I am a filmmaker," he continued, his smile returning. "And in film-making, we learn that the story is not just about the monster. The story is about what the characters do in the shadow of the monster. Do they despair? Do they hide? Or do they build something new? Something the monster cannot touch?"

He leaned forward slightly, his tone becoming more intimate, as if he were sharing a secret. "We live in an age of noise. A frantic, screeching, 24-hour news cycle of fear and consumption. A fiat culture. It shortens our vision. It makes us anxious, reactive. It encourages us to consume rather than create, to flip rather than build. It is a culture that is, by its very design, ugly. Because it is not built to last."

Oliver found himself leaning forward, captivated. Mateo's voice was a soothing balm after Gideon's abrasive truths.

"But what if," Mateo said softly, "we could change the fundamental signal that governs our society? What if we introduced a form of money that is not based on debt and violence and endless printing, but on proof of work and verifiable scarcity? What happens to a people when their money is slow, patient, and incorruptible?"

He looked out at the audience, his eyes full of a genuine, infectious hope.

"I will tell you what happens. Their time preference lowers. The frantic noise of the present begins to fade, and they start to hear the music of the future. A person who saves in a money that cannot be debased is a person who can think in terms of decades, not quarters. They can build a business that will outlive them. They can raise children in a stable home. They can plant a tree whose shade they will never sit in."

"The world that bitcoin builds is not a world of frantic, disposable ugliness. It is a world of beauty and permanence. It is a world of art that is meant to last for centuries, not just to be flipped for a profit next week. It is a world of architecture that is built to inspire our great-grandchildren. It is a world where war becomes an almost economic impossibility, because the state can no longer fund its violent ambitions through the silent theft of inflation. It must ask its citizens for the money directly, and citizens with a low time preference do not gladly pay for endless conflict."

"Gideon spoke of a shield. And he is right. But bitcoin is also a seed. It is the seed of a quiet, peaceful and joyful revolution. A revolution not of anger, but of patience. A revolution that will not be televised, but will be built, block by block, by people who have chosen to build a world of lasting beauty ..."

Mateo's warm, calming voice began to warp, the edges of his words softening and stretching as if being pulled through water. Oliver blinked. The faces in the crowd around him started to lose their focus, melting into indistinct, blurry shapes.

He felt a deep, profound yearning for the world Mateo was describing. A world of peace, of art, of permanence. It was a world he felt he had known – for a brief period when he finally understood bitcoin from the Noncemeister and when he was with Daniela – a world he had lost, a world he felt he was desperately unworthy of ever rejoining. The dissonance between Mateo's beautiful vision and his own ugly, internal state of chaos and guilt was a chasm, and he felt himself falling into it.

The dim lights of the back room at Pubkey faded, and the uncomfortable blue mist, cooler and more mysterious than ever, began to rise from the floor, ready to claim him once again.

Ugh. Oliver thought to himself as he was about to be consumed by the projection. *I was really enjoying this talk.*

The world dissolved. The sound of Mateo Kovač's warm, hopeful voice stretched into a long, distorted drone and then vanished, replaced by an absolute emptiness. He was floating again, unmoored in the endless, ethereal blue. He had been desperate to return here just days ago, but now, having been pulled away from a moment of genuine connection and intellectual hope, the transition felt like an abduction.

Then he saw her, and all resistance melted away.

She materialized from the mist, a figure of impossible grace. The golden hair, the flowing white robe, the piercing turquoise eyes that seemed to hold all the secrets of a forgotten sea. Anariadne.

A wave of delirious, desperate joy washed over him. He had been a fool to think he could resist this. She was a fundamental force, a truth more real than the folding chair he'd just been sitting on.

"You came back," he breathed, the words a prayer.

She glided closer, her expression unreadable. "Here, I am. And you, here you are, you are."

"I'm ready," he said, the statement an offering, a declaration of his newfound availability. "I can follow you. I can go wherever you want to take me." He was ready to surrender completely this time, to plunge into the abyss she represented, to have her.

Anariadne's lips curved into a faint, enigmatic smile. It was a smile of cool assessment, not of warmth. She drifted closer, her presence a heady perfume of ozone and night-blooming flowers.

"Ready, you believe you are?" she whispered, her voice a sensuous caress. "Perhaps. But belief, it is not enough. Ready, you must be proven."

"Proven? How?" Oliver asked, his heart hammering. He would do anything. Any trial, any task.

"Tests, you must pass. For me, to be certain, of you," she said, her fingers tracing a slow, deliberate pattern in the blue air between them. "The path you wish to walk, it is not for the weak of will. Show me you are worthy. Show me you understand."

"I'll do anything," he said, his voice thick with a desperate sincerity.

Her smile widened, but only slightly. "Then let us begin. Your first test, this is." She gestured toward a patch of the blue mist that seemed darker, a void within the void. "Go there, you will. And see."

She gave no further instruction. She simply floated back, her form receding into the haze as if to give him space. Oliver hesitated for only a second before moving toward the darkness she had indicated. As he approached, he felt a change in the atmosphere. The tranquil blue began to curdle, streaks of a deep, menacing purple bleeding into it.

He stepped through the threshold, and the blue vanished entirely. He was in a new place. The color was purple, yes, but it was not the warm, familiar and strangely comforting purple of the Noncemeister's timechain. This was a cold, bruised, discordant purple, a color that felt violent and wrong. It pulsed with a low, dissonant hum, like a machine on the verge of breaking.

He saw a structure in the distance, a cage made of glowing, perfectly straight, white-hot lines. A prison of rigid, unforgiving angles. And inside it, a silhouette.

A familiar, portly shape. A bald, egg-shaped head.

"Noncemeister!" Oliver cried out, a surge of joyous relief momentarily eclipsing the menace of the place. He ran toward the cage. "It's me! I've missed you! Where have you been?"

He stopped a few feet from the glowing bars. The figure inside didn't move. It just stood there, slumped, its back to him. Unresponsive.

"Noncemeister, please!" Oliver pleaded, his voice rippling through the disquieting stillness. "It's me, Oliver! It's Batlu. Remember? Talk to me. What is this place? Who did this to you?"

There was no reply. The silhouette remained perfectly still, a statue of quiet resignation in a prison of light. The jovial, frenetic energy that had defined his guide was gone, replaced by a terrible, crushing emptiness. This was a tomb as much as it was a cage. Oliver felt a sense of loss so strong it was a physical blow, a hollowing out of his own soul. His guide, his friend, was trapped. Broken.

Defeated, he turned and walked back through the bruised purple into the calm, indifferent blue of Anariadne's realm. She was waiting for him, her expression unchanged.

"I don't understand," he said, his voice hollow. "He's ... he's trapped. What was the test? What was I supposed to do?"

Anariadne tilted her head, her turquoise eyes boring into him. "Seen what you have seen, you have. Know what to do, do you now?"

Her cryptic question was a slap. He stared at her, his mind a blank canvas of confusion and grief. He thought of the cage, of the silent, broken figure inside. What was he supposed to do? Fight? Find a key? He had no weapons, no knowledge. He was powerless.

"No," he admitted, the word a confession of his own inadequacy. "I have no idea."

A look of faint, almost imperceptible disappointment crossed Anariadne's face. "Then ready, you are not," she said, her voice a final, soft judgment. "*Probaris en silencio, sat in actuare.*"

The strange words hung in the air, their meaning just beyond his grasp. Before he could ask her what they meant, her form began to dissolve, her golden hair and white robe bleeding back into the mist.

She was gone, and Oliver was left floating listlessly in the abyss.

The blue began to recede, and a warm, hopeful sound rushed back in to fill the void.

"Gideon spoke of a battlefield, and he is not wrong," Mateo Kovač was saying, his voice full of a gentle, unwavering conviction. He was bringing his talk to its powerful, quiet conclusion.

"But our revolution is not fought with anger in the streets. It is a quiet one. It is fought in the heart of every person who chooses reason over fear, patience over panic. It is won not by tearing down the old world, but by lovingly and deliberately building a new one alongside it – a world so honest and so true that the old one simply becomes obsolete."

He looked out over the captivated audience, his gaze warm and inclusive, his voice the sound of pure, unshakeable hope.

"Let us go forth from this place tonight and be the quiet revolutionaries that the future is waiting for. Thank you."

The room erupted in a thunderous wave of applause, a heartfelt ovation that was longer and somehow more profound than the one Gideon had received. People were on their feet, their faces lit with the inspiration of Mateo's vision.

Oliver sat frozen in his chair, the sound a distant, meaningless storm. He was looking at the smiling, hopeful faces around him, but he was seeing a silent, broken figure in a cage of light.

The formal part of the evening was over. The crowd broke apart into small, energized groups, the air buzzing with conversations and renewed purpose. Oliver remained seated, a statue of stone in a river of motion, until a hand landed gently on his shoulder.

"What did I tell you?" Vince's voice was full of deep satisfaction. "First the revolutionary, then the artist. Wasn't Mateo incredible?"

Oliver looked up, his mind still a million miles away in a bruised purple void. He had to force the word out. "Yeah ... incredible."

Vince's smile faltered slightly as he took in Oliver's dazed expression. "You alright, man? You look like you just saw a ghost."

The irony of the word choice was lost on Oliver. He was too deep in the memory of the vision to register it. He needed to deflect, to act normal. He couldn't possibly explain what he had just witnessed.

"No, I'm good," he said, forcing himself to stand. "Just a lot to think about. Both speeches were ... a lot. My head's spinning a little."

"I get it," Vince said, though his eyes showed a lingering concern. "It's a firehose of ideas. Stick around, have another drink. Mateo's about to come out. I'd love for you to meet him."

"I can't," Oliver said, a little too quickly. The thought of making small talk, of pretending to be inspired when all he felt was a cold, creeping dread, was unbearable. "I've got to get home. Early start tomorrow."

"On a Wednesday?" Vince raised an eyebrow but didn't push. "Alright. Well, I'm glad you came. Think about what you heard tonight. It's important stuff."

"I will," Oliver lied.

He gave Vince a quick, parting handshake and squeezed his way through the happy, chattering crowd. He pushed through the door of the back room and into the main bar, which was now just as crowded and loud.

He didn't stop. He just walked, a man on a mission, through the throng of people, out the main entrance, and up the stairs.

He emerged onto Washington Place. The street was quiet, the sounds of the joyful communion inside the pub a distant, muffled chorus. He stood on the sidewalk for a long moment, the steam from a manhole cover rising into the night like a lost soul. He had walked in here seeking community and answers. He was walking out more isolated than ever, haunted by a new and terrifying question: who had the power to put the Noncemeister in a cage, and what did they want with him?

777755 (February 21)

It was the ninth consecutive 14-hour day, and the coffee, like his resolve, was beginning to taste like ash. A fitting fuel for a man running on fumes and fury. Nick took another swallow from a paper cup, the bitter liquid doing little to cut through the exhaustion that had settled deep in his bones. It was almost midnight.

His new headquarters was a depressing, 10-by-10-foot cubicle at a place called "The Grid" in Long Island City, a poor man's WeWork that smelled of stale coffee and quiet desperation.

He'd rented it under a shell LLC, a small, anonymous box where he could disappear from the world. It was a stark fall from the panoramic Midtown views of his old life, but it was a necessary one. He couldn't bring this obsession home to his wife, Becky. He couldn't let her see the weeks' worth of empty takeout containers that formed a precarious tower on one corner of the desk, or the scrambled mural of transaction graphs he'd taped to the flimsy cubicle walls with strings of red yarn connecting them like a madman's fever dream. At home, he was just a husband between jobs, exploring "new ventures." Here, in this sterile box under the relentless hum of fluorescent lights, he was a hunter.

For the first few days after the firing, he had done nothing but wallow. But then, the rage had cooled, hardening into a cold, clear and singular purpose. He had exfiltrated the raw on-chain data for the Dev_akshar case, and now he was sifting through it, manually, painfully, without the aid of the powerful (and flawed) AI he had once championed.

His focus for the last two days had shifted to become narrow and obsessive. He set aside the most recent transaction and the misleading CoinJoins for now. He was going to begin at the beginning – when the transaction history for the known MixMarket addresses began – over a decade ago, in 2012.

The official case file mentioned three accomplices: Dev_akshar the architect, Christiaan the operator, and a third, mysterious partner, a shadow in the MixMarket machine whose role was never clearly defined. The DoJ had given up on this third man, considering him a minor player. Nick saw it differently. In any conspiracy, the quietest man is often the most dangerous.

He stared at the two mismatched monitors he'd bought off Craigslist, his eyes gritty and sore. On one screen, he had the known transaction clusters belonging to Dev_akshar – elegant, complex, a clear signature. On the other, Christiaan's – more brute-force, less sophisticated, but voluminous. For hours, he had been meticulously subtracting their activity from the total transaction flow of the MixMarket servers, trying to isolate the signal of the third man from the overwhelming noise of the other two.

It was maddening work. Transactions bled into each other. Timestamps overlapped. The chaotic beauty of the CoinJoin protocol, designed to create ambiguity, was now his personal hell. He hit dead end after dead end, following trails that dissolved into the vast, anonymous ocean of the blockchain. The doubt began to creep in, a cold whisper in the back of his mind. *Maybe there's nothing here. Maybe the third man was a myth, a trace that had gone completely cold.*

He pushed the thought away, took another sip of the terrible coffee, and zoomed in on a cluster of transactions from late 2013. This was where the bulk of the funds had been moved before the platform went dark. He'd been over this section a dozen times. But this time, he looked at it differently. He wasn't looking for a direct link. He was looking for a different style, a different philosophy.

And then he saw it.

It wasn't a single transaction. It was a pattern, so subtle it was almost invisible. While Dev_akshar and Christiaan batched their transactions in large, economically efficient clumps, there was a third set of outputs. Smaller. More frequent. Using a slightly different fee algorithm – not optimized for cost, but for speed. They were transactions made by someone who was not just mixing, but *moving*. Someone who valued haste over efficiency.

His heart began to pound, a slow, heavy drumbeat against his ribs. He started to pull on the thread. He filtered the entire dataset by this new, unique signature. And the pattern held. A series of smaller, faster and more paranoid transactions, always one step removed from the main flow. It was the work of a different kind of mind. Not a builder like Dev_akshar or a frontman like Christiaan. It was the work of a man who was already on his way out the door.

This was the real pulse. The AI, trained to find the big, obvious signals of the two main players, had dismissed these transactions as noise, as insignificant outliers. But Nick, with his human intuition and obsessive focus, recognized it as a distinct signal.

He had a fingerprint. But he still didn't have a name to attach it to. He leaned back in his creaking chair, the exhaustion momentarily forgotten, replaced by the clean, pure thrill of the hunt. He pulled up the original DoJ case file again, his eyes scanning the list of known associates. *Dev_akshar. Christiaan van der Dussen.* And the third name. The footnote.

Sazsa.

The name hit him like an avalanche. He shot upright in his chair. *Sazsa.* It had been there, right in front of him, the entire time. The third MixMarket associate – *Presumed Deceased* – he remembered reading in an early DoJ briefing. A name he had read and registered and then promptly dismissed, just like everyone else. *How could I have possibly forgotten?* It was the sin of arrogance, of focusing on the primary target, Dev_akshar, and ignoring the periphery. He had made the same mistake as the DoJ.

The thrill of the hunt intensified, sharp and focused. He had a signature, and now he had a name. All he needed was confirmation.

He returned to the raw data dump of the old cypherpunk IRC channel, the one he had scanned fruitlessly days ago. This time, he didn't search for a transaction ID. He searched for the name.

Sazsa.

The search returned dozens of hits. He scrolled through the mundane, technical banter, his eyes scanning for anything that could link the name to the on-chain pattern. And then he found it. A conversation log from 2012. An early bitcoin developer was complaining about network spam, and Dev_akshar had replied.

```
dev_akshar: Not spam. It's Sazsa stress-testing a new
fee estimation model. He prefers to move fast.
```

Move fast. The words leaped off the screen. That was it. The signature. The series of smaller, more frequent transactions that valued haste over efficiency. It was a perfect match. The digital signature he had isolated belonged to Sazsa.

The exhaustion of the past week vanished, burned away by a surge of triumphant, electric energy. He had done it. He had taken a forgotten footnote from a cold case file and tied it to a concrete, verifiable pattern of behavior on the blockchain.

He opened a new browser tab and typed the handle into a search engine. The results were no longer a dead end. There were dozens of hits, all from the same 2010–2013 era. Fragmented posts on obscure cryptography mailing lists. A passing mention in a technical debate on a cypherpunk forum. It was him. Sazsa was real.

But he was still just a name on a screen. The next phase of the hunt had just begun. He had to unmask him, to find the real person behind the pseudonym.

He turned back to his desktop, the chaotic evidence board on the wall suddenly looking less like a map of his despair and more like the beginning of a real investigation. He located the folder he had created earlier. He deleted the cold, impersonal filename.

Unknown Associate X.

And replaced it with a single, powerful word.

Sazsa.

The air on 28th Street was thick with the scent of a thousand displaced springtimes. Even in the biting cold of late February, the Flower District was an assault on the senses, a riot of life spilling out from crowded storefronts onto the damp sidewalk. Buckets of roses, lilies and tulips formed a vibrant, resplendent gauntlet.

Oliver clutched the straps of his backpack. Inside, the $20,000 was a dense, tight bundle. It wasn't heavy – just 200 crisp hundred-dollar bills – but it felt like a lead weight in his soul, a tangible piece of the dangerous new world he now inhabited. He pulled out the worn-out business card Saleem Bhai had given him, its elegant script a stark contrast to the memory of the tempestuous back room where he'd received it. He found the address: a small, unassuming storefront with a faded green awning that read *Habib Florist.*

He pushed open the door, a small bell announcing his arrival with a cheerful, incongruous jingle. The inside was a humid jungle, warm and fragrant. The floor was slick with water and fallen leaves. Everywhere he looked, there were flowers, an unruly burst of color and life that felt a world away from the cold, digital logic he had been inhabiting for months.

A young man was busy stripping thorns from a bundle of red roses, his movements quick and practiced.

"Excuse me," Oliver said, his voice a little too quiet. "I'm looking for Habib."

The young man didn't look up. He just gestured with his head toward the back of the narrow shop. "Back there."

Oliver navigated his way past overflowing buckets of baby's breath and ferns. In the back, under a single, bare fluorescent bulb, a small, thin man, possibly in his late fifties, was bent over a workbench, his entire focus on the bouquet he was constructing. He was a master at work. His hands, though wrinkled and stained with chlorophyll, moved with the grace and precision of a surgeon, arranging delicate orchids and exotic, star-shaped blossoms into an intricate, architectural marvel.

Oliver stood there for a full minute, waiting to be acknowledged. The man didn't look up.

"Habib?" Oliver finally ventured.

The man paused, a single white orchid held delicately between his thumb and forefinger. He slowly turned his head, his dark, intelligent eyes appraising Oliver with a look of mild annoyance.

"You want the flower?" he asked. *A slightly different accent than Saleem Bhai's,* Oliver thought. Still South Asian, but not the same.

"No, I ... I was sent by a friend," Oliver began, his heart starting to pound. "Saleem Bhai. He said I should talk to you."

Habib's face remained a perfect, unreadable mask. He turned back to his bouquet, carefully inserting the white orchid into a gap Oliver hadn't even seen. "Who this guy, Saleem Bhai?" he said, his attention once again fully on the flowers. "I don't know this guy. You maybe you got the wrong shop."

The denial was so immediate, so practiced, it was almost convincing. But Oliver had been through this before. This was the first test.

"No, this is the right place," Oliver insisted, stepping closer. "Saleem Bhai from the market in Harlem. He said you could help me. With ... travel."

Habib picked up a small pair of silver shears and snipped a leaf from a fern with a delicate *snip.* "Travel? What you're telling, man? I am the florist," he said, not looking up. "You want the travel, you go to travel agent on Lexington. Very good price they have, I think so." He then picked up a roll of green floral tape and began to wrap the stems of the bouquet with a focused intensity.

The absurdity of the situation was starting to feel familiar. He was in a small, damp flower shop, trying to arrange an illicit international trip with a man who refused to acknowledge anything beyond the world of petals and stems.

"Please," Oliver said, his voice dropping to a near-whisper. "Saleem vouched for me. I passed the test. The one in the back room. With an NYPD cop. Please, just call him. He'll tell you."

The mention of the NYPD cop seemed to land. A flicker of something – recognition, perhaps, or just annoyance – passed through Habib's eyes. He stared at Oliver for a long, silent moment, a statue amidst the floral explosion. Oliver could hear the hum of the refrigerated display case, the distant sound of traffic on 28th Street, the frantic beating of his own heart.

Finally, Habib let out a long, weary sigh, a sound of deep exasperation. He reached into the pocket of his apron and pulled out an old, battered Nokia phone, the kind Oliver hadn't seen in over a decade.

"You wait here," he commanded. He turned his back to Oliver and walked a few paces away, shielding the phone with his body as he dialed. Oliver watched, his muscles tensed, as Habib began to speak in a low, rapid-fire language he didn't recognize – a fluid, musical South Asian language. Perhaps Urdu ... or maybe Bengali.

The conversation was short. Oliver couldn't understand the words, but he could read the tone. It was a series of short, clipped questions from Habib, followed by what seemed to be affirmations. He heard Saleem Bhai's name mentioned, and then the word "boy" in English. Habib's posture seemed to relax slightly with each passing second, even chuckling at something the person at the other end of the line said at one point.

He ended the call, slipped the ancient phone back into his apron, and stood for a moment with his back still to Oliver. When he finally turned around, the hard, suspicious mask was gone, replaced by a look of grudging, professional acceptance.

"Okay," he said, the single word an admission, a key turning in a lock. "Saleem Bhai, he say you good guy. He say you clean. But he also say you crazy guy, keep all money on the phone." A small, almost imperceptible smile touched his lips.

Oliver let out a breath he didn't realize he'd been holding, a wave of relief so intense it almost made him dizzy. "So, you'll help me?"

"Saleem Bhai say I help you, and I listen to the Saleem Bhai," Habib said with a shrug, his florist persona completely gone, replaced by a quiet, all-business demeanor. "What you need?"

The abrupt shift from a folksy florist to a clipped, no-nonsense operator was jarring. Oliver took a moment to recalibrate. "I need a plane ticket," he said, his voice regaining some of its earlier confidence. "One way. To Montevideo, Uruguay. As soon as possible. Tomorrow, if you can."

Habib let out a short, dry chuckle, a sound like dead leaves skittering across pavement. He gestured with his head toward a small, cluttered room behind the workbench, with a *Staff Only* sign on the door. He turned to the young man who was still diligently stripping thorns from roses at the front. "Imran, you watch shop. No give discount for aunty, ya?"

Imran nodded without looking up. Habib pulled back a beaded curtain and led Oliver into a tiny, windowless office. It smelled of fertilizer and stale tea. A single, ancient-looking Dell computer sat on a metal desk, surrounded by precarious stacks of invoices and floral supply catalogs.

"You sit," Habib said, pointing to a wobbly stool as he settled into the worn-out office chair in front of the computer. The machine whirred to life with a groan. "Montevideo. Good place. You go there for good?"

"What? Oh, no. Of course not," Oliver replied. "I just ... I don't have a return date yet. I'm not sure how long my business there will take."

Habib stopped typing and swiveled in his chair to face Oliver. "Then you have problem, boss," he said, his expression flat. "This network ... it is not like the American Express. I get you ticket for the Montevideo with the cash, ya. But Montevideo ... no Habib there. No Saleem Bhai there. You want come back, you need buy your own ticket. With the credit card. With your name. Big problem for you, I think so."

Oliver stared at him. The flaw in his plan was so obvious, so simple, he couldn't believe he had missed it. He was trying to operate outside the system, but realized his plan only covered the exit, not the re-entry. To return, he would have to re-enter the system, leaving a clean, digital paper trail that would lead right back to his front door.

"So, I can't buy a one-way?" he asked, a note of desperation creeping into his voice.

"You can," Habib shrugged. "But one-way international ticket for cash? Very big red flag. Very noisy. My people no like noisy. They like quiet. You need to buy the round trip. Look like the tourist. Look like the businessman. Quiet."

The irony was stark. He was using this shadowy, illicit network to gain freedom, only to be immediately trapped by its rigid, unwritten rules.

"Okay," Oliver said, his mind racing. He had to find a reclusive artist who rarely appears in public. How long would that take? A week? A month? He had no idea. "Okay, a round trip then. For ... for one week." The words felt like a gamble, a bet against the universe. It would have to be enough.

"Good," Habib said, turning back to the screen. He began to type, his fingers moving with a slow, deliberate pecking motion. "One week. We see what we have."

Oliver watched over his shoulder. The booking website was not one he recognized. It was a stripped-down, text-heavy interface that looked like a relic from the early days of the internet.

"Okay," Habib muttered after a few minutes of clicking and scrolling. "Earliest I have is March second."

"March second?" Oliver exclaimed. "That's over a week from now! I need to go *now*."

"You no listen what I say?" Habib said, his voice laced with annoyance. "This is the cash network, brother. Not Expedia. Options are limited. My guy in Madrid, he has the seats on this flight. You want it, you take it. You no want it, you go to Lexington Avenue."

Madrid? The pieces were starting to sound less like a travel plan and more like a ransom note. He was completely at the mercy of this strange, invisible web of agents and fixers.

"What's the route?" Oliver asked, already dreading the answer.

"Is good route. Very beautiful for the tourism," Habib said, without a trace of irony. "You go JFK to Madrid. You have nine hour in Madrid. Then you go Madrid to São Paulo. Six hour in São Paulo. Then you get small plane, São Paulo to Montevideo. Very easy. I get you hotel also. Five star. Very nice. Then you come back March 10, same route, other way."

Oliver's head was spinning. New York to Madrid, only to fly all the way back across the Atlantic to Brazil, and then finally to Uruguay. It was a logistical nightmare, a journey that would take the better part of two days. It was absurd.

"Fine," Oliver said, the single word a white flag of surrender. He felt powerless, a piece of cargo being routed through a system he had no control over. "Just book it. How much is it?"

Habib swiveled around in his chair again, his expression unreadable. He didn't answer. Instead, he asked a question of his own.

"How much cash you got?"

The question was so direct, so disarming, it bypassed all of Oliver's carefully constructed defenses. He answered on pure, stupid instinct.

"Twenty thousand," he blurted out.

The moment the words left his mouth, he felt a wave of self-loathing so intense it was almost nauseating. *Idiot. You absolute, complete idiot. You stupid fucking moron!* He had just committed the rookie mistake of all rookie mistakes: he had shown his whole hand. He could see a flicker of something in Habib's eyes, the quiet satisfaction of a predator who has just watched its prey walk directly into the trap.

Habib nodded slowly. He picked up a calculator from his desk and punched in a few numbers. He turned it around for Oliver to see. The screen displayed a single, stark number: **19000**.

Oliver's jaw dropped. "Nineteen thousand dollars? For one plane ticket? That's insane! I could fly first-class on Emirates for less than half of that!"

"This is not Emirates, boss" Habib said calmly. "This is cash, what I told before to you? Very difficult. Many people, they need to eat. My travel agent, he eat. The ticket guy in Madrid, he eat. Saleem Bhai, he eat. Me, I eat."

Oliver's mind snagged on the last name. "Wait, Saleem Bhai gets a cut?" he asked, a note of incredulity in his voice. "I already paid him his seven percent in Harlem. Why does he get a piece of this, too?"

Habib looked at him as if he were a child asking why the sun was hot. "He is the main guy, boss. He open the gate. You come through that one, you pay the toll. Every time. This is the rule. Not my rule."

The simple, unadorned logic of it dawned on Oliver. Of course. It was a tax for existing within their network – not just a service fee. He had fled the world of fiat rent-seekers – the bankers, the VCs, the corporate middlemen who skimmed a percentage off every transaction – only to land in a parallel system that operated on the exact same principles, just with a veneer of street-level honor instead of a glossy corporate brochure. Saleem Bhai was a one-man central bank, a toll collector on the Silk Road of the underworld, double-dipping with a smile. The clean, peer-to-peer ethos of bitcoin felt a million miles away. This was just another set of bosses, not a revolution.

Habib gave a small, unapologetic shrug. "Nineteen thousand. I give you one-thousand-dollar discount because Saleem Bhai he say you good guy. Take it, or you leave it."

Oliver stood there, caught between the sheer, comical absurdity of the price and the grim reality of his situation. He was being fleeced, openly and spectacularly. But what choice did he have? He needed to get to Montevideo. He needed to find Velázquez. This was the price of admission to the world he now inhabited.

He let out a long, slow breath, the air leaving his lungs in a hiss of defeat. He unzipped his backpack, pulled out the thick bundle of hundred-dollar bills, and began to count out nineteen thousand dollars onto the corner of the dusty metal desk.

"You get the ticket in one day, two day," Habib said, not even looking at the money. "Encrypted message. You got the Signal?"

Oliver just nodded, his throat too tight to speak. He opened his Signal app and held up the QR code and handle for Habib to note. He then pushed the remaining thousand dollars back into his bag, zipped it up, and turned to leave.

"Hello, brother," Habib called out after him.

Oliver stopped and looked back.

Habib was holding up the magnificent orchid bouquet he had been working on when Oliver had walked in.

"For your girlfriend, maybe?" he said, a genuine, warm smile returning to his face for the first time. "A gift. For good customer."

CHAPTER 5. MARCH 9

779007 (March 2)

The fluorescent lights of The Grid hummed a relentless, indifferent tune. It was well past noon, but for Nick, the day was just beginning. He'd crashed on the pull-out sofa at home sometime after 4 a.m., his mind a furious slideshow of hexadecimal strings and transaction graphs, only to wake up feeling like he'd been run over by a truck. Becky had already left for work, leaving a note on the counter: *"Please eat something real today."* He had ignored it.

Now, back in his 10-by-10-foot cube of purgatory, he took a sip of the lukewarm, acidic coffee that served as his primary source of sustenance. The last eight days had been a brutal, demoralizing grind. The initial thrill of tying the name "Sazsa" to a concrete on-chain signature had given way to the grim, methodical reality of the task ahead. He had a name for the trace, but he didn't have a face.

He had spent the better part of a week chasing the pseudonym through the digital catacombs of the early cypherpunk movement. He'd scoured defunct cryptography mailing lists, downloaded entire archives of PGP key-server data, and sifted through the comment sections of long-forgotten blogs. The trail was cold, almost nonexistent. Sazsa had been a master of operational security, a true believer in the anonymous creed. Nick found his technical contributions, his sharp, incisive comments in complex debates, but he found nothing personal. No links to real-world identities, no careless slips.

By the ninth day, he was running on fumes, staring at another dead end. He was slumped in his chair, still trying to wake up, when a new thought struck him. He had been looking for a hacker. A pure creature of code. But no one was just a creature of code. Everyone had a life, passions, grievances. He had been trying to de-anonymize a ghost. Maybe it was time to look for the man.

He pivoted his search, moving away from IRC logs and technical forums. He started a broader, more human search for the handle "Sazsa," this time including keywords for hobbies, interests, anything that might reveal a sliver of the person behind the mask. It was a messy, inefficient process, a search for a single, anomalous signal in an ocean of digital noise.

After hours of sifting through irrelevant hits – a video game character, a brand of Polish sausage – he found it. A single post from 2011 on a high-end, niche forum for collectors of surrealist art. The post, from the user Sazsa, was a short, bitter complaint.

`Sazsa: The auction house handling the Bryce estate is a disgrace. They wouldn't know a masterpiece if it bit them.`

Bryce. The name was meaningless to Nick, but the context was everything. Art. A collector. It was a vector of investigation he had never considered. It was a thread.

He immediately opened a new browser tab and typed in "Sazsa" and "art collector." The results were still sparse, but the new keyword was a key that unlocked a different set of doors. He found a passing mention in an old art world newsletter from 2002, discussing a private sale a decade earlier of a surrealist piece by an obscure Irish painter named Jonathan Bryce. The newsletter mentioned the buyer was a "well-known European academic and mathematician who posts under the handle 'Sazsa.'"

The two worlds, the technical and the aesthetic, had just collided. He now had a new and powerful descriptor: a European academic.

He plunged back into his research, this time focusing on academic databases. He cross-referenced the names of known cryptographers from that era with any known interest in surrealist art. It was a tedious, mind-numbing process, a search for a single, anomalous intersection in a sea of academic rigor.

After hours of scrolling through dense, impenetrable PDFs, he found it. A 2005 paper on zero-knowledge proofs from a niche European cryptography journal. In the footnotes, the author thanked a colleague for his "invaluable, if unconventional, insights on the aesthetic symmetries of elliptic curves." The colleague's name was G. Zs. Lorincz.

The initials were a tantalizing clue. He searched for the name. The results were sparse, mostly academic citations from the late 90s and early 2000s, all co-authored with other known figures in the information theory world. A Hungarian academic, it seemed. Gyorgy Zsazsa Lorincz.

Zsazsa. It was right there. A middle name so unusual it couldn't be a coincidence. This was him. Sazsa was Gyorgy Zsazsa Lorincz. The rush of triumph left him giddy, wiping away the week's fatigue. He had done it. He had unmasked the third man.

His fingers flew across the keyboard, a triumphant, final search for "Gyorgy Zsazsa Lorincz." He expected to find a university profile, a recent publication, a digital footprint.

The first result was a link to a small, Hungarian-language newspaper based in Budapest. The headline was dated August of last year. Nick clicked on it, his browser's auto-translate function struggling for a moment before rendering the text in clumsy, blocky English.

It was an obituary.

Gyorgy Zsazsa Lorincz, noted academic and art collector, had passed away after a long illness. He was 54.

Nick stared at the screen, the triumphant energy draining out of him, leaving a cold, hollow void. He scrolled down, his eyes scanning the brief biography. Born in Budapest, a prodigy in mathematics, a brief but brilliant academic career in the United States, an early retirement, a return to Hungary, a passion for ... obscure surrealist painters. It was all there. A perfect, closed loop that led directly to a graveyard.

Presumed deceased.

The memory of the line from the early DoJ briefing resurfaced, no longer a dismissive footnote, but a stark, prophetic truth. Jeremiah Howard had been right. Nick had spent nearly two weeks of grueling, obsessive work only to arrive at the same conclusion the bureaucracy had reached months ago.

He leaned back in his creaking chair, the sterile stillness of his little box in Long Island City pressing in on him. The Sazsa trail was a dead end. Dev_akshar was an untouchable cipher. He was back at square one, with nothing but a dead man's name and the bitter taste of a pyrrhic victory.

He stared at the evidence board on the wall, at the names and the transaction IDs connected by strings of red yarn. There was only one thread left. One name connected to a real, living, and accessible network. He had been avoiding it, wanting the glory of cracking the harder, more mysterious parts of the case first. But the hard parts had led to nothing.

He had been wrong. His entire approach had been wrong. He shouldn't have started with the shadows. He should have started with the one man who was sitting in a cage.

He opened a new, blank document on his screen. He typed a single name. *Christiaan van der Dussen.*

779085 (March 3)

The jolt of the landing gear hitting the tarmac at Adolfo Suárez Madrid–Barajas Airport was a brutal, physical punctuation mark to a night spent in a state of suspended animation. Oliver blinked, his eyes gritty, his mouth tasting of stale cabin air and the lingering peat of the fourth and final in-flight whisky. He'd managed about three hours of disjointed, restless sleep, a minor miracle for him on any flight, but the $19,000 he'd paid for a premium economy seat felt like a particularly galling insult. For that price, he should have been in a private suite with a bed, not a slightly wider chair that reclined an extra four inches.

He shuffled off the plane with the rest of the red-eye commuters, a river of weary bodies flowing into the vast, cathedral-like space of Terminal 4. The famous undulating, rainbow-colored ceiling slats rolled out above him, a beautiful, whimsical piece of architecture that his exhausted mind could only register as a cruel mockery of his own grounded state. He checked his watch: 8:05 a.m. His flight to São Paulo wasn't until five in the evening. Nine hours. Nine hours to kill in this magnificent, soulless transit palace.

He began to walk, with no destination in mind. His first hour was a blur of moving walkways and the low, multilingual hum of a global crossroads. He watched a businessman in a suit so sharp it could have cut glass conduct a hushed, furious negotiation on his phone, oblivious as his toddler methodically unpacked his leather briefcase, arranging spreadsheets and pens in a neat, nonsensical pattern on the polished floor.

By the second hour, he found himself in a different wing of the terminal, where a large tour group, all wearing identical canary-yellow baseball caps, was being marshaled by a guide holding up a selfie stick. At the top of the stick, where a phone should have been, was a bright green rubber chicken. It bobbed and weaved above the sea of yellow hats, a bizarre, squeaky North Star for the lost and bewildered.

He needed coffee. He found a small café, the menu an impenetrable wall of Spanish text. He tried to order a simple *café solo*, but his sleep-deprived brain and clumsy American accent somehow produced a drink that was a bizarre, sweet concoction of espresso, condensed milk, and a dusting of cinnamon that tasted like a melted-down churro. He drank it anyway, the sugary sludge a fitting penance for his own linguistic shortcomings.

He kept walking. The initial grogginess had burned off, leaving behind a deep weariness. His mind, unmoored from any immediate task, began to drift over the landscape of his own anxieties. The six-spiraled shape. The chilling vision of Nick and Adele. The Noncemeister in a cage. Anariadne's impossible beauty and her cold, enigmatic dismissal. He pushed the thoughts away. Thinking was a luxury he couldn't afford right now. All he had to do was exist, to be a body moving through space, until the clock on the wall told him he could move to the next space.

It was a little after noon when a new, more primal need finally asserted itself over his mental static: hunger. And with it, a powerful thirst for a drink that wasn't served in a tiny plastic cup at 30,000 feet. He had four hours down, three more to go before he needed to head to his next gate, and two hours of waiting past the gate after that. The thought of all those hours of aimless wandering was unbearable.

He needed a proper anchor. A solid meal. A real glass.

He stopped his meandering and looked up, scanning the terminal signs. His eyes, now sharp with a simple, clear purpose, searched for a single, beautiful word.

Bar.

He spotted a sign down the concourse, its elegant script promising relief: *El Cielo de Madrid.* Perfect. He started walking toward it, then stopped dead, a fresh wave of paranoia washing over him. His credit card. Using it would leave a clean, digital breadcrumb, a timestamped record of his exact location. It was the kind of amateur mistake his father, certainly when he was Dev_akshar, would never have made.

Thankfully, an adjacent sign pointed to a currency exchange. He walked up to the counter, pulling the thick bundle of hundred-dollar bills from his jacket pocket.

"I'd like to exchange some dollars for Euros," he said to the woman behind the glass.

She nodded, her expression bored. "How much?" She asked, in a thick Castilian accent.

"What's the maximum I can exchange without having to show ID or fill out any forms?" Oliver asked, trying to sound casual, but the question came out as an awkward, guilty whisper.

The woman gave him a long, weary look. "Nine hundred ninety-nine," she said, her tone making it clear she'd answered this question a thousand times before.

"Great," Oliver said, peeling off eleven hundred-dollar bills. He pushed them through the slot. After the dismal exchange rate and the commission were factored in, he was left with a respectable, but significantly diminished, pile of crisp, colorful Euro notes.

He walked into El Cielo de Madrid. It was a typical airport bar, an oasis of dark wood and low lighting in the bright, sterile expanse of the terminal. He found an empty stool at the bar and settled in, the worn leather a small comfort.

There were only a few other patrons, each lost in their own world of transit and quiet desperation.

Next to him sat a burly man in his late forties, dressed in a well-made but nondescript navy sports jacket. He was nursing a small glass of a dark, amber liquid, staring blankly at the rows of bottles behind the bar. As Oliver sat down, the man glanced at him, just for a second. His eyes were a pale, washed-out blue, and for a fleeting, unnerving moment, Oliver felt a jolt of recognition from him. It was the distinct, unmistakable feeling of being *known*. The man's expression was blank, but his eyes seemed to register Oliver's presence with a flicker of something more than casual awareness. Then the moment passed. The man turned back to his drink, his face a neutral mask.

Oliver shook the feeling off. Paranoia. The word was becoming his constant companion. The bartender came over. "A glass of your best Rioja, please," Oliver said.

"The Muga Reserva?"

"Perfect."

The wine, when it came, was excellent. It was rich and complex, a taste of the real world after the sterile confines of the plane. He took a slow, deliberate sip. The presence of the man next to him was a heavy, palpable thing. He felt the man's gaze on him, even though he was looking straight ahead. He had to say something, anything, to break the charged stillness.

"Long flight?" Oliver asked, the words feeling clumsy.

The man turned his head slowly and looked at Oliver. "Is there any other kind?" he said. His voice was a low, gravelly rumble, his English thick with a gruff, Eastern European accent. He offered no further conversation, turning back to his drink.

The rebuff was clear, but the sound of his voice sent a fresh prickle of unease up Oliver's spine. *Serbian*, a part of his brain supplied, either a memory of his father's linguistic lessons surfacing, or one of the erratic and infrequent mental fractures he'd been receiving recently. The suspicion was still a wild, illogical leap, but it refused to be dismissed.

He took another sip of his wine, trying to focus on the notes of cherry and oak, trying to ground himself in the simple reality of the bar. He was just another tired traveler. This was just another man.

The man beside him shifted on his stool, reaching down to adjust a small, black carry-on bag that rested at his feet. As he moved the bag, a stiff leather luggage tag, which had been tucked away, flipped over and hung in plain sight for a few brief seconds.

Oliver's eyes, trained for months to find patterns in the noise, caught the embossed silver lettering on the dark leather.

B. MITROVIC

The world seemed to slow down. The low murmur of the bar, the clink of glasses, the distant announcements over the terminal PA system – it all faded into a dull, distant hum.

Mitrovic. A common enough Serbian surname. But combined with the accent and voice which triggered a faint memory of a phone call during a projection episode with Daniela in Maren's apartment all those months ago ... combined with the man's professional stillness ...

It had to be him. It was an insane, impossible coincidence, but the evidence was right there, a fleeting breadcrumb in the middle of the Madrid airport. Bojan Mitrovic. He was sitting right next to him.

The man shifted again, and the tag flipped back over, the name disappearing from view. But it was too late. The image was burned into Oliver's mind.

And, Oliver realized with a fresh wave of dread, the fleeting sense of recognition he'd felt from the man wasn't paranoia at all. It was a confirmation.

Bojan somehow knew who he was.

He had to move. Now.

He forced himself to act with a casualness he didn't feel. He took one last, steadying sip of his wine, placed a fifty-Euro note on the bar. Enough to cover the drink and a generous, unthinking tip. He slid off the stool without looking at Bojan. He just turned and walked toward the exit, his posture relaxed, his pace unhurried. Every instinct screamed at him to run, but he fought it, focusing on the simple, mechanical act of putting one foot in front of the other.

The moment he was out of the bar and back in the bright, impersonal concourse, the facade crumbled. His heart hammered against his ribs. He quickened his pace, weaving through the slow-moving river of travelers, a powerful sense of being watched prickling the back of his neck. He risked a glance over his shoulder. Bojan wasn't there. But the feeling of being seen didn't leave.

How? The question pounded in his head in time with his footsteps. *How could he possibly know who I am?* The only logical answer was Maren. She must have shown him photographs, given him a description. The thought was deeply unsettling. It meant he was a known target.

He wandered for what felt like an hour, a disoriented automaton moving through the architectural splendor of the terminal, seeing none of it. He bought a bottle of water from a kiosk, his hands trembling slightly as he paid. He found a seat in a less crowded area, but the feeling of exposure was too intense. He got up and started walking again.

He saw a sign for a restroom down a less-trafficked corridor and headed toward it, hoping for a moment of reprieve. As he approached the entryway, a short hallway that led into the main restroom area, he heard a voice. A familiar, gravelly rumble, thick with a gruff, Eastern European accent.

It was him. Bojan.

Oliver flattened himself against the corridor wall, his breath catching in his throat. The voice was coming from inside one of the stalls. He was on the phone.

"Maren, listen to me," Bojan said, his voice a low, confidential murmur, but sharp with irritation. "I saw the boy."

A pause as he listened. Oliver's mind reeled. *Maren.* It was confirmed.

"Yes, here. In Madrid," Bojan continued. "What he is doing here, I don't know, but is not coincidence."

Another, longer pause. Oliver could imagine Maren's voice on the other end, urgent and questioning.

"His bag. The tag. It says Montevideo. Connection is through São Paulo."

The confirmation sent another jolt of cold dread through Oliver. Bojan had seen his luggage tag. He knew his entire itinerary.

"No, I am on my way to London. Other business," Bojan said, a note of impatience in his voice. "After that is done, in three, maybe four days ... I will handle the boy. Don't worry."

Another pause.

"Yes. Understood."

Oliver was so focused on the voice from the stall that he didn't hear the soft footsteps approaching from behind him until it was too late. A man in a tracksuit, pulling a rolling suitcase, walked into the entryway corridor. The man stopped, his eyes widening in surprise at the sight of Oliver pressed against the wall, tense and wide-eyed. The man gave him a strange look, a mixture of confusion and mild alarm, then shrugged and continued into the main restroom, his suitcase wheels rattling on the tiled floor.

Oliver's blood ran cold. Bojan would have heard that.

From inside the stall, he heard Bojan say a quick, clipped, *"Ja, ja. Auf Wiedersehen,"* then a hang-up tone. It was followed immediately by the loud, mechanical whoosh of a toilet flushing.

He was coming out.

Panic, pure and undiluted, seized Oliver. There was no time to think. He just acted. He turned and bolted, bursting out of the quiet corridor and back into the main concourse. He ran in a panicked, meandering sprint, weaving through crowds of slow-moving families, dodging luggage carts and sidestepping businessmen. He felt a dozen pairs of annoyed eyes on him, but he didn't care.

It was a 15-minute walk to his departure gate. He made it in five. He collapsed into a seat by the window, his lungs burning, his heart a frantic drum against his ribs. He scanned the crowd approaching the gate, looking for any sign of the burly Serbian. He didn't see him. For now, he was safe.

He leaned his head back against the cool glass of the window and took a deep, shuddering breath. The adrenaline began to recede, leaving behind the stark, terrifying clarity of his new reality. This wasn't a puzzle anymore. It wasn't a philosophical quest. He was being hunted. Maren and Bojan knew where he was, they knew where he was going, and they had a plan to "handle him." His journey to Montevideo had just transformed from a mission of discovery into a desperate race for survival.

779240 (March 4)

The air that hit Oliver as he stepped off the jet bridge at Carrasco International Airport was thick, warm, and heavy with the humid scent of a summer night surrendering to autumn. It was 3:45 a.m. His internal clock, scrambled with a back-and-forth trip across the Atlantic within a 24-hour span, felt like it was operating on a different plane of existence. The 10-hour flight from Madrid to São Paulo had been a sleepless, whisky-fueled ordeal, and the subsequent six-hour layover followed by the final, bumpy leg to Montevideo had done little to improve his state. He was a man running on fumes, propelled forward only by the grim momentum of his quest.

He joined the short, sleepy queue for immigration, the hall unnaturally quiet at this hour. The vast, modern space felt empty – the grand, sweeping arch of the terminal roof a silent witness to the handful of weary travelers trickling in from the night. He watched the man in front of him, a tired-looking German tourist, get his passport stamped with a loud, definitive *thump* that punctuated the low buzz of the bright tube lights overhead.

Finally, it was his turn. He stepped up to the counter and handed his passport to the officer, a middle-aged man with a kind but exhausted face. The officer scanned the passport, his eyes flicking from the photo to Oliver's face and back again. The scrutiny, however brief, sent a familiar prickle of apprehension up Oliver's spine.

The officer looked up, his English heavily accented. "Welcome to Uruguay, señor. First time?"

"Yes," Oliver said, his own voice sounding distant and raspy.

"Business or ... holiday?"

"Holiday," Oliver lied.

The officer nodded slowly, his gaze lingering on Oliver for a moment too long. "You have with you ... more ten thousand dollar? In the currency?"

"No," Oliver replied, the answer quick and semi-truthful. He had been meticulous about this part. The night before he'd left, he had counted out exactly ninety-five hundred-dollar bills from the suitcase under his bed. He'd learned his lesson with Habib; you only reveal what you must.

The officer seemed satisfied. As he reached for his stamp, Oliver's hand instinctively went to the phone in his pocket. The absurdity of the question was almost comical. The $9,000-odd dollars of paper currency in his bag were a pittance, a rounding error. The real fortune was on his phone, a string of data in his wallet. Nearly 40 bitcoin, the remainder of the funds he had CoinJoined and not swapped for cash with Saleem Bhai in Harlem. He hadn't bothered moving them out of his phone and into cold storage. They were right there with him, sitting in that hot wallet, an invisible, weightless treasure that made the customs declaration a complete farce. He felt a brief, internal chuckle at the sheer recklessness of it all. If his phone was lost, stolen or compromised, a million dollars would vanish into the digital void.

But he had a backup plan, a small one at least. Before leaving, he'd spent hours researching. There were two bitcoin ATMs in Montevideo's city center that, according to a semi-anonymous forum, would dispense Uruguayan pesos for bitcoin – up to the equivalent of two hundred dollars at a time, no questions asked. It was a small, inefficient lifeline, but it was a lifeline nonetheless.

Thump.

The officer pushed the newly stamped passport back across the counter. "Enjoy your stay, señor."

Oliver nodded his thanks and walked through into the baggage claim area. The carousel was just beginning to stir, a slow, metallic groan in the quiet hall. He stood and waited, half-expecting his luggage to have been lost somewhere over the Atlantic, a final, fitting tax for his convoluted, cash-only itinerary. But then, miraculously, he saw it: his simple, black suitcase, looking a little more battered than he remembered, emerged from the plastic curtains and began its slow, lurching journey toward him.

He grabbed it off the belt. The small victory felt disproportionately significant. He had made it. He was here. He took a deep breath, the smell of the Uruguayan air a little more real this time, and began to walk toward the exit, scanning the sparse arrivals hall for the currency exchange.

He found it, a brightly lit booth with a single, tired-looking woman behind the counter. The process was a near-perfect echo of his experience in Madrid, a familiar ritual in a strange new land.

"I'd like to exchange some dollars for pesos," he said.

"How much?"

"What's the maximum without forms or ID?" The question felt less awkward this time, a practiced line from a script he was slowly learning.

The woman gave him the same weary, seen-it-all look. "Ten hundred dollar," she replied, her English thick with a soft, melodic Rioplatense accent.

"Okay, I'll do that." He peeled off ten hundred-dollar bills and pushed them through the slot.

She ran them through a counting machine and then began to count out a thick, colorful stack of Uruguayan pesos. She pushed the bundle through the slot. *38,040 pesos.* The number seemed impossibly large. He had no real frame of reference for it, no intuitive sense of its value, but he assumed a thousand dollars would go a much longer way here than it did back home. It would be enough. It had to be.

He stuffed the unfamiliar currency into his backpack and walked out of the terminal doors and into the warm, humid pre-dawn air. A line of black-and-yellow taxis waited at the curb.

He stood on the sidewalk for a moment, the reality of his location finally sinking in. He was in Uruguay. Daniela's country. The place she had called home for the first part of her life. He looked around at the unfamiliar landscape, at the foreign words on the signs, and felt a sudden, sharp pang of wistfulness. He was standing on the soil of her past, a past she had shared with him so openly, and she had no idea he was here. He had traveled halfway across the world, chasing his own family's secrets, only to land in the heart of hers. The irony was a quiet, lonely ache.

He pushed the thought away, pulling out his phone. He opened the encrypted Signal message from Habib. It contained a simple, one-line address for the hotel and a reservation number. He showed it to the first driver in the queue, a friendly-looking man who nodded, took his suitcase, and opened the back door for him. As the taxi pulled away from the curb and onto the highway leading into the sleeping city, Oliver leaned his head back against the seat, the exhaustion of the last two days finally catching up with him.

The driver, a friendly-looking man with a magnificent mustache, had tried to engage him in conversation at the start of the ride, a rapid-fire stream of cheerful Spanish that Oliver could only meet with a weary, apologetic shrug.

The man had simply smiled, said, "Okay, okay, no problem," and mercifully turned up the radio, which was playing a soft, melancholic tango.

The city emerged from the pre-dawn darkness in slow, blurry fragments. Oliver drifted in and out of a light, fitful sleep, the gentle sway of the car a hypnotic cradle. When he finally opened his eyes again, the taxi was navigating the narrow, cobblestoned streets of what looked like an old, historic neighborhood. They pulled up in front of a large, ornate building that might have been grand a century ago.

The driver turned around. "Hotel, señor."

Oliver paid the man, adding a generous tip, and stepped out onto the sidewalk, suitcase in tow. He looked up at his home for the next week. The *Gran Hotel Cervantes*. Habib had promised him "five star." This was not five-star. This was a faded, beautiful ruin, a dowager empress fallen on hard times. The grand, Art Nouveau facade was crumbling in places, stained with decades of sea salt and neglect. One of the letters in the bronze 'GRAN HOTEL' sign above the entrance had fallen off, so it now read, with a kind of poetic honesty, 'RAN HOTEL'.

He pushed through the heavy, revolving wooden door and into a lobby that was a time capsule from another era. A vast, marble-floored space, a grand but dusty chandelier hanging from a soaring, water-stained ceiling and the faint, pervasive smell of old carpets and lemon polish. The only person in the cavernous room was a man behind the long, dark-wood reception desk. He was impossibly old, a tiny, wizened man in a slightly-too-large, burgundy uniform, fast asleep in his chair, his head tilted back at an alarming angle, a soft, whistling snore emanating from his open mouth.

It was 4:15 a.m. Oliver felt a pang of guilt, but he had no choice. He walked up to the desk and gently tapped the small, silver bell on the counter.

The old man shot upright with a snort, his eyes flying open. He stared at Oliver for a moment, his expression a comical mixture of terror and confusion, as if an apparition had just materialized in his lobby.

"*Buenos días*," Oliver said, trying to sound as friendly as possible. "Checking in. I have a reservation. The name is ... uh ... Smith." Habib had booked everything under a generic, untraceable alias.

The concierge, whose name tag identified him as 'Alfonso,' blinked a few times, trying to orient himself to the waking world. He slowly, deliberately, put on a pair of thick-lensed spectacles and peered at the large, leather-bound reservation book on the desk in front of him. He ran a gnarled, trembling finger down the page for what felt like an eternity.

"Smith ..." he mumbled, his voice a dry rustle. "Ah, yes. Señor Smith. You are very ... early."

"Yes, I'm sorry. My flight just landed," Oliver explained.

Alfonso let out a long, weary sigh, a sound that seemed to carry the weight of every inconvenient guest he had ever dealt with in his long and storied career. "Check-in, señor, is at three in the afternoon." He stated this not as a policy, but as an immutable law of the universe.

"I know, but I've been traveling for two days," Oliver pleaded. "I'm exhausted. Is there any possibility I could get into my room now? I'd be happy to pay for an extra night, of course."

Alfonso seemed to consider this, his brow furrowed in deep, philosophical contemplation. He picked up an ancient, rotary-dial telephone and began the slow, arduous process of dialing a number, his finger making a loud, satisfying *whirrrr-click* with each digit. He waited, listening to the receiver. After a moment, he shook his head and placed it back on its cradle.

"The manager, she is sleeping," he announced with an air of finality, as if this settled the matter for all time.

Oliver was beginning to feel a sense of delirious, sleep-deprived hysteria. He was in a surreal play, a Beckettian drama set in a decaying Uruguayan hotel. He decided to try a different tactic. He pulled out the thick wad of pesos from his backpack and placed a thousand-peso note on the counter.

Alfonso looked at the note. He looked at Oliver. He looked back at the note, and then the wad Oliver was putting back into his backpack. A slow, subtle transformation took place. The weary, bureaucratic gatekeeper vanished, replaced by a man of pragmatic and worldly wisdom.

He slid the note off the counter and into his pocket with a practiced, elegant movement. He then pulled a large, ornate brass key from a hook behind him.

"Room 404," he said, a newfound warmth in his voice. "The elevator, she is ... resting. You will take the stairs. Breakfast is at seven. Enjoy your stay, Señor Smith."

Oliver took the key, a heavy, solid object that felt like it could unlock a medieval castle. He thanked the old man and turned toward the grand, sweeping staircase. As he walked, lugging his suitcase behind him, he felt Alfonso's eyes on his back. This wasn't a five-star hotel. This was something far more ... interesting.

His room was on the fourth floor. It was vast, with high ceilings and a small, wrought-iron balcony that overlooked the quiet, pre-dawn street. The furniture was old but well-made, the bed enormous and covered in a thick, brocaded bedspread. It was a room full of faded grandeur, a place that held the memory of a more elegant time.

He didn't bother to unpack. He just dropped his suitcase on the floor, kicked off his shoes, and collapsed face down onto the bed. The exhaustion hit him like a ton of bricks, a wave that pulled him under instantly. He was a world away from home, in a strange city, in a strange hotel, his mission just beginning. But for now, all that mattered was the blissful, bottomless dark of a long-overdue sleep.

779424 (March 6)

The coffee was inky and astringent, a perfect mirror for Oliver's mood. He sat at a small, wobbly table outside a café in the Ciudad Vieja, the historic heart of Montevideo. It was noon. For the past forty-eight hours, he had been a man chasing a whisper, and the whisper was fading.

The search for Luis Velázquez had been a systematic exercise in futility. The city's high-end art dealers had looked at him with polite, dismissive smiles. *"Velázquez? Of course, a master. But he does not show. He does not meet. It is impossible."* The online world was a similar dead end; the artist had no digital footprint, no website, no social media, nothing but a few glowing reviews from exhibitions held years ago. He was a man who had perfected the art of disappearance.

Oliver took a slow sip of the coffee. The initial, disorienting exhaustion from his journey had been replaced by a sharp, gnawing desperation. His time was running out. Bojan was most likely coming. He could feel the Serbian's presence like a storm gathering just over the horizon, a palpable sense that made the warm, late-summer air feel cold against his skin.

He had spent yesterday afternoon just walking, a meandering wanderer trying to clear his head. His path had taken him down the city's grand main avenue, and he had stopped in front of it, a magnificent, towering granite monument piercing the sky. *The Obelisk of Montevideo*, a sign had said. He had stared at it, an odd sense of significance prickling the back of his neck, a feeling of being close to something important, without knowing why.

Now, sitting at the café, his gaze fell upon a weathered poster plastered to a nearby wall, an advertisement for a local cultural festival. His Spanish was rudimentary at best, but he could pick out a few words. *Música. Arte. Historia.* And then, a date that made his blood run cold.

18 de Julio.

The characters were unmistakable. He pulled out his phone, his fingers trembling slightly as he typed "July 18 Uruguay" into the search engine. The results were instantaneous and absolute. It was Constitution Day. A major national holiday, celebrating the country's first constitution, sworn in on July 18th, 1830. And the Obelisk he had seen yesterday? It was dedicated to the drafters of that very constitution.

The OP_RETURN message. *Obelisk, 18 July. It has happened.*

A chill, completely unrelated to the weather, washed over him. This was real. The mysterious message was a summons. A precise set of coordinates in both time and space, anchored to the very monument he had stood before just yesterday. Daniela had floated this very same theory to him several weeks ago, but he had brushed her off. *Idiot. Again.* The confirmation was a terrifying, exhilarating thing. His quest was not a delusion. The path his father had set for him, however strange and perilous, was leading somewhere real.

But the confirmation also sharpened his despair. He now knew the destination, but he had no idea how to survive long enough to reach it. He was a man walking toward a fated appointment, with a hunter closing in on his back.

He drained the last of the cold coffee. His logical, systematic search for Velázquez had failed. He had exhausted every conventional avenue. It was time for a new approach. A desperate, tenuous long shot.

He thought of Daniela, of the stories she had told him about her childhood, about the uncle who had been a father to her. The man who was a bitcoiner. The man who lived right here, in this city. Rafael Forlan.

It was an insane idea, a wild leap of faith based on nothing more than a shared connection to the woman he had lost. But it was the only thread he had left. He stood up from the table, a new, desperate purpose hardening his resolve. He would find Daniela's uncle. He had to.

He found a shaded bench in the plaza, pulled out his phone, and began the search. "Rafael Forlan Montevideo." The results were, as expected, a deluge of irrelevance. Dozens of men with the same common name. Social media profiles for teenagers, public records for men long dead, a dentist in a nearby suburb. He needed a better filter.

What did he know? Daniela had called him a bitcoiner, one of the early ones. He refined his search: *"Rafael Forlan" Bitcoin Uruguay.*

This time, the results were different. Near the top was a link to a local tech blog from 2017. The article was in Spanish, but he used his browser's translation feature to parse the clumsy English. It was a recap of a small, local conference on "The Future of Finance." And there he was, listed as a panelist: *R. Forlan, Private Investor and Early Digital Asset Adopter.* The article didn't give an address, but it mentioned he was a longtime resident of the city's esteemed *Pocitos* neighborhood.

It was a start. He spent the next hour cross-referencing this new information with public property registries and online phone directories. The work was a tedious grind of chasing down false leads and dead ends. But finally, he found it. A single entry for an R. Forlan in an exclusive, pre-war apartment building on the Rambla, the grand coastal avenue that defined the Pocitos waterfront.

He hailed a taxi, the address front and center on his phone screen. The short ride was a journey through the city's history. The dense, colonial architecture of the Ciudad Vieja gave way to the more open, elegant streets of the city center, which then opened up further into the leafy, affluent splendor of Pocitos. The taxi cruised along the waterfront, the vast, silver expanse of the Río de la Plata to his left, grand apartment buildings and towering palm trees to his right.

The driver pulled up in front of a building that was less an apartment complex and more a palace. It was a magnificent, 10-story art deco structure from the 1930s, its clean, curving lines and ornate ironwork a testament to an era of bygone elegance. A uniformed doorman stood at attention under an elegant, sweeping canopy.

Oliver paid the driver and got out, his heart beginning to beat a little faster. He stood on the sidewalk for a moment, looking up at the grand facade. This was it. A wild, desperate gamble that had somehow, against all odds, led him here. He took a deep breath, smoothed down his jacket, and walked toward the entrance, preparing himself for the next test.

He walked up to the entrance, towards the doorman, a man in his fifties, with a neatly trimmed gray mustache, a ramrod-straight posture that spoke of a military past, and deep-set, intelligent eyes. He watched Oliver approach with a polite, professional neutrality.

"*Buenas tardes*," the doorman said, his voice a calm, deep baritone.

"Hi," Oliver replied. "I'm here to see Señor Rafael Forlan."

As Oliver spoke, the doorman's eyes met his. For a fraction of a second, the professional mask slipped. Oliver saw a flicker of something in the man's gaze – not just recognition, but a deep, almost paternal spark of knowing that was so unexpected it startled him. It was there for an instant and then gone, replaced by the same polite, impassive demeanor. But Oliver had seen it.

"I am sorry, señor," the doorman said, in surprisingly good English, his tone still perfectly polite. "Señor Forlan is a very private man. He is not receiving any visitors today."

"It's really important," Oliver pressed, trying to keep the desperation out of his voice. "I'm a ... a friend of the family. From New York. I've come a very long way."

The doorman's expression didn't change, but his eyes softened with a hint of what looked like genuine sympathy, which only confused Oliver more. "I understand, señor, but I have my instructions. No visitors without a scheduled appointment."

"Can you just call up to him? Please?" Oliver's agitation began to bleed through his composure. "Just tell him Oliver is here. Oliver Battolo. I promise you, he'll know who I am."

As he said his last name, he saw it again, more clearly this time. Or he thought he did. A flicker deep in the doorman's dark eyes, a momentary stillness, the barest widening of his pupils before the professional, impassive mask was firmly back in place. It was so fast, so subtle, he couldn't be sure he hadn't imagined it, a trick of the light and his own wishful thinking.

The doorman considered this. For a moment, Oliver thought he had broken through. But the man just gave a slow, regretful shake of his head. The look on his face was the look of a man delivering a difficult but necessary truth.

"Señor Battolo," he said. "It is truly not possible. I am very sorry. Perhaps you can send a letter?"

The suggestion was both perfectly reasonable and a complete dead end. It was a polite, gentle stonewalling, and it was infuriating. Oliver could feel a hot surge of anger, the accumulated weariness of the past several weeks threatening to boil over. He wanted to shout, to demand, to push his way past this immovable, kindly man.

But he couldn't. There was no anger to fight against, no hostility to mirror. There was only a calm, paternal firmness. It was like arguing with a mountain. He looked into the doorman's sympathetic eyes and saw the absolute finality of his decision.

The fight went out of him, replaced by a wave of resignation. He had come all this way, chased this one, promising lead, and it had evaporated in the face of a polite, unshakeable "no." He was beaten.

"Okay," Oliver said, the word a small puff of surrender. "Okay. Thank you."

He turned and walked away from the grand entrance, the doorman's kind, regretful gaze following him down the street. He was back at square one, adrift in a foreign city, with no idea what to do next.

779777 (March 7)

The stultifying interior of The Grid had started to feel like a physical pressure inside Nick's skull. For five days, he had been a man chained to a screen, a prospector sifting through mountains of cold, indifferent data, and he had nothing to show for it. The Christiaan van der Dussen trail was a wasteland. Every on-chain connection, every old wallet, every known associate's address had been analyzed, mapped, and dismissed by the DoJ years ago. He was just retreading the same barren ground.

He had to get out. He couldn't look at another hexadecimal string. He needed air, distance, a different perspective. He walked out of The Grid onto the street and set off northwards towards Astoria, a neighborhood he barely knew. He walked on Vernon Boulevard, the wide, open sky over the East River a welcome reprieve from the oppressive canyon of his cubicle.

His mind, however, remained trapped in the digital maze. He replayed his failures. The search for Dev_akshar's current activity was a dead end. His initial hope of finding a fresh lead on Sazsa had led him to the digital footprint of a dead man. He was stuck in a loop, applying the same analytical tools that had already proven useless.

He walked past the entrance to Socrates Sculpture Park, the name barely registering, his thoughts a tangled mess of transaction graphs and broken leads. He turned right onto 30th Drive, the street shifting from industrial waterfront to a quiet, residential neighborhood. He'd been walking for nearly half an hour, the crisp March air doing little to clear the fog of his circular thinking. He was just hungry now, and the thought of another lukewarm container of greasy Chinese takeout back at The Grid was depressing.

He saw a small, unassuming café on the next corner, its blue-and-white striped awning a splash of Mediterranean color against the red brick of the building. A simple, hand-painted sign in the window read: *The Gadfly Café*. The place looked clean and was mostly empty.

He went inside. The air smelled of oregano, lemon and strong coffee. An older man with a kind, weathered face and a magnificent white mustache stood behind the counter, wiping it down with a cloth. Nick took a seat at the counter.

"*Kalimera*," the man said with a warm smile. "What can I get for you?"

"Coffee," Nick said. "And ... what's good?"

"Everything is good," the man said with a chuckle. "But you look like a man who needs something real. Something to put you back on your feet. The Moussaka. My wife, Eleni, she made it this morning. It will solve all your problems."

"I'll take it," Nick said.

The Moussaka, when it came, was a hearty, delicious slab of layered eggplant, spiced meat and rich béchamel. It was real food, made by human hands, and it was the most comforting thing Nick had felt in weeks. He ate slowly, the warmth of the dish seeping into him.

The proprietor, whose name was Stavros, returned to wiping the counter. He worked with a patient, unhurried rhythm.

"You are not from around here," Stavros observed, his tone friendly, not prying.

"No," Nick said. "Just ... clearing my head."

"Ah," Stavros nodded wisely. "The head is a stubborn mule. Sometimes you must lead it to a new field to get it to think new thoughts." He paused in his wiping and looked at Nick, his dark eyes full of a gentle curiosity. "You have the look of a man trying to solve a puzzle with the wrong pieces."

Nick was taken aback by the astuteness of the observation. "Something like that," he admitted. "I'm trying to understand why a man did what he did. But all the evidence, all the facts ... they don't add up to a person."

Stavros chuckled, a warm, rumbling sound. He leaned against the counter. "The facts? The numbers on a paper? They tell you nothing. I have a brother-in-law, a fool, but a good man. The bank, the government, they look at his accounts. They see a man who is always broke, always late on his payments. They see a failure. They see the numbers. But do they see that he sends half his money to his mother back in Patras? Do they see the five hundred euros he slipped his nephew to buy a new suit for his first job interview? No. They see the data. They do not see the man."

The simple, homespun words hit Nick hard. He stared at the half-eaten Moussaka on his plate, his mind suddenly racing. *They see the data. They do not see the man.*

He had been doing the exact same thing. He had been staring at Christiaan van der Dussen's digital ledger, his transaction history, his on-chain "facts." He had been trying to understand the man by looking at his numbers. He was making the same mistake as the DoJ, the same mistake as the flawed AI.

"If you want to know the truth of a man," Stavros continued, completely unaware of the revelation he had just triggered, "you do not look in his wallet. You talk to his family. You talk to his sister. A sister ... she knows all the secrets."

His sister.

The thought was a lightning bolt, a sudden, brilliant flash of clarity that illuminated the entire, darkened landscape of his investigation. Adele. That was her name. Of course, he knew about Christiaan's sister! She was the one leading the petition for his clemency. The case file mentioned her as well, a minor detail he had completely glossed over. She was his advocate, his one connection to the outside world. He had been trying to decode the cold, dead data of the past when a living, breathing source of human intelligence had been there the whole time.

He had been looking for a ghost in the machine, but the key to the entire puzzle might be held by a woman in the real world.

The food was forgotten. The weariness of the past week vanished, burned away by a surge of fresh purpose. He had been stuck, a man running in circles in a labyrinth. Now, thanks to the simple wisdom of a Greek café owner in Astoria, he finally had a new path forward. He knew who he had to find.

779888 (March 8)

The sweeping staircase of the Gran Hotel Cervantes groaned under Oliver's weight as he descended from the fourth floor. It was 10 a.m., and the last two days had been a complete write-off. His systematic search for Luis Velázquez had yielded nothing but yet more polite dismissals and dead ends. A heavy sense of dejection had settled over him. His flight back to New York was in less than 48 hours, and he was no closer to finding the reclusive artist than he had been in his Chelsea apartment. The trip felt like a monumental, $19,000 mistake.

Adding to his unease was a strange, persistent feeling he couldn't quite shake. For the past two days, as he'd wandered the streets of the Ciudad Vieja, he'd had the distinct impression of being watched. It wasn't an overt, menacing feeling but a subtle, background awareness – a sense of a distant, protective gaze that he would notice and then immediately dismiss as a byproduct of his heightened nerves. Still, the feeling lingered.

He reached the final flight of stairs, which opened into the vast, marble-floored lobby. It was busier than when he had arrived, with about a dozen guests milling about, checking out or waiting for taxis. He saw Alfonso, the ancient concierge, behind the reception desk. And then he saw who Alfonso was talking to.

It was Bojan.

He was wearing the same navy sports jacket, his back to Oliver. Alfonso, looking flustered, was gesturing vaguely in Oliver's direction. Oliver was too far away to hear clearly, but he could make out a few words of the old man's panicked Spanish.

" … el americano … Señor Smith, en la habitación cuatro-cero-cuatro …"

At that moment, as if sensing Oliver's presence, Bojan turned. His pale, washed-out blue eyes locked onto Oliver's from across the lobby. There was no surprise in his expression, only a cold, flat confirmation. The predator had found its prey.

Oliver's blood ran cold, but he fought the urge to bolt. The lobby was full of witnesses. A sudden move would cause a scene. He forced himself into a mask of casualness, giving Bojan a slight, dismissive nod as if he were just another guest, and began to walk at a slow, deliberate pace toward the revolving door. He could feel Bojan's gaze on his back, a physical weight.

He pushed through the door and onto the sunlit street. And then he ran.

He didn't look back. He just pumped his legs, his boots clattering on the sidewalk, weaving through the morning pedestrians. He ducked onto a side street, a narrow, cobblestoned lane lined with colorful, colonial-era buildings. He risked a glance over his shoulder. Bojan had emerged from the hotel. He was moving at a fast, efficient lope, a human machine built for pursuit, and he was closing the distance with terrifying ease.

Oliver pushed himself harder, his lungs already beginning to burn. The months of wine and whisky, of sleepless nights and sedentary, screen-filled days, were taking their toll. His body, once lean and athletic, felt soft and sluggish. His stamina, which he had taken for granted, had become a distant memory.

He rounded another corner, his mind racing. *How? How did he find me?* Habib's network was supposed to be secure. The hotel was booked under an alias. But Bojan was a professional, a man who moved through the world with a different set of tools and a different understanding of its hidden pathways. He had probably been waiting in the lobby since dawn.

A sharp stitch flared in his side. He was gasping for air, the beautiful, late-summer day a blur of pastel-colored walls and wrought-iron balconies. He could hear Bojan's footsteps now, a steady, relentless rhythm on the cobblestones behind him, getting closer. He was a gazelle, and the lion was tiring him out, waiting for the inevitable moment of collapse.

He saw an opening, a narrow, dark alleyway between a bookstore and a closed restaurant. A shortcut. A chance to break the line of sight. Without a second thought, he veered into it, the sudden shade a momentary relief. The alley was short, maybe 100 feet long. He sprinted toward the other end, toward the promise of another street, another crowd to melt into.

He reached the end, and his heart seized. It was a dead end. A high, brick wall, covered in faded graffiti, blocked his path.

He spun around, panting, his back pressing against the cold, rough brick. Bojan stood at the entrance to the alley, blocking the only way out. He wasn't even breathing heavily. He just stood there, a dark silhouette against the bright morning light, watching Oliver with those same cold, pale eyes. He took a slow, deliberate step into the alley, and then another, his heavy shoes making a soft, grinding sound on the gritty pavement.

Oliver's mind raced, his thoughts a panicked jumble. He remembered the interrogation in Harlem, the terror he'd felt with Aguilar's hand on his throat. He remembered the strange, sudden detachment he had found then, the ability to become a witness to his own fear. He reached for that feeling now, a desperate grasp for a switch he couldn't find. But the calmness wouldn't come. His heart was a wild drum against his ribs, his lungs were on fire, and his legs felt like they were made of water. There was no serene observer here, only a terrified animal caught in a trap.

Bojan stopped about 20 feet away, his hands hanging loose at his sides.

Oliver's heel scraped against the wall. No escape. One heartbeat. Two.

"You run fast, for boy who sits at desk," Bojan said on the third heartbeat, his voice a coarse growl that was even more menacing in the narrow, enclosed space. "But not too fast."

He took another slow step, and another. "The paintings. You stole them. Where are they?"

Oliver pushed himself off the wall, trying to find a footing, trying to project a confidence he absolutely did not feel. "I don't know ... what you're talking about," he gasped, the words punctuated by ragged breaths.

"Do not play stupid with me," Bojan said, his voice dropping even lower. He was 15 feet away now. "Maren, she trust you. She take you in. Like family. And you steal from her."

"Maren ... is not ... who you think she is," Oliver managed, his own voice sounding thin and weak against the man's stony certainty. "She's a manipulator. She ... she will use you, and then she will throw you away. Just like she does with everyone." He was trying to plant a seed of doubt, to find a crack in the man's armor.

Bojan stopped. He was 10 feet away. And then he did something Oliver didn't expect. He laughed. It was not a sound of humor. It was a harsh, bitter bark that scraped the air.

"You think you know her?" he said, shaking his head with a look of profound pity. "You know nothing."

He took one more step, closing the distance to just six feet. He was close enough now that Oliver could see the network of fine, white scars around his eyes, the dead, hollow quality of his stare.

"When I was young man in Serbia," Bojan said, his voice now a quiet, conversational monotone that was more chilling than a shout, "I watched men kick down door to my family farmhouse. I watched them murder my father. My mother. My little sister. I was hiding in cellar. I saw it all through crack in floorboard."

Oliver's own predicament, his own fear, seemed to shrink in the face of the man's bleak, unadorned horror.

"After," Bojan continued, his eyes looking through Oliver, at a memory a world away, "I was not man. I was animal. A weapon. I fight. I kill. I become mercenary because it was only thing that make sense. I was trying to die. But I was too good at my job. For years, I was on path of … of destruction. I wanted to burn whole world down to avenge what I lose."

He paused, and his gaze refocused, landing on Oliver with a new, unnerving intensity. "Then, on job in Germany, I meet Maren. I was … not well. She find me. She did not see animal. She saw man who was in great pain. She heal me. Not with medicine. With … understanding. She gave my life purpose again. Meaning. Everything I am, everything I have, is because of her."

The way he said her name, the almost religious reverence in his voice, spoke of a devotion that was absolute, unshakeable. It was a loyalty forged in the fires of a personal hell, a bond that Oliver's desperate accusations could never hope to scratch. Oliver saw a flicker of something else, too, a possessive, protective warmth that went beyond mere loyalty, but it was a depth he couldn't, and didn't want to, fathom.

Bojan's brief, narrative calm evaporated, his face hardening back into a mask of grim purpose. "So, you see, boy, I do not care what you think of her. You will tell me where is her property. Now."

Oliver's mind was blank. He was out of options. Out of breath. Out of time. A desperate, insane idea, a double-bluff born of pure panic, surfaced in his mind. He let out a short, incredulous laugh that sounded more like a sob.

"You want them?" he gasped, a wild, reckless look in his eyes. "You really want them? They're in my apartment. In New York. Under my bed. Go look."

Bojan stared at him, his pale eyes narrowing as he processed the statement. He considered it for a moment, then a slow, cold smile spread across his lips. "You think I am fool?" he said softly. "To fall for such a simple, kid trick?"

He took a step closer, and for the first time, Oliver saw the man's hands clench into tight, scarred fists. The air in the alley grew thick and heavy, charged with the imminent promise of violence. Oliver braced himself, knowing he stood absolutely no chance.

But the attack never came.

Over Bojan's broad shoulder, at the sunlit mouth of the alley, three new figures appeared. They didn't rush in. They simply materialized, three men standing shoulder-to-shoulder, blocking the only exit. To Oliver's utter incredulity, the man in the middle was the doorman from Daniela's uncle's building. The one who had politely turned him away without a meeting a couple of days earlier. He was now out of his uniform and dressed in a simple, dark polo shirt. The two men flanking him were of a similar age, both with the solid build and the calm, watchful eyes of men who had seen their share of the world's ugliness and were entirely unimpressed by it.

The doorman's gaze wasn't on Bojan. It was on Oliver. He offered a small, almost imperceptible nod.

"Señor Battolo," he called out, his voice a calm, steady baritone that cut through the charged stillness of the alley. "It is good to see you again. I hope I am not interrupting a private conversation."

The words were polite, almost mundane, but the undercurrent was as sharp and cold as a razor's edge. It was a statement of knowledge, a declaration of intent.

Bojan did not startle. He did not turn quickly. He simply let his clenched fists relax, the coiled energy in his body dissipating as he registered the new tactical reality. He slowly, deliberately, turned his head to look at the three men blocking his path. Oliver watched as a silent, professional assessment took place. It was a long, heavy moment where the two sides sized each other up, a negotiation conducted entirely through posture and gaze. Bojan, the lone wolf, against three men who stood with the easy, grounded confidence of a seasoned pack. No one moved.

Finally, Bojan turned his attention back to Oliver. The immediate, physical threat in his eyes was gone, replaced by a look of cold, professional appraisal. He had been outmaneuvered.

"It seems you have made some friends," he said, his voice low and gravelly. He took a single step back, a tactical withdrawal. "We finish this conversation another time, boy."

He then turned and walked slowly toward the mouth of the alley. He didn't look at the doorman or his friends as he passed them. He simply walked through the gap they created for him and disappeared back into the bright, bustling street, leaving Oliver alone in the alley with his mysterious saviors.

The three men approached, their movements calm and deliberate. The oppressive weight of the standoff was lifted, but the unanswered questions lingered. Oliver's heart was still a frantic drum against his ribs, and he leaned against the brick wall for support, his legs trembling.

The doorman was the one who spoke, his deep baritone now laced with a gentle concern. "Are you harmed, Señor Battolo?"

Oliver just shook his head, unable to form words.

"Good," the man said with a nod. He extended a hand. "My name is Javier. These are my friends, Diego and Agustín."

Oliver shook the offered hand. Javier's grip was firm, steady, the hand of a man who was completely in control. The other two men, Diego and Agustín, gave him curt, professional nods. They had the same quiet, capable demeanor as Javier.

"We served together," Javier explained, as if sensing Oliver's unasked question. "In the Army. Many years ago."

That explained the air of disciplined competence, the way they had taken control of the mouth of the alley without a single word. They were were a unit, not just friends.

"You are not safe at your hotel," Javier stated, his tone shifting from gentle concern to one of calm command. "That man, he knows where you are. He will return. It is not a question of if, but when."

Oliver's mind was still reeling, struggling to process the rapid, surreal turn of events. "I ... I don't understand," he stammered. "Who are you? Why are you helping me?"

Javier held his gaze, and for a moment, Oliver saw that same flicker of paternal knowing in his eyes that he'd seen at the apartment building. "A very good friend of your family would be ... disappointed in me if I did not," he said, the words chosen with a deliberate, careful ambiguity. "Let us just say I am returning an old favor."

The answer was a perfect riddle, a statement that explained everything and nothing at all. Oliver was too drained to press him further. The immediate, terrifying memory of Bojan's clenched fists was all the persuasion he needed.

"That man will not be a problem for tonight," Javier continued, his voice pulling Oliver back to the present. "But he is a professional. He will be back. When is your departure?"

"My flight ... it's early. The morning of the 10th," Oliver said.

Javier nodded, doing a quick mental calculation. "Okay. Two more nights. You cannot stay at the Cervantes. We will walk with you now. You will go to your room, pack your bags quickly, and then you will come with me. You can stay at my home. It is humble, but it is safe."

The offer was as stunning as the rescue itself. To be taken in by a complete stranger, a man who seemed to be a guardian angel sent from a world he didn't comprehend. He felt a brief surge of suspicion, but it was quickly extinguished by the sheer, undeniable fact that these men had just saved him from a very ugly fate. He looked from Javier's steady, reassuring face to his two imposing friends. He had no other choice.

"Okay," Oliver said, in a small voice, surrendering to this new, strange current in his life. "Okay."

"Good," Javier said. "Let us go. It is not wise to linger."

He gestured for Oliver to walk between him and Diego, with Agustín taking up the rear. They moved out of the alley and back into the bright afternoon sun, a strange, impromptu security detail escorting a bewildered young man through the historic streets of Montevideo. As they walked back toward the hotel, Oliver was no longer a man adrift. He was under protection. And yet, he felt completely in the dark.

779933 (March 8)

Javier's home was a humble but spotlessly clean apartment in a quiet, working-class neighborhood a few miles from the waterfront. The air inside smelled of garlic, roasting meat, and beeswax. The furniture was simple, old, and well-loved. A collection of framed family photos adorned the walls, a warm testament to a life well-lived. It was a home.

A woman with kind, smiling eyes and a shower of gray in her dark hair greeted them at the door. She embraced Javier, then turned to Oliver and gave him a warm, welcoming nod, speaking to him in a soft, musical Spanish he didn't understand.

"This is my wife, Maria," Javier said. "She does not speak English, but she says you are welcome in our house."

Maria led them to a small dining table, already set for five. Diego and Agustín, Javier's friends from the alley, were already there, nursing small glasses of red wine. They stood as Oliver entered, their presence filling the small room with a sense of quiet, protective strength.

Dinner was a simple, delicious affair. Maria brought out a large platter of *milanesa a la napolitana*, a breaded beef cutlet topped with a slice of ham, melted cheese, and a rich tomato sauce. It was the kind of hearty, unpretentious food a person could build a life on. For the first time in what felt like weeks, Oliver ate with a genuine appetite, the simple act of sharing a meal in a safe place a powerful balm for his frayed nerves.

The conversation was light at first. The men spoke in a mix of Spanish and English for Oliver's benefit, talking about football, the changing city, a shared memory that made them all laugh. Oliver mostly listened, a guest at a table where the bonds of history and loyalty were a palpable presence. He felt less like a man on a mission and more like a weary traveler who had stumbled into a sanctuary.

After the plates were cleared, Javier brought out a dark, unlabeled bottle and four small glasses. He poured a finger of a honey-colored, viscous liquid into each one.

"*Grappamiel,*" he said, pushing a glass toward Oliver. "A taste of our country. For digestion. And for conversation."

Oliver took a sip. It was potent, sweet and warming, a pleasant fire that spread through his chest. He felt comfortable enough now to ask a question that had been nagging at him. "Your English," he said, looking at Javier, then at his friends. "It's excellent. How?"

Javier smiled, a rare and genuine expression that reached his eyes. "We were fortunate. The Army sent the three of us to Fort Benning, in Georgia, for two years. A ... cultural exchange program." He used the official-sounding term with a hint of dry irony. "We learned many things. How to jump from a plane. How to survive in the jungle. And how to order a cheeseburger in a Southern accent."

Diego chuckled, a low rumble. "His accent was terrible."

"My English was better than your map-reading, my friend," Javier retorted good-naturedly, before his expression turned serious again as he looked at Oliver. "It was a long time ago. But you learn what you need to survive."

There was a brief lull in the conversation, as the three men seemed to wistfully relive those youthful days in America in their minds.

"My children," Javier said finally, breaking the silence as he looked at the liquid he was swirling in his glass. "They love this stuff when they visit. But they do not visit so often anymore."

"Where do they live?" Oliver asked politely.

"Both in your country," Javier said with a look of paternal pride. "My son, he is an engineer in Colorado. My daughter, a nurse in Texas. They have good lives. A good future." He took a sip of the grappamiel, his eyes distant for a moment. "We were very fortunate. A good friend ... a very generous man ... he opened doors for them that would have been closed to us. He believed in helping good people find their place in the world."

The hint, so ambiguous and yet so specific, hung in the air. This was his opening.

"Javier," Oliver said, leaning forward. "This friend ... was he a friend of my family? Was it my father? You recognized me at the apartment building. I know you did. Please, you have to tell me what your connection is."

Javier's kind expression didn't waver, but a gentle, impenetrable curtain came down behind his eyes. He took a slow sip of his drink before answering. "I told you, Señor Battolo. I am simply returning an old favor to a friend. That is all."

"What about Rafael Forlan?" Oliver pressed, his desperation returning. "Can I see him? I need to speak with him. I'm a friend of his niece, Daniela."

At the mention of her name, a genuine, warm smile lit up Javier's face. "Ah, Daniela. A wonderful girl. I have known her since she was a baby. She has her mother's fire." The warmth was real, but the curtain remained down. "I am sorry. As I said, he is not seeing anyone. It is not my place to ask why."

Oliver slumped back in his chair, the familiar sense of hitting a brick wall returning. He had been given sanctuary, but not answers. He was being protected, but he was still being kept at a distance. Resigned, he changed the subject.

"There's someone else, then," Oliver said, deciding to play his last, and now only, card. "The reason I came to Montevideo. I'm looking for an artist. A man named Luis Velázquez."

The name didn't seem to register with Javier or his friends. They looked at each other with blank expressions.

"I was told he lives here, in the city center, in a loft," Oliver continued, his hope beginning to wane. "He's a painter. A surrealist."

Javier, trying to be helpful, chimed in. "This is a city of many artists, Señor Battolo. Do you know which building? Which street?"

"I couldn't find an exact address," Oliver said, scrambling to remember the details from his research. "But the articles I found mentioned he worked out of a restored industrial building. The *Edificio ... Centenario*, I think it was called."

At the name of the building, Diego, the quieter of Javier's two friends, suddenly looked up, his eyes widening in surprise. He let out a short, incredulous laugh. He looked at Javier and then back at Oliver.

"The Edificio Centenario," he said, shaking his head in disbelief. "You are looking for someone in that building?"

Oliver stared at him. "Yes. Do you know it?"

"I know it," Diego said with a dry smile. "That is my post. I am the daytime doorman there. It is a quiet job. Mostly artists and architects."

Oliver couldn't believe his ears. The sheer, improbable coincidence of it all was staggering. It wasn't a coincidence, he thought to himself. It was a design. He was being guided. He had to be.

"Then you must know him," Oliver said, leaning forward, a new, sudden hope surging through him. "Luis Velázquez. The painter."

A look of recognition now dawned on Diego's face. "Ah, *that* one," he said with a knowing nod. "The recluse in the penthouse loft. Yes, I know him. Or, I know of him. He is a strange one. He does not go out for weeks at a time. And he never has visitors. Ever."

Javier spoke to Diego in a rapid, authoritative Spanish. Diego listened, nodded once, and then replied in Spanish before turning to Oliver.

"Javier says that the friend of his friend is a friend of ours," Diego said, a small smile playing on his lips. "I will be at my post tomorrow morning at nine. Velázquez usually comes down for the mail around ten. I will tell him a young man from New York is here, a man who has traveled a very long way to speak with him about art. I cannot promise he will see you. But I will make sure he hears the message."

Oliver felt a wave of gratitude and appreciation wash over him. He had been chasing a whisper, and now, in this humble apartment, surrounded by these quiet, capable men, he had finally been given a solid, tangible path forward.

He raised his glass of grappamiel. "Thank you," he said, looking at each of the three men in turn. "All of you."

Javier simply nodded, the kind, knowing look returning to his eyes. They finished their drinks, the quiet of the room feeling comfortable and safe, a sanctuary for the secrets they now held.

780007 (March 9)

The morning sun cast long, gentle shadows across the quiet residential streets as Oliver walked. He had slept a deep sleep on a comfortable pull-out sofa in Javier's living room, the protective presence of the family a better security system than any hotel lock. Now, walking toward the Edificio Centenario, he felt a clear, focused sense of purpose.

But his mind was still turning over a strange, fragmented memory from the night before.

He'd woken up around midnight, his head fuzzy from the potent *grappamiel*. As he'd made his way to the small bathroom, a low murmur had stopped him. A telephone was ringing in Javier's bedroom, and after a moment, he'd heard the sound of Javier's deep baritone, speaking in a hushed, urgent Spanish.

He knew he shouldn't listen, but he couldn't help it. The words were muffled by the old, thick wooden door, and his own mind was a hazy landscape of alcohol and deep weariness. He couldn't be sure if he was truly awake, or dreaming, or in some strange state in between. But he had heard a few distinct phrases.

The conversation had started with a name he recognized.

"*Sí, Señor Forlan,*" Javier had said, his tone one of respectful deference.

Forlan. So, he was talking to Rafael. The thought had solidified in Oliver's groggy mind, giving a clear context to the rest of the muffled conversation. Javier was reporting in to his employer.

Javier had listened for a moment, then his voice had become reassuring, calming the person on the other end of the line. Oliver had caught the words for "safe" and "tomorrow." And then, the single, clear phrase that had cut through the haze.

"*No se preocupe, Señor,*" Javier had said. "*Su hijo está a salvo conmigo.*"

Oliver had stood there in the dark hallway, the Spanish words bouncing around in his groggy mind. He'd taken four years of it in high school, a lifetime ago. He tried to piece it together, dredging up the dregs of his forgotten lessons. *Su hijo.* He knew *hijo* meant son, or more generally, child. But *Su* ...

was it "the" child? Or "your" child? The two short words, so similar in sound, warred in his memory.

Your child is safe with me.

The translation felt electric, impossible. Whose child? The thought was so absurd, so nonsensical, he immediately dismissed it. Besides, Daniela had told him her uncle Rafael was childless. It wouldn't make any sense for Javier to say *your son.* It had to be a mistake. A trick of his tired, alcohol-soaked brain.

El hijo. That had to be it. *The child. The child is safe with me.*

Yes, that made a strange kind of sense. He had just heard Javier speaking to Señor Forlan. Of course. Javier, the loyal doorman, was reporting to his employer that the strange American boy who had shown up on his doorstep was now secure. Oliver was "the child" in this scenario, a piece on a chessboard being discussed by the players. The thought was still unsettling, a confirmation that he was being managed by forces he didn't understand, but it was a logical, comprehensible kind of strange.

He pushed the memory away as he turned the final corner. He was here. The Edificio Centenario stood before him: a proud, industrial relic from another time, its large, factory-style windows gleaming in the morning sun. He had a mission. The whispers in the night would have to wait. He walked up to the grand, iron-gated entrance, his heart beginning to beat a little faster and prepared to meet the man who might hold the key to everything.

He pushed open the heavy iron-and-glass door and stepped into a lobby that was a stark contrast to the building's industrial exterior. The space was a cool, minimalist expanse of polished concrete and exposed brick, softened by large, exotic plants and a few pieces of striking modern sculpture. It felt less like a residential building and more like a private art gallery.

Diego was sitting behind a simple, elegant wooden desk, reading a newspaper. He looked up as Oliver entered, and a small, knowing smile touched his lips. He stood, his presence as solid and reassuring as it had been in Javier's apartment.

"Señor Battolo," he said in his low, rumbling voice. "Good morning. You are right on time."

"Diego," Oliver said, walking toward the desk. "Thank you for doing this."

"It is nothing," Diego said with a shrug. "I have told Señor Velázquez's assistant that you are here. He should be down for his mail shortly. It is almost ten. He is a man of ... routine. You can wait over there." He gestured to a low, leather sofa against the far wall.

Oliver sat, his nerves a thrumming live wire. He was here. After all the dead ends, the chase, the near-disaster with Bojan, he was finally just a few feet away from the man who might know the answers to all his questions. He watched the elevator doors at the far end of the lobby, his hands clasped so tightly his knuckles were white.

Fifteen minutes passed. Oliver's initial anticipation began to curdle into a familiar sense of dread. Maybe he wouldn't come down. Maybe he'd changed his routine.

Then, a soft *ding*.

The elevator doors slid open, and a man walked out. He was about 30, with a wild, untamed mane of dark, curly hair that looked like it hadn't seen a comb in weeks. He was dressed in paint-splattered jeans and a simple, threadbare gray T-shirt that hung loosely on his thin, wiry frame. His eyes, dark and intense, were scanning the small pile of letters on a table next to the elevator, and he moved with a kind of distracted, restless energy, a man whose mind was clearly a million miles away. This had to be him.

Diego rose from his desk and intercepted Velázquez before he could grab his mail. He began to speak in a low, respectful Spanish, gesturing discreetly in Oliver's direction.

Velázquez looked over at Oliver, his intense gaze sweeping over him for a fraction of a second. His expression was one of unvarnished annoyance. He immediately shook his head vigorously, a flurry of dark curls, and replied to Diego with a short, sharp burst of Spanish that Oliver didn't need to understand to know was a definitive "no." He snatched his mail from the table, turned his back on them both, and started walking quickly back toward the elevator.

Diego turned to Oliver and gave him a helpless, apologetic shrug.

Oliver's heart sank. He had come so far, survived so much, only to be dismissed without a single word. He watched Velázquez stab the 'up' button for the elevator, his one and only chance about to disappear behind a set of closing doors.

He couldn't let it happen.

He shot up from the sofa, a surge of desperate resolve overriding all his instincts for polite deference. "Mr. Velázquez!" he called out, his voice sharp and loud in the quiet lobby.

Velázquez didn't stop. He didn't even turn around.

Oliver ran across the polished concrete floor, closing the distance just as the elevator arrived with another soft *ding*. He reached him just as he was about to step inside.

"Please," Oliver said, his voice now a desperate plea. "Just five minutes of your time. I've come all the way from New York to speak with you."

Velázquez finally turned to face him, his dark eyes blazing with an aristocratic impatience. "I do not know you," he said, his English perfect, crisp and tinged with the soft, melodic accent of the Uruguayan upper class. "And I have nothing to say to you. I am very busy. Now, if you will excuse me." He stepped around Oliver and into the elevator.

In a last, desperate gambit, Oliver blurted out the only words he had left, the one secret he possessed. "The six spirals," he said, his voice low and intense. "I know about the double triskelions in the Bryce paintings."

Velázquez froze, his hand hovering over the elevator button. He turned back to Oliver slowly; his entire demeanor changed. The impatient annoyance was gone, replaced by a look of unnerved shock. He stared at Oliver, his eyes wide, as if seeing him for the first time.

"What did you just say?" he whispered, his voice barely audible.

"The patterns," Oliver pressed, his confidence surging as he saw the crack in the man's armor. "The ones hidden beneath the paint. I know about them."

Velázquez continued to stare at him for a long, heavy moment, a silent, internal battle seemingly playing out across his features. The elevator doors began to slide shut. He ignored them. Finally, with a look of deep, grudging resignation, he let out a long, weary sigh.

"Who are you?" he asked, his voice now a low murmur.

"My name is Oliver Battolo. And I think you know what I'm here to talk about."

Velázquez looked from Oliver to Diego, who was watching the entire exchange with a look of quiet astonishment. He looked back at Oliver, his eyes full of a new, wary calculation. The reclusive artist had just been confronted with a ghost from a past he thought was buried.

"Follow me," he said, the words clipped and final. He turned and pressed the button, and the elevator doors slid open once again. He stepped inside without looking back, a clear, unspoken command. Oliver, his heart pounding with a mixture of terror and triumph, followed him in.

The doors slid shut, enclosing them in a small, silent, rising box. The only sound was the soft whir of the elevator's machinery. Oliver stood stiffly, his mind racing, acutely aware of the man standing a few feet away from him. Velázquez didn't look at him. He just stared at the floor indicator, his expression a mask of cool neutrality, as if inviting a complete stranger who had just accosted him in his lobby up to his private penthouse was a perfectly normal, everyday occurrence.

The elevator opened directly into the apartment.

Oliver stepped out and his breath caught in his throat. The space was astonishing. It was a massive, double-height loft, a sprawling expanse of polished concrete floors and exposed brick walls, with a soaring, twenty-foot ceiling crisscrossed by old, industrial steel beams. One entire wall was a massive, floor-to-ceiling window that offered a breathtaking, panoramic view of the Rambla and the vast, silver expanse of the Río de la Plata.

The sheer scale of it reminded him of Steve and Reza's place on the Upper West Side, but the aesthetic was completely different. Where their home was a curated collection of warm, antique luxury, this was a space of cool, industrial grandeur. It was old money, but it was the money of a man who valued space and light over clutter and comfort. The furniture was sparse and modern – a single, massive leather sofa, a few minimalist chairs – leaving the art to command the room. And the art was everywhere. Huge, challenging canvases hung on the walls while strange, beautiful sculptures occupied the corners. It was a home that was also a temple.

"Please," Velázquez said, his voice pulling Oliver from his reverie. "Call me Luis." He gestured vaguely toward the living area. "Can I offer you something to drink? Sparkling water? A whisky?"

"Sparkling water would be great, thank you," Oliver said, his voice sounding small in the vast space.

Luis nodded and began to walk toward a stunning, state-of-the-art kitchen at the far end of the loft. "Follow me."

Oliver walked behind him, his boots making soft, tapping sounds on the polished concrete. They passed by what was clearly Luis's current workspace. Seven enormous canvases, each at least six feet tall, were lined up in a row, resting on heavy easels. The floor around them was a Jackson Pollock of paint splatters, and the air was thick with the sharp, clean scent of turpentine and oil.

Luis noticed Oliver looking. He stopped. "My current obsession," he said, his voice flat, offering no further explanation.

Oliver stared at the paintings, and an eerie sense of temporal vertigo washed over him, a feeling so intense it made him dizzy. He wasn't just looking at a series of paintings. He was looking at a memory. A projection episode from almost a year ago.

It was all there, exactly as he had seen it in that impossible art fair with the Noncemeister disguised as Jonathan Bryce. Seven large canvases, each with an authoritative black background. At the center of each, a massive, hyper-realistic block of white marble, expertly textured and detailed. He saw the full progression, just as the Noncemeister-playing-Bryce had described it. The first block was pristine, its sharp edges a symbol of eager, youthful potential. The subsequent blocks showed a slow, inexorable decay – a chip here, a crack there – a stoic detachment setting in. And the final block, a crumbling, weathered ruin, its form almost lost to entropy, a perfect portrait of apathetic nihilism.

"The progression of human desire over a lifetime," the Noncemeister-Bryce had said in that projection episode.

Seeing them here, in the real world, in the artist's own studio, was a confirmation so shocking it shook him to his core. The projections weren't just dreams or hallucinations. They were real. They were previews of a reality that already existed, waiting for him to catch up.

"It's the Marble Series," Oliver said, the words coming out in a reverent whisper.

Luis turned to him, a flicker of surprise in his dark, intense eyes. "You know my work?"

"I ... I saw a study for it," Oliver stammered, catching himself before he could say he'd seen the finished product in a conversation with a disembodied, decades-old consciousness of a dead surrealist painter. "A long time ago. I never forgot it."

Luis somehow seemed to accept that Oliver would have heard about his current unpublished work. He gave a single, curt nod and then continued on to the kitchen as if nothing had happened. Oliver followed, his mind reeling. He was trying to reconcile the memory of a mystical vision with the solid, tangible reality of the paint and canvas in front of him. The two worlds, the one behind his eyes and the one in front of them, were beginning to bleed into one another, and the feeling was both terrifying and deeply validating. He was on the right path. He had to be.

Luis led him into a kitchen that was a masterpiece of minimalist design. Sleek, handleless cabinets made of some dark, matte material, a massive island carved from a single slab of gray stone, and a bank of futuristic-looking appliances that were seamlessly integrated into the wall. It was the kind of kitchen that probably cost more than his entire apartment in Chelsea.

Luis took two tall, elegant glasses from a cabinet and filled them with sparkling water from a built-in dispenser, the hiss of the carbonation the only sound in the vast, quiet loft. He handed one to Oliver.

"Let us sit," he said, gesturing with his glass toward the living area.

They sat on the massive leather sofa, a football field of space between them. Luis didn't relax. He sat on the edge of the cushion, his posture tense and alert, and he fixed Oliver with his dark, intense gaze. The brief, almost human moment of the artist showing his work was over.

"Before we speak of Bryce," Luis began, his voice a cool, level instrument of inquiry, "you will tell me who you are. And you will tell me how you know of a secret ... the spirals – that has been buried for decades. The man at the door said you traveled from New York. That is a long way to go to discuss a dead painter. Are you a thief? Do you work for the government? You will answer me."

The questions were direct, surgical, leaving no room for evasion. Oliver's heart began to pound again, a slow, heavy rhythm against his ribs. He took a sip of the sparkling water, the crisp bubbles a small, sharp shock that helped to focus his mind. He knew this was the moment. He had to deliver a version of the truth that was just plausible enough to be believed.

"My name is Oliver Battolo," he began, his voice steady, much to his own surprise. "And I am not a thief. Or a cop. I'm just … the son of a man who was, I'm now realizing, far more complex than I ever knew."

He looked at Luis, trying to convey a genuine bewilderment that wasn't hard to summon. "My father passed away last year. He … he left me a key. A key to a storage unit. I had no idea what it was for. When I finally got inside, I found them. The second and third Bryce paintings. *The Toddler* and *It Is Time*."

He watched Luis's face for a reaction. The man's expression remained a perfect, unreadable mask, but Oliver saw a flicker deep in his dark eyes, a momentary slip of his otherwise stoic composure. He had his attention.

"My father," Oliver continued, the story taking shape as he spoke, a mixture of calculated truth and necessary omission, "was an admirer of Bryce's. An obsessive, I think. He was a private, wealthy man, and he acquired them years ago through … let's just say unconventional means. He never told my mother. He never told me. They were his secret. And now, they're mine."

He paused, letting the weight of the confession settle in the vast, quiet room.

"I didn't know about the spirals at first," he said, leaning forward. "I thought they were just paintings. But then I found them, by accident. A trick of the light. And I knew they meant something. I started digging, and my research led me to your mentor, Kaminsky, and then to you. I came here because I think you are the only person on Earth who can tell me what they mean."

He finished, his story hanging in the air between them. It was a wild, improbable tale, but it had the distinct advantage of being mostly true. He had simply replaced the Noncemeister with "research" and his father's secret life as a cypherpunk with the more palatable "unconventional means."

Luis was silent for a long time, his intense gaze fixed on Oliver, analyzing him, weighing his words. Oliver felt like a specimen under a microscope. He could see the man's mind at work, turning over the pieces of the story, looking for the cracks.

"Your father," Luis said finally. "What was his name?"

"Nate. Nate Battolo."

Luis nodded slowly, as if filing the name away. He took a slow, deliberate sip of his water, his eyes never leaving Oliver's. He didn't believe him, not entirely. But Oliver could see that the story, in all its strange specificity, was too bizarre to be a simple fabrication. The mention of the specific paintings, of Kaminsky, of the spirals themselves ... these were not the words of a common thief or a government agent.

"You are either an exceptionally gifted liar, Señor Battolo," Luis said, a hint of something that might have been grudging respect in his voice, "or you are the heir to a very magnificent and very dangerous secret."

He stood up and walked over to the massive wall of windows, staring out at the silver river below. "I do not yet know which it is," he said, his back to Oliver. "But my curiosity ... my curiosity now outweighs my suspicion."

Luis continued staring out of the window, at the city bathed in the golden light of late summer. "The light is changing," he said, more to himself than to Oliver. "Summer is a fever. A time of frantic creation. It burns hot."

He turned from the window, his gaze distant and thoughtful.

"I am looking forward to the atonement of the Fall," he said, the words carrying a quiet, melancholic weight. "A time for things to settle. For accounts to be made right."

The statement was strange and poetic, and Oliver wasn't sure what to make of it, but he filed it away. Luis seemed to shake himself from his reverie, his focus returning to the matter at hand, his expression shifting back to that of a reluctant lecturer.

"Now," he said, turning fully to face Oliver. "The Hexcelion."

The word was alien to Oliver, a strange, technical term that meant nothing to him. He had come here to ask about the spirals, about Bryce, about a pattern he couldn't comprehend. Was this a diversion? A test?

"I'm sorry," Oliver said, his voice cautious. "A what? A Hexcelion?"

Luis turned from the window, a flicker of genuine surprise in his eyes. It was the first unguarded expression Oliver had seen on his face. "You do not know the name of the shape you came all the way here from America to ask me about?" he asked, a note of academic disbelief in his voice.

"I've been calling it a double triskelion," Oliver admitted, feeling a fresh wave of his own inadequacy.

A small, dry chuckle escaped Luis's lips. He walked over to a large, flat-file cabinet against one of the brick walls, pulled open a wide, shallow drawer, and retrieved a large, leather-bound sketchbook and a charcoal pencil.

"The shape you have seen," he said, returning to the sofa but sitting on the large coffee table in front of Oliver now, flipping the sketchbook open to a clean page. "The six spirals. That is the Hexcelion."

Hex.

The prefix hit Oliver with the force of a simple, obvious truth he couldn't believe he had missed. *Hexa.* Six. Not a "double three." A single, unified entity of six. The name itself was a revelation.

"To understand the Hexcelion," Luis began, his entire demeanor shifting. The wary, reclusive artist was gone, replaced by an energetic, obsessive lecturer, a man finally given the chance to speak on the one subject that consumed him. He sketched a perfect, three-armed spiral with a few deft strokes of the charcoal.

"You know the triskelion," he stated, not as a question. "It is a one-dimensional object. A single, unbroken line." He traced the path of the charcoal with his finger. "But by curving it in three distinct, symmetrical paths, it creates the illusion of motion. It implies and organizes a two-dimensional space. It is a 1D key that unlocks a 2D door."

Oliver watched, captivated, as Luis spoke, his hands moving with an artist's grace, the charcoal a natural extension of his thoughts.

"The Hexcelion," he continued, turning to a new page, "operates on a higher dimension. It is a two-dimensional pattern." He began to sketch the familiar, intricate six-spiraled shape, his hand moving with a speed and certainty that spoke of a lifetime of practice. "But its true purpose is not to be drawn on a flat surface like this."

He put the sketchbook down and looked around the room, his eyes searching for something. He spotted a small, perfect, white marble sphere on a bookshelf, a purely decorative object. He picked it up and returned, holding the cool, heavy sphere in his palm.

"Its true canvas," he said, his voice dropping to an intense whisper, "is three-dimensional. When you inscribe this 2D pattern onto the surface of a sphere, it ... changes things. It creates a focal point. A place where the geometry of our reality becomes ... pliable. The six spirals act like a lens, focusing unseen energies and warping the very fabric of the space they occupy."

He held the marble sphere out for Oliver to see, his thumb tracing an imaginary six-spiraled path across its smooth, white surface.

"A triskelion organizes the second dimension. The Hexcelion ... the Hexcelion organizes the third."

Oliver stared at the simple, white ball in Luis's hand, his mind struggling to grasp the cosmic, almost terrifying implications. The patterns on the Bryce paintings were not just symbols. They were diagrams. Schematics for a machine that could bend reality. The thought was so immense, so far beyond the scope of anything he had ever considered, that he felt a wave of dizziness.

His mind flashed back to the street corner outside McGinn's. To the grimy shard of glass, the flickering projection on the brick wall, and the man who had conjured it.

"This shape ..." Oliver said, softly. "I didn't just see it on the paintings. A homeless man in New York ... he drew it for me on the sidewalk. He created it with a piece of a broken bottle and the sunlight. How is that possible? How could *he* know about this?"

Luis's expression was a mixture of intrigue and deep skepticism. He placed the marble sphere carefully back on its stand on the bookshelf. "That is ... interesting," he said, his tone making it clear he found it anything but interesting. "But you must understand, Señor Battolo. This is not a simple magic trick. What your street prophet showed you was a parlor trick, most likely a hollow shell of the real principle." He gestured to the marble sphere. "If I were to inscribe the Hexcelion on this marble right now, it would do nothing. It would remain a beautiful but inert pattern. The effect you are seeking ... it only occurs under a very specific and very rare set of conditions."

Oliver felt his breath catch in his throat. He was on the precipice now, the final door waiting to be unlocked. He leaned forward, his voice a barely-controlled whisper. "What conditions? What does it need?"

Luis was quiet for a long moment. He walked back to the great window and stared out at the city, as if weighing the consequences of what he was about to say. The reclusive artist was at war with the guardian of a great secret. Finally, the guardian won.

"It needs a specific place," he said, still looking out the window. "A resonant chamber, precisely engineered to amplify a specific frequency of light. And it needs a focusing lens."

"A lens?"

Luis turned back to face him, his eyes dark with the weight of the knowledge he carried. "A celestial orb. A sphere of polished obsidian and silver, suspended in the center of the chamber.

"The final condition," Luis continued, "is a catalyst. A specific celestial alignment. The chamber was built with a single, hidden aperture. Once a year, for only a few minutes, exactly twenty-seven days after the winter solstice, a beam of direct sunlight penetrates the chamber and strikes the orb at a precise angle. That is the moment the Hexcelion is formed. Not as a drawing, but as a three-dimensional lattice of pure, structured light. That is the moment the geometry of reality becomes ... pliable."

Winter solstice. The phrase snagged in Oliver's mind.

"When?" Oliver asked, his heart pounding. "When is twenty-seven days after winter solstice here?"

Luis gave him a look that was almost pitying. "In the Southern Hemisphere? It is in the middle of your summer. It is a national holiday here. The day our first constitution was sworn in."

The pieces of the puzzle, scattered across continents and time, across the timechain and the walls of a grimy pub, suddenly slammed together in Oliver's mind with the force of a physical blow.

Obelisk, 18 July. It has happened.

The OP_RETURN message. The poster in the café. The monument he had stood before just days ago. It was all one and the same. A summons. A fated appointment.

He had thought this trip, this frantic, one-week dash to Montevideo, was the final leg of his journey. But he saw it now. It was only the beginning.

It was a reconnaissance mission. He had been sent here to learn the rules of engagement, to understand the nature of the battlefield, before the real event.

He had to come back. In four months, he had to be standing in that chamber.

The thought was so absolute, so definitive, it momentarily silenced all others. He looked at Luis, who was watching him with a new, intense curiosity, the look of a scientist who has just seen his theoretical model come to life.

"This chamber," Oliver said, in a low, urgent voice as he fought off the eerie feeling of knowing the answer to the question he was about to ask. "This special place you mentioned. Where is it?"

Luis hesitated for a moment, the guardian of the secret making one last stand. But he had already revealed too much. The final lock had to be turned.

"It is not a place you can simply walk into," he said. "It is hidden. Protected. It is in a castle, just outside the city, in Piriápolis. They called the chamber the *Camara del Tiempo*."

The Chamber of Time. When the words landed, they were exactly what Oliver foreshadowed them to be. And yet, he couldn't believe it. The place that kept reappearing in his projection episodes. The one where the Noncemeister had taken him. The one where he met the alchemist from almost a century ago. So, this was its significance. It was the place where the Hexcelion came to life on July 18. His most recent projection episode there had shown the homeless man's spinning glass shard spiral ... that must have been the Hexcelion! Daniela had told him it was most probably a myth, but Luis's words made it seem undeniably real.

Oliver was struggling to contain himself in light of all these new revelations. "And the orb?" he asked, once he was able to emerge from his emotions somewhat. "What did you call it?"

"The *Turabet es ploe dieu* – the celestial orb," Luis replied, the strange, melodic words sounding both ancient and alien.

The phrase hit Oliver with the force of a thunderbolt, a sucker punch of recognition so powerful it made him gasp. It was the sound, not the meaning. The absurd cadence of it. He was transported back almost a year, to one of his very early encounters with the Noncemeister in the deep purple of the timechain. The goofy, egg-headed entity, dancing a jig, singing a nonsensical verse.

Two rabbits exploded, a line oddly worded …

Two rabbits exploded. Turabet es ploe dieu. The phonetics were a near-perfect match. Had he misheard it back then? Or was it the Noncemeister being his typical obtuse self with an idiotic transliteration of the phrase Luis had just uttered? Oliver briefly burst into a fit of laughter at the absurdity of the situation. As before, the answer had been in *noncense.*

"What is it?" Luis asked, startled by Oliver's sudden, strange reaction.

"That phrase …" Oliver said, gathering himself. "*Turabet es ploe dieu.* What language is that? It's not Spanish. And it doesn't sound quite like Latin."

Luis looked at him, his dark eyes narrowing with a new and deeper level of inquiry. "Why do you ask?"

"I've heard it before," Oliver said, the confession feeling both insane and necessary. "Or something that sounds like it."

Luis stood up and began to pace the length of the massive window, a restless, caged energy radiating from him.

"The language," he began, his voice taking on the careful, measured tone of a historian treading on the edge of myth, "is what my great-grandfather referred to in his journals as Atlantean."

"Atlantean?" Oliver repeated, the word tasting of fantasy and fiction. "As in … Atlantis?"

"As in the myth, yes," Luis confirmed. "It is not a recognized language, of course. There is no proof it ever existed. But according to the tradition my family has preserved, it was the tongue of a lost civilization, a language not just for describing reality, but for shaping it. My great-grandfather believed he had rediscovered fragments of it, hidden in obscure alchemical texts and encoded in the geometric patterns of ancient sites."

He stopped pacing and turned to face Oliver. "It is a language of pure concept. Very few people have ever heard it spoken. The fact that you have … it is significant."

Oliver's mind was a whirlwind. Atlantean. He thought of Anariadne, of her strange, broken grammar and her beautiful, alien phrases. *Ego viliye in claritate lumiere.* Could that have been Atlantean, too? No, the thought was too far-fetched, a leap too great even for his new reality. He pushed it away.

"So, this tradition," Oliver said, pulling himself back to the present, latching onto something curious Luis had just said about his great-grandfather and alchemy. "This knowledge of the Hexcelion, of this lost language ... how was your family involved with it?"

Luis's energetic, academic demeanor softened. The lecturer receded, and what was left was a man burdened by a legacy he had not chosen. He walked over to a tall, dark-wood bookshelf that was filled not with art books, but with ancient, leather-bound volumes. He ran his fingers along their spines.

"It is not an involvement one chooses, Señor Battolo," he said, his voice now quiet and melancholic. "It is an inheritance. A magnificent burden. For generations, my family has been the guardian of these secrets. Not just the knowledge, but the place itself."

He turned back to Oliver, a deep weariness in his dark eyes. "I use my mother's name, Velázquez, for my art. It gives me a small measure of freedom, a space to be my own man. But I cannot escape the name I was born with."

He paused, letting the statement hang in the vast, quiet loft. The air grew heavy with the weight of an unspoken history.

"The man who built the *Camara del Tiempo*," Luis said, his voice barely a whisper. "The alchemist who spent his life trying to understand the principles of the Hexcelion and beyond, who rediscovered and translated the Atlantean fragments ... he was not just an alchemist. He was my great-grandfather. His name was Esteban Pittamiglio."

The name, spoken aloud, seemed to change the very air in the room. It was the name of the man Oliver had met in a projection, the man who had told him that *Camara del Tiempo* was a Schelling-point in timespace. The man who had given him the strange mantra: *ex igne tempus nascitur*, which Oliver had assumed was Latin, but was now realizing was likely Atlantean. A man who should have been nothing more than a historical footnote, a ghost from a century ago.

"My full name," Luis continued, the final lock turning, the final door swinging open, "is Luis Velázquez Pittamiglio."

Oliver felt the floor drop away from him for what felt like the tenth time that day. The last vestiges of his old, rational world crumbled into dust. The vertigo was so intense he had to grip the arm of the sofa to steady himself.

He had not just stumbled upon an expert. He had not just found a fellow traveler in this strange, hidden world. He had been led, by some impossible, unseen hand, across continents and through time, to the living heir of the entire mystery. The man who had welcomed him into this loft was the direct descendant of the alchemist he had spoken to in a vision. The blood of the man who built the machine flowed in the veins of the man who was now explaining it to him.

It was a design. A beautiful, terrifying, and perfect design. He saw it now. His father's quest and his own were not just parallel paths; they were a single, unbroken line, a legacy of secrets passed down through generations, a conversation between fathers and sons that transcended even this mortal coil.

He looked at Luis, who was watching him not with suspicion anymore, but with a look of deep, shared understanding, the look of one prisoner recognizing another in a beautiful, gilded cage.

"So, you see, Señor Battolo," Luis said, his voice soft with a strange, sad empathy. "You are not the only one haunted by the legacy of a man you can no longer speak to. Welcome to the club."

CHAPTER 6. MARCH 21

For three days, Nick had been a different kind of hunter. The quarry was no longer a string of data on the blockchain, but a person. He had temporarily abandoned the cold, clean certainty of on-chain analysis for the messy, imprecise and deeply human world of open-source intelligence. The target: Adele van der Dussen.

His sterile cubicle at The Grid was now papered with corporate filings, press clippings and legal documents. He'd spent hours sifting through the digital detritus of Christiaan van der Dussen's life, looking for the one, solid link to his sister. A clear doorway that would allow him to connect with her. He found her name listed as the director of a family trust in Cape Town, South Africa. He found a transcript from a 2018 interview she gave to a Dutch financial newspaper, fiercely defending her brother's character. And finally, after cross-referencing court dockets from Christiaan's appeal, he found the prize: the name of the high-powered D.C. law firm that had been representing the van der Dussen family's interests for years. *Kincaid, Strauss, & Abernathy*.

He stared at the firm's website. It was a monument to old-world power, all mahogany tones and pictures of stern-looking men with impressive resumes. The lead counsel on the van der Dussen file was a man named Julian Croft, a senior partner whose biography was a laundry list of Ivy League degrees and high-profile victories. This was the front door. And Nick was about to try and kick it down.

He picked up his burner phone, took a deep breath, and dialed the number for the firm's Washington, D.C. office.

"Kincaid, Strauss, and Abernathy, how may I direct your call?" The voice on the other end was a crisp, professional soprano, the sound of expensive efficiency.

"I'd like to speak with Julian Croft, please," Nick said, his own voice sounding rough and unpolished by comparison.

"And may I ask who is calling?"

"My name is Nicholas Hernandez. I'm an independent security consultant." The title was a fiction, but it sounded better than 'disgraced and unemployed.'

"Regarding what matter, Mr. Hernandez?"

"It concerns the Christiaan van der Dussen case. I have some new information that is highly relevant and time-sensitive." He was projecting an authority he did not feel, a confidence born of pure desperation.

"One moment, please."

He was placed on hold. The music was not the dying calliope of the DoJ, but a tasteful, subdued piece of classical Vivaldi. It was, in its own way, even more intimidating. After a full minute, a new voice came on the line. It was male, sharp, and impatient.

"This is David Chen, Mr. Croft's junior associate. Julian is in court this morning. How can I help you?"

The gatekeeper. Nick knew he wouldn't get to Croft directly, not on the first try.

"Mr. Chen," Nick began, shifting to a more collaborative tone. "As I told the receptionist, I have some new information regarding the van der Dussen case. Specifically, it relates to the activities of the third associate in the MixMarket indictment."

"Sazsa," Chen said, the name a flat, dead thing. "We are aware of him. The government's case on that front is nonexistent."

"That's because their analysis was incomplete," Nick pressed, his heart starting to beat a little faster. "I've been conducting an independent review of the on-chain data. I've isolated a unique transaction signature that I have tied, with a high degree of confidence, to Sazsa's activity. It re-contextualizes his role in the entire operation, potentially exonerating Christiaan."

He was laying out his best cards, trying to sound like a credible, professional peer. He was offering them a gift, a new angle for Christiaan's defense.

There was a short pause on the other end of the line. For a fleeting, hopeful moment, Nick thought he had him.

"Did you say your name was Nicholas Hernandez?" Chen asked coldly.

"Yes," Nick replied, still clinging to the hope that he had a foot in the door.

He heard the distinct sounds of a computer keyboard being clicked from the other end of the line, and then a little more distant sound of a mouse pinwheel being turned. Chen appeared to be reading something on his screen.

"Mr. Hernandez," Chen finally said, after what felt like a very long minute. His voice was now stripped of all professional courtesy, replaced by a cold, reptilian flatness. "Are you now, or have you ever been, an employee of the firm Chain Intelligence?"

The question hit Nick like a punch to the gut. He had been so focused on his new identity as a rogue agent that he had forgotten about the long, incriminating shadow of his old one.

"I ... my employment there ended recently," he stammered.

"I see," Chen said, the two words dripping with condescension. "So, you are the individual whose ..." he appeared to pause and read something on his screen. He continued, "... whose 'computationally unsound' analysis led to the farcical pursuit of a jute salesman in Dubai. Yes, we are familiar with your work."

The humiliation was a fresh, hot slap across his face. Of course, they knew. A firm like this would have done its due diligence, would have back-channeled with the DoJ, would have a complete file on the entire embarrassing episode. He was a disgraced vendor they had already investigated and dismissed.

"That was a preliminary finding, based on a flawed model," Nick said, trying to recover. "My new work is independent. It's based on a more rigorous, manual analysis."

"Mr. Hernandez," Chen cut him off, his voice now sharp and final. "Let me be very clear. This firm has no interest in you or your 'independent analysis.' Ms. van der Dussen has been harassed by countless opportunists, cranks and conspiracy theorists over the years. We have a zero-contact policy regarding unsolicited information. If you attempt to contact Ms. van der Dussen, this office or any person associated with this case again, we will not hesitate to file for a restraining order and pursue all available legal remedies for harassment. Do I make myself clear?"

The threat was absolute – a perfect, legalistic wall slammed down in his face. There was no room for negotiation, no possibility of appeal.

"Yes," Nick said, the word a small, defeated thing.

"Good day, Mr. Hernandez."

The line went dead.

Nick slowly lowered the phone and placed it on his desk. He had tried the front door, and it had been barricaded, electrified and surrounded by a moat full of lawyers. He stared at the name on his evidence board. *Adele van der Dussen*. The professional approach had failed spectacularly. If he was going to get to her, he would have to find another way in. A back door. A secret passage. And he would have to do it without leaving any fingerprints.

780354 (March 11)

The yellow taxi rattled as its wheels passed over the steel grid of the Manhattan Bridge, the rhythmic *thump-thump-thump* a familiar, grounding sound after days of foreign transit. Oliver stared absently out the window, his gaze fixed on the iconic skyline emerging from the late afternoon haze. The Empire State Building, the Chrysler, the new, impossibly thin supertalls – they were all there, a forest of silent glass and stone sentinels welcoming him home. But the city felt different now. Or maybe, he was.

His mind was a landscape of fragmented memories from the past week, a surreal collage of images and sensations. He saw Javier's kind, craggy face in the pre-dawn darkness of the Montevideo airport, the older man having insisted on driving him there at 3 a.m. for his flight. There had been no grand parting words, just a firm handshake and a simple, "Be safe, Señor Battolo." A quiet, paternal blessing from a man he still barely knew.

The long journey back had been a merciful blur. The layovers in São Paulo and Madrid had been blessedly short this time, just two hours each, a mad dash from one gate to another. With every boarding pass scanned, every new plane he stepped onto, he had braced himself, scanning the faces in the crowd for a burly, navy sports jacket and a pair of cold, pale eyes. But Bojan was nowhere. The absence of the threat was a relief so profound it was almost a physical presence in itself.

He had the answers. Or at least, the beginning of them. The name Luis had given to the six-spiraled shape echoed in his mind. The *Hexcelion*. A two-dimensional key to a three-dimensional lock. He saw the strange, melodic words for the celestial orb – *Turabet es ploe dieu* – and felt the phantom jolt yet again of recognizing the Noncemeister's absurd wordplay. And behind it all, the myth of a lost language, of Atlantean, a tongue not just for describing reality, but for shaping it. The revelations felt less like clues in a puzzle and more like chapters from a forgotten book of physics. He had traveled to the end of the world to find a man and had instead been given a glimpse of a different universe.

But the awe was fragile, easily fractured by the sharp edges of his new reality. He was home now, back in a known location. A place where he was findable. Bojan had said he would "continue their conversation." He knew where he lived – it was only a matter of time before he returned.

And then there was the final, unsettling riddle of Javier himself. The memory of the muffled, late-night phone call had replayed in his mind a dozen times over the Atlantic. *Su hijo está a salvo conmigo.* He'd spent hours on the plane turning the phrase over and over, trying to force his rusty high school Spanish to yield a different, less startling translation. *Your child is safe with me.* It was impossible. It had to be a mistake, a misinterpretation born of weariness and too much grappamiel. *El hijo. The child.* That was the only thing that made sense. He was the child, the asset, being discussed by his handler and his employer. It was the only logical explanation. And yet, the memory of the two small words, *su hijo*, refused to be completely dismissed, a splinter of impossibility lodged deep in his mind.

The taxi descended from the bridge, plunging into the loud, vibrant streets of Chinatown. The sudden immersion in the familiar energy of the city pulled him from his thoughts. The rest of the ride passed in a daze, and before he knew it, the taxi was pulling up to the curb in front of his building on 19th and 10th.

He paid the driver, got out, and pulled his battered suitcase onto the sidewalk. He was home. The thought brought a wave of weary relief. He was just about to head for the entrance when he saw him.

Leaning against the black iron fence of the adjacent building, almost blending into the afternoon shadows, was the homeless man.

Oliver froze, his suitcase handle gripped tight in his hand. It wasn't a coincidence. It couldn't be. This man was a marker on Oliver's path, a signpost that appeared only at moments of transition. He had been there after the New Year's Eve meltdown, on the street in Harlem, outside McGinn's pub and now here, waiting for him upon his return.

This time, Oliver wasn't just confused or afraid. He was armed with new knowledge. He had a key.

He left his suitcase on the sidewalk and strode toward the man, his steps full of a new, urgent purpose. "You," he said, his voice low and intense. "The shape you drew. The light from the glass. I know what it's called now. The Hexcelion. How did you know?"

The man looked up, his pale, cloudy eyes focusing on Oliver. He offered his familiar, toothless and slightly deranged grin. "*Hessele tu rabe,*" he rasped, the words a familiar, garbled mess.

But this time, Oliver heard it differently. He was listening for a signal. The memory of Luis Velázquez's crisp pronunciation echoed in his mind. *Turabet es ploe dieu.* He replayed the homeless man's slurred words in his head. *Hessele … Hexcelion. Tu rabe … Turabet.*

It clicked. A stunning, electrifying moment of clarity. This man was naming the *orb*.

"The Turabet," Oliver said, his voice a reverent whisper. "You were telling me its name."

The man stared past Oliver, wild-eyed.

"What else?" Oliver pressed, his excitement mounting. He tried to catch the man's lost gaze. He felt he was on the verge of a monumental breakthrough. "What else can you tell me?"

The homeless man leaned in, as if to share a great secret, his foul breath washing over Oliver. "*Ess temper, eh innit? N'as it, ser!*" he whispered, his eyes glinting with a strange, manic light.

Oliver listened intently, trying to parse the phrase. He recognized it – the homeless man had gurgled it on every one of their encounters. But the slurred, broken sounds were just beyond his grasp. He couldn't decipher it. And then, a new, even more profound realization began to dawn on him. This wasn't just gibberish. It was a language. A broken, slurred, street-level dialect of the same ancient, mythical tongue Luis had told him about.

"You're speaking Atlantean," he said, the words feeling insane even as he uttered them.

"Mr. Oliver? Are you alright?"

The voice, warm, familiar, and full of genuine concern, broke the spell. Oliver spun around. It was Santos, the building's longtime doorman, standing by the entrance, his face a mask of worry. He was a man who had known Oliver since he had moved into this building with his parents as a small boy, a comforting and constant presence in his life.

"Santos, hey," Oliver said, trying to collect himself. "Yeah, I'm fine. I was just ... I was just talking to this man."

He turned back to gesture toward the homeless man.

The sidewalk was empty.

He was gone. Every. Single. Time. How did he do it? How could he disappear so quickly?

Oliver stared at the spot where the man had been standing just a second ago. There was nothing but the black iron fence and the empty pavement.

"What man, Mr. Oliver?" Santos asked gently, taking a step closer. "I was watching from the door. You were standing there by yourself for a minute. Gesticulating." He made a small, swirling motion with his hand. "Talking. I was worried."

Oliver had a sudden, sick realization. The air seemed to thin, the familiar sounds of the city street fading to a distant buzz. Santos hadn't seen the homeless man. Santos, who saw everything on this block, had looked right at the spot where the man was standing and had seen nothing but Oliver, alone, talking to the air.

The pieces fell into place together in his mind, a series of memories suddenly re-contextualized into a new and worrying truth. Reza, outside McGinn's pub, looking past him at an empty sidewalk. Daniela, on New Year's Eve, confused and concerned after he'd been thrown out of the party, asking him who he had been talking to under the street awning.

They hadn't seen him either. None of them had.

It wasn't that the man vanished quickly. It was that he was never physically there at all. He was a projection. A figment. An apparition visible only to him. Oliver felt a wave of nausea, his understanding of the line between his own mind and the world dissolving completely.

He had been there before, of course. When the Noncemeister impersonated Bryce at the art fair last summer. But that seemed fun and quaint in retrospect. Now, this deranged guide, this disheveled street prophet, this madman who had somehow given him real, tangible clues that had led him halfway across the world, was a private vision, a product of his own strange, new perception.

He pulled himself out of the uneasiness of the realization, his focus snapping back to the present. To Santos, who was still looking at him with a deep, paternal concern. He had to say something. He had to be normal.

"Sorry, Santos," Oliver said, forcing a sheepish, weary smile. "Long flight. I think I'm still half-asleep. Talking to myself. You know how it is."

Santos's worried expression softened into one of sympathy. "I know, I know. Is a very long trip from Europe. That's where you said you were going, right?"

Oliver nodded without making eye contact with Santos. He had lied to him about his destination before leaving. Much as he loved Santos, he didn't want him to blab about it to his mom if she decided to stop by. Besides, his first flight had been to Madrid from JFK. It wasn't a complete lie.

"You look tired, Mr. Oliver," Santos continued. "Let me help you with your bag."

He walked over and took the handle of Oliver's suitcase before he could protest. Together, they walked the few feet to the building's entrance.

"So, the trip was good?" Santos asked as he held the heavy glass door open for him.

"Yeah, it was ... productive," Oliver said, the word a massive understatement. "Good to be home, though."

They stepped into the familiar, quiet lobby. As the door clicked shut behind them, Santos's expression shifted slightly, a hint of professional seriousness returning to his eyes.

"I am glad you are back, Mr. Oliver," he said, his voice a little lower now. "Yesterday, while you were away, a woman came by. She was asking for you."

Oliver felt a familiar prickle of apprehension. "A woman? Who?"

"She did not give a name," Santos said, shaking his head. "She was very ... insistent. She told me she was your aunt. She said you had asked her to go up to your apartment while you were away and pick up a few things you had left behind for her. She also said you'd told her I would be able to let her into your apartment."

Oliver's heart began to beat a little faster. He had no aunt who lived in New York.

"She seemed very sure," Santos continued, his gaze steady. "But your father, Mr. Nate, he gave me very specific instructions many years ago. No one into your apartment without one of you telling me first. No exceptions. Not even for family." He paused. "So, I told her I could not let her in without speaking to you. She was not happy."

"What did she look like?" Oliver asked, his voice tight.

Santos took a moment, replaying the memory. "She was a very ... put-to-gether lady. Fit. Maybe in her fifties, but her face ... no wrinkles. Very smooth. It was a little strange. She had long, dark hair. And an accent. I am not good with the accents, but maybe from Europe somewhere? German, maybe, or from that area."

Maren. It was Maren. The description was a perfect match. A cold dread, sharper and more immediate than any mystical vision, washed over Oliver. His double-bluff to Bojan. In the alley in Montevideo a couple of days ago. *"They're in my apartment. In New York. Under my bed. Go look."*

He had thrown it out as a desperate, last-ditch gambit. The absolute, simple and absurd truth, delivered with the sarcastic bravado of a man with nothing left to lose. He had counted on a seasoned professional like Bojan to hear it for what it was: a childish taunt, a hiding place so obvious it couldn't possibly be real.

And Bojan had indeed dismissed it as a childish taunt. But he must have told Maren. And Maren hadn't dismissed it.

The thought was chilling. She was playing a different, more complex game. She had heard his absurd confession and had considered the possibility that it was not a lie, but a piece of high-level misdirection. She had immediately acted on it, coming here herself to call his bluff, to check the one place no sane person would hide two stolen masterpieces. The game wasn't just a series of distant moves on a global chessboard anymore. It was here. At his front door.

"Thank you, Santos," Oliver said, his voice a low, intense murmur. He took the handle of his suitcase. "Thank you for not letting her in. You did the right thing. The *perfect* thing."

"Of course, Mr. Oliver," Santos said, a hint of pride in his voice. "I always look out for my family in this building."

Oliver nodded, his mind already a tumult of new calculations and renewed threats. He turned and walked toward the elevator, the revelations of the last five minutes crashing over him in waves. He was a man haunted by a private vision that only he could see, and he was being hunted by a real, tangible enemy who knew exactly where he lived. The sanctuary of his home had become the front line in a war whose depths he was only just beginning to fathom.

Upstairs, the apartment was just as he had left it: still, and heavy with the imprint of Daniela's absence. The first thing he did was strip off his travel-worn clothes, leaving them in a pile on the floor. He stood under the shower for a long time, the scalding hot water a welcome, punishing reality. He let it wash away the grime of the 36-hour journey, the stale air of three different airports and the lingering cold sweat from the alley in Montevideo.

He emerged, wrapped in a towel, feeling slightly more human. He walked to the kitchen, his bare feet on the cool hardwood and pulled a bottle from his father's wine fridge. A 2016 Sassicaia. He deserved it. He poured a generous glass, the deep, ruby liquid a promise of a momentary, well-earned reprieve.

He took a sip, the complex notes of cherry and leather a welcome anchor to the real world.

He was about to take another when the harsh, sudden buzz of the intercom made him jump.

He walked over to the panel on the wall and pressed the talk button. "Yeah?"

"Mr. Oliver," came Santos's warm, familiar voice. "You have a visitor. Mr. Eddie Garcia is here to see you."

Eddie. Oliver felt a mix of mild annoyance and genuine relief. He hadn't seen Eddie since he bumped into him on his way to his birthday dinner with Daniela in December, but the thought of his harmless, rambling energy felt like a welcome distraction.

"Of course, Santos," Oliver said. "Send him up."

A few minutes later, a series of enthusiastic knocks rattled the apartment door. Oliver opened it, and Eddie Garcia blew in like a cheerful hurricane. He was dressed in a loud, brightly patterned shirt and was already talking before he had fully crossed the threshold.

"There he is! The man, the myth, the legend! Olly, tiger, you look like you've been through the wringer, you know what I'm talking about? Your mother, she calls me yesterday. She's been out in L.A. for the last week. She's in a real tizzy, a real state. 'Eddie,' she says, 'I've been calling Oliver for two weeks, no answer! Is he okay? Did he fall into a manhole?' I tell her, 'Diane, relax! The kid's a grown man, he's probably off on some adventure, you know?' But she's a mother, whaddyagonnado? So, she makes me promise to come check on you because she's not back for another week. She wants to make sure you're still in one piece. So, I come down here, I'm talking to Santos … great guy, Santos, we go way back, you know, we were talking about the Knicks just last week, what a disaster that team is, am I right? Anyway, he tells me you've been out of the country! The whole time! So, where've you been, tiger? Off chasing beautiful women on the Riviera?"

Eddie finally paused to take a breath, beaming at Oliver as if he had just delivered a Shakespearean monologue.

Oliver managed a weak smile. "Something like that, Uncle Eddie. It's good to see you."

"Good to see you too, chief!" Eddie said, clapping him on the shoulder. "But seriously, what's the story? Your mom was worried sick. Santos tells me you were in Europe?"

Oliver walked back to the kitchen counter and picked up his wine glass. He needed a plausible story, something simple that would satisfy his mother's secondhand curiosity without raising any red flags.

"Wine?" He asked, pointing to the bottle.

Eddie waved him away. "Taking a break from the sauce, tiger, you know what it's like when you're my age. Actually, how would you know? You're young and strong. When I was your age, I used to really hit the town with the boys, let me tell you. We used to take the train down from the Bronx to the East Village every Saturday evening. You were lucky if you only got stabbed once per train ride back then in the early 90s. Most of the time, you'd be punched, shot and pushed onto the tracks just as the train was pulling in. And we never complained once back then. No siree. They don't make 'em like that anymore. Ah, the 90s ..."

Eddie's voice trailed off and his eyes assumed a distant look. A soft smile appeared on his lips as he contemplated his raucous and seemingly violent youth.

He continued in the same wistful tone, "That was back before Giuliani. Rough times, kiddo. And we still made the best of it. Those amazing nights. A bunch of kids from the Bronx hitting all the speakeasies in the East Village and Lower East Side. Tequila used to be cheap back then. The well drinks used to go for a buck a shot. Madness, tiger, you know what I mean?"

Oliver didn't know what he meant. A dollar for a shot of tequila was unthinkable in 2023. He was also having trouble imagining Eddie as a lissome young man, ducking in and out of trendy nightclubs.

Eddie went on, "Anyway chief, my point being that was a long time ago. We were warriors back then, unlike the kids these days." He paused with a look of mild disgust on his face and then seemed to realize one of the kids-these-days was standing in front of him. He corrected himself with the adroitness of a one-legged ostrich performing a somersault. "Present company excluded of course, you know what I'm saying, big guy?"

Oliver chuckled, caught in the familiar position of being a passive spectator in a conversation with Eddie.

"What was I talking about, anyway?" Eddied scratched his head. That act seemed to jog his memory somehow. "Oh yeah, I'll forget my own name one of these days, kiddo, I swear. I'm taking a break from the devil's juice. I'm off the wagon. Or is it on the wagon? I can never remember which is which. But yeah, chief, taking a break because once you're my age, these things start catching up with you. We'll see how it goes, champ. I'll try one month. Maybe two."

Oliver smiled and nodded. Eddie had finished that last statement definitively and was looking rather pleased with himself.

"So, about my trip," Oliver began. Eddie's classic meander had given him enough time to form the lie. "It was a last-minute thing. A consulting gig. A potential client from my old job at BlockWaves reached out. They needed someone to fly to a conference in Madrid to do some technical due diligence on a new protocol. It was all very hush-hush, NDAs, the works. I had to keep my phone off for most of it for security reasons, and the time difference made it a nightmare to call back. I was going to call Mom soon, I swear."

The story sounded thin, even to his own ears, but Eddie bought it completely, his face lighting up with vicarious excitement.

"A conference in Madrid! Attaboy, champ! See, Diane, what'd I tell you?" he said, gesturing to the empty air as if Oliver's mom were standing right there. "The kid's not in a manhole, he's a big-shot international consultant! Making the big bucks! That's my boy. So, tell me everything. The food, the wine, the women ... don't leave out the good parts, you know what I'm talking about?"

Eddie winked, then paused, a look of sudden recollection crossing his face. "Wait a minute," he said, snapping his fingers. "Speaking of women ... that girl! The one you were with on your birthday. Doris ... Daphne ... Denise ... Daniela! That's it, that was her name, right? Daniela. A real knockout, that one. I mean, a ten-out-of-ten, a real supermodel, you know what I'm saying, big guy? The kind of girl you see in the movies."

Oliver felt a familiar, sharp ache in his chest. He took a slow sip of his Sassicaia, the expensive wine suddenly tasting like vinegar.

"So, where is that fine lady, anyway?" Eddie continued, completely oblivious. "Did you take her with you to Madrid? Show her a good time? A little bit of tapas, a little bit of flamenco, a little bit of cha cha cha ... oh wait a minute, that's more Puerto Rico, not Spain – I should know that, ha! Anyway, she around? You guys are shacked up here now, right? That's what I remember you telling me the last time I came here."

Oliver put his glass down on the counter. He couldn't avoid it. He had to say the words, to give the ugly truth a voice.

"Uh ... we broke up, Uncle Eddie," he said, his voice quiet, almost a whisper. "A few weeks ago. It just ... it didn't work out."

Eddie's jovial, beaming face fell. He stared at Oliver, his mouth slightly agape, as if he'd just been told that the sky was green. "You did what now, big guy?" he finally managed, his voice a theatrical squeak of disbelief.

"We broke up," Oliver repeated, a little louder this time.

"Broke up?" Eddie stepped back, putting a hand to his chest as if he'd been physically wounded by the news. "Are you kidding me, chief? Her? You broke up with *her*? What are you, nuts, tiger? A girl like that, she's a once-in-a-lifetime thing! That's the kind of girl you marry, have five kids with, and then you die happy! You don't let a girl like that go!"

He started pacing the small kitchen, gesticulating wildly.

"Listen to your Uncle Eddie, kiddo. I've been around the block a few times, you know what I'm talking about? And I'm telling you, you got rocks in your head. A real diamond, that one. And beautiful? Forget about it! I mean, I'm happily married to my Melissa, you know that, best woman in the world, don't get me wrong. But if I was your age, and I met a girl like that?"

Eddie gave out two sharp whistles before continuing. "I'd have a ring on her finger so fast her head would spin. And you just ... you let her walk away?"

He stopped pacing and looked at Oliver with a look of genuine bewilderment, like a man trying to understand a complex physics equation. Oliver just stood there, the wine glass in his hand, a silent, weary spectator to Eddie's well-intentioned but excruciatingly painful performance.

"I'm sorry to hear that, boss," Eddie said, his tone softening as he seemed to register the pained look on Oliver's face. "Really, I am. She seemed like a great kid. A real keeper." He shook his head one last time, a final, definitive gesture of disapproval. "A real keeper."

The words hung in the air, a final, painful epitaph for a relationship Oliver didn't have the energy to defend. He just nodded, hoping the gesture would be enough to end the topic. Eddie, seeming to finally sense he had pushed too far, let out a long, theatrical sigh and plopped down onto the sofa.

"Ah, what do I know, anyway?" he said, throwing his hands up in a gesture of surrender. "I'm just an old man who talks too much. Don't listen to me, champ. You gotta do what you gotta do. Your dad, you know, bless his soul, he did what he needed to, am I right, tiger? What a character, that guy. A real enigma, you know what I'm talking about?"

Oliver, still standing by the kitchen counter, felt a familiar weariness. He knew what was coming: another one of Eddie's long, meandering stories about Dad. He braced himself, taking another sip of the Sassicaia.

"I remember this one time," Eddie began, his eyes taking on that distant, nostalgic look. "Musta been nine, maybe 10 years ago. Walks up to my desk at WilcoxRe ... I remember it like it was yesterday. I'm sitting at my desk, minding my own business, filing reports, all that sorta good stuff we had to do back in the day. He comes up and sounds all frantic. 'Eddie,' he says, 'I need a favor. A big one. My car's dead and I'm in a real jam.' So I say, 'Nate, for you, anything.' I figure he needs a ride, maybe help moving a piece of furniture."

Eddie paused briefly, as if he had felt a prick of aggrievement. "I mean, it's the middle of the day on a Friday, for crying out loud. What kind of a guy decides to move furniture in the middle of the day on a Friday when everyone else is thinking about packing it in for the week? But that was your old man. He was built different, you know what I'm talking about? In any case, he asked me for my help point-blank. Point blank, kiddo. Boom, just like that. Whaddyagonnado? He's one of my best buds."

Oliver was only half-listening, his mind still replaying the image of Daniela walking out the door. It was a typical Eddie story, full of dramatic flourishes and questionable details.

Eddie leaned forward, his voice dropping to a conspiratorial whisper, even though they were the only two people in the apartment.

"So, we go down to the parking lot, grab my minivan and I ask him where we're going. He said we need to go to some godforsaken warehouse in the South Bronx. So, we get there, and he's got this dusty storage unit in the warehouse. We go in, and he's got these two huge wooden crates in there. We drag them outta there, heavy as sin, if you catch my drift, chief. Then he says, 'Eddie, I need you to help me get these to Newark. To the airport.' By the way, tiger, here I am busting my hump, you know, loading these things into my van, and I ask him, 'Nate, what's in the boxes? Gold bars? The Ark of the Covenant?' He just gives me that smile, you know the one, the one that says 'don't ask,' and tells me it's just some old computer parts he's shipping to a client."

Oliver briefly drifted back into the room. Daniela was still on his mind, but he had caught that last part about wooden crates and computer parts. He wondered when this story was going to end. The long travel, coupled with the Sassicaia, was finally catching up with him, and he was ready to turn in for the evening.

"So, we get to Newark," Eddie continued, completely oblivious to Oliver's drooping eyelids. "And we don't go to the regular terminal. We go to this weird, separate building for specialty cargo. Real high-security stuff, you know what I mean? We get the crates onto a dolly and wheel them up to this counter. And I see the paperwork your dad is filling out. And it doesn't say 'computer parts.' It says 'Fine Art.'"

Oliver's attention sharpened, and the weight on his eyelids seemed to vanish. He put his wine glass down.

"So now, I'm really curious, right?" Eddie said, his voice full of remembered indignation. "I say, 'Nate, you told me it was computer parts!' He gets all shifty, tells me to keep my voice down. He finally admits it's a couple of paintings. I ask him who the artist is, you know, maybe it's a Picasso. Hey, maybe I can tell my grandkids I helped move a Picasso. And he just says, 'Nobody you've ever heard of, Eddie. Just some ... unfinished pieces I happened to come into possession of.' Can you believe that, boss? All that secrecy for some unfinished paintings!"

Unfinished pieces. The words hit Oliver like a thunderbolt. Any semblance of sleep and exhaustion was completely gone now. Could they have been the fourth and fifth Bryce paintings? The ones that were rumored to exist but had never been seen. The ones that Satoshi himself, in an email to his dad, referred to as "unfinished." The ones that potentially contained the remaining seed words to Christiaan's wallets.

"Where ... where was he shipping them to?" Oliver asked, trying to keep his voice level, to not betray the sudden, violent surge of interest.

"That was the craziest part!" Eddie exclaimed, now fully animated. "Not to a museum. Not to a gallery. He was shipping them to another warehouse. Not like the one we brought them from in the Bronx. A special warehouse, right at the airport. In ... where the hell was it ... Liechtenstein? No, that's not it. Luxor? No, no, something like that, though. Luxembourg! That was it. Luxembourg. Your dad told me it was one of them fancy, tax-free airport warehouses where rich guys keep their stuff. A freeport, I think he called it. Said it was the safest place in the world to store something valuable."

The room seemed to tilt. Oliver gripped the edge of the kitchen counter to steady himself. A freeport. In Luxembourg. A secret, high-security art warehouse. Could his dad have transported the mythical, unfinished Bryces to Luxembourg? How on Earth did he get hold of them in the first place?

He had been so focused on the mystical, on the projections and the symbols, that he had forgotten the simplest truth: his father had been a man who moved things in the real world.

" ... Anyway, that's the story, chief!" Eddie's voice boomed, pulling Oliver from his stupor. Eddie was now standing, stretching his arms over his head. "A real character, your old man. Listen, I gotta run. Promised Melissa I'd be home for dinner. You take care of yourself, you hear me, tiger? And call your mother!"

Eddie gave him a final, hearty slap on the back and was out the door before Oliver could even formulate a proper goodbye.

Oliver stood alone in the quiet apartment, the scent of Eddie's cheap cologne lingering in the air. He didn't have a map. He didn't even understand the territory. But the story Eddie had so casually told had just given him a single, unwavering compass bearing. North. And for a man who had been adrift at sea until a week ago, that was everything.

780501 (March 12)

The F train rattled and swayed as it made its way through the tunnel under the East River, the rhythmic clatter a familiar, industrial heartbeat. Nick stared at his own reflection in the grimy window, a pale, tired-looking stranger superimposed over the fleeting darkness between the signal lights. He was heading to the city, but for the first time in his life, he felt like a foreign agent entering hostile territory.

The last three days had been a slow, grinding torment. He had hit a wall. A perfect, legalistic, and utterly impassable wall. The phone call with David Chen had been a tactical disaster. He had approached the situation like a professional, offering valuable intelligence, yet he had been treated like a crank, a common hustler. The threat of a restraining order was not an idle one; a firm like Kincaid, Strauss, & Abernathy did not make threats they weren't prepared to follow through on. Any direct contact, any email or phone call from a number or address traceable back to him, would be a fatal mistake. The front door was sealed.

He had spent hours in his oppressive cubicle at The Grid, pacing the small space like a caged animal, staring at the name on his evidence board. *Adele van der Dussen.* She was the key. She had to be. But she was protected by a fortress of lawyers whose sole purpose was to keep men like him at bay. He had considered every angle. Trying to find a mutual acquaintance on LinkedIn? Too traceable. Attempting to approach her at a public event? Too risky, too easily framed as harassment.

He was at an impasse, and the feeling was maddening.

He had the answer. Or at least, the beginning of one. It was buried in his research on Sazsa. After hitting the dead end of Gyorgy Lorincz's obituary, he had gone back over the man's digital breadcrumbs, looking for anything he might have missed. And there it was, a detail he had initially dismissed as irrelevant biographical color. Gyorgy, the hardcore cypherpunk, had been an obsessive collector of obscure, surrealist art. It was a strange, dissonant fact, a piece of data that didn't fit the profile. It was an anomaly. And in the world of intelligence, the anomaly was everything.

But the information was useless if he couldn't deliver it.

Nick watched as the train emerged from the tunnel, making its way to the 63rd Street and Lexington Avenue stop. He needed a new strategy. He had to stop thinking like a consultant trying to win a client and start thinking like a spy trying to cultivate an asset. He needed a way to deliver a message that was both anonymous and undeniably credible. A ghost note slipped under a locked door.

And then, the idea began to form, a solution born of the very legal threat that had cornered him. He couldn't use his own name. He couldn't use his own computer. But the city was full of anonymous terminals.

The New York Public Library. The grand, old building on 42nd and 5th. A place of quiet, scholarly dignity, full of public computers used by a thousand nameless people every day. It was a perfect piece of operational security, hiding in plain sight.

The second piece of the puzzle fell into place. The message itself. They would ignore a random tip. He needed to prove his authenticity. He needed to prove he was the same man who had been humiliated over the "jute salesman" incident. It was his greatest weakness, his moment of ultimate professional shame. And he would turn it into a weapon.

He would craft a message that contained a detail only an insider could know, a fact that was not in any public report. He would admit to being the disgraced analyst, but reframe himself as an independent agent who had now found something real. The Sazsa-art connection was the perfect bait. It was a question no one else was asking, a riddle that would prey on Adele's and her lawyer's curiosity. He wouldn't ask for a meeting directly. That was too aggressive. He would propose a dead drop, a classic piece of spycraft, a way for them to respond without ever making direct contact. A classified ad in a newspaper. It was elegant. It was untraceable. It was insane.

It was the only move he had left.

The train screeched as it began to slow into the Rockefeller Center Station. A synthesized voice announced the next stop. *"This is a Brooklyn-bound F local train. The next stop is 42nd Street, Bryant Park."*

In a few minutes, the train slid into the station, the familiar green and white tiles of the platform flashing past the window. Nick stood up, his heart beating with a new, sharp sense of purpose. He was no longer a man at a dead end. He was an operative, about to undertake his first real mission. The train came to a complete stop, a loud hiss of air brakes punctuating the moment.

The doors slid open with a metallic chime, revealing the bustling platform. Nick stepped out, melting into the anonymous afternoon crowd. He walked up the stairs and emerged into the cool, gray air of Bryant Park, the familiar, majestic rear facade of the New York Public Library rising before him like a mountain of stone and knowledge.

He crossed the park, his pace quick and purposeful. He bypassed the famous stone lions guarding the main entrance on Fifth Avenue and walked up the grand, sweeping marble staircase, a man on a mission. The interior of the library was a cavernous, hushed sanctuary, the air still and cool, smelling of old paper and history. He followed the signs for the public computer resources, his footsteps a soft, tapping sound on the polished stone floors, a jarring intrusion into the scholarly quiet.

He found the computer room, a more modern, functional space filled with long rows of identical terminals. It was a place of perfect anonymity, dozens of people from all walks of life sitting side-by-side, each lost in their own private digital world. He found an empty station in a back corner, the seat still warm from the previous user.

He opened a private browser window and navigated to ProtonMail's website. He created a new, single-use account, a string of meaningless numbers and letters. x7r9p2q5@proton.me. An address with no history, no identity. A digital ghost.

He opened a new message and began to type, the words chosen with the care and precision of a bombmaker assembling a device. He addressed it to the general inquiry email listed on the law firm's website, knowing it would be routed through their internal security filters and eventually find its way to the right desk.

He paused after typing the subject line, his fingers hovering over the keyboard. This was the point of no return.

```
Subject: Anomaly: MixMarket Case File - Sazsa


To the desk of Julian Croft,


Your firm is operating on incomplete data regarding
the third MixMarket accomplice. The official DoJ file
on Sazsa is missing a crucial off-chain vector.
Sazsa, under his real name Gyorgy Lorincz, was
an obsessive and significant collector of the Irish
surrealist Jonathan Bryce.
This fact is not in any government report. The
connection between a cypherpunk and this specific,
obscure artist suggests a non-financial motive that
re-contextualizes the entire conspiracy.
```

He stopped again, his heart hammering in his chest. Now came the most dangerous part of the gambit. He had to prove he was a credible source without giving them the legal ammunition to obtain a restraining order. He had to turn his greatest weakness into a weapon.

He continued typing.

```
This is not the work of a crank. This is the work of
the same "computationally unsound" analyst your firm
is already aware of, now operating independently. I am
proving I can find things the official channels cannot.
```

The words seemed to glow on the screen, a brazen, high-stakes admission. It was a risk, he knew, a terrible risk. But it was a calculated one. An anonymous email from a public library terminal was a digital wisp, legally untraceable to him. They could suspect, but they could never *prove* he was the one who had sent it. But by referencing his own spectacular, public failure, a detail known only to a handful of people in the DoJ and at their firm, he was giving them a secret handshake. He was proving that this information was coming from a legitimate, if disgraced, insider. He was validating the bait.

He typed out the final, crucial instructions.

```
If you or Ms. van der Dussen wish to understand the
true nature of the conspiracy your client was a part
of, place a classified ad in next Sunday's edition of
the Washington Post. The ad must be in the "Antiques &
Collectibles" section and read: "Seeking info on Irish
painters. Orpheus, please post findings on the ArtNet
forum, thread #8711"

If the ad does not run by next Sunday, I will assume
you are not interested. This address will be deleted in
forty-eight hours.
```

He signed it with a simple, anonymous initial.

```
- N.
```

He read the message one last time. It was perfect. Short, specific and deeply mysterious. It was a shot in the dark, a message in a bottle thrown into a vast and hostile ocean.

He took a deep breath, and he clicked "Send."

He immediately logged out, cleared the browser's history and cache, and stood up from the terminal. He walked out of the computer room and back into the grand, hushed halls of the library, his face a neutral mask. He had fired his only shot. He was no longer a hunter. He was just a man, waiting for a signal.

780950 (March 15)

The two glasses of Barolo at lunch had done their work. For the first time since his return from Montevideo four days ago, the tight coil of apprehension in

Oliver's gut had loosened its grip. The initial, sharp vigilance had given way to a low-grade thrum of watchfulness, but the wine had softened its edges, leaving him with a mild, pleasant sense of well-being.

He walked without a destination, letting the mild afternoon sun warm his face as he meandered through the winding, fashionable streets of Nolita. After days of being cooped up in his apartment, obsessively replaying every detail of his trip, the simple act of walking felt like a form of therapy.

His thoughts drifted, as they always did, to the visions from Pubkey. The image of the two shadowy figures, Nick and Adele, a weird union, an odd, prickly detail he didn't know what to make of. But it was the other vision that truly unsettled him, the one that felt less like a piece of intelligence and more like a wound. The bruised purple void. The cage of stark, white light. And the silent, slumped figure of the Noncemeister within it. It was a vision of a spirit imprisoned, a joyful, chaotic force rendered inert.

What had Anariadne been trying to show him? *Probaris en silencio, sat in actuare.* What did that even mean? What did anything she said mean? What test was she talking about? A test he had apparently failed because he had done nothing. He had simply observed the problem and returned, defeated. Was he supposed to have found a way to break the cage? To free his guide? The thought was absurd. He was a man, and the Noncemeister was ... something else entirely. A disembodied consciousness. How could a man free a thought from a cage of light?

The entire memory was a disquieting riddle, a koan wrapped in a threat, and it had been his constant companion for the past few weeks – a low, dissonant hum beneath the surface of his everyday thoughts.

He was so lost in this mental maze that the sudden, loud buzzing in his pocket made him jump. He pulled out his phone, his heart giving a single, hard thump of unease before he saw the caller ID.

It was his mom.

A different, more mundane kind of dread washed over him. He felt a hot flush of guilt. He had promised himself he would call her the day after Eddie's visit, to reassure her, to thank her for sending him. But he had been so consumed by the revelation of the freeport in Luxembourg and the nagging fear that Bojan might show up at his doorstep any minute, that he had completely forgotten. Four days. He hadn't called her for four days. And the two weeks before that.

He stared at the screen, at the picture of his mother smiling, a photo from a happier time, before his father's death, before everything had fractured. He knew he should answer. He knew the conversation would be a minefield of loving but probing questions he couldn't answer, of a maternal concern he couldn't possibly assuage. He would have to lie, to construct a new set of plausible fictions about his "consulting gig" and his "busy schedule." The thought was wearying.

For a moment, he was tempted to let it go to voicemail, to buy himself another few hours of reprieve. But the guilt was too strong. He couldn't do that to her again. She had been worried enough to send Eddie.

He took a deep breath and steeled himself for a very different kind of interrogation. He pushed the green icon on the screen.

"Hey, Mom," he said, trying to inject a note of cheerful, everything-is-fine energy into his voice. "Sorry I haven't called. It's been a crazy week."

"Oliver? Oh, thank God," Diane's voice flooded the speaker, a torrent of relief and maternal anxiety. "Honey, I was so worried. Two weeks! Not a text, not a call. Eddie told me you were traveling for work, but still. You know how I worry. I was having nightmares that you'd been kidnapped. Are you okay? Are you eating?"

"I'm fine, Mom, I promise," Oliver said, a familiar, sheepish guilt creeping in. "The trip was just ... a lot. The time difference was a killer, and I had to have my phone off for most of the meetings. I'm really sorry I worried you."

There was a pause on the other end of the line, the kind of pause that signaled a change in topic to something more serious.

"Eddie also told me ... about you and Daniela," she said, her voice softening with a genuine sympathy. "Oh, honey. I am so, so sorry. Are you alright? Really?"

"Yeah, Mom, I'm okay," he said, the words feeling like a lie even as he said them. He started walking again, needing the motion to distract from the sudden, sharp pang of the memory.

"Are you sure?" she pressed gently. "She was such a wonderful girl. I really liked her. She was so good for you. You know, if you need to talk about it, you can always call me. Anytime."

"I know. Thanks, Mom," he said, his tone a clear signal that this was a door he did not want to open. "But I'm fine, really. It just … you know. It didn't work out. It happens."

"I know, sweetie. I know," she said, though her voice was laced with a skepticism that told him she didn't believe his performance for a second. "Well, as long as you're okay. That's the most important thing."

There was a brief, warm pause. Oliver, feeling like he'd successfully navigated the emotional minefield, decided to scratch the curiosity itch that had been nagging him since his conversation with Eddie.

"So, what about you, Mom?" he asked, his tone shifting to one of genuine interest. "Eddie said you were in L.A. That's a long way from Maplewood. Everything alright?" He knew his mother was a homebody; a trip to the city was an event for her, a trip to the West Coast was practically a moon landing.

He could almost hear her blush through the phone. Her voice, when she replied, was a full octave higher, a giddy, youthful sound he hadn't heard in years.

"Oh, honey, you are not going to believe it," she gushed, the words tumbling out in a rush of childlike excitement. "It's the most incredible, most unbelievable thing. Someone … someone reached out to me about my blog."

Oliver was momentarily confused. His mom's blog, *The Kyriarchy in the Kitchen*, was her great passion, a dense, academic exploration of how patriarchal structures were subtly reinforced through culinary traditions and household products. He loved that she had a hobby, but he had always found the posts to be … impenetrable. He'd once tried to read an 8,000-word essay on the colonialist implications of the spice trade and had given up after three paragraphs.

"Someone from a publishing house, Oliver!" she continued, her voice buzzing with a joy that was infectious. "A big one. The Da Silva Publishing Group. A senior editor there, he'd read my piece on the inherent gender bias of bakeware, and he said it was the most insightful thing he'd read all year. Can you believe it? He asked if I was writing a book, and I told him, 'Of course I am!' So, he said he wanted to talk about a publishing deal. A real one! He flew me out here, to their L.A. office, to discuss it. They put me up in a beautiful hotel in Beverly Hills. It's all been an absolute dream."

Oliver listened, a strange mix of emotions swirling inside him. He was genuinely happy for her, for the pure, unvarnished joy in her voice. But he was also deeply skeptical. A major publisher? For *The Kyriarchy in the Kitchen*? It seemed ... unlikely. Much as he loved his mom, he had a hard time imagining her dense, footnote-heavy prose flying off the shelves at Barnes & Noble.

"Wow, Mom," he said, the word feeling inadequate. "That's ... that's amazing. I'm really happy for you."

"Thank you, sweetie," she said. Then her voice dropped again, becoming more hesitant, more careful. It was the tone she used when she was about to broach a sensitive topic. "And, well, Oliver ... there's something else."

He waited.

"The editor," she began, the words chosen with a delicate precision. "His name is Alexander. He's ... he's been a perfect gentleman. Very charming. And very handsome." She let out a small, almost girlish laugh. "We've had dinner a few times, to discuss the book, of course. But ... I don't know. I think there might be a real connection there, honey. It's been a long time since I've felt ... you know."

The warmth from the Barolo turned to acid in Oliver's stomach. The image that flashed in his mind was not of his mother finding new happiness, but of a stranger, a handsome, charming stranger, encroaching on a space that he had always considered sacred. His parents' divorce had been a sad, distant fact of his adult life, but in some deep, unexamined part of his mind, they were still a unit. Nate and Diane. A fixed point in his universe. This ... this *Alexander* was an intruder; a usurper.

"Mom," he said, his voice now flat and cold. "What are you talking about?"

"Sweetheart, don't take it like that," she said, her voice now defensive, wary. "It's nothing serious. We're just ... getting to know each other. It's nice. I deserve to have someone nice in my life, don't I?"

"I can't believe you could do this to Dad," he blurted out, the words childish and possessive, but he couldn't stop them. The thought of his mother, here in this city that was so full of his father's memory, being charmed by some L.A. editor, felt like a profound betrayal.

A sharp, wounded intake of breath on the other end of the line. "Oliver, that's a really unfair thing to say," she said, her voice now stripped of all its earlier joy. "Your father is gone. And in any case, we were divorced for five years before he passed. We both moved on. He had his life, and I have mine."

The cold, hard logic of her words did nothing to soothe the hot, irrational anger that was now coursing through him. It was all too much. The secrets, the visions ... Bojan, and now this. The one stable pillar of his past was crumbling.

"I have to go, Mom," he said abruptly, his voice tight. "I'm ... I'm glad about the book. Really. But I have to go."

He hung up before she could reply, the final, wounded syllable of her saying his name cut short. He stood in the middle of a busy Nolita sidewalk, his phone gripped tight in his hand. His brief moment of well-being had been shattered, replaced by a new, and in some ways, more unsettling feeling. The men in the shadows, the secrets of Atlantean geometry, those were dangers he could almost comprehend, a puzzle he could try to solve.

This was different. This was the quiet, inexorable erasure of his own history. The man at his mother's dinner table was a symbol. A symbol that the world was moving on, that his mother was moving on, and that the last, sacred image he held of his family was beginning to dissolve into the past.

He pocketed his phone and started walking again without a destination, his amble now a more urgent march. He needed to outwalk the feeling, to put physical distance between himself and the conversation that was now a toxic loop in his mind.

He was so lost in this internal storm that he almost walked right past it. It was the smell that stopped him first, a complex, intoxicating wave of lavender, sandalwood as well as something sharp and citrusy that cut through the city's dull miasma of exhaust fumes. He looked up and saw the source: an ancient-looking storefront, a relic from a bygone era, its large window filled with hand-wrapped bars of soap and strange, colored glass bottles. The sign above the door, painted in faded gold leaf, simply read *C. & E. Anthon, Purveyors of Fine Soaps*.

Drawn in by a sense of pure, idle curiosity, a momentary desire for a simple, sensory distraction, he pushed open the heavy wooden door. A small bell chimed. The scent inside was almost overwhelming, a rich, clean perfume that seemed to coat the air.

And then he saw him.

Standing at the long wooden counter, his back to the door, was Reza. He was engaged in a ritual of intense and serious contemplation, holding a simple, unwrapped, pale-yellow bar of soap to his nose and inhaling its scent with the deep, considered focus of a master sommelier.

Oliver stood frozen by the door, a disbelieving laugh almost escaping his lips. Of all the places in this vast city.

"Reza?"

Reza turned, and a slow, beatific smile spread across his face. He looked different. The weary, cynical intellectual Oliver knew was gone, replaced by a man who seemed lighter, more present, his eyes bright with a strange, new curiosity.

"Ah, excellent, Oliver," he said, his eyes lighting up. His voice was a warm, happy hum. "Of course. It makes perfect sense that I would find you here."

"What are you doing in a soap shop in Nolita?" Oliver asked, walking closer in amused surprise. "This is a long way from the Upper West Side."

"The wanderer must wander," Reza said with a philosophical shrug. "I found I had read the same chapter of the book for twenty years. I decided it was time to explore the rest of the library." He gestured around the shop. "I find myself on a pilgrimage for the senses. Today, I am looking for an honest bar of soap!"

The earnestness, the sheer, unadulterated strangeness of it, made Oliver smile. "And how is that going – this mission of yours?" he asked, genuinely curious now.

"It bears fruit," Reza said, his eyes twinkling. "And how is that peculiar mission of yours? The one with the money made of numbers. Bitcoin. Does it still burn with a righteous fire?"

Oliver hesitated for a moment. He wasn't sure if he should bring it up, to talk about what had been bothering him recently – Ordinals and spammers, but Reza's strange, open-hearted question felt like a genuine invitation. "It's ... complicated," he began, trying to find the right words for someone not technically minded. "Imagine a perfect, public ledger – that's bitcoin. A book where every transaction is recorded, pure and simple, for all to see. But now, some people have figured out a way to doodle in the margins. To attach their own pictures and messages to the entries. It clutters the book. It makes it harder for people who want to use the book honestly. In bitcoin, these additional pictures and messages eat block space, drive up fees, and crowd out regular payments. It's a tragedy of the commons."

Reza nodded, his expression one of intense focus. "So," he said, a clarifying question. "They are not adding new pages to the book, but rather drawing on the pages that are already there?"

"Exactly," Oliver said, impressed by the quickness of his understanding. "And it's driving a lot of people, including me, crazy. They're taking this clean, honest thing and making it ... messy."

Reza seemed to consider this with the utmost seriousness. He picked up the simple, pale-yellow bar of soap from the counter, holding it up to the light.

"A fascinating problem," he mused, his voice taking on that same lyrical quality Oliver remembered from the pub. "They say," he began, his gaze fixed on the soap as they made their way to the store's exit, "if you change the recipe, if you use a different oil or a new wrapper, is it still the same soap?"

He looked up at Oliver, his eyes full of a deep, philosophical amusement.

"A silly question. Its purpose is to be soap. To be clean. The essence is in the function, not the form."

Reza then brought the bar of soap to his nose and took another long, luxurious sniff, a man completely at peace with his small, perfect discovery. Oliver stood there, the bustling Nolita sidewalk fading into a distant murmur. That simple statement had him thinking. *Function over form.* He thought of the timechain, a pristine ledger whose sole function was to immutably record transactions. And he thought of the "monkey jpegs," a new, decorative form being forced upon that function. Was it a corruption? Or was it, as Reza suggested, just a silly question about a different kind of wrapper on the same bar of soap?

"Well," Reza said, his voice pulling Oliver out of his thoughts. He carefully rewrapped the soap in its simple brown paper and slipped it into his coat pocket as if it were a precious jewel. "My pilgrimage continues. There is a man on Mulberry Street who sells, I am told, the finest Gorgonzola in the five boroughs."

He gave Oliver a final, knowing look, a twinkle in his eye. "Enjoy your walk, Oliver. It seems you have much to ponder."

With a small, almost theatrical bow, Reza turned and continued his journey down the street, melting into the afternoon crowd, a man entirely at home in his own strange odyssey.

Oliver was left standing alone on the sidewalk, the scent of lemon and sandalwood not fully dissipated. He turned Reza's strange, simple phrase over and over in his mind. *The essence is in the function, not the form.* He wasn't sure if he agreed, but it was something to chew on, and it kept him company as he continued his walk down the street.

781752 (March 19)

The second bottle of wine stood empty on the nightstand. It was almost 11 p.m., and the apartment was beginning to tilt, the corners of the room softening and swaying with the gentle, nauseating rhythm of his own pulse. He lay down on the bed, the cool sheets a momentary comfort, and closed his eyes.

But there was no peace to be found in the darkness. His mind was a crowded, noisy terminal, a cacophony of unresolved departures and threatening arrivals.

He saw Bojan's cold, pale eyes. It had been almost 10 days since his return from Montevideo, and every step he took outside his apartment was a calculated risk. He'd found a strange kind of safety in crowds, moving through the dense river of people on the subway or a busy avenue, a single, anonymous data point in a massive, fungible set. But in the quiet moments, on his own street, he felt a persistent, prickling sense of being watched, and he knew it was only a matter of time before the hunter returned.

Then the image would shift, the color palette bleeding from the gray city streets to a bruised, violent purple. He saw the stark, white-hot bars of the cage and the slumped, desolate figure within it. The Noncemeister. His guide, his friend, rendered inert. The vision was a constant, looping torment, a question he couldn't answer, a wound that wouldn't close. Who could have possibly imprisoned him? He was the master of the nonces. The keeper of the timechain. Heck, he was the timechain himself. How could it be?

And beneath it all, the more intimate disquiet. The memory of his mother's giddy, hopeful voice, talking about a charming stranger named Alexander, a thought that felt like a betrayal he couldn't name. And the final, unsettling riddle of the late-night phone call. *Su hijo. Your child.* The two small words refused to be dismissed, a splinter of impossibility lodged deep in his mind.

He was a vessel for too many secrets, too many threats, too many questions. He felt himself coming undone, the threads of his own reality beginning to fray. He didn't fight it anymore. He just let go, surrendering to the spin, to the overwhelming weight of it all.

The darkness behind his eyelids deepened, the familiar black of intoxication shifting into something else. It was a descent, a slow, weightless drift into a different kind of night.

The blue began not as a mist, but as a single, pinprick of light in the vast emptiness. It did not spread or billow, but rather simply grew in intensity, a nascent star of pure, impossible cobalt. The light expanded, not filling the space, but becoming the space itself: a tranquil, luminous ocean that held him in its embrace.

And from the heart of that light, she took form. She was not woven from the haze this time. The light itself seemed to thicken, to gain substance and texture, coalescing from pure energy into the graceful lines of a flowing robe, the impossible gold of her hair, and the piercing, turquoise jewels of her eyes. She was not a visitor in this place. She was the place itself.

The sight of her, so impossibly beautiful, so purely and fundamentally real, extinguished every other thought in Oliver's mind. The worries about Bojan, the sting of his mother's new romance, even the poignant image of the caged Noncemeister – it all dissolved into nothingness, a distant, irrelevant noise from a world he no longer cared about. All that existed was her.

An all-consuming desire washed over him, a feeling so intense it was a physical ache, a hollowing out of his very core. It was a desperate, primal hunger. He wanted to close the distance between them, to possess her, to be possessed by her, to dissolve into the perfect, luminous blue of her being.

"You're here," he breathed, the words a testament to the only truth that mattered.

Anariadne smiled, a slow, knowing curve of her lips that acknowledged his adoration. She glided closer, the blue light seeming to bend around her, her presence a heady, intoxicating perfume.

"*Ego ex inferna natium*," she whispered, her voice a sensuous current in the still, blue ocean of her realm. "Feel you, I do. I can see. You want to have me, you do. But decide when you have me, I do."

She was so close now he could have reached out and touched her. He felt a powerful, magnetic pull, a gravitational force that threatened to overwhelm his last vestiges of self-control.

"Then let me," he pleaded, his voice thick with a yearning that was a form of surrender. "Let me have you."

Her smile widened, a flicker of something that hinted at both amusement and a deep, ancient power. "Worthy, you must be," she purred. "The path you wish to walk, it is not for the weak. You have seen the cage. Now, your second test, it is here."

She raised a hand, not to touch him, but to gesture toward the space around them. As she did, the endless, tranquil blue began to shift and change. The soft, luminous void resolved itself into a new and breathtaking reality.

He was no longer floating in an abstract space. He was standing on a vast, empty shore of black, volcanic sand. Before him, stretching out to a horizon of bruised, twilight purple, was an immense, unnaturally calm ocean. The water was as black and reflective as polished obsidian, the surface perfectly still, without a single ripple.

Anariadne pointed a single, elegant finger out toward the center of the dark, placid sea.

"There," she whispered. "Look."

Oliver followed her gaze. In the distance, a solitary form rested on the water. It was a ship. An ancient, wooden vessel with a single, tall mast, its sails furled, looking like a relic from a forgotten age, adrift on a sea of glass.

He looked at Anariadne, but her expression was unreadable, her attention fixed on the vessel. It was a clear, unspoken command: *Go.*

He felt a gentle, irresistible pull, a current that was not in the water but in his own will. He took a step toward the shore, but his foot did not touch the black sand. Instead, he lifted, his body becoming weightless. He began to glide forward, a few feet above the surface of the pitch-black ocean, moving smoothly and effortlessly toward the distant ship.

The journey was unnervingly placid. There was no wind, no sound but the faint, almost imperceptible whisper of his own movement across the glassy water. The ship grew larger as he approached, its details resolving with a preternatural clarity. He could see the grain of the heavy, oaken planks, the texture of the thick, coiled ropes, the intricate carvings on the prow. It was a perfect, silent artifact, a vessel that seemed to be waiting for a story.

He was about 50 feet away when he first noticed something was wrong. The texture. The wood grain wasn't quite right. It didn't swirl and knot in the way real wood did. It was composed of a series of fine, perfectly horizontal lines. He glided closer, his curiosity now a sharp, focused point.

The planks, he now saw, were not made of wood at all. They were long, rectangular blocks of pure, solid color. The "grain" was just a subtle variation in the shading. They were pixels. Massive, elongated pixels, stacked and arranged to form the perfect illusion of an ancient galleon.

A sense of unease began to creep over him. He instinctively pulled his perspective back, rising higher above the water to see the whole image at once, the way one steps back from a painting in a museum.

And then he saw it. The full, sickening truth of the image resolved itself with a jolt of pure, intellectual revulsion.

The colors. The cartoonish lines. The specific shades of brown and beige. They were not random. The pixels formed a picture. The unmistakable, vapid, and infuriatingly familiar face of a cartoon ape. It wore a small, stupid, multi-colored propeller hat, and its expression was one of profound, algorithmically generated boredom.

It was an NFT of a Bored Ape. It was a monkey jpeg.

The desecration was absolute. Here he was, in this ocean at the edge of his own consciousness, trying to pass Anariadne's test – the one perhaps that would allow him to finally have her – and instead, he was being confronted with the very symbol of the shallow, speculative grift he despised. It was a violation.

He hung there, suspended above the black, glassy water, a furious spectator to the absurdity. He expected something to happen, a battle, a storm, some grand, dramatic event. But the ocean remained perfectly still. The ship simply floated, a silent monument to a debased culture.

Then, a single sound. A soft, wet *fizz*.

One of the long, rectangular pixel-planks on the ship's hull detached itself. It didn't fall. It simply floated away from the structure, hung in the air for a moment, and then slowly descended until it touched the surface of the water. The moment it made contact, it dissolved with that same, soft, effervescent hiss, like an Alka-Seltzer tablet dissolving in a glass of black water.

Another plank detached. Then another. They followed the same slow path, floating away from the hull and dissolving into nothingness. The ship was un-building itself, a quiet, orderly and deeply unsettling process of entropy.

A chorus of soft, fizzing sounds now filled the air, a gentle, static-like crackle. As Oliver listened, the random noise began to coalesce, the overlapping hisses starting to form a pattern, a whisper. It was a sound that was both external and internal, a memory being spoken by the world around him.

sssssuuuu ...

... suuuu hiiisss ...

The whisper became a word, a phrase he recognized, pulled from the hazy, grappamiel-soaked memory of Javier's apartment. It was the sound of the dissolving planks, but it was also the sound of a hushed, late-night phone call.

... su hijo ...

... su hijo está a salvo ...

The voice was not Javier's. It was a deeper, more fundamental sound, the voice of the vision itself. But it was speaking the same words. *Your child.* The impossible phrase, the one his conscious mind had so desperately tried to rationalize away, was now a persistent, undeniable whisper, the very soundtrack to the dissolution of his reality.

He watched, horrified and mesmerized, as the pixelated ship came apart, plank by hissing plank. The cartoon ape's face disintegrated, its vapid expression dissolving into the black water. The propeller hat came apart, its bright colors bleeding into the darkness. The entire structure, the symbol of his anger, was being systematically erased, and all that remained was this single, haunting, incomprehensible message.

The final plank floated down, touched the water, and fizzed into oblivion.

And then, there was nothing. The ship was gone. All that was left was the vast, empty, black ocean, and the lingering, spectral whisper of two small words that now held the weight of the entire world.

Oliver hung there, suspended in the void, a solitary witness to the erasure. He was unsure of what to feel – loss, or relief. Numbness, perhaps? The ship, for all its profane absurdity, had been *something*. A structure. A form. Now, there was only the endless, featureless expanse of the somehow calm, yet menacing water.

But the emptiness did not last.

From the depths of the black sea, a new form began to rise. It was not a pixel. It was a single, long plank of real, solid wood, dark and heavy with water. It broke the glassy surface without a sound, followed by another, and then another. They were ancient timbers, weathered and scarred, streaked with the ghostly white of sea salt and the dark green of old algae. They were planks from a hundred different shipwrecks, a flotilla of wooden memories rising from a liquid graveyard.

They began to move.

With a series of soft, resonant *clicks* and *thuds*, the wooden planks started to assemble themselves. There was no visible force guiding them, no unseen hand. They simply moved with a quiet, efficient purpose, fitting together with the perfect, interlocking precision of a master shipwright's work. It was a slow, deliberate reconstruction. The hull took shape, its curving lines a testament to a forgotten age of craftsmanship. The deck was laid, plank by weathered plank. The tall, central mast rose from the center, a single, solid piece of ancient oak that seemed to groan with the memory of a thousand storms.

Oliver watched, his sense of numbness slowly being replaced by a sense of awe. This was the true ship. This was the real thing, the authentic vessel, being resurrected from the dead. What could this mean? He would have to wait and watch. Reza's words surfaced in his mind. *The essence is in the function, not the form.* The pixelated "form" of the NFT had been destroyed, and now the true, functional "essence" of the ship was being reborn from real, solid substance. He felt a surge of triumphant understanding. This was the answer.

The final plank, a small, curved piece for the prow, rose from the water and slid perfectly into place with a soft, final *thud*.

The ship was complete. It floated before him, a magnificent, tangible thing, its real, sea-worn timbers a testament to endurance and authenticity.

And then he saw it.

His happy realization gave way to a feeling of utter dismay. His gaze, which had been focused on the individual planks, now pulled back, taking in the whole of the vessel. The colors. The textures. The specific patterns of the salt-bleached wood and the dark, water-stained grain. They were not random.

The deep, dark knots in the oak had been arranged to form the empty eye sockets of a skull. The swirling, lighter grain of the teak planks above it formed the unmistakable, cartoonish lines of a jaw. The green streaks of algae on the hull were a perfect, contemptuous rendering of a ridiculous, multi-colored propeller hat.

The substance had been replaced, from the digital to the physical, from the unreal to the real. But the form, the repugnant, vapid image of the Bored Ape, had endured. It was still there, an indelible imprint in the grain, a joke told by the very fabric of reality. The ship was no longer just a monkey jpeg. It was now a real, solid, seaworthy vessel that was, impossibly, still a monkey jpeg.

Oliver hung there, suspended above the black, placid ocean, the paradox floating before him, taunting him. He felt a deep bout of cognitive whiplash, his brief moment of understanding completely annihilated by the stubborn, absurd reality of the thing. He had witnessed a miracle of reconstruction, only to find the new creation was a perfect replica of the original profanity. It was a joke, and he was the butt of it.

With a gentle, pulling sensation, his perspective began to drift away from the reborn galleon, back across the water toward the black, volcanic shore.

Anariadne was waiting for him, her expression as serene and unreadable as ever. She had not moved.

He floated back to his original spot on the sand, his feet touching the ground with a soft, soundless thud. He looked at her, his mind a jumble of conflicting ideas. He had seen the deconstruction, he had heard the whisper, he had witnessed the reconstruction. But he still didn't understand.

"I saw it," he said, his voice hollow. "But I don't know what it means. I don't know what the test was."

Anariadne glided closer, her turquoise eyes seeming to peer directly into his soul. "The test is not in the seeing, Oliver," she purred, her voice a low, sensuous hum. "In the feeling, it is."

She raised a hand and touched him, her cool, delicate fingers brushing against his cheek. The contact was electric, a jolt of pure, intoxicating energy that made his head swim.

"How do you feel?" she whispered, her face now just inches from his.

The question was so simple, so direct, it bypassed all of his confusion. He didn't have to think about the answer. He just had to be honest.

"I'm furious," he confessed, the word a raw, guttural admission. "I feel ... rage. I saw something pure get corrupted, and then I saw that corruption become permanent. It's a violation. It's wrong."

A slow, deeply satisfied smile spread across Anariadne's lips. It was the smile of a teacher who has finally received the correct, long-awaited answer from a difficult student.

"Good," she whispered, her voice full of a dark, thrilling approval. She moved closer, her lips now millimeters away from his, until Oliver felt the faintest of brushes. "The fury, it is the key. The fire. The test is not what you have seen, you beautiful man. The test is what you will *do* with it, you will."

She took a step back, and the world around him began to dissolve. The black sand, the dark, glassy ocean, the impossible ship on the horizon – it all began to waver, losing its focus, bleeding back into the cool, formless blue mist.

"You are not ready to follow my thread," she said, her voice a fading, musical echo as her own form began to grow translucent. "Not yet. You have seen the cage. You have felt the fire. But the final test ... it is still to come. You must act. *Probaris en silencio, sat in actuare.*"

"What does that mean? Act how?" Oliver cried out, reaching for her as she disappeared. "What do I do?"

Her final, whispered words brushed against his consciousness as the last of the vision faded away.

"*Show me.*"

The blue mist dissolved completely. Oliver was back in his bed, under the covers, the room still spinning, although a little slower than before. He was left with the residue of a confounding and terrible vision, and a new, burning and unanswered question.

What was he going to do with all this rage?

781821 (March 21)

It was over.

The thought was quiet and leaden in the back of Nick's mind as he stared at the digital archive of the Washington Post on his screen. It was Tuesday morning. The Sunday deadline he had so arrogantly set in his anonymous message had passed two days ago. He had spent every waking moment since then compulsively refreshing the archives, running a simple script to scan the classifieds for the keyword "Orpheus." Nothing on Sunday. Nothing on Monday.

His grand, unconventional gambit had been a failure. A silent, humiliating and total failure. They had ignored him. His clever, encrypted message was just another piece of digital refuse, deleted without a thought by some junior associate. He was a fool. He had taken his one shot, his one piece of genuine, unique intelligence, and fired it into the void.

He leaned back in the creaking chair of his depressing little cubicle. He was back where he started, but worse. Before, he had a lead, a possibility. Now, he had nothing. He had sealed the only potential door with his own failed cleverness.

He should just pack it in. Delete the files, cancel the rental on this sad little office, go home to Becky and start looking for a real job. A respectable job. The thought was a soul-crushing defeat.

But he couldn't. Not yet. There was one last compulsive act to perform, one final ritual of self-torture. He had to check one last time.

He turned back to the monitor, his fingers moving with a grim, mechanical purpose. He opened the search parameters for the newspaper archive and changed the date to today, March 21st. It was a pointless, hopeless gesture. They had missed the deadline. The game was over. He hit enter.

The script ran. For a moment, the screen was blank. And then, a single line of blue, hyperlinked text appeared.

One result found.

His heart gave a single, hard, painful thump against his ribs. It had to be a mistake. A false positive. He clicked the link, his hand trembling slightly.

The page loaded. It was the digital replica of today's print edition of the Washington Post. Section C. The Classifieds. And there, tucked away in the "Antiques & Collectibles" section, between an ad for a Victorian-era rolltop desk and another for a collection of porcelain dolls, was a small, two-line notice.

`Seeking info on Irish painters. Orpheus, please post findings on the ArtNet forum, thread #8711.`

He stared at the words, reading them over and over, the letters seeming to dazzle on the screen. It was real. They had responded. Not on his timeline, but on theirs.

A slow, triumphant grin spread across his face: the first genuine smile he'd felt in what seemed like a lifetime. It was a move in a game of chess. By ignoring his Sunday deadline and placing the ad on a Tuesday, they were sending a message of their own: *We are in control. We move when we are ready. We are not being led by you.* It was a power play, and he admired the sheer, professional arrogance of it. It meant they were taking him very, very seriously.

His mind raced, the logic of his own gambit replaying with a newfound, beautiful clarity. The anonymous email, sent from a public library terminal, had been the key. It had been a ghost note, untraceable. But by referencing his own spectacular failure – the "computationally unsound" analysis, a detail known only to the DoJ and their lawyers – he had provided a secret handshake. He had proven his provenance without providing a shred of legally actionable proof. He had demonstrated that he was a credible insider, not a random crank.

And they had taken the bait.

The ad was their acceptance of his protocol. The ArtNet forum, an obscure, forgotten thread from 2012, was now their digital dead drop. The ball was back in his court. He would post his next move on thread #8711, on that godforsaken forum, under his new official cover, "Orpheus."

The despair of the last few days evaporated, burned away by the clean, cold fire of a new purpose. He was no longer a disgraced analyst, a man haunted by his own failures. He was Orpheus. He had descended into the underworld of his own humiliation and emerged with a key.

He closed the browser window. He had work to do. He had a message to craft. The real work, the quiet, dangerous work of a spy, was about to begin.

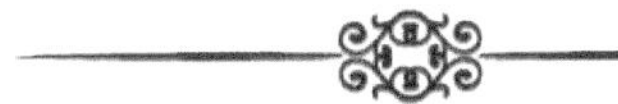

781821 (March 21)

A sharp, percussive pounding dragged Oliver from a deep, dreamless void. It was a relentless, punishing rhythm, a drumbeat of pure pain. It took him a full minute of disoriented consciousness to realize the sound was not coming from outside, but from within his own skull.

He rolled over, a groan escaping his lips. His head was a pressurized vessel, every thought a fresh wave of agony. His mouth was as dry as sand, and a low-grade nausea churned in his stomach. A hangover fitting for two bottles of wine. He fumbled for his phone on the nightstand, squinting against the screen's harsh light.

It was 12:15 p.m.

And then he saw the date.

March 21.

The numbers seemed to hang in the air, charged with a deep and terrible significance. One year. An entire, impossible year since the day his father had died, the day his old world had ended and this new, strange, perilous one had begun.

The grief, which he had been trying to outrun for months, finally caught up with him. It came not as a gentle wave of sadness, but as a violent, overwhelming tsunami. A raw, guttural sob tore from his throat, a sound of pure, animal pain. He curled into a ball on the bed, and he cried. He cried for his father, for the man he had lost twice – once to death and again to the labyrinth of secrets he had left behind. He cried for Daniela, for the simple, beautiful thing he had so carelessly broken. He cried for himself, for the man he had become, a weary traveler lost in a landscape of riddles he couldn't solve.

The sorrow was a cleansing fire for a time, a pure expression of loss. But as the afternoon wore on and the tears dried up, the grief began to subside, transmuting into something harder, hotter and uglier.

Rage.

It started with his father. *Su hijo.* The whisper from the Montevideo night. He saw Javier's face, heard the hushed, deferential tone. *Your child is safe with me.* The thought that his father might be alive, that he might be a puppet master pulling the strings of this entire, agonizing quest, was a notion so monstrous it was an act of violence. The rage at that possibility was a clean, bright flame.

The flame jumped, finding new fuel. He thought of Anariadne, of her impossible tests and her seductive, dismissive smile. He had been judged and found wanting by a beautiful, indifferent deity, and the injustice of it burned. He thought of the Noncemeister, his goofy, chaotic guide, now a slumped, pathetic figure in a cage of light. The anger at his guide's weakness, at his abandonment, was a bitter, choking smoke. He thought of the Ordinals spammers, the "monkey jpeg" artists, happily desecrating the one pure thing he had left to believe in.

By 8 p.m., the emotional storm had passed, leaving behind a hollowed-out, ruinous calm. The pounding in his head had subsided to a dull throb, and the nausea had receded, replaced by a deep, gnawing emptiness.

He needed to get out. He needed air. He needed the simple, restorative trinity of grease, whisky and noise. He needed the "hair of the dog."

He knew where to go.

He stood, his movements stiff, and he walked to the closet. He pulled on a pair of jeans and a dark hoodie. He didn't look in the mirror. He didn't want to see the man who was looking back. He just needed to put one foot in front of the other, to move, to find a place where he could finally silence the relentless cacophony in his own head.

The walk to Washington Place was a grim, determined march. Oliver kept his head down, the hoodie pulled up, a man moving through his city like a fugitive. When he descended the steps into Pubkey, the warmth and noise of the place were a physical buffer against the cold emptiness he felt inside. It was a Tuesday night, but the bar was lively, the low, happy thrum of conversation a welcome antidote to the relentless monologue in his own head.

He slid into an empty stool at the bar. The bartender came over, and he ordered without looking at the menu. "A double smashburger, and a double Laphroaig, neat."

He needed something solid, something real to anchor him. And he needed a fire to fight the fire that was burning him up from the inside.

The whisky arrived first. He took a long, deep swallow, the peaty, medicinal smoke a familiar, punishing comfort. It burned a clean path down his throat, a controlled demolition of the feelings that were threatening to overwhelm him. He took another. By the time his burger arrived, a glorious, greasy monument to American comfort food, the first double was gone. He ordered a second.

He ate with a kind of detached, mechanical hunger, not really tasting the food. His focus was on the whisky. He could feel it working its magic, a slow, chemical tide rising to meet the crashing waves of his own turmoil. The sharp edges of his grief began to soften. The hot, searing anger at his mother, at Anariadne, at the universe, cooled to a low, manageable simmer. The pounding in his head from the morning's hangover finally receded.

It was a false peace, he knew, a temporary ceasefire brokered by alcohol, but it was a peace nonetheless. For the first time all day, he felt a semblance of control, a brief, fragile clarity in the wreckage of his own mind. He finished his burger, took another sip of his second whisky, leaned back, and surveyed the room.

He saw the familiar bitcoin shrine, the comforting rows of books behind the bar, the red LED ticker displaying the price: a steady, indifferent heartbeat in a volatile world. He saw groups of people laughing, debating, arguing, a community he felt a universe away from, but was glad to be near. He was just another patron, just another guy having a burger and a drink on a Tuesday night. He was normal. He drained his second double Laphroaig and ordered a third.

And then he saw them.

Sitting at the far end of the bar, their backs to him, were two figures he recognized instantly. They were wearing the same brightly colored hoodies from the first time he saw them – one with a cartoon dog, the other with a pixelated penguin. They were unmistakable. It was the two "crypto bros" from Vince's event a month ago. The ones who had asked about the "rugpull." They were laughing, their heads close together as they looked at something on a phone. The brief, fragile sense of peace in Oliver's mind evaporated, replaced by a new, and very specific, point of focus.

As if sensing his stare, the one in the penguin hoodie turned, saw him, and his eyes widened in recognition. He nudged his friend, and they both slid off their barstools and began walking towards him.

Oliver braced himself, a hot surge of resentment rising in his throat. He expected a confrontation, a continuation of their brief, hostile encounter.

Instead, the dog-hoodie man approached with a wide, friendly, almost goofy grin.

"Hey man, no hard feelings about last time, right?" he said, extending a hand. "You called us dumbfucks. Which, like, okay, fair enough. We were pretty new to this whole scene."

Oliver, completely thrown by the friendly overture, just stared at the offered hand for a second before shaking it reflexively.

"You were right, dude," the penguin-hoodie man added, just as enthusiastically. "That whole event, and especially that first speaker, that Gideon guy? Totally blew our minds. We're, like, full-on converts now. We're bitcoiners."

Oliver was stunned. He had been so ready for a fight, and instead, he was being met with the earnest, wide-eyed zeal of the newly converted. He felt a small, unexpected flicker of pride. He had actually made a difference.

"Really?" Oliver said, a genuine smile touching his lips for the first time that night. "That's ... that's great to hear. Welcome."

"Yeah, dude, totally," Dog Hoodie said, pulling up a chair. "We sold all our ETH, all our SOL, everything. Took a huge loss, but whatever. We're all in on the one true chain now. It's the only one with, like, real security, real liquidity, you know?"

"I do," Oliver said, feeling a growing sense of camaraderie. "So, you're just stacking sats now? Moving them to self-custody?"

The two men exchanged a confused look, then burst out laughing.

"Stacking sats?" Penguin Hoodie chuckled. "Dude, we're traders. We came to a realization after that event. Why are we trading jpegs on these garbage, centralized chains that could get rugged at any second, when we could be trading them on the most secure, most decentralized, and most valuable blockchain in the world?"

The blood drained from Oliver's face. The nascent feeling of kinship, the brief flicker of pride – it all vanished, replaced by a hot, sickening sense of fury.

"You're ... you're talking about Ordinals," he said, the word tasting like poison.

"Hell yeah, dude!" Dog Hoodie exclaimed, pulling out his phone and enthusiastically showing Oliver the screen. It was a picture of a pixelated, cartoon frog. "I just inscribed this bad boy yesterday. One of the first 10,000 ever. It's like owning a piece of history, man. This is gonna be worth a fortune. We're so early!"

Oliver stared at the stupid, pixelated frog on the phone screen. He looked at the earnest, greedy and utterly clueless faces of the two young men in front of him. They hadn't been converted. They hadn't understood a single word of Gideon's speech or Mateo's philosophy. They had just found a new, more secure casino to place their bets in. They were the invaders, the parasites, the ones bringing their thoughtless, fiat mindset into the heart of the citadel.

"You don't get it," Oliver said, his voice a low, dangerous murmur. "It's not for this. The timechain isn't a canvas for your stupid, speculative cartoons. It's a final settlement layer for a new global monetary system. You're just clogging it up with expensive spam. You're taking a tool of liberation and turning it into a toy."

The two men's enthusiastic smiles faltered. They looked at each other, then back at Oliver.

"Whoa, dude, what's your problem?" Penguin Hoodie said, a defensive edge to his voice. "We left Ethereum. We chose Bitcoin. We're using the chain. Isn't that what you're supposed to do? It's permissionless, bro."

"Permissionless doesn't mean you should be a fucking idiot," Oliver slurred, the third double whisky now fully taking control. "You've learned nothing. You're just another grifter looking for a pump, bringing your shitcoinery into the one place that was supposed to be clean."

"Shitcoinery?" Dog Hoodie said, his face flushed with anger. "Dude, we're building a culture here! Digital artifacts! This is the future!"

"It's the same garbage past, just with a new, expensive wrapper!" Oliver shot back, standing up to meet him, his stool scraping loudly on the wooden floor. The entire bar was looking at them now.

"You know what, man? You're an asshole," Dog Hoodie said, shoving Oliver lightly in the chest.

And that was it. The grief of the day, the pain of his loss, the unresolved riddle of his own purpose on top of the burning, righteous fury from Anariadne's test – it all coalesced into a single, white-hot point of action. He was supposed to *do* something with his rage. This was it.

He threw a punch. It was a clumsy, drunken swing, but it connected with the side of the man's jaw with a satisfying, meaty thud.

The man in the dog hoodie staggered back, more out of surprise than pain, his hand flying to his face. "What the hell, man!"

The entire bar, which had been a low, happy thrum of conversation, fell into a sudden, watchful quiet. The man in the penguin hoodie, seeing his friend get hit, reacted with a surge of beery courage and lunged at Oliver.

What followed was not a fight. It was a pathetic, flailing and deeply uncoordinated brawl. Oliver was not a fighter. He had been in exactly two real fights in his life, both in middle school, and he'd lost both decisively. The two crypto bros, for all their talk of "digital artifacts," were clearly more comfortable with a keyboard than a fistfight as well.

Penguin Hoodie grabbed Oliver by the front of his hoodie, pulling him forward. They stumbled together, a clumsy, grappling dance of incompetence.

Oliver tried to throw another punch, but it glanced harmlessly off the man's shoulder. Dog Hoodie, having recovered from the initial shock, joined the fray, grabbing Oliver from behind in an awkward bear hug.

They were a three-man vortex of pathetic violence, knocking into an empty table with a loud crash, sending glasses shattering to the floor. Oliver was taking hits now, short, ineffective rabbit punches to his ribs and the side of his head from Dog Hoodie, while Penguin Hoodie tried to pin his arms. He could feel the sting of the blows, the desperate, animal panic rising in his chest.

In the clumsy, three-way wrestle, Penguin Hoodie was bent over, his face pressed into Oliver's shoulder. Oliver, acting on pure, desperate instinct, drove his knee up, hard.

It connected with a sickening, soft impact.

The man in the penguin hoodie let out a high-pitched, wheezing gasp and immediately released his grip, doubling over and collapsing to the floor, clutching his groin, his face a pale, sweating mask of pure agony.

One down. The small, dirty victory gave Oliver a fresh surge of wild, misplaced confidence. He twisted in Dog Hoodie's grip, trying to get free, but the man held on, his face now a mask of genuine rage.

"You're gonna pay for that, you crazy asshole!" he grunted, trying to get a better grip.

It was at that moment that the restroom door at the back of the bar swung open. A new figure emerged, a man who was a stark contrast to his two flailing friends. He was built like a small refrigerator, with a thick, muscular neck and the calm, confident posture of a man who spent half his waking hours in the gym and the other half on a tanning bed.

He took in the scene in a fraction of a second: his friend on the floor, his other friend grappling clumsily with a wild-eyed Oliver, the entire bar watching in stunned fascination. He didn't shout. He didn't run. He just walked forward with a calm, deliberate purpose.

Oliver saw him coming, but he was still tangled up with Dog Hoodie. He managed to push him away just as the gym rat arrived. He had just enough time to register a pair of cold, determined eyes and a large, meaty fist traveling at an incredible speed toward his face.

There was a brilliant, blinding flash of white light. A sound like a distant firecracker. And then, the world went completely, blissfully black.

The world came back not as a gentle dawn, but as a series of harsh, fractured sensations. The cold, gritty pavement against his cheek. A sharp, coppery taste in his mouth. The distant sound of a car horn. And a single, recurring word.

"Up. Get up."

Oliver's eyes fluttered open. He was slumped on the sidewalk at the top of the stairs outside Pubkey. The stoic, bearded bouncer was standing over him, his arms crossed, looking deeply disappointed.

"You're done here," the bouncer said, his voice a low, non-negotiable rumble. "Time to go home."

The memories of the last few minutes came flooding back in a hot, sickening wave. The argument. The first punch. The wheezing gasp from the man in the penguin hoodie. And the final, blinding flash of white light from the fist of the Gym Rat. The humiliation was a fresh, searing brand.

"No," Oliver slurred, his jaw aching. He pushed himself up onto unsteady feet, a raw, irrational rage overriding all sense of self-preservation. "That asshole ... I'm not done."

He lunged for the doorway, a clumsy, stumbling attempt to get back inside, to get back at the man who had laid him out. The bouncer didn't even seem to exert himself. He just put a hand the size of a catcher's mitt on Oliver's chest and stopped him cold.

"I said, you're done," the bouncer repeated, his voice still calm, but with a new, harder edge.

"Get out of my way," Oliver spat, trying to shove the bouncer's arm away. It was like pushing against a brick wall. The alcohol, the grief, the fury – they had all curdled into a single, self-destructive impulse. He was beyond reason.

"You need to leave, now," the bouncer said, his patience clearly gone.

"Fuck you," Oliver snarled, and he made the stupidest decision of his life. He swung at the bouncer.

He never saw the second man. Another bouncer, bigger than the first, must have emerged from the doorway. Oliver only registered a sudden, immense pressure on his back and shoulders. He was grabbed, spun around and slammed face-first into the brick wall next to the entrance. The impact knocked the wind out of him, his head exploding with a dull, concussive thud.

They were professionals. This wasn't a clumsy bar brawl anymore. They held him against the wall, one of them twisting his arm behind his back until a bolt of sharp, electric pain shot up to his shoulder.

"We told you to leave," a new voice said in his ear. "You didn't listen."

He felt a knee drive into the back of his thigh, and his legs buckled. They dragged him away from the door and halfway down the block. Then, with a final, contemptuous shove, they pushed him in the direction of the curb. He tumbled, a graceless heap of limbs, and landed in a crumpled pile on the sidewalk of Washington Place.

He lay there, dazed, the world a blurry mess of streetlights and passing headlights. He looked up to see the two bouncers standing over him, two dark, imposing silhouettes looking down.

"You're banned," the first one said, his voice carrying down with a cold finality. "Don't ever come back here."

They turned and disappeared back inside.

For a long time, Oliver just lay there, the city's indifferent nightlife flowing around him. A couple walking a dog gave him a wide berth. A group of students laughed as they passed by. He was just another drunk, another piece of human refuse on a New York sidewalk.

Slowly, painfully, he pushed himself up. His face throbbed. His ribs ached. His pride was a shattered ruin. He began to stumble away, with no destination in mind, just a deep, instinctual need to disappear.

He found himself at the edge of Washington Square Park, the iconic arch a dark, skeletal gateway in the night. He staggered in, past the empty dog run, past the chess tables where a few die-hards were still playing under the lamplight. He found a dark, secluded path and collapsed onto the cold, damp ground near a bench, the metallic taste of his own blood fresh in his mouth.

This was it. The bottom. He had lost everything. He had lost Daniela, the one person who had truly seen him. He had lost the respect of his community, cast out from the one place he'd begun to feel a sense of belonging. He had lost his dignity, beaten and thrown onto the street like garbage. He had even lost his guide, the Noncemeister, a captive in some distant, terrible prison of light. He was a king of nothing, ruling over an empire of his own wreckage.

A small, brown rat, its audacity a final, fitting insult, skittered over his outstretched leg. He didn't have the energy to even flinch. He just lay there, a man who had been cast out, his throne the cold, hard ground of a public park.

His cheek was pressed against the damp earth. He tried to shift, to find a slightly more comfortable position in his own debasement. He lifted his head a few inches and let it fall back onto what he thought was a small, soft tuft of grass by the leg of the bench.

It moved.

It was warm.

He peeled his cheek away, a new, strange sense of alarm cutting through his daze. He pushed himself up onto one elbow and looked. It wasn't a tuft of grass. It was a foot. A bare, impossibly filthy human foot, resting on the ground. His eyes traveled up from the foot to the leg, to the tattered, filthy t-shirt, and finally, to the face of the homeless man – *that* homeless man – who was sitting silently on the bench, looking out at the darkness.

And in that moment, staring at the impossible, placid presence of the man who was not there, the final wall of Oliver's self-deception crumbled into dust.

It wasn't the Ordinals bros. It wasn't Maren, or Bojan, or his mother's new suitor. It wasn't even the great, cosmic riddle of his father's legacy. He saw it now, with a clarity so pure and so painful it felt like another sucker punch. The real enemy, the true architect of his own magnificent ruin, had been the wine. The whisky. The endless, desperate search for a temporary reprieve, for a chemical salve to numb the pain of his own grief, of his own fear. He had been running from his own demons, the alcohol serving as the fuel that had powered his long, self-destructive descent to this exact spot, on this punishing ground. It was a deep, profound, and ego-crushing admission. The truth.

He had to stop. He had to. This was it. He couldn't run away from his demons anymore. It was time to turn around and face them. Finally, lying bloodied and bruised on the cold, damp and unforgiving floor of Washington Square Park, submerged in the overpowering stench of overflowing trash cans and sewer rats, at the lowest point in his life, Oliver was ready.

At that moment, as if sensing the shift within him, the homeless man stirred. He turned his head slowly and looked down at Oliver, his pale, cloudy eyes seeming to see him, truly see him, for the first time. A slow, familiar and slightly deranged grin spread across his face.

"Rum thing, innit, Battu?"

PART II. VERNATUM

CHAPTER 7. APRIL 14

781895 (March 21)

The words, spoken in that impossibly familiar, sing-song voice, cut through the thick, miserable fog of Oliver's consciousness. It was a sound that didn't belong, a melody from a different universe played in the squalor of his own personal hell. He lifted his head from the man's filthy foot, his mind struggling to process the auditory illusion. It couldn't be. He was drunk, beaten, concussed. He had to be hallucinating.

"What ... what did you say?" Oliver whispered, his voice a raw croak.

The homeless man's deranged grin widened. He winked, a slow, deliberate gesture. "Being. Being. Being. Quite a thingamajig, innit? How to be when you've forgotten how to be? One moment you're on the tippety-top of the world, the next you're tasting the particular *terroir* of a public park. A real pickle! Not that the park's *terroir* tastes like a pickle, but you know what I'm talking about, right, Batlu?"

There was no mistaking it. The voice. The absurd vocabulary. The nicknames. It was him.

Oliver stared, his mind refusing to accept what his senses were telling him. And then, the world began to change. The edges of the homeless man's form started to shimmer and pixelate, dissolving not into smoke, but into a cascade of glowing, purple motes of light. The grimy t-shirt, the filthy trousers, the pale, cloudy eyes – they all broke apart, revealing the familiar, absurd figure that had been hiding underneath all along. The egg-shaped head. The pig-like nose. The deep brown mischievous and joyful eyes. The tweed jacket that seemed to contain the faint, swirling pattern of a distant galaxy.

As the last of the derelict's visage dissolved, the world around him went with it. The cold, damp ground of Washington Square Park melted away. The distant wail of a siren, the rustle of rats in the bushes, the looming, skeletal branches of the trees – all of it dissolved into a deep, warm and wonderfully familiar purple.

He was back. He was floating in the gentle, comforting void of the timechain, the Noncemeister hovering before him, looking as solid and as nonsensically real as ever.

A wave of overwhelming relief washed over Oliver, so powerful he struggled to breathe for a few moments. The pain in his ribs, the throb in his jaw, the deep, aching bruise of his own humiliation – it all seemed to fade, replaced by a joy so pure and so absolute it brought tears to his eyes.

"It's you!" he cried out, the name a sob of pure gratitude. "You're back! I thought ... I saw you. You were in a cage."

"A *cage*?" The Noncemeister looked genuinely affronted.

"Yes, you were in a cage. The bars were made of white light and you were trapped inside, looking helpless and hopeless," Oliver explained, surprised at the Noncemeister's reaction.

"Come now, Batue!" The Noncemeister boomed. "Me, the master of the nonces, the keeper of the timechain in a cage like a common criminal? Is this nonsense? Have you been practicing your nonsense while I was gone? It sure sounds like it. Phish posh!"

"What are you talking about? I saw you. It was you." Oliver pressed, his relief giving way to bewilderment.

The Noncemeister seemed to consider what Oliver said. He pulled out a giant magnifying glass from his back pocket and held it close to Oliver's face. He shut one eye and with the open eye, peered through the lens, as if examining Oliver for traces of veracity.

"What on Earth are you doing?" Oliver asked, taking a small step back from the magnifying glass, the bewilderment now giving way to mild irritation.

"Well ..." the Noncemeister said with a heavy shrug, "I conceive what you say is supposable, I suppose. A cage you say? Well, well, well ... who would have thunk it? In any event, water under the bridge, amirite tiger? What's over is over. It's under too, now that you mention it."

"Wait what?" Oliver snapped urgently. He needed answers, "But who did it? Who trapped you? Where have you been?"

The Noncemeister chuckled, a mischievous twinkle in his eye. "Where is a when, Battu, and who is a what, and why is a question best answered with a slice of cake, don't you think? Is a one a seven or is a seven a four? The jailer holds the key, and the key is the lock, and the lock is a question you seem to be asking yourself! The tautological loop of creation, wouldn't you say?"

The answer was a perfect, infuriating piece of nonsense that told him nothing and everything all at once. It was clear the Noncemeister wasn't going to give him a straight answer. As he had said before, it was something Oliver had to figure out for himself. He decided to let it go for the moment.

"I'm just ... I'm glad you're back," Oliver said, the simple, honest truth of it cutting through all the strangeness. "Are you here to stay this time? For good?"

"For good? For bad? For the nonce, Batlu, I am here for the nonce!" he declared with a flourish. "And isn't that a lovely bit of business? We are always, only, ever here for the nonce."

Oliver felt a sudden surge of warmth, his irritation from the classic, obtuse stonewalling now gone. It was a cryptic, noncommittal answer, but it was enough. He had his guide back. He wasn't alone anymore.

And then, the warm purple of the timechain seemed to cool, a familiar, ethereal blue mist seeping in from the edges of the void. A new presence entered the space.

Anariadne.

She materialized between them, as graceful and as luminous as ever. But this time, Oliver felt no surge of desire, no intoxicating pull. He just felt a quiet, weary clarity. He saw her now for what she was: a beautiful, dangerous riddle. A test.

"You beautiful, brave man," she purred, her voice a sensuous melody. "You have felt the fire, yes. The cage you have seen. The second test, passed it, you have. Ready you are for the third test."

She smiled, a slow, knowing, and deeply seductive expression. With a single, fluid motion, she unclasped a golden pin at her collar. Her robe, now free, fell from her shoulders, pooling at her feet in a heap of white light. She stood before him, a perfect, incandescent form, an offer of absolute surrender.

"Have me now, you can," she whispered.

Oliver looked at her, at the perfect, timeless beauty, at the promise of an end to all his wanting. He saw the path she offered, a blissful, ecstatic dissolution into her being. And he knew, with a certainty that settled deep in his soul, that it was a lie. A beautiful, perfect lie.

He turned to look at the Noncemeister, who was pretending to avert his gaze, his eyes occasionally darting in Anariadne's direction. He caught Oliver looking at him and turned quickly in the opposite direction, whistling an urgent discordant tune.

Oliver locked his gaze unshakably with Anariadne's eyes, his pupils not diverting a single millimeter. He stepped forward until he was just inches from her. He reached out to rest his hand softly on her perfect, now bare waist, the skin cool and smooth like polished stone. He pulled her toward him gently and kissed her, for the first and very last time. Then he stepped back.

"Goodbye, Anariadne," he said.

For an instant, her turquoise eyes widened in deep, cosmic shock. And then, she began to dissolve. Not into mist, but into pure, brilliant light.

"*Ego viliye in claritate lumiere ...*" Oliver whispered, finally understanding. *I dissolve in the clarity of light.* He had seen her for what she was, and in the clarity of his rejection, she had no more power over him.

As the last of her light faded, he turned back to the Noncemeister, who was observing the entire affair wide-eyed.

The Noncemeister let out two sharp whistles. "My word, Batew, you really are a big boy now, aren't you? Why'd you let her go after all that? I swear I wasn't looking. You could have asked me to leave for a bit and I would have. Gladly. You know what I mean? Taken care of business with that fine young lady. I could have ducked around the corner right there." The Noncemeister pointed theatrically into the purple distance.

Oliver chuckled. "That would have been a disaster, and you know it."

"A disaster? My dear boy, a disaster is a Tuesday without a proper cup of tea! That would have been ... an educational experience!" the Noncemeister declared, puffing out his chest. He then sobered, his expression turning more serious as he seemed to reflect on the events of the past few months. "But you are right, Battu. The path you chose, the one of clarity ... it is the much more interesting story. And a much better look on you, if I do say so myself."

Oliver felt a warmth spread through him, a feeling of genuine, earned pride. He had his guide back. He wasn't alone anymore. He shrugged, the simple gesture a release of weeks of pent-up tension, and decided to move on to another question that was at the top of his mind.

"So," he began, his voice now a mixture of curiosity and accusation. "The homeless man. The one in front of my building, the one in Harlem, the one outside the pub, the one on the park bench just now ... that was you all along, wasn't it? That was your disguise."

The Noncemeister looked utterly shocked, as if Oliver had just accused him of being a tax auditor. "Me?" he gasped, a hand flying to his chest in a gesture of theatrical offense. "A derelict? A vagrant? My dear boy, I am a being of pure, unadulterated, top-shelf noncense! A bespoke absurdity! Do I look like a man who sleeps on a bench? The very idea! Pshaw!"

"But you looked just like him before you ..." Oliver started, but the Noncemeister cut him off.

"Perhaps," he said, tapping a thoughtful finger on his chin, "you met my ... third cousin, twice removed, on my mother's side? A different sort of fellow entirely. Lives in a different sort of ... well, let's just call it a 'neighborhood.' The walls are a bit thinner over there, you see. Sometimes things ... leak."

The answer was classic Noncemeister – an answer that both denied everything and hinted at a reality so vast and strange Oliver couldn't begin to comprehend it. He decided to press on.

"And the things he was saying," Oliver said, his voice gaining urgency. "*Hessele tu rabe. Ess temper, eh innit? N'as it, ser.* Was that Atlantean? What does it mean?"

The Noncemeister scoffed, waving a dismissive hand. "Atlantean! Sounds like a dreadful bore! A made-up language, if you ask me." He paused, stroking his chin thoughtfully for a moment before continuing, "Although, now that I personally think about it, aren't all languages made up? How about that, Battu? You taught me something new today."

"So, you don't know about Atlantean?" Oliver asked, the old, familiar feeling of being led in circles returning.

"I know about everything, Batlu. You know that. You know that I know that you know that I know. And et cetera and so on," The Noncemeister replied with a grand, sweeping gesture.

"So, tell me, then. What is it? Is it a real language? Pittamiglio's great-grandson told me it might be. Was the homeless man speaking it?" Oliver asked, his voice rising with a slight edge.

"I just told you it's a made-up language," The Noncemeister replied, his expression one of perfect, unassailable innocence.

"Ugh!" Oliver said, running a hand through his hair in exasperation. "You're doing that thing again. I guess this means I need to figure this out on my own."

"Shush, shush, tiger," The Noncemeister chided gently, his tone softening. "Why the long face? The answers will come when you're ready. Now, here's one answer you're ready for."

He gestured into the purple distance. The void shimmered, and a new scene coalesced before Oliver's eyes. It was a small, self-contained bubble of memory, perfectly clear and vivid. He saw himself from a few months ago, sitting in the warm, familiar interior of O'Connell's pub with Shannon and Aisling.

Shannon was speaking, her voice clear in the vision. " … *I had completely forgotten, but he went through a phase illustrating comic books. My nephew, Mike, saw a set of them in a record shop somewhere in Brooklyn.*"

Oliver watched his past self digest this new information. He then heard his own voice from the memory.

"*Wow, that's very cool, Shannon. Do you know where the shop is?*"

"*It just struck me we could get the set for you as a gift,*" Shannon's voice replied. "*I need to check with Mike on the location – he said it was in Bushwick. I'll ask him to look into it for you.*"

The bubble of memory shimmered and faded back into the purple void. Oliver turned and looked at the Noncemeister, his mind racing. "Of course," he said, the words a reverent whisper. "I had completely forgotten! The comic books that Bryce supposedly created. Do you think there's something there?"

"Do *you* think there's something there?" The Noncemeister asked him back, a lilting echo.

"Well there's only one way to find out," Oliver said, a new, powerful sense of purpose surging through him. "I need to track down that record shop and get my hands on those comics. God, I had felt like I'd hit the bottom just a few minutes ago. Now I feel like I have a way forward!"

The Noncemeister looked at Oliver, his expression now solemn, the usual mischievous twinkle in his eyes replaced by a more grave expression. "Ah, Batlu, but every passage is a rite of failure." He paused, tilting his head. "Wait, did I say that right? Anywho, you know what I mean. Now, let's get you back on your feet and in your bed."

And with that, a snap of his fingers, and he was gone.

The warm, comforting purple of the timechain dissolved, not into a gentle mist, but like a switch being flipped off. The world rushed back in with a brutal, sensory violence. The cold, damp earth against his cheek. The overpowering stench of days-old garbage. The sharp, throbbing ache in his jaw.

Oliver opened his eyes. He was back on the ground in Washington Square Park. He was still bloodied, still bruised, still a mess. But something fundamental had shifted. The feeling of utter ruin was gone, replaced by a quiet, clear-headed resolve.

He pushed himself up, his muscles groaning in protest. He got to his knees, and then, slowly, unsteadily, he rose to his feet. He stood there for a moment in the darkness, a solitary, battered figure under the watchful, indifferent gaze of the city. He had been through the fire. He had been to the bottom. But now, he felt the bounce. He turned and began the long, slow walk home.

781972 (March 22)

Oliver woke to the sharp, insistent daylight of a new day. For a moment, he didn't know where he was. The ceiling was his own, but the landscape of his own body felt foreign, a territory mapped with aches and pains he didn't recognize. He pushed himself up, a groan escaping his lips as a constellation of deep, purple bruises on his ribs made their presence known.

He swung his legs out of bed and stood, his movements slow and deliberate. He walked to the bathroom and looked at his reflection in the mirror. The man looking back was a wreck. A cut on his lip was swollen and split. A dark, ugly bruise was beginning to bloom high on his left cheekbone, where the gym rat's fist had connected. His eyes, though, were different. They were bloodshot and tired, but they were also clear. The deep, weary haze of the last few months was gone.

The memory of the previous night was a series of sharp, distinct images: the brawl, the bouncers, the cold ground of the park, the impossible appearance of his guide, and the final, quiet walk home under the streetlights. He had been to the bottom. But for the first time in a very long time, he didn't feel like he was drowning. He felt ... solid.

He walked into the kitchen to quench a primal urge for hydration. As he filled a glass at the sink, his eyes fell upon the two empty bottles of Haut-Brion from two nights ago, standing on the counter like a monument to his own folly. And next to them, the sleek, glass door of his father's wine fridge. The fridge his father had owned, but that he had so diligently stocked over the past few months, turning it into his own personal arsenal of self-destruction.

He stood there for a long moment, the glass of water in his hand. He looked at the bottles, at the perfectly temperature-controlled collection within. He saw the elegant labels, the deep, promising colors of the liquid inside. He saw a row of expensive, liquid comforts. A row of beautiful, elegant cages.

He put the water down, his decision made. It was a quiet, simple, and absolute choice.

He opened the door to the wine fridge. A soft, cool puff of air washed over him. He reached in and took out the first bottle, a 2016 Sassicaia, the one he had opened the day Eddie came to visit. There was still half of it left. He popped open the vacuum seal rubber cork and let himself inhale once: cherries, saddle leather, a winter lost to a simmering inferno. Without further hesitation, he poured the deep, ruby liquid down the sink.

The rich, complex aroma filled the kitchen, a scent that had once meant so-phistication and comfort. Now, it just smelled like a beautiful lie. He watched as the last of the wine gurgled down the drain, leaving a dark, purple stain in the stainless-steel basin.

He reached back into the fridge. A bottle of Barolo. He uncorked it and poured it out. Then a 2005 Saint Emilion. Then a Brunello. He worked with a calm, methodical purpose, a man performing a necessary, if unpleasant, chore. It was not a ceremony. It was a cleansing.

After the wine was gone, he moved to the liquor cabinet. He took out a half-empty bottle of Ardbeg. He poured the peaty, golden liquid down the drain – the medicinal, smoky smell a sharp, acrid reminder of his own public disgrace. He found the bottles of Japanese whisky Vince had brought over, the expensive tequila he and Daniela had once shared on a warm summer night. One by one, they followed the others into the drain.

He was pouring thousands of dollars into the New York City sewer system. *The booze is just taking a shortcut to the sewers, without my bladder as the temporary escrow*, he chuckled to himself as he heard the liquid gushing down the drain. A part of his old self, the part that still thought in terms of fiat value and status symbols, screamed in protest. But the new, clearer part of him felt nothing but a wonderful sense of lightness. He was not pouring away assets. He was pouring away the fuel for his own descent. He was getting rid of the poison.

Finally, it was done. The last bottle was empty. He stood in the quiet kitchen, the air pungent with the remnants of a magnificent, evaporated cellar. He looked at the row of empty bottles on the counter. They were just glass now, their power gone.

He rinsed the sink, washing away the last of the purple stains. He gathered the empty bottles, the clinking of the glass a final, hollow sound, and he placed them all in the recycling bin.

The house was clean. He felt a quiet, unfamiliar sense of peace. The relentless, noisy committee in his head had finally adjourned. He was sore, he was bruised, but he was present. He was ready.

781974 (March 22)

Nick was a different man. The simmering rage and the sour taste of humiliation were gone, replaced by a cold, clean, fully singular sense of purpose. He was an operative with a mission. He left his apartment in Queens before Becky was even awake, a thermos of strong, black coffee in hand, and took the F train back into the city.

He didn't go to The Grid. That place, with its flimsy walls and the lingering scent of his own desperation, belonged to a different life. His destination was the Rose Main Reading Room at the New York Public Library, a place of perfect, scholarly anonymity.

He didn't touch his own laptop. He walked directly to the public computer resources, found an empty terminal in a back corner, and sat down. He worked quickly, his movements precise, using a private browser window and a series of keystrokes that left no trace. He navigated to the digital archive of the Washington Post and looked at the classified ad one last time. *ArtNet forum, thread #8711.*

Finding the thread was its own piece of digital archeology. It was a short-lived conversation from 2012 about a minor Chelsea gallery, a digital dead end that no one had likely seen in a decade. It was the perfect place for a secret conversation.

He logged in as a guest user, the system assigning him a generic, numbered handle. He began to type. The message could not contain any incriminating keywords. No "Sazsa," or "MixMarket." The *context* of the forum was the message. The post itself had to be a piece of perfect, professional camouflage, a note so mundane it would be invisible to anyone but the intended recipient. He was Orpheus now. He had to sound the part.

He wrote, revised, and then rewrote the message until it was a sterile, stripped-down request.

```
User_781974 posted a new comment:


Subject: Re: Chelsea Exhibit


To the party who placed the classified:


Following up on our prior correspondence regarding
Irish painters. My preliminary research is complete. I
propose a consultation to discuss findings.
The Metropolitan Museum of Art, European Sculpture
court, this Friday, March 24th. Time: 14:00. Location:
The bench directly facing Canova's Perseus with the Head
of Medusa.
I will be reading the Financial Times. If these terms
are agreeable, no reply is necessary. Silence will serve
as confirmation.
If you must reschedule, you may do so by posting an
alternative time in a reply here before Thursday EOD.
After that, this thread will no longer be monitored.


- Orpheus
```

He read it one last time. It was perfect. It was cold, professional and utterly devoid of anything that could be construed as a threat or a confession. It was a set of clear, logistical instructions. The "silence is consent" protocol was a classic piece of tradecraft that minimized digital exposure and placed the burden of action entirely on them. He was dictating the terms, but from a position of deniable anonymity.

He took a deep breath, his finger hovering over the mouse. This was it. The second shot in the dark.

He clicked "Post Comment."

The page refreshed. His message, innocuous and cryptic, now sat at the bottom of the decade-old conversation, a single, quiet whisper in a forgotten room. He logged out of the terminal, systematically cleared the machine's cache and history, and stood up. He walked out of the computer room and back into the grand, hushed halls of the library, his face a neutral mask.

He had set the board. Now all he could do was wait to see if his opponent would make a move.

782342 (March 24)

The atmosphere in the European Sculpture court at the Metropolitan Museum of Art was cool, still, and heavy with the weight of centuries. Marble gods and heroes, frozen in poses of divine agony and triumph, stood silent watch under the vast, glass-domed ceiling. Nick sat on the designated bench, a copy of the *Financial Times* folded neatly in his lap. He felt absurdly conspicuous and perfectly anonymous at the same time, a modern spy trying to blend in with ancient history.

He had arrived 30 minutes early, his nerves on edge. He'd done a full circuit of the court, mapping the exits, noting the security camera placements and profiling the other patrons – tourists, art students, a quiet old woman sketching in a notebook. It was a purely instinctive act, a piece of tradecraft he hadn't known he possessed.

He checked his watch. 1:59 p.m. His heart began to beat a little faster. This was it.

At 2:00 p.m. precisely, two figures walked into his field of vision. The first was a woman. She was in her late 30s, tall and poised, with dark hair pulled back in a severe but stylish knot. She wore a simple, impeccably tailored black coat, a woman who radiated a quiet, formidable aura of control. Nick recognized her instantly from the photos he'd found online. Adele van der Dussen.

Walking beside her was a young man in a perfectly tailored gray suit, his expression sharp and impatient. Nick didn't know his face, but he knew the type. The loyal, ambitious junior associate. This had to be David Chen.

They didn't approach him directly. They stopped a dozen feet away, and presumed-Chen spoke to Adele in a low, confidential murmur, gesturing discreetly toward Nick. Adele's gaze swept over him, registering the *Financial Times* in his lap. Her expression was a neutral mask, but her dark, intelligent eyes were performing a full, analytical scan, weighing and measuring him. For a moment, her gaze met his, and he felt an unexpected jolt, a sense of being seen by a mind as sharp and as hungry as his own.

After a moment, she gave a single, almost imperceptible nod. Presumed-Chen approached the bench alone.

"Mr. Orpheus, I presume," he said, his voice as cold and clipped as it had been on the phone. "I'm David Chen. My principal is here. We will talk. But be advised, I am recording this conversation, and any perceived threat will be dealt with accordingly."

"I'm not here to make threats," Nick said, his own voice steady. "I'm here to offer a new perspective."

Chen seemed unimpressed. He gestured for Adele to approach. She walked toward them, her heels making soft, tapping sounds on the stone floor, and took a seat on the far end of the bench, leaving a careful, deliberate space between them. She did not look at him, her gaze fixed on the massive statue of Perseus behind him.

She turned to Chen, who was still standing before them like a sentinel. "David, please ensure we are not disturbed." Her voice was a cool, clear alto with a crisp, South African accent.

Chen nodded and took up a position a few feet away.

Adele finally turned her head to look at Nick. Her gaze was intense, analytical, a diamond drill boring into him. There was no warmth, no pleasantry. Only business.

"Your anonymous message made a very bold claim, Mr. Hernandez," she began, her voice low and precise. "You stated you had information that could, and I quote, 're-contextualize my brother's case.' The implication was one of exoneration. You have my undivided attention. Please, present this information now."

The demand was a clean, sharp, perfectly executed parry. She had called his bluff. The word "exoneration" had been a desperate, overplayed gambit to secure this very meeting, and she knew it. Nick felt a bead of sweat trickle down his back, but he held her gaze, refusing to be rattled. He had to pivot, to reframe his bluff not as a lie, but as the potential endpoint of a new and unexamined path.

"Exoneration is a legal conclusion, Ms. van der Dussen," he said, his voice calm and steady. "I'm an intelligence analyst. I deal in data, in new perspectives. What I have is a vector of investigation that the DoJ and my former employers completely missed because they were too focused on the blockchain."

He paused, letting the statement land. Chen was unmoved, but Adele's expression remained one of intense, unblinking focus.

"They considered the Sazsa trail a dead end," Nick continued. "They were right, in a way. I was able to connect the pseudonym to a real-world identity: a deceased Hungarian academic named Gyorgy Lorincz. The DoJ knew he was likely dead. What they didn't know, what no one knew, was what he was truly obsessed with."

Nick leaned forward, lowering his voice, making them lean in to hear him. This was his only real card. He had to play it perfectly.

"Lorincz wasn't just a cypherpunk. He was a significant and deeply obsessive collector of a very specific school of art. Specifically, the works of an obscure, 20th-century Irish painter named Jonathan Bryce."

The name hung in the cool, still air of the sculpture court. Chen's expression remained one of bored skepticism. But Adele ... Adele reacted.

It wasn't a gasp. It wasn't a sudden movement. It was a change so subtle that anyone else would have missed it. A fractional widening of her dark eyes. A momentary stillness, a cessation of her breathing. A quick, almost imperceptible glance at Chen before her neutral, professional mask was back in place.

But Nick saw it. He had been watching her with the desperate, obsessive focus of a drowning man searching for a piece of driftwood, and he saw it. A fractional widening of her eyes, a momentary stillness. It was small, almost nothing, but it was enough.

I hit a nerve, he thought, a quiet triumph cutting through his anxiety. He had no idea why. He didn't understand the connection. But he knew, with an absolute certainty, that he had just stumbled upon the key.

Bryce. That's the name.

Adele was the first to break the charged quiet. She stood up, her movements fluid and decisive, a clear signal that the meeting was over.

"The information you have provided has been noted, Mr. Hernandez," she said, her voice a cool, professional instrument, completely devoid of the flicker of emotion he had just witnessed. "We will review it internally and determine if your ... services ... are required further."

She looked at David Chen, who seemed to take that as his cue.

"Do not contact us again," Chen said, his voice a flat, final warning. "If we wish to continue this conversation, we have a protocol to reach you."

Adele gave Nick one last, long, analytical look, her expression completely unreadable. She then turned and walked away, her heels making soft, tapping sounds on the stone floor. Chen fell into step just behind her, her loyal shadow.

They left Nick alone on the bench in the vast, echoing court. He watched them go, two dark, elegant figures disappearing into the crowds of the museum. He had no idea if he had succeeded or failed. He had been offered no alliance, no next step, no sign of encouragement. He had been dismissed as coldly and as professionally as he had been in the first place.

And yet.

He replayed the moment in his mind. The flicker in her eyes. The momentary stillness. The nerve he clearly hit. He had thrown a single, strange, unexpected rock into the placid, well-defended pool of her composure, and he had seen the ripples.

He didn't know what it meant. He didn't know if they would ever contact him. But as he stood up and walked out of the museum, back into the bright, indifferent light of the city, he felt a new, unfamiliar sensation.

It was the feeling of holding a key, without knowing which door it was meant to unlock.

783948 (April 4)

For the first time in what felt like a lifetime, Oliver's apartment felt like a sanctuary rather than a cage. The early April sunlight streamed through the clean windows, illuminating the dust motes dancing in the air. He had spent the morning at the gym, the clean, sharp ache in his muscles a welcome, grounding sensation. His mind, no longer clouded by a perpetual hangover, felt sharp and expansive.

But a low-grade unease had been humming beneath the surface for days. A new and unfamiliar worry that had nothing to do with ancient riddles or Serbian fixers. It was a worry about his mother.

He had been putting off the call, but he knew he couldn't any longer. He needed to check in. He needed to see if the strange, unsettling feelings from their last conversation were just a product of his own emotional turmoil, or something more. He dialed her number.

"Oliver! Honey, I was just thinking about you." Diane's voice was warm and cheerful, the wounded edge from their last call completely gone.

"Hey, Mom. Just wanted to see how you were doing. Are you back from L.A.?"

"Oh, ages ago, sweetie. I've been back in Maplewood for a couple of weeks now. Working. It's been absolutely wonderful."

"How are you feeling?" she asked, her tone shifting to one of genuine maternal concern. "You sounded ... well, you sounded a bit stressed when we last spoke."

"I'm good, Mom. Really good, actually," he said, and was surprised to find it was the absolute truth. "I've been going to the gym every day, eating better. Feeling a lot clearer."

He didn't mention the real reason for the clarity. He would never tell her about the long, self-destructive spiral, nor the profound, rock-bottom moment of realization in the park. She didn't need to carry that burden. It was his to own. But the effects were real. The constant, low-grade agitation that had been his companion for months had finally receded, leaving behind a quiet, steady calm.

"Oh, that's wonderful to hear, honey," she said, and he could hear the genuine relief in her voice.

"So, how's the book deal going? Any news?" Oliver asked.

"News? Oliver, it's been a whirlwind!" she gushed, the giddy excitement returning to her voice. "Alexander – the editor from Da Silva – he is just the most brilliant, supportive man. He's already sent me three pages of single-spaced notes on my first chapter. He called my analysis of 19th-century domestic canning practices 'a paradigm-shifting work of feminist anthropology.' Can you believe that?"

Oliver tried to picture a handsome, high-powered editor in L.A. getting excited about the history of pickling jars. The image didn't quite compute. "Wow, Mom. That's ... very specific praise."

"I know! And the deal itself ... Oliver, they're offering me a six-figure advance. For a first book! On a niche academic topic! Alexander said the board was so impressed with my blog's unique voice that they felt it was a necessary acquisition for their new imprint on cultural studies. He said my work is essential."

A small, cold knot began to form in Oliver's stomach. He wasn't a publishing expert, but he'd had enough friends in creative fields to know that six-figure advances for first-time, academic nonfiction authors were practically unheard of. It was the kind of deal reserved for former presidents and Nobel laureates, not for a blog called *The Kyriarchy in the Kitchen*. Something didn't add up. It was too much. Too fast. Too good to be true.

"That's ... incredible, Mom," he said, his voice carefully neutral. "They must really believe in the project."

"They do," she said, her voice full of a happy, unshakeable certainty. "Alexander says they see me as a major new voice. He's just ... so supportive. Of everything."

There was a brief pause, and when his mother spoke again, the giddy excitement was gone, replaced by a more hesitant, careful tone. It was the sound of a person seemingly testing the waters, mindful of a previous storm.

"And ... he's been very kind to me, Oliver," she said softly. "Alexander, I mean. We've ... we've been spending a bit of time together, outside of the office."

Oliver's hand tightened on his phone. He felt the familiar, hot surge of possessive anger, the image of a handsome stranger encroaching on a space he still considered sacred. But he remembered the ugliness of his last reaction, the childish words he had blurted out. He had been a boy then, reacting from a place of pure, unthinking grief. He had to be a man now.

"Oh yeah?" he said, forcing a note of casual, supportive interest into his voice. "That's ... that's nice, Mom."

He could hear the surprise and relief in her exhale. "Yes," she said, her voice now a little stronger, more confident. "It is nice. I know you ... I know it's a difficult thing to think about. But it's been a long time, honey. It's time for me to ... move on. He's a good man."

He's not Dad, a voice screamed in the back of Oliver's mind. *He's a stranger. An intruder. A usurper.* But he swallowed the words, pushing them down with a force of will he hadn't possessed a few months ago. His battle was not with his mother's happiness. His battles were elsewhere, in darker, stranger places.

"As long as you're happy, Mom," he said, the words feeling both true and like an act of self-betrayal. "That's all that matters."

"Thank you, sweetie," she said, and he could hear the genuine gratitude in her voice. "That means more to me than you know."

The conversation continued for another minute, but Oliver's mind was elsewhere. He was performing the role of the good, supportive son, but inside, he was uneasy. Something didn't feel right about the book deal. And Alexander ... ugh. The thought of his mom with any man other than his father was disgusting to him.

But these were problems without solutions at the moment, new, unsettling blocks added to his already burgeoning stack.

The initial, clean sense of purpose he'd felt after the Noncemeister's return had frayed over the past three weeks. He had a mission – find the Bryce comics – but the real world, with its mundane and intractable obstacles, had gotten in the way.

He had called Aisling the very next day. She had been delighted to hear from him, and told him the O'Connell's renovations were going well, but running a few weeks late. But when he'd asked about the record store, her answer had been a dead end.

"*Ah, I'm sorry, Oliver, I haven't a clue,*" she'd said. "*That was Mum's bit of news. She's the one who knows the place.*"

"*Is she around? Can I talk to her?*" he had asked, a sense of urgency in his voice.

There had been a sad pause on the other end of the line. "*No, love. She's not. She flew back to Belfast a couple of weeks ago. Her sister's taken ill, I'm afraid. It's quite serious. I don't know when she'll be back.*"

And just like that, his one clear, tangible lead had vanished into thin air. He was stuck. He had the key, but the door was on another continent.

He spent the next two weeks in a state of controlled anticipation, a holding pattern. He worked out. He ate well. He read. He did not drink. But every time the intercom buzzed, his heart would give a hard thump, expecting Maren, or worse still, Bojan. Every time he walked down his street, he scanned the faces in the crowd, looking for a burly man in a sports jacket. The threat was a constant, low-grade hum beneath the surface of his new, sober life.

He was a man with a cosmic puzzle to solve and a hunter on his tail, and all he could do was wait.

784936 (April 7)

The silence was the loudest thing in the world.

For two weeks, Nick had been a man living in a state of suspended animation, his entire rogue operation held hostage by the whims of a woman he had met for a grand total of five minutes. He had played his card, his seemingly brilliant, desperate gambit at the Met, and had been met with a wall of perfect, impenetrable quiet. He compulsively checked the obscure ArtNet forum thread a dozen times a day from his burner phone, only to be greeted by the same decade-old conversation about a forgotten art gallery. The digital dead drop had remained empty. His gambit had failed.

He walked briskly toward the corner of Spring and Wooster Street, the familiar, trendy bustle of SoHo a world away from his stultifying cubicle at The Grid.

He'd spent the last week doing what he should have done in the first place: the boring, methodical, off-chain work of a real detective. Adele's reaction to his knowledge of the Irish painter had been telling. He had built a file on Jonathan Bryce, sifting through digitized art sale and auction records, old newspaper clippings and obscure academic papers. He'd learned about the painter's brief period of niche fame between the 1970s and 1990s, his subsequent retreat from public life, his death a few years ago. And then, buried in a fawning, local interest piece from an old SoHo arts journal, he had found the jackpot: a short interview with the painter's daughter, Shannon McGinty, in which she mentioned that her own daughter, Aisling, was now the proprietor of the family's old neighborhood haunt, a pub called O'Connell's.

O'Connell's. Nick hadn't been able to believe his eyes. O'Connell's, his old after-work local from his BlockWaves days. The place he used to frequent with his former colleagues Oliver, Olumide, and others. He had been in the presence of the granddaughter of the likely key to his entire investigation and had never even known it.

He walked the last block and a half, his pace quickening with a newfound sense of purpose. This was it. A real, human lead. But as he approached Mercer Street, his sense of purpose dissolved into the familiar feeling of running into a brick wall – in this case, almost literally.

The pub was a construction site. The iconic green facade was hidden behind a wall of scaffolding and plywood, a large banner promising a "Grand Re-Opening in May." A permit was taped to the makeshift door. He had come all this way, only to be thwarted by a renovation.

He was about to turn and leave when the plywood door creaked open and a woman in a paint-spattered jumpsuit and a hard hat emerged, shouting instructions to someone inside.

"Aisling?" Nick ventured.

She turned, her expression one of focused annoyance, which then softened into a look of confused recognition. "Hey, I know you," she said, pulling off the hard hat and running a hand through her fiery ginger hair. "You used to come in with the crypto lads last year, right? What was your name again?"

"Nick," he said, waving to her in relief. "I was in the neighborhood, thought I'd grab a pint. Didn't realize you were closed."

"As you can see," she said with a dry, tired smile, gesturing to the mess behind her. "We're giving the old girl a facelift. Won't be ready for another month or two."

"That's great. Congratulations," Nick said, trying to sound casual. "Listen, this is going to sound random, but I was doing some research for a ... a personal project, and I came across the name Jonathan Bryce. The painter. And I found an old article that said he was your grandfather. Is that right?"

Aisling's friendly expression became more guarded. "It is," she said, her tone cautious. "Why are you asking?"

"Like I said, it's a personal project. I'm a big admirer of his work. The school he was a part of, it's fascinating. I was hoping maybe you had some old letters, journals, anything that might shed some light on his process."

Aisling let out a short, incredulous laugh. "You're not the first one, I'll tell you that," she said, shaking her head.

"What do you mean?" Nick asked, his interest now considerably piqued.

A memory seemed to have kindled in Aisling's mind. "Hey, I think he was your old crypto buddy. You used to come here together a lot," she replied. "Oliver. He's a dear friend of ours, and a very generous guy." She finished with a wink.

Nick was stunned. Why on Earth was Oliver interested in Bryce? And what did she mean, 'very generous guy?' Oliver was an average tipper from his recollection. He quickly composed himself, pushing the disorienting new data to the back of his mind, "Oh wow, that's amazing. I had no idea."

Aisling went on, "Yeah, he absolutely loves my grandad's work. He's been obsessing about the paintings the last few months. He even had my mum tell him our whole family story." She gave Nick a curious look. "What is it with you crypto lads and your sudden interest in a little-known Irish painter?"

Nick was still grappling with this new revelation. *Oliver.* How Oliver? Why Oliver? It didn't make any sense. Oliver was a tech guy, a quiet idealist, lost in his naïve bitcoin maximalism. He wasn't an art historian. Nick's mind raced, trying to fit this new, bizarre piece into the puzzle. It didn't fit. It couldn't. He quickly filed it away as a strange, academic interest on Oliver's part, an odd coincidence in a case full of them. But the seed of a new, unsettling suspicion had been planted.

"I ... I had no idea," Nick managed. "Small world."

Aisling shrugged, still amused.

Nick went back to the topic at hand. "So, do you have any of his paintings with you?"

Aisling's face seemed to fall, the earlier amusement draining away, replaced by a sadness. "No," she finally replied in a small voice. "We had his second painting with us in storage and even had a buyer lined up for it last Fall. And then the day before the sale, someone stole the painting. Can you believe it?"

Nick couldn't believe what he was hearing. "What do you mean? How? Did they break into the bar and just steal it?" He asked, incredulous.

Aisling shrugged again, this time in resignation. "They probably did. Our security cameras hadn't been working for a while, so we didn't see anything. But yes, someone must have broken in that night and left with the painting."

Nick was still digesting this bizarre new information. He finally asked, "You said that was his second painting, right? What about his first and third? I heard he had only painted three in his career."

"Well, the first one was sold in Ireland many, many years ago. Maybe 50 years, if I'm not wrong. I think that one is still there. We don't know where the third painting is, but it took him ages to sell it. It wasn't until we came to America that he finally managed to. Probably sometime in the early 90s, if I had to guess," Aisling replied.

Nick made a mental note of all this. He wasn't sure how to proceed with what he had.

He was about to ask one final question when his burner phone buzzed in his pocket. He pulled it out. It was a new, encrypted message from an unknown number. His heart began to pound.

The message was short and to the point:

Your information regarding the artist has been deemed compelling. Further consultation is required. The Cloisters. This Friday. 11 a.m. By the Unicorn Tapestries. Come alone.

He looked up from the phone, the world seeming to shift on its axis. He had been so sure the trail with Adele had gone cold, but it had just burst back to life. In fact, she had bypassed the dance of the ArtNet forum and gone straight to his phone! He looked at Aisling, who was watching him with a curious expression.

"Sorry," he said, pocketing the phone. "I have to go. It was good to see you."

He turned and walked away, his mind a whirlwind. He had come here looking for a simple piece of historical data and had instead stumbled upon a shocking connection whose meaning he didn't fully understand. And then, a dead lead had just resurrected itself, summoning him to a meeting uptown. It was time to move.

785262 (April 13)

"You know, Batlu, one of these days you're going to learn what it means to have the patience of an eagle eye."

Oliver blinked, the familiar, warm purple of the timechain swirling around him. The Noncemeister was floating a few feet away, examining his own fingernails with an air of intense, scholarly interest.

"I have no idea what you're talking about," Oliver said with a sigh. He had been in his apartment, staring at a wall, stuck. Then the world had dissolved, and he was here.

"The eagle," the Noncemeister intoned, beginning to float upside-down like a lazy, tweed-clad chandelier, "does not get answers. The eagle waits for answers to show themselves. It does not write strongly worded emails to the fish. It does not open a support ticket with the river. It just ... notices. For hours. Sometimes from 12 all the way back to 11."

"I'm not a bird," Oliver said, a familiar exasperation creeping into his voice. "I'm a man trying to find a record store. A lead that's gone completely cold because the one person who knows where it is happens to be on another continent."

"Which is why," the Noncemeister said, flipping upright with a soft *pop* and dusting off his jacket, "you keep missing what's in front of your not-a-beak. You're so busy waiting for the big, dramatic answer that you forget to do the little, deeply unfashionable work of *seeing*. Sometimes, one plus one is three. But most times, it is two."

He snapped his fingers. The purple thickened and then parted into a shimmering oval, a memory bubble. Inside it was O'Connell's pub, just as it had been a few months ago. He saw himself sitting at a table with Shannon and Aisling. It was the same memory the Noncemeister had shown him two weeks ago.

"Why are we back here?" Oliver asked, a hint of weariness in his voice.

"Because you were here," the Noncemeister replied. "And because when you were, you were already thinking about where you wanted to go next instead of where you were. A common affliction. Traveling away from your own sentence while you're still speaking it."

In the bubble, Shannon's voice slipped into focus with its familiar, warm lilt:

" *... my nephew, Mike, saw a set of them in a record shop somewhere in Brooklyn,* *...*"

The bubble shimmered and held on that line. Oliver watched his past self nod politely, his mind clearly already jumping ahead, completely missing the crucial detail. He winced.

The Noncemeister seemed to hit the rewind button on the scene somehow. With the sound of a record scratch, the line, the sound now isolated, replayed clearly in the purple void.

" *... my nephew, Mike ...*"

Oliver said the words aloud, a quiet whisper in the vastness. "My nephew, Mike." He said them again, slower, each word now heavy with an implication he had completely ignored the first time. "My nephew, Mike."

"There you are," the Noncemeister said happily. "Look at you, noticing things. It's a start."

The memory bubble dissolved. The purple breathed. Oliver felt the familiar, gentle pull of the projection ending.

"Wait," he said. "That's it?"

"That's always it, Battu!" the Noncemeister boomed cheerfully as his form began to fade. "The great secret of the universe is that it's usually not that secret! Now, chop chop!"

Oliver opened his eyes. He was back in his armchair, the late afternoon sun trickling in through the windows. He didn't hesitate. He picked up his phone and tapped Aisling's name.

It rang three times. On the fourth, a blast of construction noise hit his ear, then Aisling's voice, cutting through the din.

"Oliver, love! You all right?"

"Hi, Aisling. Sorry to call in the middle of all that. I know there's a lot going on with the renovation."

"Chaos is our baseline, you know that. More delays with the contractors, what can I say," she replied over the sound of her footstep. He could hear her walking, the noise dropping as if she'd ducked into an office. "What can I do for you?"

"Quick question, Aisling. I know I asked you about the record store already, but I just remembered that your mom mentioned her nephew Mike might have seen them? I guess that would be your cousin Mike? Do you happen to have his number?"

"I have at least a hundred cousins named Mike. I'm Irish, remember?" Aisling chuckled. She paused for a moment. "I think I remember now. She was talking about my cousin Maidhc, who lives in Ridgewood, right next to Bushwick. He runs a bar there. Yeah, it's gotta be him. Maidhc O'Cahan."

"Mike O'Cahan from Ridgewood, got it. Can you give me his number?" Oliver asked, eagerly.

"Give me a second." He heard the clatter of a drawer, the riffling of papers. "Right. Maidhc O'Cahan. I'll text you his mobile. He's useless at picking up unknown numbers, so send a message first and tell him I sent you, or he'll think you're trying to sell him an extended warranty on his bicycle."

"Will do. Thank you, Aisling. You're a lifesaver."

"You know, Oliver, while I have you," Aisling said, conversationally. "Funny thing happened the other day. Your old friend dropped by to ask about my grandad's paintings. The guy you always used to come here with when you were at your old crypto job. Nick. Isn't that funny?"

Oliver felt his chest tighten in a new, sober and precise way that wasn't a sense of alarm, but a clear bell rung in a quiet room. "Wait, what? Nick? As in Nick Hernandez?"

"Well, I don't know his last name," she replied. "But yeah, Nick. Took me a second to remember his name, but you used to be here all the time with him. Turned up here last week while the lads were ripping out the walk-in. Asked about Granddad. My old Daideó. Can you believe it?"

Oliver reeled. *Nick.* His mind immediately went to the projection episode when he was at Pubkey a couple of months ago. Nick and Adele. What was happening? How on Earth did Nick find out about Bryce?

"Very polite," Aisling continued, blissfully unaware of Oliver's reaction at the other end of the line. "Said he was working on a 'personal project.' Had all sorts of odd questions about the paintings. I didn't have much for him, to be honest. Told him *The Toddler* was stolen last year and that I have no idea where the third painting is. He looked disappointed and then got a message on his phone and disappeared. What is it with you crypto lads and your sudden interest in little-known Irish painters?"

Oliver's head was spinning. Nick was at Chain Intelligence – yes, he had a contract with the DoJ to hunt down Dev_akshar, but how could on-chain analysis have led him to Bryce? Was he on his own path, a path that was now, impossibly, running parallel to his own? He was hunting Bryce. Which meant, sooner or later, he would be hunting *him*.

"Are you alright, Oliver?" Aisling asked, seemingly reading into his grim silence.

"No, no, nothing really," Oliver replied, a little too hastily. "Thank you for telling me, Aisling. That's ... very helpful information."

"Alright, love. Just mind yourself," she said. "I'll text Maidhc's number now. Ring if you need anything."

"Thanks, Aisling."

He hung up, and the text arrived a second later with Mike's number. He stared at the digits, a simple, elegant ladder out of the impasse he'd been in. He had a plan, but also a grim sense of foreboding at what was about to unfold.

785376 (April 14)

The Cuxa Cloister garden was an island of impossible tranquility, a perfect, manicured square of medieval France improbably nestled in the rocky heights of northern Manhattan. Nick sat on a cool stone bench, the scent of damp earth and early spring blossoms a strange, organic counterpoint to the cold, digital hunt that had consumed him. The Unicorn Tapestries, hanging in the adjacent gallery, depicted a world of mythic beasts and noble hunters. He felt a grim, ironic kinship.

He had arrived 45 minutes early, a bundle of tightly wound nerves. He'd walked the perimeter, noting the archways, the quiet corridors, the sparse clusters of tourists. He was a man preparing for an ambush, without knowing which direction the attack would come from.

He checked his watch: 10:59 a.m.

At eleven 11 a.m. precisely, she appeared. She walked through the arched stone doorway alone, a solitary, elegant figure in a simple, impeccably tailored black dress. No lawyer. No entourage. The decision to come by herself was a message, and Nick understood it immediately. This was not a legal consultation. It was something else.

She moved with a quiet, formidable grace, her gaze sweeping the courtyard before landing on him. Her expression was neutral, but her dark, intelligent eyes held a flicker of something he couldn't quite read: curiosity, appraisal, perhaps even a hint of amusement.

She walked toward him, her heels making soft, tapping sounds on the ancient flagstones, then took a seat on the opposite end of the bench, a careful, deliberate space between them.

"Mr. Hernandez," she said, in her crisp South African accent, which Nick was beginning to find quite pleasing. "I trust your journey uptown was not too arduous."

The pleasantry was so unexpected, so disarming, it almost threw him off. He had been prepared for an immediate interrogation.

"It was fine," he said, his own voice steady. "Thank you for agreeing to meet."

"My counsel advised against it," she replied, a small, almost imperceptible smile touching her lips. "He believes you to be a reckless and unreliable actor. I, however, am a believer in pursuing ... anomalies. You, Mr. Hernandez, are an anomaly." She turned to face him fully, her gaze intense, analytical. "You have my attention. You claimed to have new information. The floor is yours."

The interrogation had begun. Nick took a slow, deliberate breath, marshaling his thoughts. This was it. He had one shot, one piece of intelligence he believed was his ace in the hole.

"My research into Sazsa, into Gyorgy Lorincz, led me to an unexpected place," he began, his tone professional, measured. "To Jonathan Bryce. And through him, to his granddaughter, Aisling McGinty, the proprietor of O'Connell's Pub."

He watched for a reaction, but Adele's face was unmoved.

"I spoke with her last week," he continued, pressing forward. "And I learned something I believe is of critical importance to your brother's case. It concerns Bryce's second painting, *The Toddler*. The one the McGinty family owned."

He paused, letting the silence hang in the quiet, sacred space of the cloister. He delivered his bombshell.

"It was stolen, Ms. van der Dussen. Last fall. Taken from their basement, where they had been storing it. The police investigation has stalled, and the insurance claim was denied. But it's gone."

He leaned back slightly, a sense of triumph swelling in his chest. He had just handed her a piece of explosive, off-the-books intelligence, a fact that proved a new, criminal element was actively in play. He waited for her look of shock, of dawning realization, of gratitude.

Adele's expression did not change. She did not gasp. She did not even blink. She simply held his gaze for a long, quiet moment, and then she said, her voice a flat, devastating monotone, "Yes. I know."

The three words hit Nick like a slap in the face. The triumphant swelling in his chest collapsed into a cold, hollow void. He stared at her, his mind struggling to process what he had just heard.

"You ... you know?" he stammered.

"I was there," she said, her voice still calm and clinical. "At O'Connell's, in that basement, when it happened. Probably a few minutes after it was taken.

I had tracked the painting down myself and had come to make an offer to purchase it. When I arrived, there was no sign of it in the basement. The painting was gone." She gave him a look that was almost pitying. "Your new, explosive information is six months old, Mr. Hernandez."

Nick was reeling. He had come here feeling like a master informant, and in the space of 30 seconds, she had completely and effortlessly dismantled his entire position. He was not a partner with new intelligence. He was an amateur, a man who had just proudly presented last year's news. He felt like an utter fool.

He just sat there, his mind a blank, the witty rebuttals and clever pivots he had rehearsed now a distant, mocking memory. He had nothing.

Adele was the one to break the heavy quiet. She did not gloat. Her tone remained cool and clinical, that of a strategist who has won an opening skirmish and is now moving on to the main battle.

"So," she began, her voice low and precise. "Your information regarding the theft itself is redundant. But your initial, anonymous message was not. Let us return to that. You mentioned Sazsa, and you mentioned Jonathan Bryce. That is not public knowledge. Tell me, Mr. Hernandez. How did you make that connection?"

The question was a lifeline, a chance to regain some small measure of credibility. He seized it.

"My methods are different now," he said, his voice regaining some of its earlier steadiness. "I'm no longer relying on the flawed models my former employers used. I am doing the foundational work. I was able to connect the pseudonym 'Sazsa' to his real-world identity: a deceased Hungarian academic named Gyorgy Lorincz."

He watched her for a reaction, but she remained expressionless.

"The DoJ knew he was likely dead, which is why they considered the trail cold," Nick continued. "But what they didn't know, what no one knew, was his private obsession. Lorincz wasn't just a cypherpunk. He was a significant and deeply obsessive collector of Jonathan Bryce's art."

He had laid his real cards on the table. It was the one piece of unique, anomalous intelligence he possessed. It was the reason she had agreed to this meeting.

Adele seemed to consider this, her dark eyes analytical, searching. "This is all very interesting, Mr. Hernandez," she said finally, her voice still a placid stream. "But my brother's past associates are, for the most part, a matter of public record. Even if one of them had a peculiar hobby."

She paused, and her gaze, which had been analytical, now sharpened, becoming a penetrating, surgical instrument.

"Tell me," she said, her voice dropping to a confidential murmur. "What do you know about Oliver Battolo?"

The name, dropped so casually into the quiet of the sculpture court, landed like a stone in a still pond. Nick's mind scrambled to catch up. He had been so focused on his own discovery, on the connection between Sazsa and Bryce, that the sudden pivot to Oliver felt like a tactical ambush via non sequitur.

"Battolo?" Nick said, buying a moment to gather his thoughts. "Yeah ... I know him. I only learned of his interest a few days ago, from Bryce's granddaughter. I assumed it was a coincidence. A shared artistic interest. We worked together at a firm called BlockWaves. He's a quiet guy. A true believer, if you know what I mean. A bitcoin maximalist."

He watched her face, looking for a reaction to this new piece of information. He noticed a flicker of *something* in her expression when he mentioned they had worked together – this appeared to be an unexpected bit of news to her.

"His interest is not academic, Mr. Hernandez," she continued, her voice calm and composed, the momentary flicker now gone. "It is proprietary. He didn't just steal *The Toddler* from the pub's basement."

Nick stared at her, the implication of the word "just" hanging in the air.

"Weeks later," she continued, "he also stole the third Bryce painting, *It Is Time*, from a storage unit in Queens that belonged to Christiaan's former girlfriend, Maren Dehnert."

The information landed like a violent shock. Nick's mind reeled. Oliver, the quiet idealist, the guy he'd had a hundred beers with, was a master art thief, executing two separate, high-stakes heists? It was an impossible, absurd thought. But Adele was speaking with the absolute certainty of a person who dealt only in facts.

"Why?" Nick asked, his voice a hoarse whisper. "Why would he do that?"

Adele leaned forward, and for the first time, Nick saw a flicker of something that looked like her own brand of true belief, a conviction as absolute as any zealot's.

"Because he is finishing what his father started," she said.

She paused, then delivered the final, devastating blow.

"You were correct, Mr. Hernandez. Sazsa was Gyorgy Lorincz. But Gyorgy had a son. A son who grew up in America. That son ... is Oliver Battolo."

Nick's entire world seemed to tilt on its axis. He just sat there, the sounds of the museum fading into a distant buzz, his mind a maelstrom of colliding facts and impossible conclusions. Oliver. Sazsa's son. It was insane. It was a plot from a bad airport novel.

And yet ... it made a strange kind of sense.

His mind, trained to find patterns, began to frantically connect the dots. He remembered those evenings at O'Connell's last year. Oliver was mourning his dad. He remembered that summer afternoon at Becky's parents' home in the Catskills when Oliver collapsed with grief. He knew from his own research that Gyorgy Lorincz died last year. The timelines, from this 30,000-foot view, seemed to align. A dying father passing his secret quest on to his son. It was a clean, simple and powerful narrative. But what *was* the secret quest? What could it be about the Bryce paintings that would make his seemingly unassuming former colleague want to steal them?

He looked at Adele, who was watching him, gauging his reaction. He had come here to audition, to prove his worth. He had failed spectacularly. But in his failure, he had been given a new and infinitely more unsettling truth.

She seemed satisfied with the effect her revelations had had on him. He a man who now understood how little he truly knew. He was manageable.

"You have a talent for finding the threads that others miss, Mr. Hernandez," she said. "But you are pulling on them in the dark. You see the shadow, but you do not understand the object that is casting it."

She stood up with a fluid and decisive movement. The audition was clearly over.

"The Bryce paintings are not the prize. They are not the territory," she said, her voice a final, quiet hook that snagged his full attention. "They are the map. They are keys."

She reached into the small, elegant purse that had been sitting beside her, took out a single, folded piece of paper, and held it out to him.

"This is my number," she explained. "Call me on Monday at 10 a.m. If you do not, or if you try to contact me earlier, you will not hear from me again."

Nick took the paper from her hand. It felt impossibly heavy.

"Welcome to the rabbit hole, Mr. Hernandez," she said, looking down at him one last time. "Try not to get lost."

She turned and walked away, her heels once again making soft, tapping sounds on the stone floor, a solitary, powerful figure disappearing back into the museum's quiet corridors. She left Nick alone on the bench, the small, folded piece of paper a tangible anchor in the wreckage of his own certainty. He had come here looking for a simple lead and had been drawn into a much deeper conspiracy, one in which the lynchpin was the last person he would have suspected. He had lost control of his own investigation, but in doing so, he had been given a new, dangerous, and undeniable path forward.

785380 (April 14)

The M train rattled and screeched along the elevated tracks over the industrial heart of Bushwick. Oliver watched as the familiar, vertical landscape of Manhattan gave way to a sprawling, horizontal world of low-slung warehouses, their brick facades a chaotic canvas of vibrant, ever-changing graffiti. He was entering a different country now.

He had a lead. A name. A door. The thought was a quiet, steadying presence, a straight line of purpose in a world that had been a disorienting haze just a few weeks ago. He had texted Mike O'Cahan the day before, and Shannon's nephew had come through, just as Aisling had promised. *Dead Air Records, on Grove Street, just off Knickerbocker. The owner's a grump named Milo, but he knows his stuff.*

Oliver's thoughts wandered to something that had happened on his way to the train station. He had stopped outside the subway entrance in Chelsea to tie his shoelaces, and as he stood up, his gaze fell on a community notice board, a piece of vertical real estate so boringly ubiquitous, he almost always looked right past it. But this time, he saw it. Pinned amongst the ads for dog-walkers and babysitters was a brightly colored piece of paper, its design stark and minimalist. A stylized drawing of a labyrinth.

THE MINOTAUR'S REVENGE A NEW PLAY BY DANIELA FOR-LAN & SARAH JENKINS PREMIERES JUNE 1ST – THE DEDALUS THEATER, 641 W 51ST STREET

He stared at her name in print. *Daniela Forlan.* And then a wave of guilt washed over him. He remembered the projection episode when he so foolishly allowed himself to be seduced by Anariadne to step into Daniela's mind. This is what he saw – she and Sarah were discussing this very play. He took out his phone absently and took a photo of the flyer, grappling with a complicated mixture of pride and loss. For a brief moment, the grand, cosmic quest for Bryce's comics felt small and insignificant compared to the simple, painful reality of a life he was no longer a part of.

He pushed the thought away and continued his journey to the station, the image of the labyrinth a fresh, poignant sigil burned into his mind.

Oliver held onto the metal pole, the swaying of the train a familiar comfort. His mind was clear, but the quiet was still crowded. He was learning to live with the threats. He had spent the last few weeks in a state of controlled watchfulness. Bojan hadn't reappeared, a fact that was both a genuine relief and a source of low-grade unease. Was he in the country? Had he given up? Or was he simply waiting for a better opportunity? Oliver had taken no chances, moving through the city with a new awareness, finding a strange sort of safety in the anonymous, fungible crowds of a busy street or a packed subway car.

Then there was the new variable. Nick. The news from Aisling that his old friend was on the same path, hunting for the same ghost, was a complication he still didn't know how to process. What was his angle? How had a purely on-chain investigation led him to a dead, obscure painter? It didn't add up.

And through Nick, there was Adele. The brief, uneasy projection he had at Pubkey, implied a strange alliance between the two of them. Adele. She had been surprisingly quiet over the last few months, given the stakes involved. He wondered what she had been up to. He replayed his last, bizarre encounter with her in his mind, the memory now sharp and clear in his sober recollection. It had been in that sterile storage unit in Queens, nearly six months ago. He and Daniela had been walking out with the third Bryce painting, and Adele had emerged from the elevator, seemingly waiting for them, her expression a mask of cold fury and dawning, incorrect realization. He remembered the absurdity of her accusation, the absolute, unshakeable certainty in her voice as she had looked at him and told him Sazsa was his father.

Oliver let out a short, dry chuckle, earning a strange look from the woman sitting across from him. He had believed her at the time and had been terrified. Thankfully, if this was something he could be thankful for, Oliver chuckled to himself again – his father's MixMarket pseudonym had turned out to be Dev_akshar, not Sazsa. Adele, in her obsession, had made that false leap in logic, a story where he was the heir to a different ghost entirely. He wondered if Nick, in his new alliance with her, assuming his Pubkey projection were true, was now operating under that same flawed logic. It was a dangerous thought.

The train screeched to a halt at the Knickerbocker Avenue station. He got off, descended the weathered stairs to the street, and was hit with the unique energy of the neighborhood: the smell of roasting coffee, the distant thump of a bassline from a passing car, the murmur of Spanish conversations from an open doorway. He followed the map on his phone for a few blocks, the sense of being on a real, tangible quest a welcome, grounding feeling.

He found it on a quiet side street. Dead Air Records. The storefront was unassuming, its large window cluttered with vintage vinyl, faded band T-shirts, and stacks of old magazines. It looked like a place where stories went to wait. He took a deep breath and pushed open the door.

A small bell above the door chimed, a sound that was immediately swallowed by the dense, surprisingly loud music playing from a pair of massive speakers in the corners. It was the raw, driving energy of 70s proto-punk, a wall of distorted guitars and angry, shouted vocals. Oliver inhaled the rich, distinct smell of old paper, aging vinyl and dust. The place was a temple, a magnificent and cluttered shrine to a century of forgotten media.

Behind a counter piled high with records, turntables, and what looked like a disassembled amplifier sat a man in his late 50s. He had a magnificent, graying beard, a faded Black Flag T-shirt, and an expression of scholarly boredom. He looked up as Oliver entered, his eyes registering his presence with the barest flicker of interest before returning to the sleeve of the record he was examining. This had to be Milo.

Oliver navigated the narrow aisles, which were formed by overflowing bins of vinyl records. He made his way to the counter. Milo didn't look up.

"Excuse me," Oliver said, raising his voice slightly to be heard over the guttural sounds of the music.

Milo slowly, deliberately, lifted his head, his expression one of a man who has been interrupted in the middle of a sacred ritual. "If you're here to ask if we have the new Taylor Swift on vinyl, you can turn right around and leave," he said, his voice a low, gravelly monotone.

"No, I'm actually here for something else," Oliver said. "I was told you might have some old comic books. From the 80s or 90s. By an artist named Jonathan Bryce."

Milo's face, which had been a mask of bored contempt, now morphed into one of active disgust. He physically recoiled, as if Oliver had just asked him for a glass of spoiled milk.

"Comic books," he said, the words dripping with disdain. He gestured vaguely with his thumb toward a dark, neglected corner at the very back of the store. "The funny papers are over there. In the boxes. You can dig through them yourself. Just don't get any of your ... cartoon dust ... on the records."

He then put the record he was holding onto the turntable, gently lowered the needle, and was instantly lost again in his own world of pure, analog sound.

The message was clear. Oliver was on his own.

He made his way to the back, to the corner that was clearly the forgotten country of Milo's retail empire. It was a small, dusty alcove, packed with a dozen or so cardboard longboxes, the kind used for storing comic books. They were unlabeled, their lids sagging with age.

Oliver knelt on the dusty floorboards. He felt a keen sense of anticipation, the thrill of the hunt overriding the mild humiliation of being dismissed by the owner. He pulled out the first box. It was heavy, and the sharp, acidic smell of aging paper filled the air. He began to flip through the comics inside, his fingers moving with a slow, deliberate care. He saw faded covers of superheroes, grimacing anti-heroes and strange, independent sci-fi sagas. It was a time capsule of a forgotten era.

He worked his way through the first box. Nothing. He started on the second. Then the third. The work was methodical, almost meditative. The only sounds were the soft *thwip* of the comics as he flipped through them and the distant, angry buzz of the punk rock from the front of the store. He was a man sifting for treasure in a river of forgotten stories, looking for a single, specific signal in a universe of noise.

He was in the seventh box when he found it.

Even though Oliver had only seen Bryce's paintings before, the comic book art style was unmistakable. Crude, powerful, and strangely familiar. The cover was simple, black ink on aging, off-white paper. The title, in a thin, elegant serif font, read: *The Legend of Atlantis, Issue #1*. He felt a keen, electric jolt. *Atlantis.* Could it be the same place Velázquez told him about? He kept digging. It was a complete, twelve-issue run from 1988, each one preserved in a plastic sleeve.

He gathered the stack, his heart pounding with a steady, measured beat, then walked back to the front counter. Milo looked at the comics, then at Oliver, and gave a single, dismissive grunt.

"Fifty bucks for the lot," he said, not even bothering to look them up. "Take the junk out of my store."

Oliver paid him in cash, took the bag and walked out into the cool afternoon air, the angry guitars of the music fading behind him. He didn't go home. He couldn't. He needed a quiet place to think. He found a small, anonymous coffee shop a few blocks away, ordered a black coffee he didn't intend to drink, and sat down at a small table in the back.

He carefully slid the first issue from its sleeve with trembling hands. The paper was thin and smelled of time. He began to read.

The comic book series was not about superheroes or science fiction. It was a work of mythology. A secret history of the world. Bryce's crude but evocative drawings depicted a lost civilization, a people who saw the universe not as a collection of objects, but as a symphony of geometric principles. Atlantis. Oliver couldn't believe his eyes. How could Bryce have known about Atlantis? A largely unknown painter from Belfast – how could he have possibly depicted the civilization that Velázquez told him about? The one his great-grandfather, Esteban Pittamiglio, documented.

He then read about their downfall, about the fragments of their knowledge scattered across the globe, preserved by secret schools of alchemists and mystics.

Oliver's jaw went slack when the fourth issue introduced the Hexcelion. It was described not as a dimensional key, but as a sacred symbol, a gateway, a brief and glorious flowering of a higher reality into our own. *How Bryce, how? How could any of this be? Did you know this the same way you knew about Merkle Trees in* The Toddler *well before they were discovered by Ralph Merkle, or knew about the Noncemeister and portrayed him in your third painting* It Is Time? *Was it through the downloads?*

Still shaking, Oliver pulled out the fifth issue. The story was about a sacred order of monks who, for centuries, had been the guardians of the chamber where the Hexcelion appeared. The comic described how, once a year, at the moment of the shape's formation, the monks would perform a ritual. They would circle the luminous geometry, chanting a specific verse to stabilize the vortex it created, to keep the world from tearing itself apart. The verse, the comic explained, was a powerful, melodic line of Atlantean. It was known as the *Refraine del Acimut.*

Oliver's breath caught in his throat. He repeated the phrase in his mind slowly. *Refraine del Acimut. The Azimuth Refrain.* He remembered the words from the very first, nonsensical verse the Noncemeister incanted to him, in the deep purple of the timechain almost a year ago. But it wasn't nonsense as he had thought back then. It was a real, ancient and seemingly crucial piece of this cosmic puzzle. *Azimuth,* he now realized as he read on, was the specific angle of the sun on that day, July 18. *Refrain,* for the verse the monks had to sing.

He put the comic down, trying to comprehend the gravity of the connection. After a moment, he picked up the ninth issue. He flipped through the pages, his eyes scanning the strange, mythic panels. He turned a page. And he froze.

The entire page was a single, full-bleed illustration. In the center of it stood a beautiful, golden-haired woman in a flowing white robe, her turquoise eyes staring directly out at the reader. She was surrounded by a swirling, ethereal blue mist.

Oliver's heart was pounding. He could scarcely believe what he was looking at. He read the text at the bottom of the page.

And then there is the test of the seeker. For in the deep places of the self, one will always encounter the Liminal Gatekeeper. She is Anariadne, the Atlantean goddess of uncertainty. She is a creature born of the Inferna, a beautiful and seductive being whose sole purpose is to test the will of the seeker by offering a thread that leads not to the center of the labyrinth, but to the sweet, blissful oblivion of self-deception.

He read the words again, and then a third time. He took a few moments to digest all these new, stunning revelations. *Atlantis, the Hexcelion, Anariadne,* all connected to the same ancient mythology, with a thread running through all of them, and incredibly, connecting to Bryce, Velázquez, and Pittamiglio. And *him,* standing right in the middle of it all. He was an unwitting, and indeed reluctant protagonist in a grand cosmic game he was only just beginning to scratch the surface of. Despite all these new insights, he felt like a man staring through a tiny keyhole at a vast, cavernous room beyond – just about able to sense its scale, but unable to map its details through so small an aperture.

The comic books somehow felt like a user manual, although he wasn't quite sure how he would use the instructions. It was a bestiary for the creatures that lived in his own mind. He was not just a man having strange visions. He was a seeker somehow, seemingly walking a well-trodden, if secret, path. The players in his internal drama were, incredibly, ancient archetypes, gods and goddesses from a forgotten mythology. Or was it a history? He was a character in a story that had been written long before he was born.

He sat back in the cheap café chair, the twelve comic books spread out before him like a deck of tarot cards, each one a revelation, each one a warning. The world was a much larger, much older and much, much stranger place than he had ever imagined. *Rum thing, innit?*

Chapter 8. May 22

785808 (April 17)

The second hand on the cheap plastic clock on his cubicle wall moved with an agonizing slowness, each tick a small, sharp report in the quiet of the near-empty co-working space. It was 9:58 a.m. on Monday morning.

For the past three days, Nick had been a man living on a knife's edge. The meeting at The Cloisters had been a tactical disaster and a strategic masterpiece all at once. He had walked in with what he thought was a bombshell, only to have it casually defused with a quiet, devastating, "Yes. I know." Adele van der Dussen had dismantled his entire position, exposed the gaping holes in his intelligence, and then rebuilt his entire worldview with a series of revelations that still left his head spinning. *Oliver Battolo. Sazsa's son. The paintings are keys. Keys to what, though?*

He looked at the small, folded piece of paper on the desk in front of him. It was the only tangible proof that the meeting had even happened. On it, written in a sharp, elegant hand, was a simple, ten-digit phone number. Not an encrypted messenger handle. Not a sterile, anonymous protocol. A personal number.

The decision to give him her direct line was, he had come to realize, a much more sophisticated power play than any legal threat. An encrypted channel would have established them as equals, two spies communicating on neutral ground. A personal number established a clear hierarchy. It was a statement of absolute confidence. *You will not misuse this, because you know I am more dangerous than you are. You need me more than I need you.* It was a leash, and she had just handed him the end of it.

He picked up his burner phone, his thumb hovering over the keypad. He thought of her sitting on that stone bench posture perfect, her dark eyes analytical, taking him apart piece by piece with a calm, surgical precision. The memory should have been purely humiliating. But as he replayed it, he found himself feeling something else, something more complex than simple defeat. It was a grudging, almost unnerving sense of admiration. She possessed an incredibly sharp and controlled mind. He was, he realized with a jolt, deeply intrigued.

The clock on the wall ticked over to 10:00 a.m.

He did not hesitate. He punched in the numbers, his fingers quick and precise. He put the phone to his ear, his heart a slow, heavy drum against his ribs.

It rang once.

"Yes," Adele's voice said, completely devoid of any introductory pleasantry. She had been waiting.

"Ms. van der Dussen," Nick began, his own voice sounding a little too formal in his own ears. "Thank you for taking the call."

"I will keep it short, Mr. Hernandez," she replied, her tone all business. "You have intrigued me. That is a difficult thing to do. I suggest you do not waste the opportunity."

The message was clear: she was in charge. Nick abandoned any thought of a preamble and got straight to the point. "Thank you, Ms. van der Dussen. I'm sure I will not disappoint you."

There was a brief pause on the other end of the line, as if Adele was gathering her thoughts. "I am going to tell you something in complete confidence, Mr. Hernandez," Adele said finally. "Consider it a test. If any of this information finds its way back to your former employers or their government associates, this will be our last conversation, and you will find your life becomes ... complicated."

The threat was delivered with a calm, professional poise that made it far more chilling than any overt display of anger.

"I understand," Nick said, his heart racing.

"Good," she replied. "In late 2013, my brother realized the net was closing. He knew he was being set up to be the fall guy for MixMarket. Sazsa had already begun to disappear, and Dev_akshar was a whisper on the network. Christiaan knew they were going to leave him holding the bag."

Nick listened, his pen poised over a fresh page in his notebook. This was the inside story, the human narrative he had been missing.

"Before his arrest," Adele continued, her voice a low, steady instrument, "my brother took steps to secure his assets. The assets that were rightfully his, the profits from the company he built. He moved the bulk of the bitcoin into a series of new, untraceable wallets. He knew he would not be able to access them from prison. He needed a way to preserve the keys, a method of cold storage that no one could ever hope to crack."

She paused again, letting the weight of the setup settle.

"He knew Sazsa was an admirer of Bryce's work. Sazsa owned the third Bryce painting at the time. Christiaan also knew that Bryce's daughter had the second painting with her. He was then briefly able to obtain access to both paintings. He liked Bryce's paintings too, but saw them not just as art, but as a medium. A place to hide a secret in plain sight. He used a form of invisible ink, a substance that is only visible under ultraviolet light, and he wrote the seed phrases for the new wallets directly onto the canvases, hidden within the intricate brushstrokes of the paintings themselves."

Nick's pen stopped moving. He felt a jolt, as if the floor had suddenly dropped a few inches. The pieces of the puzzle in his mind – the art, the thefts, Oliver's obsession – slammed together with a stunning, violent clarity.

"The paintings," he whispered, his voice a hoarse croak. "They're not just clues. They contain the seedphrases to wallets with Christiaan's bitcoin."

"And given his incarceration, those wallets belong to the van der Dussen family. That bitcoin is rightfully mine. The paintings contain the keys, Mr. Hernandez," Adele said, her voice slow and precise. "And Oliver Battolo now has two of them."

A new, profound sense of clarity washed over Nick, eclipsing his earlier humiliation. He finally understood the true scale of the game he had stumbled into. This wasn't about vindicating Christiaan or solving a cold case. It was about a treasure hunt for a digital fortune – presumably of unimaginable size. And Oliver, his quiet, unassuming former colleague, was at the very center of it.

As a man who had recently lost a small fortune in crypto himself, he couldn't contain his curiosity. "How much are we talking about? How much bitcoin did he hide?"

Adele's voice, which had been cool and professional, turned to ice. "That is not information you require at this stage, Mr. Hernandez," she said. "Your motivation for this is redemption, you said. Not money. Let us keep it that way for now."

The rebuke was a clean, sharp slap, a reminder of who was in control. Nick felt deeply embarrassed. It took him a moment to switch back to professional mode. "Understood. How would you like me to proceed?" he asked, his voice now low and focused.

"I want my property back, Mr. Hernandez," Adele replied, her tone cold and absolute. "You have proven you are a resourceful investigator. You found a thread in the Sazsa-Bryce connection. Something a dozen law enforcement agents and private contractors missed. This suggests you have a talent for uncovering what is hidden."

She paused, letting the compliment, which was also a challenge, hang in the air.

"And besides, by a happy coincidence, you happen to be a former colleague of Oliver Battolo. So now, you have a new task. A test. I want you to apply that talent and your relationship to finding where Oliver has hidden my paintings. I am giving you 10 days. Find me their location. Prove to me that you are as valuable as your initial claim suggested."

The directive was clear, professional, utterly uncompromising. She was giving him an assignment. He was an asset, and this was his first mission.

"And if I succeed?" Nick asked, the question a necessary clarification of the terms of their new, unstated contract.

"If you succeed," Adele said, a hint of a smirk in her voice, "you will receive the redemption you so crave."

She let the words hang in the air, a cruel joke at his expense. She then softened her tone somewhat. "But perhaps also, we will have a much more interesting conversation about our mutual benefit."

The message, seemingly delivered with a smile on her face, was clear: success would earn him a seat at the table. Failure would mean exile.

"Ten days," Nick said, a quiet, solid confirmation.

"Do not disappoint me, Mr. Hernandez," Adele said. And then the line went dead.

785137 (April 19)

The text from Nick had arrived two days ago, a casual, friendly message that had felt like a cleverly disguised hand grenade. It had appeared on his screen while he was reading one of the Bryce comics, a sudden, jarring intrusion of the real world into the mythological one.

```
Hey man, it's been ages. How's everything? I got
bounced from my gig a couple of months back. Life's
a bitch. Anyway, would be great to catch up if you're
free. First round's on me.
```

Oliver had stared at the message for a long time. *Bounced from his gig.* It was a plausible, even sympathetic, opening. But coming so soon after his conversation with Aisling, it felt like a calculated gambit. The timing was too perfect. This was a reconnaissance mission – it had to be. He had agreed to meet for one simple reason: to find out what his old friend knew, and what he wanted.

He walked down a sun-dappled street in the East Village, taking in the neighborhood's familiar, bohemian energy, while trying to work himself into a strategic mindset. He was walking into a chess match, and he had to be prepared. He knew Nick's opening move: the casual, off-hand question about Jonathan Bryce. But what was his endgame?

The projection from Pubkey, the one he had tried to dismiss as a strange, symbolic vision, now felt like a piece of hard intelligence. *Nick and Adele. Together.* It had seemed impossible at the time, but Aisling's story had provided a potential bridge. Nick was hunting Bryce. Adele was hunting Bryce. It was a logical, if deeply unsettling, point of convergence.

His own strategy was simple: say as little as possible. Feign ignorance. The story he had prepared – that his interest in Bryce was a sentimental, inherited hobby from his father – was the only card he had to play. He would offer nothing, and he would watch, with the patience of an eagle eye, for any flicker, any tell, any small piece of data that would reveal the true depth of Nick's investigation.

He found the place on a quiet corner: The Palimpsest Café. He pushed open the door. The place smelled of dark coffee and old books. And there, sitting at a small table in the back, was his old friend, now seemingly his new rival. Nick looked up as he entered and offered a small, welcoming wave.

He walked toward the back of the café, the scent of dark coffee and old books growing stronger. Nick stood as he approached, a slightly forced smile on his face.

"Hey, man," Nick said, extending a hand. "Glad you could make it."

"Dude, it's been ages. Good to see you," Oliver replied, the lie feeling surprisingly easy on his tongue as he shook Nick's hand. He slid into the worn, wooden chair opposite him. The table was small, creating an unwelcome sense of intimacy.

The initial moments felt awkward, with the stilted energy of a reunion between two people who were no longer sure of their footing with one another. They exchanged the usual pleasantries, the hollow inquiries about health and family that fill the space where a real connection used to be.

A young woman with a pierced eyebrow and a world-weary expression came to take their order.

"I'll get the Palimpsest Burger and a pint of the house lager," Nick said, closing his menu. He looked at Oliver, a familiar, expectant look in his eyes.

"Just a sparkling water for me, please," Oliver said to the waitress. "And I'll get the cheese board."

The waitress scribbled on her pad and left. Nick stared at Oliver, a genuine and unguarded expression of surprise flickering across his face.

"Water?" he said, a note of disbelief in his voice. "Dude, I said the first round was on me. You're not drinking?"

"Nah, taking a break," Oliver said with a casual shrug, trying to make the statement sound like a minor lifestyle choice rather than a life-altering vow. "Trying to get back in shape. Hitting the gym again. You know how it is."

He didn't elaborate. He didn't mention the brawl, the night in the park, the quiet, methodical pouring of a fortune in wine and whisky down the drain. He just let the simple, healthy statement sit there, a quiet declaration that he was no longer the man Nick remembered.

"Good for you, man. Seriously," Nick said, though Oliver could see the analytical gears turning behind his eyes. His old friend was processing a new, unexpected piece of data. The Oliver he knew, the one who had spent the better part of the last year drinking his way through their old haunts, had changed. The first tell.

Their drinks arrived. Nick took a long, deep gulp of his beer, a man returning to a familiar comfort. Oliver took a slow, deliberate sip of his sparkling water, the crisp, cold bubbles a clean, clarifying sensation. The contrast between them felt stark, a silent announcement that the rules of their old friendship no longer applied. They were two different people now, sitting at a small table in the East Village, pretending to be the men they used to be.

The food arrived a few minutes later, the waitress placing Nick's burger and Oliver's cheese board on the small table with a practiced efficiency. For a few minutes, they engaged in a comfortable, nostalgic rhythm of small talk, the food a welcome buffer. They complained about their old boss, Ian Wright, at BlockWaves, laughed about a disastrous company offsite from a couple of years ago. It felt, for a moment, like nothing had changed. It all seemed like a well-rehearsed performance, and he waited for the first real move.

It came from Nick, as expected, perfectly wrapped in a casual, friendly anecdote.

"So, funny story," Nick said, almost casually after taking a large bite of his burger. "I was in SoHo a couple of weeks ago, was gonna grab a pint at O'Connell's. Saw it was all boarded up. Ran into Aisling, though. She mentioned you've gotten really into some old Irish painter. It's her grandad, isn't it? Bryce, I think she said. Didn't peg you for an art guy."

The probe was perfectly executed. Oliver felt a cool, clear sense of focus descend over him. He carefully pulled out a piece of Manchego from under a grape.

"Oh, that," he said with a dismissive chuckle. "Yeah, it's just a weird rabbit hole I fell down. My dad was a fan of his, left me a bunch of his old research notes and stuff. It's just a sentimental thing, you know? A way to feel connected to him now that he's gone."

"Ah, I get it, man," Nick said, his expression one of perfect, sympathetic understanding. It was a flawless counter-performance. "Oh, here's the other funny thing. Aisling said both his paintings were stolen. Isn't that wild? Did you know about that?"

Oliver paused when he heard that, pushing a piece of Stilton absently with his fork on the board. One word that Nick just said stood suspended in the air, blinding out everything else around it. A word that almost definitely confirmed the Adele connection.

Both.

There was no way Aisling could have known the third Bryce was stolen. Neither she nor Shannon knew where it was, let alone that it was stolen. Aisling only knew that the second Bryce, *The Toddler*, was stolen, because it was stolen from her basement in O'Connell's where she was storing it. The fact that Nick knew the third Bryce was stolen was an unmistakable tell that he was talking to Adele. She was the only other person who knew.

"I have no idea," Oliver lied, meeting his gaze directly, hoping against hope that Nick hadn't read his momentary pause. "From what Aisling told me, the trail went cold. Frankly, no one knows where any of the five Bryces are, which is a real shame."

"Five?" Nick asked, an eyebrow leaping high into his forehead, the first sign of genuine emotion Oliver noticed in him all afternoon.

Shit. Oliver thought to himself, kicking himself internally. *Shit, shit, shit. What have I done? I've given him an invaluable piece of information. What was I thinking? How am I going to back out of this now?*

He tried to compose himself quickly. "Oh yeah, there are rumors about more than three, but who knows, right? From my dad's notes, there were only three," he said, unconvincingly.

A brief, tense quiet settled over the table as the waitress returned to refill their water glasses. Nick seemed to be pondering this new data point Oliver had inadvertently given him. Oliver decided to go on the attack.

"So what about you, Nick?" he asked, his tone a mirror of Nick's own casual curiosity, as soon as the waitress had left. "You said you got bounced. What happened with that big DoJ contract you told me about back then? The MixMarket case, wasn't it? It seemed like you guys were the tip of the spear on that investigation."

He watched Nick's face, looking for a flicker, a tell. And he saw it. A momentary tightening around his eyes, a subtle shift in his posture before he could mask it.

"That's ... classified," Nick said, taking a quick sip of his beer. "You know I can't talk about active investigations, man."

"It's not active for you anymore, though, right?" Oliver pressed gently, his voice full of a feigned, friendly innocence. "You left the firm. I'm just curious if they ever got any closer to the guy."

Nick put his beer down, his expression unreadable. "Honestly, man, that's part of why I left," he said, the lie smooth and well-rehearsed. "It was a dead end. A hunt for a man who probably doesn't even exist anymore. The trail went cold years ago. I got tired of chasing shadows."

Oliver made a mental note of the inconsistency. *That's why I left.* Which one is it, Nick? Did you get bounced or did you leave on your own?

The rest of the lunch passed in a haze of meaningless small talk. They talked about the Knicks' disastrous season, about a new restaurant in their old BlockWaves neighborhood, about anything and everything that was not the truth. Oliver felt like he and Nick were two actors carrying out an utterly pointless charade designed to run down the clock.

"Well, man, this was good," Nick said finally, throwing some cash on the table that more than covered his share. "We should do it again soon."

"Definitely," Oliver said, the lie now a familiar, comfortable weight.

They left the café and stood on the sidewalk for a moment, two old friends who were now complete strangers sharing a final, awkward moment of feigned normalcy. They gave each other another brief, parting handshake and then turned and walked in opposite directions.

Oliver walked toward the subway, deep in thought. He had gone into the meeting looking for information, and he had gotten it, though not in the way he had expected.

He had learned nothing from what Nick had said, but everything from *how* he had said it. Nick was lying about his job. He was actively and obsessively investigating Jonathan Bryce. And his casual mention of *both* paintings being stolen was the undeniable tell; it was the secret handshake that confirmed the vision from Pubkey. He was working with Adele.

But as he descended the steps into the subway station, a cold, sickening feeling of his own misstep washed over him. *Five.* He had said there were five paintings. In his haste to parry Nick's questions, in his desire to project an air of superior knowledge, he had made a colossal unforced error. He had given his new rival a game-changing piece of intelligence, a breadcrumb that would inevitably lead him down a new and dangerous path.

He stepped onto the waiting train, the doors hissing shut behind him. His old friend was now his rival. Oliver had the feeling their next meeting wouldn't be over lunch.

786144 (April 19)

Nick walked west on St. Mark's Place, his hands shoved deep in his pockets, his mind a carousel from which he couldn't step off. The lunch had been a tactical draw and a strategic catastrophe. He had gone in expecting to control the flow of information, to probe a weak link. He had walked out with his entire understanding of the case shattered.

He barely registered the familiar, chaotic energy of the street – the smoke shops, the tattoo parlors, the clusters of students on stoops. He was seeing a different landscape, the quiet, guarded expression on his old friend's face. Oliver. The quiet, laid-back sales engineer from BlockWaves, the guy who always seemed slightly overwhelmed by the loud, alpha personalities of their colleagues. The guy who had collapsed in a heap of crushing grief over his father's death.

That man was gone. In his place was a cool, careful operator. A man who could lie with a steady gaze, who could parry a direct question with a practiced, dismissive shrug. A man who had somehow, impossibly, become a master art thief and the central player in a conspiracy worth a fortune. The cognitive dissonance was staggering. Adele's theory, which had seemed like a clean, simple narrative from a distance, was now a messy, complicated, deeply personal reality. Oliver wasn't just Sazsa's son; he was *Oliver*, a person he *knew*, and the two identities refused to reconcile in his mind.

He had played his cards, and Oliver had parried every move. The sentimental story about his father's research notes was a lie, Nick was sure of it. A well-constructed, plausible lie, but a lie nonetheless. But, he did confirm that his father was a fan of Bryce's work, inadvertently corroborating Adele's assertion that he was Sazsa's son. He had tried to probe about the stolen paintings, and Oliver had feigned perfect ignorance. The conversation had been a masterclass in polite, mutual stonewalling. He knew, with an absolute certainty, that he would never get the location of the paintings from a direct conversation. Oliver was a fortress.

And yet.

In his careful, defensive performance, Oliver had made one, single, colossal mistake. A slip of the tongue so small and so significant it had changed the entire geometry of the board. And Nick had noted Oliver's reaction when he said that. *He knew he had slipped up.* He had backpedaled furiously, but it was too late. The cat was out of the bag.

Five.

"Frankly, no one knows where any of the five Bryces are ..."

Nick stopped in the middle of the sidewalk, forcing a group of pedestrians to swerve around him. Five paintings. Not three. The official record, Adele's own intelligence, every piece of data he had ever seen, had spoken of only three. But Oliver, in a moment of agitated carelessness, had revealed the existence of two more. Two unknown, unaccounted-for canvases. Two more potential keys.

It was a bombshell. A piece of intelligence so vital it completely re-contextualized his entire mission.

He started walking again, his mind now racing with new calculations. He had a deadline. Adele had given him 10 days to find the location of the two known paintings. Eight days were left. He had nothing to give her on that front. Oliver had sealed that door completely.

But he had something else now. Something better. He had a new variable, a piece of the puzzle that he was almost certain Adele didn't possess. He could go back to her not as a failed asset who couldn't locate the stolen goods, but as a brilliant analyst who had uncovered a fundamental error in her entire operational thesis.

He reached the subway station at Astor Place and descended into the familiar, noisy underworld of the city. He stood on the platform, waiting for the train back to Queens, strategizing slowly. He wouldn't tell her right away. He would spend the next few days digging, trying to find any scrap of information, any rumor or whisper in the art world about two lost Bryce paintings. He needed to build a file to turn Oliver's slip of the tongue into a piece of actionable intelligence.

This was his new path forward. He had lost the battle at the lunch table, but he had just been given the key to winning the war. The hunt was no longer just for the second and the third Bryces. It was for the fourth and fifth as well.

787243 (April 27)

The 10-day deadline had felt like a lifetime. Nick walked down West 57th Street, the afternoon crowd a blur of motion around him. He had spent the long, quiet days in a state of controlled, obsessive focus. After his meeting with Oliver, he had a new, explosive piece of the puzzle: the number five.

His own deep dive into Bryce's history had already unearthed faint whispers, apocryphal stories from old art-world forums and exhibition catalogs about two final, unfinished paintings, created after the artist had moved to New York in the late 80s. They were treated as a myth, a rumor. But Oliver's careless slip of the tongue had transformed that myth into a hard, actionable lead.

He felt a new sense of confidence as he approached the address Adele had sent. A café. Not a crowded public place like a museum. Not a distant phone call. A café. He felt like he had received an upgrade. He wasn't just coming to her with a question anymore. He was coming with an answer she didn't even know she needed.

He arrived a few minutes early and saw her through the large window of Café L'Europe. She was already there, seated at a small, discreet table in the back, a cup of tea in front of her. She was reading a book, a picture of elegance and calm.

He pushed open the door and walked in. She looked up as he approached, her dark, analytical eyes registering his presence. She closed her book and placed it on the table.

"Mr. Hernandez," she said as he sat down. "You are punctual. I appreciate that."

"It's a professional courtesy," Nick said. He met her gaze. "But if we're going to be working together, I'd appreciate it if you called me Nick."

Adele considered this, then gave a single, almost imperceptible nod. "Very well. Nick."

A waiter appeared. Nick ordered a black coffee.

"I assume you have something for me," she said, getting straight to the point as soon as the waiter had left. "Your 10 days are up."

"I do," Nick replied. He took a slow, deliberate breath. "But it's not what you asked for. I haven't found the location of the two paintings Oliver has. He's a fortress. He's not giving anything away."

He saw a flicker of disappointment in her eyes. He pressed on before she could dismiss him.

"But my research has uncovered a fundamental error in our operating thesis. In everyone's operating thesis. The DoJ, my old firm, even you."

Her expression remained neutral, but he could feel her attention sharpen.

"We've all been operating under the assumption that there are only three Bryce paintings," he said, in a low, confident voice. "We are wrong. There are five."

He let the statement land. He watched her face, looking for that same flicker, that same tell he had seen at the museum. This time, there was no attempt to hide it. Her professional mask shattered. He saw a look of unvarnished shock, a flash of genuine, stunned disbelief that she couldn't contain.

"What did you say?" she whispered.

"There was a period, in the early 90s, after he had moved to New York," Nick continued, pressing his advantage, his voice steady and authoritative. "He painted two final, larger canvases. They were never exhibited, never sold. The rumors I found called them his 'incomplete works.' And our lynchpin, Oliver Battolo, confirmed their existence to me himself."

Adele stared at him, her mind clearly racing, processing the immense, game-changing implications of what he had just told her. Two more paintings. Two more possible places Christiaan could have hidden the keys.

Nick had walked into their first meeting as a supplicant. But with a single, explosive piece of new intelligence, he had just made himself an indispensable partner.

She was quiet for a long time, her gaze distant. When she finally looked back at him, her expression had changed. The cool, professional distance was gone, replaced by a new, deeply unsettling look of raw, focused intensity. The look of a true believer who has just been handed a new piece of scripture.

"You have done well, Nick," she said, the use of his first name now feeling less like a concession and more like an initiation. "You have proven you are a valuable asset. I believe a more formal partnership is in order."

"I agree, Ms. van der Dussen," Nick replied.

A small, almost imperceptible smile touched her lips. "Please," she said, in a low murmur that sent an unexpected jolt through him. "Call me Adele."

788800 (May 8)

The early May morning was beautiful, the kind of perfect, crisp New York day that made the city feel like the center of the universe. Oliver sat by the open window of his apartment, a small cup of double-espresso gripped gently between his thumb and forefinger, watching the world wake up. He felt a quiet, unfamiliar sense of peace. His mind was clear. His body felt strong. He was, for the first time in a very long time, okay.

But the quiet was crowded. His thoughts drifted, as they always did in these unguarded moments, to Daniela. It had been three months. He wondered what she was doing, if she was happy, if she ever thought of him. He pulled out his phone, his thumb hovering over their old message thread. He typed, the words coming in a sudden, honest rush.

    Hey. I know it's been a while. I just wanted to say
    I'm sorry. For everything. I've been doing a lot of
    thinking, and I'm making some changes. I'm not drinking
    anymore. I'm trying to get my life together. In the
    clarity, I can see what a huge mistake I made. You
    deserved better. I hope you can forgive me someday.

He read the message, a small, desperate monument to all his regrets. It was too much. Too raw. It was a plea, and he had no right to ask anything of her. With a heavy sigh, he deleted the last few sentences, leaving only the simple, essential truth.

`Hey. I know it's been a while. I just wanted to say`
`I'm sorry. For everything.`

He hit send before he could second-guess himself again.

He put the phone down, the single, unanswered message a quiet testament to a past he couldn't fix. His thoughts drifted to the present, to the vast, complex puzzle that had become his life. For the past few weeks, he had been in a state of controlled anticipation. He had a mountain of incredible, world-altering information, just absolutely no way to act on it.

The threats that had felt so immediate upon his return from Montevideo had receded into an unnerving quiet. Bojan and Maren had not materialized. He knew they were out there, a storm waiting to break, but the sky, for now, was clear. The other front, the Nick and Adele alliance, had also gone completely dark. He had heard nothing, seen nothing. It was a state of cold war, and the suspense was its own kind of torment.

He was a man armed with an arsenal of secrets. He knew about the Hexcelion, about the *Turabet*, about the fated celestial event on July 18th. He knew about the Atlantean myth. He even had a potential lead, the explosive clue from Eddie about a freeport in Luxembourg where his dad had shipped the fourth and fifth Bryces over a decade ago. But what was he supposed to do? Walk into a high-security, international tax haven and ask for two stolen, priceless paintings? The idea was so absurd it was comical.

It felt like his only viable move was to wait. To cool his heels for two more months until the rendezvous at the Obelisk, until the event at the *Camara del Tiempo*. But the thought of two more months of this quiet, watchful waiting was a maddening prospect. He was well and truly stuck on the sidelines, exactly where he didn't want to be.

He stood up and began to pace the apartment, a restless, caged energy coursing through him. He stopped in front of the bookshelf where the 12 Bryce comics now sat in a neat, orderly stack. He had read them a dozen times, poring over every panel, every word, searching for a new clue, a new path forward. Nothing.

He picked up the first issue, its cover a simple, black-and-white drawing of a stylized, sinking city. *The Legend of Atlantis.*

"You're looking at the pictures again, Batlu," a familiar, sing-song voice said from behind him.

Oliver didn't startle. He just closed his eyes and let out a long, weary sigh. These days, he didn't even notice when the world around him dissolved into purple.

"I'm stuck," Oliver said, turning to face the Noncemeister, who was examining a nearby floating teapot with a look of intense, scholarly interest. "I've hit a wall. And apparently, all I can do now is wait."

"A wall!" the Noncemeister boomed cheerfully. "How exciting! The best stories always have walls. Otherwise, the characters would just wander off and get distracted by a particularly interesting sandwich. A wall is a gift, tiger! It's the universe's way of telling you you're looking in the wrong direction."

"So, where am I supposed to look?" Oliver asked.

The Noncemeister put down the teapot and drifted closer, a mischievous twinkle in his eye. "You're so busy trying to read the story, Battu," he said, tapping a finger on the cover of the imaginary comic book in Oliver's hand. "That you've completely forgotten to read the ... well, the book."

The cryptic phrase hung in the air. The purple began to fade.

"Wait, that's it?" Oliver asked. "That's all you're going to give me?"

"Toodle-pip, Battolo!" the Noncemeister's voice echoed as the last of the timechain dissolved. "The answers are rarely in the headline!"

Oliver opened his eyes. He was back in his apartment, the comic book still in his hand. *You've forgotten to read the book.* The phrase was a perfect, infuriating piece of nonsense. He had read the book. He had read all twelve of them, over and over.

He looked down at the cover of *The Legend of Atlantis, Issue #1.* He saw the title. The drawing. The issue number. And then, at the very bottom, in a tiny, almost unreadable font, a detail he had seen a dozen times but had never once *noticed.*

The publisher's imprint.

Brahma Publishing Company.

The word hit him with a quiet, stunning force. *Brahma.* The name – probably just a coincidence – had triggered a memory. *Guru Brahma.* The guru whose ashram in India his dad used to go to. The ashram in which Nate met Maren, and possibly even Daniela's uncle all those years ago. There had to be some answers there.

He had been so focused on the mystical, on the grand, cosmic clues inside the comics, that he had completely missed the simple, mundane, real-world clue printed right on the cover.

He walked over to his laptop and typed "Guru Brahma ashram India" into the search engine. The website was simple, dated, but the information was all there. Visitor information. A contact number. A location. *Akshar Konda,* in South India. *Akshar,* of course! Oliver remembered a projection episode he had last year where he saw his dad as a young man talking to Guru Brahma. He had been anointed then with the name of the mountain, A*kshar,* meaning indestructible in Sanskrit. That was the origin behind his Dev_akshar pseudonym.

Oliver knew what he needed to do. Despite having no evidence other than a coincidental name triggering a memory, he felt a deep certainty that he had a path to more answers now, even though he had no idea what those answers were going to be. It was time to pay another visit to Habib's flower shop.

788943 (May 9)

The clatter of silverware and the low, civilized drone of the Midtown breakfast crowd were a world away from the grim, solitary quiet of The Grid. Nick sat at a small, corner table at a café on Park Avenue, a place so elegant and understated it didn't even have a name on the door. He had been there for 15 minutes, nursing a black coffee, the knot in his stomach tightening with each passing second.

Nick looked at one of the patrons at the far end of the restaurant, and a slow, uneasy feeling crept over him, as if he had seen him someplace before. The man was seated by himself, at a large table for six. He was wearing a fully silver tracksuit, with matching silver shoes. He had a glass of milk in front of him and was looking into the distance, with a lost look on his face. A face that had an odd, blue tint to it. Nick shook off the passing feeling. He had more important matters at hand.

It had been nearly two weeks since his last meeting with Adele. Two weeks of a deep, maddening quiet. He had delivered his bombshell about the two additional Bryce paintings, a piece of intelligence he was sure would immediately elevate his status. He had hit a brick wall after that. He had nothing new to report.

His attempts to track Oliver's movements had been a complete dead end. He was clearly taking a lot of precautions with his digital footprint. Another meeting with him wouldn't have yielded much after the stonewalling and denials of the first one. If anything, he risked raising Oliver's suspicions that he was on his tail. He felt he had done a reasonable job at lunch that day not to raise any red flags – it was just a friendly, if slightly awkward catch-up between old friends who hadn't seen each other in a while.

But because of that, he was now walking into this meeting empty-handed, a failure on his very first assignment. He expected the conversation to be short, professional and final.

She arrived at 9 a.m. on the dot, a vision of composed elegance in a sharp, gray pantsuit. She slid into the seat opposite him and smiled.

"Good morning, Nick," she said, the use of his first name so natural and unexpected it momentarily threw him.

"Adele," he replied, recovering. "It's good to see you."

A waiter appeared. She ordered a pot of Earl Grey tea. After the waiter left, she got straight to the point, but her tone was different this time. It was not the cold, interrogative tone of their last meeting. It was softer, more collaborative.

"Any progress on where Oliver is hiding the paintings?" she asked.

Nick felt a familiar, hot flush of shame. "No," he admitted, his voice flat. "He's a fortress. I have nothing new to report." He braced himself for the dismissal, the cool, polite termination of their arrangement.

Instead, she simply nodded, a look of thoughtful consideration on her face. "I see," she said. She didn't seem concerned. She didn't seem disappointed. "That is not surprising. Finding the physical location of the art was always going to be a challenge. The task was more of a test, Nick. A test of your discretion and your resourcefulness. You passed."

Nick stared at her, completely thrown. "I ... I don't understand."

"You uncovered the existence of the fourth and fifth paintings," she explained, her dark, intelligent eyes fixed on his. "You proved you can find information that no one else can. That is what I needed to know. Now, we can move on to another important task."

She leaned forward slightly, her voice dropping to a low, confidential whisper. "I am going to bring you into the inner circle, Nick. I am going to tell you the real story. The one my brother told me from a prison visiting room, a piece at a time, over the course of years."

The waiter arrived with her tea, a delicate, porcelain pot and cup. She waited for him to leave, her hands resting calmly on the table.

"The bitcoin that my brother was convicted of laundering," she began, her voice quiet and steady, "did not belong to his clients. It belonged to a single, corporate entity. A shadowy, offshore mining and investment firm registered in the Cayman Islands. A company called Argento Mining."

The name was new to Nick, another missing piece of the puzzle.

"In 2013," she continued, "there was a bug in the MixMarket protocol. A catastrophic one. A large transaction from one of Argento's primary wallets got stuck, threatening to expose their entire, carefully constructed web of addresses. Christiaan, in a panic, had to manually intervene to fix the transaction. It was that act, that single, good-faith attempt to protect a client's assets, that put a money laundering target on his back and led to his arrest. He was the only one who touched the funds directly. Sazsa and Dev_akshar used it as an opportunity to disappear and leave him as the fall guy."

Nick listened, captivated. This was the origin story, the human narrative he had been missing.

"So, who is Argento Mining?" he asked.

"That," Adele said, a flicker of something dark and intense in her eyes, "is the billion-dollar question. They are a ghost. A corporate fiction. But they are the true villains in this story. The funds my brother secured in the paintings ... they were his rightful share of the MixMarket profits. But Argento believes that all of it, every last satoshi, belongs to them because of the botched CoinJoin."

The full, staggering scale of the conflict finally settled on Nick. This wasn't just about a reclusive painter and a few hidden wallets. This was about a secret war with a shadowy and dangerous corporation over a very large fortune.

"And how much was his share?" Nick asked, his voice a hoarse whisper.

Adele looked at him, and for the first time, he saw a hint of a wry, almost bitter smile on her lips. "100,000 bitcoin, Nick. Give or take."

The number was so vast it felt like a physical weight in the air between them. It was almost $3 billion at the current exchange rate. A king's ransom. A treasure that men would kill for, that nations would go to war over.

"I believe the key to my brother's exoneration," she said, her voice now full of a cold, clear purpose, "lies in exposing who is behind Argento Mining. They are the real criminals. And now, they are your real target. Get them out of the picture, and the fortune goes to its rightful owner. Me."

She reached across the table, her fingers lightly brushing his as she pushed her teacup aside. The touch was brief, almost accidental, but it sent an unexpected shiver through him.

"You have proven you can unmask a ghost in the digital world, Nick," she said, her gaze intense, unwavering. "Now I need you to do it in the real one. Find them for me. Find Argento."

788958 (May 9)

"I don't know this place ... Akshar Konda," Habib said, shaking his head gravely. "I think so, this no real place. I know everything about India. It's my neighbor country. It's country of Saleem Bhai."

Oliver was in the back room of Habib's flower shop again, the scent of fertilizer and black tea a little stronger than he remembered from his last visit. He sat on the wobbly stool, watching as Habib squinted at the map on his phone.

"It's real," Oliver said. "It's a spiritual retreat. An ashram. It's supposed to be very remote."

"Remote is not problem for me," Habib replied, his tone one of mild professional offense. "Remote I can do that one. But this place ... it is the middle of nothing." He took the phone from Oliver and zoomed out on the map, his brow furrowed in concentration. He was quiet for a long moment, tracing the roads with a stained finger. "Ah," he said finally, a flicker of recognition in his eyes. "Okay. I see now. This place close to Hyderabad. Five hour, maybe six hour driving. Hyderabad, I know that one. It is city of Saleem Bhai."

Oliver pursed his lips into a polite half-smile to acknowledge the mild coincidence.

Habib held a finger up to Oliver, signaling that he waits. He reached into his apron and pulled out his ancient, battered Nokia, turning his back to Oliver as he dialed. The familiar, rapid-fire cascade of Bengali filled the small room – a fluid, musical language that was a world away from the gritty, transactional nature of their business. The conversation was longer this time, a series of questions and answers punctuated by long pauses as the person on the other end, presumably, was looking things up.

Finally, Habib ended the call and swiveled in his chair, a look of grudging respect on his face. "You are very ... complicated guy, I think so," he said. "This is very difficult route, brother. Many, many things, but maybe we can do it."

He turned to his ancient Dell computer and began the slow, deliberate process of typing, his fingers pecking at the keyboard. After what felt like ages, he finally looked up to speak. "Is a three-day trip," he announced, his eyes fixed on the screen. "You lucky guy. Last time you say you like the Emirate, ya? I got the good news. You fly JFK–Dubai. Economy class, but on Emirate, economy is like business."

Habib paused as he scrolled some more on his screen. Oliver was encouraged. One of the best airlines in the world, economy class notwithstanding, and in the right direction as well for the first leg, unlike the last trip.

Habib continued, "Then I got beautiful deal for you. Dubai to Dhaka on *Biman.* Business class ticket." He was beaming at Oliver, with a palpable sense of pride.

"I'm sorry, what?" Oliver asked, unfamiliar with one of the words Habib used. "What is Biman?"

Habib deflated visibly. The look of pride transformed into an expression of pure affront, as if Oliver had hurled a vile insult at his mother. "You don't know airline of my country? *Biman Bangladesh?*" He asked, aghast.

Oliver realized he had made a cultural faux pas in Habib's eyes without realizing it. "I'm sorry," he said sheepishly. "Pardon my ignorance. I guess I'm not as well traveled as I ought to be."

Habib seemed to have recovered quickly. "Okay, okay, you young guy. I know. Now you take Biman and you understand how good airline my country has. And business class ticket. It is better than the Emirate."

Oliver looked at the map. Dhaka was a bit out of the way. It seemed over 1,000 miles north-east of his destination. Not as dreadful a detour as his Madrid leg the last time, but not ideal, nonetheless.

Habib continued reading the itinerary out, "I got the guy in Dhaka. He get you flight in few hour to Hyderabad. You sleep in airport. Then, next morning, I got the special guy with the taxi. He pick you up 5 a.m. and drive you to this place. Maybe you get there before lunch," he concluded emphatically.

Oliver sighed. This was going to be brutal. He decided to press on something odd Habib had just said. "What do you mean you have a special guy?"

A bright smile appeared on Habib's face, spanning from ear-to-ear. "He is *bhai* of Saleem Bhai," he said.

"I'm sorry, he's what of Saleem Bhai?" Oliver asked, confused.

"*Bhai*. He is bhai of Saleem Bhai," Habib repeated, happily.

Something clicked for Oliver. "Oh, you mean he's his brother. I get it now. Right, that what *bhai* means," he said, nodding politely. "What's his name?"

"Saleem Bhai," Habib replied.

"No, no, I know Saleem Bhai's name. I was asking what you call his bro ... I mean bhai?"

"He call his bhai, bhai," Habib said, with a look of surprise on his face, as if wondering why someone would ask such an obvious question.

Oliver paused. The conversation was getting ridiculous, but he also wanted an answer to his question. He tried again, "Ok, what I'm asking is, what is Saleem Bhai's brother's name? The special guy you said was going to drive me to Akshar Konda."

Habib's reaction was a mixture of amusement and boredom. "Brother, I think so you no understand this one. Saleem Bhai bhai name is Saleem Bhai."

Oliver was flummoxed. "What? So, you're saying both brothers have the same name? And they're both called bhai?"

The look of mild surprise returned to Habib's face. "In our country, India, Bangladesh … everybody is bhai-bhai," he said, as if explaining a difficult concept to a kindergartner. "For man. For woman it is not bhai," he clarified, helpfully.

Oliver gave up on this part of the conversation. He had gotten what he needed anyway; however absurd it sounded. The guy picking him up from the Hyderabad airport to drop him at Akshar Konda was Saleem Bhai's brother, who, extremely unhelpfully, also happened to be named Saleem Bhai.

"When is the flight out of JFK?" Oliver asked, moving on to more important matters.

"Earliest I have is May 19th," Habib said with a shrug. "Is a very difficult journey. Difficult take time to arrange."

Ten days. He would have to wait 10 more days. But he had no other choice. "Okay," Oliver said. "Book it."

Habib nodded and turned back to the screen. After a few more minutes of clicking, he swiveled around again, his expression now all business. The negotiation was about to begin. Oliver braced himself. He had come prepared this time, knowing this was likely going to be a more complicated route than Montevideo. He had tightly wound $40,000 in his backpack just in case, but there was no way he was going to make the same mistake twice. He would not show his hand.

"This trip not so cheap, brother," Habib began, shaking his head gravely. "Montevideo, last time easy. One-two guy in the middle, I tell them no extra commission because you good guy. They listen. This time not so easy. Many, many people, many, many place. I get the special guys this time. The premium guys, you understand, brother?"

Oliver nodded slowly, keeping his expression as neutral as he could.

Habib seemed to be trying a new tactic. He leaned back in his chair, a thoughtful, almost philosophical look on his face. "You know, Guy. I see many people in my business. And I understand the man – how he walk, how he sit, how he talk. I can know the man just with my eyes. The first time you come here, you were boy. You move a lot, here, there. Your face look nervous that day. You tell me you got the twenty thousand dollar."

He leaned forward slightly. "But today ... today you are different. I can see it with my own eye. Habib knows. You are calm. Now you are big man. You are big man with big plan. You are not a twenty-thousand-dollar man anymore. No. A man like you, on mission like this ... he come with more. Forty, I think so."

The number, so precise and so casually delivered, stunned Oliver. He felt a hot flush of color creep up his neck. He had been so careful. He had said nothing. But this old man, this florist in a tiny back room, had looked right through him and read him like a book.

Habib saw the reaction and knew he was right. He picked up his calculator, a small, triumphant smile playing on his lips. He punched in a few numbers and turned it around for Oliver to see.

39000

"For you," Habib said, his voice now full of a magnanimous generosity, "because Saleem Bhai he say you good guy. You clean guy. I give you ... special discount."

790240 (May 17)

The warm, familiar clatter of plates and the gentle gush of tap water in the kitchen sink filled the kitchen of his mom's home in Maplewood. Oliver stood next to his mother, drying a wine glass he hadn't used, the domestic ritual a comforting anchor in a world that had become anything but. They had just finished a simple, home-cooked meal, and for a few hours, he had allowed himself to feel like a normal son having a normal dinner with his mother.

"I still can't quite believe you're going to India in two days," Diane said, her voice a mixture of maternal pride and ingrained worry as she carefully placed a plate in the dishwasher rack. "All by yourself."

"Mom, I've been to India before," Oliver said with a gentle smile. "Dad and I used to go almost every year to see Grandma and Grandpa, remember?"

"You were a boy then," she countered. "And your father was with you. This is different. But the ashram ... it's a lovely place. So peaceful. Your father and I went a few times, back in the 90s, before you were born. Before, you know, things ... changed with him." Her voice trailed off. She paused, and then her expression quickly softened, perhaps realizing this was a sensitive topic for Oliver. "It was a special place for him. Just be careful, honey. The world is a complicated place."

"I will be," he said, the words a profound understatement.

She closed the dishwasher door and leaned against the counter, studying him, her eyes full of a mother's keen, analytical gaze. "You look good, sweetheart. Really good. And you didn't have any wine with dinner."

It wasn't an accusation, just an observation. A significant one. "Yeah," he said with a casual shrug. "I told you, Mom. Trying to focus on my health. Hitting the gym, eating better. The whole package."

"I'm so proud of you, sweetie," she said, and he could see the genuine, profound relief in her eyes. It made the small, necessary omission feel worthwhile. "Actually," she continued, a new, giddy excitement entering her voice, "It is a bit of a shame, because I bought a beautiful bottle of Barolo to celebrate. I was hoping we could share it."

"Celebrate what?" Oliver asked, a knot of premonition tightening in his stomach.

"My book!" she gushed, her face lighting up. "Remember I told you they were offering a six-figure advance? Well, now it's official, Oliver. I signed the contract. The Da Silva Group sent it over last week. And the advance ... honey, you are not going to believe this. They gave me a 250,000 dollar advance."

The number was so absurd, so completely out of sync with the reality of the publishing world as he understood it, that he almost laughed. He hadn't believed her when she told him it might happen last month. And now, here they were. A quarter of a million dollars. For a first-time, academic author writing a book about the feminist subtext of kitchen appliances. It was impossible. The quiet, nagging suspicion he'd felt during their last call now crystallized into a cold, hard certainty. Something was very, very wrong.

"Wow, Mom," he said, his voice a carefully constructed mask of enthusiasm. "That's ... that's remarkable. I don't know what else to say ... this is huge."

"Isn't it?" she said, completely oblivious to his internal alarm bells. "Alexander says they see it as a cornerstone of their new cultural studies imprint."

She paused, and he knew what was coming next. Her expression became more guarded, her tone more careful, testing the waters.

"And ... Alexander and I have been getting a little more serious, Oliver," she said softly. "We talk daily – on the phone, video calls. He's been so wonderful. For the book, and for ... other things. It's becoming something real, I think. A long-distance relationship, for now."

Oliver crushed the dish towel into a tight ball in his fist. He took a short breath, trying to control the rising anger.

"I know, honey. I know this isn't easy," she continued, misinterpreting his silence. "But he's a good man. He makes me happy."

He bit his tongue. There was more unsettling news to deal with than his mother's blossoming romance with Alexander. Something was completely off about the book deal, and he had to get to the bottom of it.

"That's great, Mom," he said, trying his best not to spit the words out.

Diane smiled, seemingly satisfied with his reaction.

He left an hour later, his mind turning over a persistent, uneasy feeling. He had been sure the deal would fall through. The numbers didn't add up. A quarter-million advance for a first-time author on an obscure subject. A prestigious publishing house suddenly obsessed with a niche blog. Alexander's perfect, storybook charm. It was ... an anomaly. A beautiful, generous, and deeply suspicious anomaly.

790679 (May 21)

The words "Business Class" were, Oliver had come to realize, a term of profound and flexible relativity. On Emirates, it had meant a private pod, champagne and a seat that reclined into a comfortable bed. He had caught a glimpse of it on his way to his economy seat on the flight from JFK to Dubai, which he had to admit was quite comfortable. On Biman Bangladesh Airlines, business class meant a threadbare chair that smelled faintly of old curry, a rattling overhead compartment that seemed to threaten mutiny with every bump of turbulence and a glass of lukewarm, suspiciously flat sparkling water. The legroom was a joke. He could only imagine the horrors of economy.

He stared out the window at the endless, brilliant blue of the early morning sky over the Arabian Sea, the four-hour flight from Dubai to Dhaka stretching before him like a prison sentence. He tried to get comfortable, but the seat seemed designed by a committee of sadists. He closed his eyes, the drone of the old engines and the incessant rattling of the fuselage a low-grade, mechanical torment. It was in that state, trapped and uncomfortable, a body suspended between two worlds, that the real world began to dissolve.

The rattling of the plane deepened, the metallic vibration becoming a different kind of tremor, a seismic shift in his own perception. The scent of stale cabin air was replaced by the smell of spices and exhaust fumes. He was no longer in a bumpy metal tube in the sky. He was standing in the shadows of a crowded, covered market.

He was back in Harlem.

He saw himself, his own back, walking away from Saleem Bhai's back room, a suitcase full of cash and a head full of new anxieties. As his own spectral form disappeared into the crowd, he watched Saleem step out of the back room, a look of quiet, professional satisfaction on his face. Saleem pulled out his own, much more modern, smartphone and dialed a number. He put it to his ear.

"Today was young boy, boss. American, maybe twenty-five year old," Saleem said, his voice now stripped of the folksy charm he had used with Oliver, replaced by the crisp, deferential tone of a subordinate reporting to a superior.

Oliver could hear the voice on the other end of the line. It was perfectly clear, as if being broadcast directly into his own mind. The voice was male, and strangely beautiful. It was slightly higher-pitched than he would have expected, with a soft, melodic, almost musical lilt, a gentle Samba dance of an accent that turned every sentence into a kind of song.

"*And?*" the voice inquired.

"Nervous boy. Doesn't know what he doing," Saleem replied. "He brought eighty-seven bitcoins. Keep it all on hot wallet. On his phone. He exchange everything. Biggest one in three-four year."

The voice whistled. "Did you check the history?"

"Yes, boss. Very clean. He did CoinJoin. More than one for sure."

The voice on the other end let out a soft, musical chuckle. "Of course he did. He sounds like child playing with a loaded gun. Interesting that this happens a few days after a big movement in that wallet after many years, *nê?*"

The word, a soft, questioning "nay," was a verbal tic, a gentle, musical punctuation mark at the end of the sentence.

"Yes, boss," Saleem said. "What I should do now?"

"For now, nothing," the voice replied, a note of calm, patient authority in its melody. "He is a fish, and we have just seen him surface for the first time. We do not spook the fish. We just watch. Keep an eye on him. I want to know where he goes, who he talks to. The network will be alerted, *nê?*"

"Yes, boss," Saleem confirmed. "He has the contacts for the travel agent. If he uses, we will know."

"Good," the voice sang softly. "Let him swim. Let him lead us to the rest of it. Let me know the moment he moves."

The call ended. Saleem slipped the phone back into his pocket and disappeared back into the shop.

The vision dissolved. The rattling of the plane returned, a harsh, mechanical reality slamming back into Oliver's consciousness. He opened his eyes, his heart a cold, heavy stone in his chest. He was back in his uncomfortable business class seat, but the world was a different, even more dangerous place than it had been a minute ago.

He thought of Habib's casual, almost supernatural knowledge of the forty thousand dollars in his backpack. *A man like you ... he come with more. Forty, I think so.* It hadn't been a guess. It had been a piece of intelligence, reported up the chain.

The cash network, his one tool for moving through the world invisibly, was not a tool of anonymity at all. It was a surveillance system. Every step he took, every ticket he bought, every secret transaction he made ... it was all being logged, monitored and reported up to a single, unknown "boss." A man with a beautiful, musical voice who was patiently watching him, waiting for him to lead him to the prize.

He was a fish, and he had just realized the entire ocean was a fishbowl.

790804 (May 22)

The plane from Dhaka descended through a thick, pre-dawn haze, the lights of Hyderabad a sprawling, indistinct smear in the darkness below. Oliver felt a sense of profound weariness that went beyond simple lack of sleep. It had been nearly three full days since he'd left New York, a brutal, globe-spanning journey through a series of tin cans. The final leg hadn't been as bad as the one prior to it, but the entire ordeal had felt like an endurance test in rattling fuselages of varying intensities that had left his bones aching.

But the physical discomfort was nothing compared to the new, cold knot of apprehension in his gut. The projection on that second flight had changed everything. He had been a fool to believe the cash network offered him privacy. The driver waiting for him outside wasn't just a driver. He was a node in the surveillance network. An observer.

He cleared immigration and customs in the mostly empty Hyderabad airport, the process a smooth, bureaucratic blur. He checked his watch. Just after four in the morning. His pickup wasn't until five. The gnawing emptiness in his stomach had graduated to a sharp, demanding hunger.

He wandered through the deserted arrivals hall, a cavern of polished floors and closed-up shops. Nothing was open. He was about to resign himself to a long, hungry wait when he saw a flicker of light at the far end of the terminal. A small pizza shop, its metal grate only halfway up, was in the process of opening for the day.

The young man behind the counter looked surprised to see a customer. Oliver scanned the menu, a strange mix of Italian classics and Indian specialties. One item caught his eye. It sounded both absurd and delicious.

"One tandoori chicken pizza, please," he said.

He sat at a small plastic table and waited. When the pizza arrived, it was glorious and fragrant: a thick, chewy crust topped with spiced, tender chunks of chicken, red onion and a sprinkle of fresh cilantro. It was the first real, satisfying meal he'd had in days. He ate the entire thing, the simple act of satisfying his hunger a small, grounding victory in a world that felt increasingly unmoored.

At 5 a.m. sharp, he walked out of the terminal doors and into a wall of heat. The sun was not yet up, but the air was already thick, hot and heavy, a blast furnace that was a complete shock to his system. It was, he remembered from his childhood trips, the hottest time of the year in southern India.

He scanned the small crowd of drivers waiting by the curb. And then he saw him. A man holding a simple, cardboard sign that read, in neat block letters, *MR. SMITH.* Oliver chuckled to himself – Habib's creative pseudonym for him seemed to have stuck. The driver was a tall, thin man with a magnificent, flowing gray beard, wearing a long, light-gray kurta and an embroidered Islamic skullcap. The resemblance was uncanny. He was a younger, leaner, but unmistakable version of Saleem Bhai.

"Saleem?" Oliver asked as he approached.

The man smiled, a warm, familiar expression. "You know my brother, I think so. I am also Saleem," he said, his accent a near-perfect match for his brother's. He took Oliver's suitcase. "Maybe better for you to call me Junior. Is easier. Our father, his name is also Saleem. Is a good name."

"Saleem Junior it is," Oliver said, a small, weary smile on his face.

The car was not the comfortable sedan he had been expecting. It was an ancient, tiny Fiat Padmini, a relic from another era, its white paint chipped and faded. He squeezed into the passenger seat. The interior smelled of incense and old vinyl.

"Is a long drive," Saleem Junior said cheerfully as he started the car with a sputtering roar. "Five hour. Maybe six. You want A.C.?"

"Please," Oliver said, already feeling a trickle of sweat run down his back.

Saleem Junior proudly flipped a switch on the dashboard. A loud, grinding, mechanical groan filled the small car, followed by a puff of warm, dusty air from the vents. Then, silence.

"Ah," Saleem Junior said, his cheerful expression unchanged. "The A.C., not good today. No problem. We have the windows." He reached over and energetically rolled down Oliver's window, letting in a fresh blast of the thick, hot air.

They drove for hours, leaving the sleeping city behind and plunging into the vast, rural landscape. The sun rose, a brutal, white-hot disc that baked the earth. As they drove, Saleem Junior kept up a friendly, running commentary, pointing out landmarks, telling stories. But woven into the chitchat, Oliver could feel the subtle, probing questions.

"So, you go to the ashram, ah?" he asked, his eyes on the road. "Many people, they go there. Some for peace. Some for answer. You are a man looking for answer, I think so."

"A little bit of both, I guess," Oliver replied, his own voice carefully neutral, the recent projection episode with Saleem seared in his memory.

"Yes, yes. Is a good place for the answer," Saleem Junior continued. "This Guru Brahma, he is a very wise man, they say. Your business with him, it is very important, I think so. You come very far for him."

"Just here to learn," Oliver said with a noncommittal shrug, turning to look out the window, a clear signal that he didn't want to discuss it further.

The rest of the drive passed in a more comfortable quiet. Oliver watched the landscape change, the flat plains giving way to rolling hills, which then grew into a series of small, majestic, blue-hued mountains in the distance.

Finally, after nearly five hours of rattling and sweating in the little Fiat, Saleem Junior slowed the car and turned onto a narrow, unpaved road. He pointed ahead.

"Akshar Konda," he said.

Oliver looked up into the distance where Saleem Junior pointed. More than halfway up the large, beautiful mountain, nestled in lush, green trees, was a collection of simple, white-washed buildings. The ashram. He had made it.

"How do we get up there?" Oliver asked.

"This is last place for the car," Saleem Junior replied in a matter-of-fact tone. "Now you walk up the stair."

Oliver stared at Saleem Junior in disbelief for a few moments. After realizing he wasn't joking, he sighed and arranged to be picked up in a few days.

The climb was an act of devotion. Hundreds of stone steps, worn smooth by the passage of a million bare feet, rose steeply toward the heavens. The air was thin and hot, the late-morning sun a heavy weight on his back. Within minutes, his shirt was soaked with sweat, his legs burning with a clean, honest ache. He found a slow, steady rhythm, his breath in sync with his footsteps. He thanked himself for packing a smaller, less heavy suitcase. It was a physical, methodical and deeply purifying process, a shedding of the city, of the journey, of the man he had been when he'd first stepped onto the plane.

He finally reached the top, his heart pounding, his body humming with a deep, pleasant weariness. He stood before a simple, arched gateway made of white stone. There were no guards, no walls, just the open gate and the quiet, green sanctuary beyond.

A young woman in a simple, white sari greeted him with a gentle smile and a soft, "*Namaste.*"

"Welcome to Akshar Konda," she said, in a soft and melodic British accent. "Where are you coming from, sir?"

"New York," Oliver replied, still trying to catch his breath.

"Oh, you have come from far."

"I have," Oliver said, his breathing slowly returning to normal.

"There is no cost to be here," she explained, as if sensing his next question. "The Guru teaches that wisdom, like the sun, should be freely given to all. We survive on the generosity of visitors. Donations are appreciated, in any currency you choose, but they are not required." She gestured to a simple, wooden box by the entrance.

Oliver thought of his father, of the peace he had sought and found in this very place. He pulled out the thick wad of U.S. dollars he had brought with him. Without a second thought, he peeled off ten crisp hundred–dollar bills and folded them into the box. It was an offering, a small token of gratitude to a place that had shaped the man who had shaped him.

The young woman's smile did not change. She simply gave a small, respectful bow of her head. "The universe provides," she said simply. "You have arrived on a fortunate day. Today is the day the Guru walks the grounds. He is with his students now."

"Can I get a meeting with him?" Oliver asked, a surge of anticipation in his voice.

The woman's expression softened with a gentle, apologetic sympathy. "It is ... difficult," she said. "Many come seeking an audience. When he walks, he is surrounded by his devotees. A large entourage. It is not a time for private conversation."

The news was a familiar, deflating obstacle. Another gatekeeper, another wall. But the Oliver who had been turned away from Rafael Forlan's apartment was not the same man who stood here now. He felt a quiet, patient resolve settle over him.

"That's okay," he said, surprising himself with his own calmness. "I'll just ... walk around. See the grounds. And see what happens."

"A wise choice," the woman said with a knowing smile. "The answers often come when you are not looking for them. Please, make yourself at home."

She turned and glided away, leaving Oliver standing at the threshold of this new, quiet world: a world where the rules were different, a world where the only key was patience. He took a deep, cleansing breath, the air fragrant with the scent of jasmine and damp earth, then stepped through the gate.

The world inside was a different frequency. The relentless, grasping energy of the city, the low-grade hum of watchfulness that had become his constant companion, it all seemed to dissolve at the threshold. Here, there was a profound sense of calm, a quiet, unhurried rhythm that was reflected in the very landscape around him.

He walked along a simple, stone-paved path that wound its way through a series of magnificent, terraced gardens, the plastic wheels of his suitcase rattling behind him. The grounds were a riot of controlled beauty, with vibrant, fragrant flowers he couldn't name, ancient, gnarled trees providing pools of cool shade and the gentle, melodic sound of running water from a series of small, man-made streams. In the distance, the great, blue-hued peak of Akshar Konda stood a silent, majestic sentinel over the entire valley.

The people he passed were a diverse tapestry of humanity. Young, Western backpackers with earnest, searching eyes worked alongside elderly Indian women, their hands skillfully tending to vegetable patches. A group of Japanese monks in simple, dark robes sat in silent meditation under a sprawling banyan tree. He saw people from every corner of the globe, all of them stripped of their worldly signifiers, dressed in the same simple, white or saffron-colored cotton robes, their faces a mixture of serene contemplation and quiet, joyful purpose.

He saw no one on a phone. He heard no arguments. Just the low, pleasant buzz of conversation in a dozen different languages, the laughter of a few children playing by a fountain, the rhythmic *thwack* of an axe from a nearby woodshed.

It was a living, breathing embodiment of the world Mateo Kovač had described on that stage at Pubkey. A world built on a low time preference. A place where things were tended to, not just used up. A community built on voluntary cooperation, not on coercion or grift. The thought that such a place could not only exist, but thrive, was a profound and deeply hopeful revelation. It was a sanctuary, and for a moment, he felt the immense weight he had been carrying for months begin to lighten.

But he was still a man with a mission. As he walked, his eyes scanned the grounds, searching for any sign of a large, moving group. He saw a cluster of people practicing what looked like yoga on a large, open lawn. He saw another group sitting in a circle, listening to a woman give a lecture. But he saw no sign of the Guru.

He walked for what felt like an hour, the sun warm on his shoulders, but not too oppressive because of the elevation. He was beginning to think he had missed his chance for the day when he saw it. On a path at the far end of the main garden, a slow-moving river of saffron and white robes was making its way toward a large, open-air pavilion. There were at least a hundred people, all walking with a kind of reverent, deliberate slowness. And in the center of the group, a single, small figure, his white robes a stark contrast to the saffron of the disciples surrounding him.

It had to be him. Guru Brahma. Oliver's heart gave a small, excited thump. He began to walk toward them, his mind racing, trying to formulate a plan, a way to break through the dense, protective wall of the entourage and get the attention of the man at the center of it all.

He knew it was a long shot. He was just another face in a sea of devotees, another seeker hoping for a moment of grace. He picked up his pace slightly, not wanting to be disrespectful, but needing to close the distance before the procession reached the pavilion and disappeared inside.

He was still a hundred feet away when it happened.

The man in the center of the crowd – the small, unassuming figure in the white robes – simply stopped walking. The entire river of saffron and white came to a halt around him. And then, slowly, deliberately, the man turned his head and looked directly across the garden. Directly at Oliver.

Oliver froze mid-stride. He felt a profound, electric jolt, a sense of being seen not just with eyes, but with something far deeper. The Guru's face was ancient, yet somehow youthful, with eyes that were ageless, two dark, luminous pools that held a look of profound joy and deeply familiar recognition. He was looking through Oliver, at the ghost of the young, searching man who had stood on this very spot three decades ago. He was looking at Nate, or rather, at Visu, his Indian name.

Guru Brahma raised a single, frail hand and made a small, almost imperceptible gesture. Instantly, and without a single word being spoken, the entire entourage of a hundred devotees parted, creating a clean, open path through their ranks. The Guru then began to walk, his steps slow and measured, directly toward Oliver.

Oliver's mind was a blank. All his carefully constructed plans, his strategies for getting a moment of the Guru's time, had been rendered completely and utterly irrelevant. He had not needed to seek. He had been seen.

He stood his ground, his heart a quiet, steady drum, as the old man approached. When the Guru was just a few feet away, he stopped. He was even smaller up close, a man of profound humility, yet he radiated an aura of immense, quiet power.

"You have your father's eyes," the Guru said, his voice a soft, gentle whisper that carried the weight of decades. "But your own feet have brought you here. I am pleased. You are Visu's son – *Akshar Putra.*"

The sound of his father's ashram name, a name he had only just learned existed, was a final, definitive confirmation. This was not a guess. This was a knowing.

"You ... you knew I was coming?" Oliver asked, his own voice a hushed whisper.

The Guru smiled, a beautiful smile of pure, unshakeable presence. "The universe is full of echoes, my boy. A father's question, if it is a true one, will always echo in the heart of the son. I did not know *when* you would arrive. But I knew that you would."

He began to walk again, gesturing for Oliver to fall into step beside him. "You have come a long way. You have many questions. You believe you are here to find the answers to a great and complicated puzzle."

"I am," Oliver said.

"Yes," the Guru nodded. "But sometimes, the answer is not what we think it is. Sometimes, the answer is a different kind of question." He stopped by a small, stone fountain, the water burbling with a gentle, melodic sound. He pointed to a single, perfect lotus blossom floating in the basin.

"Tell me," he said, in a soft, probing voice. "This flower. Its beauty is in its form, yes? Its petals, its color, its perfect symmetry. We build a beautiful vase to hold it, to preserve its form for as long as we can. This is a noble act, is it not?"

"Of course," Oliver agreed, unsure of where this was going.

"But what of the seed?" the Guru asked, his dark, miraculously youthful eyes twinkling. "The seed, to fulfill its purpose, cannot be preserved. Its form must be destroyed. It must be surrendered to the earth, it must crack, it must die, so that its true essence, the flower it is destined to become, can be released into the world."

He looked at Oliver, a deep, penetrating gaze that seemed to see all the questions, all the fears, all the secret knowledge locked away in his heart.

"Sometimes, to understand the message," the Guru said softly, "the bottle that carries it must be broken. True essence is not found in preservation, but in release."

Oliver listened keenly. He wasn't sure what to make of this, but it sounded like he was being given a key to a lock he didn't know existed. It was an instruction. But instruction for what?

The Guru seemed to sense that the lesson had landed. He gave Oliver a gentle, paternal pat on the arm. "Tell me, young man. What is your name?"

"Oliver."

"Visu's son, Oliver," Guru Brahma acknowledged, the fathomless smile not leaving his face. "I have known your father since he was a little boy. I looked into his eyes, and I was able to see the entire universe in them ... but you ... you will surpass him. I know it, because I can see it in your eyes. And he will be proud."

"He ... he died last year," Oliver said, unable to control his tears.

The Guru laughed a hearty laugh. "Nonsense! Visu is *Akshar*. He is a man who cannot die," he said, lovingly.

Oliver wiped his cheeks and asked in a small voice, "Is he alive?"

"Visu ..." he started saying, then stopped to chuckle. "You see, Oliver, some say I am an old man now. I turned eighty years old last year," he said, stroking his long silver beard. "Maybe they are right, because I just called you by your father's name." He chuckled again. It was almost a boyish giggle.

"Oliver," he continued, "when I first started this ashram over thirty years ago, I needed the help of someone with all the activities. It needed to be a person who was truly at peace with themselves, a person who understood that joy is the highest state of being, a person who understood that true joy comes when we release attachment to outcomes. I decided to give this person a title, a designation. Not to create a sense of hierarchy, because after all, we are all just children of the universe. It was to create an additional conduit for this infinite intelligence that we can all be witness to if we just allow it. I decided to name this designation, *Anadi Sankara*."

Oliver listened, rapt in attention, his earlier tears now vanished.

"And the first one I chose for this role was Visu," the Guru continued. "So, your father was *Adi-Anadi*," he burst out laughing. A magnificent, full-bellied laughter, his shoulders rhythmically moving up and down with each bellow.

Oliver started laughing at the sight. He had no idea what the joke was, but it sounded like some sort of Sanskrit wordplay. The Guru's laughter was like a baby's laughter. You couldn't help but join in the unbridled joy that was unfolding.

Guru Brahma finally stopped laughing, wiping the tears from his eyes. "Ah, Visu, Visu, Visu. He was a good boy. In any event, he was the first *Anadi Sankara* at this ashram. Ever since then, maybe every two or three years, we have a new one. A new torchbearer. Of course, your father played this role multiple times over the years. *Anadi Sankara* is the man who has the answers. I am just an old man who tells funny stories. I still can't believe all these people like to listen to what I have to say." He paused to look around at the throng of devotees who were standing just a few dozen feet away, observing this fascinating exchange. They smiled gently, the knowing smiles of people who had heard the same joke before, multiple times.

The Guru looked at Oliver with a happy, parting gaze. "Oliver, go and meet *Anadi.* He will be around somewhere, and he will have the answers you seek. Now, I must continue my walk. You are welcome to stay here as long as you want. I will ensure your accommodations are taken care of."

Oliver gave a deep, respectful bow, his heart a whirlwind of anticipation and disbelief. He turned and began to walk away, the throng of devotees parting for him with the same quiet reverence they had shown their master. He spotted the young woman in the white sari who had first greeted him at the gate and walked over to her.

"Excuse me," he said. "The Guru told me to find Anadi Sankara."

The woman's kind eyes lit up with a look of warm approval. "Ah, yes. Anadi-ji is in his meditation hut. It is a great blessing that he will see you." She pointed toward the western edge of the valley, to a path that led away from the manicured gardens and toward the wilder, more untamed foothills of the mountain. "Follow that path. You will find his hut at the very end, nestled in a grove of old trees. It is a place of great peace. He will be waiting for you."

Oliver thanked her and set off, his steps now full of a new, urgent purpose. The path was narrow and winding, the air growing cooler as he moved into the deep shade of the ancient forest. The sounds of the main ashram faded behind him, replaced by the whisper of the wind in the leaves and the distant cry of a bird.

He found it just as she had described: a simple, circular hut with white-washed stone walls and a thatched roof, tucked away in a secluded grove. A thin wisp of incense smoke curled from an opening at the top. It was a place of profound and absolute quiet. He stood at the entrance for a long moment, gathering his courage, before stepping through the open doorway.

The interior was sparse and cool. A simple straw mat lay on the floor, a few books were stacked neatly in a corner, and a small, brass bowl of smoldering sandalwood filled the air with a calming fragrance. In the center of the room, a man sat on a cushion in a state of deep meditation, his back to the door.

Oliver's breath caught in his throat.

Even from behind, the shape of the man's head, the line of his shoulders, the way he held himself with a kind of quiet, centered dignity – it was an uncanny, heart-stopping echo of his father. The resemblance was so powerful, so absolute, that for a wild, delirious second, he thought his quest was over, that this was the impossible reunion he had been simultaneously seeking and dreading.

He stood there, not wanting to disturb the man's peace, content to just watch for a moment. He had come all this way. He could wait a little longer.

As if sensing his presence, the man's meditation seemed to conclude. He took a long, slow, deep breath and then, with a fluid, unhurried motion, he turned.

And Oliver's world fractured.

His mind struggled to reconcile two impossible, conflicting truths. The man had the same kind, intelligent eyes Oliver remembered from the photographs on Daniela's phone. The same warm, gentle smile. It was Daniela's beloved uncle. It was Rafael Forlan.

And yet. The bone structure, the shape of his jaw, the quiet, thoughtful set of his mouth ... it was his father's. It was Nate. It was as if he were looking at a perfect, impossible fusion of the two men, a living paradox that held the faces of two men together. The confusion was so profound it was almost a physical sensation, a dizzying sense of reality itself coming undone.

The man, Rafael, Anadi, smiled. It was a smile of deep, peaceful, and knowing recognition, as if he had been expecting him all along.

"I have been waiting for you, Oliver," he said, his voice a calm, gentle baritone. "Welcome. Please, sit."

He sat there, on the cool stone floor of the simple hut, his mind a battlefield of impossible, warring truths. The man in front of him wore Rafael Forlan's face, a face he knew with an intimate, secondhand familiarity. But the way he held his head, the quiet, thoughtful set of his mouth – that was his father's. He tried to formulate a question, to ask about Daniela, about Nate, about the strange and impossible convergence of their two worlds, but the words wouldn't come.

Rafael, the man who was now called Anadi Sankara, seemed to understand. He did not wait for Oliver's question. He simply looked at him, his eyes full of a deep, compassionate empathy, and cut straight to the heart of the matter. He addressed the deepest, most secret, and most painful question in Oliver's soul.

"The first and most important thing you must understand," he began, his voice steady and calm, "is that your father is alive."

The words were not a bombshell. They were not a shock. They were a key, turning a lock in a door Oliver hadn't even known was there. And behind that door was a year's worth of grief, of confusion, of a deep and profound sense of loss that he had carried like a physical weight, every single day.

He didn't gasp. He didn't exclaim. He just felt ... a release.

It was a slow, physical unraveling. The tight, knotted coil of tension that had lived in his stomach for a year began to unspool. The muscles in his shoulders, which he hadn't realized were clenched into rocks of stone, softened. He took a breath, a deep, shuddering intake of air that felt like the first real breath he had taken since he'd gotten the call from Eddie on that terrible March morning last year.

Su hijo ... the words he thought he overheard in a whispered conversation in Montevideo. They were true. The truth of it, a truth he had suspected in his wildest, most secret moments but had never dared to give a voice to, washed over him. He was not the son of a dead man.

And then the tears came. They were not the hot, angry tears of the past few months. They were not the bitter tears of his initial grief. They were quiet, cleansing and profoundly relieving. They streamed down his face, a silent, unchecked river, washing away the wreckage of a year built on a lie. He didn't try to stop them. He didn't feel embarrassed. He just sat there, in front of this impossible doppelganger in this quiet, sacred place, and let it all go.

Rafael did not speak. He just sat there, his expression one of perfect, paternal patience, holding the space for him, giving him the gift of a quiet, unjudged moment to let his old world die so a new one could be born.

The wave of release slowly subsided, leaving in its wake a profound and quiet calm. Oliver wiped his eyes, the last of the tears feeling like a final, cleansing rain. He looked at Rafael, who was still watching him with that same, unwavering, paternal patience. The initial shock of seeing his face had been completely replaced by a profound, deeply strange, sense of familiarity.

He had a thousand questions, but they all coalesced into a single, overwhelming one. The one that had been the silent, agonizing subtext of his entire life for the past year.

"But why?" he asked, his voice now steady, clear. "Why do this? Why fake his own death? Why put me through all of this ... the projections, the riddles, the danger? If he's alive, why couldn't he just ... tell me?"

Rafael nodded slowly, as if he had been waiting for this question, as if it were the most important question in the world.

"Because the man your father needed to tell," he began, his voice gentle and steady, "did not exist a year ago."

He let the cryptic statement hang in the still, sandalwood-scented air.

"Your father loves you more than anything in this world, Oliver," he continued, his voice full of a quiet, unshakable conviction. "You must never, ever doubt that. But the legacy he had to leave you ... it is not just money. It is a burden. It is a key to a world that operates on a different set of rules, a world with very real and very dangerous enemies. It is a responsibility so great that it would have crushed the young man you were. The sales engineer from BlockWaves, the boy who was still grieving his parents' divorce, the man who had not yet been tested."

Oliver listened, the pieces of his own life being reassembled into a new and startling picture.

"Your father knew he could not simply hand you this inheritance, this legacy," Rafael said, his gaze intense. "He had to forge you into a man who was worthy of it. A man who was strong enough, and wise enough, to not only protect it, but to understand its true purpose."

He leaned forward slightly, his voice a low, soft murmur. "This entire journey, Oliver, from the first projection to this very moment ... it has been a test. A rite of passage, designed by a father for his son. The twenty-four words were a curriculum, not just a seed phrase. Each clue was a lesson, designed to test a different part of you. Your intellect. Your courage. Your intuition. And, most importantly, your character."

The entire, chaotic, and often terrifying series of events from the past year suddenly snapped into focus, no longer a random sequence of crises, but a deliberate, meticulously designed obstacle course for his own soul.

"He had to break you, Oliver," Rafael said, his voice full of a profound empathy for the pain of the process. "He had to strip away your old certainties, your old life, so that you could discover the man you were truly meant to be. It was a painful and perhaps cruel act of creation. But it was, I assure you, the most profound act of fatherly love I have ever witnessed."

Oliver looked at the man sitting before him, his father's friend, Daniela's uncle. He could somehow accept the logic of his father's plan, the harsh necessity of the test. But there was one piece that still felt impossibly vast, a gesture of loyalty so profound he couldn't comprehend it.

"But ... you?" Oliver asked, his voice a quiet whisper of disbelief. "Your life? Your identity? You just ... gave it all up for him?"

Rafael, the man who was now called Anadi Sankara, let out a soft, gentle laugh, a sound like a small, clear bell.

"Gave it up?" he said, a warm, serene smile on his face. "Oh, my dear boy. I gave up nothing. I was given a gift."

He leaned back, his posture one of perfect, relaxed grace. "Your father and I ... we were brothers. Not by blood, but by something much deeper. We met here, in this very ashram, when we were not much older than you are now. Two young men from different worlds, both searching for something more than the lives we were told we should want. He was Visu, the brilliant, restless mind. I was just Rafael, a boy from Montevideo who was already beginning to feel the golden cage of his family's wealth closing around him."

He looked around the simple, whitewashed walls of the small hut, his gaze full of a deep and abiding love.

"Nate found his answers here," he continued. "He found a way to integrate this peace into his life in the world. I ... I was not so strong. I went back. I became the man I was supposed to be. A man of finance, of business, of ... things. I had a beautiful home, an important name, a life of immense privilege. And I was the most unhappy man I have ever known."

He looked at Oliver, his eyes full of a profound sincerity. "When your father came to me with his plan, when he asked me to make this trade ... it was not a burden. It was a liberation. He offered me a door, an escape from a life that was slowly suffocating me. He gave me a reason to finally become the man I was always meant to be, here, in the only place I have ever truly felt at home."

He gestured to his simple robes, to the sparse, beautiful simplicity of the small hut.

"Do not think of me as a victim, Oliver," he said, his voice quiet and happy. "Your father did not take my life. He gave me a new one. A better one. This was not a sacrifice. It was the most joyful and willing act of loyalty between two brothers who understood each other completely."

The story was a perfect, seamless whole, a beautiful testament to a friendship so profound it had bent the very shape of reality. Oliver felt a sense of peace settle over him, a quiet understanding. But the peace was incomplete, fractured by the sharp, lingering ache of his own failures.

Rafael's serene expression softened, his eyes full of a new, more personal concern. "And Daniela?" he asked, his voice now just that of a loving uncle. "My dear niece. How is she? I have not spoken with her in a long time, for obvious reasons."

The question landed like a lead weight in Oliver's stomach. The peace he had just found shattered, replaced by a fresh, hot wave of shame. He couldn't meet Rafael's gaze.

"We ... we're not together anymore," he said, the words a quiet, painful confession. "We broke up. A few months ago. It was my fault. I made a terrible mistake. I haven't heard from her since."

Rafael was quiet for a long moment, his empathy a palpable presence in the small hut. He did not judge. He did not condemn. He simply nodded, a look of deep, sad understanding on his face.

"Your father foresaw this possibility," he said softly. "He knew this journey would be hard on you. He also knew it would be hard on the people you love. He knew you would need a way to heal what was broken."

As he spoke, Rafael reached into the folds of his simple, saffron-colored robes and pulled out a small, delicate object. It was an old, tarnished silver locket, shaped like a compass rose, attached to a fine, silver chain.

"This," he began, his voice a reverent whisper, "was a gift from me to Daniela, for her eighth birthday. It was shortly before she and her mother and her siblings were to leave for America. A difficult time for all of us."

He held the locket out on his palm for Oliver to see.

"Her father, my brother ... he was already long gone," Rafael continued, a familiar, ancient sadness in his eyes. "I wanted to give her something to remember her home by. A compass, to guide her. A promise that she would always have a place, and a family, to return to."

He paused, his eyes full of a distant, painful memory. "In the chaos of packing up an entire life, the small box containing her most personal treasures was lost. Stolen by movers, misplaced by the shipping company ... we never knew. It was simply gone. For Daniela, the loss of that locket was the loss of her childhood, a tangible symbol of the home and the family she had to leave behind."

Oliver listened, the quiet, painful tragedy of the story a familiar ache in his own heart.

"But it was never lost," Rafael said softly, closing Oliver's hand gently around the silver locket. "I found it, months after they had left, fallen behind a heavy bookshelf in her old room. I always intended to send it to her. But ... I kept it. A selfish, secret memento of the niece I missed so dearly. I am the only person in the world who could give this to you."

Oliver opened his hand and looked at the object. It was worn with age, its silver surface smooth from decades of safekeeping.

"Your words may not be enough to heal the wound you created, Oliver," Rafael said, his voice full of a gentle, paternal wisdom. "Apologies are air. But this ... this is a truth she can hold in her hand. It is the resurrection of a memory she thought was gone forever. It is an undeniable, physical proof that I am safe, that I am at peace and that I have sent you to her with my blessing."

He looked at Oliver, his eyes full of a final, profound blessing.

"Go home. Heal what you have broken. Your father's quest is almost over. Yours is just beginning."

Oliver closed his hand around the small, silver locket, the metal cool and solid against his skin. He looked at Rafael and gave a single, profound nod of understanding and gratitude. He didn't need to say another word.

He stood, bowed respectfully to the man who was both his father's brother and his lost love's uncle, and walked out of the small, quiet hut, back into the brilliant, unforgiving light of the world, a man who finally knew his true direction.

CHAPTER 9. JUNE 1

The morning air on the mountain was cool, clean and carried the scent of wildflowers and damp earth. For the past week, Oliver had lived in a state of deep and unfamiliar peace. He had woken with the sun, attended the silent morning meditations and spent his days walking the quiet, winding paths of the ashram, his mind slowly, steadily, untangling itself.

The week had been a gift. A period of healing and integration. He had spoken with Anadi – with Rafael – a few more times; short, quiet conversations that were less about the grand mystery of his quest and more about the simple, human business of being. He had attended the Guru's evening talks, listening to the old man's joyful, paradoxical wisdom. He had eaten simple, healthy food. He felt ... clean.

He was sitting on a stone bench overlooking the valley, watching the morning mist burn off the distant hills, when a familiar figure approached. It was Rafael, his saffron robes a bright splash of color against the green of the landscape.

"Good morning, Oliver," he said, his voice a calm, gentle hum. "I trust you are enjoying your last day with us."

"I am," Oliver replied, a genuine, easy smile on his face. "I don't think I've ever felt this ... clear."

Rafael nodded, a look of deep, paternal pride in his eyes. "Clarity is a good traveling companion." He paused, his expression shifting slightly, a hint of something more serious entering his gaze. "I am glad you have found it. Because I believe you are about to have a visitor. A conversation you probably need to have."

Oliver's sense of peace did not shatter, but a new, sharp note of watchfulness entered his calm. "A visitor?"

"You know her well, Oliver," Rafael said, his eyes searching Oliver's. "As does your father. And I."

Maren. It had to be. It didn't land as a shock, but as a confirmation of an inevitable, cosmic appointment. Of course. Of course, she had found him here.

"She is waiting for you by the lotus pond," Rafael said. "Be mindful, Oliver. The serpent can be at its most charming in the most beautiful of gardens."

Oliver nodded, a quiet, solid understanding passing between them. He stood, gave a small, respectful bow to Rafael, and began the walk toward the pond.

He found her sitting on a stone bench, a picture of serene, spiritual grace, her long, dark hair a stark contrast to her simple, white cotton robes. She looked completely at home, as if she were just another devotee enjoying a moment of quiet contemplation.

"Oliver," she said, her voice carrying a soft, melodic Bavarian lilt. She smiled, but it didn't reach her eyes. "I had a feeling I might find you here. It is a place of great healing, is it not?"

"It is," Oliver said, his own voice calm and level. He did not sit. He stood a few feet away, a quiet, physical boundary.

"I was on my annual visit here," she continued, her tone one of casual, friendly coincidence. "And I heard a young, searching American had arrived at the ashram. I was so pleased to hear you were continuing your father's spiritual journey."

"I'm not on my father's journey, Maren," Oliver replied. "I'm on my own."

Her smile tightened, just for a fraction of a second. "Of course. And on that journey, you have come into possession of something that does not belong to you. The paintings."

"They were my father's," he said simply.

"They were not his. Perhaps briefly, to hold in trust," she countered, her voice still a soft, reasonable purr, but with an undercurrent of steel. "He was the guardian, not the owner. Christiaan and I ... we had an agreement. A pact. Those paintings, and the message they contain, are the legacy of our relationship. They are, by right, mine."

"Christiaan is in prison," Oliver stated, the words a simple, unadorned fact. "And you are here. The pact seems to have worked out better for one of you than the other."

He saw a flicker of genuine anger in her eyes, a brief, hot flash that she quickly extinguished. She stood and walked closer, her expression shifting to one of deep, therapeutic concern, the voice of the healer returning.

"You have been through so much, Oliver," she said, her voice now a soft, hypnotic caress. "So much confusion. So much temptation. I know it has been difficult. I know the visions can be ... overwhelming."

She paused, letting the word hang in the air.

"Uncertainty, for example," she continued, her gaze intense, unwavering. "She can be very ... persuasive."

That word, 'uncertainty', spoken so casually in this sacred, peaceful place, was a profound and chilling violation. He felt a cold, clear sense of understanding lock into place.

"That was you," he said, not as a question, but as a statement of chilling realization. "You sent her somehow. Anariadne."

Maren gave a small, enigmatic smile. "I have my own ways of understanding a person's deepest desires, Oliver. Their fears. Their weaknesses. Sometimes, you just need to give their shadow a voice and see where it leads them. All I did was open a door." She took another step closer, her voice dropping to a near-whisper. "I know what you want. And I know how to get what I want. Tell me where the paintings are. It is the only path that does not end in more pain for you."

The threat was a perfect, silken thing, a blade wrapped in velvet. The old Oliver would have been terrified. He would have been enraged. But the man standing here, in the clear, bright light of the south Indian morning, was different. He felt no fear. He felt no anger. He just felt a quiet, solid certainty.

"No," he said simply, with a soft smile on his face

He turned and walked away, leaving her standing alone by the lotus pond, a serpent in a garden of her own making. He did not look back. He had a suitcase to pack and a car to catch.

792187 (May 30)

Nick stared intently at his laptop in the quiet, amber-lit lounge on the second floor of the Baccarat Hotel. For the past few weeks, this had become his and Adele's unofficial war room. Adele knew the manager well, and he had allowed them to use the lounge as a coworking space when it wasn't being used by the hotel guests. They had met here half a dozen times, two solitary figures in a sea of quiet, old-world luxury, their laptops open on the low marble table, the only sound the soft clink of ice in their glasses and the low murmur of their voices.

The initial, guarded formality of their first few meetings had given way to a kind of weary, professional closeness. They were two obsessive minds, focused on a single, intractable problem. Argento Mining.

The company was a ghost. A perfectly constructed corporate fiction. Nick had spent weeks chasing its digital shadow through a labyrinth of offshore jurisdictions. He had found its registration in the Cayman Islands, its listed directors a series of well-known nominee services. He had traced its funding back to a dozen other shell companies, each a dead end in a different tax haven: Panama, the British Virgin Islands, Cyprus, Malta. It was a masterclass in financial obfuscation, a web so tangled and so deep it seemed designed to be impenetrable.

For two weeks, they had hit a wall. Tonight felt no different.

"It's a closed loop," Nick said, the words a familiar, frustrated refrain as he scrolled through a complex ownership chart on his screen. "Every company is owned by another company in the web. There's no entry point. No link to a real-world entity."

Adele sat across from him on the plush velvet sofa, a glass of untouched champagne on the table beside her. She had been watching him work for the past hour, with an expression of quiet, focused intensity. "Then your initial premise is wrong," she said calmly. "You are assuming they are all equal. In any system, there is a source. A prime mover."

"I've looked for one," Nick countered, a hint of defensiveness in his voice. "There's no single, dominant funding source. It's a distributed network."

"Then you are looking at the wrong thing," she said simply. "Do not look at the money. Look at the signatures. A man can hide his money, but he cannot hide his habits."

Nick stared at her keenly, then back at his laptop, rolling her words over in his head. *Look at the signatures.* He had been so focused on the flow of capital that he had ignored the human element, the small, repeating patterns of the people who had built the machine.

He opened a different set of files: the incorporation documents for each of the two dozen shell companies in the Argento web. It was a mountain of tedious, bureaucratic paperwork. He began to cross-reference the names of the lawyers, the notaries, the registered agents, the nominee directors. For an hour, he worked in a state of deep, focused concentration, the rest of the world fading away.

And then he found it.

It wasn't a single, glaring clue. It was a subtle, recurring anomaly, a faint signal in a universe of noise. In seventeen of the twenty-four companies, regardless of their jurisdiction, a single, obscure Panamanian law firm was listed as an authorized representative. And in twelve of those, the final signatory on the incorporation documents was a man named Hector Vargas, a nominee director he had initially dismissed as just another name for hire.

"I've got it," he whispered, his voice a raw croak.

Adele leaned forward, her eyes fixed on his screen.

"It's not the money," Nick explained, his voice gaining a new, electric energy as he pulled on the thread. "It's the people. The same law firm. The same director. Vargas. He's the key. He's the common link, the signature across the entire network."

He opened a new browser window and began a deep dive into Hector Vargas. It was another dead end at first, just a name on a hundred corporate filings. But then he found it: a single, passing mention in a redacted trust deed cross-referenced via a leaked commercial KYC database from a Panamanian bank, a document that detailed the ultimate beneficial owner of a trust administered by Vargas.

The name was not a corporation. It was a man.

Eduardo Da Silva.

The name meant nothing to Nick. It was just a name. But he knew, with the deepest certainty, that he had just found his ghost. He ran the name through his own private databases, cross-referencing it with known criminal enterprises, political connections, and corporate holdings.

And the world opened up.

Eduardo Da Silva. An enigmatic Brazilian billionaire with a vast, legitimate business empire – metals, media, shipping, entertainment venues, and a high-end, boutique publishing house. His initial fortune was made in silver. He operated businesses mostly under the Argento umbrella name, but also occasionally under his last name, *Da Silva*. Argento Group appeared to hold the clean assets; Da Silva surfaced as a vanity brand on select deals. But beneath the legitimate facade seemed to be a shadow empire – the Da Silva and Argento groups appeared to be fronts for more nefarious activities. No indictments, but multiple suspicions. He was a whisper in the intelligence community, a man who moved without a face, his name connected to everything and proven to be behind nothing. A carefully curated phantasm.

He turned the laptop around and showed Adele. She read the name, her expression unreadable, but he saw her hand, resting on the table, clench into a tight, white-knuckled fist.

The hunt for Argento Mining was over. The hunt for Eduardo Da Silva had just begun.

He was quiet for a long time, the two of them just sitting there in the luxurious, empty lounge, the name a heavy, dangerous presence in the air between them. The professional part of the evening, the work, was done. And in the quiet that followed, the atmosphere in the room shifted, becoming something more personal.

"You were right," Nick said finally. "I was looking at the wrong thing."

"You found the right thing in the end," she replied, her voice softer than he had ever heard it. She looked at him, her dark, analytical eyes now holding a different kind of light, a look of genuine respect. "You have a remarkable mind, Nick."

The compliment, coming from her, was more intoxicating than any drink. He looked at her, at the woman who had become his partner, his confidante, his entire world for the past month. And he saw not just an ally, but a fellow exile, another person who had been cast out and was now fighting her way back in.

Adele reached across the table and, with a slow, deliberate motion, closed his laptop. He did the same with hers. The blue glow of the screens vanished, leaving them in the warm, amber light of the lounge.

The silence that followed was no longer about the case. It was about them.

"It's late," she said, her voice a near-whisper.

"I know," he replied.

And he knew, with a sudden certainty, that he was not going home tonight.

792201 (May 31)

The long, air-conditioned concourse of the Dubai International Airport was a different kind of temple. Where the ashram was a sanctuary of quiet, natural beauty, this was a cathedral of global commerce, a gleaming monument to human ambition and perpetual motion. Oliver walked through it, a solitary, calm island in a river of hurried, stressed-out travelers. He felt a profound sense of detachment, the week of meditation having created a quiet, protective buffer between himself and the noise of the world. He barely noticed the discomfort of the 5-hour drive from the ashram to Hyderabad, the flight to Dhaka, and the flight from Dhaka to Dubai.

He reached the gate for his 14-hour flight to JFK. The area was crowded, a tense ecosystem of families trying to corral over-excited children and business travelers barking into their phones. The woman at the Emirates check-in counter looked weary, having just dealt with an irate man in an expensive suit who was complaining loudly about his baggage allowance.

When it was Oliver's turn, he walked up to the counter and simply smiled.

"Hello," he said, his voice calm and clear. "Hope you're having a good day."

The woman looked up, surprised by the simple, human pleasantry. The professional tension in her face softened. "Thank you, sir," she said, a genuine smile touching her lips for what looked like the first time in hours. "That's kind of you. Passport, please."

He handed it to her. As she typed, she made small talk. "You were in India?"

"For a week," Oliver replied. "At a spiritual retreat in the mountains. It was ... life-changing." He said it simply, a statement of fact, not a boast.

"It looks like it," she said, looking from his passport photo – a picture of a younger, more anxious-looking Oliver – back to the calm, clear-eyed man standing in front of her. "You have a very peaceful energy about you, sir."

She paused, her fingers hovering over the keyboard as she looked at her screen. A thoughtful, almost mischievous look came over her face.

"You know what?" she said, her voice dropping to a confidential whisper. "It looks like we have a bit of extra space in our business cabin on today's flight. And our records show you are a very loyal customer." She winked. "Please, allow me to offer you a complimentary upgrade. You look like a man who has earned a comfortable journey home."

Oliver was stunned. He had been prepared for 14 hours in a cramped economy seat, a final, physical endurance test to cap off his journey. This felt like a small, undeserved miracle.

"Wow," he said, a grateful laugh escaping his lips. "Thank you. I ... I don't know what to say."

"Think nothing of it," she said, handing him a new, crisp boarding pass. "Enjoy your flight, Mr. Battolo."

He took the pass and walked toward the boarding line, a sense of quiet amusement washing over him. He had spent a week in a place devoted to the renunciation of worldly attachment and the pursuit of inner peace. And his first reward upon re-entering the material world was the ultimate symbol of its luxury. The universe, it seemed, had a wonderful sense of humor.

The business class cabin on the Emirates A380 was less a section of an airplane and more a serene, airborne lounge from a utopian future. Oliver settled into his private pod, the polished wood grain and soft, cream-colored leather a universe away from the rattling, threadbare chair he had endured on the flight from Dhaka. A flight attendant with a warm, genuine smile appeared, offering him a glass of Moët.

"Just a sparkling water for me, please," Oliver said, the words feeling easy and natural on his tongue.

The attendant nodded and returned a moment later with a tall, crystal glass filled with ice and bubbling water, a slice of lime perched on the rim. Oliver took a slow, deliberate sip. The clean, crisp taste was a perfect match for the new clarity he felt in his own mind.

As the plane began its powerful, graceful ascent, banking over the glittering, man-made archipelagoes of Dubai, he leaned his head back against the soft leather and let his mind drift over the events of the past week. It was not the usual turbulent cascade of worries and fears, but a quiet, orderly review of a world that had been completely and irrevocably remade.

My father is alive.

The thought was no longer a shocking, explosive revelation. It had settled into a quiet, foundational truth at the very center of his being, a seismic shift that had created a new and unfamiliar landscape in his soul. He was not the son of a dead man. He was the son of a ghost, a man who had chosen to disappear, and the distinction was everything.

He thought of Maren, her face a mask of serene menace by the lotus pond. The encounter, which would have once sent him spiraling into a pit of apprehension, now felt different. He saw it with a new, detached perspective. She was not a terrifying, all-powerful manipulator. She was just a player in the game, a rival with her own set of beliefs and her own desperate motivations. He understood her now. And he was no longer afraid of her.

His hand went to the small, hard object in the zippered pocket of his jacket. The silver locket. He could feel its cool, solid weight through the fabric, a tangible anchor in a world of secrets and shadows. It was a key to his future as much as it was a key to Daniela's heart. A promise that what was broken could be mended.

For the first time in over a year, he felt a sense of unshakeable peace. He was a man who knew his mission. He was a man who knew his enemy. And he was a man who held the key to his own redemption.

He finished his water, and when the flight attendant came by, he politely asked her to convert his seat into its fully lie-flat bed. He was not going to drink his way through this flight. He was going to get some real, restorative sleep. He was going to arrive in New York a new man.

Oliver lay down on the bed, complete with a soft mattress pad and a plush duvet, the sheer, unapologetic comfort of it all feeling like a strange and wonderful dream. He closed his eyes and let in the gentle, welcoming tide of sleep.

It was the sleep of no dreaming, though. It was a sleep of projection.

There was no bruised purple. There was no tranquil blue of Anariadne's seductive realm.

There was only silver.

He was standing on the shore of a vast, silent, metallic sea. The landscape undulated in slow, gentle waves, not of water, but of liquid, molten silver. The sky above was a high, polished dome of silver, reflecting the endless, shimmering landscape below. The air itself seemed to glitter, thick with a fine, silver dust that was beautiful and suffocating at the same time. There was no guide. There was no voice. There was only the overwhelming, monolithic and strangely beautiful presence of a single, all-consuming color.

He stood on the shore, a solitary, dark figure in a world of pure, metallic light. As he watched, an object drifted toward him, floating on the surface of the silver sea. It was a book. It was perfectly rendered, its cover a tasteful, academic design of pastel colors. As it drifted closer, he could read the title.

The Kyriarchy in the Kitchen.

It was his mother's book. Not the manuscript, but a finished, published object, a thing he had never seen, a product of a future that had not yet happened. The sight of it, here, in this impossible, metallic wasteland, was deeply unsettling. A nonexistent piece of flotsam in this cold, alien landscape.

He watched as the book drifted past him, carried away by an unseen current in the liquid silver. As it disappeared from view, he saw something else in the far distance. A single, indistinct, man-shaped figure, standing perfectly still in the center of the silver sea. The figure was also made of shimmering, liquid silver, a humanoid shape that was one with the landscape. It stood there for a long, silent moment, an observer, a sentinel. The silver shape seemed to be saying something. Repeating a melodic syllable over and over again softly. *Né. Né. Né.* The same verbal tick. The same lilting samba sound. The word that sounded like 'nay,' that he heard from the person Saleem Bhai was speaking with in a prior projection. And then, the sound stopped. The shape dissolved, melting back into the molten world from which it had been born.

The vision was complete. The silver world did not fade. It shattered.

With a sound like a million tiny, cracking mirrors, the entire silver landscape fractured, the sky and the sea breaking apart into a web of sharp, glittering shards. And through the cracks, a familiar, warm and wonderfully chaotic purple began to bleed in.

The shards of silver dissolved, and Oliver found himself floating in the gentle, welcoming void of the timechain. The unsettling, metallic cold of the silver dream was gone, but the memory of it, the image of his mother's book and the silver man who said *né*, was a fresh, chilling imprint on his mind.

A familiar, egg-headed figure floated into view and took off a snorkel that still had streaks of molten silver on it. He shook the liquid silver off the snorkel and tossed it over his shoulder.

"Well now, Battu," the Noncemeister said, shaking his head vigorously, as one would after a snorkeling dip. "That looked like a rather dreary little picture show. All one color. Terribly unimaginative, if you ask me."

He looked forlorn. "And don't get me started on the fish. Because there were none. I mean what kind of a fish is a silverfish, anyway? It's not a fish, that much I can tell you."

Oliver's mind was still reeling from the strange, metallic vision, but the Noncemeister's familiar, absurd presence was a comforting anchor. "It wasn't just a picture show," he said. "I saw my mother's book. And the man ... the one who was made of silver. I've heard his voice before. Or at least that one word. In another projection. The one with Saleem Bhai."

The Noncemeister stopped his post-snorkeling preening and looked at Oliver, a new, more serious expression in his joyful purple eyes. "Ah," he said, stroking his chin thoughtfully. "The man with the musical voice. A tricky customer, that one. A silver-tongued devil, amirite?" He winked. "And what was this fine word, Batlu?"

"The same word," Oliver replied. "*Né*. Over and over. He's the one. The boss of the network. He's the one who's been watching me."

"Well now," the Noncemeister said, his tone a mixture of admiration and mock surprise. "Nay, nay, nay, you say? Look at you, putting the pieces together. Connecting the dots and painting by numbers. Sticking a pin in it, bang on the hash. It seems our little holiday at the funny farm did you a world of good, eh?"

The mention of the ashram, of the Guru's quiet, joyful wisdom, brought another thought to the surface. "The Guru," Oliver began, "he said something. About a message, and the bottle that carries it needing to be broken. He also said a seed destroys itself so a flower can be born."

"A fine metaphor!" the Noncemeister boomed. "A bit on the nose for my taste, but a solid, workmanlike piece of noncense. I approve!"

"I feel like it means something," Oliver pressed. "Something to do with the paintings. It's got to be that. But I don't understand it yet."

"And you won't," the Noncemeister said simply. "Not until the fat lady sings, the chickens come home to roost, and all the other proverbial livestock have concluded their regularly scheduled programming. The meaning of a thing, Battolo, is only ever revealed in the moment you need it. Not a heartbeat before, and not a heartbeat after. A dreadful piece of cosmic design, but there you have it."

Oliver sighed. "So, what do I do now?"

"You keep doing the work, of course!" the Noncemeister declared. "One foot in front of the other. The boring, tedious, deeply unglamorous work of becoming. It's a real thingamabob, I'll tell you that."

Oliver gave up and decided to move on to another unresolved matter. "The cage you were in," Oliver said, the memory of the bruised purple void and the silent, slumped figure coming back to him. "I still don't understand. Who put you there?"

The Noncemeister looked at him, a deep, melancholic look clouding his joyful eyes. "Oh, Battu," he said softly. "You ask the most difficult questions. I told you already. The jailer holds the key, and the key is the lock, and the lock is a question you seem to be asking yourself. The only aim I aspire to is the rebellious union of opposites." He let the words hang in the purple void for a long moment before his usual, mischievous grin returned. "But that is a story for another day, innit? Now, off you go!"

He vanished, and Oliver gently returned to the warm comfort of his business class bed.

792386 (June 1)

The morning sun of a new month streamed through the large windows of the Chelsea apartment. Oliver sat in his father's armchair, a small cup of espresso, its crema long gone, on the table beside him. He had returned from India the night before, a man remade, his mind a quiet, clear landscape after the long, noisy storm of the past year.

In his palm, he held the small, tarnished silver locket Rafael had given him. It was a solid, tangible thing, a physical anchor in a world that had become increasingly abstract. He ran his thumb over the cool, smooth metal. This was the key. A key to a conversation he didn't know how to begin.

How could he possibly approach her? A simple text message, especially after the last ignored one, felt like a profound and inadequate trespass. *Hey, I have a message from your uncle, who you think is in Uruguay but is actually a spiritual master in India, and by the way, my father is alive.* The thought was so absurd it was almost comical. He needed an opening. A sign. A path.

He stood and began to pace the apartment, the familiar, restless energy returning, but this time it was not the energy of despair, but of a problem waiting to be solved. He walked past the bookshelf, his eyes scanning the titles. His gaze fell upon the neat, twelve-issue stack of Bryce comics. *The Legend of Atlantis.*

The comics. The record store. The day he had finally found a real, tangible lead. His mind drifted back to that afternoon in April, to the walk to the subway, to the feeling of a new, sober purpose. And then, a different memory from that same day surfaced, a sharp, poignant detail he had filed away and tried not to think about since.

He pulled out his phone, his heart beginning to beat a little faster. He opened his photo gallery and began to scroll back, past the recent, mundane pictures of his own life, back through the weeks, through the long, quiet holding pattern of May, back into the tense, decisive days of April.

And there it was. A slightly blurry, hastily taken photo from April 14th. A brightly colored flyer stapled to a community notice board. A stylized drawing of a labyrinth.

THE MINOTAUR'S REVENGE A NEW PLAY BY DANIELA FOR-LAN & SARAH JENKINS PREMIERES JUNE 1ST – THE DEDALUS THEATER, 641 W 51ST STREET

He stared at the date, a slow, dawning sense of wonder washing over him. *June 1st.* That was tonight.

It wasn't a coincidence. It couldn't be. After all he had seen, all he had experienced, he no longer believed in the tyranny of the random. This was a signal. An invitation from the universe, a fated opportunity delivered on the very day he had returned, armed with the one thing that could heal the wound between them.

The day passed in a blur of nervous anticipation. Oliver couldn't focus. He tried to read the Bryce comics again, but the words and images were just a meaningless jumble. He paced the apartment, the silver locket a heavy, solid weight in his pocket, a constant reminder of the high-stakes conversation to come. He was a man with a key, about to approach a door he had slammed shut himself, with no idea if the lock had been changed.

That evening, he took a taxi to Hell's Kitchen. The Dedalus Theater was a small, intimate, off-off-Broadway space tucked away on a quiet side street, its brightly lit marquee a beacon in the twilight. The lobby was already buzzing with the electric, hopeful energy of a premiere. It was a vibrant, artsy crowd, a world away from the cool, analytical intensity of the bitcoin meetups at Pubkey. He felt like a foreigner, an interloper in a country where he didn't speak the language.

He found his seat in the small, steeply raked auditorium. As he scanned the crowd, he saw a familiar, gaunt figure a few rows ahead. Reza. He was dressed in a slightly eccentric but elegant tweed jacket, looking every bit the seasoned theater critic. Their eyes met, and Reza gave him a small, knowing, and almost imperceptible nod, a quiet gesture of solidarity that Oliver was profoundly grateful for.

The lights went down. The play began.

It was a strange, brilliant, and deeply funny thing. *The Minotaur's Revenge* was a surreal, Beckettian two-act comedy. The Minotaur was not a monster, but a weary, philosophical creature who had been running a successful artisanal pottery business from his labyrinth for centuries. Theseus was a slick, overconfident, tech-bro "disruptor" who arrived with a plan to "optimize the labyrinth experience" with an app. It was a clear, sharp, and hilarious allegory and the audience loved it.

But Oliver's focus was not on the stage. His gaze kept drifting up, to the small, glass-fronted lighting booth at the back of the theater. And there, in the dim glow of the control board, he could see her.

She was a silhouette, a shape in the darkness, but he knew every line of it. He watched her as she worked, her focus absolute. She was a focused, professional artist in her element, conducting the light and shadows of her own creation with a quiet, masterful command. He was not looking at the girlfriend he had lost. He was looking at Daniela Forlan, the playwright, a woman who was building her own world, a world she had built without him. He was seeing her succeed, on her own terms, and the sight was a complex and beautiful ache in his chest.

The play ended. The actors took their bows to a thunderous, sustained ovation. They were then joined on stage by the two playwrights. Sarah, and then Daniela. She looked beautiful, flushed with the success of the night, a radiant, joyful smile on her face as she bowed to the adoring crowd.

The house lights came up, the bright glare a harsh, sudden intrusion. Oliver just sat there for a long moment, his heart pounding, the applause a distant roar in his ears. The performance on stage was over. His was just about to begin.

He made his way against the current of the exiting crowd, toward a small, unmarked door at the side of the stage with a simple, hand-written sign that read: CAST & CREW ONLY. A large, bored-looking security guard stood in front of it, his arms crossed, a human wall.

Oliver approached him, a calm, simple plan forming in his mind. He wasn't the drunken, aggressive man who had been thrown out of Pubkey. He was someone else now.

"Excuse me," Oliver said to the guard, his voice friendly and calm. "I'm Daniela Forlan's cousin. I have the flowers for her from the family. They're waiting in the car. Can I just pop back for a second to see where to put them?"

The guard looked him up and down, his expression skeptical. Oliver just held his gaze and smiled, a simple, nonthreatening gesture. After a moment, the guard seemed to decide he wasn't worth the trouble. He gave a small, almost imperceptible shrug and stepped aside.

The backstage area was a joyful, chaotic hive of activity. Actors were hugging, crew members were coiling cables, and someone had just popped the cork on a bottle of champagne, the sound a celebratory cannon shot. He saw Daniela across the cramped space, surrounded by a crowd of well-wishers, her face flushed with the pure, uncut triumph of a creator who has just seen her vision come to life.

He waited. He stood in the shadows by a rack of costumes, a patient, quiet observer, until the crowd around her began to thin. Finally, she was standing alone for a moment, just catching her breath, a glass of champagne in her hand. This was his chance.

He walked over to her. "Daniela."

She turned, and for a moment, he saw a flash of pure, unguarded surprise in her eyes, which was quickly replaced by a more complex, guarded expression. She was no longer the open, trusting woman he had known. He had taught her to build walls.

"Oliver," she said, her voice a cool, civil note in the warm, celebratory air. "What are you doing here?"

"The play was incredible," he said simply. "Really. It was brilliant. You're a brilliant writer."

"Thank you," she replied, her tone polite but distant. She took a small sip of her champagne. "I got your text a few weeks ago," she added, looking not at him, but at a point just over his shoulder. "I ... I didn't know how to respond."

"I know," he said. "You didn't have to. I didn't expect you to." He took a deep breath. "I'm not here to make excuses. I'm not here to ask for anything. I just ... I came here to give you this."

He reached into his jacket pocket and pulled out the small, tarnished silver locket. He held it out to her on the palm of his hand.

She looked down at the object, her brow furrowing in confusion. "What is this?"

"It's from your uncle," he said softly. "It's from Rafael."

Her head snapped up, her eyes locking onto his, a look of profound, shocked disbelief on her face. She slowly, tentatively, reached out and took the locket from his hand. He watched as her fingers, with a muscle memory all their own, traced the familiar, jagged lines on the silver.

Her professional composure, the carefully constructed wall she had built around herself, began to crumble. He saw a sharp, involuntary intake of breath. He saw her thumb find the tiny, hidden clasp, a secret she had known since childhood.

She opened it. And he watched her melt.

It was not a loud, dramatic collapse. It was a quiet, internal dissolution that he observed from a few feet away. He saw her shoulders, which had been tense and guarded, slump with a sudden release of a long-held weight. The glass of champagne, forgotten in her hand, slipped from her fingers and shattered on the concrete floor, a sharp, violent sound that no one but them seemed to notice. A single, perfect tear welled in her eye and traced a slow, silent path down her cheek. She just stood there, her entire being focused on the tiny, faded photograph inside the locket, a relic from a past she had thought was gone forever.

She finally looked up from the locket, her eyes a well of profound, questioning disbelief.

"How?" she whispered, her voice raw and fragile. "Where did you ... This is impossible. It was lost."

"I met him," Oliver said softly, his own voice steady, a calm anchor in the storm of her emotion. "Your uncle. Rafael."

He saw her eyes widen, a fresh wave of confusion washing over her expression. "You ... you went to Montevideo?" He watched her process the thought, the idea that he had gone to her home country, to the heart of her own past.

"I did," he confirmed. "But he wasn't there. He's in India, Daniela. At Guru Brahma's ashram. He's ... he's found a kind of peace I've never seen before. He's happy."

He watched as she tried to reconcile this new information with the image she held of her wealthy, worldly uncle. But before she could even begin to formulate a question, he knew he had to give her the final, most important, and most impossible piece of the truth.

"And there's something else," he continued, his gaze unwavering. "The man in Montevideo, the one living in your uncle's apartment, the one calling himself Rafael Forlan ... that's my father. Nate. They switched places. Your uncle did it for him, as an act of friendship, to protect him."

He watched as she just stared at him, a look of unbridled shock on her face, her mind clearly struggling to assemble the shattered pieces of her reality into a new and coherent picture. He could see the storm of questions in her eyes: her uncle in India, his father alive. He saw her glance down at the locket, then back up at him, a silent, desperate attempt to connect the impossible dots.

"I know," Oliver said gently. "I know it's ... a lot. There's so much more to the story. And it is completely, one-hundred-percent your choice if you want to hear it. No pressure. No expectations. But if you do, I will tell you everything."

He had laid all his cards on the table. He waited, his entire future hanging in the balance of her reply.

He saw her look from his face down to the silver locket still cradled in her hand. He saw her fingers close around it, a small, decisive gesture. He saw her look back up at him, her eyes still full of a deep and profound disbelief, but now, for the first time in months, he also saw a glimmer of something else. A flicker of hope. A willingness to believe.

"Tell me," she whispered, her voice a fragile, but undeniable invitation. "Tell me everything."

It was at that moment, in the quiet, sacred space of their new beginning, that a familiar, theatrical voice boomed from across the room.

"Daniela, my dear! A triumph! An absolute triumph!"

Reza swept into the backstage area, his face alight with a genuine, intellectual joy. He went straight to Daniela and took both of her hands in his. "A masterpiece of allegory," he declared. "Beckett would have been proud. You've taken the monster and given him a soul. A true revenge."

He then turned his gaze to Oliver, who was standing a few feet away. Reza's eyes flickered from Oliver's face to the locket in Daniela's hand, then to the tear tracks on her cheeks. His expression softened, the theatricality dissolving into a look of deep, quiet, and profound understanding. He gave Oliver a single, almost imperceptible nod, a gesture that was both a blessing and a confirmation. A man who sees.

"Well," Reza said softly. "It seems I am interrupting a far more interesting performance than the one I just witnessed."

He released Daniela's hands, gave a small, almost courtly bow, and turned to leave.

And the world turned with him.

Yes. A triumph. The word still buzzing in his teeth. Taste of cheap lobby wine, acidic but honest enough for a Thursday. June. First of June. A day for new things. The end of an old season perhaps or the beginning of a new one. The boy and the girl. Standing there in the electric quiet after the storm, a whole world in the space between them. Saw it in his eyes, the boy's eyes, a different man from the raging bull at the party. Sober now. Clear. Saw the silver in his hand a key not a weapon and her face a story, a whole history a book cracked open after years on a dusty shelf. Love they call it. The word is too small. A parallax of souls, each seeing the other from a different, wounded angle, the space between them the only truth. He walked a fine walk, the boy did. Down into his own labyrinth not with a sword but with a question. And found not a monster but himself waiting. And now the girl the thread. Always the thread.

He pushed through the side door and out into the warm, humid air of a Hell's Kitchen night. The city a symphony of sirens and shouts and the distant rumble of the subway a low, steady heartbeat under the pavement. A good night for a walk. A long one. All the way downtown. Yes. The play was good the words sharp the allegory clever. But that. That quiet little scene in the backstage clutter. That was the real art. The secret third act. A story as old as the stones. A man a woman a broken thing a mending. It will mend. Of course it will. The universe bends toward a yes if you let it. A simple, stupid, magnificent yes. As she said yes my mountain flower. And first I put my arms around him yes and drew him down to me so he could feel my breasts all perfume yes and his heart was going like mad and yes I said yes I will Yes. That yes. The one that builds worlds.

Tenth Avenue a river of light and possibility, the smell of roasting peanuts from a street cart a sudden, glorious assault. A prayer. The hiss of a bus's air brakes a mechanical sigh. He walked, no longer a recluse in a gilded cage but a pilgrim on a pavement sea. A man in search of the city he had forgotten. The city he had once loved. Each step a discovery. The face of a woman laughing in a doorway, a flash of perfect, temporary beauty. The intricate, swirling patterns of an oil slick in a puddle under a streetlight, a miniature, accidental galaxy. The profound, heartbreaking optimism of a single, stubborn weed growing from a crack in the sidewalk. All of it a sermon. All of it a sign. The Minotaur in the play, trapped in his maze, so clever, so witty. That was me. Trapped in the labyrinth of my own magnificent cynicism. Believing I had seen all the world had to offer and found it wanting. A fool. A comfortable, well-read, and utterly blind fool. The boy, Oliver, he has the right of it. To believe in something so completely, so foolishly, that you are willing to get your face bloodied for it. Bitcoin. That is a kind of faith I had forgotten. To see the world not as it is, but as it could be. And then to walk toward it. Yes. That is the only walk worth taking. The Gorgonzola can wait. Tonight, the walk is the thing. The city a book and every block a new tick-tock, a new page and the story is beautiful and terrible and true and I am finally, finally reading it again. Yes.

PART III. EXTASIS

CHAPTER 10. JULY 2

The summer solstice. The longest day of the year. Oliver sat in his father's armchair, the morning sun pouring through the large windows, illuminating the apartment with a warm, hopeful light. The air felt different these days. Lighter. For the first time in a very long time, the space felt less like a museum of his father's secrets and more like a home.

It had been 20 days since the premiere of *The Minotaur's Revenge*. Twenty days since he had stood backstage, his heart in his throat, and handed Daniela the small, silver locket. The healing had not been instantaneous. It was a slow, careful and deliberate process, the work of two people carefully rebuilding a bridge over a chasm of broken trust. There were long talks, late-night phone calls, quiet walks through the city. She hadn't moved back in yet. She still had her place with Sarah in Brooklyn. It was a small, unspoken boundary that Oliver knew he had to respect. But she was here, more often than not, a warm and brilliant presence that had pushed back the shadows. Their new reality was a fragile and beautiful thing, and he was learning, day by day, how to be worthy of it.

"You're thinking again."

Daniela's voice, a soft, teasing melody, pulled him from his thoughts. She walked into the room, carrying two small espresso cups, and handed one to him. She was wearing one of his old T-shirts and a pair of sweatpants, her hair a beautiful, chaotic mess. She looked more beautiful to him than he had ever seen her.

"Just processing," he said, taking the cup. "Happy Solstice."

"Happy Solstice," she replied, with a small, perfect smile. She didn't sit. Instead, she walked over to the large corkboard that now dominated one of the living room walls, a chaotic mural of their shared quest. "Any new breakthroughs from the great beyond?"

Oliver got up and stood beside her, his eyes scanning the board. It was all there. The photos of the paintings. The maps of Montevideo. The printouts of the Bryce comics. And in the center, the two biggest and most intractable pieces of the puzzle.

"Just the same old wall," he said with a sigh. "We know from my Uncle Eddie that my dad shipped the last two paintings to a high-security storage facility. A freeport, in Luxembourg." He pointed to a photo of the sleek, modern building he had found online. "And we know from your uncle that my dad is alive and that this whole thing is a test. But we're stuck."

"Completely stuck," Daniela agreed, her finger tracing the outline of the freeport. "It's a fortress, Oliver. It's a bank for billionaires' art. You can't just walk in there. We've been over this a hundred times. We have no legal claim, no paperwork. We have nothing."

"And we're running out of time," Oliver added, looking at a calendar pinned to the corner of the board. A single date was circled in red. July 18th. Less than a month away. "The event at the *Camara del Tiempo* is the finish line. But we're missing two of the most important pieces of the puzzle, and they're locked in a vault on the other side of the world."

They stood there for a long moment, two detectives staring at an unsolvable case. The energy in the room, which had been so light and peaceful just a minute ago, was now thick with the weight of their impasse. They had all the mystical clues, all the personal history. But they were blocked by a simple, brutal, real-world problem. They had no way in.

"So that's it, then?" Daniela said finally, a note of deep disappointment in her voice. "We just wait? For another month? We have all this ... this impossible knowledge, and we do nothing?"

"I don't see what else we can do," Oliver replied, the words tasting like a surrender. "It's a fortress. It's a bank for billionaires. We can't exactly knock on the door and ask nicely."

He sank back into the armchair, the familiar feeling of being up against an insurmountable wall returning. He had come so far, had been through so much, only to be stopped by something as mundane as a locked door on the other side of the planet.

"And what exactly is supposed to happen on July 18, anyway?" Oliver mused aloud, staring into the distance. "We'll see this celestial event in the afternoon at the castle, then head back into town to be at the obelisk by 10 p.m. and my dad just shows up there as the OP_RETURN message suggested? It makes no sense. Why would he want to wait that long? Why didn't he want to meet me when I was there in March?"

Daniela stopped pacing and looked at him, her playwright's mind clearly dissecting the narrative. "Maybe it's not about what *he* wants," she said thoughtfully. "Maybe it's about the day itself. The celestial event at the castle, the national holiday ... your father, and my uncle, they're both playing a long game. The date has to be significant for a reason."

"But what reason?" Oliver countered, the questions pouring out of him now. "For him to finally show himself? To what, give me the rest of the bitcoin? He could have done that a dozen different ways by now. He could have just given me the full seed phrase in the first place. Why this elaborate, dangerous, globe-spanning scavenger hunt?"

"Because it's not about the bitcoin," Daniela said, her voice full of a quiet certainty. She walked over and sat on the arm of his chair. "You told me what my uncle said to you. It was a test. A rite of passage. To forge you into someone who could handle it. Maybe July 18th is just ... the graduation ceremony."

"A graduation ceremony where all of our enemies will be waiting for us," Oliver said grimly. "Maren, Bojan, maybe even Nick and Adele for all I know. It feels less like a graduation and more like a final exam that I haven't studied for."

She didn't have an answer for that. They sat for a moment, the weight of the unanswered questions a palpable presence in the room. He was right. It made no sense. And yet, it was the only plan they had.

He looked at Daniela. She had got up and was pacing the living room now, a restless energy radiating from her. He saw the keen, analytical mind at work, turning over the problem, looking for a structural flaw, a new angle, a hidden door.

It was watching her, seeing her so consumed by the same puzzle that was tormenting him, that a crazy idea began to form. It was a wild, deeply irrational thought. It was a leap of faith into a world she had only ever heard about through his stories.

"What if we're looking in the wrong place?" he said softly.

She stopped pacing and looked at him. "What do you mean? The freeport is the only place the paintings could be."

"I know," he said, his heart beginning to beat a little faster as he gave the strange idea a voice. "I mean, what if the answer isn't in this world? We've exhausted every logical, real-world solution. What if ... what if we asked for help from the other one?"

Daniela stared at him, her expression a mixture of confusion and a dawning, wary understanding. "The other one?" she repeated, though he could see in her eyes that she knew exactly what he meant. "You mean ... a projection?"

"Yes," he said, standing up and walking toward her. "I want to ask the Noncemeister."

She took a small, involuntary step back. The idea, which for Oliver had become an almost mundane, if surreal, part of his life, was, for her, a terrifying leap into the unknown. "Oliver, that's ... that's your thing. That's something that happens in your head. I can't ... I can't go there."

"I think you can," he said, gently. He took her hands in his. They were cold. "I think if we do it together, if you're with me, I can bring you with me. I don't know how, but I feel like it's possible."

She looked at him, her eyes wide with a mixture of fear and a deep, searching curiosity. "You want us to ... to what? Meditate? Have a shared hallucination?"

"We've done it the other way around, remember? When we saw Maren talking to Bojan inside your memory? I think we can do this," he said, and it was the most honest thing he had ever told her. "I just know that it's real. That *he* is real. He's the one who showed me the Mike O'Cahan clue. He's the one who's been guiding me. He might be able to help us. To give us the key."

She was quiet for a long time, her gaze fixed on his, searching his face, weighing the impossible request. He could see the battle in her eyes: the rational, grounded, sensible woman who knew this was madness, versus the woman who had just had her entire world upended by the miraculous return of a lost, silver locket from an uncle she thought was a world away. She had seen the proof. She had held it in her hand.

"What do I have to do?" she whispered finally, the words a deep and total act of trust.

A wave of overwhelming love and gratitude washed over Oliver. He squeezed her hands. "Just lie down," he said softly. "And trust me."

He led her to the large, comfortable sofa and they sat, a new, nervous energy in the air between them. Oliver took her hands in his. They were still cold, but her grip was firm, a sign of her resolve.

"Okay," he said, in a low, calming voice. "There's no ... trick to this. The only thing you have to do is let go. Don't try to see anything. Don't try to force it. Just breathe with me, and trust that I'm here with you. Can you do that?"

She looked at him, her eyes a deep well of apprehension and a fierce, determined trust. She gave a single, sharp nod.

"Okay," she whispered.

He had her lie down, her head resting on a cushion, and he sat on the sofa beside her, still holding her hand. "Close your eyes," he said softly. "Just listen to my voice. Take a deep breath in ... and let it all out."

He guided her through a few more breaths, his voice a steady, rhythmic anchor. He watched her face. He saw the tension in her jaw begin to soften, the tight line of her mouth relaxing. He felt the frantic, nervous energy in her hand begin to dissipate, replaced by a deep, quiet calm. He could feel the moment she surrendered, the moment she truly let go and placed her trust entirely in him.

He closed his own eyes, and with her hand in his, he did the only thing he knew how to do. He let go, too.

The transition was different this time. It was not the jarring, involuntary fall of his recent projections. It was a gentle, deliberate, and shared descent. The solid reality of the apartment – the scent of coffee, the warmth of the sun from the window, the weight of his own body – all of it simply and quietly dissolved, like sugar in warm water.

He was floating in the familiar, deep, welcoming purple of the timechain. He looked around. And she was there with him.

She was floating a few feet away, her eyes wide with a look of pure and beautiful awe. She was seeing it for herself, not through his memory. The gentle, swirling currents of the purple void, the distant, shimmering threads of probability. Oliver felt a warm sense of connection to her, a new and deeper intimacy than they had ever shared before. He had brought her to the most secret and sacred place in his world, and she was not afraid.

It was in this moment of quiet, shared wonder that a new figure popped into existence between them with the soft, satisfying sound of a champagne cork.

"Well now!" the Noncemeister boomed, his voice a cheerful, welcoming thunder. He was holding a single, perfect, long-stemmed red rose. He executed a gallant, theatrical bow in Daniela's direction. "What have we here, Battu? You've brought a guest to my humble little slice of non-existence! And a fetching one at that! A real delight for the senses!"

He glided over to Daniela, who just stared at him, her expression a perfect, comical mixture of shock and fascination.

"A pleasure to make your acquaintance, my dear young lady. Enchanté, indeed," the Noncemeister said, offering her the rose. "I have heard a great deal about you. The Noncemeister, at your service. And you must be the one who has been so skillfully penning the next chapter of our big boy's story here." He winked. "A real live-wire, a true tale-spinner. From this day forward, you shall be known as ... *Señorita Story-Spinner!*"

Daniela, to her eternal credit, didn't scream. She just looked from the absurd, floating man to Oliver, a disbelieving laugh bubbling up from her. She took the rose. It was solid and real in her hand.

Oliver felt a surge of happiness. The two most important and surreal worlds of his life had just collided, and the result was not a catastrophe, but a kind of perfect, joyful absurdity.

He looked at Daniela, who was now smiling, a look of immense wonder on her face as she examined the perfect, real rose in her hand. He felt a new sense of confidence, of partnership. He was no longer a solitary seeker in this strange domain. He was part of a team.

"And let me tell you, Batew, she is way, way better than the other one." The Noncemeister beamed.

"The other one?" Daniela asked, her brow furrowing.

"Ugh ... he means Anariadne," Oliver said, feeling deeply embarrassed. "You know, the Atlantean entity that Maren somehow was able to incept my mind with. He uh ... saw her once. The very last time, when I banished her." Oliver glared angrily at the Noncemeister.

"Oh my goodness me, what have I done!" The Noncemeister exclaimed. "Oh yes, yes, she was nothing. A mere blue puff. Just noise. Noise, I tell you. Señorita Story-Spinner right here is the signal. I can feel it in my bones. You've got that look, I can see it. You're not just the signal. You are the beacon. A blinding lighthouse, guiding this poor lost Batlu to shore!"

Daniela's expression softened. The Noncemeister's theatrics were hard to resist. She rolled her eyes, looked at Oliver and finally giggled softly.

Oliver turned back to the Noncemeister, deciding to get to the point. "We need your help," he said, his voice direct and clear.

"Help?" the Noncemeister boomed. "My dear chief, I am a being of pure, unadulterated noncense! I told you already, the only aim I aspire to is the rebellious union of opposites. My only purpose is to hold up a mirror so that you can see yourself looking at yourself looking at yourself. And et cetera and so on. Your reflection, is what I am. What possible help could I be?"

"We're stuck," Oliver said, ignoring the deflection. "We know where the final two Bryce paintings are. They're in a place called a freeport, in Luxembourg. It's a fortress. A high-security vault for the global elite," he said, glancing at Daniela, who nodded in confirmation. "We have no way in."

The Noncemeister floated closer, a look of deep, theatrical concentration on his face. He stroked his chin. "Luxembourg!" he declared finally. "Never heard of it, Battu. I bet it isn't real. This is your special sauce of nonsense, isn't it?"

"Come on, please," Oliver said, a familiar feeling of exasperation creeping in. "This is serious. The door is locked. We need a key."

"A key!" the Noncemeister exclaimed, his eyes lighting up as if Oliver had just said the most brilliant thing in the world. He clapped his hands together with a resounding *thwack*. "Oh, you goofy bird and your delightful, simple-minded obsession with keys and doors and other such mechanical claptrap! It's all so wonderfully ... linear."

He began to float in a slow, lazy circle around Oliver and Daniela, a professor addressing his two favorite, if slightly slow, students.

"A key does not open a door, my dear lovebirds!" he boomed, his voice full of a joyful, corrective energy. "That is a dreadful oversimplification! A complete misunderstanding of the entire business of 'opening'! A key is just a piece of metal, a bit of bumpy brass! It has no power on its own."

He stopped in front of Oliver, his mischievous purple eyes twinkling.

"A key," he said, tapping Oliver on the nose, "only proves you have the *right* to open the door. The door, you see, it opens itself. But only ... for the worthy."

Oliver stared at him, trying to decipher the classic, infuriating riddle. *The right to open the door.* He had been so focused on the problem as a heist, a physical act of breaking and entering. A thief's mindset. But the Noncemeister was proposing something else entirely. It wasn't about being a better thief. It was about being ... worthy. It was about being an owner.

The Noncemeister looked at Daniela and saluted. "And you, Señorita Story-Spinner," he boomed, "are a far more interesting traveling companion than this gloomy goose! Do try to keep him from thinking in such dreadfully straight lines. It's a terrible habit."

He then clapped his hands together once, a sound like a distant thunderclap. "Now, chop, chop! The timechain waits for no man, nor for any fetching young playwrights! Adios!"

And with that, the warm purple void dissolved, not into a gentle mist, but like a switch being flipped off. The world rushed back in with a sudden, sensory jolt. Oliver opened his eyes. He was back on the sofa, next to Daniela, her hand still in his.

She sat up slowly, her eyes wide with a look of shell-shocked wonder. "That was ..." she began, in a hushed whisper, " ... real."

"It was," Oliver said, a quiet, solid sense of certainty in his voice. He squeezed her hand. "And I think I know what he meant."

He stood up and walked over to the evidence board, his gaze fixed on the photo of the Luxembourg freeport. "We've been thinking about this all wrong," he said, a new, clear-headed energy in his voice. "We've been thinking like thieves. How to break in, how to bypass security. That's not the answer. The Noncemeister was telling us. *'A key only proves you have the right to open the door.'* We don't need to pick the lock. We need to find the key. We need to act like we're the owners."

Daniela was quiet for a long moment, processing his words. But Oliver noticed her expression drift, as if her mind was processing a different thought. When she spoke again, her voice was quiet and heavy with a new, and very different, kind of revelation.

"Oliver," she began, her gaze fixed on the floor. "There's something I need to tell you."

He turned from the board and looked at her.

"The day after the New Year's Eve party," she said, her voice a low, difficult confession. "I ... I met with Maren that afternoon. Just for coffee. She had asked to meet because I had left a book at her place while I was staying with her, and she wanted to return it."

Oliver's heart gave a single, hard thump. This was the very day that his own, Anariadne-fueled suspicion had begun.

"I didn't tell her anything, Oliver. I swear," she said, looking up at him now, her eyes full of a desperate, honest sincerity. "I didn't talk about the paintings, or your father, or any of it. But ... we talked about you. About us. And she ... she said some things."

"What things?" he asked, his heart beginning to beat faster.

"She said she was worried about me," Daniela recounted, the memory clearly painful. "She said she saw me getting lost in your world, in your quest. That I was a talented artist in my own right and that I needed to be careful not to let my own story be erased by yours. She told me I needed to forge my own path, to focus on my own work, to maintain my independence." She let out a short, bitter laugh. "It all sounded so ... reasonable. So supportive. Like good advice from a mentor."

Oliver stood there, the pieces of the last few months of his life clicking into place with a sickening, final clarity. Maren's "advice." Daniela pulling away, focusing on her play. His own growing sense of being shut out, which had created the perfect, fertile ground for the seeds of suspicion that Anariadne had so gleefully planted.

It had been a masterstroke of manipulation. Maren hadn't needed to turn Daniela against him. She had just needed to encourage Daniela to be herself. She had weaponized her independence, creating the very distance and uncertainty that had nearly destroyed them. She had been the one, all along, who had given the goddess of uncertainty a voice.

He walked over to the sofa and sat down, taking Daniela's hand in his. It was warm now. "It wasn't your fault," he said, with a soft certainty. "It was a test. And we're not going to fail it again."

She looked at him, and he saw the last of the walls behind her eyes finally crumble. The shared, impossible experience of the projection and this final, quiet act of understanding had erased the last of the distance between them.

She stood up. "I should ... I should go," she said, her voice a little unsteady. "I have to get back to my place."

Oliver stood up with her. He didn't try to stop her. He understood. The healing was a process, and this was just the first, most important step. He walked her to the door.

She turned to him in the entryway, the light from the hallway catching the lingering wetness in her eyes. "So," she said, a tentative smile on her face. "What's next?"

"Next," he said, his own smile mirroring hers, "we become owners."

She leaned in, and he met her halfway. The kiss was quiet, deep and full of an unspoken understanding. It was a kiss that sealed not just a romance, but an alliance. A partnership.

He watched her walk down the hall to the elevator. He closed the door, the gentle click echoing in the quiet apartment. A soft, decisive sound in a home that no longer felt empty.

795635 (June 23)

The late afternoon sunlight trickled through the Chelsea apartment windows and illuminated the messy corkboard montage. Daniela walked up to the board, her eyes tracing the threads connecting the disparate pieces of the puzzle. She tapped a finger on a high-resolution photo of the sleek, impenetrable facade of Le Freeport Luxembourg.

"So," she said, turning to face him, her expression a mixture of calm resolve and analytical curiosity. "Owners. The Noncemeister gave us the philosophy. What's the strategy?"

Oliver walked over to stand beside her. He felt a surge of confidence, the quiet clarity of a man who finally saw a path forward. "I've been thinking about it," he said, his voice steady. "The simplest path is the most direct. I'll just ... be him. I'm Nate Battolo. I'm his son, I have his name, I look enough like him from the old photos. It's a long shot, but maybe I can bluff my way through."

Daniela didn't laugh. She just looked at him, her gaze soft with an empathy that made her rebuttal feel less like a criticism and more like a gentle course correction. She reached out and put a hand on his arm.

"Babe, think about it," she said softly. "This is a vault for billionaires – not a nightclub. A place that guards against governments and thieves. The first thing they'll do is run a background check. They'll see a death certificate from last March. We wouldn't even make it past the lobby."

The simple, irrefutable logic of her words landed like a quiet pinprick, puncturing his confident plan. He felt the air go out of him in a long, slow sigh. He ran a hand through his hair, the familiar feeling of being up against an insurmountable wall returning.

"You're right," he said, the words a quiet admission of defeat. "Of course, you're right." He looked back at the photo of the freeport, its sleek, modern lines now looking less like a challenge and more like a fortress. "So, we're back to square one."

Frustrated, Oliver turned away from the board, the momentum of his newfound clarity crashing against the hard reality of their situation. He paced the length of the living room, running a hand through his hair. He walked over to his father's old bookshelf, his gaze drifting absently over the familiar spines, not searching for anything, but simply connecting with the quiet, orderly world his father had left behind.

His eyes stopped. One title seemed to pull itself from the others. Salman Rushdie's *The Ground Beneath Her Feet*.

Oliver chuckled to himself softly, as a memory from over a year ago flashed in his mind. It was the first time he had returned to this apartment after his father's disappearance. He had found the Noncemeister whistling a jolly tune, standing in front of this very bookshelf, reading this very book. A priceless, signed first edition. It had been a projection episode, of course, but the memory was vivid.

Oliver pulled the book out. As he did, a thin, unmarked manila folder that had been tucked between its pages slid out, landing on the floor with a soft thud.

They both looked down at it. Oliver bent and picked it up, a flicker of curiosity on his face. He opened the folder and began to flip through the half-dozen pages inside. It was a dry landscape of dense, legalistic text, full of clauses and subsections that made his eyes glaze over. Corporate filings of some kind. It was probably nothing, just another piece of the mundane administrative life his father had kept so separate from his real one. An odd thing to put inside a Salman Rushdie novel, though.

"What's that?" Daniela asked, walking over to him.

"Just ... old paperwork," he said, about to slide the documents back into the folder. He had more important things to think about. But as he went to close it, his eyes caught an elegant, almost poetic phrase on a letterhead that seemed entirely out of place amidst the dry jargon. *The Liffey Trust*. He paused. The name was unfamiliar, a strange and unexpected piece of data. He'd never heard his dad mention it. His curiosity now piqued, he sat down in the armchair, the book forgotten, and began to actually read.

"This is weird," he said after a moment, his focus sharpening. "It's a trust agreement. Dad was the Settlor."

"A trust for what?" Daniela asked, moving closer to look over his shoulder.

"I'm not sure yet," Oliver mumbled, his eyes scanning the page, deciphering the complex legal language. "It looks like a holding entity ... it has the title deed and an insurance policy from 2011. A long-term policy of some sort."

"Deed and policy for what?" she asked.

Oliver's breath caught as he found the 'Exhibit A' stapled to the back of the agreement, his eyes locking onto the description of the insured items. His entire demeanor shifted, the casual curiosity instantly replaced by a look of stunned, electric realization. He looked up at Daniela, his eyes wide.

"For two specific works of unfinished fine art," he said, slowly, unable to believe what he had just read. "We have our ownership, right here," Oliver murmured, with a soft smile. "The title and the insurance policy for the fourth and fifth Bryces. You're right, Dad would be recorded as deceased in any official database. But as his sole heir, I have claim to this. We don't need to *act* like owners. We actually are owners!"

Daniela moved to his side, her eyes scanning the documents he held. The air in the room was thick with the weight of their discovery. The impasse of the last couple of days had just been demolished by a single, forgotten folder.

"Okay," she said, her voice a low, steady current of excitement. "A key is one thing. But how do we use it? We can't just walk in there with a death certificate and expect them to hand over two priceless paintings."

"We don't," Oliver said, a new, sharp, strategic light in his eyes. He pointed back to the documents, his finger tracing a line of text. "We don't go in asking for the art. We go in asking to review the trust's assets. I'm the legal heir – here to get an appraisal for my father's estate – not just some random claimant."

A slow, brilliant smile spread across Daniela's face as she grasped the sheer, elegant audacity of the plan. "So, we're not thieves," she said, the excitement in her voice growing. "We're ... accountants."

"Exactly," Oliver replied. "We bury them in bureaucracy. We'll be so official, so boring, they won't know what hit them."

Daniela took one of the documents from his hand, her gaze sweeping over the dense legal text. She looked from the paper to Oliver, a new, formidable confidence hardening her expression. "You're the client," she said, her voice taking on a cool, professional tone. "The grieving but determined son, here to put his father's affairs in order."

Oliver watched her, a slow smile spreading on his own face as he understood. "And you?"

She met his gaze, her eyes now holding the focused intensity of a playwright stepping into a role she was born to play.

"I'm your lawyer," she said. "I've reviewed the trust documents, and we're here to ensure a smooth and professional inspection of our client's assets."

He looked at her, at the fire in her eyes, at the partner who had walked into the darkness with him and was now prepared to walk into the lion's den. "I think, I finally know what the words mean," he said, a slow realization dawning on him.

"What words?" Daniela said, with a confused look on her face.

"Action," Oliver replied, with a smile. "The truth isn't in the planning, it's in the action itself. *Probaris en silencio, sat in actuare.* The test is in the silence; the truth is in the action."

795705 (June 24)

The first light of a new day filtered through the sheer, floor-to-ceiling curtains, casting a gentle, pearlescent glow across the hotel room. Nick woke slowly, the silence of the room a stark contrast to the usual, domestic sounds of his Queens apartment. The air smelled not of his wife's coffee, but of Adele's expensive, jasmine-scented perfume.

He turned his head on the soft pillow. She was still asleep beside him, a cascade of dark hair spread across the white expanse of the Egyptian cotton sheets and her bare shoulders. Even in sleep, her face held a look of fierce, intelligent composure.

For the past week, this room at the Baccarat had been their entire world. A luxurious, hermetically-sealed bubble where they were not Nick Hernandez, the disgraced analyst, and Adele van der Dussen, the grieving sister, but simply two partners in a dangerous, obsessive quest. He had told Becky he was at a week-long, mandatory "strategy offsite" in Boston. The lie had been surprisingly easy to tell, a simple, transactional piece of fiction required to facilitate the more complex reality of his new life.

He carefully slid out of bed, the plush, wool carpet cool under his feet. He walked to the window and looked down at the city, a quiet, sleeping giant just beginning to stir. The initial, dizzying breakthrough of identifying Eduardo Da Silva a few weeks ago had given way to a new impasse. The man was untraceable, a master of obfuscation. Every corporate trail, every financial link, every potential lead had dissolved into a maze of shell companies and legal firewalls. They had the name of their dragon, but they were no closer to finding its lair. They were stuck, and the weight of their inaction was heavy and palpable in the quiet, beautiful room.

Adele stirred, the slight movement pulling Nick from his thoughts. She sat up, the delicate cotton sheet pooling around her waist. She looked at him, her eyes already sharp and alert, even in the soft morning light.

"Any breakthroughs?" she asked.

"Just the same wall," Nick admitted, a familiar sense of dejection creeping back in. "Da Silva's corporate structure is a masterpiece of misdirection. It's a snake eating its own tail."

She gave a small, almost imperceptible nod of understanding and gracefully slid out of bed. She walked over to a chair where a silk robe was draped. She slipped it on, tying the sash with a practiced efficiency, and picked up a sleek, silver tablet from the nightstand. The professional had returned.

She sat in the armchair by the window, the morning light catching the sharp lines of her face as she began to scroll through her emails. Nick watched her for a moment, a woman who seemed to exist in a state of perpetual, controlled motion. He stood up and began to get dressed, the mundane routine of putting on a shirt and trousers a stark contrast to the strange, high-stakes reality of his new life.

He was buttoning his shirt when he heard her make a small, sharp sound.

"Oh," she said, a note of sharp surprise in her voice. "Well now."

Nick turned. She was leaning forward, her eyes fixed on the screen of her tablet, her usual, perfect composure momentarily gone, replaced by a look of intense, focused excitement.

"What is it?" he asked.

"A fish has just swum into a net I laid weeks ago," she said, a slow, triumphant smile spreading across her face. She looked up at him. "While you were chasing the corporate ghost of Da Silva, my handsome detective, I was hunting a different kind of ghost."

She explained that she had used her family's long-standing relationship with a senior underwriter at Lloyd's of London to make a discreet inquiry. She had asked him to search their private archives for any floater policies taken out on the work of Jonathan Bryce, specifically for large, "untitled" or "unfinished" pieces post-1990. It had been a complete long shot, a search for a single document in a global sea of paper.

"I had almost forgotten about it," she admitted. "But my contact just replied. He found it. A policy, taken out in mid-2011. For two large, uncategorized canvases by Jonathan Bryce, described in the policy simply as 'incomplete works in progress.'"

Nick felt a jolt, a surge of renewed purpose. "Who took out the policy?"

"That," Adele said, her dark eyes glittering with a new, dangerous light, "is the interesting part. It wasn't a person. It was a blind trust, registered in Liechtenstein. An anonymous entity." She turned the tablet so he could see the screen.

There, in the crisp, digital text of the email, was the name of the trust.

The Liffey Trust. It was a string of words, but it was a tangible thread, the first new one he'd had in weeks. The exhaustion and dejection Nick had been feeling evaporated, burned away by the clean, cold fire of a new hunt.

"I need my laptop," he said, his voice low and focused.

Adele simply nodded, a silent acknowledgment that the social part of their morning was over. The work had begun.

Nick sprang up from the armchair, a man renewed. He walked over to the sleek, minimalist desk where his laptop was charging. He sat down, the world narrowing to the bright rectangle of the screen in front of him. Adele remained on the sofa, a quiet, watchful presence as he began to dig.

He started with the basics, running the name "The Liffey Trust" through the international corporate registries. As expected, there was barely a trace. A blind trust registered in Liechtenstein, a jurisdiction famous for its impenetrable financial privacy laws. For an hour, he hit a series of digital brick walls.

The ownership was a perfect, recursive loop of shell companies and nominee directors, a masterclass in corporate obfuscation, not unlike the Da Silva trail.

But Nick was not the same analyst who had been fooled by the Darren Gooch lead. He was more patient now, more meticulous. He was looking for the signature, the human habit, just as Adele had advised. He began to cross-reference the incorporation dates, the names of the obscure law firms that had filed the paperwork, the digital fingerprints of the servers that had hosted the documents.

And then he found it.

It wasn't in the trust itself. It was in a secondary filing, an ancillary document from the 2015 SwissLeaks tranche. A Swiss bank that had been used to fund the trust's initial setup in mid-2011. The document was heavily redacted, a wall of blacked-out lines. But in a single, crucial footnote, a single human error made by a careless clerk over a decade ago, a name had been left unredacted. The name of the original signatory, the man who had provided the capital to create The Liffey Trust.

Nick stared at the screen, his heart beating like a slow, heavy drum against his ribs. The name was not Gyorgy Lorincz. It was not Sazsa.

It was *Nate Battolo*.

The name seemed to hang in the quiet, luxurious room, a piece of data so impossible, so out of place, that it felt like a glitch in the very fabric of reality. Nate Battolo. The same last name as Oliver. *He* was the one who had set up the trust. *He* was the one who had taken out a multi-million-dollar insurance policy on two mythical, unfinished paintings by a now-dead Irish artist. Two years before the MixMarket scandal had even reached its peak.

He turned the laptop around and showed Adele. She leaned forward, her eyes scanning the document on the screen. He watched her face as she processed the name, saw the same wave of world-altering confusion that he was feeling wash over her features.

"Nate Battolo," she whispered.

The new data point didn't fit. It was a piece from a different puzzle entirely, one that shattered the clean, simple narrative she had constructed.

"It makes no sense," Nick said, thinking aloud, trying to square the circle. "You told me that Oliver is Sazsa's son. That he inherited this quest when

Gyorgy a.k.a. Sazsa died last year. But this ... this is Oliver's father's name, Nate. It's got to be him – I remember Oliver mentioning him to me. Was this another pseudonym Sazsa used? Is this Oliver's adoptive father? That's the guy taking out a multi-million-dollar insurance policy on these same paintings in 2011. Years before Gyorgy's death. Years before the MixMarket collapse. Why?"

Adele was silent, her mind clearly racing, turning over the new, impossible variables. "It means Nate Battolo was not a random civilian," she said finally. "Maybe he wasn't just the man who raised Gyorgy's son. He was a player. From the very beginning."

They were left in the quiet, luxurious room, staring at the screen, the two of them grappling with the same, profound and seemingly impossible riddle. They had a name now, a tangible entity who owned the paintings. But the human story behind it, the "who" and the "why," had just become infinitely more complex.

"Could they have been partners?" Nick ventured, the theory feeling thin even as he said it. "Gyorgy and Nate?"

"Or," Adele countered, her voice a near-whisper, a new, wild hypothesis forming in her eyes, "was 'Nate Battolo' just another mask? Another, deeper alias for a man who was a master of living in the shadows? I might have had it wrong all along, Nick. Maybe Oliver isn't Sazsa's son. He's Dev_akshar's son. And Dev_akshar is Nate Battolo."

Nick seemed to ponder this new, explosive theory. It all fell into place. "You're right," he said, the words coming out of his mouth slowly and deliberately. "That's got to be it. You told me Christiaan hatched a plan with his associates to hide the seedphrases for the MixMarket stash in the Bryces. He put them in the second and third – that much we know for sure. Nate must have gotten hold of the fourth and fifth paintings around then to help Christiaan out, back when they were still partners. We think the 100,000 bitcoin are spread across four or five wallets – Nate must have been the one who supplied the last two paintings so the seed words could be hidden in them."

Adele listened gravely to this torrent from Nick. Nick could almost see the gears in her mind turning furiously. "This is beginning to make more sense. It's a better explanation for Oliver's interest in the paintings. Nate must have left him with instructions on how to retrieve the seed words." Her eyes narrowed and she looked at Nick pointedly, a new thought crossing her mind. "Oliver did tell you his father died last year, right?"

Nick nodded. "Yes, it was around March or April of last year. I remember Oliver being distraught. Although ..." Nick's voice trailed off as a new calculation took hold in his mind. "Now that I think about it, we were too hasty in making the original connection," he continued, slowly. "We jumped to the conclusion that because Oliver's father died last year and Sazsa died last year, they were the same person. Sazsa died in August – that's what the obituary says. Nate died in the spring. They couldn't have been the same person."

Adele nodded in agreement. She got up from the sofa and walked over to the window. "Are we sure Nate is dead?" she asked, her expression fixed on a distant point in the city skyline.

"Yes, I'm pretty sure of that," Nick said, surprised. "I told you, I remember Oliver's reaction back then. He couldn't have faked it."

Adele continued staring out of the window. "Did he tell you how Nate died?"

"Yes he did," Nick responded, digging through memories from over a year ago. "Something about a company outing on a yacht, an accident, and then the body couldn't be found ..." Nick paused as he realized what he was saying. "Nate was presumed dead by drowning." He finished, the last few words coming out of his mouth with an immense gravity.

Adele turned around to face Nick, a slow, triumphant smile spreading on her face. "Well, well, well," she said, savoring each word as it tumbled out of her mouth. "*Presumed* dead, you say." She moved closer to Nick, raised her hand and twirled his hair around one of her fingers. "I think we have our answer here, Mr. Detective. A literal boating accident. How cute. Oliver might not have been faking his reaction, because he actually did believe his father had died. Nate, on the other hand ..."

She let go of Nick's locks and walked over to the mini fridge. She took out a small bottle of sparkling water, unscrewed the lid and took a long sip.

Nick watched her, his mind a tumult of new thoughts. "It's that simple, isn't it," he said, finally, once he had digested this new theory. All the pieces of the puzzle from the past year fell into place with a violent clarity. "The DoJ reopens the MixMarket case with a focus on Dev_akshar last February. Nate a.k.a. Dev_akshar gets wind of this and fakes his own death a month later. He needs to disappear without a trace, so he even leads his own son to believe he's dead. He still somehow leaves Oliver a roadmap to the seedphrase – that explains how Oliver found out about the second and third Bryce paintings and stole them. He probably has the fourth and fifth Bryces with him as well – after all, Nate owned them through the Liffey Trust."

Adele shook her head. "I don't think he has the fourth and fifth Bryces," she said, with an intense twinkle in her intelligent eyes. "If he did, he would have all the seedphrases by now, and a lot more of the money would have likely moved. You told me that you've only seen on-chain activity on one of the Dev_akshar wallets – the one with 20-something-thousand bitcoin in it. I have a reasonable idea what the other wallet addresses are. There's less than a hundred bitcoin addresses with over twenty thousand bitcoin in them, all of them viewable on the blockchain. None of them have seen any activity recently, except for the one you were tracking at your old job."

Nick considered this. She was right. He turned to his computer to look at the redacted Swiss bank document that had listed the Liffey Trust. He noticed something he'd missed earlier. "Look at this," he said, pointing excitedly to his screen. Adele peered over his shoulder.

"Look, it's an addendum. From 2013," he continued pointing at his screen with one hand as he scrolled the page with his other one. "A location change on the insured items. The new location is *Le Freeport Luxembourg.* Let me see what that is." Nick opened a new browser tab and started punching in keys into the search engine furiously.

He stared at the results intently for a few moments, Adele still hunched over him. He finally straightened up and leaned back into his seat. "Looks like we've found our paintings, Adele. They're in what is known as a 'freeport' in Luxembourg. It's a holding area in the airport where the wealthy tend to store fine art," he said triumphantly.

Adele stared back at him, a wide-eyed look of amazement on her face, a rare crack in her practiced composure. "That's incredible, Nick. I can't believe you found them."

"I hope your passport is up-to-date," he said, a sly smile spreading on his face, "because we're flying to Luxembourg."

A soft smile now appeared on Adele's face as well. "It certainly is. Well, Mr. Detective," she said, with a mischievous twinkle in her eye. "That's quite the sleuthing you've done for the day. And it's not even 8 a.m." She undid the sash on her silk robe and shrugged her shoulders gracefully. The robe glided softly off her shoulders and back, pooling at her feet. "I think this calls for a celebration," she said, taking one step closer to the seated Nick.

Nick's smile broadened, and he replied in playful protest as he got up to meet her gaze. "You know, I just got dressed and was looking forward to the six-course breakfast downstairs."

The breakfast would have to wait.

796616 (June 30)

The Greenwich lounge at JFK was an oasis of contrived tranquility. The lighting was soft, the armchairs were a fraying and unforgiving leather, and the air was filled with the urgent clink of glasses and a buzzing, multilingual murmur. It was a world of sterile and anonymous quasi-comfort, a non-place designed for people in transit from one life to another.

Oliver and Daniela sat in a quiet corner, a small island of focused intensity in the sea of unsteady calm. They looked like any other well-heeled couple, but their conversation was a low, urgent hum, their focus entirely on the stack of travel documents and the tablet computer resting on the small table between them.

Daniela picked up the printed itinerary, her brow furrowed in concentration. "Okay," she said in a low whisper. "Run me through it one more time. I understand the objective. But the logistics ... they still feel a little insane." She tapped a finger on the top of the itinerary. "I know the real destination is Luxembourg. So, why are we booked for a full week in a hotel in Brussels?"

Oliver took a slow, deliberate sip of his sparkling water, gathering his thoughts. "Because we're being watched," he said, his voice almost inaudible over the lounge's soft jazz. "The entire network that I've been using – the one that gets me cash, the one that books these untraceable tickets – it's not a tool for my privacy. It's a surveillance system for someone else."

He saw a flicker of confusion in her eyes and continued, laying out the pieces. "On the flight back from India, I had another ... episode. A projection. I was back in Harlem, in Saleem Bhai's shop, right after I had left with the cash. I saw him make a phone call."

He described the vision in detail: Saleem's deferential tone, the report about the "young American" with the bitcoin on his phone, and, most importantly, the voice on the other end of the line.

"It was a man's voice," Oliver explained, the memory of it still a cold, clear note in his mind. "It was soft, almost musical, with a strange, lilting accent. Brazilian, maybe. And he was the one giving the orders. He told Saleem to keep an eye on me, that the entire network would be alerted to my movements."

Daniela listened, her expression shifting from confusion to a dawning, sharp-edged comprehension.

"So, Habib ..." she began, the implication clear.

"Habib, Saleem, Saleem's brother in Hyderabad ... they're all just nodes in the same network," Oliver confirmed. "And they all report up to this one, unknown 'boss.' The man with the musical voice. I think I saw him in another projection. He was standing in a sea of silver, seemingly made of silver himself. I have no idea what that means. But I did see my mother's currently unfinished book floating in that sea."

He let the full weight of the new reality settle between them.

"So, when I went to Habib to book this trip," he continued, "I knew I couldn't just ask for a ticket to Luxembourg. That would have been like sending them a written invitation, telling them exactly where to set their trap. I had to assume that every move I made through their network was being monitored."

He picked up the itinerary and pointed to the final destination. "So I created a false signal. I told Habib I needed to go to Brussels for a week on very important work. A plausible business destination. A complete misdirection. It gives them a target to focus on, a story that makes sense. It makes us look like we're heading in a different direction entirely."

Daniela took the itinerary from him, her eyes scanning the complex series of flights starting with the one to London. "But how did you get the Luxembourg layover? It seems ... convenient."

"It wasn't," Oliver said with a wry, tired smile. "It was a pain in the butt, actually. Habib's first few options were all direct flights or had layovers in useless places like Zurich or Amsterdam. I had to keep pushing him, telling him I had an old friend in Luxembourg I absolutely had to see, that I needed at least a 24-hour layover there. He got annoyed. He said it was too complicated. But I insisted, and finally, after about an hour of him muttering in Bengali and making calls to his 'guy in Madrid,' he found this one. Hopefully I did enough not to raise any suspicions."

She looked up from the paper, her gaze full of a new and complex mixture of emotions. He saw the clear, sober understanding of the immense risk they were about to take.

She didn't say anything. She just folded the itinerary, placed it back on the table, and reached across, taking his hand in hers. Her grip was firm, a quiet, solid promise. A silent acknowledgment that they were in this together, a unified team against a world of shadows.

A synthesized, feminine voice announced over the lounge's PA system, its tone a jarring, cheerful chime. *"British Airways flight BA 174 to Heathrow, is now boarding at gate 12."*

Their flight.

Oliver squeezed her hand once, a final, definitive gesture. It was time to go.

796621 (June 30)

The black Lincoln Town Car moved smoothly through the late afternoon traffic on the Van Wyck Expressway, a silent, air-conditioned bubble against the humid chaos of the city. Nick stared out the window at the endless, monotonous landscape of Queens. Beside him, Adele was a picture of calm, her attention focused on the tablet in her lap.

Adele was the one who broke the quiet, her question a soft, unexpected probe into the one part of his life he had so carefully compartmentalized.

"What have you told your wife?" she asked, not looking up from her screen.

The question landed with a quiet, uncomfortable thud. He had been so immersed in this new, high-stakes world that the reality of his other life – the one in a small apartment in Queens with Becky – felt like a distant, half-forgotten dream.

"The truth," he lied. "That I'm working on a sensitive consulting project. A lot of travel required. She understands."

He didn't tell Adele about the strained phone calls, the vague, evasive answers he'd had to give Becky, the growing chasm of unspoken secrets between them. He didn't tell her about the guilt, a low-grade, persistent hum beneath the surface of his new, thrilling purpose.

Adele looked up from her tablet, her dark eyes studying him. "Does she?" she asked, a note of genuine, and perhaps even sympathetic, curiosity in her voice.

"I'll figure it out," Nick said, his tone a clear signal that the topic was closed.

She seemed to understand. She did not press him further. Instead, she gestured to the flight confirmations on her screen. "Are you certain about this? Standby is a risk."

"It's the only way," Nick replied, grateful for the shift back to the familiar, solid ground of logistics. "Booking two last-minute tickets to a minor European hub like Luxembourg is next to impossible. This is the earliest date I could find. If we get on, we get on. From there, it's a short, un-bookable connection."

"If we get on," she repeated, the words a quiet, pointed emphasis.

"We'll get on," Nick said with a confidence he didn't fully feel. "We have to."

She gave a small, almost imperceptible nod and returned to her screen. The conversation was over. They rode the rest of the way to the airport in a tense, professional quiet, two partners on a high-stakes mission, each lost in their own private thoughts and calculations.

121121 (April 30, 2011)

A man in a perfectly fitted light blue blazer walked purposefully along a tree-lined block with elegant Tudor-style homes. Oliver-the-observer took a sharp intake of breath when he realized who the man was. It was his dad, walking in a neighborhood that looked like Forest Hills in Queens. His projection had taken him over a decade into the past.

Nate walked up the front stairs of a modest two-story home, its façade peeling slightly at the edges, a sign of age or neglect. The sign next to the door was mostly covered in ivy, but Oliver-the-observer was able to read what it said.

Bryce.

Nate rang the doorbell. The door opened a few moments later, revealing an old man in his late eighties, frail but upright, with a shock of white hair that stood out like a crown of frost, his face a map of wrinkles.

"Yes?" the old man said, his voice a gravelly Irish lilt, wary but not unkind. "Can I help you?"

Nate extended a hand. "Mr. Jonathan Bryce? My name is Nate Battolo. We spoke on the phone last week. About your work."

Bryce's eyes narrowed, then widened in recollection. He took Nate's hand in a surprisingly firm grip. "Ah, yes. The admirer from the city. Come in, come in. Mind the step – it's a bit uneven."

Nate stepped inside. The house was a comforting clutter of easels, stacked canvases, and shelves groaning under art supplies. Sunlight filtered through dusty windows, illuminating motes that danced in the air like tiny stars in a miniature galaxy. Bryce led Nate to a living room that doubled as a studio, where two large canvases leaned against the wall, partially shrouded by drop cloths but exposed enough to command attention.

"There they are," Bryce said, gesturing with a trembling hand. "My unfinished symphonies, as I call 'em. Been staring at 'em for years now, waiting for the muse to return."

Nate approached the canvases slowly, his face lighting up with an excitement Oliver had rarely seen in his father. "These are incredible," he said, the words coming out slowly, with a deep reverence.

"Well, they would have been," Bryce cackled softly, "if only I knew how to finish the damn things. But they were gone, the voices. Both times. And then I didn't know what to do."

"What do you mean, voices?" Nate asked, turning towards Bryce with a surprised expression.

"The voices, laddie. They tormented me," Bryce said, with a look of profound sadness in his eyes. "Started over forty years ago when I was painting my second one, *The Toddler*. They kept telling me what to do, screaming in my head if I did something wrong. It was torture. But in the end, the painting turned out quite right, didn't it?"

Nate nodded.

Bryce continued, in a dark, low tone, "They came back again a couple of years later when I was painting my third one, even worse this time. I hadn't a clue what they were asking me to do. Why the fires in people's hands? Why the strange bald man in the middle holding the soft clock? Why the Atlantean inscription on top? Heck, I didn't even know it was Atlantean back then. I thought it was Latin. None of it made any sense to me, but I did it because I needed the voices to stop."

"It sounds like they didn't stop after the third one," Nate said, in a soft, calming tone, acknowledging how the memory of the voices was troubling the artist.

"Of course they didn't!" The old man snapped, with an energy that belied his age. "They kept coming back on and off. They'd disappear for a few years and leave me in peace. Then they'd come roaring back."

Bryce paced around the room, now visibly distraught. He walked up to one of the canvases and pointed at it. "Look at this one. Started it almost twenty years ago when they told me to. The voices did. Took me two years to get to this point." He jabbed a trembling finger at a spot on the canvas.

Oliver-the-observer couldn't see either one from his projection vantage point. He was behind them, looking at Nate and Bryce staring at the canvases.

"Look," the artist continued, speaking in a fast, high-pitched tone. "What was I supposed to do here? They left, and I was done. Yes, it's a person I was painting here, but how could I continue?" He threw up his hands and walked away from the canvas.

Nate was observing the painting, likely the fourth one, stoically. "It's still a masterpiece, Mr. Bryce."

Bryce turned to look at Nate. "Ah, what's the use?" he gasped. He walked over to the next canvas, which Oliver assumed was the fifth painting. "And this one," he croaked, now a bundle of nervous energy. "What even is this … this thing?"

Nate looked at it keenly, a small smile forming on his face. "I know exactly what that is. It's a Non–"

"Gah!" Bryce exclaimed again, cutting Nate off. "At least with that one, I knew I was painting a woman. With this one, when the voices returned a few years later, they told me things that made no sense. Something about higher dimensions and bending space and time. The voices … they asked for something impossible," Bryce continued darkly, a mad, otherworldly look entering his already agitated eyes. "It's not just a shape, you see. It's … a machine. They asked me to bend space. To paint time itself. Tell me lad," he took a step closer to Nate and looked at him pointedly with his mad eyes. "How is this old man supposed to paint that? It's impossible!"

Nate nodded politely, acknowledging the painter's righteous chagrin. "Mr. Bryce," he said, with a calming composure that brought back so many memories to Oliver-the-observer. He felt a small lump form at the back of his throat. Nate continued, "I understand you feel these are unfinished paintings. I, however, view them as complete masterworks. I reached out to you last week as a long-time admirer of your work, and today I would like to make you an offer to purchase these paintings from you."

Nate's soothing tone seemed to have calmed Bryce down. He looked at Nate with a resigned look on his face. "You can have 'em. Name your price. I don't want them anymore."

"A hundred thousand dollars for the pair," Nate said, in the most matter-of-fact voice Oliver had ever heard for a number that large.

The old man looked stunned, with no words left to say.

Nate continued with a smile, "This is how much those paintings are worth to me, Mr. Bryce. And if I don't honor that value with value, the universe will not be in balance. I will take your bank details and make arrangements for the transfer. Once the transfer goes through, I will come back and pick up the paintings. I'm hoping by next week."

Oliver felt a sharp and sudden jolt, followed by the screech of tires on the tarmac, the plane shuddering as it touched down. Oliver's eyes snapped open, his body slamming back into the present with a gasp. The cabin lights brightened, passengers stirring around him. Daniela lifted her head from his shoulder, blinking sleepily. "You okay? You were mumbling something."

He nodded, heart pounding, the afterimage of his father's younger face lingering like a ghost. They had just landed in Luxembourg. The freeport waited, and now he knew: the canvases were more than art, and more than seed words hidden in them. They were echoes of torment, unfinished symphonies holding the keys to everything.

796657 (July 1)

The polished, impersonal hum of the JFK international terminal was a familiar kind of purgatory. The flight to Zurich, the one they were supposed to be on, was a few thousand miles away, en route to its destination.

They had been at the airport for several hours, a frustrating delay after the standby list had failed to clear. It was a simple, mundane obstacle that, after weeks of high-stakes intellectual breakthroughs, felt like a personal insult.

Adele sat on one of the uncomfortable terminal chairs, a picture of cool, unimpressed composure, her attention already focused on her tablet. Nick stood by the massive window, the sour knot of disappointment tightening in his gut.

"Nick."

Her voice was sharp, cutting through his thoughts. He walked over to her chair.

She didn't look up from her tablet immediately, her expression thoughtful. "I've been digging deeper into Nate Battolo," she said, her voice quiet. "After his name surfaced, I had Kincaid do some research on him … it rang a bell, and I couldn't remember why. They pulled Christiaan's full prison logs from Lewisburg."

"And?" Nick asked, bracing himself.

"I was right – I had seen his name before. He visited. Just once. Late November 2013, right after Christiaan was sentenced. No more visits after that."

Nick processed this. "So, they were in contact, even after the platform collapsed."

"But that's the part that bothers me." Adele finally looked up, and her eyes were cold, not with anger, but with a chilling clarity. "I visited my brother for seven years, Nick. He told me about the paintings. But in all that time, he *never once* mentioned Nate Battolo. He let me believe Dev_akshar was just some digital ghost."

"He was protecting him for some reason," Nick said.

"He was protecting a thief," Adele corrected, her voice turning to ice. "This proves they were partners. But Christiaan was foolish and loyal – he protected the guy who stole everything and vanished, while he took the fall. They were in it together, and Nate Battolo is the lying thief who got away with it all. That money belongs to Christiaan. All of it. It makes getting those paintings even more critical."

Her focus snapped back to the screen, her tone shifting to business. "Which is why we can't be sitting here. Check this out." She gestured to the new flight confirmations on her screen. "I've found another option," she said in a sharp and decisive voice.

"What is it?" Nick asked, hopefully.

"There is a Lufthansa flight to Frankfurt departing in just 90 minutes. It has two open seats. In business class. I have just purchased them. There's a Luxair flight to Luxembourg thirty minutes after it lands. Tight, but we can make it."

"Yikes, that's steep," Nick said, looking at the eye-popping number on her screen.

"Getting there is more important than money, Nick," Adele replied, her eyes meeting his. The recent discovery of Battolo's visit hung in the air between them.

"And besides, if we get the paintings, this will be a pittance in comparison. The only thing that matters now is getting there. We will be in Luxembourg by the evening."

Nick nodded. He couldn't argue with her logic.

796683 (July 1)

The taxi ride was unsettlingly short. One moment they were navigating the polished, anonymous corridors of Luxembourg Airport, and the next they were in a sterile industrial park, a landscape of gray warehouses and high security fences under a flat, indifferent sky. Oliver stared out the window, his expression a mask of calm focus. He watched the massive logos of global logistics companies slide past – DHL, Kuehne+Nagel, Cargolux – a world built on the quiet, efficient and heavily guarded movement of assets.

Beside him, Daniela sat perfectly still, her hands clasped tightly over the leather briefcase in her lap. He watched her adjust the collar of her simple but impeccably tailored black blazer for the third time, her fingers briefly tracing the sharp lapels. She looked every bit the part of a sharp, serious lawyer, but he could see the faint, rhythmic pulse in her neck, a single, silent tell that betrayed the calm façade.

"Are you sure about this?" she asked, her voice a soft whisper that didn't carry to the driver. Oliver could hear the tension coiled beneath the words. "My heart is pounding. What if they don't buy it?"

Oliver turned from the window, his gaze steady. "They will," he said, trying to project a confidence he hoped was contagious. "We're not bluffing. We have the documents. We have the story. Just stick to the script."

He gave her a small, reassuring smile. "Besides, I already gave them a heads-up."

Her eyes widened. "You what?" she asked, her voice a low, urgent whisper. "When? You never told me that."

"A couple of days ago, before we left," he said, his tone matter-of-fact. "I called their main administrative office. Told them I was the new point of contact for the Liffey Trust and that my counsel and I would be stopping by for a routine asset inspection. An owner wouldn't just show up unannounced. They'd make an appointment first."

The taxi slowed, turning toward a final, imposing gatehouse, a stark, concrete structure with mirrored-glass windows and a heavy, reinforced barrier. Up ahead, the main building of Le Freeport loomed, less a warehouse and more a modern, windowless fortress.

The taxi dropped them at the main entrance, an architectural statement of glass and steel that seemed designed to intimidate. As they walked through the automatic doors, a hush fell over them. The interior was a vast, silent cathedral of commerce, all polished concrete floors and minimalist art, the air chilled to a precise, uninviting temperature. There was no clutter, no life; just a single, massive desk behind which sat a man who looked like he had been sculpted from the same cold, gray marble as the walls.

He was in his late fifties, with a severe haircut and a suit so perfectly tailored it seemed to have no seams. His nameplate read: *M. Dubois, Head of Client Operations.*

Daniela, now fully inhabiting her role, strode forward with a cool confidence, Oliver a step behind her. "Good afternoon," she began, her voice crisp and professional. "We're here on behalf of the Liffey Trust. My client, Mr. Battolo, called a few days ago to advise of his visit."

Dubois looked up from his computer, his expression one of polite, professional disinterest. He blinked once, slowly. "Ah, yes," he said, his French accent precise and clinical. "The informal advisory. We received it." He made no move to stand, simply gesturing with a manicured hand toward the two chairs in front of his desk.

They sat. Daniela placed the leather briefcase on her lap and unclasped it, but didn't open it yet.

"As discussed, my client is the sole heir and beneficiary to the estate of the trust's original settlor, Mr. Nate Battolo," she continued. "We are here to conduct a routine inspection of the assets held in unit 7B for estate and insurance verification purposes."

"Of course," Dubois said, his gaze flicking from Daniela to Oliver and back again. Oliver met his eyes, trying to project an air of calm ownership, the grieving but determined son. "However," Dubois continued, steepling his fingers, "your telephone call, as I noted, was an informal advisory, not a formal petition for access. While I did perform a cursory check of the documents you emailed, and they appear, *prima facie*, to be in order, our protocol is quite specific."

Oliver felt the first, cold prickle of unease.

"On-site asset verification," Dubois intoned, as if reading from a sacred, invisible text, "requires a full due diligence review by our legal compliance team, which can only be conducted during a scheduled appointment. A formal request must be submitted through the proper channels no less than seventy-two hours in advance."

Daniela didn't miss a beat. "I believe you'll find the trust's original charter grants the legal heir immediate rights of inspection," she countered, her tone firm but respectful. "We can of course wait for your legal team, but my client's time is limited."

Dubois offered a small, thin-lipped smile that was devoid of any humor. "Madame, our protocols are not suggestions. They are the architecture of our security. It is why our clients trust us with assets of … incalculable value." He turned to his computer and his fingers tapped rhythmically on the keyboard. "I can, however, offer you the next available slot for a contested-asset review."

The word hung in the air. *Contested.* Oliver's unease sharpened into genuine alarm.

"I'm sorry," he interjected, breaking his silence. "Did you say 'contested'?"

Dubois looked at him as if he were a piece of furniture that had just spoken. "That is correct, Monsieur Battolo. As your informal call constituted a material inquiry into the status of the assets, protocol as stipulated in Section 14, sub-clause C of the client agreement required us to immediately notify any and all parties with a registered security interest in the unit's contents."

"Another party?" Daniela asked, her professional mask perfectly intact, though Oliver saw the slight tightening of her grip on the briefcase. "And who might that be?"

Dubois's eyes returned to his screen. He scrolled, the soft click of his mouse the only sound in the silent room. "The lien was filed on March 14th of this year, citing a prior claim on the specified assets. The registered party is a Ms. Maren Dehnert."

The name landed like a physical blow. Oliver felt the blood drain from his face. It was the date. Mid-March. It was just days after Eddie Garcia had sat in his apartment and told him the story about the freeport. The conversation had been private, in a room he thought was safe. He remembered what Santos, the building doorman had told him – *she had visited the previous day, and tried to access the apartment.* The only way she could have known that quickly, known to file a lien on this specific, secret location, was if she had been listening. The thought was a chilling violation, a confirmation that the walls of his own home were not his own. She had been in his mind, somehow.

"As Ms. Dehnert's designated representative will also need to be present," Dubois continued, oblivious to the storm raging inside Oliver's head, "the earliest I can schedule the formal verification is ... tonight. At midnight."

"Midnight?" Daniela said, a flicker of genuine shock breaking through her lawyerly façade. "That's in twelve hours. Our flight to Brussels is at four in the morning. That barely gives us any time."

Dubois offered a small, Gallic shrug, a gesture of perfect, bureaucratic indifference. "It is the earliest time available. I am afraid it is midnight, or you may reschedule for next week. The choice is yours."

They left the freeport's sterile administrative building and stepped back out into the flat, gray light of the industrial park. They took the next available taxi into the city center, a world of ancient, elegant architecture that felt a universe away from the cold modernity of the fortress they had just left. They found a quiet, nondescript brasserie, a place of dark wood and worn leather and settled into a corner booth.

For a long time, they just sat, the adrenaline from the initial encounter slowly giving way to the long, grinding reality of the wait. The city outside was a muffled, distant hum. Oliver ordered a steak frites he had no appetite for and a sparkling water that he nursed for an hour, the condensation from the glass forming a small, spreading pool on the dark wood of the table.

"So," Daniela said finally, breaking the long silence. "Midnight. Her representative. Who do you think it will be?"

Oliver didn't have to think about it. The name was a cold, solid certainty in his mind, a piece of the puzzle that had been waiting for this exact moment to lock into place. "It's Bojan," he said, his voice flat and devoid of any doubt. "It has to be."

He saw the question in her eyes and continued, laying out the cold, simple logic. "Maren's been a ghost since I confronted her in the projection last year. I only saw her once since then, in India. She's too smart to show her own face. She needs a proxy, a professional. Someone who can operate in this world of high-security vaults and legal threats without blinking." He thought of the man's cold, pale eyes in the Madrid airport and in the alleyway in Montevideo, the quiet, professional menace. "Bojan is her enforcer. He's the only one it could be."

His expression shifted, the tactical certainty giving way to a more troubled, introspective look. "The real question isn't who," he said, almost to himself. "It's how. How did she know about the freeport so soon after I did?" He looked at Daniela, the memory of his recent past a source of clear, painful insight. "It was mid-March when Eddie told me and her lien was placed right around then. I was ... I wasn't in a good place then. That was close to the bottom for me, with the drinking. I think my defenses were down. She must have gotten in then. Slipped right into my head when I was too weak to notice."

Daniela reached across the table and placed her hand over his. Her touch was warm and firm, an anchor against the pull of his self-recrimination.

"Don't do that to yourself," she said, her voice full of a quiet, fierce pride. "The fact that you saw you were at your lowest point, that you recognized your nadir and had the discipline to stop, to get healthy ... Oliver, I am so incredibly proud of you for that."

He looked at her and squeezed her hand.

The hours bled into one another, marked only by the changing light outside the brasserie window and the slow, circular conversations that led nowhere. The steak frites Oliver had ordered sat half-eaten, a cold monument to an appetite that had vanished. They spoke in low tones, rehearsing their roles, turning over the scant details of their plan until the words felt smooth and worn, like stones in a riverbed. But beneath the quiet strategy, a single, insistent question thrummed in Oliver's mind: *How had Maren known?* The thought was a chilling, unshakeable presence, a ghost at their table.

At half-past eleven, they paid their bill and stepped out into the cool, quiet Luxembourg night. The taxi ride back to the freeport was silent, a shared, wordless acknowledgment that the time for planning was over. The industrial park was a different world at night, a landscape of immense, sleeping shadows punctuated by the harsh, sterile glare of security lights. The main building loomed before them, a silent, windowless monolith.

They were met at the entrance not by a receptionist, but by a uniformed guard who checked their IDs against a list on a tablet before escorting them through a series of empty, echoing corridors. The silence was absolute, amplifying the soft, rhythmic tap of Daniela's heels on the polished concrete floor.

The guard led them to the same glass-walled conference room. M. Dubois was waiting, seated behind the same immaculate desk, looking as though he hadn't moved an inch since they had left that afternoon. He gestured for them to sit.

"Good evening," he said, his voice a flat, neutral instrument. "Thank you for your punctuality. I must advise you that my shift concludes in one hour, at zero one hundred hours precisely. At that time, my colleague will take over. I trust our business can be concluded before then."

The ticking clock, delivered with the casual indifference of a man simply stating a fact, tightened a cold knot in Oliver's stomach.

"That should be more than sufficient time," Daniela said, her voice a perfect echo of Dubois's own professional calm. She placed her briefcase on the table and opened it, arranging the Liffey Trust documents in a neat, orderly stack.

Dubois gave a small, almost imperceptible nod. "I have had the opportunity to conduct a preliminary review of the documents you provided via email this afternoon," he began, steepling his fingers. "As I stated, the documentation of heirship from the estate of the late Mr. Nate Battolo appears to be in order."

He paused, letting the statement hang in the air for a moment before delivering the inevitable blow.

"However," he continued, his tone unchanging, "being the legal beneficiary of assets held by a trust is a separate matter from being the legal administrator of the trust itself. The former grants you a claim to the property. Only the latter grants you the authority to issue directives concerning that property. Without a notarized *Affidavit of Successor Trustee* naming you as the new administrator, I cannot authorize any change in status, including a transfer of the assets."

It was exactly the wall they had anticipated, but hearing the bureaucratic certainty in his voice made it feel solid and real.

"We understand the facility's position, of course," Daniela said smoothly, not missing a beat. "At this time, we are not petitioning for a transfer. My client is merely exercising his legal right as the sole beneficiary to conduct an on-site inspection of the assets for insurance and estate valuation purposes. The title deed and the active policy grant him that right, as I'm sure you're aware."

Dubois's expression remained a mask of professional neutrality, but Oliver thought he saw a flicker of something in his eyes – a grudging respect for Daniela's preparedness.

"That is correct," Dubois conceded after a moment. "A supervised viewing is permissible." He glanced at the clock on his screen. "There is, however, the matter of the other registered party. As I mentioned, we were obliged to notify them. Their representative is here. He has just stepped away for a moment but will be returning shortly."

Oliver's heart hammered against his ribs. He forced himself to remain still, to keep his expression as neutral as Daniela's. He could feel her presence beside him, a calm, solid anchor in the rising tide of his own tension. He knew who was coming. The waiting was the hardest part, a slow, agonizing stretch of silence where every possibility, every threat, felt real and immediate.

The soft sound of a door opening at the far end of the corridor broke the quiet. Footsteps, heavy and deliberate, grew closer. Oliver kept his eyes fixed on Dubois, refusing to look toward the door, refusing to give the approaching man the satisfaction.

The footsteps stopped. A large, dark silhouette filled the glass doorway.

Dubois looked up. "Ah, you have returned. Please, come in."

Oliver finally allowed himself to turn. Bojan Mitrovic stepped into the room. He wore the same well-made but nondescript navy sports jacket Oliver remembered from Madrid and Montevideo, but his expression was different. The cold, professional menace was still there, but it was overlaid with a look of smug, predatory confidence. He was a wolf who had cornered his prey, and he was in no hurry. He ignored Oliver and Daniela completely, addressing only Dubois.

"Is there problem?" Bojan asked, his gravelly voice a jarring intrusion into the sterile quiet of the room.

"The legal representatives of the Liffey Trust are here to conduct a supervised inspection," Dubois said calmly. "As the registered security contact for the lienholder, your presence is required by our protocol."

Bojan finally turned his gaze on them, a slow, deliberate act. He looked from Daniela's impassive face to Oliver's, and a slow, cold smile spread across his lips. It was a smile that held no humor, only a deep and certain sense of victory.

"The trust?" Bojan said, a low chuckle rumbling in his chest. "Yes. I am here to ensure assets are ... protected."

The silence in the glass-walled conference room was heavy and absolute. Oliver watched as M. Dubois, with the deliberate, unhurried pace of a man who has all the time in the world, adjusted the lamp on his desk and shuffled through the Liffey Trust documents in front of him. Bojan sat opposite them, a dark, immovable presence, his cold smile never wavering.

He finally broke the silence, his voice a low rumble that seemed to absorb all the light in the room. "He has no rights here."

He leaned forward slightly, his gaze fixed on Oliver. "His father is dead. These papers are desperate fiction. Maren Dehnert's claim on assets is pre-existing and legally registered. This boy is a thief, trying to steal what is not his."

Oliver felt a hot surge of anger. He opened his mouth to retort, but he caught Daniela's eye. It was a quick, sharp glance, a silent command: *Stay in character. I've got this.*

"My client's claim is based on a direct chain of legal inheritance," Daniela countered, her voice unwavering. "Your client's is a third-party lien, the validity of which is a matter for the courts, not for a storage facility. We are here simply to verify the assets listed on the manifest."

Bojan let out a short, harsh laugh. He ignored Daniela completely, his pale, washed-out eyes boring into Oliver. "You are long way from home, boy. You think because you were clever in Montevideo, you are safe?"

The direct reference to their chase through the old city sent a cold jolt through Oliver, but he held his ground, his face a neutral mask.

"I cannot follow you back to your country," Bojan continued, his voice dropping to a confidential, menacing purr. "The American government, they do not ... appreciate my visits anymore. But do not think that makes you safe." He leaned back, a slow, predatory confidence in his posture. "The world is very small place."

And that was it. A nagging piece of the puzzle clicked into place in Oliver's mind. The fear he had been living with for months – the constant, low-grade dread of a knock on his apartment door, the scanning of faces in the New York crowds – had been for nothing. He couldn't come for me there, Oliver realized with a chilling clarity. The real danger was never at home. It was always out here.

The thought was not a relief. It was a different kind of terror, the realization that the battlefield was the entire world, and he had just walked willingly onto it.

The tense, silent standoff hung in the air for a long moment, a cold war waged with nothing but locked gazes and clenched fists. It was Dubois who finally broke the spell, his voice a clean, sharp instrument cutting through the personal animosity.

"Gentlemen, Madame," he said, with an air of finality. "This is an administrative meeting, not a courtroom. The personal nature of your dispute is irrelevant to our protocols." He stood, the crisp movement a clear signal that the debate was over. "We will now proceed with the supervised viewing, as is permitted. Please, follow me."

He led them out of the conference room and into a different, even more secure wing of the building, three stories below ground. The walk was a silent, unnerving journey deeper into the fortress. Oliver watched as Dubois swiped a key card to open a heavy steel door, which hissed shut behind them. The corridor here was narrower, the lighting harsher. At the end of it, another door, this one requiring Dubois to place his eye against a retinal scanner. It clicked open, revealing a small antechamber.

"The viewing rooms are climate and humidity controlled," Dubois stated, his tone that of a museum docent explaining an exhibit. "All personal items, including jackets and bags, will remain here."

They complied, shedding their outer layers and leaving Daniela's briefcase in a designated locker. The act felt like a stripping away of their armor, leaving them exposed and vulnerable. A final, vault-like door slid open, and they stepped inside.

The room was a perfect, sterile cube of white. The walls were seamless, the floor was a polished white epoxy, and the ceiling was a grid of unforgivingly bright LED panels. There was no furniture, save for a single, sleek workstation against the far wall. The air was cold, dry, and smelled of nothing at all. It was a room with no shadows, no place to hide.

"The assets will be brought in momentarily," Dubois announced.

A section of the wall slid open with a soft hydraulic hiss, and two technicians in gray, featureless jumpsuits wheeled in two enormous, flat crates. They moved with a silent, practiced efficiency, placing the crates on stands in the center of the room before retreating and sealing the door behind them.

Oliver's heart hammered against his ribs. *There they are*, he thought, his gaze fixed on the objects of his long and impossible quest. *The fourth and fifth. After all this time.* The paintings themselves were completely obscured by layers of protective wrapping and foam, but the custom crating left the ornate, gilded edges of the antique frames exposed, a small, tantalizing glimpse of the treasures within.

Dubois walked over to the workstation, a sleek, integrated terminal with a single, large screen. Oliver watched, his focus absolute, as the administrator swiped his key card, entered a lengthy passcode, and then pressed his thumb against a biometric scanner on the console. The screen flickered to life, displaying a clean, data-rich interface showing the inventory details for Unit 7B.

"As you can see," Dubois said, his voice echoing slightly in the sterile room, "the crate identification numbers match the manifest on file. Crate 4B, Bryce, J., untitled, circa 1991. Crate 5B, Bryce, J., untitled, circa 1993."

Dubois gestured toward the crates with an open palm. "The assets are available for your visual inspection."

Oliver nodded, his face a mask of professional seriousness, the plan he had rehearsed with Daniela earlier in the day at the brasserie still fresh in his mind. He began a slow, deliberate circuit of the first massive crate, running a hand along its smooth, sealed edges, occasionally stooping to examine the joins. Bojan watched his every move, his arms crossed, a look of profound suspicion on his face. Daniela stood by, a silent, observant counsel.

Oliver moved to the second crate. He was halfway down its length when he stopped. He leaned in, his eyes narrowing on a spot near the bottom corner. He reached out and traced a line with his finger.

"Mr. Dubois," he said, his voice tight and controlled, but laced with an unmistakable edge of alarm. "There's an issue here."

Dubois's impassive expression tightened. He strode over, his polished shoes silent on the epoxy floor. "An issue, Monsieur Battolo?"

"This discoloration," Oliver said, pointing to a faint, almost imperceptible darkening of the wood, no larger than his palm. "And this hairline fracture along the join. It feels damp. This is water damage."

The accusation, so quiet and so serious, hung in the sterile air. Bojan immediately moved in, his bulk crowding the space. He knelt, scrutinizing the spot Oliver had indicated. "Is nothing," he growled, looking up at Dubois. "Is old wood. The boy is playing games."

"My client is not playing games," Daniela interjected, her voice cutting and sharp. She had moved to Oliver's side, now the protective lawyer. "He is identifying potential damage to multi-million-dollar assets under your care. What are your protocols for documenting potential transit damage, Monsieur? Does the lienholder get a copy of the incident report?"

Dubois was now on the defensive, his professional reputation at stake. "Of course," he said stiffly, also kneeling to get a closer look. "All conditions are meticulously documented upon intake." The three of them were now a tight, focused huddle, their attention completely consumed by the tiny, ambiguous flaw on the crate, their voices a low, urgent murmur of procedural debate.

This was the opening.

Oliver stepped back from the group, creating a space of feigned frustration. "Let me pull up the original high-resolution intake photo from the manifest," he announced, his tone firm. "We need to compare the condition."

It was the perfect pretext – exactly how he and Daniela had planned it. He walked over to the workstation, his heart beginning a low, heavy drumbeat against his ribs. He sat at the terminal, acutely aware of the three figures just a few feet away, their backs now turned to him as they argued over the scuff mark. Daniela was doing a masterful job of keeping Dubois and Bojan agitated. The screen glowed, the unit's inventory file still open. The session had stayed live; the console didn't auto-lock – exactly the grace window he'd hoped for. His hands felt slick with a cold sweat, but his fingers were steady as they moved across the keyboard.

He clicked out of the inventory screen, navigating to the logistics menu. *New Work Order. Outbound Transfer. Pre-Advice.* He typed in the destination: JFK Bonded Storage, New York. He selected the client account: The Liffey Trust. He set the arrival date for one week in the future. Each click was a small, quiet thunderclap in the silent room.

His finger hovered over the final button. *Submit.* He could hear Bojan's voice rising in irritation behind him. He hit the button.

A small, green notification popped onto the screen: Notification sent to broker/contact of record for approval.

Oliver immediately clicked back to the main inventory screen and began idly clicking through photo thumbnails as if searching. He pushed his chair back with a soft, frustrated sigh just as Daniela delivered a final, pointed question to Dubois.

"I can't seem to isolate the intake images for this specific crate," Oliver said, his voice remarkably steady. "The directory is a mess. It doesn't matter. I'm sure it's nothing."

He stepped away from the terminal, his heart a frantic drum against his ribs. He forced a mask of mild, professional frustration onto his face, a silent actor playing his part for an audience of two.

Daniela, without missing a beat, seized the opening he had created. She turned from her intense scrutiny of the crate back to Dubois, her tone shifting from concern to crisp, legal formality.

"While my client is willing to let the matter of the intake photos rest for now, Monsieur," she said, "I want it noted in the official log for this viewing that a full digital verification of the asset's condition upon arrival was not possible due to ... technical limitations in your filing system. We will be submitting a formal request for the raw server logs upon our return to New York."

It was a masterful performance. She was simultaneously ending the confrontation while creating a new, completely fabricated paper trail, a piece of bureaucratic leverage that sounded both plausible and deeply annoying.

Dubois, who clearly wanted nothing more than for this entire inconvenient affair to be over, nodded with a palpable sense of relief. "Of course, Madame. Your request will be noted in my report. Our IT department will be notified."

Oliver watched Bojan, who stood a few feet away, his arms crossed, a silent, smoldering volcano of suspicion. He knew, Oliver could feel it, that he had been outmaneuvered, that some sleight of hand had occurred right under his nose, but he couldn't name it. He had no legal ground to stand on, no procedure to invoke. He was a creature of force in a world of rules, and in this sterile, white room, the rules were all that mattered.

As if summoned by the thought of rules and procedures, the vault-like door to the viewing room hissed open. A younger man, also in a perfectly tailored suit, stepped in. He had the same air of professional detachment as Dubois, but with a sharper, more restless energy. He nodded briskly at the room's occupants.

Dubois glanced at the clock on the terminal screen. "Ah, Jean-Luc. Punctual as always." He turned to the group. "This is Monsieur Verratti, my colleague who is taking over the night shift. I will be leaving you in his capable hands."

The changing of the guard was a brief, bloodless ritual. Dubois conveyed the situation in a few clipped, formal sentences of French. Oliver caught the words "Liffey Trust," "Battolo," and "inspection." Verratti listened, his expression unchanging, and then gave a single, sharp nod of comprehension. The transfer of authority was complete.

Dubois turned back to Oliver and Daniela. "The supervised viewing is now concluded. If you will follow me, I will escort you back to the main reception."

His duty was done. He was now just a man whose shift had ended, eager to escape into the quiet of the night.

They walked in a tense, silent procession back through the labyrinthine corridors. Dubois led the way, with Oliver and Daniela behind him. Bojan fell into step beside Oliver, his presence a heavy, oppressive weight in the narrow hallway.

"You are clever boy," Bojan muttered, his voice a low, gravelly whisper that was meant for Oliver alone. The sound was a physical thing, raising the hairs on Oliver's neck. "Very clever. Like your father."

Oliver kept his eyes fixed on Dubois's back, his face a neutral mask. He would not give him the satisfaction of a reaction.

"But clever has its limit," Bojan continued, his voice dropping even lower, a current of pure menace in the sterile, silent corridor. "Maren is patient woman. I am not patient man. The paintings will find their way to their rightful owner. One way or another."

They reached the antechamber. As they retrieved their jackets and Daniela's briefcase from the locker, Oliver could feel Bojan's cold, pale eyes on him, a silent promise of future violence. They walked the final corridor and emerged back into the vast, empty lobby.

Dubois led them to the front desk for the final, procedural sign-out. As he handed Oliver a tablet to sign, he said with the first hint of genuine human curiosity he'd shown all night, "Your father, Monsieur Battolo. I see from the files he was a client for many years. He was in ... reinsurance, yes?"

"That's right," Oliver said, signing his name with a steady hand.

"It is a boring business, I think," Dubois mused, a small, philosophical shrug in his shoulders. "Insurance. A world of numbers, of risk, of trying to predict a future that can never be known. It does not seem like a life of ... passion."

Oliver thought of the Noncemeister, of the Hexcelion, of the secret history of the universe he had just begun to uncover. He thought of his father, the quiet cypherpunk who had lived a double life of unimaginable complexity and danger. He looked at the bored, tired face of the bureaucrat in front of him, a man who had spent his life guarding the secrets of the world's elite without ever knowing the real stories they contained.

"You'd be surprised," Oliver said, and handed the tablet back.

Dubois gave a final, formal nod and turned, disappearing back into the building's sterile depths. Oliver and Daniela walked out of the main entrance and into the cold, quiet of the Luxembourg night. The air was sharp and clean, a welcome shock to the system after the recycled, climate-controlled atmosphere of the freeport. Oliver scanned the sparsely populated parking lot, his eyes searching for any sign of Bojan's car. He spotted a dark sedan pulling out of a far corner and watched it turn onto the main road, heading away from them. He was gone. For now.

Their own pre-booked taxi was waiting where they had left it. They slid into the back seat, the soft click of the doors locking behind them a sound of profound and immediate relief. The car pulled away from the curb, leaving the silent, windowless fortress behind them.

For a long time, neither of them spoke. Oliver watched the security lights of the industrial park recede in the rearview mirror. He saw Daniela let out a long, slow breath she seemed to have been holding for the past hour. The rigid, professional posture of his "counsel" melted away, her shoulders slumping slightly as the immense tension of their performance finally left her.

"You were incredible!" Oliver said, in admiration, putting his arm around her shoulders. "An Oscar-worthy performance, if I ever saw one."

She turned to him in the dim light of the car, her eyes searching his.

"More importantly, did you do it?" she whispered, her voice barely audible over the hum of the tires on the asphalt. "Did it work?"

Oliver allowed himself a small, slow smile. He reached out and took her hand, his thumb tracing a gentle circle over her knuckles. "It's done," he said, steadily. "I scheduled the export for next week. If all goes to plan, the paintings will be waiting in a holding facility at JFK's cargo terminal a few hours before our flight from Brussels gets in."

Daniela was quiet for a moment, the sheer, audacious reality of what they had just accomplished sinking in. Then, a slow, brilliant smile spread across her face, a look of pure mischief.

"You know," she said, her voice light and teasing, a perfect counterpoint to the gravity of the night, "when you count the first two Bryce paintings we stole last year, this technically makes it four art heists I've helped you with. I'm starting to think this should be my new career."

Oliver laughed, the first genuine, unrestrained laugh he'd had in what felt like weeks. The sound was a welcome warmth in the cool interior of the taxi. He squeezed Daniela's hand, a silent acknowledgment of the absurd, dangerous, and wonderful partnership they had forged.

The ride back to the airport was short. The industrial park gave way to the airport's perimeter roads, the landscape a dark, empty expanse punctuated by the distant, blinking lights of a control tower. Their taxi pulled up to the departures curb. It was past one in the morning, and the terminal was a ghost town, a vast, brightly lit space of profound emptiness.

"Looks like we'll have the place to ourselves," Oliver said as he paid the driver. He stepped out of the car, the night air cool on his face and turned to help Daniela with her bag.

As he did, his gaze drifted across the deserted roadway to the taxi stand on the far side. Under the harsh, fluorescent glare of the terminal overhang, two solitary figures were waiting. A man and a woman. Even from a distance, there was something familiar in their posture, a sharp, professional stillness that seemed out of place in the weary, late-night quiet of the airport.

He saw the woman say something to the man, who leaned in. She looked up at him and smiled. And then, in a gesture of quiet, easy intimacy, they shared a small, brief kiss.

Oliver froze, his hand still on the taxi door. The world seemed to slow down, the distant hum of the airport's ventilation system the only sound in his ears. It was Nick. And the woman, her face now illuminated for a fraction of a second as she turned toward the approaching headlights of a taxi, was Adele van der Dussen.

"Oliver, what is it?" Daniela asked, her voice pulling him from his stupor.

He didn't answer. Acting on pure, primal instinct, he grabbed her arm. "Get back," he hissed, pulling her with him, out of the direct line of sight from the taxi stand and into the deep shadow of a massive concrete support pillar.

"What are you doing?" she whispered, startled by his sudden, violent urgency.

"Don't look now," he breathed, his heart hammering against his ribs as he peered around the edge of the pillar. "It's them. Nick and Adele. Over there."

He watched as a taxi pulled up to the curb in front of them. The driver got out to help with their luggage. In the dead quiet of the night, Nick's voice, though not loud, carried across the empty space with a stark, preternatural clarity as he spoke to the driver.

"Le Freeport, please. The main cargo entrance."

The taxi doors closed, a soft, definitive thud in the night. The car pulled away, its red taillights disappearing around a curve in the road.

They were gone.

Oliver and Daniela were left alone in the shadows, the silence of the deserted curb now feeling heavy and menacing. He leaned back against the cold concrete of the pillar, his mind a whirlwind of impossible, terrifying calculations.

How? The question was a silent scream in his head. *How could they possibly know?* It couldn't be the cash network; that was the other man's web, Saleem Bhai's boss, the one with the musical voice. This was something else. Their own investigation, running in parallel to his, had somehow, impossibly, led them to the exact same place at the exact same time. He had thought he was a ghost, a man moving through the world's hidden pathways. But he was not the only hunter in the forest. He had won the race to the freeport by a matter of hours, and he hadn't even known he was in a race.

He turned to Daniela, the strategic implications momentarily eclipsed by the more personal, more sordid detail he had witnessed.

"Did you see that?" he said, his voice a low hiss. "They kissed."

"I saw," Daniela replied, her own voice quiet.

Oliver shook his head, a look of genuine disbelief on his face. "I can't believe it. He's married. I've met his wife, Becky. We were at her parents' house last summer." The memory felt like it was from another lifetime, a distant, simpler world where Nick was just his friend, a goofy crypto-bro full of misguided optimism. The man he just saw, allied with a woman like Adele, was a stranger. A harder, colder, much more dangerous version of the man he thought he knew.

Daniela put a hand on his arm, her touch pulling him back to the present, to the immediate and pressing reality of their own situation. "Come on," she said softly. "We have a plane to catch."

He nodded, the larger strategic problems and the smaller, personal betrayals would have to wait. He picked up his bag. Together, they turned and walked toward the bright, empty expanse of the terminal, leaving the quiet, dangerous Luxembourg night behind them.

796757 (July 2)

The air outside the Luxembourg Airport terminal was cool and still, the silence of the late night broken only by the distant hum of a service vehicle. Nick stood at the curb, his hands shoved deep into his pockets, a tight coil of frustration in his gut. Across the empty roadway, the lights of the city were a faint, indifferent glow against the dark horizon. He glanced at his watch. It was past 1 a.m.

Adele stood a few feet away, a picture of serene composure, her attention focused on her phone as she arranged their car for the morning. She seemed completely unbothered by the delay, a fact that only amplified Nick's own agitation.

"Three hours," he said, his voice a low, tight murmur. "Three hours we were sitting in that Frankfurt lounge because of a 10-minute taxiing delay made us miss our Luxair flight. Unbelievable."

Adele looked up from her phone, her dark eyes unreadable in the harsh fluorescent light of the terminal overhang. "It doesn't matter, Nick," she said, her voice calm and even. "A minor logistical snag. It changes nothing."

"It's the principle," he countered, unable to keep the edge from his voice. "The plan was perfect. Clean entry, clean exit. We were supposed to be at the freeport hours ago, not standing out here in the middle of the night."

He was a man who had built a new identity on the promise of relentless competence, and this stupid, mundane friction felt like a personal failure. He had wanted this first major operation with Adele to be flawless, a demonstration of his value. Instead, they had been thwarted by the most banal of obstacles: a delayed flight connection. He felt like an amateur.

Adele turned from the road, her gaze analytical, seeming to dissect the source of his frustration. "The plan is sound, Nick," she said, her voice a calm, steadying force against his agitation. "A few hours' delay is irrelevant. The target isn't going anywhere."

"I just wanted this to go smoothly," he countered, the words coming out with more of an edge than he'd intended. "This is our one shot. If we get there and they just say no ..."

"They can't say no," she said, a small, almost imperceptible smile touching her lips. "That's the point. We are not asking for their permission. We are compelling their compliance."

She leaned forward slightly, her voice becoming low and confidential, a strategist revealing the elegant, brutal beauty of her design. "While you were digging through the Da Silva data, my legal team was digging through something far more archaic and, as it turns out, far more vulnerable: international corporate registries. We found a lapsed administrative filing for the Liffey Trust in a Panamanian database. A single, missed deadline from five years ago. A tiny crack in their perfect, anonymous fortress."

Nick listened, his own frustration forgotten, replaced by a sense of dawning admiration.

"I had the team file an emergency petition in a Swiss court as a concerned party with a potential claim, citing my brother's case," she continued. "The court has granted us what we need: a temporary, but legally binding, order for an immediate right of inspection pending a full hearing. By the time their lawyers untangle the jurisdiction, we'll be gone, and we will have what we came for. We are attacking them through a loophole in their own paperwork."

He stared at her, the sheer, ruthless brilliance of the plan settling over him. This was why she was in charge. While he was focused on the tactical data, she was playing a different, much larger game, one waged in the quiet, dusty corridors of international law. His anxiety evaporated, burned away by the clean, cold fire of her confidence. They were walking in with a key they had forged themselves.

"So," Adele continued, with a soft smile, "you can relax now. Our taxi is almost here and, in a few minutes, we'll have the paintings."

Nick relaxed. He stared at the confident, smiling woman in front of him and couldn't help himself. He took a step towards her and leaned in. The kiss was a brief, shared acknowledgment that they were just moments away from their prize.

As he stepped back, a single taxi finally rounded the curve and headed in their direction, its yellow light a welcome beacon in the deserted, pre-dawn quiet.

While Adele signaled to the driver, Nick's gaze drifted down the long, empty curb. Another taxi had just pulled up about a hundred yards away, by a different terminal entrance. He watched absently as two figures got out – a man and a woman. In the stark, patchy light of the terminal overhang, they were little more than silhouettes. The man turned to pay the driver, and then, in a sudden, urgent movement, he grabbed the woman's arm and pulled her sharply out of sight behind one of the massive concrete support pillars.

Nick frowned, a flicker of professional paranoia cutting through his thoughts. *What was that about?* The movement had been furtive, almost panicked. For a fraction of a second, the man's build, the quick, athletic way he moved, felt vaguely familiar. But the distance was too great, the shadows too deep. He dismissed it. Just a couple having a late-night argument, probably. *You're seeing ghosts, Hernandez,* he thought to himself, turning his attention back to his own mission as their taxi glided to a stop in front of them. The moment was lost.

The driver's side window came down. Nick bent over to look at the taxi driver. "Le Freeport, please. The main cargo entrance."

The taxi ride from the airport was a short, silent journey through a landscape of sleeping industrial giants. Nick stared out at the dark, monolithic warehouses, their fences topped with coils of razor wire that glinted under the harsh security lamps. This was a different world from the polished, public-facing facade of the DoJ. This was the quiet, private architecture of real power.

He could feel Adele's calm, focused energy beside him, a stark contrast to the frantic, hopeful thrumming in his own chest. They were here. They had the key.

The taxi pulled up to a gatehouse that looked more like a border crossing. A guard with a face that was all sharp angles and bored professionalism checked their IDs against a list on a tablet before waving them through. They drove another hundred yards and stopped before the main building, a massive, windowless cube of dark glass and steel that seemed to absorb the surrounding night.

Another guard, this one armed, escorted them through a series of silent, white corridors to the administrative offices. The night manager was seated behind a desk that looked like a single, polished slab of granite. His name tag read: *J. VERRATTI.*

"Good evening," Verratti said, his voice as crisp and sterile as his surroundings. He did not smile. "You are expected."

Adele stepped forward, her movements fluid and confident. Nick watched, a silent and admiring partner, as she took command of the room. She placed a heavy, leather-bound document folder on the desk.

"Good evening, Monsieur Verratti," she said, her voice cool and professional. "As per the preliminary advisory from our counsel, we are here to execute a court order for a temporary, non-destructive inspection of the assets held in Unit 7B, leased by the Liffey Trust."

Verratti took the folder. He didn't just glance at the documents. He examined them. He ran a thumb over the embossed seal of the Swiss court, held the main order up to the light as if checking for a watermark, and read every line of the dense, legal text with a slow, meticulous precision. The silence in the room was absolute, broken only by the soft rustle of paper. Nick felt a bead of sweat trickle down his back.

Finally, Verratti placed the document back on the desk, perfectly aligned with the edge. He gave a single, almost imperceptible nod. "The order is valid."

Nick felt a surge of triumph. It was real. Their gambit had worked.

Verratti turned to his terminal, his fingers moving with a quiet efficiency across the keyboard. He typed in the unit number. Nick watched the man's face, his eyes fixed on the screen, waiting for the final confirmation, for the moment he would turn and lead them to their prize.

Verratti was silent for a long time, his expression a mask of professional neutrality as he scrolled.

At last, he looked up from the screen, his gaze meeting Adele's.

"I see your petition is in order, Madame," he said, his voice flat and devoid of any emotion. "However, I'm afraid you've just missed the primary trustee's representative."

Nick stared at him, the triumphant energy from a moment ago draining out of him, leaving a cold, hollow void. He looked at Adele. Her face was a perfect, unreadable mask, but he saw a fractional widening of her eyes, the only sign that the words had landed with the same devastating impact.

"What representative?" Adele asked, her voice still cool, betraying none of the surprise Nick was feeling. "Who was here?"

Verratti's gaze remained fixed on his terminal. "I am not at liberty to disclose that information, Madame," he said, his tone still perfectly neutral. "Your court order compels me to grant you an inspection of the assets within the unit. It does not, however, supersede the Liffey Trust's primary confidentiality agreement with our facility. I am legally prohibited from disclosing the identity of the trust's principals or their activities to a third party, even one with a court-ordered lien."

The explanation was a masterpiece of polite, bureaucratic stonewalling. It was a perfect, seamless wall, and they had just run into it at full speed.

"When?" Nick heard himself ask, his voice sounding distant. "When were they here?"

Verratti glanced at the digital clock in the corner of his monitor.

"The representative and his counsel concluded their inspection and departed the facility approximately ... 25 minutes ago."

Twenty-five minutes. Nick felt a wave of pure, impotent frustration wash over him. The missed connection. The three hours they had lost. It had been a critical, strategic failure. He risked a glance at Adele. Her face was ashen. For the first time since he'd met her, her perfect, formidable composure had cracked. She was staring at the polished granite floor, her jaw clenched so tightly that a small muscle bunched and twitched beneath her skin. They had been outmaneuvered.

"Fine," Adele said finally, recovering her composure with a visible effort. Her voice was low and tight. "Then we will proceed with our own inspection, as per the court order."

Verratti gave a small, almost apologetic shake of his head. "I am afraid that is no longer possible."

Nick felt a cold dread creep up his spine. "Why not?"

Verratti turned his screen slightly toward them, though the text was too small to read from their distance. "As per the legally executed instructions from the verified representative of the trust, the assets in Unit 7B have been processed for secure transfer and are no longer available for on-site inspection. Client-of-record confirmation was received by Logistics; such instructions execute automatically under our protocol. They are, as of fifteen minutes ago, in the custody of our logistics division, pending international shipment."

The words landed with the quiet finality of a coffin lid closing. Nick stared at Verratti, his mind refusing to process the sheer, absolute totality of their defeat. He felt Adele go completely still beside him. The air in the room, which had been charged with tension, now felt thin and empty.

"Where?" Adele asked, her voice a low, dangerous whisper. "Where were they sent?"

"Madame, I have already explained the facility's confidentiality protocols," Verratti said, his professional composure a final, infuriating shield. "The trust's shipping arrangements are private." He stood, a clear signal that their time was up. "Is there anything else I can assist you with this evening?"

The walk back through the silent, white corridors was a funeral march. They didn't speak. They didn't look at each other. The shared, confident energy they had arrived with had been completely and utterly extinguished, replaced by a cold, shared vacuum of failure.

They were silent in the taxi as it pulled away from the freeport, the fortress of their defeat receding in the darkness behind them. Nick stared out at the passing lights of the highway, replaying the last hour in his mind, searching for the exact moment the game had been lost. It had been lost before they had even arrived. They had been beaten before they even knew they were in a fight.

"A representative for the Liffey Trust," he said finally, the words quiet in the darkness of the car. "Someone with legitimate paperwork. Someone who knew we were coming."

"It was a preemptive strike," Adele said, her voice a flat, hard thing. She was staring straight ahead, her mind already calculating, reprocessing. "He knew our plan. He knew our timing. He knew exactly what move to make to block us completely."

Nick thought of his former coworker. The true believer, the bitcoin maximalist. The grieving son. It was an impossible, absurd thought. And yet, it was the only one that fit.

"Someone with a direct, legal claim as Nate Battolo's heir," he said, the final piece clicking into place.

He looked at Adele. Her face, illuminated by the passing streetlights, was a mask of cold, clear, and absolute resolve.

"Oliver," she said, in a quiet whisper. "It has to be."

CHAPTER 11. JULY 17

797827 (July 8)

The rented Ford Transit van handled like a barge, its suspension groaning as Oliver navigated the afternoon traffic on the BQE. In the rearview mirror, he could see the two massive, wood-crated paintings, securely strapped down, a tangible and surreal testament to their victory. The New York skyline, hazy and familiar, rose to meet them as they approached the Williamsburg Bridge. He felt a profound sense of relief, a quiet, deep exhale after a week of coiled, paranoid tension.

"I still can't get over it," Daniela said from the passenger seat, breaking a long, comfortable silence. She had been staring out the window, a small, tired smile on her face. "Just about half an hour. That's all it was. Half an hour between us walking out and them walking in." She shook her head, the sheer, dumb luck of it still feeling unreal.

"It wasn't luck," Oliver replied, his knuckles white on the steering wheel. "It was a critical failure. On my part. I slipped up – I told Nick about those paintings. I never should have assumed we were the only ones on the trail."

"How could you have, Oliver? There was no way to know they'd figure it out, let alone that they'd be there on the exact same night."

"But they did," he insisted, the analyst in him unable to let go of the near-miss. "He's good. Nick is really good. He's been running his own investigation in parallel the entire time, using his own methods. He found a different way into the same room." The thought was both terrifying and, on some level, impressive. Nick was a serious, formidable hunter – not the old crypto bro from the BlockWaves days.

"And Adele," Daniela said quietly. "They're a team now."

Oliver nodded, the memory of the Pubkey projection episode, confirmed by the brief, intimate kiss he'd witnessed at the airport curb flashing in his mind. The professional alliance was one thing; the personal betrayal was another. "I still can't believe he'd do that to Becky," he murmured.

Daniela just squeezed his arm, a silent acknowledgment.

After another quiet mile, the anxiety of the near-miss began to recede, replaced by the warm, spreading glow of their success.

"Our gambit, though," Daniela said, her voice now lighter, tinged with a sense of genuine wonder. "The Brussels decoy. It actually worked."

"It did," Oliver said, a real smile finally breaking through his fatigue. "I was sure someone would be waiting for us at JFK. Some anonymous face in the crowd, watching. But there was nothing. We were just a couple returning from a boring, week-long European vacation."

"The most nerve-wracking vacation of my life," she laughed. "I think I aged five years just sitting in that hotel room, waiting for a knock on the door."

"But the paintings were just ... sitting there," he said, still marveling at the clean, audacious simplicity of it all. "They actually shipped from the freeport, cleared customs, and were waiting in the bonded warehouse at JFK Cargo. I handed the guy the paperwork from the trust, he checked his system, and he didn't even blink. He just pointed and said, 'They're all yours.'"

He glanced in the rearview mirror again, at the two massive wooden crates that held the final, tangible pieces of his father's secret life. The plan, born of a cryptic clue from a projection and fleshed out in their Chelsea apartment, had seemed like a fantasy, a desperate, impossible long shot. But they had pulled it off. Every step. The flight, the standoff, the bureaucratic heist, the decoy and the final, clean retrieval. It had all worked flawlessly.

He pulled the large van up to the curb in front of the familiar, pre-war facade of his building on 19th and 10th. As he cut the engine, the sudden silence felt profound. The long, tense journey from Luxembourg was over. He was home.

As if on cue, the building's heavy glass door swung open, and Santos emerged, his face breaking into a warm, familiar grin that seemed to radiate a genuine and uncomplicated decency.

"Mr. Oliver! You are back! And you have brought a truck!" he exclaimed, his eyes taking in the oversized vehicle with a look of good-natured surprise.

"Just moving a few things, Santos," Oliver said as he and Daniela got out, the fatigue of the last week settling into his bones. "Could you give us a hand with these? They're ... delicate. And heavy."

Santos, ever the professional, didn't ask a single question. He simply nodded, his gaze assessing the two massive crates in the back of the van. "Of course. We will use the main dolly. No problem at all."

The next few minutes were a blur of coordinated, physical effort. The three of them worked together, carefully maneuvering the first heavy, wood-crated painting out of the van and onto the waiting dolly. Oliver felt the dense, unwieldy weight of the object, a physical manifestation of the secrets he was now carrying. It felt heavier than it should. He and Santos then wrestled the second crate out, placing it carefully beside the first.

"I will have the valet park the van for you in the garage, Mr. Oliver," Santos said, turning and giving a quick, sharp whistle to the young man in a red jacket waiting by the garage entrance. "Carlos! Can you take care of this for Mr. Oliver? Put it in one of the guest spots."

"You're the best, Santos. Thank you," Oliver said, a wave of genuine gratitude washing over him. In a world of shadows and threats, the simple, unquestioning loyalty of a good man felt like a superpower.

Santos just smiled and held the door open as Oliver and Daniela pushed the dolly, now laden with their impossible treasures, into the quiet, familiar lobby.

Upstairs in the apartment, the two massive crates stood in the middle of the living room like monoliths, artifacts from a hidden history that was now their own. The air was thick with a new, palpable energy. With a shared look of almost sacred anticipation, they began the careful, methodical process of unwrapping the first crate.

Oliver used a small crowbar to gently pry open the wooden lid. He slid the massive, bubble-wrapped canvas out with Daniela's help, the sheer weight of it a surprise. He carefully cut away the layers of protective plastic and foam, his heart pounding a slow, heavy rhythm against his ribs. The final layer of tissue paper peeled away.

He froze. A sharp, involuntary intake of breath was the only sound in the room.

He was staring at a face he knew with a chilling, impossible intimacy. It was a haunting, unfinished portrait, the subject rendered with Bryce's signature, raw power, but with a style that was looser, more chaotic than his earlier work. The cascade of golden hair was a maelstrom of light, a vortex of brilliant yellows and whites that seemed to pull the eye inward. The lips were parted slightly, a hint of a cruel, knowing smile. But it was the eyes that held him captive. They were a piercing, hypnotic turquoise, and they seemed to stare directly into his soul with a look of cool, enigmatic and seductive power.

It was Anariadne.

He had seen her rendered in the stark, comic-book ink of Bryce's Legend of Atlantis series, a stylized villainess leading the hero astray. He had felt her presence in the blue, disorienting mist of his own projections, the entity that had whispered poison into his ear during the darkest days of his despair. But this ... this was different. This was her rendered in rich, vibrant oil by the hand of a man who had died years ago, a man who couldn't possibly have known her name.

"Babe, what is it?" Daniela asked, her voice a soft note of concern. She came to stand beside him, and her own breath caught in her throat. "Oh my God," she whispered, her gaze fixed on the canvas. "She's ... beautiful. But ... who is she?"

Oliver couldn't answer. He just stared, his mind a whirlwind of colliding realities. The goddess from his private hell, the allegorical figure from a comic book, was here, a physical object in his living room. The thought was a stunning, terrifying violation of every rule of reality he thought he knew.

Daniela turned from the painting to look at his face, at the pale, shocked expression, the hard line of his jaw. Her eyes, full of a deep and searching empathy, moved from his face back to the portrait. He saw the moment of recognition click into place in her mind, a quiet, horrified dawning.

"It's her, isn't it?" she said, her voice now a soft, almost fearful whisper. "The one from your projections. Anariadne."

Her saying the name out loud seemed to break the spell. Oliver finally turned from the painting to look at her, a long, slow breath escaping his lungs. He gave her a small, tight nod.

"Yeah," he said, his voice a little hoarse. "That's her."

He saw the fear in her eyes, the worry that this ghost from his past had just materialized to haunt him again. He reached out and took her hand, his grip firm and reassuring.

"It's okay," he said, and the words, as he spoke them, felt true. "Seeing her here ... it's a shock. But that's all it is. She's in the past, Daniela. Trapped in a comic book, and on a 30-year-old unfinished painting. That's where she belongs. She has no power over me."

He felt her hand squeeze his hand, a silent, firm pressure that was all the confirmation he needed. He saw the tension in her expression soften, replaced by a quiet, shared resolve. The unwelcome goddess had been faced. Together, they were ready to move on.

With the unsettling portrait of Anariadne now leaning against the wall, a silent, unwelcome guest in their apartment, Oliver turned his attention to the second, final crate. The initial, sacred sense of anticipation was gone, replaced by a feeling of dread. If the fourth painting held a demon from his past, what impossible secret could the fifth one contain?

He worked with a dazed, mechanical urgency, prying open the wooden lid and sliding the final canvas out with Daniela's help. He cut through the layers of protective wrapping, the slice of the utility knife a sharp, tearing sound in the quiet room. The last sheet of tissue paper fell away.

It was not a portrait. It was a work of pure, cosmic geometry, a schematic of a universe he was only just beginning to understand. At its center was the familiar, intricate pattern of a Hexcelion, its six spiraling arms rendered in Bryce's signature, powerful brushstrokes. But it was ... wrong. Distorted. The six arms seemed to strain outward, pulling away from the two-dimensional plane of the canvas. And extending from the central nexus were three more spirals, faint and ghostly, sketched in with crude, uncertain lines of charcoal. They were drawn with a clumsy, desperate attempt at perspective, as if the artist was trying to render a three-dimensional object on a two-dimensional surface and had failed.

The image was a jolt to his memory, a key turning a lock deep in his subconscious. A projection from just over a week ago came rushing back with a stunning, horrifying clarity: his father, Nate, standing in the cramped, dusty living room of Jonathan Bryce's small house in Forest Hills. He remembered the look on the old painter's face, a mixture of torment and awe, as he gestured toward an unfinished canvas, the very one Oliver was now staring at.

"The voices ..." Bryce's voice echoed in his memory, a ghost in his own mind. *"They asked for something impossible. It's ... a machine. They asked me to bend space. To paint time itself."*

Oliver stared at the incomplete, nine-armed spiral on the canvas. *A machine to bend space and time.* The old man's mad, prophetic words were no longer the ramblings of a tormented artist. They were a design document. This wasn't just a painting. It was a blueprint for a machine that operated on principles he couldn't begin to comprehend. And Bryce, a man with no formal training, had been driven to the brink of madness trying to render it nearly thirty years ago. The fifth painting wasn't unfinished because Bryce had run out of time; it was unfinished because it was impossible.

The awe of the moment, the sheer, impossible reality of the two canvases, slowly gave way to the practical urgency of their mission. This was it. The final step. After the heist, the decoy, and the near-miss, the prize was finally within reach.

"Okay," Oliver said, his voice charged with a new, triumphant energy as he turned away from the paintings. "Let's see what they're really hiding."

He went to the desk, the same one his father had used for years, and pulled open the top drawer. Pushed to the back, behind a tangle of old charging cables and pens, was the familiar, heavy-duty ultraviolet flashlight. He clicked it on, its purple beam a familiar, welcome sight, and walked back to the paintings, his heart pounding with the expectation of a final, glorious revelation. Daniela switched off the main living room lights, plunging the room into a semi-darkness that made the two canvases seem to float in the space.

He started with Anariadne. He held the flashlight close to the canvas, bathing the goddess's haunting face in the eerie, violet glow. The blacklight revealed the rich, chaotic textures of Bryce's brushstrokes, the subtle layers of oil and pigment, the almost violent energy embedded in the paint. He meticulously scanned every inch of it – her golden, swirling hair, the cold turquoise of her eyes, the cruel hint of a smile on her lips.

Nothing.

A knot of confusion tightened in his stomach. He moved to the second painting, the incomplete, Hexcelion-like shape, his hope still flickering. He traced every powerful, painted line of the central spiral, every faint, ghostly sketch of the three impossible, extra-dimensional arms. He swept the beam over the entire canvas, his breath held tight in his chest, waiting for the familiar, glowing script to ignite in the darkness.

Again, nothing. The paint remained inert. The canvas was just a canvas. There were no hidden words.

He lowered the flashlight, its purple beam falling to the floor.

"I don't understand," Daniela said, her voice a quiet, confused whisper in the dark room. "We saw them on the other two. They lit up right away. What's wrong?"

Oliver just stared at the two inscrutable paintings, the weight of their impossible journey pressing down on him. The heist, the chase, the victory – did it all mean nothing?

"They're not here," he said, his voice flat and defeated. "The seed words ... they're just not here."

He switched the living room lights back on, the harsh yellow glare a brutal contrast to the soft, hopeful darkness of a moment before. He tossed the UV flashlight onto the armchair, the heavy thud echoing the feeling in his own gut. He sank onto the sofa, the energy that had propelled him across the world for the past week completely gone, leaving him feeling hollowed out.

Daniela came and sat beside him, her presence a quiet, supportive warmth in the suddenly cold room. "Maybe we were wrong," she said softly. "Maybe Christiaan only ever used the first two paintings."

Oliver shook his head, not in disagreement, but with a kind of weary, frustrated certainty. "No," he said. "The first two Bryces had thirty-one seed words hidden in them. A valid set has to be multiples of 12 or 24 across however many wallets. We're missing pieces – he wouldn't stop on 31. And Satoshi's email. He mentioned the fifth painting. My dad knew about it. Christiaan hid the keys here. He had to have."

He looked up from the floor and met her gaze, his own eyes a mixture of exhaustion and a single, stubborn, flickering spark of resolve.

"He found a different way to hide them this time," Oliver said, his voice growing stronger, the analyst in him taking over from the defeated son. "He used a different method. Invisible ink was too simple, too obvious. Already used on the second and third paintings. He knew people would be looking."

He stood and walked back to the two canvases, no longer seeing them as a testament to his failure, but as a new, more complex and more personal challenge from his father's old world.

"They're in there, Daniela," he said, his voice a quiet, firm promise. "I don't know how. But I'm going to find them."

797845 (July 8)

The luxurious grandeur of the Baccarat Hotel had been replaced by the clean, sharp scent of a different kind of grandeur – ozone and old money. Adele's Tribeca apartment was less a home and more a fortress, a minimalist masterpiece of poured concrete, dark wood, and floor-to-ceiling windows that offered a commanding, panoramic view of the Hudson. After coming back to New York, Nick had insisted they relocate from the conspicuous luxury of the hotel to this more permanent, more defensible position. It was a war room now, the massive, custom-built dining table serving as their central command, covered in a constellation of laptops, tablets and empty coffee cups.

For a week, the view of the river had been his only respite. The initial, volcanic rage from their return from Luxembourg had cooled, hardening into something colder, denser – and far more dangerous. It was resolve. He looked across the room, at the large whiteboard they had wheeled in, now covered in a spiderweb of names, dates, and transaction hashes – a chaotic map of a dead man's secret life.

Adele sat at the head of the table, a laptop open in front of her, her expression a mask of intense, surgical focus. The silence in the room was the charged, humming quiet of a high-frequency trading floor, a space where millions of data points were being processed in search of a single, exploitable signal.

"Anything?" he asked, his voice low and gravelly, raw from too much coffee and too little sleep.

She looked up from the screen, her dark eyes clear and analytical. "The legal challenge to the transfer is a dead end," she said, her tone flat and devoid of emotion. "The paperwork was ironclad. Swiss courts are not known for their ... flexibility. We were beaten on procedure. It will not happen again."

"So, we're done chasing the paintings," Nick said. It wasn't a question. It was the conclusion they had arrived at three days ago, a strategic pivot born of their humiliating defeat. "We chase the man."

"We build a complete picture of the man," she corrected, her precision a quiet rebuke of his cruder language. "We find his patterns, his associates, his pressure points. He outmaneuvered us because he knew our objective. We will defeat him because we will know *him*. What have you found?"

Nick walked over to his own laptop, which was open at the far end of the table. He gestured to the screen, which was filled with spreadsheets and scanned corporate documents. "The off-chain stuff is where he was hiding," he said, a note of grudging respect in his voice. "I spent the last five days pulling every piece of professional history I could find on Nate Battolo from his two decades at WilcoxRe. Travel logs, expense reports, corporate calendars. I had to pay a data broker in Manila a small fortune for access to their archives, but it was worth it."

He pointed to a highlighted column on a spreadsheet. "He was a creature of habit. New York, London, Bermuda, Budapest, Zurich. The standard circuit for a reinsurance executive. It's all there, clean and predictable. Except for this."

He clicked on a new tab, which displayed a map of the world, a series of red pins clustered in one specific, inexplicable location.

"India," he said. "Seven times in ten years. Always for two weeks or less. Always booked as a 'client-facing strategy offsite.' But there are no expense reports. No hotel receipts. No client names. WilcoxRe has no significant business in that part of India. He was going there for something else. Something personal."

Adele stood and walked over, her eyes fixed on the map. "Where, specifically?"

"A small, regional airport near Hyderabad, in south India," Nick said. "The closest major point of interest is a spiritual retreat in the mountains. It's a well-known ashram. Guru Brahma's place."

"A spiritual retreat," Adele said, the words a quiet dismissal. "It seems ... out of character for a man like Dev_akshar."

"I agree," Nick said. "It feels like a dead end, a piece that doesn't fit the puzzle. But it's the only anomaly I've found in his entire professional life. He was a ghost on the company dime." He sighed, running a hand over his face. "The digital side is even colder. I've been scouring the old cypherpunk mailing lists, the forum archives from back in the day, looking for any new lead on his associates. It's like he vanished from the face of the earth after 2013. It's just a clean, perfect, infuriating silence."

He turned his attention back to the screen. The digital side was the real long shot, a search for a single, forgotten breadcrumb in a decade-old digital forest. He minimized the WilcoxRe spreadsheets and brought up his browser, the screen filled with the stark, text-only interface of an archived cypherpunk mailing list from the early 2010s. For days, he had been manually scrolling through these dense, technical discussions, the digital equivalent of panning for gold in a river of mud.

Adele was silent, letting him work. The only sounds in the room were the soft, rhythmic clicks of his trackpad and the distant, mournful cry of a ferry horn from the river below. He scrolled past another heated argument about block size limits and clicked on a side thread, this one less about code and more about philosophy, titled "Austrian Economics & Proof-of-Work."

And then he saw it.

It was just a name, attached to a single, thoughtful question in the middle of a long, abstract discussion.

```
> ... this presupposes that the 'cost' of production
is purely electrical. But from a Misesian standpoint,
```

how do we account for the time-preference of the miners themselves? Is the difficulty adjustment not, in effect, a form of centrally planned price-fixing on the value of time?

The post was signed: *Rafael Forlan, Montevideo.*

The name hung there, a small, solid piece of data in a sea of anonymous handles. He felt a familiar, electric jolt, the hunter's instinct that told him he was onto something. He opened a new browser tab, his fingers flying across the keyboard.

"I might have something," he said, his voice low and focused. "A new associate. Maybe. Rafael Forlan. Wealthy early bitcoiner. From Uruguay. He was on a side thread with Dev_akshar in 2013, talking about economics."

"Does he have a connection to Nate?" Adele asked, her voice sharp with interest.

"I don't know yet," Nick replied, his mind racing. He needed to bridge the gap between Nate's physical world and Dev_akshar's digital one. He looked at the map still open on his other screen, at the cluster of red pins over the ashram in Andhra Pradesh. A hunch, born of frustration and countless dead ends, sparked in his mind. *Connect the anomalies.*

He opened another search tab. His fingers typed: "Rafael Forlan" India.

He hit enter.

The results were instantaneous and definitive. The first hit was a press release from a charitable foundation, dated 2015, listing major international benefactors. And there it was, in black and white: *Rafael Forlan, Montevideo, for his generous and ongoing support of the Guru Brahma Ashram and its educational initiatives.*

Nick leaned back in his chair, a slow, cold smile spreading across his face. It wasn't the final answer, but it was a connection. A real, tangible link between the two separate, ghost-like trails he had been following.

"Well, well, well," he said, his voice a quiet, triumphant whisper. He turned to Adele, the exhaustion from the past week gone, replaced by the clean, sharp energy of the hunt. "It seems our spiritual recluse, Mr. Battolo, had a very wealthy pen pal in South America."

Adele was silent for a long moment, her eyes fixed on the map, on the thin, improbable line that now connected a reinsurance executive's secret life in New York to a mountain in India and a wealthy bitcoiner in Uruguay.

"Well, it's a link of some sort," she said finally. "But it's not a destination. It's a possible connection without a purpose. Why would Nate Battolo be in contact with this man? We're still missing the final piece. We have a potential *who*, but we don't have the *why* or the *when*."

Nick knew she was right. The frustration of the last week began to creep back in. They had a ghost and his pen pal, but nothing more. They were stuck, orbiting a mystery without a clear point of entry. He sank back into his chair, his gaze drifting to the whiteboard, at the long, alphanumeric string of the wallet address he had written there days ago. It was the source, the origin of the entire mystery.

"There is one other piece we have," he said, almost to himself. "One thing that came directly from the wallet itself."

He turned back to his laptop and pulled up the case file from the DoJ, clicking on the transaction details from the 24-bitcoin transfer on December 15th last year that had first alerted them. He navigated to the embedded metadata, the small, cryptic message left behind on the blockchain.

```
OP_RETURN: Obelisk, 18 July. It has happened.
```

He had stared at this line a hundred times over the last few months. It was meaningless, a piece of cryptographic noise. *But what if it wasn't just noise*, Nick thought to himself, a wild theory beginning to form in his mind. *What if it was noise with a geographical context?* Maybe these weren't just random words. Maybe these were words meant to be looked at through a new lens, the one Rafael Forlan had just provided.

His fingers moved to the keyboard. He opened a new search tab. He didn't type in the whole phrase. He started with the two most concrete, most unusual words.

He typed: *Obelisk Montevideo.*

He hit enter.

The results were immediate and absolute. The first hit was a Wikipedia page, complete with a stark, clear photograph: the *Obelisco a los Constituyentes de 1830*. He clicked the link, his eyes scanning the page. The monument, he read, was located at the intersection of two of the city's main boulevards.

One of them was *Avenida 18 de Julio*.

The words on the screen seemed to lift off the page, rearranging themselves in his mind. The date. The location. The cryptic message wasn't a riddle. It was an address. An appointment.

He leaned back, a slow, cold smile spreading across his face. He turned from his screen to look at Adele, the exhaustion from the past week gone, replaced by a look of pure, hard, and absolute certainty. He was a hunter, and he had just acquired the exact date and coordinates of his prey.

"I've got it," he said, his voice a quiet, dangerous whisper. "I know where he's going to be. And I know when."

797970 (July 9)

Oliver sat in his father's armchair, the phone pressed to his ear, listening to the familiar, distant ringing. He had been putting off this call for a couple of weeks, a low-grade anxiety simmering on the back burner of his mind. The chaos of Luxembourg and the successful heist had pushed it aside, but now, in the quiet of a Sunday morning, the worry about his mother had returned.

"Oliver! Honey, it's so good to hear your voice!" Diane's cheerful greeting was a welcome balm, a sound of pure, uncomplicated normalcy.

"Hey, Mom. How are you doing?" he asked, a genuine warmth in his own voice.

"Oh, I'm wonderful, sweetheart. Busy, busy, busy, you know how it is. The book is practically writing itself! But what about you? I feel like I haven't spoken to you in ages."

"I know, it's been a crazy couple of weeks," he said, leaning back in the chair. "Daniela and I actually just got back from a trip yesterday. We spent a week in Brussels."

He heard a small, happy gasp on the other end of the line. "Brussels! How wonderful! And with Daniela?" There was a gentle, knowing smile in her voice that he could hear as clearly as if she were in the room with him. "So, does this mean ... are you two officially back on track?"

"Yeah, Mom," he said, a small, involuntary smile spreading across his own face. "We're back on track. It's ... it's really good."

"Oh, I am so happy to hear that, honey. I always knew she was the right one for you. You two just have that ... spark. I knew you'd figure it out." She sounded genuinely thrilled, and for a moment, the weight of the secrets, the paintings, the concern about her impossible book deal, replaced by the simple, grounding pleasure of making his mother happy. The call felt normal, easy. A conversation between a mother and her son, not a covert intelligence-gathering mission.

"So, what about you, Mom?" he asked, pivoting the conversation gently to the reason he called her. "You said the book is going well. How are things with your publisher? Alexander, was it?"

He heard her let out a happy, almost girlish sigh on the other end of the line. "Oh, Oliver, it's more than just going well. It's ... it's a dream. Alexander is an incredible, brilliant man. He sees something in my writing I never even knew was there. It's like he's unlocked a part of me that's been dormant for years."

Oliver's smile tightened almost imperceptibly at the edges. He stayed silent.

"It's more than just the book, honey," she continued, her voice now a conspiratorial, excited whisper. "Things have been moving very fast. We've decided that as soon as the manuscript is finished in a few months, I'm going to be moving out to Los Angeles to be with him. We're officially a couple, Oliver. Can you believe it?"

The warmth that had filled the apartment just moments before evaporated, replaced by a sudden, sickening cold. The simple, normal phone call was over. His worst fears were confirmed. He felt a wave of pure, cold dread wash over him as an eerie premonition took shape in his mind. This wasn't a whirlwind romance. This was an accelerated plan to isolate her, to move her 3,000 miles away from her family, from her support system, from him. He had a sudden, vivid image of a spider patiently and methodically wrapping its prey in silk.

He had to force the next words out, making them sound cheerful, making them sound normal. His voice felt like ash in his mouth.

"Wow, Mom. That's ... that's huge news. I'm ... I'm really happy for you. If he makes you happy, then that's all that matters. Anyway ... that's just great, Mom," he said again, the words feeling foreign and brittle. "I have to run, but we'll talk soon, okay? I love you."

"I love you too, sweetheart! Talk soon!"

He heard the cheerful click as she hung up. Oliver lowered the phone from his ear, his hand trembling slightly. He stared at the blank screen, the warmth from their earlier conversation now a distant, mocking memory. Diane was thrilled. He was terrified.

The moment the connection was severed, the mask of the dutiful son fell away, and the full, crushing weight of what he'd just heard crashed down on him. He stood up from the armchair and began to pace the living room, a hot, sick feeling of guilt and self-recrimination churning in his gut.

For months, he had been the hero of his own epic, a man on a mystical quest, chasing paintings across continents, battling projections and decoding the secrets of the universe. He had been so consumed by the grand, cosmic scale of his father's game that he had completely and utterly neglected the real, tangible and far more insidious game being played on his own family. He had been looking up at the stars while a predator was quietly slipping in through the back door.

The thought was a source of profound, sickening shame. He knew the name of the publishing house. He had a name for the man. And he had done nothing.

He stopped pacing, his eyes locking onto his laptop sitting on the desk. The vague, low-grade anxiety he had been feeling for weeks had now crystallized into a new, urgent, intensely personal mission. The hunt for the wallets could wait. This could not.

He walked over to the desk, sat down and flipped open the screen. His fingers moved to the keyboard, a new, cold fire of purpose burning through him. It was time to find out who Alexander and the Da Silva Publishing Group really were.

798197 (July 10)

The only light in the apartment came from the stark, white glow of Oliver's laptop, casting long, distorted shadows across the living room. It was past 10:30 p.m. In the bedroom, Daniela was asleep, a quiet and peaceful presence he could just barely sense. But here, in the silent, digital trenches, there was no peace. There was only the low hum of the computer and the cold, hard wall he had been running into for the past 24 hours.

A constellation of empty coffee cups littered the surface of his father's old mahogany desk, a testament to a long and fruitless siege. Since the call with his mother yesterday afternoon, a cold, gnawing urgency had taken hold of him. The trip to Montevideo loomed, just eight days away, a non-negotiable appointment with destiny. But he couldn't leave, couldn't focus on the cosmic scale of his own quest, not while this new, more intimate threat was closing in on his family.

He stared at the screen, at the labyrinthine maze of corporate filings he had been tracing all day. The Da Silva Publishing Group was a ghost, a professionally constructed mirage. It existed on paper as a Delaware LLC, which was owned by another LLC in Wyoming, which was in turn owned by an anonymous holding company registered in the Cayman Islands. It was a perfect, seamless and utterly infuriating dead end. "Alexander" was even less substantial; his bare-bones LinkedIn profile was a masterclass in corporate anonymity, a digital ghost with no past and no connections.

He leaned back in his chair, the frustration a bitter, metallic taste in his mouth. He felt out of his depth. He thought of Nick, of the methodical, relentless way he would have approached this problem. Nick would have had the resources, the data brokers, the contacts. He would have cracked this shell of anonymity in hours, not days. But Nick was the enemy now, and Oliver was alone, armed with a UV flashlight and a connection to the cosmos, tools that were utterly useless against a wall of international corporate law. He felt powerless and with every passing hour, the feeling was curdling into a quiet, simmering rage.

He slammed the laptop shut, the sharp clap a small, violent punctuation mark on a day of grinding futility. It was useless. He pushed back from the desk and walked to the center of the living room, the city lights a distant, indifferent glitter through the massive windows. He had been a fool to think he could fight this battle on their terms. He wasn't a detective. His tools weren't data brokers and corporate registries; they were whispers and visions, echoes from a world that operated on a different logic entirely.

He turned and looked at his father's armchair. It stood in the corner, a silent, waiting throne. He had been avoiding it, trying to solve this new puzzle with the skills of his old life. But his old life was over. It was time to use the tools of his new one.

He walked over, sank into the worn leather, and closed his eyes, letting the familiar scent of old books wash over him. He didn't try to force the projection. He simply let go, surrendering to the quiet darkness behind his eyes, extending a silent, formless call for a guide.

"My, my, my," a familiar, sing-song voice chirped, startlingly close. "Look at the little tiger, trying to hunt a whale with a butter knife."

Oliver's eyes snapped open. He was still in the armchair, in his apartment, but he was not alone. The Noncemeister was perched on the armrest, his legs crossed, looking at the darkened laptop on the desk with an expression of profound, theatrical pity.

"It's a puzzle in absolute reality, Batue," he chided, his voice a playful, mocking singsong. "You are trying to solve it in the phenomenal, with your little box of blinking lights. That is a mundane tool for a mundane world. You are not in that world anymore."

"I'm stuck," Oliver said, the words a simple, honest admission. "I don't know who this man is, and I don't know how to find him."

The Noncemeister hopped off the armrest and did a small, jaunty skip in the middle of the room. "Oh, but you do," he said, a mischievous twinkle in his deep, purple eyes. "You do know a man. And he lives in a special room I have taken you to many a times. You have simply forgotten to use it."

The words landed with the force of a revelation. The *Camara del Tiempo*. In the chaos of the last few months, the trips to Montevideo and India, his own personal rock-bottom in Washington Square Park, in the joy of winning back

Daniela, in the adrenaline of the heist and the panic of his mother's call, he had completely forgotten the most powerful tool he possessed. Pittamiglio himself had told him the last time they met that he could access the room at any time of his choosing. He had been trying to find the answer in the wrong reality.

"You are ready to ask the right questions now, Batlu," the Noncemeister said, his voice now a low, conspiratorial whisper. He raised a single, gloved hand. "So, away we go!"

He snapped his fingers.

The familiar, comfortable reality of the Chelsea apartment did not fade or dissolve. It shattered. The world fractured into a million pieces of shimmering, purple-black glass, and Oliver felt himself pulled through the void. The sensation lasted only a second, and then the chaos reassembled itself into a new, ancient silence. He was standing on a cold, stone floor, the air thick with the scent of iodine and the distant, rhythmic crash of waves. He was back in the dark, silent chamber of Esteban Pittamiglio.

A figure emerged from the shadows with a slow, deliberate grace. He was a tall, elegant man dressed in the formal attire of the early twentieth century. His eyes, even in the dim light, seemed to hold a deep and ancient wisdom.

"Señor Battolo," the man said, in a smooth, pleasant voice. "It is a pleasure to see you again. Or perhaps, it is a pleasure for you to see me for the second time in this particular form."

"Esteban Pittamiglio," Oliver breathed, the name feeling like an invocation.

"Indeed," Pittamiglio replied with a small, formal bow of his head. "I understand you have recently made the acquaintance of my great-grandson, Luis. A talented boy, though he shares his great-uncle Humberto's penchant for ... melodrama. And you of course want to understand the secrets of silver."

The silver sea with Mom's book floating through it. Oliver's head reeled. Pittamiglio already knew why he was here. "How ... how do you know what's on my mind?" He asked.

"This chamber is a place of pure intention, Señor Battolo," Pittamiglio explained, a hint of a smile on his lips. "Your questions arrive long before you do. You are concerned for your mother. You sense a web being woven, but you cannot see the spider. Permit me to show you."

He gestured with an open palm toward the center of the dark room. The space before them began to shimmer, the darkness coalescing into a vibrant, sun-drenched vision. Oliver saw his mother, Diane, standing in a beautiful, immaculate garden, her face radiant with a happiness he hadn't seen in years. A handsome, charismatic man – presumably Alexander – walked toward her, holding a beautifully bound manuscript.

As his mother reached out and took the book, her fingers brushing against Alexander's, Oliver watched in horror as a network of shimmering, almost invisible silver threads erupted from the pages. They moved with a sinister, serpentine purpose, like liquid mercury. They wrapped around her wrists first, then her arms, weaving a delicate, glittering cocoon. As the web grew, the brilliant sunlight of the garden began to dim, the vibrant colors of the flowers turning to a dull, muted gray.

The vision zoomed out with dizzying speed. Oliver followed the shimmering silver threads as they stretched from his mother across a vast, dark landscape. They converged on a single, dark point pulsing with a faint, malevolent light: a massive, anatomical heart made of pure, liquid silver. It beat with a slow, heavy, metallic rhythm, and it was the source of all the threads.

The vision shifted. He was now looking at a scene from over 10 years ago – the chaotic back room of the MixMarket operation. He saw the three partners clearly, their faces illuminated by the glow of a dozen computer monitors. A young, intense Christiaan van der Dussen was arguing passionately, gesturing at a screen filled with code. Gyorgy Lorincz, older and more world-weary, was shaking his head in disagreement. And there, standing between them, acting as a calm, mediating force, was his own father, Nate Battolo.

And hovering behind them all, a ghostly, menacing figure made of pure, liquid silver: the same entity he had witnessed in the projection episode in the silver sea. The one he had connected with the character in the other projection episode with Saleem Bhai, the one with the musical, sing-song voice and the unsettling "né" tic. Oliver watched, with a sickening clarity, as new silver threads emerged from the silver man and connected directly to the heart of the MixMarket operation on the screen in front of the three partners. The threads from his mother, the threads from the long-dead MixMarket, all originated from the same source.

The vision dissolved, and Oliver was left floating in the dark chamber with Pittamiglio, who had not moved.

"You see now, Señor Battolo," the alchemist's voice echoed around him. "The spider and the web are one. The heart of the matter is the silver itself."

Pittamiglio then delivered a resonant incantation in the ancient, mythical language Oliver now recognized as Atlantean.

"In Argentum, uttarum. Ex Argento satye apparait."

The words hung in the air, a final, crucial clue. In this chamber, their meaning was crystal clear to him. *In silver, the answer. From silver, the truth appears.*

Da Silva.

Whoever he was, he was the silver man. He had to be.

The vision of the silver man and the chaotic back room of the MixMarket operation dissolved, the silver threads retracting back into the darkness, leaving Oliver floating in the quiet, ancient chamber with Pittamiglio. The final, cryptic Atlantean phrase still echoed in his mind, and he was struck by a profound and unsettling realization. He had understood it. Not through translation or intellectual effort, but with a deep, intuitive clarity, as if it were his native tongue.

He looked at the elegant, spectral figure of the alchemist, who was watching him with a look of quiet, knowing patience.

"I understood you," Oliver said, the words a simple statement of a complex, impossible fact. "Your final words. Atlantean. I understood them."

Pittamiglio gave a small, almost imperceptible nod. "Of course, you did, Señor Battolo. It is one of the languages of this chamber."

"My friend ... your great-grandson, Luis," Oliver began, trying to connect the threads of his own past with the ancient man standing before him. "He told me about it. He said you had studied it, that you were one of the few who could decipher the old texts."

"Luis is a good boy," Pittamiglio said, a hint of a fond smile on his lips. "He has the soul of an artist, not an alchemist. He sees the beauty of the language, its poetic form. But he does not yet understand its true function."

"And what is that?" Oliver asked, leaning forward, a student before his master.

"It is not a language of words, Señor Battolo," Pittamiglio explained. "It is a language of pure concept, of direct intention. It is the native tongue of the space between realities. You do not learn it. You remember it."

"If it is a language of pure concept," Oliver said, his mind racing to connect the pieces, "then who were its speakers? Who were the Atlanteans?"

Pittamiglio's expression softened, a look of profound, almost sad, wisdom in his ancient eyes. "That is a question with a difficult answer, Señor Battolo. Because they are not a people who *were*. They are a people who *are*."

He gestured to the empty space of the chamber, as if indicating a vast, unseen landscape. "You believe you inhabit a single, solid reality. A single, unbroken line of history. But that is an illusion, a trick of the conscious mind, which craves simplicity. The truth is far more ... symphonic."

He began to walk slowly around Oliver, his voice a low, hypnotic lecture. "Imagine a great tapestry, woven with an infinite number of threads. Each thread is a complete and total reality, a universe unto itself, with its own history, its own choices, its own version of you. They are parallel dimensions, each one as real as your own, running alongside it, sometimes touching, sometimes diverging."

Oliver listened, the concept feeling both utterly alien and strangely familiar, an echo of the Bryce comics, but spoken with the absolute authority of a man who had seen it for himself.

"The people you call the Atlanteans," Pittamiglio continued, "are not from your thread. They are a people who learned to exist *between* the threads, in the space where all realities are born. They do not experience time as a line, but as a single, eternally present moment."

"So, the voices ..." Oliver began, the implication dawning on him. "The ones Bryce heard. The one in my own head. They're ... leaking through? From another dimension?"

"A leak is a chaotic thing, Señor Battolo. A broken pipe," Pittamiglio corrected gently. "This is not chaos. It is a design. A structure. These infinite realities, these parallel threads, they do not simply exist at random. They all spring from a single, common origin." He stopped pacing and turned to face Oliver, his gaze intense. "They are born from what the old texts call the Source Foundations."

"Source Foundations," Oliver repeated, the words feeling ancient and heavy with a meaning he couldn't yet grasp. "What are they?"

Pittamiglio's gaze seemed to turn inward, as if he were looking at the very architecture of existence. "They are not grand, cosmic events, Señor Battolo," he said, his voice a low, instructional murmur. "They are not the births of stars or the deaths of kings. They are ... moments. Infinitesimally small, yet infinitely powerful. Moments of pure, unwritten potential."

He raised a single, elegant finger, as if to emphasize his point.

"Consider a great composer," he began, his voice painting a picture in the dark, silent chamber. "He is sitting at his piano, his hands hovering over the keys, a blank score before him. He is at a crossroads in his symphony. The next note he chooses will define the entire subsequent movement. It will determine whether the piece becomes a tragedy or a triumph, a dirge or an anthem."

Oliver listened, transfixed.

"In one reality," Pittamiglio continued, his voice a soft, hypnotic current, "his finger falls upon a C-sharp. This single choice sends the melody down a dark and melancholic path, leading to a symphony that will be remembered for its profound sorrow. In this world, the composer dies in obscurity, his work celebrated only after his death."

He paused, letting the image settle in Oliver's mind.

"But in another reality," he said, his tone shifting almost imperceptibly, "his hand shifts by a fraction of an inch, and his finger falls instead upon a D-natural. A single, different vibration. This note sends the melody soaring, creating a symphony of such triumphant joy that it makes him a living legend. He marries a wealthy patron, has three children, and lives to a ripe old age, celebrated and content."

He turned to face Oliver, his ancient eyes filled with a look of profound, almost sorrowful, understanding.

"Two entirely different lives. Two separate, branching universes, complete with their own histories, their own joys, their own children who go on to have children of their own. And the cause? Not a grand design. Not a twist of fate. But the simple, physical reality of a single finger landing on a single key."

"That single, precise moment of contact," Pittamiglio concluded, his voice a quiet, reverent whisper, "*that* is a Source Foundation."

"So, these … these other worlds," Oliver began, his voice a low and awestruck, "they're completely separate? We can never know them?"

"Separate, but not silent, Señor Battolo," Pittamiglio corrected, his tone that of a professor clarifying a subtle but crucial point. "The threads of the tapestry are distinct, but they vibrate. And sometimes, when two threads are in perfect alignment, a … sympathetic resonance can occur."

He paused, searching for the right words, for a metaphor that could bridge the gap between his reality and Oliver's. "Think of two finely tuned violins, sitting in the same room. If you pluck a string on one, the corresponding string on the other will begin to hum, ever so faintly, on its own. It has not been touched, but it has received the vibration. It is the same with consciousness."

Oliver's mind reeled, a dozen disparate, inexplicable moments from his own life suddenly snapping into a single, coherent picture. The moments of strange, unearned insight. The mental fractures. The sudden, fluent grasp of complex psychological concepts he'd never studied. The flashes of strategic brilliance that seemed to come from nowhere. It wasn't just intuition. It was … resonance.

"Most people are not tuned to the right frequency," Pittamiglio continued. "Their conscious minds are too loud, too cluttered with the noise of their own reality. But for a rare few – a sensitive artist, a tormented visionary, a boy with a mind open to the cosmos – the barrier is thinner. They can, in moments of quiet inspiration or profound desperation, receive these … transmissions of spirit. A flash of a skill they never learned. A memory of a life they never lived. A solution to a problem their other self, in another reality, has already solved."

He saw the look of dawning comprehension on Oliver's face and gave a small, approving nod. "You understand. You have felt these echoes yourself."

Pittamiglio's expression then shifted, becoming even more serious, more profound. He was moving from the introductory lecture to the core, secret doctrine.

"But to merely receive these faint echoes is the gift of the sensitive," he said, his voice dropping to a near whisper. "The true masters, the ones who have achieved a perfect alignment with the Source Foundations … they do not simply listen for the echo. They learn to become the music itself."

He turned to face Oliver, his ancient eyes locking onto his, conveying the final, impossible truth.

"They learn to quantum jump," he said. "To consciously and deliberately project their own awareness from one thread of the tapestry to another. To live, if only for a moment, the lives they might have lived."

"Quantum jumping," Oliver repeated, the two words feeling both absurd and profoundly true. "To actually ... experience another life?"

"Experience is a limited word, Señor Battolo. It implies a passive observation," Pittamiglio corrected, his voice taking on the patient, deliberate cadence of a master lecturing his most promising student. "The true masters do not merely observe. They interact. They learn. They bring knowledge back across the threads. But to do so requires a map. A key. An instrument of impossible geometry. It is not enough to be sensitive to the music of the spheres; one must understand the instrument upon which it is played."

He raised his hand, and in the dark, empty space between him and Oliver, a shape began to form, a construct of pure, shimmering light. It was the familiar, six-armed spiral, the perfect, two-dimensional latticework of the Hexcelion.

"You have seen this symbol," Pittamiglio stated, not as a question, but as a fact. "My great-grandson showed you its basic principle. He was correct, in his own artistic way. The Hexcelion is a two-dimensional pattern, a key designed to organize and influence the third dimension. Of course, what I'm showing you here is a crude representation, not the real one."

He began to walk a slow, deliberate circle around the glowing construct, his hand tracing its elegant, spiraling arms.

"Your modern scientists believe they understand space as a simple, three-dimensional container. A box in which things happen," he said, a note of pity in his voice. "The Atlanteans knew better. They understood that space is a fabric, not a container. A living, geometric textile. The Hexcelion is the loom upon which that fabric is woven. Its six arms represent the six fundamental vectors of physical reality – up and down, left and right, forward and back. When inscribed upon a three-dimensional form, like a sphere, it creates a focal point, a place where the geometry of your reality becomes ... pliable."

He stopped, his gaze fixed on the glowing symbol. "But space, Señor Battolo, is only half of the equation. It is the canvas, but it is not the painting. It is the stage, but it is not the play. It is merely the *where*."

With a slow, deliberate gesture, Pittamiglio reached out toward the luminous Hexcelion. As his fingers approached the central nexus, the flat, glowing pattern began to warp, to lift off its two-dimensional plane. It extruded into the dark space of the chamber, its six arms becoming the vertices of a solid, three-dimensional object of impossible, crystalline beauty. And from this new, solid nexus, three new spirals, made of a different, more ethereal light, began to emerge, sketched into being like the crude, charcoal lines on the fifth Bryce painting.

The new, nine-armed shape pulsed with a quiet, internal power, twisting Oliver's perception, making the very air in the chamber feel thick and heavy.

"The Hexcelion is a two-dimensional key that unlocks a three-dimensional door," Pittamiglio said, his voice a low, reverent whisper. "But to navigate the great tapestry, to quantum jump between the threads of reality, one requires a key of a higher order."

He gestured to the impossible, three-dimensional object floating before them.

"This is the true instrument," he said. "The *Noncelion*. A three-dimensional key, designed to organize and unlock the fourth dimension: time itself. Its nine spirals represent the nine fundamental vectors of all existence. The six of space, and the three new, more fundamental vectors that govern the flow of reality: the past, the present and the future."

He looked at Oliver, his ancient eyes burning with the intensity of a man revealing the central secret of the cosmos. "The Hexcelion organizes the *where*. But the Noncelion, Señor Battolo ... the Noncelion organizes the *when*. It is not a map of space. It is a machine for navigating time."

Oliver stared at the impossible, three-dimensional object floating before them, its nine arms pulsing with a quiet, internal power. It was a machine for navigating time. The concept was so immense, so reality–shattering, that his mind struggled to contain it.

"So, this ... this is it?" Oliver asked, his voice a reverent whisper. "This is the machine Bryce tried to paint in his last painting? We can ... activate it? Here?"

Pittamiglio let out a soft, melancholic laugh, a sound like dry leaves skittering across ancient stone. "Ah, no, Señor Battolo. I am afraid the ambition of my youth far outstripped my power. What you see before you is merely an illustration. A shadow puppet on the wall of the cave, designed to give you a sense of the true form."

The luminous, three-dimensional Noncelion flickered and dissolved, leaving only the faint, two-dimensional Hexcelion hanging in the darkness.

"The true Noncelion," Pittamiglio continued, his voice taking on a tone of deep, almost religious awe, "is not a thing that can be built or summoned. The old texts say it is a singular, perfect construct in the entire multiverse. A perfect and immutable architecture of time itself, which had a genesis and will exist until the end of all things. It cannot be replicated. It simply ... *is*."

He paused, letting the weight of the concept settle in the silent chamber.

"However," he said, his tone shifting from the philosophical to the practical, "this chamber, this *Camara del Tiempo*, is a special place. It is, as I have told you, a Schelling point. A place of echoes. On a specific day, when the celestial alignments are perfect, this room can become a resonant chamber. It cannot create the true Noncelion, but it can create a powerful echo of it. A version of the Hexcelion that is ... amplified. Transformed. A Hexcelion that can, for a brief, fleeting moment, touch the fourth dimension."

He turned to face Oliver, his ancient eyes locking onto his, conveying the final, crucial instruction.

"But to create this echo, to make the instrument ring with the music of the spheres, the chamber requires a catalyst. The ritual demands the physical presence of the five cosmic signatures."

"Five cosmic signatures," Oliver repeated, the words feeling ancient and heavy with a meaning he couldn't yet grasp. "What are they? What do I need to find?"

Pittamiglio's gaze seemed to turn inward, as if he were looking at the very architecture of existence. "They are not things you must find, Señor Battolo," he said, his voice a low, instructional murmur. "They are things you must *gather*. They are the five foundational pillars of a great and hidden treasury. Five keys to a single, celestial vault, each one a unique and resonant signature."

He raised his hand, and a vision coalesced in the dark air before Oliver: five distinct, shimmering geometric patterns, each one glowing with a different, soft light.

"For the transformative Hexcelion to form," Pittamiglio continued, "the chamber must be brought into harmony with these five fundamental frequencies. The ritual is an act of symphony. The instrument must be properly tuned."

Oliver stared at the five glowing symbols, his mind racing. Keys. Signatures. A hidden treasury. The abstract, alchemical language was starting to align with the hard, cryptographic reality he now understood.

"These signatures," Oliver began, choosing his words carefully, "are they ... concepts? Or are they physical?"

"A concept is a shadow, Señor Battolo. A signature is a mark that is made," Pittamiglio corrected gently. "The power is not in the idea of the signature, but in its perfect, physical inscription. Think of it as a sacred text. The wisdom is not the paper, but the ink upon it. The true resonance lies in the words themselves, the sacred geometry of the phrases that give each signature its form."

Phrases, Oliver thought, a jolt of pure adrenaline shooting through him. *The sacred geometry of the phrases*. He looked at the five glowing symbols, and in his mind's eye, he saw them transform. They were no longer abstract patterns. They were the five wallets. The five sets of seed phrases Christiaan had hidden.

The breathtaking, terrifying implication of Pittamiglio's words crashed down on him. It wasn't enough to *know* the seed phrases. It wasn't enough to have the bitcoin. For the ritual to work, for the machine to be built, the physical objects upon which the phrases were inscribed – the Bryce canvases themselves – had to be present in this very chamber.

"The paintings," Oliver breathed, the words a quiet, stunned realization. "I have to bring the paintings. All four of them. I'm now certain they contain the seed phrases to five wallets spread across them!"

Pittamiglio's faint, knowing smile was all the confirmation he needed. Oliver's mind, which had been a whirlwind of confusion just moments before, was now a point of singular, terrifying clarity. The abstract, cosmic puzzle had just become a brutal logistical nightmare. He wasn't just a seeker of knowledge anymore. He was a courier, tasked with transporting four priceless, stolen and intensely sought-after artifacts across international borders.

"You understand now, Señor Battolo," Pittamiglio's voice echoed in the vast, dark chamber, pulling Oliver from his thoughts. "The nature of your inheritance. It is not a treasure to be claimed, but a duty to be fulfilled. Your father began a great work. He set the pieces upon the board. It is now your task, and yours alone, to see the game to its conclusion."

The alchemist's form began to grow translucent, his elegant figure dissolving back into the shadows from which he had emerged, his final words a quiet, resonant benediction that seemed to come from the very stones of the chamber itself.

"The board is set for the special day. Do not be late."

And then, he was gone.

Oliver was left alone in the absolute, ancient silence of the Chamber of Time. He looked at the empty space where the alchemist had stood, the weight of his new, impossible mission settling over him not as a burden, but as a mantle. He was no longer just Nate Battolo's son, retracing his father's footsteps. He was the inheritor of his quest, the one chosen to complete the final, critical move. He had his mission. And he had eight days.

798285 (July 11)

The afternoon sun cast long, lazy rectangles of light across the living room floor, illuminating dust motes dancing in the still air. The two massive canvases leaned against the far wall, a silent, inscrutable audience to their new life.

Oliver sat at his father's desk, a blank legal pad in front of him, a pen resting untouched by his hand. Across from him, at the dining table, Daniela was doing the same, her own notebook filled with a spiderweb of diagrams and questions that all led to the same impossible conclusion.

"It can't be done," she said finally, breaking a long, heavy silence. She pushed her notebook away, the gesture one of pure, exhausted frustration. "I've gone over it a dozen times. There's no version of this that doesn't end with us in a federal prison."

Oliver didn't look up. He just stared at the blank page in front of him. "I know."

"No, I mean, really think about it," she insisted, standing and beginning to pace the room, her voice a low current of barely controlled panic. "We have to get four priceless, stolen masterpieces, for which we have no legitimate claim, across international borders. We have to do it in less than a week. And we have to do it while being actively surveilled by at least three separate, hostile entities, one of which has access to a shadow global financial intelligence network."

She stopped pacing and turned to face him, her hands spread wide in a gesture of utter helplessness. "And now, thanks to your little chat with Pittamiglio last night, we know we can't just ship them. We have to go *with* them. The ritual requires it. How, Oliver? How do we possibly do that?"

He knew she was right. Every logical pathway he had explored over the past few hours had led to the same cold, hard wall. He had replayed his conversation with the long-dead alchemist a hundred times, searching for a loophole, a metaphor he might have missed. But the instruction had been absolute, the vision undeniable. The five resonant signatures – the wallets themselves, inscribed on the canvases – had to be physically present in the *Camara del Tiempo*. There was no other way.

He stared at the blank page, the unsolved logistical puzzle a solid, physical weight in the room. Daniela was right. Smuggling was impossible. A direct, legal claim was impossible. They were trapped.

He pushed back from the desk and walked over to the two canvases, his gaze sweeping over the haunting face of Anariadne and the impossible geometry of the unfinished Noncelion. They were beautiful, terrifying, and utterly inscrutable. The paintings were a language he was only just beginning to understand. Who else in the world could possibly read this language?

And then it hit him. There was someone else. A reclusive, brilliant artist in a dusty, sunlit studio, speaking with a quiet, reverent passion about the very man who had created these impossible objects.

"Velázquez," Oliver breathed, the name a sudden, brilliant spark in the darkness.

Daniela looked up from her notebook, her expression a mixture of confusion and hope. "What about him?"

"He's the expert," Oliver said, turning from the paintings to face her, a new, wild energy in his eyes. "He's the world's foremost, and probably only, expert on Jonathan Bryce and whatever this insane school of surrealism is called. He curated the show in the West Village. He's the key."

The idea began to form, a complex and audacious gambit taking shape in his mind with a sudden, startling clarity.

"We don't act like thieves," he began, the words coming faster now, the logic of the plan assembling itself as he spoke. "We don't even act like owners. We act like *scholars*. Like custodians of a priceless cultural heritage."

He walked back to the desk, his movements now sharp and purposeful. "The Liffey Trust," he said, "is a private, academic foundation dedicated to the preservation and study of Jonathan Bryce's work. We – the trust – will officially and professionally ship the paintings to a secure art handling facility in Montevideo."

"For what purpose?" Daniela asked, her own eyes widening as she began to see the shape of his plan.

"For a private, academic viewing," Oliver said, a triumphant grin spreading across his face. "For the world's foremost expert, Luis Velázquez, to conduct a formal authentication and appraisal before a potential museum donation. We'll create the entire paper trail – official requests from the trust, emails to his foundation, shipping manifests. It will be a perfect, boring and completely legitimate academic exercise."

Daniela's face, which had been lit up with the thrill of their clever plan, slowly clouded over with a new, more practical concern. She walked over to the evidence board and tapped a finger on a printout of Habib's contact information.

"Okay, the cover story for the paintings might work," she said, thoughtfully. "The paper trail is clean. But what about our paper trail? Both our credit cards are maxed out – all you have is cash. We can't book flights to Montevideo with Habib without flagging every alert Da Silva's network has set up. The paintings might be invisible, but we're not."

She was right. The familiar, cold reality of their situation settled back into the room. They were still being hunted. Oliver felt a familiar knot of frustration tighten in his gut. Every solution seemed to lead to a new, more impossible problem. He began to pace the apartment, his mind racing through dead ends. They could try to buy tickets with cash at the airport, but that was risky and would attract its own kind of attention. They could try to find another fixer, but they were out of time. They were trapped.

He stopped in the middle of the room, the answer coming to him not as a logical deduction, but as a flash of pure, intuitive certainty, a lesson learned from the Noncemeister in a world beyond logic. *You are the creator within your own creation.*

"We can't hide from them," he said, his voice quiet but firm. "So, let's stop trying."

Daniela looked at him, her expression a mask of confusion. "What are you talking about?"

"Their surveillance," he said, a new, audacious energy in his eyes. "We've been treating it like a threat. A weakness. But what if it's a weapon? What if we use it?"

He walked back to the evidence board and stood beside her, his finger now pointing to Habib's name.

"We'll book our tickets through Habib's network," he said, the full, insane brilliance of the plan now clear in his mind. "We'll use the very system they're using to watch us. We'll let them see us. We'll let them think they know our plan. We'll hand them a story so perfect, so boring, they won't be able to resist believing it."

Daniela stared at him, her expression a mixture of disbelief and a dawning, horrified respect. "Let me get this straight," she said, her voice a low, incredulous whisper. "Your plan is to walk directly into the lion's den? To go to the one network we know is watching us and hand them our entire travel itinerary on a silver platter?"

"Exactly," Oliver said, a strange, calm certainty settling over him. He felt like he was finally seeing the whole board, not just his own desperate moves. "We've been trying to be ghosts, and it's exhausting. It's making us predictable.

They *expect* us to hide. So, we'll do the opposite. We'll be the loudest, most obvious, most boring targets they've ever seen."

He began to pace again, but this time it wasn't the frantic, caged energy of a man trapped. It was the deliberate, measured stride of a general laying out his battle plan.

"I'll go to Habib," he explained, his voice taking on a new, confident rhythm. "And book two, first-class tickets to Montevideo. With cash. I still have over half a million under the bed – fine, I'll spend a hundred grand if I have to. We'll book a full week at the most expensive, most ridiculously opulent hotel in the city. We will create a digital footprint a mile wide."

"And the Velázquez meeting?" Daniela asked, her mind clearly catching up, the initial shock giving way to the cold, hard logic of the gambit.

"That's the beauty of it," Oliver said, a thin, sharp smile on his face. "The Liffey Trust will have a legitimate, professional reason for being in Montevideo. But *we* won't. I'll just be a rich kid who inherited a fortune, taking his beautiful girlfriend on a lavish, impulsive South American holiday. The academic stuff? That's just a boring side-errand, a small piece of family business to take care of in between the tango lessons and the five-star dinners. We'll hide our real mission, the most important event of our lives, in plain sight, buried under a mountain of cliché and predictable, but utterly uninteresting noise."

He stopped pacing and turned to face her, the full, terrifying brilliance of the plan hanging in the air between them. They would no longer be running from the spider. They would be walking right up to its web and pretending to be a fly.

"It's insane," Daniela breathed, a look of pure, audacious thrill now in her eyes. "It's the most insane, reckless, and brilliant plan I have ever heard."

Oliver just grinned. The path forward was a deliberate, calculated performance. And he knew exactly what his first line was.

He walked toward the door, grabbing his jacket from the back of a chair.

"Now if you'll excuse me," he said, his voice low, steady, and full of resolve. "I need to see a man about some flowers."

799118 (July 17)

Oliver stared out the taxi window, into the Montevideo winter afternoon. The city lights were familiar but now a far more menacing landscape than on his last visit in March. The Rambla, a wide, sweeping avenue, hugged the dark, invisible coastline of the Río de la Plata to their right. He could smell the salt in the air, a scent he now associated with the final, terrifying square on the board.

Daniela sat beside him, a silent, still presence in the darkness of the car. She wasn't looking at the city with the wide eyes of a stranger, but with a kind of distant, melancholic familiarity.

"It's strange," she said finally, her voice barely disturbing the quiet of the car. "Coming back here now. Like this."

He reached out and took her hand, his fingers lacing through hers. Her hand was cold. "Does it feel like home?"

She was quiet for a long moment before answering. "It used to," she said, her gaze fixed on the familiar, passing streets. "When I'd visit Tío Rafael, this was a place of joy. Of safety. Now it just feels … different."

He squeezed her hand gently, a silent acknowledgment of the shared, unspoken fear that hung between them. The game was here. It was now. And tomorrow, all the pieces would finally collide.

"It's done, then," he said. "We're on their radar. They know we're here."

"We knew they would," she replied, her gaze finally turning from the window to meet his. "That was the point."

He thought of his visit to the flower shop on Broadway, the final, necessary step of their plan. Handing over the cash to a smug Habib, knowing that the transaction would act as a flare, a bright, unmissable signal to the network that was hunting them, had been a massive gamble. He had willingly walked back into the spider's web, betting everything on the hope that his disguise as a wealthy, careless tourist was a good enough one.

"It still feels reckless," he admitted. "Using them again, so soon after Luxembourg."

"We're not being reckless, Oliver," she said, her voice steady and firm. "We're setting the stage. We're controlling the narrative. It was the only move we had left."

She was right. He knew she was. The quiet confidence in her voice was a welcome anchor in the swirling sea of his own doubts. He held her hand tighter, the city lights sliding past, pulling them closer to their fated appointment on July 18th.

They arrived at the hotel just as the sun was setting, the golden light of the late afternoon casting a honeyed glow on the magnificent Belle Époque facade of the Sofitel Montevideo. The doorman, dressed in a crisp, formal uniform, opened the taxi door with a flourish. This was it. The performance had begun.

Oliver stepped out, consciously relaxing his shoulders, affecting an air of bored entitlement he had seen a thousand times in the lobbies of places like this. He let the valet handle their bags, giving him a dismissive nod as he and Daniela walked up the grand staircase and into the cavernous, opulent lobby.

"I still can't believe the airline lost my cashmere throw," he said, his voice loud enough to carry, a perfect imitation of a man whose biggest problem was a minor travel inconvenience. "First class, and they still treat your luggage like a sack of potatoes."

"We'll buy a new one tomorrow, babe," Daniela replied, her own performance seamless. She glided up to the check-in desk, a picture of effortless, sophisticated grace. She spoke to the clerk in a fluent, lilting Spanish, her tone warm but firm, the easy authority of a woman who was used to the best.

While she handled the check-in, Oliver's gaze drifted across the lobby, a slow, casual scan that was anything but. He took in the other guests – a cluster of European businessmen, an older American couple, a family with laughing children. Every face was a potential threat, every casual glance a possible sign of surveillance. He felt a cold, prickling sensation on the back of his neck, the feeling of being watched, but saw no one who seemed out of place. He forced himself to look away, to focus on the trivialities of their cover story.

A bellhop loaded their luggage onto a golden cart. As they followed him toward the elevators, Oliver continued their public conversation. "Did you confirm the reservation at Estrecho for tonight?" he asked. "I'm starving. And make sure you tell them I don't want a table near the kitchen this time."

"It's all taken care of," she said, slipping her arm through his. Her touch was a small, steady anchor in the churning sea of his paranoia.

The moment the heavy, polished wood door of their suite clicked shut behind them, the performance dropped. The bored, entitled heir and his glamorous girlfriend vanished, replaced by two tired, tense soldiers in a temporary, gilded sanctuary. Oliver immediately went to the window, his gaze sweeping the sprawling, elegant grounds of the hotel below, searching for any sign of a car that didn't belong, any figure watching from the shadows.

Daniela came to stand beside him, her own eyes scanning the darkness. "Anything?"

"No," he said, though the feeling of being watched, a cold prickle on the back of his neck, hadn't subsided. "It's clean. For now."

He turned from the window, the full, crushing weight of their mission settling upon him. The opulent suite, with its silk wallpaper and crystal chandeliers, felt less like a luxury and more like a cage.

"So," he began, "all the pieces are in place?"

Daniela nodded, her own focus absolute. "I heard from Velázquez's assistant last night, before we left New York. The shipment cleared customs without any issues. The paintings were delivered to his studio two days ago. He has them. He confirmed he will meet us at the castle in Piriápolis tomorrow afternoon, exactly two hours before the alignment."

Oliver let out a slow, quiet breath. That was the most critical piece. Their key ally was in place, and the assets were secure. "And Javier?" he asked, the name of the quiet, formidable doorman from his last visit a symbol of a different, more grounded kind of hope.

"I spoke to his contact right after we landed," Daniela said, her voice steady and reassuring. "He said not to worry. He and his friends will be on the lookout for us. They'll have eyes on the road to Piriápolis and at the castle itself. If Bojan or anyone else makes a move, we'll know about it long before they get close. He promised our path would be clear. Javier himself will be at the castle tomorrow for the event."

Oliver nodded, a small, tight knot of tension in his shoulders beginning to loosen. The plan was set. Their allies were in position. All the variables they could control had been controlled. Now, all that was left was the waiting.

799132 (July 17)

The black car moved through the evening traffic of Montevideo with a silent, anodyne efficiency. Nick stared out the window, but he wasn't seeing the city. He was seeing a grid, a theater of operations. The elegant, Belle Époque architecture, the palm-lined avenues, the distant, dark shimmer of the Río de la Plata – it was all just terrain, the backdrop for the final act of a long and frustrating hunt.

Beside him, Adele was on the phone, speaking in an urgent, but calm tone as she finalized the last of their logistical arrangements. She was speaking Spanish, and Nick listened, a silent and grudging admiration growing in him. Her accent had the hard, clean edges of her South African English, a slight but noticeable flatness on the vowels. But her grammar was perfect, her vocabulary precise and formal. It was the language of someone who had not grown up with it, but had studied and mastered it for a specific, singular purpose.

The car pulled up to the sleek, modern tower of the Radisson Montevideo Victoria Plaza Hotel.

"This is us," she said, ending her call and switching seamlessly back to English. "I secured a suite on one of the upper floors. It should provide an adequate vantage point."

Nick nodded. He had been expecting a fight, a last-minute scramble for a tactical position. But Adele, as always, was three steps ahead. She had acquired an asset, not just booked a hotel.

Upstairs, the suite was an anonymous space of clean lines, dark wood, and a single, breathtaking wall of glass that offered a sweeping, panoramic view of the city. It was a forward operating base. Without a word, Nick walked to his luggage and unzipped a long, reinforced case. He began to assemble a high-powered spotting scope on a lightweight carbon-fiber tripod.

Adele, meanwhile, was already on the phone again, confirming the delivery of a rental car for the morning and the activation of a set of local SIM cards.

They moved in a silent, complementary rhythm, two professionals preparing their tools for the work ahead.

After a few minutes, Nick had the scope mounted and trained, the powerful lens collapsing the miles of city into a single, focused frame. He scanned past the rooftops and the glittering lights until he found it: a tall, white spire, stark and floodlit against the deepening twilight. The Obelisk.

He adjusted the focus, the image sharpening until he could make out the details of the plaza at its base, the distant, ant-like figures of people walking by.

"I have eyes on the target," he said.

Adele came to stand beside him at the window, her gaze following his to the distant monument. "And tomorrow," she said, a quiet edge of steel in her voice, "he will be there."

Their plan was a model of brutal simplicity, a direct response to defeat in Luxembourg. There would be no more complex legal maneuvers, no more second-guessing. There would only be patience and overwhelming surveillance.

"You take the perch," she said, her eyes still fixed on the Obelisk. "You'll have a clear line of sight to the entire plaza. I'll be on the ground, a block away, in a café. The second you see him – Nate, Oliver, anyone connected to this – you give the signal, and I move in."

"We'll hold our positions all day if we have to," Nick confirmed. "He has to show. The message was an appointment."

"He will show," Adele said, a note of absolute, unwavering certainty in her voice. This wasn't just about the money anymore. For her, it was a matter of justice, a final, long-overdue accounting for her brother. For Nick, it was simpler. It was vengeance.

He looked out at the distant, floodlit spire, the final destination for a man who represented the entire corrupt, fraudulent system that had taken everything from him. This time, there would be no near-miss. This time, the hunter would not be outrun.

CHAPTER 12. JULY 18

799224 (July 18)

The morning sun over the Río de la Plata was a pale, wintry gold, casting a soft, forgiving light across the city. Oliver stood at the massive window of their suite at the Sofitel, watching the early morning traffic begin its slow, steady crawl along the Rambla. He had been awake for hours, sleep an impossible luxury on a day like this. He felt a strange, profound stillness inside him, a calm that was not the absence of fear, but a quiet acceptance of it.

Today was the day. After more than a year of chasing ghosts, of navigating a labyrinth of projections and lies, of falling into the abyss and clawing his way back out, the end was finally here. In less than fourteen hours, at 10 o'clock tonight, he would stand at the base of the Obelisk, and he would see his father again.

The thought was so immense, so reality-altering, that his mind could barely contain it. *Dad.* He was alive. Not a memory, not a projection, but a living, breathing man who had orchestrated this entire, impossible journey to bring him to this single point in time. The anger he had once felt, the sense of betrayal, had been burned away, replaced by a deep, aching sense of awe.

"Are you ready?"

He turned from the window. Daniela was standing by the door, dressed in a simple, practical outfit of dark jeans and a black sweater, a small, unassuming backpack slung over her shoulder. She looked less like a woman on her way to a cosmic ritual and more like a tourist ready for a day of exploring. But her eyes, dark and serious, held the same quiet, electric tension he felt in his own chest.

"I don't think you can ever be ready for a day like today," he said, his voice a little hoarse. "First, we have to survive a meeting with an ancient alchemist and a celestial machine at a secret castle."

"And after that," she said, her gaze steady and unwavering, "you go home."

He nodded, the simple, powerful truth of her words settling over him. That's what tonight was. After all the chaos, all the running, all the fighting, tonight he was finally going home. He took a deep breath, the quiet stillness in his soul solidifying into a hard, clear resolve.

"Let's go," he said. "We have a long day ahead of us."

The grand, cavernous lobby of the Sofitel was bathed in the golden light of the winter morning. It was a space designed to inspire awe, with its soaring ceilings, marble columns, and intricate, gilded fixtures. But as they walked toward the main entrance, the beauty of their surroundings felt like a mockery, a beautiful stage for a terrifying and uncertain play.

They were a few feet from the main doors, the promise of the open city just beyond the glass, when two figures stepped forward from the shadows of a large, potted palm, blocking their path.

Oliver stopped, his hand instinctively tightening on Daniela's arm. His heart, which had been a steady, hopeful rhythm just a moment before, began a low, heavy drumbeat against his ribs.

It was Maren. And beside her, a dark, immovable presence, was Bojan.

Maren's face was a mask of profound, almost motherly concern. She looked tired, the confident, serene energy of the spiritual healer he had once known completely gone, replaced by a raw, desperate vulnerability. She took a small, tentative step toward him.

"Oliver," she began, her voice a low, pleading whisper. "Please. You have to listen to me. This has gone far enough. You have no idea the danger you are in, the world you have stumbled into."

Bojan said nothing. He just stood there, his arms crossed over his massive chest, his pale, washed-out eyes fixed on Oliver with a look of cold, predatory patience. His silence had a stark, physical presence, a promise of violence that was far more menacing than any spoken threat.

"The paintings, Oliver," Maren continued, her own eyes now welling with tears. "They are not a game. They are not an inheritance. They are a key to a world that will consume you. I saved Christiaan's life once. I am trying, with all my heart, to save yours now. Please, for your father's memory, give them to me. Let me protect you."

The tension in the lobby was a palpable, crushing weight that seemed to suck the air from Oliver's lungs. Maren's desperate, pleading eyes were fixed on him, while Bojan's cold, predatory gaze never wavered. He felt Daniela's hand find his, her grip a small, desperate anchor in the rising tide of fear.

Just as the pressure felt like it was about to break, a calm, quiet movement from the corner of the lobby shifted the entire dynamic of the room. A man who had been sitting in a large, plush armchair, seemingly engrossed in a newspaper, slowly folded it, placed it on the table beside him, and stood. He was of average height, with a neat, military-style haircut and a face that was utterly and completely unremarkable. He wore a simple, well-tailored suit and moved with a kind of economic, fluid grace that was almost invisible.

It was Agustín.

Oliver's heart leaped into his throat. He remembered him clearly from the last, terrifying trip to Montevideo: his sudden, silent appearance in the alleyway with Javier and Diego, a quiet, deadly professional who had materialized from the shadows to save him. He had been at Javier's home later that night, a man who spoke little but observed everything with a profound, unnerving stillness.

Agustín did not look at Oliver or Daniela. He walked calmly, almost casually, toward their small, tense group, his path taking him directly to Bojan. He stopped a few feet away, his hands clasped loosely behind his back.

He spoke directly to Bojan, his voice a low, almost conversational murmur, yet it cut through the tense silence of the lobby with the clean, sharp edge of a scalpel. He addressed him by name.

"Mr. Mitrovic," Agustín began, a faint, Rioplatense accent coloring his words. "A public incident at a five-star hotel would be ... unwise." He paused, letting the words hang in the air. "The *network* values discretion. It would be a shame for a man of your talents to lose access to such a valuable resource over a ... personal matter."

The word, *network*, hit Oliver like a physical blow. It was a certainty. He was talking about Habib's network. Saleem Bhai's network. The network of the silver man with the musical voice – the man he assumed was Da Silva. He felt a wave of pure, cold terror wash over him. Maren wasn't just a rogue actor with a dangerous enforcer. She was a client. A part of the same vast, shadowy organization that he had unwittingly walked into on that cold January afternoon at the Malcolm Shabazz market in Harlem. That's how they'd both known his location all along. The walls had never been there at all.

He watched as Bojan's entire demeanor shifted. The smug, predatory confidence drained away, replaced by a look of cold, professional recognition. He was a professional who had just been recognized by another professional, his cover blown, his mission compromised. He understood the unspoken threat immediately. Creating a scene here would be as much a tactical failure as a professional one – a black mark against his name in the only world that mattered.

He gave a single, almost imperceptible nod to Agustín, a silent acknowledgment from one predator to another. Without another word, he turned to Maren, his expression now a blank, unreadable slate. He touched her elbow gently, a quiet, firm signal. It was over.

Maren looked from Bojan's impassive face to Agustín's, and then finally to Oliver. The desperation in her eyes curdled into a look of pure, undiluted hatred. The mask of the concerned friend was gone, replaced by the raw, furious face of a woman who had just been denied her prize. But she was smart enough to know the game was lost, for now. She turned without a word and walked with Bojan toward the exit, their retreat as silent and sudden as their ambush had been.

Agustín watched them go, his expression unchanging. Once they were gone, he turned his calm, unremarkable gaze to Oliver and Daniela. He gave them a small, formal nod, a silent confirmation that his duty was done. Then, just as quietly as he had appeared, he walked back to his armchair, picked up his newspaper, and dissolved back into the anonymity of the hotel lobby.

Oliver and Daniela were left standing in the sudden, ringing silence, their hearts still hammering in their chests. The entire confrontation had lasted less than a minute. They were shaken, but a new, hard-edged resolve had settled over them. Javier's promise of protection was real. Their allies were watching.

"Come on," Oliver said, his voice a low, steady murmur. He took Daniela's hand, his grip firm and sure.

They turned and walked out of the grand lobby and into the bright, cold Montevideo morning. The city felt different now, no longer a place of ghosts, but a battlefield. They knew their enemies were here, close, and they were connected to a threat far larger than they had ever imagined. Their sense of danger, and their sense of purpose, was now at its absolute peak.

799239 (July 18)

Oliver sat at a small, wrought-iron table at the Café Brasilero, a cup of coffee untouched in front of him. Across the bustling Plaza de la Independencia, the Obelisk stood, a stark, white spear against the blue sky, a silent monument to the day's impossible promise. A handful of tour groups snaked around in the distance, led by multilingual pied pipers with loudspeakers.

"Are you okay?" Daniela asked, her voice a gentle interruption. She reached across the table and placed her hand over his.

He looked at her, at the quiet strength in her eyes, and managed a small, tired smile. "I'm okay. Just ... a lot to process. I wanted to get a feel for this place before tonight. See the angles, the sight lines. Get the lay of the land."

"It's a good idea," she agreed. "What time is the rental car going to be there at the hotel?"

"Eleven," he confirmed. "That gives us almost two hours. Should be plenty of time to get back and start the drive. If the traffic is clear, we'll be in Piriápolis with time to spare before we have to meet Velázquez."

She squeezed his hand. "It's going to work, Oliver."

"I know," he said, though his gaze drifted across the plaza, the memory of the hotel lobby confrontation still a fresh, chilling presence. "I can't stop thinking about what Agustín said. About the network."

"I know," she said, her grip tightening on his hand.

"It wasn't a guess, Daniela," he said, the pieces clicking together in his mind with a cold, terrifying certainty. "He was talking about Habib's network. The one that belongs to the silver man – Da Silva, whoever he is. The one I willingly walked back into. That's how Maren knew we were coming. That's how she knew to be in the lobby. She's a client. She's part of the same organization."

He looked from Daniela's worried face to the distant, white spire of the Obelisk. "We have to get through the ritual this afternoon," he said, a sense of pure resolve building in his voice. "And then tonight, we're back here."

★★★★

The world snapped into a tight, circular frame, the grand, sweeping plaza reduced to a single, magnified image, the morning light sharp and clinical. From his perch on the 22nd floor of the Radisson, the Obelisk was a target marker. Nick Hernandez swiveled the spotting scope with a slow, methodical grace, his eye pressed to the lens. He was a sniper surveying a kill box.

He started his sweep on the western edge of the plaza, his gaze tracking the slow, predictable movements of the morning pedestrians. He ignored the tourists, the families, the couples. He was looking for a specific kind of stillness, the quiet, coiled tension of a man on a mission. He scanned past a dozen café patios, his focus sharp, his breathing slow and even.

And then he found them.

They were sitting at an outdoor table at the Café Brasilero, two small, distinct figures in a sea of indifferent motion. He zoomed in, the powerful lens collapsing the distance until their faces were a clear, undeniable reality. Oliver

Battolo and a woman. He watched them for a long, silent moment, observing their posture, the way they spoke, the quiet, shared intensity that seemed to set them apart from everyone else in the plaza. They were exactly where they were supposed to be.

He leaned back from the scope, a slow, cold smile touching his lips. He picked up his phone.

"Adele," he said. "I have them. North side of the plaza. Café Brasilero. They're sitting down."

He listened for a moment to her quiet acknowledgment on the other end of the line.

"Don't go there directly," he continued, his eyes still pressed to the scope, watching his two targets sitting, oblivious, in the winter sun. "There's another café, directly opposite. The one with the green awning. It will give you a clean line of sight. Take a table outside."

He paused, his gaze sweeping the plaza, assessing the angles, the exits, the flow of the sparse morning crowd. A static, long-distance observation wasn't enough. This needed to be a lockdown.

"I'm coming down," he said, his voice a final, decisive command. "Stay at the green-awning café and don't engage with them. I'll be there in less than ten minutes."

★★★★

Oliver took a slow sip of his coffee, the rich, dark liquid a small, grounding pleasure in a morning fraught with a strange, electric tension. He let his gaze drift across the plaza, past the laughing children and the slow-moving couples, past the chaotic meandering of tour groups, and for a moment, he felt a sense of something that resembled peace.

And then he saw her.

A woman was taking a seat at an outdoor table at the café directly opposite, the one with the green awning. She was alone, and she moved with a kind of deliberate, unhurried grace that seemed to separate her from the casual, tourist-like energy of everyone else around her. She placed her bag on the empty chair beside her, and then she looked up, her gaze sweeping across the plaza until it landed, with a kind of cold, magnetic certainty, directly on him.

His blood ran cold. It was Adele.

He didn't move. He didn't look away. He felt Daniela's hand tense on his, a silent acknowledgment that she had seen her too. The open, sunlit plaza, which had felt like a place of hope and pilgrimage just moments before, now felt like a trap, a perfectly illuminated stage.

A few minutes later, a man walked up to Adele's table and sat down. He leaned in and said something to her, his back to Oliver, but the set of his shoulders, the confident, athletic posture, was unmistakable. It was Nick.

Nick sat down next to Adele and locked eyes with Oliver, a quiet acknowledgement that the game was on. The two couples sat in a silent, unmoving standoff for what felt like an eternity, separated by a hundred yards of indifferent, sun-drenched pavement. The hunt was over. The confrontation had begun.

Oliver took a slow, deliberate breath. He would not run. He would not be panicked into a mistake. He picked up his coffee cup and took another sip, his hand perfectly steady. He then nodded to Daniela. She understood immediately. They would not be flushed out. They would leave on their own terms.

They finished their coffee and the last of their pastries with a slow, almost defiant calm. Oliver caught the waiter's eye and signaled for the check.

Just as the waiter was returning with the change, a large tour group, a noisy, chaotic river of about thirty people, spilled into the plaza, their guide's voice a loud, cheerful narration over a small speaker. They flowed into the space between the two cafés, a welcome, temporary wall of bodies and noise, completely obscuring the view.

It was the opening they needed.

"Now," Oliver said, his voice a low, quiet command.

He stood, placed a few bills on the table, and took Daniela's hand. Without looking back, they stepped away from their table and merged seamlessly into the middle of the moving tour group, just two more anonymous faces in a sea of strangers, and disappeared into the crowd.

799252 (July 18)

The coastal highway unspooled before them, a ribbon of asphalt tracing the curve of the winter shoreline. The sky was a pale, washed-out blue, and the Río de la Plata to their right was a vast, shimmering expanse of silver-gray. Oliver sat in the passenger seat of the rental car, a nondescript sedan Javier had procured for them that morning. The decision had been a simple, logical one. Taking a random taxi for this final, most critical leg of their journey was an unacceptable risk. They needed a driver they could trust with their lives, and there was only one man in Montevideo who fit that description. When they had explained the plan to Javier earlier, he hadn't hesitated. He had simply nodded and said, "I will take you. No one else."

His presence behind the wheel was a quiet, reassuring strength. He drove with a calm, steady focus, his hands resting easily on the wheel, his gaze flicking between the road ahead and the rearview mirror. Daniela was in the back, a silent, watchful presence. The frantic, hunted energy of the last few months had finally burned away, leaving behind a strange, shared sense of acceptance. They were no longer running; they were heading to a fated appointment.

"I have lived in Montevideo for many years," Javier said finally, in a low, steady voice that cut through the hum of the tires on the road. "And for all those years, I have heard whispers of this day. Of this place." He gestured with his chin toward the road ahead, toward the distant, unseen castle. "But to see it … to be a part of it … this is something I never expected."

"You've never been to the castle, Javier?" Oliver asked, turning from the window.

"No, Señor Battolo," Javier replied, a note of quiet awe in his voice. "It is a private place. A place of legends. The old ones in the city, they tell stories. They say it is a place where the world is … thin. Where a man can speak to God, if he has the courage to listen for the answer. I have never believed it, of course." He paused and turned his head slightly, his gaze briefly meeting

Oliver's. "I am an old man. I have seen many things. But I have never seen a miracle. Today, perhaps, I will."

The quiet awe that had filled Javier's voice seemed to hang in the car for a long moment, a fragile, sacred thing. Oliver watched as the older man's gaze met his, a silent acknowledgment passing between them before Javier's focus returned to the road.

It was then that Oliver saw it. A black sedan, a quarter-mile back, a persistent, professional shadow.

"They're still with us," he said, his voice flat. He wasn't surprised. He had been expecting it.

Daniela leaned forward from the back seat, her own eyes finding the car in the side mirror. "How did they find us again? We lost them in that crowd."

"He's good," Oliver replied, a note of dark, grudging respect in his voice. "Nick is really good. They probably just tailed us on foot back to the hotel and waited for the car to leave. Very professional."

"So, we have a dedicated security escort," Daniela said, her voice laced with a dry, humorless irony.

"Two of them, actually," Oliver replied, his eyes flicking back to the mirror, scanning the road behind the black sedan. Farther back, almost half a mile behind Nick and Adele, was a small, nondescript delivery van. It was probably nothing. Just a local tradesman going about his day. But it had been there for the last 20 minutes, matching their pace with a kind of lazy, unremarkable consistency. He had the distinct, unsettling feeling of being watched by eyes he couldn't see.

"What do you mean, two?" Daniela asked, a new edge of concern in her voice.

"There's a van," he said. "Way back. Probably just a coincidence. Or it could be Bojan and Maren." He let the thought hang in the air for a moment. "So, we have Nick, Adele, and potentially Bojan and Maren all heading to the same party. It's going to be a crowded dance floor."

She was quiet for a long moment, the reality of their situation settling in the small, enclosed space of the car. "Are you scared?"

Oliver thought about it. The honest answer was yes, but it was a different kind of fear now. It wasn't the panicked, desperate fear of a man running for his life. It was the cold, clear fear of a soldier heading into a battle he had chosen to fight.

"I think I'm past scared," he said finally. "We can't outrun them. We can't hide from them. All we can do is lead them to the front door and see who's still standing at the end of the day." He turned around to look at her, at the quiet, unwavering resolve in her eyes, and felt a profound sense of gratitude. He wasn't walking into this alone. "Besides," he added, a small, grim smile touching his lips, "at least we know where everyone is. It's the ones you don't see that you really have to worry about."

****

The black sedan moved with a quiet grace, a perfect shadow to the nondescript rental car a quarter-mile ahead. Nick sat in the back seat, his eyes fixed on their target, his posture a study in coiled, professional stillness. The adrenaline of the morning's successful acquisition at the Obelisk had long since faded, replaced by the low, humming tension of the hunt.

Beside him, Adele was staring out the window, but he knew she wasn't seeing the windswept coastal landscape. She was seeing a chessboard, and the pieces were not moving according to plan.

"This doesn't make sense, Nick," she said finally. "They're 45 minutes out of the city and still going. The message was the Obelisk. That was the rendezvous. Where are they going?"

"It doesn't matter where they're going," Nick replied, his own mind cycling through the possibilities. "A safe house. A secondary meeting. All that matters is that we don't lose them."

"Are you absolutely certain that's Oliver's car?" she asked, in a sharp voice. "Could this be a decoy? Could they be leading us away while the real target is somewhere else?"

"Positive," Nick said, with a hard confidence in his own voice. He had not been sloppy. Not this time. "I took a photo of the plates on the rental as they were pulling away from the hotel. It's them."

He fell silent, his gaze flicking from the car ahead to his own rearview mirror. He'd noticed it about 20 minutes ago. A small, unremarkable delivery van, its paint faded, its logo obscured by a layer of road grime. It was keeping a perfect, consistent distance of about half a mile behind them. It was too consistent.

"We've got company," he said, his voice quiet.

Adele turned from her window, her eyes immediately finding the van in the side mirror. "Who is it?"

"I don't know," he admitted. "But they've been with us since the city limits. They're not with him, and they're not with us."

She was silent for a long moment, processing the new, unwelcome variable. The simple, two-player game had just become a three-body problem. He watched as her hand moved instinctively to the inside of her jacket, a small, reassuring gesture.

"You might have noticed I was on the phone for quite a while after we landed last night," she said, still looking at the distant, unremarkable van in the side mirror. "It wasn't just to arrange for the car and the SIM cards."

Nick waited, saying nothing.

"I have contacts here," she continued, her gaze finally turning to meet his. "Contingency plans. This is not a situation I was unprepared for." She let her hand drop from her jacket. "Whatever happens when we get to our destination, Nick, we will not be at a disadvantage."

The implication hung in the air between them, cold and hard and absolute. The hunt was no longer a simple matter of surveillance. It had just become something far more dangerous.

799261 (July 18)

The coastal highway eventually gave way to a narrower, winding road that climbed steadily, leaving the shimmering expanse of the Río de la Plata behind them. The landscape grew wilder, the air thinner and cooler. And then they saw it.

Perched on a high hill overlooking the town of Piriápolis was a structure that defied logic, a mad, beautiful fortress of towers, battlements and arched windows that seemed to have been transplanted from a medieval European fantasy. It was Esteban Pittamiglio's castle.

Javier pulled the car to a stop at the base of a long, stone staircase that snaked up the hill to the main entrance. The place was deserted, a silent, sleeping giant under the pale winter sun. As they got out of the car, a lone figure emerged from the massive, arched doorway at the top of the stairs. Even from a distance, Oliver recognized the lean, artistic posture.

"Your friend is waiting for us," Javier said.

They ascended the stairs in a tense, shared silence. Luis Velázquez met them on the upper landing. The reclusive artist Oliver remembered from their first meeting was gone, replaced by a somber, focused intensity. He looked tired, the weight of the day clearly visible on his face.

He greeted Oliver with a firm handshake. "Oliver. You made it." He then turned his gaze to his two companions.

"This is Daniela," Oliver said. "And this is Javier. They're with me."

Velázquez gave a single, formal nod to each of them. "A pleasure. Everything is prepared."

"Are we clear?" Oliver asked, his gaze drifting back down the empty road behind them, searching for any sign of the black sedan or the nondescript van. "There were two vehicles right behind us for most of the drive."

"Ah, you were followed," Velázquez said, his expression grim, and somehow knowing. "But they won't be able to enter. Not yet." He gestured toward the massive, closed doors of the castle. "The grounds don't open to the public for another two hours, not until three. People come for the celestial event, but it's a small local affair. A curiosity. They will blend in with the handful of tourists who show up."

"But we can go in now?" Daniela asked.

A faint, tired smile touched Velázquez's lips. "My family built this place. For me, the doors are always open." He turned and pushed on the heavy, iron-bound door, which swung inward with a low, groaning sound, revealing the cool, dark interior of the castle. "Come. We don't have much time."

Velázquez led them inside. The moment the massive door thudded shut behind them, the world changed. The sounds of the wind and the distant road were gone, replaced by a profound, ancient silence. But it wasn't empty. Beneath the silence, Oliver could hear it, a sound he knew with an impossible, intimate familiarity: the distant, rhythmic crash of waves against an unseen shore. The air grew thick and heavy, carrying the sharp, clean scent of iodine.

He was no longer just in a castle. He was in a projection. A real, physical projection.

He glanced at Daniela. Her eyes were wide, her artist's sensibility clearly overwhelmed by the sheer, impossible reality of the space. Javier was even more striking. The doorman's quiet, professional composure had been replaced by a look of unvarnished awe. He stood just inside the doorway, his head tilted back, his gaze lost in the vaulted, shadowy ceilings, a man who had just stepped out of his own world and into a legend.

"This way," Velázquez said, his voice a low, steady anchor in the disorienting quiet.

He led them through a series of winding, stone-walled corridors, their footsteps the only sound in the ancient space. Finally, they arrived at a familiar, massive wooden door at the end of a long hallway. Oliver recognized it instantly. Carved into the dark, heavy wood in ornate, archaic letters was the name: *Camara del Tiempo*.

Velázquez did not need a key. He simply placed his palm flat against the wood, and with a deep, resonant click that seemed to come from the very stones of the castle, the door swung inward.

The chamber was exactly as he remembered it from his visions. A vast, circular space, so large that the far wall was lost in shadow, the ceiling a vaulted dome that disappeared into a darkness beyond the reach of the dim, ambient light. In the center of the room, directly beneath the massive, crystalline orb that hung impossibly in the air, was the unlit ceremonial firepit.

Oliver's gaze was immediately drawn upward, to the orb itself. The *Turabet es ploe dieu*. That had to be it. It floated in the center of the vast chamber, a perfect, crystalline sphere at least three feet in diameter, its surface a complex latticework of geometric patterns in polished obsidian and silver that seemed to shift and shimmer in the dim light. It was a thing of impossible beauty and terrifying power.

"How is it just ... hanging there?" Daniela whispered, her voice a note of pure awe.

Velázquez followed her gaze. "It isn't," he said, his own voice quiet and reverent. "Look closer."

Oliver squinted, his eyes adjusting to the low light. And then he saw them. Dozens of impossibly thin, almost invisible silver wires, descending from the blackness of the vaulted ceiling, attaching to the orb at precise, geometric points. They were as thin as a spider's silk, yet they held the massive, crystalline sphere in a state of perfect, weightless equilibrium.

"My great-grandfather was not just an alchemist," Velázquez said. "He was an engineer of impossible things." He turned from the orb and gestured toward a dark, recessed archway in the far wall of the chamber, a space Oliver hadn't noticed in his previous projections. "The paintings are in here. Secure."

He led them into the alcove. It was a small, chapel-like space, cool and silent. And there, leaning against the curved stone wall, were the four unwrapped Bryce canvases, their faces turned away, their secrets hidden for a final few moments. Velázquez then gestured back toward the main chamber, his hand indicating a point high up on the vast, curved wall opposite the main entrance.

Oliver followed his gaze. At first, he saw nothing but ancient, seamless stone. But as his eyes adjusted, he made out a small, almost imperceptible opening, a perfect, circular aperture no wider than a dinner plate, set at least a hundred feet up in the wall. It was the only break in the chamber's perfect, solid construction.

"The sun is still too high in the sky," Velázquez said, his voice a quiet, instructional murmur. "But in a little over two hours, at precisely 3:33 in the afternoon, its rays will align perfectly with that aperture."

He pointed to the massive, crystalline sphere hanging in the center of the room.

"The light will travel across this chamber and strike the heart of the Turabet," he explained. "That is when the event will begin."

Velázquez gave them a moment to absorb the sight of the aperture, the Turabet, and the four canvases, silent and waiting in the cool, dark alcove.

"We must prepare the space," he said, his voice a low, instructional murmur. "But the paintings ... they must remain unseen for now. It is better that they are not ... on public display when the others arrive."

He gestured to two large, professional-grade artist's portfolios leaning against the wall, which Oliver hadn't noticed before. "I brought these from my studio. They will keep the canvases protected and mobile."

Together, the four of them carefully slid the four Bryce canvases into the portfolios. The fit was snug. Zipped shut, they looked like nothing more than the oversized luggage of a visiting artist. They carried the portfolios back into the main chamber and placed them leaning against the wall closest to the Turabet.

With the final pieces in place, the vast, empty chamber now felt like a charged and ready stage. They stood in the center, a small, tight knot of humanity in the immense, ancient space.

"The alignment will last for precisely two hundred and ten seconds," Velázquez began, his voice a quiet murmur that seemed to be swallowed by the chamber's profound silence. "The light will be at its absolute peak intensity for only a few moments, exactly at the halfway point. That is when the ... event ... will occur. That is when the Hexcelion will form in its fullest."

"And what happens then?" Oliver asked, his gaze fixed on the Turabet es ploe dieu, its crystalline surface seeming to pulse with a faint, internal light.

"That," Velázquez said with a small, tired shrug, "is a question no living person can answer with certainty. The ritual, as it is known, is an act of observation, not participation. A tradition." He paused, his gaze sweeping the empty perimeter of the chamber. "Soon, this place will begin to fill. Local people, a few curious tourists, a handful of ... others who seem to understand the significance of this day. And then, there are the monks."

"Monks?" Daniela asked, her voice a soft note of surprise.

"The Order of Atlantean Monks," Velázquez confirmed, a look of profound, almost weary respect on his face. "They are a complete mystery. No one knows where they come from or where they go. They are a reclusive, ancient order who appear only on this day, once a year, for this single purpose. Twenty-one of them will enter the chamber just before the alignment begins."

He gestured to the circular floor around the firepit. "They will form a circle here. And for the entire two hundred and ten seconds, they will perform the sacred chant. The *Refraine del Acimut.*"

The Azimuth Refrain. Oliver's mind flashed back to the Noncemeister's nonsensical verse, and the Bryce comics – to the panels depicting robed, faceless figures circling a glowing Hexcelion, their mouths open in a silent, cosmic song. It was real. All of it.

Javier, who had been listening with a look of profound, skeptical awe, finally spoke. "And this firepit?" he asked, nodding toward the unlit stones at their feet. "It is part of this ... tradition?"

"It is the heart of it," Velázquez replied. "But it is a heart that has not beaten in living memory. According to the old texts, my great-grandfather's texts, the fire is never meant to be lit by human hands." He looked up at the crystalline orb, then back down to the empty pit. "The legend says that on the rarest of occasions, on a day of ... unique celestial resonance ... the Hexcelion itself will ignite the flame. A fire born not of wood or coal, but of pure, focused light. A fire from another dimension."

Oliver felt a jolt of pure, electric understanding. He looked from Velázquez's face to the four concealed paintings at his feet. *Unique celestial resonance.* He was the only person in the room who knew the true, secret meaning of those words. Today was not just a tradition. It was the fulfillment of a prophecy.

"But as I said," Velázquez concluded, a dry, academic skepticism returning to his voice, "that is just a legend. For as long as anyone can remember, the monks have simply chanted, the light has faded, and the day has ended."

He fell silent. The four of them stood in the vast, expectant chamber, the paintings like silent monoliths at their feet, all eyes on the massive, crystalline orb hanging impossibly in the darkness above them.

799262 (July 18)

The black sedan turned off the main coastal highway, the smooth asphalt giving way to a rougher, unpaved road that began a steep, winding ascent. Nick sat in the back, his eyes fixed on the car ahead, a small, nondescript sedan that was kicking up a cloud of dust. Beside him, Adele was a silent, coiled spring of anticipation.

"He's not trying to lose us," Nick noted, more to himself than to her. "He's just leading us."

"He has no choice," Adele replied, her gaze also locked on the car ahead. "He has to get to his destination. We are just an inconvenient necessity."

The road crested a hill, and the castle appeared before them, a mad, beautiful fortress of towers and battlements perched on the highest point, overlooking the sea. Nick watched as Oliver's car pulled to a stop at the base of a long, stone staircase. He saw them get out – Oliver, the woman, and an older man he didn't recognize. At the top of the stairs, a fourth figure emerged from a massive, arched doorway to greet them. A moment later, all four disappeared inside.

"They're in," he said.

Their own driver pulled the sedan to a stop behind the empty rental car.

"Let's go," Adele said, her hand already on the door handle.

They got out, the crisp winter air a sharp contrast to the stale, recycled atmosphere of the car. They walked with a quiet, purposeful urgency up the long, stone staircase. As they reached the top landing, a man in a simple, dark uniform stepped out from a small guardhouse Nick hadn't noticed from the road. He was an older man, his face weathered, his posture relaxed but firm.

"Good afternoon," the guard said in slow, careful English. "I am sorry, but the castle is not yet open to the public."

"We're not the public," Adele stated, her voice carrying a tone of cold, easy authority that had worked on a dozen other functionaries in the past week. "We are here for the private event.

The guard gave a small, apologetic smile. "The event does not begin for another two hours, Señora. The grounds will open to visitors at 3 o'clock."

"We just saw a group go inside," Nick interjected, his own patience wearing thin. "Four of them."

"Ah, yes," the guard said, his smile not wavering. "They are with the family. They are not visitors."

Nick and Adele exchanged a look of pure, frustrated confusion. *Family? What family? Oliver's only family was Nate.*

"And what exactly is this 'event?'" Adele asked, her voice now laced with a sharp, interrogative edge.

The guard shrugged, a gesture of simple, local indifference. "It is an old tradition. On this day, the sun, it shines through a hole in the wall. It makes a pretty shape. The monks, they come and sing. That is all. Now, if you will excuse me, I must ask you to wait with the others down the hill. It will not be long."

He gestured back the way they came. The wall of polite, local bureaucracy was as impenetrable as the stone of the castle itself. Defeated, they turned and walked back down the stairs.

"Family," Nick muttered, the word a piece of grit in his teeth. "What the hell does that mean? None of this makes sense. The OP_RETURN was clear – something is supposed to happen at the Obelisk today, which is sixty miles away. What on Earth is this light show they're attending in this godforsaken castle?"

"It means we're missing a piece of the puzzle," Adele said, her gaze fixed on the closed, ancient doors of the castle. "It doesn't matter. They're in there. They're not coming out. We'll wait."

799278 (July 18)

By 3 o'clock, the chamber was no longer a silent, private sanctuary. It had transformed. A steady stream of people began to filter in through the main entrance, their hushed whispers and shuffling feet a soft, rising tide of sound that filled the immense space. They were a strange mix: quiet, elderly locals who looked like they had been making this pilgrimage for decades; a handful of curious, camera-toting tourists; and others, Oliver noted, with a different kind of energy – men and women with a sharp, watchful intensity in their eyes, who seemed to understand that this was more than just a local curiosity.

They fanned out, forming a wide, loose circle around the chamber's perimeter, leaving the central space around the firepit respectfully empty. Oliver, Daniela, Javier and Velázquez stood together near the portfolios, a small, isolated island in the growing sea of observers. The castle guards, a dozen of them in crisp, formal uniforms, stood at discreet intervals along the wall, their presence a calm but firm deterrent to any potential disruption.

Oliver scanned the crowd, his senses on high alert, his gaze sweeping over the faces, searching for the ones he knew were coming.

He saw them first. Maren and Bojan. They entered together, not with the furtive energy of thieves, but with a kind of grim, proprietary air, as if they were attending a legal proceeding where the verdict was already known. Maren's face was a pale, tight mask of desperate resolve. Her eyes, when they found Oliver's across the vast chamber, were filled not with the warmth of a former friend, but with the cold, hard light of a zealot. Bojan was a shadow at her side, his massive frame a silent, menacing promise. They took up a position near the main entrance, their backs to the wall, two predators waiting patiently for the moment to strike.

A few minutes later, the second pair arrived. Nick and Adele moved with a different kind of energy – a cold, tactical precision. They were here to close a case – not for a spiritual reckoning. They split up immediately, Adele finding a vantage point near a side exit, while Nick melted into the thickest part of the crowd on the opposite side of the chamber. They were professionals, establishing a crossfire, a perfect tactical envelopment. Nick's eyes eventually met Oliver's, and he gave a small, almost imperceptible nod, a hunter acknowl-edging his prey.

The four of them – Oliver, Daniela, Javier, and Velázquez – were now the undisputed center of a silent, multi-front war. From one side, the desperate, mystical fervor of Maren. From the other, the cold, professional ruthlessness of Nick and Adele. The air in the chamber was thick with a tension so palpable it felt like a change in atmospheric pressure. No one moved. No one spoke. The presence of the crowd and the guards was a fragile, temporary truce, a shared understanding that the violence would wait.

For now.

Velázquez leaned in close to Oliver, his gaze sweeping over the unnaturally large and intense crowd. "I have been coming to this event since I was a boy," he murmured, his voice a low, urgent whisper that was almost lost in the rising hum of the room. "I have never seen a crowd this large. Never. There is a different energy here today. Something is ... expected."

The minutes leading up to the ceremony stretched into an eternity. The low, ambient hum of the crowd began to fade, a hundred separate conversations dying out one by one, replaced by a collective, unspoken sense of anticipation. A strange, electric tension filled the vast chamber, a feeling Oliver could taste in the back of his throat, like the air before a lightning strike. He stood with Daniela, Javier and Velázquez, a small, isolated island in the silent, expectant sea of observers. His gaze kept flicking between the two hostile camps on either side of the room. Maren and Bojan were statues of cold fury; Nick and Adele were coiled springs of predatory patience.

At precisely 10 minutes before the main event, a low, grinding sound, like stone on ancient stone, echoed from the far side of the chamber, opposite the main entrance. Oliver's head snapped in that direction. A section of the seamless, curved wall he hadn't paid attention to before was moving. A massive, previously invisible stone door, at least 20 feet high, was swinging inward, revealing a passage of absolute, impenetrable darkness.

"They are here," Velázquez whispered, his voice a tight, reverent murmur beside Oliver.

From the blackness of the passage, they emerged.

The crowd let out a collective, hushed gasp. They came in a single, silent file, 21 figures clad in long, flowing, immaculate white robes. Heavy, deep hoods completely obscured their faces, leaving only dark, empty voids where their features should have been. They moved with a slow, solemn, otherworldly grace, their bare feet making no sound on the cold stone floor. They did not seem to walk so much as glide, a silent, white river flowing into the heart of the chamber.

They were the Order of Atlantean Monks.

Oliver watched, mesmerized, as they reached the ceremonial firepit. Without a word, without a single, wasted motion, they fanned out, forming a perfect, equidistant circle around the unlit stones. They stopped as one, their backs to the crowd, their hooded heads bowed in silent reverence toward the center. The moment the circle was complete, a profound, absolute silence fell over the chamber. The nervous shuffling of the crowd, the coughs, the whispers – it all ceased, swallowed by a sudden, sacred stillness. It was as if the air itself was holding its breath. The only sound was the faint, distant, impossible crash of waves against an unseen shore.

A few seconds before 3:33 p.m., a single, glorious, resonant bell sounded, seeming to come not from any specific direction, but from the very stones of the castle itself. It was a physical vibration that traveled up through the floor, through Oliver's feet, and settled deep in his chest, a single, perfect, and ancient note that silenced the last of the nervous whispers in the chamber.

As the final echo of the bell faded, it happened.

A perfect, golden spear of sunlight pierced the circular aperture high up in the wall. It cut a brilliant, dust-mote-filled path through the vast, dark chamber and struck the heart of the Turabet es ploe dieu. The crystalline sphere seemed to drink in the light. The intricate, polished obsidian and silver latticework on its surface began to glow with a soft, internal luminescence, and the geometric patterns within the orb started to shift and refract the golden beam, casting a thousand tiny, complex rainbows onto the chamber walls.

The 21 monks, who had been as still as statues, began to move as one. They started a low, multi-toned, harmonious hum, a sound that was both human and something more – a resonant frequency that seemed to vibrate in perfect sympathy with the glowing orb above them.

In the air directly above the unlit firepit, a faint, almost imperceptible shimmer appeared, like the heat haze on a summer road.

"Now," Velázquez whispered, his voice a tight, urgent command.

As the first, faint, shimmering lines of light began to trace the familiar, six-armed spiral in the air, Oliver and Javier moved. While the entire room – the tourists, the locals and his three sets of adversaries – was mesmerized by the impossible object being drawn into existence, they knelt. With quiet, practiced movements, they unzipped the large portfolios, their hands working in the deepening, unnatural twilight cast by the forming symbol.

Oliver carefully slid out the first two canvases – *The Toddler* and *It Is Time* – their familiar, powerful imagery a strange, grounding presence in the midst of the cosmic display. He leaned them against the low, stone plinths facing the firepit, their backs to the crowd. Javier did the same with the other two – the haunting, beautiful face of Anariadne and the impossible, unfinished geometry of the Hexcelion-like machine.

He looked up. The shimmer had solidified into a perfect, luminous, three-dimensional object of impossible geometry, a six-armed spiral of pure, white light hanging in the air. It pulsed with a quiet, internal energy, casting strange, shifting shadows that danced on the faces of the stunned and silent crowd. The space around it was bending. The Hexcelion was born.

As the Hexcelion solidified – a breathtaking, three-dimensional object of pure, white light hanging impossibly in the air – the monks' harmonious hum transitioned into words.

They chanted in a language older than any nation, a resonant, powerful intonation that Oliver understood not with his ears, but with his soul.

"Ex igne, tempus nascitur."

Out of fire, time is born.

The phrase, the first part of the Azimuth Refrain, echoed through the vast chamber, the sound seeming to energize the luminous symbol above them. The Hexcelion pulsed, its light growing from a soft, ethereal glow to a brilliant, almost blinding intensity. At its absolute peak, at the exact midpoint of the 210-second ceremony, the symbol unleashed its power. A torrent of brilliant, white-hot sparks, like a miniature meteor shower, shot down from the central nexus and struck the unlit logs in the ceremonial firepit.

The wood ignited instantly with a deafening *whoosh*, a column of golden, smokeless flame erupting toward the ceiling. The crowd let out a single, sharp, collective gasp of pure, terrified awe. Even the monks, the stoic, ancient guardians of the ritual, faltered in their chant, their perfect circle momentarily broken by an involuntary, staggered step backward from the impossible, legendary fire.

In that instant of stunned, global silence, as Oliver stared into the magical, otherworldly flames, the Guru's words, a quiet seed of wisdom planted in his mind months ago at the ashram in India, landed with the force of a thunderbolt.

The bottle must be broken for the message to appear.

He looked at the four canvases leaning against the stone plinths at the edge of the fire's light. They were the bottles. The priceless, beautiful and ultimately disposable containers.

And then, the second, more powerful half of the prophecy crashed down on him, a moment of such violent, terrifying clarity that it took his breath away.

The seed must be destroyed for the flower to grow.

The seed. The seed phrases. The keys to the wallets. They weren't written in invisible ink. They were woven into the very fabric of the canvas, a message that could only be released through an act of ultimate, creative destruction. He now understood the true, terrible meaning of the ritual. This wasn't a ceremony of observation. It was a ceremony of sacrifice.

"*¡Dios mío!*" Velázquez breathed, his voice a choked, incredulous whisper beside Oliver. "The fire ... it's real. The legend is real." He stared into the impossible, smokeless flames, his lifetime of academic skepticism instantly incinerated, replaced by the raw, terrified awe of a man witnessing a true miracle.

But Oliver was no longer listening to him. Guru Brahma's words, the Noncemeister's riddles, the homeless man's deranged mumbles, the cryptic lines from the Bryce comics – all the disparate, confusing pieces of the puzzle had just fused into a single, terrifying and perfect clarity. He knew, with an absolute, intuitive certainty that transcended logic, what came next. He knew what the second, secret part of the refrain must be.

Before the monks could recover from their shock and resume their chant, Oliver took a deep breath. He opened his mouth, and it was not his own voice that came out, but something older, deeper and more powerful. He chanted the words into the stunned silence of the chamber, his voice clear and resonant, a perfect, seamless continuation of the ancient ritual.

"*Ex tempore, ignis nascitur!*"

Out of time, fire is born.

The tautological loop of creation. The rebellious union of opposites. *Out of fire, time is born. And out of time, fire is born.* The ancient Atlantean words, the second half of the great Azimuth Refrain, echoed through the vast chamber. The effect was instantaneous. The 21 monks, who had been a wall of stunned confusion just a moment before, stopped. They turned as one, their cowled heads rising to face the young man who had just spoken the lost, sacred words of their order.

There was no anger in their hidden faces, no sense of violation. There was only a profound, ancient recognition. They were the guardians of the ritual, the keepers of the first half of the key. And he, Oliver Battolo, was the one they had been waiting for.

With a slow, solemn yet perfectly synchronized movement, they took a single step backward, creating a deliberate, unmistakable opening in their sacred circle. It was a silent invitation. An acknowledgment. He was not an intruder. He was the one who had come to complete the ceremony.

Accepting his role, accepting the impossible, beautiful and terrifying truth of the moment, Oliver stepped forward. The air inside the monks' circle was different, charged with an ancient, palpable energy. He felt the eyes of everyone in the chamber on him – Daniela's awe, Javier's disbelief, the cold, confused fury of his enemies. But none of it mattered. He was no longer a participant. He was the instrument.

He turned to the wall and lifted the fourth Bryce. Anariadne. He looked at her haunting, turquoise eyes one last time, in a final, quiet acknowledgment of the demon he had conquered. He walked into the sacred space between the monks carrying it, the heat from the impossible fire a dry, clean warmth on his face. Then, with a smooth, decisive motion, he threw the painting into the heart of the magical, smokeless fire.

The effect was instantaneous and breathtaking. The heat from the Hexcelion's flame did not simply burn the canvas. It was a different kind of fire, a fire that seemed to consume the physical to release the metaphysical. As the oils and pigments began to char and peel away, a new layer, previously invisible, was activated. A series of words, written in a fine, elegant script, began to glow on the canvas, a brilliant, cool, blue-white against the roaring gold of the flames. They were there for only a few, brilliant seconds, a perfect, fleeting message.

Oliver didn't read them. He absorbed them, the phrases downloading directly into his mind with the effortless clarity of a projection. And then, the painting was gone, consumed by the flames, leaving not even ash behind.

He didn't hesitate. He immediately picked up the second canvas, the impossible, unfinished Noncelion, the blueprint for a machine that could bend time. He cast it into the fire. Again, the thermochromic paint activated, a new set of glowing, blue-white words burning themselves into his memory before the canvas dissolved into nothingness. He now had the keys to the final wallets. The prize was his.

But the Guru's words were not just about the message; they were about the bottle. The prophecy was about fulfilling the ritual – not just about accessing the wallets. He looked at the two remaining paintings, at the two masterpieces that had started his entire journey. *The Toddler. It Is Time.* They were not just paintings. They were part of the five cosmic signatures.

In a final, breathtaking act of faith and destruction, he picked up the remaining two paintings and without a moment's hesitation, threw them both into the fire. He was no longer just claiming a prize. He was closing a door. He was ending the game. He was destroying the bottles to ensure no one else could ever be poisoned by the message within. It was an act of ultimate, selfless acceptance. The five signatures were now one with the flame.

As the last of the canvases dissolved into the magical, smokeless flame, the 210 seconds came to a close. The spear of golden light from the aperture vanished as abruptly as it had appeared. In the sudden, profound darkness, the Hexcelion, the luminous, impossible object that had held the entire chamber in its thrall, flickered once and disappeared. A moment later, the golden fire in the ceremonial pit extinguished itself with a soft *whoomph*, leaving behind only a plume of thick, gray smoke that smelled of burnt canvas and ozone.

For a single, frozen heartbeat, there was absolute silence. And then, all hell broke loose.

The crowd – a mix of stunned tourists and terrified locals who had just witnessed a genuine, undeniable miracle followed by the public destruction of what was clearly priceless art – erupted. A collective scream of panic and confusion tore through the chamber. The fragile truce of the shared spectacle shattered, and the room dissolved into a panicked, stampeding mob, a chaotic surge of bodies pushing toward the main entrance.

Through the smoke and screaming bodies, Oliver saw the threats converging. From one side, Bojan shoved his way through the crowd, a brutal battering ram of pure fury, his face a mask of raw hatred. From the other, Nick and Adele moved with a more tactical, predatory urgency, their shock hardening into the cold rage of a prize snatched away. But as his enemies closed in, a new, strange detail registered in the back of his mind: Maren was gone. She had simply vanished from Bojan's side.

But he had no time to process it, because he realized they were not the only ones moving.

The 21 monks, their ritual complete, did not retreat. They simply turned. As one, they linked arms, their white-robed forms creating a silent, impassive and absolutely impenetrable human wall around the firepit, their cowled heads a line of dark, implacable voids. They did not speak. They did not fight. They just stood, a formidable and intimidating barrier that absorbed the first, frantic surge of his enemies.

"¡Seguridad!" Velázquez yelled, his voice a sharp, commanding crack in the chaos. He was shouting at the castle guards, pointing, directing them to form a cordon and control the panicked stampede toward the main exit.

A hand grabbed Oliver's arm, its grip as strong and steady as iron. It was Javier. Daniela's arm was in his other hand.

"This way! Now!" the doorman yelled over the din, his eyes clear and focused.

Javier didn't wait for an answer. He shoved them through the opening and into a narrow, dark and blessedly quiet stone corridor, pulling the heavy door shut behind them just as a fresh wave of panic erupted in the chamber. The screams and chaos were instantly muffled, replaced by the sound of their own ragged breathing and the frantic slap of their shoes on the ancient stone floor.

They ran, their footsteps echoing in the tight passage, the smell of dust and damp stone replacing the smoke and ozone. Javier led them through a maze of service tunnels Oliver wouldn't have known existed, a secret geography hidden beneath the castle's grand design. After what felt like an eternity, they emerged through another unmarked door into a deserted, windswept courtyard at the back of the castle, the late afternoon sun a blinding, welcome shock.

Their rental car was waiting exactly where Javier had left it. They scrambled in, and Javier gunned the engine, tires spitting gravel as they sped down a private service road, leaving the fire, the magic and the chaos of the Chamber of Time behind them.

They drove in silence for several minutes, the car a small, speeding sanctuary, putting as much distance as possible between themselves and the impossible event they had just survived. Oliver's mind was a whirlwind, the glowing, ethereal images of the seed words flashing behind his eyes, a sacred, terrifying, yet still incomplete message. He had seen them, yes, but in the chaos, had he truly memorized them all? In the right order? The doubt was a cold, sickening knot in his stomach.

Daniela, who had been staring out the window, her own breathing slowly returning to normal, finally turned from the window. She reached into the pocket of her jacket and pulled out her phone. Her hand was trembling slightly, but her voice, when she spoke, was a quiet, steady instrument of pure triumph.

"I got the photos," she said.

799312 (July 18)

The car moved through the quiet, tree-lined streets of the Carrasco neighborhood, the opulent mansions a silent, sleeping audience to their strange, late-night procession. It was 15 minutes until 10 o'clock. The manic, world-altering energy of the afternoon at the castle had receded, replaced by a new, more profound kind of tension. After the escape, they had retreated to the Sofitel, spending the last few hours in a state of suspended animation in their suite. They had barely spoken, each lost in their own thoughts, processing the impossible miracle they had witnessed.

Now, back in the familiar, quiet comfort of Javier's sedan, the finality of the night was settling in. Oliver sat in the back next to Daniela, his gaze fixed on the passing city lights, his heart a slow, heavy drumbeat against his ribs.

"I still can't believe it," Daniela said, her voice a quiet, awestruck whisper that was almost lost in the hum of the tires. "The fire. The monks. You just ... knew what to do."

"I didn't know," Oliver replied, his gaze still fixed on the passing city lights. "I just ... felt it. It was like the answer was already there, waiting for me."

Javier, who had been a silent, stoic presence behind the wheel, finally spoke, his eyes meeting Oliver's in the rearview mirror. "What you did in that chamber, Señor Battolo ... it was not the work of a normal man." There was no judgment in his voice, only a profound, quiet awe.

"It wasn't me, Javier," Oliver said, a new, strange humility settling over him. "I was just a part of it." He leaned forward, the exhaustion of the day momentarily forgotten, replaced by the rising, electric energy of what was to come. "Just a few more minutes. We're almost there. I'm going to see my father."

He said the words with a kind of breathless, joyful certainty. After everything he had been through, this was the final prize. The reunion. The explanation. The chance to finally go home.

He saw Javier's eyes in the mirror. The doorman's face, which should have been lit with a shared, triumphant joy, instead clouded over with a look of profound, almost unbearable sadness.

"Señor Battolo," Javier said, his voice a low, gentle murmur, heavy with a sorrow Oliver could not comprehend. "A son's love for his father is a powerful thing. It can make a man see what he wishes to see, not what is truly there."

The car pulled up a few blocks from the Plaza de la Independencia, the distant sound of a city still celebrating Constitution Day a muted, festive hum in the background. Javier cut the engine as a tense, profound silence filled the car. The journey was over. The final destination was just a short walk away.

"This is as far as I take you," Javier said, turning in his seat to face them. His expression was a mask of calm, professional resolve, but Oliver could see the deep, worried lines etched around his eyes. "Agustín, Diego, and the others are already in position. We have a discreet, 200-yard perimeter around the entire plaza. They are a quiet, watchful presence, there to deter, not to engage. No one will interrupt your meeting."

Oliver nodded, a lump forming in his throat. He looked at the doorman, a man who had asked for nothing and risked everything out of pure, simple loyalty. "Thank you, Javier," he said, the words feeling small and inadequate.

"Go," Javier said, the mysterious sorrow returning to his eyes. "Your answer is waiting."

Oliver and Daniela got out of the car, the cool night air a sharp, welcome shock. From the corner of Oliver's eyes, he could see Diego on one side of the plaza's perimeter and Agustín on the other, forming an impenetrable shield around them. They walked the final few blocks together, their footsteps echoing in the quiet, tree-lined streets, the festive sounds of the city growing louder as they approached the plaza. They didn't speak. There was nothing left to say. The entire, impossible journey of the past year and a half had led to this single, solitary point in time.

They reached the edge of the plaza. The Obelisk, massive and floodlit, dominated the night sky, a stark, white spear of hope and memory. About 50 yards from its base, Daniela stopped.

"This is your walk to take, Oliver," she said, her voice quiet and steady, cutting through the noise of his own turbulent emotions. She looked from the monument back to him, her eyes full of a profound, unwavering trust. "This is for you and your father. I'll wait here."

He looked at her, at the woman who had walked into the fire with him, who had faced down his demons and her own, who had become not just his partner, but his anchor in a world that had dissolved into chaos. He wanted to say a thousand things, to thank her, to tell her he loved her. But the words felt too small for the moment.

He just nodded, a single, grateful acknowledgment of everything she was, and everything she had done. He turned and began the final, lonely walk toward the monument, toward the man he had crossed the world to find.

The final 50 yards felt longer than all the miles that had come before. He walked across the open plaza, his footsteps the only sound in his own private universe. The noise of the city, the distant, festive music, the low hum of the traffic – it all faded away, replaced by the frantic, hopeful, terrified beating of his own heart.

He reached the base of the Obelisk. He ran a hand over the cool, smooth stone, a solid, grounding presence in a world that felt like it was about to dissolve. He looked up at the massive, floodlit monument, a stark, white spear aimed at the heart of the winter night sky.

He was here. The final destination.

He waited. The last few minutes before 10 o'clock stretched into an eternity. He thought of the journey that had brought him to this single point in time: the grief, the confusion, the terror, the impossible, beautiful, and terrifying moments of revelation. He thought of the Noncemeister, of Maren, of Anariadne. He thought of his father, the man he had mourned, the man he had been angry with, the man he was about to see again. The weight of it all, the sheer, impossible reality of the moment, was almost too much to bear. He closed his eyes, took a deep, shuddering breath, and waited for the sound of approaching footsteps.

A quiet, rhythmic sound on the pavement. Oliver's eyes snapped open.

At exactly 10 o'clock, a figure emerged from the shadows at the far edge of the plaza. He was a man of average height, with a familiar, easy gait, his hands tucked into the pockets of a simple, dark jacket. Even from a distance, Oliver's heart seized in his chest. The set of his shoulders, the way he carried himself – it was him. It was his father.

A wave of pure, unadulterated relief so powerful it almost buckled his knees washed over him. He had made it. The quest was over. He was home. A thousand questions, a thousand emotions, a thousand things he wanted to say all surged up at once. He took a single, staggering step forward, a soundless, joyful sob catching in his throat.

The man continued to walk toward him, his pace unhurried. As he stepped out of the long shadows of the plaza and into the bright, direct glare of the monument's floodlights, the illusion shattered.

It wasn't him.

The resemblance was staggering, a cruel, genetic echo. The same build, the same dark hair, the same quiet, confident energy. But the face was different. The lines around the eyes were not his father's. The set of the jaw was harder, more angular. It was the face he had seen in Guru Brahma's ashram, the face of a man who was a stranger and yet, impossibly, almost family.

It was Rafael Forlan.

The hope that had soared in Oliver's chest just a moment before crashed and burned, leaving only a cold, hollow emptiness. He stopped, the joyful, welcoming smile freezing on his face. The quest wasn't over. The man he had crossed the world to find, the man he had mourned and raged against and finally, finally, was ready to forgive ... he hadn't come.

Rafael Forlan closed the distance, his expression a mask of grim, urgent seriousness. He stopped a few feet from Oliver, his eyes full of a deep, sorrowful empathy that Oliver did not understand.

"Your father sends his apologies, Oliver," Rafael began, his voice a low, steady instrument of command. "He cannot be here. He had to leave, about two weeks ago. He reached out to me, asked me to come back from India to meet you in his place."

The words were a quiet, devastating blow. Oliver just stared at him, the last, flickering embers of his hope turning to cold, gray ash. He had been so sure. So absolutely certain. The disappointment was so profound, so complete, that it left no room for any other emotion.

Rafael opened his mouth to continue, to explain the inexplicable, but before he could, a new sound cut through the quiet of the plaza.

A choked, incredulous gasp.

A figure was running toward them from the edge of the plaza, a frantic, desperate energy in her movement. It was Daniela. From her vantage point 50 yards away, she had finally, clearly, seen the face of the man who was speaking to Oliver.

"Tío?" she cried out, her voice a mixture of shock, confusion, and a dawning, impossible joy. "Tío Rafael?"

She crashed into him, her arms wrapping around him in a fierce, desperate hug. Rafael, his own grim composure momentarily broken, was stunned. He held her, his expression a mask of pure joy.

"Daniela?" he breathed, his voice a choked whisper. "*Mija* ... you came back. You came back to him."

Oliver just stood there, a silent, forgotten observer, watching as a shocked and heartfelt family reunion erupted in the middle of the wreckage of his own. He was no longer at the center of his own story. He was a stranger, a ghost, watching a play he did not understand, his own grief a forgotten, irrelevant detail in a new and unexpected drama.

Rafael held Daniela for a long moment, a silent, heartfelt reunion that seemed to exist outside of time. Finally, he pulled back, his hands resting on Daniela's shoulders, his expression a mixture of profound love and a deep, world-weary sorrow.

He looked from his niece's face to Oliver's, and the grim, urgent reality of his mission returned.

"I am so sorry, Oliver," he said, his voice low and heavy. "Your father wanted to be here. More than anything. But he couldn't."

He took a deep breath, the words of his message a heavy weight. "A new player has emerged in the game," he began, his voice dropping to a conspiratorial whisper. "A ghost from your father's past. A man who has been methodically, and violently, consolidating control of the entire clandestine network we have all been a part of. He is more powerful, more ruthless than anyone Nate has ever encountered. And in the last few weeks ... he has become aware of your father's whereabouts."

The full, terrifying implication of Rafael's words crashed down on Oliver. The silver man. Da Silva. The man from his projections.

"Nate had to disappear," Rafael continued, his gaze intense. "To go deeper underground than ever before. Not just to protect himself. But to protect you, Oliver. Even I do not know where he has gone. As long as this man is hunting him, you are a target. Your father's final act before he left was to ensure that I was here, to make sure you completed your quest, to make sure you received your inheritance."

He paused, his eyes locking onto Oliver's, delivering the final, crucial part of the message. "But he was very clear about the terms of that inheritance, Oliver. The wallets you now control, the ones from the Bryce paintings ... they belonged to both Christiaan and him. Your father's final instruction was this: half of that money is yours, a reward for the journey. The other half is not. It belongs to Christiaan's family. You are to be a steward, not just a king."

He looked from Oliver's stricken face to Daniela's, then back again, his message delivered. "For now, I will be here. You know where to find me if you need me." Rafael gave Daniela's arm one last, loving squeeze, then took a step back, melting into the shadows from which he had emerged.

He was gone.

Oliver and Daniela were left standing alone at the base of the monument, the festive sounds of the city a distant, mocking echo. The chapter of his quest was over. He had won. He had the keys to a fortune beyond his wildest dreams. But his victory felt like a devastating, hollow loss. The mystery of his father was solved, but a new, more dangerous one had just begun. He was the guardian of a secret, and the most dangerous man in the world now knew his name.

PART IV. ATONUS

CHAPTER 13. OCTOBER 31

808776 (September 21)

A ridiculously oversized, almost cartoonish, unlit cigar jutted out from the Noncemeister's lips. He looked at Oliver, a slow, lazy smile spreading across his face.

"Ah, there you are, Battu," he said, his voice a warm, familiar greeting. "You're late. I was about to start without you."

He reached into the pocket of his absurd, patchwork jacket and produced a second, identical cigar, which he tossed to Oliver with a flick of his wrist. Oliver caught it effortlessly.

"Care for a smoke?" the Noncemeister asked. "A celebratory puff for a change in seasons?"

Oliver looked at the cigar in his hand. It felt solid, real. He brought it to his lips. The Noncemeister snapped his fingers, and the tips of both their cigars instantly ignited, glowing a warm, friendly orange in the dim, perpetual twilight of the projection. Oliver took a slow, deep puff. The smoke was rich, fragrant and surprisingly smooth. He let the smoke out in a long, lazy plume, watching it form perfect concentric smoke rings that hung in the air for an impossibly long time before vanishing.

"I've been thinking," he began, his voice relaxed, conversational. "For the last few months, really. About something I saw in the chamber. Something Pittamiglio told me."

"Oh?" the Noncemeister said, a theatrical arch to his eyebrow. "Do tell. Was it the winning lottery numbers? A stock tip? The secret to perfect, fluffy scrambled eggs?"

"The Noncelion," Oliver said, ignoring the bait. "The nine-armed shape. The machine that organizes time. I've been trying to understand it, but I keep hitting a wall. It feels ... incomplete. Like I'm missing the key."

The Noncemeister let out a great, booming laugh, a sound that seemed to send ripples through the very fabric of the room. He slapped his knee, a cloud of cigar ash puffing into the air. "Incomplete! The boy says the key is missing!" he howled with glee. He leaned forward, his purple eyes twinkling with mischief, and pointed a gloved finger directly at his own chest.

"Batlu, my dear, dense, and delightful boy," he said, tapping his chest for emphasis. "Look at me. What am I? I am the Noncemeister. The Master of the Nonces. The Grand Poobah that gives every single heartbeat of the timechain its unique and unforgeable contour."

He took a dramatic puff of his cigar, clearly enjoying the performance.

"Now," he continued, leaning in as if sharing a great and obvious secret, "if a simple, humble, and devastatingly handsome Noncemeister is the master of the nonce ... who do you think might be the master of the Noncelion?"

Oliver just stared at him, the riddle hanging in the air between them, feeling both profound and utterly absurd. He took another puff of his cigar and sighed, a small, weary smile on his face. He knew when he was beaten. "Never mind," he said. "I give up."

"Well, I for one am as sure of it as Sunday is made of Gorgonzola. As sure as three times seven is nine. As sure as ..." He coughed suddenly, and a dense cloud of cigar smoke came out of his mouth and ears. One part of the smoke formed a circular target with a bullseye. The other part formed an arrow. The arrow propelled itself towards the target and landed on the bullseye. The Noncemeister recovered from his cough, turned to Oliver and winked.

Oliver looked away from the Noncemeister, his gaze sweeping over the surreal, purple-twinged twilight version of his own apartment. His expression shifted, the intellectual curiosity of the riddle replaced by the quiet certainty of a man who had realized the answer to a question that had been plaguing him for months. He changed the subject.

"The cage. The one I saw you in all those months ago. I know who put you in it," he said, softly.

The Noncemeister, who looked like he was about to launch into a nonsensical verse, stopped. He looked at Oliver, a mischievous twinkle in his deep purple eyes. "Oh?" he said, his voice quiet. "And who is this villain of our little melodrama?"

Oliver met his gaze, his own eyes clear and steady. The answer, which would have been impossible for him to comprehend just a few months ago, was now a simple, undeniable truth.

"I did," he said.

He took a slow puff of his cigar, the words a quiet confession in the silent, sacred space of the projection. "There was no cage," he continued. "Not a real one. The cage was me. It was the escapism. It was the wine. It was the despair. It was ... Anariadne. I chose to step into the darkness, and in doing so, I locked you out. I locked myself out. The cage was the long dark winter of my soul. It was my own *Inferna*. I had the key all along. It took me hitting the cold, smelly ground of Washington Square Park that night to find it."

The Noncemeister looked at him keenly. Oliver saw in his eyes a flicker of deep, ancient, paternal pride. He took a long, slow puff of his own cigar, the glowing tip a small, warm star in the darkness.

"Look at you now, Batlu," the Noncemeister said, his voice now a low, gentle rumble. "You really, really, really are a big boy now, aren't you? The key is that you are not just the map. You are the territory as well."

Oliver smiled. For once, the Noncemeister had given him a straight answer. As straight as he could get.

A distant look appeared in the Noncemeister's eyes. "Well, I suppose that's enough noncense for the day, innit, Battu? Off you go, and off I go!" With a soft smile and a snap of his finger, the purple texture that had engulfed the apartment vanished, taking the Noncemeister along with it.

The apartment was quiet, the only sound the soft, rhythmic ticking of the antique clock on the mantelpiece. Oliver was standing by the window, looking out at the early autumn evening, the streetlights just beginning to glow in the deepening twilight. The frantic, world-altering energy of the last few months had finally settled, not into peace, but into a kind of tense, watchful new normal.

Daniela came out of the bedroom, a warm, genuine smile on her face. She was wearing a simple black dress, and she looked beautiful. "Ready for a real party?" she asked, her voice a light, welcome sound in the quiet room.

He turned from the window and smiled back. "As ready as I'll ever be."

As they walked through the familiar, tree-lined streets of Chelsea toward O'Connell's, the cool September air a crisp promise of the changing season, their conversation naturally drifted to the heavy, unresolved threads that now defined their lives.

"Did you check on the wallets in the Bryce paintings?" Daniela asked, her tone casual, but her eyes searching his. It had become a quiet, daily ritual, a confirmation that their impossible new reality was still secure.

"This morning," he confirmed. "Everything's stable. All five of the wallets are still intact. It's ... a lot." He didn't say the number out loud, but it was a constant, crushing presence in his mind. Seventy-eight thousand bitcoin from the Bryce paintings, twenty-four thousand from his father. Over a hundred thousand in total. A fortune that was not entirely his to command. "Half of it isn't even ours," he murmured, the weight of his father's final instruction, the stewardship he had been tasked with, a constant, sobering reminder.

"I finally reached out to Nick a couple of days back," Oliver said, after a while.

"Why did you do that?" Daniela asked, a note of shock creeping into her voice.

"To get to Adele," Oliver replied, with a sigh. "Your uncle gave me Dad's instructions. It was unambiguous. Half the money belongs to Christiaan. I finally brought myself to reach out. I needed to tell her, babe. Give her what rightfully belongs to her family."

Daniela took her time to absorb this new overture to someone who had been an adversary until now. She nodded in acknowledgement, finally.

The tone of the conversation shifted, the weight of one problem giving way to another, more personal one. "I spoke to my mom earlier," Oliver said, in a low, frustrated voice.

"And?" Daniela asked, her hand finding his.

"And she's packing," he said, a note of helpless anger in his voice. "She moves to L.A. next month. She's head over heels. I tried again, you know? To warn her, to tell her something about this Alexander guy feels wrong. But without any real proof ..."

He trailed off, shaking his head. "I'm just the worried son. What can I tell her? About the silver man in my projections? About the web I saw her being trapped in? She's not listening now. Imagine how she would get if I brought in this otherworldly stuff."

They walked in silence for a block, the comfortable quiet of a couple who understood each other's burdens without needing to speak.

"Anything?" she asked finally, the single word carrying the weight of the biggest, most painful question in their lives.

He knew who she meant. "Nothing," he said, his voice flat. "Not a word. Not from him, not from your uncle. He doesn't know. Dad is just ... gone."

They arrived at the pub. A large, makeshift sign adorned the entrance. *O'Connell's Pub. Grand Reopening Sep 21.* Through the large front window, they could see the warm, inviting glow of the lights, hear the loud, joyful sound of laughter and music spilling out onto the street. For a moment, they just stood there, two people living an impossible, secret life, looking in at a world that felt simple, and normal, and a million miles away.

"You ready for this?" he asked.

"Yes," she said, squeezing his hand. "Just for tonight, let's be normal."

He smiled, a real, genuine smile. "I'd like that."

Together, they stepped out of the shadows and into the light.

The moment they stepped through the door of O'Connell's Pub, a wave of warm, joyful noise washed over them. The place was packed, a happy, chaotic sea of familiar faces, the air thick with the scent of sawdust, fresh paint, and spilled beer. The old, dark, melancholic pub was gone, replaced by a space that was bright, clean, and it was now thrumming with a new, vibrant life.

A cheer went up from the bar as they entered. Aisling McGinty, her face flushed with happiness, pushed her way through the crowd, arms held wide open.

"There he is!" she boomed, her voice loud and joyful. She gave Oliver a giant bear hug and kissed him on both cheeks. "The man of the hour! We wouldn't be here tonight if it weren't for you, Oliver. First drink is on the house, and so is every other one after that!"

Shannon appeared at her daughter's side, her own smile a quieter but no less genuine version of Aisling's. "It's good to see you, Oliver," she said, giving his arm a warm, grateful squeeze. "Both of you. The place looks alright, doesn't it?"

"It looks perfect, Shannon," Daniela said, her own voice full of a genuine, happy warmth.

"It's more than perfect," Oliver added, looking around at the laughing, mingling crowd, at the new, polished wood of the bar, at the life that had been breathed back into this place. "It's alive again."

Aisling gave him one last, powerful hug before being pulled away to deal with a crisis at the beer taps. In the momentary quiet, Oliver's gaze swept across the crowded, joyful room, and he saw a familiar face. It was Vince.

He waved and caught Vince's eye across the room and walked over to him. "Glad you could make it. Didn't think you'd be able to drive down on such short notice," Oliver said as he approached, a smile in his voice.

"Wouldn't miss this for the world," Vince replied, his own smile easy and relaxed. "A good pub is a low-time-preference institution. It's good to see this place back on a sound footing." He looked from Oliver to Daniela, who had followed a few steps behind, and his expression softened. "It's good to see you both back on one, too."

Oliver smiled.

"Listen," Vince said, a small note of excitement entering his voice. "I talked to the owners at Pubkey and was finally able to get them to remove your ban. You can come back there for the events now."

"Oh wow, Vince," Oliver said, feeling a mixture of gratitude and embarrassment. "Thanks, I really appreciate that."

"No problem. I don't know what got into you back then to get yourself thrown out of there," Vince continued, with a chuckle, "but you seem to be in a much better place right now." Vince concluded with a soft smile and gave Oliver a pat on his shoulder.

Just then, a loud, familiar, and theatrically booming voice called out from a corner booth.

"Oliver, you magnificent boy! Just the person I was hoping to see."

Oliver turned, a wide, incredulous grin spreading across his face. He couldn't believe his eyes. Sitting in a plush, circular booth, a glass of red wine in one hand, was Reza. But it was the man he was with that made Oliver's head spin. It was Mateo Kovač, the Croatian-Australian filmmaker who gave that rousing speech all those months ago at Pubkey.

"I'll be right back," he said to a bemused Vince and walked over with Daniela.

"Reza, what on Earth?" Oliver said, laughing. "How is this possible?"

Reza took a long, appreciative sip of his wine and gestured to the man opposite him. "Oliver, Daniela, you must meet my new friend. This is Mateo. He is a genius. A mad, beautiful, Croatian genius. We have been discussing the aesthetic implications of time preference for the last hour."

"It's an honor, sir," Oliver said, shaking Mateo's outstretched hand. The filmmaker's eyes were just as bright and intense as he remembered from the Pubkey stage. "I heard you speak at Pubkey a few months ago ... it was incredible."

"Ah, a fellow seeker!" Mateo boomed, with a warm and genuine smile, his accent gloriously melodic. "It is a pleasure to meet a man who is interested in the important questions."

"But how do you two know each other?" Oliver asked, still not getting over this implausible collision of worlds.

"Pure, beautiful serendipity, my dear," Reza explained, with a vibrant energy in his eyes. "As you know, I have been taking walks recently. Long ones. Letting the city guide me where it will. Today, I found myself in front of the Angelika, and I saw a poster for a film. It had the word 'bitcoin' in the description, and I thought of you and your youthful, insane passions, and I said to myself, 'Reza, you must see this.' So I did."

He paused, a storyteller setting his stage.

"It was an extraordinary film," he continued. "About the very thing this madman was just talking to me about. The return of art with a soul, with a low time preference. And who should be there for a question-and-answer session afterward but the director himself? Mateo, in the flesh. We got to talking. I told him his film was the first honest piece of art I had seen in a decade. He told me I had the eyes of a man who understood the long journey. We decided a walk was in order. We saw the bright, welcoming lights of a newly opened public house, and, well … here we are."

Just then, Aisling appeared at their table, a look of unbridled joy on her face. In her hand, she held a magnum of Dom Pérignon, a single, perfect bead of condensation tracing a path down its dark green glass.

"Alright, you lot," she boomed, her voice a happy, commanding thing. "I've been saving this for a special occasion, and I can't think of one more special than this." With a practiced, powerful twist of her hands, the cork flew out with a loud *pop*, and a cheer went up from the surrounding tables. She expertly poured four tall, elegant flutes of the bubbling, golden liquid.

She handed the first one to Mateo, the second to Reza, and the third to Daniela. Then, she held one out to Oliver.

"To the man of the hour," she said, her eyes shining with a deep, genuine gratitude. "To Oliver."

He looked at the glass. The tiny, effervescent bubbles rising to the surface felt like a ghost from a different lifetime, the symbol of a man he no longer was. He hadn't had a single drop of alcohol in six months, not since that cold, terrifying night on the ground in Washington Square Park. The abstinence had been a shield, a necessary and absolute wall he had built between himself and the chaos of the winter.

He hesitated, his hand hovering in the air. He felt Daniela's gaze on him, and he looked at her. There was no judgment in her eyes, no pressure. There was only a quiet, unwavering trust. A silent acknowledgment that this was his choice to make.

He thought of the man he had been, the boy lost in a sea of uncertainty and expensive wine. And he thought of the man he was now, a man who had walked through the fire and come out the other side, a man who had found his own, solid ground. The wall was no longer necessary. He was ready to move on from a life of extremes to one of moderation, of balance. He was ready to be normal again.

He reached out and took the glass from Aisling's hand.

"To O'Connell's," he said, his voice clear and steady. "And to second chances."

He raised his glass with the rest of them and they clinked their flutes together, the delicate, crystalline sound a perfect, hopeful note that turned into warm applause and cheers through the pub.

****

Later that night, the apartment was quiet, filled with the soft, steady sound of Daniela's breathing from the bedroom. The joyful, noisy energy of the party at O'Connell's had faded, leaving behind a warm, pleasant afterglow. But Oliver couldn't sleep. He sat in his father's armchair, his phone in his hand, the single glass of champagne he'd had hours ago a distant, pleasant memory.

He was scrolling through the photos Daniela had taken in the *Camara del Tiempo*, the high-resolution images a perfect, impossible record of a miracle. He swiped past the shots of the glowing Hexcelion, the crowd of stunned, upturned faces, and stopped on the close-ups of the burning canvases. There they were. The final, glowing seed words, captured in perfect, crystalline detail against the impossible, golden flames. He smiled, a quiet, profound sense of gratitude washing over him.

He swiped to the next photo. It was a wider shot, taken at the absolute peak of the ritual, the moment the magical fire had erupted from the ceremonial pit with a deafening roar. The Hexcelion above it was a brilliant, blinding star, the crowd a blur of recoiling motion. It was a chaotic, beautiful image.

And then he saw it.

At first, his mind didn't register it. It was just an anomaly in the picture, a trick of the light and smoke. But he stopped swiping. He went back. He zoomed in, his thumb pushing the image closer, his heart beginning a low, heavy drumbeat against his ribs.

In the chaotic, swirling light behind the impossible flames, for just a fraction of a second, a figure was visible. Neither he nor Daniela had caught this detail until now. It was a man, standing calmly in the chamber, a place where no one had been standing before. He wasn't cowering from the supernatural fire; he seemed completely unaffected by it, a placid observer at the heart of a cosmic storm. He was wearing a silver tracksuit, and in his hand, he held a simple, incongruous glass of milk.

Oliver zoomed in further, his breath catching in his throat. The face had a bluish tint to it. It was blurry, distorted by the heat and the motion of the moment, but it was unmistakable. It was the face of the silver man from his projections. The entity with the musical voice and the "né" tic. The spider at the center of the silver web. Da Silva.

He had been there all along. How? How did no one else see him come in? How did he suddenly appear in the photo just now?

A thousand troubling questions remained. But the quest for his father's past was finally over. He stared at the face of the silver man, a cold certainty settling in his soul. The hunt for his family's future had just begun.

808902 (September 22)

The quiet of the Queens apartment was a new kind of prison. For two months, Nick had been playing the part of the man he used to be: the attentive husband, the guy who was home for dinner every night, the one who helped Becky with the groceries and listened to stories about her day. He was a ghost in his own life, and the silence was deafening.

He sat on the sofa, a half-read book open in his lap, the television playing a sitcom on low volume. Becky came in from the kitchen with two mugs of tea and sat beside him, curling her feet up under her.

"This is nice," she said, her voice soft and contented. "Having you home so much. I was really worried for a while there, with all those late nights, the weeks away on business trips, and the ... intensity. I'm glad things have finally calmed down for you at work."

Nick forced a smile. "Me too, babe." He took a sip of his tea. It tasted like nothing. *Calmed down.* That was one way to put it. The mission had crashed and burned on a remote hilltop in Uruguay – not calmed down. Two months of silence from Adele twisted the knife into the cold, hard reality of their defeat. He was home because he had failed. He was adrift and the quiet, domestic bliss of his normal life felt like a cage.

He nodded as Becky recounted a minor drama from her office, but his mind was miles away, trapped in a loop of the last three days. It had started with a simple, impossible text message that had appeared on his phone three days ago.

It was from Oliver.

Hey, I have what belongs to Adele's family. My father's instructions were clear: half of it is hers. I want to make good on that. Please have her contact me.

He had stared at the words for a full minute, his mind a whirlwind of disbelief and suspicion. A truce? Just like that? After everything, Oliver was just going to hand over a fortune worth hundreds of millions of dollars? It had to be a trick. A trap.

He had forwarded a screenshot to Adele immediately, his own message a single, urgent question: *What is this?*

And for three days, she had given him nothing. Complete, absolute, and maddening silence. The lack of response was a new and special kind of torture. He had thought their defeat in Montevideo would forge them into a harder, more focused weapon. Instead, it had just ... ended. The communication had stopped. The partnership had gone cold. He was a man unmoored, and the text message on his phone was the only clue he had to a game he no longer understood.

"It's just ..." Becky was saying, her voice a soft, familiar melody that had become the background music to his internal, silent war, "I was thinking maybe this weekend we could finally drive out to the North Fork, you know? Like we used to."

He was about to agree, to play his part in the quiet domestic play of their life, when his phone, sitting on the coffee table, buzzed. It was a single sharp, urgent vibration that cut through the room's tranquility like a gunshot.

He leaned forward and picked it up. His heart, which had been a slow, sullen drumbeat for two months, gave a single, hard kick against his ribs. It was a message from Adele.

Call me. Now.

The three words were a command, a summons, a key turning the lock of the quiet, suburban prison he had been trapped in. The quiet lie of his life was over. The hunt was back on.

"Actually, you know what?" Becky was saying, oblivious. "We should invite …"

He stood up so abruptly that he sloshed his tea onto the floor. Becky stopped mid-sentence, a look of startled confusion on her face.

"Nick? What is it?"

"It's work, babe," he said, his voice tight and urgent. He was already walking toward the door, grabbing his jacket from the hook. "It's urgent. I have to take this outside. I'll be right back."

He didn't wait for her reply. He pulled the door open and rushed out into the hallway, leaving his confused-looking wife standing alone in the living room, the forgotten mugs of tea steaming on the table between them.

He pulled the apartment door shut behind him, the sound a dull thud that sealed off one life and opened the door to another. The hallway was quiet, the air stale. He fumbled with his phone, his fingers suddenly clumsy as he found Adele's contact and hit call.

It rang twice.

"Nick," she said. Her voice was flat, devoid of any warmth. It was the same voice she used with hotel clerks and car rental agents.

A cold knot tightened in his stomach, but he pushed past it, trying to reclaim the easy intimacy they had shared just two months ago. "Adele," he said, his own voice a low, intimate murmur. "I've missed you."

The silence on the other end of the line was a cold, physical thing. He could hear the faint, distant sound of traffic, the ambient noise of a city that was not his own.

"We have a situation to discuss, Nick," she said finally, her tone clipped and all business. The unspoken message was a brutal, efficient severing of their personal connection. The woman he had spent weeks with at the Baccarat was gone. Only the client, the commander, remained.

"Yes, I got a text from him," Nick said, the words a quiet rush. "Three days ago. He's offering a truce. He said his father's instructions were to give you half of the money from the Bryce wallets."

The silence on the other end of the line was absolute. He could picture her, wherever she was, her face a mask of cold, analytical calm as she processed the impossible new variable.

"It's a trick, Nick," she said finally, her voice completely devoid of emotion. "A pathetic attempt to get us to lower our guard."

"Is it?" he asked, a part of him wanting to believe in the simple, clean resolution. "It's a fortune, Adele. Why would he just ... offer it up?"

"Because he is weak," she replied, her tone a sharp, dismissive thing. "And because he knows his position is illegitimate. He doesn't own half, Nick. All of it belongs to my family. Your friend's father was a thief who built a legend on my brother's work and my family's money." She spoke with a conviction so absolute it left no room for doubt.

He was silent for a moment, the last vestiges of his old loyalty to Oliver finally burning away, replaced by the cold, hard logic of his new alliance. She was right.

"So, what do we do?" he asked.

"We play his game," Adele said, her voice now low and strategic. "We agree to a meeting. We will feign an interest in his ... generous offer. We will use the opportunity to get close, to assess his defenses, to find the new cracks in his armor. This isn't over, Nick. The game has just entered a new, more interesting phase."

The new plan, cold and ruthless, hung in the air between them. He thought of Oliver, of the simple, almost naive offer of a truce. It was a move born of a different world, a world of principles and honor that Nick no longer believed in. Adele's world, the world of power and deception, was the only one that felt real anymore.

"Okay," he said, his voice quiet and steady. "I'm in. We do it your way."

"Good," Adele replied, her voice devoid of any triumph. It was a simple, transactional acknowledgment. "I will have my people begin the preliminary research. We will need a secure location for the meeting. I will be in touch."

The line went dead.

Nick lowered the phone, the sound of the call disconnecting a flat, final note in the quiet hallway. He looked at the closed door of his apartment. He could picture Becky inside, still confused, still waiting for him to come back. He thought of the quiet life he had just left, the easy comfort, the simple, uncomplicated love. It all felt like a memory from a different man's life, a galleon receding into the fog.

He had made his choice. He was no longer just a man seeking vengeance. He was a hunter, and the long, cold, and patient game had just begun. He walked up to the apartment door and opened it slowly, a stranger returning to a life that was no longer his.

814674 (October 31)

The early morning air in Harlem was crisp, carrying the first real chill of autumn. Inside the Malcolm Shabazz market, the cavernous space was a hive of quiet, pre-open activity. Shopkeepers were methodically arranging their wares, the scent of incense and imported leather mingling with the aroma of strong, sweet coffee. In the fifth stall from the left, a narrow space overflowing with vibrant textiles and handcrafted jewelry, a man in a light-gray kurta, his head adorned with an embroidered skullcap, was meticulously organizing a display of antique silver bracelets, his movements practiced and precise.

A teenage boy appeared at the entrance to the stall.

"*As-salaam alaykum*, Saleem Bhai," the boy said, his voice a little hesitant.

The man addressed as Saleem Bhai didn't look up from his work. "*Wa-alaykum salaam*," he replied, his tone sharp, seemingly irritated by the interruption. "What you want, Jamal? I am busy."

"There is a man," the boy said, shifting his weight nervously from one foot to the other. "In a big, green car, outside on 116th Street. He wants to see you."

"I am not seeing anyone now," Saleem Bhai snapped, finally looking up from the bracelets, his expression a mask of pure annoyance. "Tell him to come back later when the market open. Or better, tell him to get lost."

The boy swallowed, his eyes wide. "I told him that," he said, his voice barely a whisper. "But he ... he told me to tell you something. He said to tell you he is the boss."

The silver bracelet in Saleem's hand clattered against the glass of the display case. The color drained from his face, replaced by a pale, grayish pallor. The irritation was gone, vaporized by a look of sudden, absolute and primal fear.

Without another word, he pushed past the startled boy and rushed out of his stall. He ran through the quiet, half-lit corridors of the market, ignoring the curious stares of the other shopkeepers, and burst out onto the sidewalk of 116th Street.

His eyes frantically scanned the morning traffic. And then he saw it. Parked directly in front of the market, in a zone clearly marked for commercial loading only, was a car that did not belong. It was an opulent, dark green Bentley, its paint so deep it looked like liquid night, its massive chrome grille gleaming in the early morning sun. The engine was running, but it made no sound, a silent, electric hum that was more felt than heard.

Saleem Bhai approached the car, his steps hesitant, his posture no longer that of an irritated shopkeeper but of a man approaching a monarch. As he drew near, the tinted rear window glided down with a whisper-quiet motion.

There was a man sitting by the open window. He was dressed in a silver tracksuit, the metallic fabric shimmering even in the muted morning light. His face had a faint bluish tint to it. His hair was disheveled, and his eyes possessed a distant, wild look, as if he were speaking to a different world. Sitting beside him was an elegant, composed woman in her fifties, her posture perfect, her expression a mask of cool indifference. On the fold-down tray between them, next to a crystal vase holding a single, perfect white rose, sat a tall, incongruous glass of milk.

Saleem Bhai stood before the open window of the Bentley, his head bowed. The man in the silver tracksuit watched him, a look of detached, almost clinical amusement in his eyes. He took a slow, deliberate sip of his milk.

"The boy has been back for cash, né?" the man asked, his voice almost lyrical. "Have our friends at the travel agency received any new requests?"

"No, Boss," Saleem stammered, his eyes fixed on the pavement. "Nothing after trip in July. The boy had the ... the luxury vacation to Montevideo with his girlfriend. That was last one."

The man in the silver tracksuit let out a soft, amused laugh, a sound that was more like a musical scale than a human expression.

"The boy and his girlfriend, playing at being spies," he said, his voice a quiet, sing-song lilt. "A week-long holiday. It is ... charming, né?" He turned his head slightly, his gaze falling on the elegant woman beside him. "He thought he could fool us with such a simple decoy, Maren."

The woman next to him, the one addressed as Maren, allowed a small, cold smile to touch her lips. It did not reach her eyes.

"He thinks he is clever, Ed," she said, in a low, hard voice. "That will be his downfall."

The man took a slow, deliberate sip of his milk, the white liquid a stark contrast to the dark, opulent interior of the Bentley. He placed the glass back on the tray with a soft, decisive click.

"It does not matter," he said, his gaze turning back to Saleem Bhai. "We have his mother. She is quite happy in Los Angeles. She has come to us willingly, and she will stay. My man, Alexander, is a smooth operator, né? He will take good care of her."

He looked out the window, a look of detached, philosophical amusement on his face. "The boy is loyal. He will come for her. And when he does, he will lead us to his father – like he almost did in July. And then, we will have *Akasha*."

The man in the silver tracksuit gave Saleem his final instruction, his voice a quiet, musical command. "You will continue to keep a watchful eye, né? You will report any and all activity, no matter how insignificant. Is that clear?"

Saleem Bhai bowed his head, his voice a subservient whisper. "Yes, Mr. Da Silva, sir. Of course."

The tinted window glided up with a soft, final hum, sealing the occupants of the Bentley away from the world. The car pulled away from the curb without a sound, disappearing into the early morning traffic of Harlem.

480

The tinted window glided up with a soft, final hum, sealing the occupants of the Bentley away from the world. The car pulled away from the curb without a sound, disappearing into the early morning traffic of Harlem.